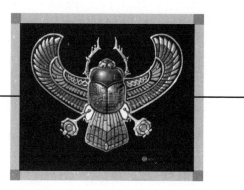

OTHERLAND

Volume Two

RIVER OF
BLUE FIRE

TAD WILLIAMS

DAW BOOKS, INC.
DONALD A. WOLLHEIM, FOUNDER

375 Hudson Street, New York, NY 10014

ELIZABETH R. WOLLHEIM
SHEILA E. GILBERT
PUBLISHERS

First printing, July 1998

1   2   3   4   5   6   7   8   9

DAW TRADEMARK REGISTERED
U.S. PAT. OFF. AND FOREIGN COUNTRIES
—MARCA REGISTRADA
HECHO EN U.S.A.

PRINTED IN THE U.S.A.

This book is dedicated to my father,
Joseph Hill Evans,
with love.

As I said before, Dad doesn't read fiction. He still hasn't noticed
that this thing is dedicated to him. This is Volume Two—let's
see how many more until he catches on.

Acknowledgements

As always: huge book, much to say, lots of blame (almost entirely mine), but also lots of credit, herewith tendered. The ever-swollen Roster of Gratitude carried over from the first doorstopping volume was:

Deborah Beale, Matt Bialer, Arthur Ross Evans, Jo-Ann Goodwin, Deb Grabien, Nic Grabien, Jed Hartmann, John Jarrold, Katharine Kerr, M.J. Kramer, Mark Kreighbaum, Bruce Lieberman, Mark McCrum, Peter Stampfel, Mitch Wagner.

It must now be amended to include:

Barbara Cannon, Aaron Castro, Nick Des Barres, Tim Holman, Nick Itsou, Jo and Phil Knowles, LES.., Joshua Milligan, Eric Neuman, Michael Whelan, and all the friendly folks on the Tad Williams Listserve.

Still starring in their long-running, long-suffering roles as my Esteemed Editors, a bazillion thanks should also be rendered unto Betsy Wollheim and Sheila Gilbert.

Author's Note

I've received an awful lot of mail, electronic and old-fashioned-with-a-stamp both, about the first OTHERLAND volume. Most, I'm pleased to say, has been extremely nice and very favorable. The only note of discomfort has been from some readers who were upset by what they felt was the "cliffhanger" nature of the first volume's ending.

I understand and apologize. However, the problem with writing this kind of story is that it's not really a series—it's one very, very long novel, which should be under one cover except that 1) it would take so long to write that my family and pets would starve, and 2) they couldn't make covers that size, unless they were adapted from circus tents. That means I have a difficult choice to make: end each part in more abrupt fashion than some readers find ideal, or create artificial endings for each volume which I believe would change the overall shape of the book, and perhaps even adversely affect the structure of the story.

Thus, I can only ask for the indulgence of kind readers. I'll do the best job I can not to end volumes in mid-sentence—"And then she discovered she was . . . oops, The End"—but please understand that what you're getting is a part of a larger work, and may reflect that. I'll still do the best I can to find some kind of closure for each individual volume.

Thanks.

For more information, visit the Tad Williams web site at:

http://www.tadwilliams.com

OTHERLAND: City of Golden Shadow

Synopsis

Wet, terrified, with only the companionship of trench-mates *Finch* and *Mullet* to keep him sane, *Paul Jonas* seems no different than any of thousands of other foot soldiers in World War I. But when he abruptly finds himself alone on an empty battlefield except for a tree that grows up into the clouds, he begins to doubt that sanity. When he climbs the tree and discovers a castle in the clouds, a woman with wings like a bird, and her terrifying giant guardian, his insanity seems confirmed. But when he awakens back in the trenches, he finds he is clutching one of the bird-woman's feathers.

In South Africa, in the middle of the twenty-first century, *Irene* *"Renie" Sulaweyo* has problems of her own. Renie is an instructor of virtual engineering whose newest student, *!Xabbu,* is one of the desert Bushmen, a people to whom modern technology is very alien. At home, she is a surrogate mother to her young brother, *Stephen,* who is obsessed with exploring the virtual parts of the world communication network—the "net"—and Renie spends what little spare time she has holding her family together. Her widowed father *Long Joseph* only seems interested in finding his next drink.

Like most children, Stephen is entranced by the forbidden, and although Renie has already saved him once from a disturbing virtual nightclub named Mister J's, Stephen sneaks back in. By the time Renie discovers what he has done, Stephen has fallen into a coma. The doctors cannot explain it, but Renie is certain something has happened to him online.

American *Orlando Gardiner* is only a little older than Renie's brother, but he is a master of several online domains, and because of a serious medical condition, spends most of his time in the online identity of *Thargor*, a barbarian warrior. But when in the midst of one of his adventures Orlando is given a glimpse of a golden city unlike anything else he has ever seen on the net, he is so distracted that his Thargor character is killed. Despite this terrible loss, Orlando cannot shake his fascination with the golden city, and with the support of his software agent *Beezle Bug* and the reluctant help of his online friend *Fredericks*, he is determined to locate the golden city.

Meanwhile, on a military base in the United States, a little girl named *Christabel Sorensen* pays secret visits to her friend, *Mr. Sellars*, a strange, scarred old man. Her parents have forbidden her to see him, but she likes the old man and the stories he tells, and he seems much more pathetic than frightening. She does not know that he has very unusual plans for her.

As Renie gets to know !Xabbu the Bushman better, and to appreciate his calm good nature and his outsider's viewpoint on modern life, she comes to rely on him more and more in her quest to discover what has happened to her brother. She and !Xabbu sneak into the online nightclub, Mr. J's. The place is as bad as she feared, with guests indulging themselves in all manner of virtual unpleasantness, but nothing seems like it could have actually physically harmed her brother until they are drawn into a terrifying encounter with a virtual version of the Hindu death-goddess Kali. !Xabbu is overcome, and Renie, too, is almost overwhelmed by Kali's subliminal hypnotics, but with the help of a mysterious figure whose simulated body (his "sim") is a blank, with no features at all, she manages to get herself and !Xabbu out of Mister J's. Before she goes offline, the figure gives her some data in the form of a golden gem.

Back (apparently) in World War I, Paul Jonas escapes from his squadron and makes a run for freedom through the dangerous no-man's-land between the lines. As rain falls and shells explode, Paul struggles through mud and corpses, only to find he has crossed over into some nether-region, stranger even than his castle dream—a flat, misty emptiness. A shimmering golden light appears, and Paul is drawn to it, but before he can step into its glow, his two friends from the trenches appear and demand that he return with them. Weary and confused, he is about to surrender, but as they come closer he sees that Finch and Mullet no longer appear even remotely human, and he flees into the golden light.

In the 21st Century, the oldest and perhaps richest man in the world is named *Felix Jongleur*. His physical body is all but dead, and he spends his days in a virtual Egypt he has built for himself, where he reigns over all as *Osiris*, the god of Life and Death. His chief servant, both in the virtual and real world, is a half-Aboriginal serial murderer who has named himself *Dread*, who combines a taste for hunting humans with a strange extrasensory ability to manipulate electronic circuitry that allows him to blank security cameras and otherwise avoid detection. Jongleur discovered Dread years before, and helped to nurture the young man's power, and has made him his chief assassin.

Jongleur/Osiris is also the leader of a group of some of the world's most powerful and wealthy people, the *Grail Brotherhood*, who have built for themselves a virtual universe unlike any other, the Grail Project, also called Otherland. (This latter name comes from an entity known as the "Other" which has some important involvement with the Grail Project network—an artificial intelligence or something even stranger. This powerful force is largely in the control of Jongleur, but it is the only thing in the world that the old man fears.)

The Grail Brotherhood are arguing among themselves, upset that the mysterious Grail Project is so slow to come to fruition. They have all invested billions in it, and waited a decade or more of their lives. Led by the American technology baron *Robert Wells*, they grow restive about Jongleur's leadership and his secrets, like the nature of the Other.

Jongleur fights off a mutiny, and orders his minion Dread to prepare a neutralization mission against one of the Grail members who has already left the Brotherhood.

Back in South Africa, Renie and her student !Xabbu are shaken by their narrow escape from the virtual nightclub known as Mister J's, and more certain than ever that there is some involvement between the club and her brother's coma. But when she examines the data-object the mysterious figure gave her, it opens into an amazingly realistic image of a golden city. Renie and !Xabbu seek the help of Renie's former professor, *Dr. Susan Van Bleeck*, but she is unable to solve the mystery of the city, or even tell for certain if it is an actual place. The doctor decides to contact someone else she knows for help, a researcher named *Martine Desroubins*. But even as Renie and the mysterious Martine make contact for the first time, Dr. Van Bleeck is attacked in her home and savagely beaten, and all her equipment destroyed. Renie rushes to the hospital, but after pointing Renie in the direction of a friend, Susan dies, leaving Renie both angry and terrified.

Meanwhile Orlando Gardiner, the ill teenager in America, is hot in pursuit of the golden city that he saw while online, so much so that his friend Fredericks begins to worry about him. Orlando has always been odd—he has a fascination with death-experience simulations that Fredericks can't understand—but even so this seems excessive. When Orlando announces they are going to the famous hacker-node known as TreeHouse, Fredericks' worst fears are confirmed.

TreeHouse is the last preserve of everything anarchic about the net, a place where no rules dictate what people can do or how they must appear. But although Orlando finds TreeHouse fascinating, and discovers some unlikely allies in the form of a group of hacker children named the *Wicked Tribe* (whose virtual guise is a troop of tiny winged yellow monkeys) his attempts to discover the origins of the golden city vision arouse suspicion, and he and Fredericks are forced to flee.

Meanwhile Renie and !Xabbu, with the help of Martine Desroubins, have also come to TreeHouse, in pursuit of an old, retired hacker named *Singh,* Susan Van Bleeck's friend. When they find him, he tells them that he is the last of a group of specialist programmers who built the security system for a mysterious network nicknamed "Otherland," and that his companions have been dying in mysterious circumstances. He is the last one alive.

Renie, !Xabbu, Singh, and Martine decide they must break into the Otherland system to discover what secret is worth the lives of Singh's comrades and children like Renie's brother.

Paul Jonas has escaped from his World War I trench only to find himself seemingly unstuck in time and space. Largely amnesiac, he wanders into a world where a White Queen and a Red Queen are in conflict, and finds himself pursued again by the Finch and Mullet figures. With the help of a boy named *Gally* and a long-winded, egg-shaped bishop, Paul escapes them, but his pursuers murder Gally's children friends. A huge creature called a Jabberwock provides a diversion, and Paul and Gally dive into a river.

When they surface, the river is in a different world, a strange, almost comical version of Mars, full of monsters and English gentleman-soldiers. Paul again meets the bird-woman from his castle dream, now named *Vaala,* but this time she is the prisoner of a Martian overlord. With the help of mad adventurer *Hurley Brummond,* Paul saves the woman. She recognizes Paul, too, but does not know why. When the Finch and Mullet figures appear again, she flees. Attempting to catch up to her, Paul crashes a stolen flying ship, sending himself and Gally to what seems certain doom. After a strange dream in which he is back in the cloud-castle, menaced by Finch and Mullet in their strangest forms yet, he wakes without Gally in the midst of the Ice Age, surrounded by Neandertal hunters.

Meanwhile in South Africa, Renie and her companions are being hunted by mysterious strangers, and are forced to flee their home. With the help of Martine (whom they still know only as a voice) Renie, along with !Xabbu, her father, and Dr. Van Bleeck's assistant *Jeremiah,* find an old, mothballed robot-plane base in the Drakensberg Mountains. They renovate a pair of V-tanks (virtuality immersion vats) so Renie and !Xabbu can go online for an indefinite period, and prepare for their assault on Otherland.

Back on the army base in America, little Christabel is convinced to help the burned and crippled Mr. Sellars with a complex plan that is only revealed as an escape attempt when he disappears from his house, setting the whole base (including Christabel's security chief father) on alert. Christabel has cut what seems an escape hole in the base's perimeter fence (with the help of a homeless boy from outside), but only she knows that Mr. Sellars is actually hiding in a network of tunnels beneath the base, free now to continue his mysterious "task."

In the abandoned facility, under the Drakensberg Mountains, Renie and her companions enter the tanks, go online, and break into Otherland. They survive a terrifying interaction with the Other which seems to be the network's security system, in which Singh dies of a heart attack, and find that the network is so incredibly realistic that at first they cannot believe it is a virtual environment. The experience is strange in many other ways. Martine has a body for the first time, !Xabbu has been given the form of a baboon, and most importantly, they can find no way to take themselves offline again. Renie and the others discover that they are in an artificial South American country. When they reach the golden city at the heart of it, the city they have been seeking so long, they are captured, and discover that they are the prisoners of *Bolivar Atasco,* a man involved with the Grail Brotherhood and with the building of the Otherland network from the start.

Back in America, Orlando's friendship with Fredericks has survived the twin revelations that Orlando is dying of a rare premature-aging disease, and that Fredericks is in fact a girl. They are unexpectedly linked to Renie's hacker friend Singh by the Wicked Tribe just as Singh is opening his connection to the Grail network, and drawn through into Otherland. After their own horrifying encounter with the Other, Orlando and Fredericks also become Atasco's prisoners. But when they are brought to the great man, along with Renie's company and others, they find that it is not Atasco who has gathered them, but Mr. Sellars—revealed now as the strange blank sim who helped Renie and !Xabbu escape from Mister J's.

Sellars explains that he has lured them all here with the image of

the golden city—the most discreet method he could devise, because
their enemies, the Grail Brotherhood, are so unbelievably powerful
and remorseless. Sellars explains that Atasco and his wife were once
members of the Brotherhood, but quit when their questions about the
network were not answered. Sellars then tells how he discovered that
the secret Otherland network has a mysterious but undeniable connection to the illness of thousands of children like Renie's brother
Stephen. Before he can explain more, the sims of Atasco and his wife
go rigid and Sellars' own sim disappears.

In the real world, Jongleur's murderous minion Dread has begun
his attack on the Atascos' fortified Colombian island home, and after
breaking through the defenses, has killed both Atascos. He then uses
his strange abilities—his "twist"—to tap into their data lines, discovers Sellars' meeting, and orders his assistant *Dulcinea Anwin* to take
over the incoming line of one of the Atascos' guests—the online group
that includes Renie and her friends—and takes on the identity of that
usurped guest, leaving Dread a mystery spy in the midst of Renie and
friends.

Sellars reappears in the Atascos' virtual world and begs Renie and
the others to flee into the network while he tries to hide their presence. They are to look for Paul Jonas, he tells them, a mysterious virtual prisoner Sellars has helped escape from the Brotherhood. Renie
and company make their way onto the river and out of the Atascos'
simulation, then through an electrical blue glow into the next simworld. Panicked and overwhelmed by too much input, Martine finally
reveals her secret to Renie: she is blind.

Their boat has become a giant leaf. Overhead, a dragonfly the size
of a fighter jet skims into view.

Back in the mountain fortress, in the real world, Jeremiah and Renie's father Long Joseph can only watch the silent V-tanks, wonder,
and wait.

Contents

Second

VOICES IN THE DARK

Third

GODS AND GENIUSES

Fourth

BEDLAM'S SONG

Foreword

THERE was snow everywhere—the world was white.

It must have been warmer in the Land of the Dead, he thought, mocking himself, mocking the senseless universe. *I should never have left.*

Snow and ice and wind and blood. . . .

The thing in the shallow pit made a terrible raw honking sound and swung its head. Antlers the size of small trees swept from side to side, gouging snow and dirt, narrowly missing one of the men who had leaned in to jab at it with his spear.

The elk was larger than anything like it Paul had ever seen in tired old London Zoo, taller than a man at its shoulders and heavy as a prize bull. It had fought with terrifying strength for almost an hour, and the points of the huge, curling antlers were streaked with the blood of a man named Will Not Cry, but the animal's shaggy pelt was also drenched with its own blood, as was the snow around the edge of the hole.

It leaped again and fell back scrabbling, hooves churning the bottom of the pit to a pink froth. Spears snagged in the elk's thick hide rattled like exotic jewelry. Runs Far, who seemed the party's most fearless hunter, leaned in to jerk one of his spears free. He missed his first stab, dodged the swinging antlers, then smashed the stone point back in again just under the creature's thick jaw. Arterial blood spurted ten feet, splashing Runs Far and the two hunters nearest to him, adding another layer of color to their ocher-and-black hunting paint.

The elk heaved up the slope once more in a last desperate attempt
to escape the pit, but failed to crest the rim before the spears of the
hunters pushed it off balance and sent it sliding backward, awkward
as a fawn.

The freshet of blood from its throat pulsed more weakly. The buck
stood on wobbly legs at the bottom of the pit, hitching as it sucked
air. One leg buckled, but it struggled upright yet again, teeth bared in
final exhaustion, glaring from beneath the spread of horn. The man
named Birdcatcher jabbed a spear into its side, but it was clearly a
superfluous gesture. The elk took a step backward, its face registering
what in a human Paul would have called frustration, then fell to its
knees and rolled onto its side, chest heaving.

"Now he gives himself to us," said Runs Far. Beneath his smeared
paint, his mouth was locked in a grin of exhausted pleasure, but there
was something deeper in his eyes. "Now he is ours."

Runs Far and another man clambered into the pit. When his companion had grabbed the antlers, holding them firm as the elk gasped
and twitched, Runs Far slashed its throat with a heavy stone blade.

In what seemed a piece of particularly cruel irony, the hunter with
the strange name of Will Not Cry had suffered not just deep antler-
gouges across his face and head, but had lost his left eye as well. As
one of the other hunters stuffed the ragged hole with snow and bound
it with a strip of tanned hide, Will Not Cry murmured to himself, a
singsong whisper that might have been a lament or a prayer. Runs
Far crouched beside him and tried to wash some of the blood from
the injured man's face and beard with a handful of snow, but the
ragged facial wounds still bled heavily. Paul was astonished by how
calmly the others reacted to their companion's terrible injuries, although all of them bore scars and disfigurations of their own.

People die easily here, he decided, *so anything less serious must seem like
a victory.*

The Neandertal hunters quickly and adroitly razored the elk carcass
into chunks with their flint knives and wrapped the skin, organs, and
even bones in the still-smoking hide for travel. The People, as they
called themselves, did not waste anything.

As work slowed, some of the men began to watch Paul again, perhaps wondering whether the stranger they had saved from the frozen
river was properly impressed by their prowess. Only the one called
Birdcatcher looked at him with open distrust, but they all kept their
distance. Having participated in neither the kill nor the dismember-

ment, Paul was feeling particularly useless, so he was grateful when Runs Far approached. The leader of the hunt had so far been the only one to speak with Paul. Now he extended a blood-smeared hand, offering the stranger a strip of the kill's deep-red flesh. Sensible of the kindness being shown him, Paul accepted it. The meat was curiously flavorless, like chewing on a bit of blood-salted rubber.

"Tree Horns fought hard." Runs Far took another piece into his mouth. When he could not fit it all in, he reached up and sliced off the remainder with his stone blade, retaining it until he had finished the first mouthful. He grinned, displaying worn and scratched teeth. "We have much meat now. The People will be happy."

Paul nodded, unsure of what to say. He had noticed a curious thing: When the hunters spoke, it was in recognizable English, which seemed a highly unlikely thing for a group of Neandertal huntsmen to do. At the same time, there seemed a slight dissynchronization between their lips and what they said, as though he had been dropped into a well-dubbed but still imperfect foreign drama.

In fact, it seemed as though he had been given some kind of translation implant, like the kind his old school friend Niles had received on entering the diplomatic corps. But how could that be?

For the fifth or sixth time that day, Paul's fingers went to his neck and the base of his skull, feeling for the neurocannula that he knew was not there, again finding only goose-pimpled skin. He had never wanted implants, had resisted the trend long after most of his friends had them, yet now it seemed that someone had given them to him without his permission—but had also managed to completely hide the physical location.

What could do that? he wondered. *And why? And more importantly, where in the bloody hell am I?*

He had been thinking and thinking, but he was no nearer to an answer. He seemed to be sliding through space and time, like something out of the more excessive kind of science fiction story. He had traveled across a boy's-adventure Mars, he remembered, and through somebody's cracked version of Alice's Looking Glass. He had seen other improbable places, too—the details were fuzzy, but still too complete to be merely the residue of dreams. But how was that possible? If someone were to build sets and hire impostors to fool him this thoroughly, it would cost millions—billions!—and try as he might, he could not find a single crack in the facades of any of these might-be actors. Neither could he imagine a reason why anyone would spend such resources on a nonentity like himself, a museum curator with no important friends and no particular prospects. No matter what the voice from the golden harp had said, this must all be real.

Unless he had been brainwashed somehow. He could not rule that out. Some kind of experimental drug, perhaps—but why? There was still a gap in his memory where the answer might lurk, but unlike the strange journeys to imaginary landscapes, no amount of concentration could bring light to any of that particular patch of darkness.

Runs Far still crouched at his side, his round eyes bright with curiosity beneath the bony brows. Embarrassed, confused, Paul shrugged and reached down for a handful of snow and crunched it between the crablike pincers of his crude gloves. Brainwashing would explain why he had awakened in a frozen prehistoric river and been rescued by what looked like authentic Neandertals—costuming and sets for a hallucination wouldn't be very expensive. But it could not explain the absolutely, unarguably *real* and sustained presence of the world around him. It could not explain the snow in his hand, cold and granular and white. It could not explain the stranger beside him, with his unfamiliar but utterly lived-in, alien face.

All those questions, but still no answers. Paul sighed and let the snow fall from his hand.

"Are we going to sleep here tonight?" he asked Runs Far.

"No. We are close to where the People live. We will be there before full dark." The hunter leaned forward, furrowed his brow, and stared into Paul's mouth. "You eat things, Riverghost. Do all the people from the Land of the Dead eat things?"

Paul smiled sadly. "Only when they're hungry."

Runs Far was in the lead, his stocky legs carrying him through the snow with surprising ease; like all the hunters, even the terribly wounded Will Not Cry, he moved with the instinctive grace of a wild beast. The others, although burdened now with hundreds of kilograms of elk parts, followed swiftly, so that Paul was already winded trying to keep up.

He skidded on a fallen branch hidden by snow, and slipped, but the man beside him caught and held him unflinchingly until Paul had found his feet; the Neandertal's hands were hard and rough as tree bark. Paul found himself confused again. It was impossible to sustain disbelief in the face of such powerful arguments. These men, although not quite the caricature cavemen he remembered from childhood flicks, were so clearly something different from himself, something wilder and simpler, that he found his skepticism diminishing—not so much fading as sliding into a kind of hibernation, to awaken when it again had a useful task to do.

What sounded like a wolf howl came echoing down the hillside. The People ran a little faster.

Nothing around you is true, and yet the things you see can hurt you or kill you, the golden gem, the voice from the harp, had told him. Whatever these men were, true or false seemings, they were at home in this world in a way that Paul most decidedly was not. He would have to rely on their skills. For his sanity's sake, he might have to trust that they were exactly what they seemed to be.

WHEN he had been a boy, when he had still been "Paulie," and still the chattel of his eccentric father and frail mother, he had spent each Christmas with them at his paternal grandmother's cottage in Gloucestershire, in the wooded, rolling countryside that the locals liked to call "the real England." But it had not been real, not at all: its virtue was precisely that it symbolized something which had never completely existed, a middle-class England of gracious, countrified beauty whose tattered true nature was becoming more obvious every year.

For Grammer Jonas, the world beyond her village had become increasingly shadowy. She could describe the complexity of a neighbor's dispute about a fence with the sophistication of a newsnet legal analyst, but had trouble remembering who was prime minister. She had a wallscreen, of course—a small, old-fashioned one framed in baroque gold on the parlor wall, like the photo of a long-dead relative. It mostly went unused, the calls voice-only. Grammer Jonas had never completely trusted visual communication, especially the idea that she could see without being seen if she chose, and the thought that some stranger might look into her house and see her in her nightgown gave her, as she put it, "the creeps, Paulie-love, the absolute creeps."

Despite her distrust of the modern world, or perhaps even in part because of it, Paul had loved her fiercely, and she in turn had loved him as only a grandmother could. Every small success of his was a glowing victory, every transgression against parental authority a sign of clever independence to be encouraged rather than condemned. When, in one of his fits of unfocused rebellion, young Paul refused to help with the dishes or do some other chore (and thus forfeited his pudding) Grammer Jonas would be at the door of his prison-bedroom later in the evening to pass him a contraband sweet, in a breathless hurry to get downstairs again before his parents noticed her absence.

The winter when he was seven, the snows came. It was England's whitest Christmas in decades, and the tabnets competed for the most astonishing footage—St. Paul's dome wearing a dunce cap of white, people skating on the lower Thames as they had during Elizabethan

times (many died, since the ice was not thick enough to be safe.) In
the early weeks, before the tabs began to trumpet "New Atlantic
Storm Creates Blizzard Horror" and run daily body counts (with
corpse-by-corpse footage) of people who had frozen to death sleeping
rough or even waiting for trains at the smaller stations, the heavy
snows brought a sense of joy to most people, and young Paul had
certainly been one of them. It was his first real experience of snow-
balls and sleds and tree branches dropping cold surprises down the
back of one's neck, of a world with most of its colors suddenly wiped
clean.

One mild day, when the sun was out and the sky was mostly blue,
he and his grandmother had gone for a walk. The most recent snow-
fall had covered everything, and as they walked slowly through the
fields there were no signs of other humans at all except for the distant
smoke from a chimney, and no footprints but the tracks of their own
rubber boots, so that the vista spread before them seemed primordial,
untouched.

When at last they had reached a place between the hedgerows,
where the land before them dipped down into a gentle valley, his
grandmother abruptly stopped. She had spread her arms, and—in a
voice he had never heard her use, hushed and yet throbbingly intense—said, "Look, Paulie, isn't it lovely! Isn't it perfect! It's just like
we were back at the beginning of everything. Like the whole sinful
world was starting over!" Mittened fists clenched before her face like
a child making a wish, she had added: "Wouldn't that be wonderful?"

Surprised and a little frightened by the strength of her reaction, he
had struggled to make her insight his own—struggled but ultimately
failed. There *was* something beautiful about the illusion of emptiness,
of possibility, but he had been a seven-year-old boy who did not feel,
as his grandmother more or less did, that people had somehow ruined
everything, and he was just baby enough to be made nervous by the
thought of a world without familiar places and people, a world of
clean, cold loneliness.

They had stood for a long time, staring at the uninhabited winter
world, and when at last they turned back—Paul secretly relieved to be
walking in their own reversed footprints, following the trail of bread
crumbs out of the worrisome forest of adult regrets—his grandmother
had been smiling fiercely to herself, singing a song he could not quite
hear.

Paul had tried and failed to share her epiphany that day, so long
ago. But now he seemed to be the one who had tumbled into the

world she had wished for, a world—thousands of generations before even his grandmother's inconceivably ancient childhood—that she could only imagine.

Yes, if Grammer Jonas could have seen this, he thought. *God, wouldn't she have loved it. It really is the beginning—a long time before the crooked politicians and the filthy shows on the net and people being so rude and vulgar, and all the foreign restaurants serving things she couldn't pronounce. She'd think she'd gone to heaven.*

Of course, he realized, she'd have trouble getting a good cup of tea.

The People were moving in deceptively ragged order along the edge of a hillside forest, heading down a long, snow-blanketed slope broken up by irregular limestone outcroppings. Slender tree-shadows stretched across their path like blueprints for an unbuilt staircase. The light was fading quickly, and the sky, which had been the soft gray of a dove's breast, was turning a colder, darker color. Paul suddenly wondered for the first time not when in the world he was, but where.

Had there been Neandertals everywhere, or just in Europe? He couldn't remember. The little he knew of prehistoric humankind was all in fragmented, trivia-card bits—cave-painting, mammoth-hunting, stone tools laboriously flaked by hand. It was frustrating not to remember more. People in science fiction flicks always seemed to know useful things about the places time travel took them. But what if the time traveler had been only an average history student? What then?

There were more limestone outcroppings now, great shelves that seemed to push sideways out of the ground, shadowy oblongs less luminous in the twilight than the ever-present snow. Runs Far slowed, letting the rest of the group jog past, until Paul at the end of the line had caught up with him. The bearded hunter fell into step beside him without a word, and Paul, who was quite breathless, was content to let him do so.

As they came around the corner of a large outcrop, Paul saw warm yellow light spilling out onto the snow. Strange, gnarled figures stood silhouetted in a wide gap in the cliff face, spears clutched in misshapen hands, and for a nervous moment Paul was reminded of folktales about troll bridges and fairy mounds. Runs Far took his elbow and pushed him forward; when he had reached the mouth of the cave, he could see that the guardians were only older members of the People, twisted by age, left behind to protect the communal hearth like Britain's wartime Home Guard.

The hunting party was quickly surrounded, not only by these aged guardians, but by an outspilling of fur-clad women and children as well, all talking and gesticulating. Will Not Cry received much sympathetic attention as his injuries were examined. Paul half-expected his own appearance to cause superstitious panic, but although all the People regarded him with interest that varied from fearful to fascinated, he was clearly less important than the meat and tales which the hunters brought. The group moved away from the lip of the cave, out of the cold winds and into the fire-flickering, smoky interior.

At first the People's home looked like nothing so much as an army encampment. A row of tents made from skins stood with their backs to the cave's entrance like a herd of animals huddled against the wind. Beyond these, sheltered by them, was a central area where a large fire burned in a depression in the floor, a natural limestone hall, low-roofed but wide. The few women who had remained there tending the flames now looked up, smiling and calling out at the hunters' return.

The rest of the People were much like the men with whom he had traveled, sturdy and small, with features that but for the pronounced brows and heavy jaws were nothing like the caveman caricatures he had seen in cartoons. They dressed in rough furs; many wore bits of bone or stone hung on cords of sinew, but there was nothing like the jewelry that bedecked even the least modernized tribes of Paul's era. Most of the younger children were naked, bodies rubbed with fat that gleamed in the firelight as they peered from the tent doorways, shiny little creatures that reminded him of Victorian illustrations of gnomes and brownies.

There was surprisingly little ceremony over the hunters' return, although Runs Far had told him they had been out for days. The men greeted their families and loved ones, touching them with probing fingers as though making certain that they were real, and occasionally someone rubbed his face against someone else's, but there was no kissing as Paul knew it, no hand clasps or hugging. Paul himself was clearly mentioned several times—he saw some of the hunters gesturing at him, as though to illustrate what a strange adventure it had been—but he was not introduced to anyone, nor was there any clear hierarchy that he could see. About two dozen adults seemed to make the cave their home, and not quite half that many children.

Even as some of the People exclaimed over the elk meat, others began preparing it in an extremely businesslike manner. Two of the women picked up long sticks and swept a portion of the firepit clear, pushing the burning logs to one side and exposing a floor of flat stones. They then spread several portions of the meat across these heated stones; within moments, the smell of cooking flesh began to fill the cavern.

Paul found himself a spot in the corner, out of the way. It was much warmer here in the cave, but still cold, and he sat with his skins pulled tight around him, watching the quick return of normal life; within a few moments after the hunting party's arrival, only the hunters themselves were not busy with something. Paul guessed that on other nights, they, too, would be at work, making new weapons and repairing the old ones, but tonight they had returned from a long, successful trip and could wait for the victors' rewards, the first portions of the kill.

One of the women lifted a sizable chunk of flesh from the fire with a stick, placed it on a piece of bark, and carried it like an offering to Runs Far. He lifted it to his mouth and took a bite and grinned his approval, but instead of finishing his meal he sawed the meat in half with his knife, then rose and carried the bark platter away from the fire toward one of the tents. No one else seemed to pay any attention but Paul was intrigued. Was he taking food to a sick wife or child? An aged parent?

Runs Far stayed inside the tent for long moments; when he came out, he was putting the last of the meat into his own mouth, chewing vigorously with his broad jaws. It was impossible to guess what had just happened.

A presence at Paul's elbow suddenly caught his attention. A little girl stood beside him, staring expectantly. At least, he thought it was a girl, although the boys were just as shaggy-haired, and positive identification was made difficult by the kirtle of fur around the child's waist. "What's your name?" he asked.

She shrieked with gleeful terror and ran away. Several other children pulled free of the general hubbub to chase her, laughing and calling in high voices like marsh birds. Moments later, another, larger shadow fell across him.

"Do not speak to the child." Birdcatcher looked angry, but Paul thought he saw something like naked panic just beneath the man's scowl. "She is not for you."

Paul shook his head, not understanding, but the other only turned and walked away.

Does he think I'm interested in her sexually? Or is it this Land of the Dead thing? Perhaps Birdcatcher thought he meant to take the girl away, back to some death-realm beyond the frozen river.

That's me, the Grim Reaper of the Pleistocene. Paul lowered his head and closed his eyes, suddenly as tired as he had ever been.

There had been a woman in his dream, and flowering plants, and sun streaming through a dusty window, but it was all disappearing now, pouring away like water down the plughole. Paul shook his head and his eyes fluttered. Runs Far was standing over him, saying something he could not at first understand.

The hunter prodded him again, gently. "Riverghost. Riverghost, you must come."

"Come where?"

"Dark Moon says you must come and talk." The hunt leader seemed excited in a way Paul had not seen before, almost childlike. "Come now."

Paul allowed himself to be coaxed to his feet, then followed Runs Far toward the tent where the hunter had taken the first cooked meat of the slaughtered elk. Paul thought he would be led inside, but Runs Far gestured for him to wait. The hunter ducked through the flap, then reappeared a few moments later, leading a tiny shape wrapped in a thick fur robe out into the firelight.

The old woman paused and looked Paul up and down, then extended her arm, the invitation—although it was more like a command—very clear. Paul stepped forward and let her clutch his forearm with hard, skinny fingers, then the three of them moved slowly toward the cookfire. As they led the woman to a rounded stone near the warmest part of the blaze, Paul saw Birdcatcher staring at him, holding the arm of the little girl who had approached Paul earlier. His grip was so tight she was squirming in pain.

"Bring water to me," the old woman told Runs Far as she slowly settled herself on the rock. When he had gone, she turned to Paul. "What is your name?"

Paul was not sure what kind of answer she wanted. "The men of the People call me Riverghost."

She nodded her satisfaction, as though he had passed an examination. Dirt lay in the wrinkles of her seamed face, and her white hair was so thin the shape of her head could be clearly seen, but the forcefulness of her personality and the respect in which the People held her was quite clear. She raised a clawlike hand and carefully touched his.

"I am called Dark Moon. That is the name they call me."

Paul nodded, although he was not quite clear why she seemed to attach so much importance to this exchange of information. *This isn't my world,* he reminded himself. *To primitive people, there's magic in names.*

"Are you from the Land of the Dead?" she asked. "Tell me your true story."

"I . . . I am from a place very far away. The People—the hunters—saved me when I was in the river and was drowning." He hesitated, then fell silent. He did not think that he could make her understand his true story since he did not understand it himself, even the parts he remembered clearly.

She pursed her lips. "And what do you mean for us? What do you bring to the People? What will you take away?"

"I hope I will take nothing from you, except the food and shelter you give to me." It was hard to talk simply without sounding like an Indian chief in a bad American Western. "I came from the river with nothing, so I have no gifts."

Dark Moon looked at him again, and this time the appraisal went on for some time. Runs Far returned with a cup made from what looked like a section of animal horn; the old woman drank enthusiastically, then turned her gaze back to Paul. "I must think," she said at last. "I do not understand what you do in the world." She turned and patted Runs Far on his shoulder, then abruptly raised her voice to address the People at large. "Hunters have returned. They have brought back food."

The others, who had been pretending with almost civilized discretion not to be listening to her conversation with Paul, now raised a few ragged shouts of approval, although most were busy chewing.

"Tonight is a good night." Dark Moon slowly spread her arms. The weight of the fur robe seemed too great for her tiny frame to support. "Tonight I will tell a story, and the one called Riverghost will think kindly of the People, who have given him food."

The tribesfolk came closer, those nearest arranging themselves near Dark Moon's feet. Many took the chance to study Paul carefully. He saw fear and concern in most faces, but it was only Birdcatcher in whom it seemed to have an edge that might become violent. The rest of the People looked at him as civilized shoppers might watch a street crazy who had happened through the store's front door, but as yet had shown no signs of screaming or knocking things about.

Some of the smaller children had already fallen asleep, worn out by excitement and bellies full of cooked flesh, but their parents and guardians simply carried them to the gathering, unwilling to miss something so clearly important. Birdcatcher, his distrust not sufficient to keep him away, stood on the outside of the circle, and though he still glared at Paul, he was listening, too.

"I will tell you of the days that are gone." Dark Moon's voice took on a kind of singsong cadence, and even Paul could feel the satisfaction of a familiar ritual beginning. *"These are days before your fathers' fathers and their fathers walked in the world."*

As she paused, he felt an unexpected thrill. Despite his reservations, his skepticism, it was hard to huddle in this cold cave and not to feel that he was close to one of the sourcepools of story—that he was about to be the privileged auditor of one of the oldest of all tales.

"Then, in those days," Dark Moon began, *"everything was dark."*

There was no light, and there was no warmth. The cold was everywhere, and First Man and First Woman suffered. They went to the other First People, all the Animal People, and asked them how to keep warm.

Long Nose told them to grow hair all over their bodies, as he had done. Because he was so large, First Man and First Woman thought he must be very old and very wise, but as hard as they tried, they could not grow enough hair to stay warm. So First Man killed great Long Nose and stole his hairy skin, and for a little while they did not suffer.

But soon the world grew colder, and even the skin they had taken from Long Nose was not enough to keep them warm. They went to Cave Dweller and asked her how they might keep warm.

"You must find a deep hole in the mountain," said Cave Dweller, "and there you can live as I live, safe from the wind-that-bites, and raise a family of cubs."

But First Man and First Woman could not find a hole of their own, so they killed Cave Dweller and stole her hole for themselves, and for a little while they did not suffer.

Still the world grew colder. First Man and First Woman huddled in their cave and pulled their skins tight around them, but knew that they would soon die.

One day, First Woman saw tiny Naked Tail running across the cave. She caught him in her hands and was going to eat him, for she was very hungry, but Naked Tail told her that if she did not swallow him, he would tell her something important. She called over First Man to hear what Naked Tail would say.

"I will tell you of a powerful secret," Naked Tail said. "Yellow Eyes, who lives out there in the great cold and dark, has a magical thing, a thing that bends in the softest wind and yet does not blow away, that has no teeth but can eat a hard tree branch. This magic is a warm thing that keeps the cold away, and it is what makes the eyes of old Yellow Eyes shine brightly out in the darkness."

"What does this matter to us?" said First Man. "He will never let us have this magical warm thing."

"We can play a trick on him and steal it," said First Woman. "Did we not take Long Nose's skin and Cave Dweller's house?"

First Man did not speak. He was frightened of Yellow Eyes, who was cruel and strong, and much more clever than Long Nose or Cave Dweller. First Man

*knew that the broken, gnawed bones of many of the other Animal People lay
outside Yellow Eyes' den. But he listened while First Woman told him the
thoughts that were in her belly.*

*"I will do what you say," he said at last. "If I do not try, we will die in any
case, and the darkness will have us."*

The flames wavered as a gust of cold air scythed through the room.
Paul shivered and pulled his furs more tightly around him. He was
becoming drowsy, and it was hard to think clearly. Everything was so
strange. He had heard this story somewhere, hadn't he? But how
could that be?

The cave grew darker, until the glow of the embers turned all the
listeners into red-lit ghosts. Dark Moon's cracked voice rose and fell
as she sang the song of stolen fire.

*First Man went to the place of many bones where Yellow Eyes lived. He saw
the bright eyes from a long way away, but Yellow Eyes saw him even sooner.*

*"What do you want?" he asked First Man. "If you do not tell me, I will
crush you in my jaws." Yellow Eyes showed his terrible teeth to First Man.*

*"I have come to make a bargain with you," said First Man. "I wish to trade
for the warm, bright thing that you have."*

*"And what do you have to trade?" asked Yellow Eyes. His eyes were shining
a little more brightly.*

*"A child," said First Man. "It is so cold that he will die anyway if we do not
have some of your warm, bright thing."*

*Yellow Eyes licked his lips and clicked his terrible teeth. "You would give me
your child for a little of my fire?"*

First Man nodded his head.

*"Then put the child where I can see him," said Yellow Eyes, "and I will give
you what you ask for."*

*First Man reached into his skins and took out the child made of mud which
First Woman had shaped with her clever hands. He set this child down before
Yellow Eyes.*

"He is very quiet," Yellow Eyes said.

"He is frightened of your teeth," First Man told him.

*"That is good," said Yellow Eyes, and opened his jaws wide. "Reach into my
mouth and you will find what you asked for."*

*First Man was very frightened, but he came close to the mouth of Yellow
Eyes, which had the smell of death.*

"Reach into my mouth," said Yellow Eyes again.

*First Man stretched his arm deep into the mouth of Yellow Eyes, past the
terrible teeth and down the long throat. At last he touched something very hot
and cupped his hand around it.*

"Take only a little," said Yellow Eyes.

First Man withdrew his hand. In it was something yellow that bent in the wind but did not blow away, that had no mouth but began to bite his skin even as he held it. First Man looked at Yellow Eyes and saw that he was sniffing the child made of mud, and so First Man began to run, the warm yellow thing held close in his hand.

"This is not your child!" screamed Yellow Eyes in anger. "You have tricked me, First Man!"

Yellow Eyes began to chase him. First Man ran as fast as he could, but heard his enemy coming closer and closer. The warm magic thing was very heavy in his hand and was biting his skin, so First Man threw it away up into the air. It flew into the sky and stuck there, and it covered the world in light. Yellow Eyes screamed again and ran faster, but First Man reached the cave where he lived with First Woman and ran inside. They pushed a stone into the opening so that Yellow Eyes could not get at them.

"You have cheated me, and I will not forget," shouted Yellow Eyes. "And when a true child comes to you, I will take it from you."

First Man lay on the floor of the cave, with no strength left in his body. First Woman saw that a little of the warm, bright thing still stuck to his hand. She brushed it off with a stick, and as it began to eat the stick it grew and warmed the whole cave. That was fire.

Ever after, First Man's fingers were not all the same, as with the other Animal People. One finger on each hand was twisted sideways from carrying the hot fire, and that is why all First Man's and First Woman's children have hands that are different from the Animal People.

The fire that was thrown into the sky became the sun, and when it shines, Yellow Eyes and his people hide from its light because it reminds them of how First Man tricked them. But when it grows small and the world is dark, Yellow Eyes comes out again, and his eye is the moon that stares down as he looks for the child First Man and First Woman promised to him. Every night since the days your fathers' fathers and their fathers walked in the world, he hunts for the children of First Man and First Woman.

Dark Moon's voice had become very still, a thin whisper that rode above the breathless silence in the cave.

"He will hunt for them even when your children's children and their children walk in the world."

He could hear a great, slow pounding, the ticking of a titan clock or the footfalls of an approaching giant, but he could see nothing but darkness, could feel nothing but icy wind. He had no hands or body, no way to protect himself from whatever lurked in the black emptiness here on the edge of all things.

"*Paul.*" The voice in his ear was soft as feathered flight, but his heart thumped as though it had shouted.

"*Is that you?*" His own voice made no sound outside his head, or he no longer had the ears to hear himself speak.

Something was beside him in the dark. He could sense it, although he did not know how. He could feel it, a swift-hearted, tenuous presence.

"*Paul, you must come back to us. You must come back to me.*"

And as though she had never left his dreams, but had only vanished from his waking mind, he could see her now in memory, could summon up the image of her absurd but beautiful winged form, her sad eyes. She had crouched, trapped in that golden cage, while he had stood helplessly on the other side of the bars. He had left her to that terrible grinding thing, the Old Man.

"*Who are you?*"

Her presence grew a little stronger, a barely-felt vibration of impatience. "*I am no one, Paul. I don't know who I am—don't care anymore. But I know that I need you, that you must come.*"

"*Come where? You said 'come to us.' To whom?*"

"*You ask too many questions.*" It was spoken sadly, not angrily. "*I do not have the answers you wish. But I know what I know. If you come to me, then we will both know.*"

"*Are you Vaala? Are you the same woman I met?*"

Again the impatience. "*These things are unimportant. It is so hard for me to be here, Paul—so hard! Listen! Listen, and I will tell you everything I know. There is a place, a black mountain, that reaches to the sky—that covers up the stars. You must find it. That is where all your answers are.*"

"*How? How do I get there?*"

"*I don't know.*" A pause. "*But I might know, if you can find me.*"

Something was interfering with his concentration, a vague but insistent pain, a sense of pressure that Paul could not ignore. The dream was collapsing from its own weight. As he felt it beginning to fall away, he struggled to cling to her, that voice in the emptiness.

"*Find you? What does that mean?*"

"*You must come to me . . . to us. . . .*" She was growing faint now, barely a presence at all, a whisper traveling down a long corridor.

"*Don't leave me! How do I find you?*" The vague discomfort was growing sharper, commanding his attention. "*Who are you?*"

From an incomprehensible distance, a murmur: "*I am . . . a shattered mirror. . . .*"

*   *   *

He sat up, his throat tight, a pain like a knifepoint of fire in his belly. She was gone again! His link to sanity—but how could someone or something so clearly mad lead him back to reality? Or did he only dream. . . ?

The pain grew sharper. His eyes adjusted to the darkness, to the glow of dim coals, and he saw the shapeless shadow crouched over him. Some hard, sharp thing was pressed against his stomach. Paul dropped his hand and felt the cold stone spearhead buried deep in his fur robe, a warm slickness of blood already matting the hairs. If it pressed in an inch farther, it would pierce through to his guts.

Birdcatcher leaned close, sour meat on his breath. The spearpoint jabbed a little deeper.

"You are my blood enemy, Riverghost. I will send you back to the Land of the Dead."

First:

THE
SECRET RIVER

. . . For here, millions of mixed shades and shadows, drowned dreams, somnambulisms, reveries; all that we call lives and souls, lie dreaming, dreaming, still; tossing like slumberers in their beds; the ever-rolling waves but made so by their restlessness.

—Herman Melville, *Moby Dick*

CHAPTER 1

Deep Waters

NETFEED/NEWS: Schoolkids Need Waiver To Avoid Helmet
(visual: children trying on helmets)
VO: Children in Pine Station, a suburban town in Arkansas, must either
wear a safety helmet during their entire school day or their parents must sign
a waiver saying they will not sue for damages should their child be injured.
(visual: Edlington Gwa Choi, Pine Station School Dist. Superintendent)
GWA CHOI: "It's quite simple. We can't afford the coverage any more. They
make nice, comfortable helmets now—the kids will hardly even notice
they've got them on. We've done tests. And if they don't want them, that's
okay too, as long as their folks take responsibility. . . ."

A beetle the size of a panel truck was bumping slowly along the shoreline, the baboon beside her was singing, and Renie was dying for a cigarette.

"*And we go down,*"

!Xabbu chanted in an almost tuneless voice,

"*Down to the water.*
Ah!
Where the fish are hiding,
Hiding and laughing . . ."

* * *

"What's that?" Renie watched the beetle hunch across the uneven stones of the beach with the mindless forward drive of one of those drone robots working to tame the surfaces of Mars and the moon. "That song you're singing."

"My uncle used to sing it. It helped him be patient while waiting for fish to pass over the rock dam so we could catch them." !Xabbu scratched at his baboon pelt in a fastidious manner far more human than simian.

"Ah." Renie frowned. She was having trouble concentrating, and for once even !Xabbu's stories about his childhood in the Okavango Delta did not interest her.

If someone had told her that she would be transported to what was for all purposes a magical land, where history could be rewritten at a whim, or people could suddenly be shrunk to the size of poppy seeds, but that at least for this moment, her most pressing concern would have been the absence of cigarettes, she would have thought them mad. But it had been two harrowing days since she had smoked her last, and the momentary leisure of floating in midstream on a huge leaf that had once been a boat had finally given her a chance to notice what she was missing.

She pushed away from the leaf's curling edge. Better to do something, anything, than stand around obsessing like a chargehead with a fused 'can. And it was not as though everything was under control, she reflected. In fact, from the moment they had reached Atasco's virtual golden city, things had gone pretty damn poorly.

Across the expanse of water, the beetle had clambered up from the beach and was disappearing into a sea of grass stems, each as tall as the palm trees back home. She walked carefully toward the center of the leaf, leaving !Xabbu to sing his quiet fish-catching song and watch the now empty beach.

Sweet William's stage-vampire silhouette stood at the leaf's farthest edge, watching the opposite and more distant shoreline, but the others sat in the center with their backs against the huge center vein, a makeshift shelter of skin torn from the leaf's outer edge draped over their heads to protect them from the strong sun.

"How is he?" Renie asked Fredericks. The young man in quasi-medieval garb was still nursing his sick friend Orlando. Even limp in slumber, Orlando's muscular sim body was a poor indicator of the frail child who animated it.

"He's breathing better, I think." Fredericks said it with real emphasis, enough so that Renie instantly doubted him. She looked down at the curled figure, then squatted so she could touch his forehead. "That doesn't really work," Fredericks added, almost apologetically. "I mean, some things show up on these sims, some don't. Body temperatures don't seem to change much."

"I know. It's just . . . reflex, I guess." Renie sat back on her heels. "I'm sorry, but he doesn't look good at all." She had only so much strength, and she could not support any more hopeful untruths, even though the things Fredericks had told her about the real Orlando Gardiner tore at her heart. She made herself turn away. "And how are you, Martine. Any better?"

The French researcher, who wore the dark-skinned, dark-haired sim of a Temilúni peasant woman, mustered a very faint smile. "It is . . . it is easier to think, perhaps. A little. The pain of all this new imput is not quite so bad for me now. But . . ." She shook her head. "I have been blind in the world for a long time, Renie. I am not used to being blind here."

"What you mean, 'here'?" The warrior-robot sim belonged to a Goggleboy-type who called himself "T4b." Renie thought he was younger than he let on, maybe even as young as Orlando and Fredericks, and his sullen tone now only deepened her suspicions. "Thought nobody come here before. What's all that *fen* back at the last place if you been here?"

"I don't think that is what she meant . . ." began Quan Li.

"No, I have not been here," Martine said. "But online—plugged in. That has always been my world. But the . . . noise since I have come here, the overwhelming information . . . it makes it hard for me to hear or even think the way I am used to." She rubbed at her temples with slow, clumsy movements. "It is like fire in my head. Like insects."

"We don't need any more insects, God knows." Renie looked up as a distant but still unbelievably large dragonfly skimmed the shoreline and started out across the river, loud as an ancient propeller plane. "Is there anything we can do, Martine?"

"No. Perhaps I will learn to . . . to live better with it when some time has passed."

"So what *are* we going to do?" Renie said at last. "We can't just drift with the current, literally or figuratively. We have no idea what we're looking for, where we're going, or if we're even heading in the right direction. Does anyone have any ideas?" She looked briefly at Florimel, who like Martine and Quan Li wore a Temilúni sim, and wondered when this woman would make her feelings known; but Florimel remained unsettlingly silent, as she had been most of the time since their shared escape had begun. "If we just wait . . . well, Sellars said there would be people coming after us." Renie looked around at the odd assortment of sims. "And we certainly are hard to miss."

"What do you suggest, dearie?" Sweet William was picking his way across the irregular surface of the leaf toward them, feathers bobbing; Renie wondered whether he wasn't finding all that simulated black leather a bit uncomfortable in this tropical warmth. "Don't get me wrong, all this can-do attitude is most inspiring—you must have been a Girl Guide. Should we build an outboard motor out of our fingernail clippings or something?"

She smiled sourly. "That would be better than bobbing along waiting for someone to come and catch us. But I was hoping someone might come up with something a little more practical."

"I suppose you're right." William levered himself down beside her, his sharp knee poking her leg. Renie thought he had changed a little since they had fled Atasco's palace, that his arrogance had softened. Even his strong northern English accent seemed a little less pronounced, as though it were as much an affectation as his death-clown sim. "So what do we do, then?" he asked. "We can't paddle. I suppose we could swim to shore—that would give you all a laugh, watching me swim—but then what? I don't think much of having to dodge yon overgrown buggy-wuggies."

"Are they big, or are we small?" asked Fredericks. "I mean, they could just be monster bugs, you know, like in that Radiation Weekend simworld."

Renie narrowed her eyes, watching the shoreline. A few flying shapes, smaller than the dragonflies, were hovering erratically at the water's edge. "Well, the trees are miles high, the grains of sand on the beach are as big as your head, and we're riding in a leaf that used to be a boat. What do you think? My guess would be 'We small.' "

Fredericks gave her a quick, hurt look, then returned his attention to his sleeping friend. Sweet William, too, glanced at Renie with something like surprise. "You've got a bit of a bite, don't you, love?" he said, impressed.

Renie felt shamed, but only slightly. These people were acting like this was some kind of adventure game, like everything was bound to turn out all right, that at the very worst they might earn a low score. "This isn't going to just end with a polite 'Game Over,' you know," she said, continuing the thought out loud. "I felt and saw a man die trying to break into this network. And whether what happened to the Atascos took place online or off, they're just as dead." She heard her voice rising and struggled to control herself. "This is not a game. My brother is dying—maybe dead. I'm sure you all have your own worries, too, so let's get on with it."

There was a moment's silence. T4b, the spike-studded robot warrior, ended it. "We ears, wo'. You talk."

Renie hesitated, the weight of their problems suddenly too much to bear. She didn't know these people, didn't have answers for them— didn't even truly understand what questions to ask. And she was also tired of pushing these strangers forward. They were an odd group, showing little of the initiative that Sellars had ascribed to them, and of the few people she trusted in the world only !Xabbu was truly here, since Martine was strangely transformed, no longer the quiet, ultra-competent presence she had been.

"Look," Renie said, "I agree we don't want to land if we can help it. Even the insects are as big as dinosaurs, and insects may not be the only animals out there. We haven't seen any birds yet, but that doesn't mean there aren't any, and we would make about a single bite for a seagull."

"So what can we do besides drift?" asked Quan Li.

"Well, I'm not saying we can make an outboard motor, but I'm not ready to give up on paddling, or maybe even making some kind of sail. What if we pulled up more of this skin from the leaf," she indicated the tattered awning over their heads, "and used that?"

"You cannot have a sail without a mast," said Florimel heavily. "Anyone knows that."

Renie raised an eyebrow: The silent woman apparently did know how to talk, after all. "Is that really true? Couldn't we make something that would at least catch some wind? What are those things they use on shuttle rockets—drag chutes? Why couldn't we make a reverse drag chute and use some of the thinner veins to tie it down?"

"I think Renie's ideas are very good," said Quan Li.

"Oh, she's a regular Bobby Wells, all right," Sweet William said. "But how long is it going to take us? We'll probably starve to death first."

"We don't have to eat, do we?" Renie looked around; the sim faces were suddenly serious. "I mean, don't you all—haven't you all arranged something? How could you go online for this long without some kind of feeding system in place?"

"I'm getting fed on an intravenous drip, probably." Fredericks suddenly sounded lost, miserable. "In that hospital."

A quick poll revealed that Sweet William's question had been largely rhetorical. All the party claimed they had some kind of resources that would allow them to be self-sufficient. Even William parted the curtain of his fabulous glamour long enough to reveal: "I'll probably be all right for a week or so, pals and chums, but then I'll have to hope someone looks in on me." But everyone was strangely reticent about their offline lives, rekindling Renie's frustration.

"Look, we're in a life-or-death situation," she said finally. "We all must have important reasons for being here. We have to trust each other."

"Don't take it personal," said William, grimacing. "I'm just not having any frigging Canterbury-let's-all-tell-our-Tales. Nobody has a right to my life. You want *my* tale, you have to earn it."

"What is it you want to know?" demanded Florimel. Her Temilúni sim displayed resentful anger quite convincingly. "We are all some kind of cripples here, Ms. Sulaweyo. You, him, me, all of us. Why else would that Sellars man choose us—and why do you think we are all prepared for a long period online? Who else would spend so much time on the net?"

"Speak for yourself," spat William. "*I* have a life, and it doesn't include a Save the World Fantasy Weekend. I just want to get out of here and go home."

"I wasn't prepared," said Fredericks mournfully. "That's why my folks have got me in a hospital. Orlando wasn't expecting this either. We kinda came here by surprise." He grew thoughtful. "I wonder where he is—I mean, his body?"

Renie closed her eyes, struggling to stay calm. She wished !Xabbu would come back from the leaf's edge, but he was still watching the shoreline slide by. "We have more important things to do than argue," she said at last. "Fredericks, you said you tried to go offline and it was very painful."

The young man nodded his head. "It was horrible. Just horrible. You can't believe how bad it was." He shuddered and crossed his arms in front of his chest, hugging himself.

"Could you communicate with anyone, Fredericks? Did you talk to your parents?"

"Call me Sam, would you?"

"Sam. Could you talk?"

He thought about it. "I don't think so. I mean, I was screaming, but I couldn't really hear myself, now that I think about it. Not when I was . . . there. It hurt so bad! I don't think I could have said a word— you just don't know how bad it was. . . ."

"I do know," said Florimel, but there was little sympathy in her voice. "I went offline, too."

"Really? What happened?" Renie asked. "Did you find a way to do it yourself?"

"No. I was . . . removed, just as he was." She said it flatly. "It happened before I reached Temilún. But he is right. The pain was indescribable. Even if there were a way to do it, I would kill myself before having that pain again."

Renie sat back and sighed. The vast orange disk of the sun had dropped behind the forest a little while before, and now the winds were freshening. A large insectoid shape flew erratically overhead. "But how can you not find your neurocannula? I mean, maybe you can't see it, but surely you can feel it?"

"Don't be naive, dearie," said William. "The information going from our fingers to our brains is no more real than what's coming in at our eyes and ears. That's what a neural shunt *does*. What have you got that's any better?"

"It's not better. In fact, it's worse." Renie smiled in spite of herself. "My equipment is old—the kind of thing you wouldn't be caught dead using. And because it's simple, I can just pull it off."

William glowered and said, "Well, hooray for Hollywood." Renie had no idea what he meant. "What good does that do the rest of us?"

"I could go offline! I could get help!"

"What makes you think you wouldn't get the torture-chamber effect yourself?" demanded William.

"Let her go," growled T4b. "Let her anything. Just want out this far crash place, me."

"Because my interface doesn't connect to my nervous system like yours does." She reached up to her face, searching for the reassuring, if invisible, contours of her mask, fondled many times in past days. But this time her fingers touched nothing but skin.

"And that brother you keep talking about," said Florimel. "Was *his* nervous system connected directly to a system? I do not think so."

"Renie?" Quan Li asked. "You are looking unhappy. Would you like us not to talk about your poor brother?"

"I can't feel it anymore." The twilit sky seemed to press down on her. She was lost and defenseless in the most alien place imaginable. "Jesus Mercy, I can't feel my mask. It's gone."

FOR a while he had been able to follow the conversation, but soon Orlando found himself sinking back down, the murmur of his companions' voices no more intelligible than the slapping of small waves against the side of their strange craft.

He felt weightless but still strangely heavy. He was motionless, stretched at Fredericks' side, but at the same time he was moving somehow, slipping down through the very fabric of the leaf, the waters rising blood-warm around him. He was sinking into the deeps. And as it had been not long ago, when he had shared the raft with Fredericks, he found he did not care.

In this vision, this trance, the water-world was all light, but a light stretched and bent and split by the water itself, so that he seemed to be passing through the heart of a vast, flawed jewel. As he sank deeper through the cloudy river, odd glimmering shapes wriggled past him, creatures whose own self-created radiance was brighter than the refracted glow of the sun. They did not seem to notice him, but went their apparently random, zigzagging ways, leaving an afterimage burned across his bemused gaze like particles mapped on their path through a bubble chamber.

They were not fish, though. They were light—pure light.

I'm dreaming again. The idea came to him gradually, as though he had begun to solve the central riddle of a mystery story that no longer interested him. *Not drowning, dreaming.*

As he sank deeper, ever deeper, the light grew fainter and the pressure increased. He wondered if this was how death would feel when it came at last, a gentle, helpless descent. Perhaps he truly was dying this time—he was certainly finding it hard to be interested in all the *living* everyone else seemed intent on doing. Perhaps the end was nothing to be feared, after all. He hoped that was true, but he had watched and studied death for so long, trying to learn its every guise so that he would be prepared for it when it came, that he could not fully trust it.

Death had been waiting for him as long as he could remember—not the far-off death of most people, a sad but necessary appointment that would have to be made one day, when life had been pursued to satisfaction and everything important had been arranged, but a very present death, as patient and persistent as a bill collector, a death that loitered outside his door every day, waiting for that one moment's distraction that would allow it to get its bony foot across the threshold. . . .

A shadow impinged on Orlando's downward-drifting reverie, and his swift clench of fear at its appearance told him that, expecting it or not, he was still not resigned to death's cold incursion. But if this was death that had come to him at last, a dark silhouette in the deepest waters, it had come in the form of . . . a lobster, or a crab, or some other many-jointed thing. In fact, the shadow seemed to be . . .

. . . a bug?

Orlando. Boss, I don't know if you can hear me. I'll keep trying, but I'm running out of time. If they catch me, I'm history.

He could see the thing slowly waving its jointed legs, movement picked out in the faint gleam from its circle of eyestalks. He tried to speak, but could not. The water was pressing on his chest like the weight of a giant's hand.

Listen, boss, last time you told me "Atasco." I think that's what you said—it was subvocal. I've played it back thirty times, done every kind of analysis I could. But I don't know what it means, boss. There was a bunch of stuff on the nets about someone named that, tons of stuff. He got killed in South America. That guy? You gotta give me some more information, boss.

Orlando felt a vague stirring of interest, but it was only a twitch beneath an immensely heavy blanket. What did this many-legged thing want of him? He was trying to drift downward in peace.

The crab-thing crawled onto his chest. He could feel its blunted legs only very faintly, as the fairy-tale princess must have dreamily sensed the sleep-disturbing pea. He wanted to shake it off, to bring back the heavy quiet again, but the thing would not go.

Your parents are going to turn me off, boss. They won't turn off the household system because they're scared to unplug you again after your vital signs dropped so bad, but they're going to have me pulled. I had to sneak my external body into your suitcase, boss, but it's only a matter of time until someone in this hospital notices me.

Orlando tried to speak again. He felt inaudible sounds form and die in his throat.

See, the only way I can resist a shutdown is if you order me to, boss. I'm just a psAI, an agent—your parents have authority unless you tell me different, but I can't pick you up online at all. Where are you?

The effort of resisting the downward tug was too much. Orlando felt a great lethargy sweep through him, a warm, compelling heaviness. The voice of the crab-thing was growing fainter.

Boss, listen to me. I can't help you if you don't help me. You have to tell me to save myself or I can't do it—they'll drez me. If you tell me to, I can pull all my stuff and hide in the system somewhere, even move to another system. But you have to tell me, boss. . . .

He wished no one ill, not even a bug. "Go ahead, then," he murmured. "Save yourself . . ."

The voice was gone, but something about its urgency lingered. Orlando wondered what could possibly have been so important. As he considered, he felt himself drifting ever downward. The abyss, dark and enveloping, lay waiting beneath him. The light was only a faint glimmer far above, shrinking every moment like a dying star.

Renie's shock and horror was such that it was hard to understand what the others were saying. The dreamlike nature of the whole experience had just taken a savage turn into an even more threatening unreality.

"Look, love, don't act so frigging surprised." Sweet William hunched his bony shoulders so that, feathers aquiver, he looked more than ever like a strange jungle bird. "It's some kind of autohypnosis or something."

"What do you mean?" asked Quan Li. The old woman had put an arm around Renie's shoulders when the tears, so unexpected, had suddenly begun to flow.

I can't feel the oxygen mask, but I can feel tears on my cheeks—naked cheeks. What's going on here? Renie shook her head and sniffed, ashamed to have lost control in front of these near-strangers, but if she could no longer feel those physical things that connected her to RL, then she could not leave this horror story, no matter how bad it got. *I'm not plugged in like the others. How can this be happening?*

"I don't know if autohypnosis is the right word. Post-hypnotic suggestion—you know what I mean. Like what stage magicians do."

"But who could do such thing? And how?" demanded Florimel. "It makes no sense." Her anger sounded like contempt, and Renie felt herself even more disgusted that she had cried in front of this woman.

"Maybe that's the same as the pain when I got unplugged," Fredericks offered. "But whatever it was, it didn't *hurt* imaginary. Imaginarily. You know what I mean. It hurt *majorly*."

"See, that would make sense, too," said William. "Something piggybacked on the carrier signal, a super-powerful subliminal. If they can mess about with our brains at all—and they *must* be able to mess about with people's brains, otherwise we wouldn't have come here looking for answers in the first place—I'll bet they can do it without us realizing it."

Renie wiped her eyes and blew her nose, trying to ignore the ridiculous, impossible aspects of the exercise. A few more insects droned unsteadily past overhead, each the relative size of a small car. The bugs seemed uninterested in the tiny humans talking so urgently below—which, Renie decided, was something at least to be grateful for.

"So what, then?" she said out loud. "I'm only imagining that I'm wiping my nose, is that what you're saying? Just like Fredericks here only imagined that he was having electrical shocks run through his spine?"

"Have you got a better explanation, chuck?"

She narrowed her eyes. "How come you know so much about all this. . . ?"

"Renie!" !Xabbu called from the leaf's edge. "There are many more of these insects near the water's edge, and they are moving out onto the river in a crowd. I have not seen this kind of insect before. Are they dangerous, do you think?"

Renie squinted at one of the round-bodied creatures as it rumbled past the leaf. Although its wings were strong and shiny, the rest of it had a curiously unformed look, legs awkward, head lumpish.

"Whatever they are, they are new-hatched," pronounced Florimel. "They eat nothing as large as us, I am sure, if they eat at all. They are looking to mate—see how they dance!" She pointed to a pair who performed a swooping *pas-de-deux* less than a hundred relative yards from where she and the others sat.

"Are you a biologist?" Renie asked. Florimel shook her head, but did not elaborate. Before Renie could decide whether to ask another question, Fredericks began waving his hands as though he had burned them.

"Orlando isn't breathing!"

"What? Are you sure?" Renie scrambled toward the still form. Fredericks was kneeling beside his friend, tugging at his thick-muscled arm in an effort to wake him.

"I'm sure, I'm sure! I just looked down and he wasn't breathing!"

"It's a sim," Sweet William said, but his voice was sharp with sudden fear. "Sims don't need to breathe."

"He was breathing okay before," said Fredericks wildly. "I watched him. His chest was moving. He was breathing, but now he isn't!"

Even as Renie reached Orlando's side, she was roughly shoved out of the way by Florimel, who knelt over the bulky form and began to push with brutal force on his chest.

"It's a *sim,* damn it!" cried William. "What are you doing?"

"If he has tactors, this will translate, at least a little," Florimel said between clenched teeth. "Giving him air will not—or I would give you something useful to do with that open mouth."

"Sorry." William waggled his long fingers helplessly. "Christ, sorry."

"Don't let him die!" Fredericks bounced up and down beside her.

"If he is in a hospital in real life, like you are," Florimel gasped, "then they will be able to do more for him than I can. But if his heart has stopped, we may be able to keep him alive until someone reaches him."

!Xabbu stood on his hind legs beside Renie, one hand on her shoulder. Time seemed suspended, each second achingly long. Renie's stomach contracted on cold nothing. It was terrible to watch Orlando's sim, head wagging limply as Florimel pounded on its chest, but she could not turn away. One of the hatchling insects buzzed loudly past just a few yards from the leaf's rim, and Renie bitterly wished she was of a size again to swat it.

"The noise is getting worse," said Martine suddenly, as though oblivious to what was happening. "The noise in my head."

"We can't do anything about the bugs now," Renie said. "You'll just have to ignore it. This boy may be dying!"

"No, it's . . . it's very loud." Martine's voice rose. "Ah! Oh, God, help me, it's . . . something is . . ."

The leaf abruptly lurched upward, as though some great fist had punched it from below. Renie and !Xabbu and the others found themselves floating in the air, weightless at the top of the sudden rise; for a brief instant, their eyes met in astonishment, then the leaf dropped back down to the surface of the river again and they scrabbled to maintain their balance.

Before they could speak a word, a vast shining shape, big as the prow of a submarine, rose from the water beside the floating leaf. It was a fish, hallucinatory in its gigantism, water streaming from its glossy, spotted back, its flat, stupid eye wider than Renie was tall. A pink cathedral miracle of flesh and cartilage was visible for an instant down the titan gullet. As the leaf rocked violently in the foaming waves of its emergence, the mouth snapped shut like a cannon crash. The hatchling insect disappeared. The fish fell back into the fountaining river.

The first waves had just spun the leaf around, sending Renie and the others tumbling across its uneven surface, when a monstrous dark shape leaped over them, then smashed into the river on their far side, smacking a huge spume of water far up into the air. The leaf, caught between waves, tipped up on one side. Shrieking, Renie felt herself skidding down the veined surface toward the seething water. At the last moment, the bottom end of the leaf was batted upward by another surfacing shape. Renie crunched into the leaf's fibrous, curling edge and fell back, stunned and breathless.

More fish were popping their heads above the water to feed on the hovering insects, so that the whole surface of the river seemed to boil. Gouts of water splashed onto the leaf, instantly filling it waist-high. Renie struggled to pull herself upright, but the leaf was rocking too boldly.

"!Xabbu!" she screamed. She could dimly see human figures being tossed like bowling pins all around her, splashing and foundering, then being dashed to one side again, but no sign of the little man's baboon sim. A shard of memory pierced her: !Xabbu's terrible fear in the water at Mister J's, his childhood terror from a crocodile attack. She tried to call for him again, but a wave running horizontally across the leaf filled her mouth and knocked her down.

"Hold on!" someone shouted. A moment later the edge of the leaf was jerked upward again as though on a string, what had been horizontal rising in a split second to the vertical. Renie found herself hanging in midair, weightless again for a fractional instant, then she was tumbling downward into dark water. It closed on her, swallowed her, like the cold jaws of Leviathan itself.

HE was down deep, deep as he could imagine being. There was no light. There was no noise, not even the familiar, old-neighbor sounds of his own body. The stillness was absolute.

Orlando was waiting for something, although he did not know what. Someone was going to tell him an important fact, or something was going to change, and then everything would be clear. One thing he knew for certain, down in the depths, down in the dream of darkness, was that he himself had nothing left to do.

He had fought so long against the weakness, against the fear, against the pain of simply being different, of feeling other people's horror and pity like a smothering weight—fighting not to care, to smile and make a joke, to pretend that really he was just as good, just as happy, as everyone else. But he couldn't fight any more. There was no strength left in him. He could not sustain the weight of another struggle against the remorseless tide, could not imagine anything that could make him care.

And yet . . .

And yet a small voice, something that almost did not seem a part of him, was still alive within the great stillness he had become. A part of him that still *wanted,* that believed things, that cared, that . . . hoped?

No. Such a voice could only be a joke, a final terrible joke. Hope had been a meaningless word for so long, a doctor's word, his mother's word, his father's brave-smile word. He had given all that up, which took more strength than any of them could ever know. Hope was a word whose purpose had nothing to do with its meaning; rather, it was a word used to keep him going, a word that wasted what little time and strength he had, disrupting the small moments of serenity with false promises. But now he had turned away, abandoned the rough current of life struggling to maintain itself. He was in deep, enveloping darkness, and he finally had the strength to look at hope squarely and dismiss it.

But the ridiculous voice would not go away. It poked him and irritated him like an argument in the next room.

Don't give up, it said, adding cliché to insult. *Despair is the worst thing of all.*

No, he told the voice wearily, *hope without meaning is the worst thing. By far the worst thing.*

But what about the others? What about the people who need you? What about the great quest, a hero's quest, just like something out of the Middle Country, but real and incredibly important?

He had to give the voice credit for sheer persistence. And, if it was a part of himself, he had to admire his own capacity to play dirty.

No, what about me? he asked it. *Enough about all those other people and what they want. What about me?*

Yes, what about you? Who are you? What are you?

I'm a kid. I'm a sick kid, and I'm going to die.

But what are you until then?

Leave me alone.

Until then?

Alone.

Only you can decide that.

Alone . . .

Only you.

It would not give ground. It would not surrender. The voice was hopelessly outmatched, but still it would not do the gracious thing and capitulate.

With a weariness he could never have imagined even on the worst days of his illness, against all the weight of the peaceful, solitary deeps, Orlando surrendered to himself and to that small, stubborn voice.

He began to make his way back.

CHAPTER 2

Greasepaint

NETFEED/INTERACTIVES: GCN, HR. 7.0 (Eu, NAm)—"Escape!"
(visual: Zelmo being rushed into surgery)
VO: Nedra (Kamchatka T) and Zelmo (Cold Wells Carlson) have escaped
from Iron Island Academy again, but Lord Lubar (Ignatz Reiner) has
activated his Delayed Death-Touch on Zelmo. 8 supporting, 10 background
open, previous medical interactive pref'd for hospital strand. Flak to:
GCN.IHMLIFE.CAST

ONE of the tires on the Zippy-Zappy-Zoomermobile had gone flat, and they were all going to be late for King Sky Monkey's fabulous Pie in the Sky Picnic. Uncle Jingle, with help from the children, was trying to comfort a weeping Zoomer Zizz when the headache came back with vengeance.

She turned down the responsiveness of her facial tactors as the pain knifed through her—it didn't really matter if Uncle Jingle wore a fixed grin for a little longer than usual. She held her breath until she could tell how bad it would be. It wasn't as serious as some of the others. She'd probably live.

"Zoomer's still crying!" one of the younger children shrieked, overcome by the pathos of a weeping zebra in a bobble hat.

Unseen beneath the electronic mask, Uncle Jingle gritted her teeth and struggled to sound halfway normal. "But that's silly—he's being silly, isn't he, children? We'll help him fix the Zippy-Zappy-Zoomer-mobile!"

The roar of agreement made her wince again. God, what was this? It felt like a brain tumor or something, but the doctors had promised that her scans were fine.

"No-o-o-o!" wailed Zoomer. "It'll be t-t-t-oo l-late! No, no, no! We'll miss King Sky Monkey's picnic. And it's *all my fault!*" The striped snout belched forth another long, nerve-searing wail of woe.

Uncle Jingle rolled her eyes. This particular Zoomer Zizz, whoever he was—Uncle J. had a vague recollection that this shift it was the new guy in Southern California—was really pushing it with all this bellowing. What did he want, a spin-off of his own? It wasn't like his legs had fallen off. (That had happened to one of the other Zoomers in an episode, and that particular actor had shaped it into a charming comic turn.) The problem was, these new people didn't know how to do real improv. They all wanted to be stars, and wanted to end everything with a punchline. And they didn't understand anything about working with children.

The headache was getting worse, a pain behind her left eye like a hot needle. Uncle Jingle checked her time. Ten minutes to go. Tired and hurting, she could not take any more.

"I guess you're right, Zoomer. Besides, they probably wouldn't want a smelly old zebra at their picnic anyway, would they, kids?"

The child-chorus cheered, but only a little, unsure of where this was going.

"In fact, I guess we better just leave you here crying by the side of the road, Mister Stripey-Butt. We'll go to the picnic without you and have fun, fun, fun. But first, let's all look at that special party invitation that King Sky Monkey and Queen Cloud Cat sent to us! Let's look at that invitation right now, okay?" She cleared her throat suggestively. "Invitation-right-*now.*"

She held her breath, hanging on until one of the engineers caught the signal and played the invitation—a recorded segment featuring the royal court, an all-feline, all-simian singing and dancing extravaganza. Uncle Jingle pushed her panic button and an engineer's voice chirped in her ear.

"What's up, Miz P.?"

"Sorry. Sorry, I have to go off. I'm . . . I'm not feeling well."

"Well, you sure put the boot to old Zoomer. Maybe we can say you were trying to show him how silly he was being—you know, feeling sorry for himself."

"Certainly. Whatever. I'm sure Roland can think of something."

Roland McDaniel was the next Uncle Jingle in the rotation, already in harness and waiting to go; he would only be filling an extra few minutes before his regular slot.

"Chizz. You gonna be systems go for tomorrow?"

"I don't know. Yes, I'm sure I will." She clicked off, pulled the Uncle Jingle plug, and became Olga Pirofsky again. She undid the harness with shaking hands and let herself down, then stumbled to the bathroom where she vomited until there was nothing left in her stomach.

When she had cleaned herself up and put on water for tea, she went to the master bedroom to let out Misha. The little bat-eared dog stared at her from his seat on the bedspread, making it quite clear that her tardiness was not going to be easily forgiven.

"Don't look at me like that." She picked him up and tucked him into the crook of her arm. "Mummy's had a very bad day. Mummy's head hurts. Besides, you only had to wait an extra five minutes."

The tail did not yet wag, but Misha seemed to be considering the possibility of forgiveness.

She opened a seal-pac of dog food and squeezed it into his bowl, then put it on the floor. She watched him eat, experiencing the first thing resembling happiness she had felt since her workday had started. The water was not yet boiling, so she walked gingerly into the front room—her head was still throbbing, although the worst was past—and turned the radio on very quietly, a classical station out of Toronto. There was no wallscreen; a framed series of St. Petersburg's riverwalk and a large picture of the Oranienburgerstrasse Synagogue of Berlin filled the space where the screen had once been. Olga got quite enough of the modern world in her job. Even the radio was an antique, with a button on the side to scan stations and red digital numbers glowing on its face like the coals of a fire.

The whistle of the kettle brought her back to the kitchen. She turned off the halogen plate and poured the water into the cup on top of the spoonful of honey, then dropped in the strainer full of Darjeeling. The one time she had visited the studio's corporate building, someone had brought her one of those pop-top, self-boiling teas, and even though she had been hoping for a raise in salary, and thus was desperately anxious to be liked, she had not been able to make herself drink the swill.

She limped out to the front room. The radio was playing one of the Schubert *Impromptus*, and the gas fire was finally beginning to heat the room properly. She settled into her chair and set the cup down on the floor, then patted her thigh. Misha sniffed the cup and her ankle, then, apparently deciding it was not an evening for grudges, vaulted up into her lap. After she had bent to pick up her tea, the tiny dog tucked his nose under the bottom hem of her sweater, paw-pushed a few times to find just the right position, then immediately fell asleep.

Olga Pirofsky stared at the fire and wondered whether she was dying.

The headaches had started almost a year ago. The first had come just at the climax of Uncle Jingle's Magic Mirthday Party, an event that had been planned for most of a season, and which had been cross-marketed with a fervor never before seen in children's interactives. The pain had come so suddenly and with such hammering intensity that she had dropped offline immediately, certain that something terrible had happened to her real body. It had been a fortunate coincidence that the Mirthday Party plotline had featured Uncle J. splitting into twelve identical versions of himself—the production company was kindly allowing all the Uncle Jingles to participate in the residuals bonanza—so her absence was not critical. In any case, it was only a short absence: The pain had come and gone swiftly, and there was nothing unusual at home to suggest that something had happened to her helpless physical body.

If the problem had stopped there, she would never have thought of it again. The Mirthday shows broke net ratings records, as expected, and provided her with a nice bonus when the accounting was completed. (A sort of living explosion named "Mister Boom," which she had invented on the spot with Roland and another Uncle, even became a bit of a short-term fad, featuring in comedy monologues and other people's online games and spawning his own line of eternally-detonating shirts and mugs and toys.)

Two months later, though, she had another attack, and this one forced her off the show for three days. She had visited her doctor, who pronounced it stress-related, and prescribed a mild course of pain-blockers and Seritolin. When the next attack came, and the others that began to follow almost weekly, and when the tests repeatedly showed nothing abnormal in her physiology, the doctor grew less and less responsive.

Olga had ultimately stopped seeing him. It was bad enough to have a doctor who could not make you well; to have one who clearly resented you for being ill in an unfathomable way was unbearable.

She scratched the little crease that ran down the middle of Misha's skull. The Papillon snored quietly. His world, at least, was as it should be.

The Schubert piece ended and the announcer began to read some interminable commercial about home entertainment units, only slightly easier to stomach for being in soft classical-radio tones instead of the usual overstimulated screaming. Olga did not want to wake the dog by getting up, so she closed her eyes and tried to ignore the advertisement, waiting for the music to start again.

It was not stress that caused these horrid pains. It couldn't be. Years had passed since she had gone through the real stresses of her life: All the worst things, the nearly unbearable things, were long past. The job was difficult sometimes, but she had been in front of audiences most of her life and the electronic interface could disguise a multitude of sins. In any case, she loved children, loved them deeply, and although the children could certainly tire her out, she could think of nothing she'd rather be doing.

Years and years and years had passed since she had lost Aleksandr and the baby, and the wounds had turned to hard, numb scars long ago. She was only fifty-six, but felt much older. In fact, she had lived the life of an old woman for so long now that she had nearly forgotten any other way to do it. She could count on one hand the number of lovers she'd had since Aleksandr, none of them in her life longer than a few months. She seldom left her apartment except to shop, not because she was frightened of the outside world—although who wouldn't be, sometimes?—but because she liked the peace and solitude of her life at home, preferred it to the hubbub of other people living their heedless lives.

So, what stress? That was no explanation. Something more organic must be eating away at her, something darkly hidden inside her brain or glands that the doctors simply hadn't spotted yet.

The commercial ended and another began. Olga Pirofsky sighed. And if she was truly dying, was it so bad? What was there to regret leaving? Only Misha, and surely some other kind soul would give him a home. He would get over her as long as someone gave him love and wet food. The only other things she had were her memories, and losing them might well be a blessing. How long could a person mourn, anyway?

She laughed, a sour, sad laugh. "How long? For the rest of a lifetime, of course," she told the sleeping dog.

Finally, the announcer-babble ended and something by Brahms began, a piano concerto. She opened her eyes so she could drink some tea without spilling it on poor trusting, snoring Misha. Her coordination was never good after one of the headaches. They made her feel decades older.

So if it were all to end, was there anything she would regret leaving? Not the show. She had not created the character, and although she thought she brought something to him none of the others could—her circus training was so unusual in this day and age it had to make a difference—it did not mean much in the end. A fancy way to sell toys and entertainments to children was really all it was. As Uncle Jingle, she could occasionally do a little teaching, perhaps bring cheer to a sad child. But since the viewers did not distinguish between one Uncle Jingle performer and another—millions of credits of gear and filters and continuity coaches and art direction went every year to make sure they couldn't—she felt very little personal contact with her audience.

And lately, since the pain had begun, she found it increasingly difficult to stay involved with her job. So hard, it was so hard to be there for the children when that pain was pecking at her skull. It sometimes seemed that it only happened when she was working.

Only happened . . .

Misha began to wriggle in irritation, and Olga realized that she had been stroking him in the same spot for at least a minute. She was quite astonished that she hadn't noticed that detail before—that the doctors and the company's medical insurance personnel hadn't spotted it either. The headaches only happened when she was hooked into the Uncle Jingle character.

But they had tested her neurocannula and her shunt circuits as a matter of routine in every company physical for years, and had tested them again when the headaches began. They weren't stupid, those company men and women. The 'can wiring had been just fine, as problem free as the scans.

So what did that mean? If the circuitry was good, then perhaps something else was wrong. But what could it be?

She scooped Misha from her lap and put him down on the floor. He whimpered once, then began to scratch behind his ear. She stood and began to pace, only remembering to set down her teacup when the hot liquid sloshed onto her hand.

If the circuitry was good, what was bad? Was it just her own faulty internal mechanisms after all? Was she clutching at exotic answers because she wasn't truly ready to face the unpleasant truth, no matter how stoic she thought herself?

Olga Pirofsky stopped in front of her mantelpiece to stare at a 3-D rendering of Uncle Jingle, an original sketch from the production company's design department, given to her at her tenth anniversary party. Uncle's eyes were tiny black buttons that could look as innocent as a stuffed toy's, but the toothy grin would have given Red Riding

Hood a lot to think about. Uncle Jingle had rubbery legs and huge hands, hands that could do tricks to make children gasp or laugh out loud. He was an entirely original, entirely artificial creation, famous all over the world.

As she stared at the white face, and as the radio played soft piano melodies, Olga Pirofsky realized that she'd never liked the little bastard much.

CHAPTER 3

The Hive

NETFEED/NEWS: Bukavu 5 Fears in Southern France
(visual: ambulance, police vehicles on airport runway, lights flashing)
VO: A small private airstrip outside of Marseilles in southern France has
been quarantined by French and UN health officials amid rumors that it
was the entry point for an entire planeload of Central African refugees sick
with what is now being called Bukavu Five. An eyewitness account claiming
that all the passengers were dead when the plane landed, and the pilot
himself near death, has appeared as actual confirmed news on some net
services, but as of now is still unconfirmed rumor. Officials of the local
French prefecture will make no comment as to what caused the quarantine,
or why UNMed is involved . . .

THE water was full of monsters, huge, thrashing shapes that in her old life, in the real world, Renie could have snatched up with one hand. Here, she would be less than a mouthful for any one of them.

A vast smooth side pushed past her and another great wave rippled out, spinning her wildly along the surface. In the backwaters, beyond the roil of the feeding madness, the water was strangely solid, almost viscous, and it dimpled beneath her rather than swallowing her whole.

Surface tension, she realized, not in words but images from nature documentaries: She was too small to sink through it.

An eye as big as a door loomed near, then slid back into the murk beneath her, but the water's cohesion was broken and she began to sink. She struggled to stay upright, fighting panic.

I'm really in a tank, she reminded herself desperately. *A V-tank on a military base! None of this is real! I've got an oxygen mask on my face—I can't drown anyway!*

But she could no longer feel the mask. Perhaps it had slipped loose, and she was dying in the sealed, coffinlike V-tank. . . .

She blew out her held breath, then sucked in air, along with far more water spray than she wanted. She had to sputter it out before she could scream.

"!Xabbu! Martine!" She threw out her arms and legs, desperately trying to keep her head above the surface as the water plunged like a giant trampoline. Just a few dozen yards away the river was seething as titan fish collided in their frenzy to reach the hovering insects. She saw no sign of the leaf or any of her fellow passengers, just tidal-wave crests and canyon troughs of river water, and the erratic movements of the hatchlings flying overhead. One of them had drawn close, and was hovering almost directly above her, the noise of its wings for a moment obscuring the first voice she had heard that was not her own.

"Hey!" someone shouted hoarsely from close by, faint but clearly terrified. "*Hey!*" Renie kicked herself as far above the river's surface as she could, and saw T4b smacking his arms against the water as he fought to keep his unwieldy robot sim afloat. She scrambled toward him, tossed and battered by the waves surging beneath her, struggling against their sideways force.

"I'm coming!" she called, but he did not seem to hear her. He began screaming again, and windmilled his arms, an explosion of activity that she knew he could not maintain for more than a few seconds. His own movements forced him down through the surface, stirring up a froth as he sank. As she increased her own effort, and finally began closing the gap, a silvery head like the front of a bullet train flashed up from the river in an explosion of spray, engulfed him, then slid back into the depths.

Renie rocked back and forth as the force of the strike spread past her and dissipated. She stared, shocked into shutdown. He was gone. Just like that.

The roaring of wings grew louder overhead, but Renie could not lift her eyes from the spot where T4b had been swallowed, even when the wings were so close above her that the water began to fly in stinging drops.

"Excuse me," someone shouted. "Do you need help?"

Trapped in a dream that was becoming more bizarre by the second, Renie at last looked up. One of the dragonflies was hovering just a stone's throw above her. A human face protruded from its side, peering down.

Renie was so astonished that the next swell knocked her under. She thrashed to the surface to find the dragonfly still above her, the goggled face still staring down. "Did you hear me?" the unlikely head called. "I asked if you needed some help."

Renie nodded weakly, unable to summon a single word. A rope ladder with shiny aluminum rungs dropped from the insect's stomach like the last unraveling thread in the weave of reality. Renie grabbed at the bottom of the ladder and clung; she did not have the strength to climb. A gigantic stretch of gleaming scales broke the surface near her and then slid under once more, at its crest a fin that looked as large as a cathedral window. Somebody in a jumpsuit was clambering down the ladder toward her. A strong hand clasped her wrist and helped her up into the belly of the dragonfly.

She sat in a small padded alcove with a mylar emergency blanket wrapped around her shoulders. It was hard to tell which was making her vibrate the most, her own exhausted shivering or the mechanical dragonfly's wings.

"It's strange, isn't it?" said one of the two jumpsuited figures perched in the cockpit seats. "I mean, using an imaginary blanket to warm up your actual body. But everything here works in symbols, more or less. The blanket's a symbol for 'I've earned being warm,' and so your neural interface gets the message."

She shook her head, feeling a pointless urge to correct this improbable stranger, to explain that she didn't have anything as high-quality as a neural interface, but every time she opened her mouth, her teeth chattered. She could not turn off the film loop that kept playing in her head—three seconds of T4b splashing, then being swallowed, over and over and over.

The bug-pilot nearest her pulled off helmet and goggles, revealing a close-cropped head of black hair, Asian eyes, and rounded feminine features. "Just hang on. We'll fix you up back at the Hive."

"I think I see something," said the other jumpsuit. The voice sounded masculine, but the features were still hidden by the goggled helmet. "I'm going to drop her down a little."

Renie's stomach remained in the place they had been for several seconds after Renie and the others had plummeted back toward the river.

"Someone hanging onto some flotsam. Looks like . . . a monkey?"

"!Xabbu!" Renie jumped and banged her head painfully against the top of the alcove. The padding wasn't particularly thick. "That's my friend!"

"Problem not," he said. "I think we need that ladder again, Lenore."

"Chizz. But if this one's a monkey, he can damn well climb up himself."

Within moments, !Xabbu had joined Renie in the alcove. She hugged the small, simian body tight.

Several passes over the roiling water turned up no other survivors.

"Too bad about your friends," said the pilot as they headed the dragonfly away from the river and into the forest of impossibly tall trees. "Win some, lose some." He peeled back his goggles, revealing freckled, long-jawed Caucasian features, then blithely spun the dragonfly on its side to slip between two mountainous but close-leaning trunks, forcing Renie and !Xabbu to clutch at the alcove wall. "But that's what happens—this river is no place for beginners."

Renie was stunned by his callousness. Lenore's expression was disapproving, but it seemed only the mild censure one might display to a little brother caught in the cookie jar.

"Give her a break, Cullen. You don't know what they were doing. It could be a real problem."

"Yeah, yeah." The skinny pilot smirked, clearly unmoved. "Life's a bitch and then some fish eat you."

"Who are you people?" !Xabbu asked about a half-second before Renie could begin shrieking at them.

"The question really is . . . who are you?" Cullen flicked a glance over his shoulder, then returned his attention to the megafoliage whipping past the dragonfly's windshield. "Don't you know that this is private property? Believe me, there are a lot better people to put on the scorch than Kunohara."

"Kunohara?" Renie was having trouble keeping up. Hadn't her companions just been killed? Didn't that mean anything to these people, even in this virtual world? "What are you talking about?"

"Look, you must have noticed that you'd crossed into another simulation," said Lenore, her voice kind, her manner ever-so-slightly impatient. "This whole place belongs to Hideki Kunohara."

"King of the bugs," said Cullen, and laughed. "It's too bad your friends are going to miss it."

Renie struggled with her outrage, remembering Atasco and the mistakes she had made in his world. "I don't understand. What are you talking about?"

"Well, your friends won't be able to get back in here—in fact, I'm not quite sure how you guys got in to begin with. Must be some kind of back door from one of the other simworlds. Not surprising, I guess—Kunohara's got a lot of weird deals going." He shook his head in admiration. "So your friends are going to have to meet you somewhere else. Don't worry, though. We can get you to wherever it is, if you've got an address." He banked the dragonfly sharply to avoid a low-hanging branch, then brought it neatly level with a flick of the steering controls.

"I'm Lenore Kwok," the woman said. "Your pilot is Cullen Geary, common asshole by day, but by night . . . well, he's an asshole then, too."

"Flattery, Len-baby, flattery." Cullen grinned contentedly.

The sky beyond the cockpit window was now a deep mauve; the trees were rapidly becoming monstrous vertical shadows. Renie closed her eyes, trying to make sense of it all. These people seemed to think that T4b and Martine and the rest were fine, that they'd just been knocked out of the simulation. But could that be true? And even if they could survive being killed here in the simworld—which she wasn't all that positive about, given what had happened to Singh—how would she and !Xabbu ever find them again? The whole grueling effort was already over, it seemed, with all Sellars' work gone for nothing.

"What is this place?" she asked. "This simulation."

"Ah-ah." Cullen wagged his finger. Twilight rushed past the view-screen. "You haven't told us who *you* are yet."

Renie and !Xabbu exchanged glances. With all their other concerns, she and her companions had not had a chance to concoct a cover story in case of a meeting like this. She decided that half-truth was the best strategy.

"My name is . . ." she struggled to recall the earlier alias, ". . . Otepi. Irene Otepi. I was doing systems analysis for a man named Atasco." She paused, watching their rescuers for a reaction. "Do you know him?"

"The anthropologist?" Lenore was checking readouts on the instrument panel. If she was hiding something, she was good at it. "Heard of him. Central American, South American, something?"

"South American," said Cullen. "Colombian, in fact. Saw him in an interview once. What's he like?"

Renie hesitated. "I didn't meet him. Something went wrong—I'm

not sure what. His simworld . . . well, there was an uprising or something. We were all on a ship, and we just kept going." Renie suspected
they were wondering why she hadn't simply dropped offline. It was a
good question, and she couldn't think of an answer other than the
bizarre truth. "It was all pretty crazy. Then we floated through to here,
I guess. The ship turned into a leaf, the leaf got tipped over, you found
us."

!Xabbu had been watching her closely, and now spoke in his most
careful English. "I am Henry Wonde," he said. "I am Ms. Otepi's student. How can we find our friends again?"

Cullen turned to observe the baboon for a long moment before a
looming tangle of branches jerked his gaze back to the viewscreen.
"Why? Are you planning to stay online? Just go back through to this
Atasco simulation or something?"

Renie took a breath. "There's something wrong with our own systems, I think. We can't go offline."

Cullen whistled, impressed. "*That's* weird."

"We'll get you fixed up at the Hive," Lenore said confidently. "Make
it all better."

Renie was less than certain, but said nothing. The dragonfly sped
on through the darkening night.

ORLANDO had one last dream before waking, a dim and fuzzy frag-
ment in which a faceless child sat in a cold, dark room, pleading with
him to stay and play a game. There was some kind of secret involved,
something that must be kept from the grown-ups, but it all streamed
away like windblown smoke as he awakened. Still, even though the
events of the next minutes pushed it quickly from his mind, the feeling of foreboding it left took much longer to fade.

In the first too-bright moments after opening his eyes he thought
he was paralyzed. His legs felt unattached, and seemed to move aimlessly; he had very little feeling below a tight band around his waist.

"Orlando?"

The voice was familiar. The feeling of being in the world was less
so. He squinted and turned toward the voice.

"You're awake!" Fredericks' face was very close. Orlando realized
after a moment that it was his friend's arm he felt around his waist,
and that Fredericks was holding on to the edge of the leaf while they
both floated chest-deep in the warm river.

"Well, cheers and welcome to the party, sunshine." Sweet William,
looking not unlike a wet black cockatoo, was clinging to the leaf-edge

a few yards away. "Does this mean he can swim now, so we don't have to keep dragging you two back on board every few minutes?"

"Leave him alone," growled Fredericks. "He's really sick."

"He's right," a woman's voice said. "Arguing is a waste of time."

Orlando craned his neck—it felt boneless as taffy—to focus on the faces beyond Fredericks' shoulder. Three female sims, the women named Quan Li, Florimel, and Martine, had clambered up to a higher part of the leaf, and were holding fast to the slope. Florimel, who had spoken, looked back at him intently. "How are you?"

Orlando shook his head. "I've felt better. But I've felt worse, too."

A vibration shuddered the leaf. Orlando grabbed at Fredericks and reached for the leaf's edge with his other hand, his heart suddenly racing. After a moment, the vibration ceased.

"I think we scraped on a root," Florimel said. "We are close enough to the bank that we should swim the rest of the way."

"I don't think I can do it." Orlando hated to admit weakness, but there wasn't much he could hide from these folks, not after they'd been watching him flounder in and out of consciousness for however long it had been.

"Don't worry your pretty little head," Sweet William replied. "We'll just carry you on our backs all the way to the Emerald City, or Mordor, or wherever the hell it is we're going. Isn't that how it works in those stories? Buddies till the end?"

"Oh, shut up," offered Fredericks.

Orlando closed his eyes and concentrated on keeping his head above water. A few minutes later the leaf shuddered again, then bumped to a halt, rocking in the gentle current.

"We do not know how long this is going to remain snagged here," Florimel pointed out. "Let us head for the shore now—it is not far."

"Everybody wants to be in charge, don't they?" Sweet William sighed theatrically. "Well, soonest muddled, soonest mended. Let's get on with it." He splashed free of the leaf and swam until he was level with Fredericks.

Orlando wondered a little dreamily what William was doing, then was abruptly jerked away from the leaf by an arm around his neck and tumbled backward into the water. He thrashed, trying to get free.

"Stop fighting, you prat," spluttered William. "Or I *will* let you swim by yourself."

When Orlando realized that the other was trying, in his idiosyncratic way, to help him to shore, he relaxed. William set out with a surprisingly powerful stroke. As Orlando floated backward, his chin in the crook of the death-clown's arm, he watched the blue tropical sky overhead, wider than anything he had ever seen, and wondered if this dream was going to continue forever.

This looks so utterly, he thought. *Here I am, in a place where I could be like everyone else—better than everyone else—and I'm still sick.*

But his muscles didn't feel as weak as they had at first, which was interesting. He made a couple of experimental kicks, just to see, and was rewarded by a wet snarl from Sweet William: "You're knocking me off-balance. Whatever you're doing . . . don't do it."

Orlando relaxed, feeling a small pleasure at the returning responsiveness of his virtual flesh.

A few moments later William dragged him up onto the rounded stones of the beach, then stood over him, sodden plumes draggled on his shoulders and head. "Now, just wait there, Hero Boy," he said. "Think good thoughts. I've got to go back and wrestle the blind lady onto shore."

Orlando was more than content to lie in the warm sun and flex his fingers and toes, working up after a few minutes to arm- and leg-stretching. His lungs still hurt if he took anything but the shallowest breaths, and all his muscles ached, but he felt almost none of the slippery, disconnected dreaminess he had experienced since commandeering Atasco's royal barge. But a bit of internal darkness remained to trouble him, a shadow he could not quite name or clearly see.

Something happened. I had a . . . a dream? With Beezle in it? And some kind of little kid? It was troubling because it seemed meaningless, while at the same time something was whispering deep in his thoughts that it was all very meaningful indeed. *Was I supposed to do something? Help someone?* Another thought, slow to coalesce, but even more chilling: *Was I almost dead? I went down into the dark. Was I dying?*

He opened his eyes to watch the rest of the group trudging ashore, Sweet William carrying Martine in his arms. He set her down beside Orlando with surprising tenderness. It was only as the others hunkered down in a small circle that Orlando suddenly realized that something else was wrong, too.

"Where are the others? Where's. . . ?" For a long moment he could not remember the names. "Where's Renie—and her friend? And the guy in the body armor?"

Quan Li shook her head but said nothing, looking down at the stones of the beach.

"Gone," said Florimel. "Perhaps drowned, perhaps washed up somewhere else." There was a false note in her matter-of-fact speech, something that might have been pain sternly repressed. "We were all washed overboard. Those you see here were able to cling to the leaf.

Your friend pulled you back and held your head above the water, which is why you are alive."

Orlando turned to Fredericks. "So take me to *Law Net Live,*" Fredericks said defiantly. "I wasn't going to let you drown just because you're an idiot." Something turned in Orlando's stomach. How many times had his friend saved his life recently?

As it to underscore the question, Sweet William added: "In fact, my duck, just before we tipped over, you stopped breathing for a bit. Flossie here gave you mouth-to-mouth whatsit."

"Florimel, not Flossie." She glowered at the bedraggled William. "Anyone would have done the same."

"Thank you." Despite another debt of gratitude, Orlando wasn't sure how he felt about the fierce woman, and for the first time he realized the magnitude of their loss. "Could we look for Renie and the others? I mean, what if they need help?"

"Some of us aren't quite as perky, because *we* didn't get a free ride," said William. "Some of us are that tired, we could lie down right here and sleep for a week."

Orlando looked along the riverbank; from his shrunken perspective it was a thing of huge brown arroyos and thin stretches of stony beach. The river, a vast stretch of green that seemed active as a storm-brushed sea, wound away into the distance. On the far side of the riverbank loomed the first of the forest trees, each one as vast as the world-ash of Norse legend, tall as Jack's beanstalk. But more than just the size of things was puzzling. "It's morning," he said. "It was evening just a little while ago. Does the time jump around here?"

"Hark at him." William laughed. "Just because he had a nice nap while the rest of us did the dogpaddle all night, he thinks time went all funny."

Orlando felt sure that somewhere his real face was flushed pink. "Oh. Sorry." He snatched at something to say. "So are we going to spend the night here? Do we need to make a fire or something?"

Martine, who had been silent since William carried her ashore, abruptly sat up straight, her eyes wide. "There is something. . . !" She brought her hands to her face, rubbing so hard Orlando feared she would hurt herself even through the tactors. "No, someone . . ." Her mouth fell open and her face distorted, as though she silently screamed. She flung out a hand, pointing down the river course. "*There!* Someone is there!"

All turned to follow her gesture. A short distance away stood a white-shrouded human figure of their own size, looking down at something along the river's edge that was invisible from where they sat. Orlando struggled to get onto his feet, but was immediately struck by a wave of dizziness.

"Orlando, don't!" Fredericks scrambled up and took his arm. Orlando wavered and tried to take a step forward, but the weakness was too much. He swayed in place, trying to find his balance.

Florimel was already walking swiftly toward the spot, picking her way over the uneven stones. Sweet William followed her.

"Be careful!" called Quan Li, then moved to take Martine's hand. The French woman's sim still gazed sightlessly, head turning slowly from side to side like a tracking dish unable to lock onto a signal.

As Orlando managed his first steps, inhibited more than helped by Fredericks' insistence on propping him up, the white-cloaked form turned toward Florimel and William as though realizing for the first time that there were others present. Orlando thought he saw a glint of eyes in the shadows of the hood, then the figure vanished.

Fredericks let out a breath. "Scanny. Did you see that? He just disappeared!"

"It's . . . VR," panted Orlando. "What did you . . . expect, a . . . puff of smoke?"

Their two companions were kneeling over something that lay in one of the shallow backwaters of the river. At first Orlando thought it was some kind of discarded machinery, but it was far too shiny to have been in the water long. When William and Florimel helped the machinery to sit up, Orlando suddenly recognized it.

"Look who we have here!" William shouted. "It's BangBang the Metal Boy!"

They helped T4b out of the water as Orlando tottered forward on Fredericks' arm; an observer might have thought that two ancient and venerable celebrities were being introduced.

"Are you okay?" Fredericks asked the warrior robot. Florimel began checking T4b in much the same way any accident victim might be checked, flexing joints, exploring for a pulse reading. Orlando wondered how much good that would do on a sim. "I mean, wow." Fredericks took a deep breath. "We thought you were dead!"

"And what *do* we call you, anyway?" fluted William. "I forgot to ask. Is just 'T' acceptable, or do you prefer 'Mr. Four Bee?' "

T4b groaned and brought a spike-gauntleted hand up to his face. "Feel pure *fenfen,* me. Fish ate me." He shook his head and one of his helmet prongs almost poked Florimel in the eye. "Puked me up, too." He sighted. "Doing that again? Never."

"It's not much, but it's home," Cullen declared. Renie could see nothing but a sprinkle of dimly-glowing lights before them.

"Hold up." Lenore's voice was sharp. "We got a bogey at 12:30 and closing."

"What is it?"

"One of those damn quetzals, I think." Lenore scowled, then turned to Renie and !Xabbu. "Birds."

"Hold tight." Cullen dropped the dragonfly into a steep dive. "Better still, grab those belts and strap in."

Renie and !Xabbu fumbled their way into the crash-belts hanging in the alcove. They fell for only seconds, then slowed so swiftly that Renie felt she was being squeezed like an accordion. They were floating downward, as far as Renie could tell, when a mechanical wheeze and bang came from underneath their feet, making her and !Xabbu jump.

"Extending the legs," explained Lenore. As the dragonfly thumped down on something, she continued to stare at the readouts. "We'll just wait until the damn bird gets bored. They can't see you if you're not moving."

Renie could not understand these people. They acted as though they were playing some sort of complex game. Perhaps they were. "Why do you have to do this?" she asked.

Cullen snorted. "So it doesn't eat us. Now there's a real waste of time."

"All clear," said Lenore. "He's circled off. Give it another few seconds to be on the safe side, but I see nothing except empty skies."

Shuddering, the wings beating hard, the dragonfly lifted off again. Cullen aimed it at the lights once more, which flattened as they drew closer into a vertical wall of gleaming points. One rectangular spill of light grew larger and larger before them, until it revealed itself as a huge, square doorway that dwarfed the aircraft as they passed through. Cullen brought the dragonfly in neatly, hovered for a moment, then landed.

"Top floor," he said. "Mandibles, chitinous exoskeletons, and ladies' lingerie. Everyone out."

Renie felt a sudden urge to smack him, but it diffused in the effort of dragging her tired body out of the crash-belt and through the hatchway behind the two dragonfly pilots. !Xabbu followed her down, climbing slowly so as not to hurry her.

The insect-plane stood in a vast hangar whose outside door was just now sliding shut with a whine of hard-working gears. Renie thought of the military base in the Drakensbergs, and then had to remind herself that the base was real but this place was not. Like all the Otherland simulations, it was incredibly lifelike, a high-ceilinged architectural monster constructed of, or appearing to be constructed of, fibramic tie-girders, plasteel plates, and acres of fluorescent lighting. All the half-dozen sims who trotted forward to begin servicing the dragonfly had individual and very realistic faces. She wondered if any of them represented real people.

She suddenly realized she had no idea whether even their rescuers were real.

"Come on." Lenore beckoned. "We'll debrief you—that shouldn't take long, although Angela may want a chat with you—then we'll show you around."

The Hive, as Lenore kept calling it, was a huge installation built into a mound of forest earth. The mound, in comparison to the tiny humans, was even larger than the mountain containing the Wasp's Nest base, but Renie thought the whole thing still seemed an eerie parallel to their RL situation. As they walked out of the landing bay into a long corridor, Lenore and Cullen in front arguing amiably, !Xabbu pacing on all fours beside her, she wondered again whether this was some kind of elaborate game-world.

"What exactly do you do here?" she asked.

"Ah, we haven't told you, have we?" Lenore smiled. "Must seem pretty strange."

"Bugs," said Cullen. "We do bugs."

"Speak for yourself, scanman," said Lenore. "Me, I *watch* bugs."

!Xabbu got up on his hind legs long enough to run his fingers along the wall, feeling the texture. "Is this a game, this place?" he asked, echoing Renie's earlier thought.

"Serious as a heart attack," Cullen countered. "It may be a playground for Kunohara, but to us entomologists it's like dying and going to heaven."

"Now I'm really curious," said Renie—and, surprisingly, she was. The fear for her companions' safety had not disappeared, but Otherland had again caught her off guard.

"Hang on a minute and we'll give you the whole thing. Let's just get you some visitor passes and then we can show you around properly."

Renie, overwhelmed by the bustling realism, had expected Lenore to lead them to some office, but instead they were still standing in the middle of the corridor, where Lenore had opened a data window in midair, when a stocky woman suddenly materialized beside them. She had an extremely serious face, well-simulated Mediterranean features, and short brown hair.

"Don't look so startled," she told Renie and !Xabbu. It sounded almost like a command. "Here in the Hive we don't have to put up with all that 'realistic' crap." As they pondered this confusing statement, she turned to Lenore. "You wanted to talk to me? About these people, right?"

"We would have checked them in before we got here, but Cully almost ran us down a bird's throat on the way in, so it was a little distracting."

"You wish," was Cully's riposte.

"They wandered in from someone else's simworld—Atasco, was it?" Lenore turned to Renie for confirmation. "And now they can't get offline."

The new woman snorted. "I hope you're getting enough water and glucose wherever you call home, sweetie, because we don't have much time to help you right at the moment." She turned back to the pilots. "That *Eciton* front has swung around, and it's about forty feet across when it's moving. I want you two to go and check it out again tomorrow morning."

"Aye-aye, Cap'n." Cullen saluted.

"Piss off." She returned her attention to Renie and !Xabbu, examining the latter with eyebrows arched. "If I had the time to waste on an old joke, I'd say 'we don't get many baboons in here'—but I don't have the time. I'm Angela Boniface. You two are a problem. We've got a very strict agreement with the leaseholder, and we're not supposed to bring in anyone without his approval."

"We don't want to be in your way," Renie said hurriedly. "We'll leave as soon as we can. If you can take us to the nearest . . ." she paused, unsure of the word, "border, I guess, we'll just get out."

"Not that easy." Angela Boniface squinted. "Damn. Oh, well—Kwok, see if you can find someone around here who might be able to figure out what's gone wrong with their gear. I have to go kick Bello's ass about something." Before she had turned halfway around, she was gone, vanished like a stage magician.

"Project administrator," said Lenore by way of explanation.

"What did she mean by 'that realistic crap'?" asked !Xabbu. Even Renie had to smile at his inflection.

"She meant in here we don't have to pretend like it's a real world," Cullen explained, extending his long arms in a catlike stretch. "Kunohara doesn't want anything disturbing the natural look of the simulation, so if we want to examine things up close, we have to interact, have to be part of the environment—but an unobtrusive part of the environment. That's why the vehicles look like big bugs. He set up all these other incredibly irritating rules we have to follow. It's kind of a little game he's got going, and he enjoys making us jump through the hoops. At least that's what *I* think."

"And when you earn your first billion or two," Lenore pointed out, "you can build your own simulation, Cully. Then *you* can make the rules."

"Well, when I do, Rule Number One is going to be 'No sixteen-hour days for the boss.' I'm going to take care of some notes, then I'm outta here. Sayonara." He flicked his fingers and disappeared.

"There really isn't any place to sleep," Lenore apologized as she left them in a conference room. "I mean, no one bothers to do that here—wouldn't make sense." She looked around at the empty space. "Sorry it's so bare. I can put something on the walls if you want, maybe make some more furniture."

Renie shook her head. "It's all right."

"Well, I'll come back to get you in a few hours. If any of the gearheads are available before then, I'll have them buzz you." She evaporated, leaving Renie and !Xabbu alone.

"What do you think?" !Xabbu had clambered onto the featureless rectangular block that served as a table. "Can we talk here?"

"If you mean in real privacy, I doubt it." Renie frowned. "It's a virtual conference room—this whole thing's just the visual interface for a multi-input, multi-output communications machine. But do I think they're listening? Probably not."

"So you do not think these people are our enemies." !Xabbu crouched on his heels, brushing at the short hair on his legs.

"If so, they've gone to a lot of trouble for very small chance of reward. No, I think they're just what they say they are—a bunch of university people and scientists working in an expensive simulation. Now the fellow who owns the place, whatever his name was, him I wouldn't be so sure about." She sighed and lowered herself to the floor, putting her back against the stark white wall. The jumpsuit her sim wore was only a little the worse for wear despite immersion in the river, but it was within the bounds of what would really happen. It seemed these Otherland simulations even took note of wear and tear.

Who were these people, this Brotherhood, she wondered again. How could they build a network this realistic? Surely money alone, even in almost unimaginable amounts, was not enough to bring about this kind of performance-level jump.

"So what do we do?" !Xabbu asked. "Have we lost the others for good?"

"I really don't have any answers." Bone-tired and depressed, Renie struggled to get a grip on her thoughts. "We can wait and hope that Sellars finds us before any of those Grail people do. We can keep moving, keep looking for . . . what did Sellars say that man's name was?"

!Xabbu furrowed his simian brow in thought. "Jonas," he said at last. "Sellars spoke to him in dreams. He set him free, he said."

"Right. Which tells us exactly nothing about where he might be. How are we supposed to find him, anyway? Follow the river? Which could go for millions of miles through virtual space, for all we know. It could be some kind of Moebius river, for God's sake, and keep changing so that it has no end at all."

"You are unhappy," !Xabbu said. "I do not think it is as bad as that. Look at this place! Remember the man Atasco's country. There cannot be enough people in the world to construct a million such complicated things as this."

Renie smiled a tired smile. "You're probably right. So that's it, is it? Back to the river, and hope we find Martine and the rest, or this Jonas fellow. Have you ever heard the expression, 'a needle in a haystack'?"

!Xabbu shook his narrow head. "What is a haystack?"

Her dreams came and went almost unnoticed, like early morning rain showers. She woke, curled on her side on the floor of the imaginary conference room, and listened to !Xabbu's gentle breathing beside her.

A memory floated through—only an image at first, an amalgam of sound and feeling. On cold mornings, when he was small, Stephen would crawl into her bed. He would mumble drowsy nonsense for a moment, then curl against her and within seconds drop back into deepest sleep, leaving Renie herself resignedly half-awake and waiting for the alarm.

It was terrible, this between-state that Stephen was now in, this unresolved nothingness. At least her mother had gone for good, to be missed and mourned and occasionally blamed. Stephen was neither dead nor alive. Limbo. Nothing to be done about it.

Nothing but *this,* perhaps, whatever "this" turned out to be—a hopeless search? A confused assault on incomprehensible powers? Renie could only wonder. But every moment that Stephen remained ill and that she did not make him better was a burning reproach.

The pain summoned another memory: When he was five or six, he had come home one afternoon full of agitation, flapping his arms as though he would fly. His wide-eyed upset had been so exaggerated that at first Renie had almost laughed despite herself, until she noticed the blood on his lip and the dirt on his clothes. Some of the older children had waylaid him on his way back from school. They had tried to make him say something he didn't want to say—one of the tired rituals of malevolent youth—and then had shoved him down in the road.

Without even pausing to wash his split lip, Renie had dashed out of the house. The little gang of ten-year-old thugs had scattered when they saw her coming, but one of them was a step too slow. Shouting with rage, Renie had shaken that boy until he was crying harder than Stephen. When she let him go, he slumped to the ground, staring at her in mortal terror, and she had been pierced by a deep shame. That she, a grown woman and a university student, should put such terror into any child. . . . She had been horrified, and still had never quite forgiven herself. (Stephen, who had watched from the doorway, had no such compunctions. He was gleeful about the bully's punishment, and did a little laughing dance as she returned to the house.)

How could someone set out systematically to injure children? What did these Grail people believe could be worth such monstrousness? It was beyond her comprehension. But then, these days, so many things were.

Her contemplative mood turned sour, Renie grunted and sat up. !Xabbu made a quiet sound and rolled onto his other side.

What could she do but go on? She had made mistakes, had done things she didn't like to remember, but Stephen had no one else. A life, a most important life, was in her hands. If she gave up, she would never see him run again in his skittery, gangly-graceful way, never hear him chortle at the painfully stupid jokes on the net shows, or do any of the things that made him uniquely Stephen.

Perhaps that bullying ten-year-old hadn't deserved such angry reprisal, but he had never bothered Stephen again. Someone always had to stand up for the weak and the innocent. If she didn't do all she could, she would spend the rest of her life beneath a shadow of failure. And then, even if Stephen died, he would always remain in limbo for her, a ghost of the most real sort—the ghost of a missed chance.

CHAPTER 4

In The Puppet Factory

NETFEED/NEWS: *Mini-Elephants Not Just A Fad*
(visual: Cannon with miniature elephant "Jimson")
VO: Business is very good indeed for Good Things Farm these days. Owner Gloriana Cannon, shown here with young bull Jimson, breeds and sells almost a hundred of the mini-elephants sometimes affectionately known as "half-a-lumps" every year. The business, which began as another mini-pet fad a decade ago, has outlasted the experts' best guesses.
CANNON: "Part of it is because these little guys are so smart. They're not just novelties, they're real companions. But they're also a lot more stable than some of the other genetic minis—their DNA just handles it better, or something. Stop that, Jimson. When you remember how unpredictable those little grizzlies were, all those accidents they had. And those small jungle cats that turned out so nasty . . . what was that stupid marketing name? 'Oce-littles' or 'Oce-lite', something like that. . . ?"

DULCINEA Anwin put her hand on the palm-reader and noticed that her nails were ragged. She frowned, waiting for the door to decide to trust her. Too much to do. She must look dreadful, but at the moment, life was even wilder and more overwhelming than usual.

The last time I went through this door, I had never killed anyone. That thought, or others much like it, had been cropping up for days. She was pretty sure she was handling it well, but she had little with which to compare it. Still, she did not feel consumed by guilt. It would have been different, she supposed, if the victim had been someone she really knew, instead of some minor Colombian gearhead Dread had hired.

Besides, she had seen this coming for years. You couldn't be successful in her business without coming into personal contact with violence, or at least you could not avoid it forever. Still, she had thought her first experience with murder would be watching someone else do it, not performing the act herself. She pushed the thought away again, but the memory of Antonio Celestino's sightless eyes, both before and after the killing shot, seemed unlikely to go away soon. . . .

The apartment door, unable to distinguish between the new Dulcie who had shot Celestino and the old Dulcie who had not, hissed open. When she had crossed the beam, the door paused exactly one point five seconds, then shut itself. Jones appeared in the bedroom doorway, stretched luxuriously, then padded across the floor toward her with no apparent haste, as though her mistress had not been gone for almost two weeks.

Dulcie dropped her bag and leaned down to stroke the cat, who bumped her shin and then turned and sauntered away. Jones' fluffy backside, Persian-wide but bearing the Siamese coloring of the other half of her heritage, showed no signs of unfashionable shrinkage. At least Charlie from downstairs seemed to have fed her properly.

The wallscreen was pulsing with a faint pink light, but Dulcie ignored it. She hadn't accessed any messages since boarding the flight in Cartagena, and she was in no hurry to do so. She felt as though she hadn't been properly clean for days, and God knew that she would be busy enough soon.

"Priority message," said a soft male voice, cued by the front door opening and closing. *"You have a priority message."*

"Shit." Dulcie flipped her hair out of her eyes and rubbed her forehead. It couldn't be Dread again already, could it? She felt positively waxy. "Play the message."

Her current employer's ugly-handsome face appeared a meter high on her wallscreen, his long hair lank and damp. He looked like someone who had been chewing khat, exalted and buzzing like a downed power line. *"Dulcie, call me as soon as you get in. It's extremely, extremely urgent."*

"Oh, Christ. No peace." She told the screen to return the call, then slumped onto the couch and kicked off her shoes.

He came on almost immediately. "We've got a problem."

"Didn't those subroutines work?" She had cobbled together a few reaction loops before leaving Dread to mind the fort in Colombia, behavior gear that would allow them to leave their puppet sim untenanted for short stretches of time, but which would keep the impostor looking occupied and alive. Nothing that would confound serious scrutiny, but enough to get through sleeping periods and the occasional distraction on the handlers' end of things.

"It's all working fine. But the group's been split up. That African woman and her monkey friend—they're lost, maybe drowned. There was some kind of fish frenzy on the river. The boat tipped over and the rest of the group are stranded on shore."

Dulcie took a deep breath, fortifying her patience. Men, no matter how intelligent or powerful, sometimes couldn't help acting like boys, so lost in their games that they forgot they *were* games. Women, on the other hand, remembered what was important—an occasional bath and clean hair. "But our sim is still with the rest of the group?"

"Yes. Everyone's together now, except those two. But they're clearly in a dangerous situation, so we could lose them all at any time. I need to get on with researching some of the things they've already talked about. I can't do it while I'm handling the sim."

"Could this possibly wait just another hour? I'm sure you're tired, but I just walked through the door and I have to eat something before I faint." Men didn't understand baths, but they usually understood food.

He stared for a long moment. The look on his face seemed to suggest imminent violence, or at least harsh criticism, but then he grinned instead, his teeth bright in his dark face. "Of course," he said. "Sorry."

Dulcie could make little sense of the man—his odd reactions, like this one, the flares of brilliance, the childishness of his nickname, did not quite add up to make a full picture. Not being able to categorize him irritated her. "I really do need a chance . . ." she began.

"Call me back when you're ready." He broke contact.

Dulcie looked down at Jones, who had returned and was sitting patiently by her stocking-clad feet. "Hurry, hurry, hurry," Dulcie told her. "Always hurrying." Jones lidded her round eyes; she seemed to agree that it was no way to do things properly.

Her curling red hair was wrapped in a towel-turban and her softest bathrobe coddled her damp but now wonderfully clean skin. She had stretched lengthwise on the couch with her feet up, a squeeze-tube of mango yogurt in her hand, and Jones resting comfortably—it was comfortable for Jones, anyway—along her thighs.

Look at me, she thought. *I've shot someone. There are a lot of men who couldn't even do that. But look at me. I'm so calm.* She made sure her pose reflected this impressive fortitude. "Now," she told the wallscreen, "you may redial."

Dread appeared thrice life-size. He seemed a little less manic. "They're all asleep, so it's not such an emergency. The puppet looks great—a little snore here, a little twitch there. You do good work."

"Thank you."

"Did you get something to eat?" His dark eyes flicked along the length of her bathrobed form in a way she found both sexual and somehow dismissive. "I'd like to take this opportunity to bring you up to date."

"I'm fine." She waved her yogurt tube. "Fire away."

Dread began where she had handed over the reins that morning, with the whole crew still floating on the river in the boat that had become a leaf, and brought her up to the present moment, with special emphasis on character continuity. "We really ought to see if we can find some agent gear that will take subvocalized notes on the fly," he said. "Otherwise, if a lot happens, we might lose some important detail after a hand-over and blow the puppet's cover."

Dulcie wondered inwardly how long he would want to keep this up, but reminded herself that with the bonus he had already credited to her account, and the salary he had promised for her share of sim-time, she could take at least a year or two off. That much freedom was worth some inconvenience.

Another part of her wondered at how quickly Celestino had become nothing more than a number in her credit account.

Aloud, she said: "Is there a chance we could find a third person to help with this? Even if those people sleep for eight hours a day, that's still a full working day for both of us, seven days a week, indefinitely. I could probably find someone to help."

Dread went silent, his face suddenly expressionless. "You have someone you want to bring in?"

"No, no." Until today, he had been so ecstatically happy about the results of the Sky God project she had almost forgotten his mood swings, but now they were again in high gear. But, she told herself, at least he wasn't boring, like most men. "No, I don't have anyone in mind. I'm just thinking about us both going crazy from overwork. And you said there's a lot of other stuff you have to do with . . . with that data." She had almost said Atasco's name: she *was* tired, she realized. She doubted anyone was actually tapping her lines—Dread himself had sent her some topflight defense gear, which she was using on top of her own precautions—but it was stupid to take any unnecessary risks, and certainly the Atasco assassination had been world news for days now.

"I'll consider it." For a moment, his stony look lingered. Then, as if someone had poured hot liquid into a cold cup, life came back into his features. "And there're a few other things we need to discuss, too . . ."

"There is someone at the door," said the house-voice. *"Someone at the door."*

Dulcie rolled her eyes. *"Intercom.* Who's there?"

"Me—Charlie," was the response. *"So you really are back!"*

"Who is that?" Dread had gone zero-degrees again.

"Just my downstairs neighbor." She got up, dislodging a silent but irritated Jones. "She feeds my cat. I can call you back if you want."

"I'll wait." Dread killed his visual and the wallscreen went blank, but Dulcie had no doubt he would be listening.

Charlie's white-blonde hair was elaborately foiled; the strands encircled her head like the electron paths of a model atom, so that the closest kiss she could bestow landed somewhere in the air a handspan from Dulcie's cheek. "Oh, God, Dulce, where's your tan? What good is going to South America if you don't get a tan?"

"Too much work." Charlie, Dulcie felt sure, would think a nuclear explosion had an upside—all those skin-darkening rays. "Any problems with Jonesie? She looks great."

"No, everything was just 'zoonly. Your mother came by one day when I was here. She's a chort."

"Yeah, she's a chort, all right. Laugh-a-minute." Dulcie's feelings about Ruby O'Meara Mulhearn Epstein Anwin at their very strongest could not be called affectionate, but other people always seemed to think her mother was a wonderful character. Dulcie wondered what she was missing. "Anything else?"

"Oh, God, you must be exhausted. I really just came up to make sure that was you I heard." Charlie abruptly twirled, catching up her silvery tesselated skirt and exposing her long, slender legs. "Do you like this? I just bought it."

"It's great. Well, thanks again for taking care of Jones."

"Problem not. Do you think you could feed Zig and Zag next week? I've got . . . I'm going out of town. You just have to give them lettuce and check their water."

Charlie had always maintained that she was an account executive for a cosmetics firm—a lie that Dulcie guessed was rooted in some briefly-held teenage job. Charlie thought Dulcie did not know that she was a call girl—and a fairly expensive one, too: her cartoony voice and schoolgirl figure were doubtless very appealing to a certain type of well-heeled clientele. Charlie believed her career was a complete secret, but Dulcie made it her business to find out everything she could about all her neighbors, and Dulcie was good at finding things out.

Charlie thinks she's so wicked. She doesn't know that her friend upstairs is an international terrorist-for-hire. She's been feeding the cat of a professional murderess.

Even when shared only with herself, the joke was beginning to wear thin. In fact, she had just decided not to think about Celestino for a while, to allow the incident to find its proper place in the Dulcie Anwin scheme of things.

When Charlie had gone posture-walking back to the elevator like an oversized, overdressed Girl Scout, Dulcie turned back to the wall-screen.

"She's gone."

Dread's face popped up immediately, as she had known it would. Of course he was listening. He'd probably been watching, too, and thinking perverse thoughts about blonde, short-skirted Charlie. But if he had been, he made no mention of it, or gave any sign at all.

"Right. Well, the first thing we need to decide is how much we can afford to lead this little group from within." Dread frowned, his eyes remote. "If I thought they had any purpose at all, I'd be happy just to sit back, but they have a golden opportunity to find things out and instead they just seem to be . . . drifting."

"A golden opportunity to find things out for *you*," Dulcie suggested.

He smirked. "Of course." His smile vanished. "You know who I work for, don't you?"

Dulcie wasn't sure what she was supposed to say. "You've never told me . . ."

"Come on. Don't lower my opinion of you. You're good at what you do, you make great money, you drive that scorching little red sports car way too fast, but you've never had a ticket—you get around, Dulcie. You must have a pretty good idea of who my boss is."

"Well, yes, I think I know." In fact, after seeing the Otherland network from the inside, she had known the rumors about Dread working for the almost-mythical Felix Jongleur had to be true. Only Jongleur and a very few other people could afford that kind of technology.

"Then you can guess how serious this is, what we're doing. We're holding back crucial information from one of the meanest, smartest, most powerful men in the world. We're right in the Old Man's back-yard here. If he finds out, I'm a dead man. Instantly." He fixed her with a stare even more intense than the one he had used earlier. "Don't misunderstand this. If you sell me out, even if I don't get to you myself before the Old Man sixes me, he won't let you live. Not someone who's found out as much as you have about this network of his. You won't even be history. In twenty-four hours, there will be no evidence you ever existed."

Dulcie opened her mouth and then closed it. She had thought about just these possibilities, all of them, but to hear Dread say them so flatly, with such certainty, brought it home to her in a way her own musings hadn't. Suddenly, she knew herself to be in a very high and precarious place.

"Do you want out?"

She shook her head, not trusting her voice at this moment.

"Then do you have any questions before we go on?"

Dulcie hesitated, then swallowed. "Just one. Where did your name come from?"

He raised an eyebrow, then barked a laugh. "You mean 'Dread'? You sure that's all you want to ask me?"

She nodded. When he laughed like that, his lips pulled away from the corners of his mouth like some kind of animal. Like something that grinned before it bit.

"It was a name I gave myself when I was a kid. This guy in this place I stayed . . . well, that doesn't matter. But he turned me on to this old music from the beginning of the century, Jamaican stuff called 'ragga.' 'Dread' is a word they used all the time."

"That's all? It just seemed . . . I don't know, kind of silly. Not really you."

For a moment she wondered if she'd gone too far, but his dark face flexed into amusement once more. "It has another meaning, too—something to make the Old Man crazy, him with all his King Arthur bullshit, his Grail and all that. The full version isn't just 'Dread,' it's 'More Dread.' Get it?"

Dulcie shrugged. All that Middle Ages stuff had always bored her to tears in school, along with the rest of History. "Not really."

"Well, don't worry your head about it. We got more serious stuff to do, sweetness." The curled-lip laugh returned. "We are going to stir it up for the Old Man—stir it up major."

Recovering her composure a little, Dulcie allowed herself the indulgence of a twinge of contempt. He thought he was so bad, so scary, so dangerous. All the men in this business were either complete psychopaths, ice-blooded technicians, or action-star wannabes, full of pithy lines and menacing glances. She was quite sure Dread would prove to be the last.

"Problem not, Pancho," she said—Charlie's favorite expression. "Let's get on with it."

Empty-eyed, self-absorbed . . . yes, she knew his type. She was willing to bet that he went through a lot of women, but that none of the relationships lasted very long at all.

CHRISTABEL had slipped and skinned her knee at school the day before, trying to show Portia how to do a special serve in foursquare. Her mother had told her to quit peeling the spray off it to look, so she waited until she was all the way down the street and around the corner before stopping her bike.

The spray was funny, a round white place on her knee that looked like spiderwebs. She sat down on the grass and scraped at the edge of the white stuff with her fingernails until it began to come loose. Underneath, the red sore spot was beginning to turn a funny yellow color and get all gummy. She wondered if that was what happened when parts of the Minglepig fell off, like on Uncle Jingle's Jungle last week, when all the Minglepig's noses came off at the same time after he sneezed. She decided that if that happened it would be very, very gross.

There were no people on the athletic field when she rode past, but she could see a few of them on the far side, wearing their army uniforms and marching back and forth, back and forth, on the dirt track. There was no music today, so the sound of her pedals was loud, sort of like music itself, going *squeak-a, squeak-a.*

She rolled down street after street, hardly even looking at the signs because she knew the way now, until she came to the part of the base with the raggedy grass and the little cement houses. She parked her bike beside a tree, pushed hard with her foot until the kickstand went down, and then took the paper bag out of the bike basket that her daddy had fixed so it wouldn't be all wobbly any more.

"Hey, weenit. *Que haces?*"

Christabel jumped and made a squeaking noise louder than the bike pedals. When she turned, someone was coming down out of the tree, and for a moment she thought it was a monkey in clothes, a scary killer monkey like that show her mother hadn't wanted her to watch but that Christabel had promised wouldn't give her nightmares. She wanted to scream, but it was like in a bad dream and she couldn't do anything but watch.

It wasn't a monkey, it was a boy with a dirty face and a missing tooth. It was the same boy who had helped her cut the fence when she was helping Mister Sellars, except he was even dirtier and he looked smaller than before. But he was inside the fence! Inside the fence, where she was! She knew that was wrong.

"Don't talk much, you." The boy was smiling, but it looked like it hurt him. Christabel took a few steps backward. "Hey, *mu'chita,* not gonna do nothin' to you. What you got in the bag?"

"It's n-not for you." Christabel held it tight against her shirt. "It's f-f-for someone else."

"*Verdad,* weenit?" The boy took a step closer, but slow, like he hardly even knew he was doing it himself. "Some food, huh? Feedin' someone, you? I saw. I been watchin.' "

"Watching?" She still couldn't understand what this dirty boy was doing here. There were inside-the-fence people, and there were outside-the-fence people, and he was not an inside person.

"Yeah, *claro,* I been watchin'. Ever since you got me to cut that fence, I been watchin'. Fence goes off, I climbed over. Get some good stuff, me, what I thought. But the fence go back on. Both of 'em. Threw a stick at it, just to see, people came running—soldier boys. I go'd up a tree, but they almost saw me."

"You can't get out." She said it as she realized it. "You can't get back over the fence, 'cause . . ." she stopped, scared. She had almost said Mister Sellars' name. " 'Cause it's turned on. 'Cause it's 'lectric."

"Got that right, *mu'chita.* I found some food, too—they throw lotta stuff away in here, man, they *locos*—major scanny, seen? But they don't throw out food always. And I'm pretty hungry, me." He took another step nearer, and suddenly Christabel was terrified he would kill her and eat her, like in the monster stories Ophelia told at sleepovers, grab her and then bite her with that dirty mouth and the hole where his front tooth was supposed to be. She turned and began to run.

"Hey, weenit, come back!"

She ran looking down at the ground flying underneath her, at her legs going up and down. It felt like something was jumping in her chest, thumping her from the inside, trying to get out. She could hear the boy's voice coming closer, then something shoved her in the back and she was running too fast for her feet. She stumbled and fell onto the grass. The boy stood over her. Her leg was hurting from where she fell down at school, and now on the other leg, too. When her breath came back, Christabel began to cry, so scared she was hiccuping, too.

"Crazy little bitch." He sounded almost as unhappy as she was. "What you do that for?"

"If you hurt m-m-me, I'll . . . I'll tell my daddy!"

He laughed, but he looked angry. "Yeah? Chizz, weenit, you tell. And then I'll tell about what you hiding out here."

Christabel kept hiccuping, but she stopped crying because she was now too busy being even more afraid. "H-hiding?"

"I told you, I been watchin'. What you got? What you hiding out here? Some kinda dog or something?" He stuck out his hand. "*Fen,* I don't care if it dog food. Gimme that bag." When she did not move, he bent over and took it from her curled fingers. He didn't pull hard, and Christabel felt more than ever like this was a bad dream. She let it go.

"*Que . . . ?*" He stared at the wrappers. "This soap! What are you, play some game with me?' With his quick, dirty fingers, he unpeeled one of the bars and held it to his nose to take a hard sniff. "*Fen!* Soap! *Mu'chita loca!*" He threw it down. The soap bounced away. Christabel could see it sitting on top of the grass where it stopped, like an Easter egg. She didn't want to look at the boy, who was very angry.

"Right," he said after a minute, "then you gonna bring me food, bitch. Right here, every day, *m'entiendes*? Otherwise, you daddy gonna know you come here. Don't know what you doin' with that soap, but I bet you washin' something you ain't s'posed to have. You got me, little *vata loca*? I know where you live, you in your Mammapapa house. I see you through the window. I come through that window some night if you don't bring me nothing to eat."

Anything would be better than having him yell at her. She nodded her head.

"Chizz." He swung his arms from side to side, so he looked like a monkey again. "And you better not forget, 'cause Cho-Cho be *un mal hombre*. You hear? Don't mess with Cho-Cho, or you wake up dead."

He went on saying things like that for a while. At last, Christabel figured out that Cho-Cho was him, the boy. It wasn't a name she had ever heard. She wondered if it meant something outside the fence.

He let her keep the rest of the soap, but even after he had climbed up into the nearest of the thick trees and scrambled away to some secret hiding place, she did not dare leave the bag for Mister Sellars. She put it back into the basket of her bicycle and rode home. Halfway there, she began to cry again. By the time she reached her street, she could hardly see the sidewalk.

And now both her knees were skinned.

DREAD rang off and settled back, extending his long legs. He called up the Otherland sim and opened its eyes briefly. All the others were still sleeping, and watching them brought a sympathetic heaviness to his own eyelids. He shook his head, then reached into his pocket for a stimulant tab—Adrenax, the real stuff from the South American black bazaars—and dry-swallowed it. He followed it up with a little drum music on his internal system, a counterpulse to make everything seem a little more exciting. When the rhythm was pumping at what seemed the proper level, cascading from one side of his head to the other, he returned his attention to business. He left the Otherland window open, but shut the sim's eyes most of the way so as not to attract undue attention should any of the others wake, then leaned back in his chair to think.

His hand stole to his t-jack; callused fingertips traced the smooth circumference of the shunt. There were so many puzzles, and so little time to spend on them. Maybe Dulcie's idea was a good one, after all. He himself couldn't keep spending nine or ten hours a day under simulation even if he had nothing else to do, and the Old Man certainly wouldn't leave him alone forever.

And what about Dulcie herself? His good opinion of her, bolstered by the unhesitating speed with which she had dispatched that idiot Celestino, had been diminished more than a little by her insistence on going back to New York. And all because of a cat—a cat! The most amazing technological advance conceivable, this Otherland network, a simulation more real than RL itself, and she was worried about leaving her cat with that pale blonde slut of a downstairs neighbor another week or two. The stupidity of it was almost enough to warrant taking Ms. Anwin off the protected species list.

What was even more irritating was that he had just sunk many thousands of his own personal credits, stringently shielded from the Old Man's notice, into building a new office to share with her in Cartagena, and now he had to worry instead whether her home system could competently carry this kind of bandwidth. When she had said she was going home, he had seriously considered just killing her and doing the whole Otherland surveillance by himself. But that would not have been practical, of course—not under current circumstances.

A pleasure deferred, then.

It was particularly galling, however, to be dependent on a woman. As a rule he never trusted anyone with more than a small piece of a job, and held all the connectors in his own hands. When you delegated, you always suffered some signal degradation. Just look at the way that pusbag of a gear man had almost blown the whole thing to bits.

Well, Celestino was landfill now, a job even *he* would have trouble screwing up.

Dread lit a thin Corriegas cigar, one of the few compensations of being stuck in South America as far as he was concerned, and contemplated his options. He had to be ready if the Old Man had another job for him; this was exactly the wrong time to show any hesitation or resistance. He also had to keep the Otherland puppet sim active, either by himself or with help from trustworthy employees. So far, Dulcie Anwin still fit that category, but bringing in someone else would just mean more management for him, more security concerns, more possible points at which something could go massively astray. . . .

He would put that decision aside for later, he decided. When Dulcie took over in four hours, and if the residual stimulants in his system would permit it, he would try to get a little sleep, and then he might be in a better frame of mind to judge something so important.

But in the interim, he needed to get on with some of his own research. What the people caught inside the Otherland simulation network had discovered told him very little so far about the Old Man's purposes; what they had unwittingly revealed about themselves, though, was more immediately useful. For one thing, if he decided to bring in other sim drivers to help, he could then look into trying to replace a second member of that merry little band of river travelers, in case his current infiltration got bounced from the system by the next giant fish attack or whatever.

However, he was even more interested in knowing who these people were and why the mysterious Sellars had brought them together, and of all the travelers, the African woman and her friend were the top priority. He had the others where he could keep an eye on them, but for all he knew Renie whatever-her-name-was had been knocked offline, in which case she was now a very loose thread indeed.

Dread notched down the intensity of the rhythm track to something more in line with careful thought, then sent a smoke ring spinning toward the low, white ceiling. The room was windowless, part of a half-untenanted office complex in the outer ring of Cartagena, but it had high-bandwidth data lines, and that was all he cared about.

This Renie was African, that much he could have told just from her accent. But someone had said that her companion was a Bushman, and some quick reference-checking suggested that most of the remnants of that people were to be found in Botswana and South Africa. That didn't mean that the woman couldn't be from somewhere else, that they might not have met online, but he liked the odds that they were both from the same place.

So, Botswana and South Africa. He didn't know a lot else about her, but he knew that her brother was in a coma, and when cross-checked with her first name and its possible variants, that would have to narrow things down considerably.

But he wasn't going to do it himself. Not the grunt work. Since the job seemed likely to be in southern Africa, he would let Klekker and his associates handle it, at least until they found a hot trail. After that, he wasn't so sure: Klekker's men were mostly thugs, which certainly came in handy sometimes, but this was a very delicate situation. He would decide when he knew more.

Dread sent up another smoke ring, then waved his hand, obliterating it. The adrenals had kicked in, and along with the rush of energy he felt a sort of blind, idiot ache in his groin and behind his eyes that he hadn't felt since the night he'd taken the stewardess. It was an itch, he knew, that would become more than that soon, but he didn't know how he could possibly find the time to hunt safely. He was right on the edge of the biggest thing ever, and for once he intended to take the Old Man's advice and not let his private pleasures compromise his business.

Dread grinned. The old bastard would be so proud.

A thought occurred to him. He lowered a hand to his crotch and squeezed meditatively. It wasn't a good time to hunt—at least not in RL. But this simulation was so realistic. . . .

What would it feel like, to hunt in Otherland? How closely would these sims imitate life—especially in the losing of it?

He squeezed again, then brought the drums back up inside his head until he could feel them buzzing in his cheekbones, the sound track for some ultimate jungle movie of danger and darkness. The idea, once kindled, began to burn.

What would it feel like?

CHAPTER 5

The Marching Millions

NETFEED/NEWS: US, China At Odds Over Antarctica
(visual: signing ceremony for Six Powers treaty)
VO: Only months after the signing of the Zurich accord, two of the Six Powers
are again squabbling over Antarctica.
(visual: American embassy in Ellsworth)
Chinese and American companies, both of which license space for
commercial exploitation from the UN, are in a dispute over who has the
rights to what is thought to be a rich vein of mineral deposits in the Wilkes
Land area. Tensions rose last week when two Chinese explorers disappeared,
and accusations were made by Chinese media sources that US workers had
kidnapped or even murdered them . . .

"CAN I come in?" a voice asked in Renie's ear.

Two seconds later, Lenore Kwok appeared in the conference room. She wore a jaunty leather aviatrix helmet and what looked like new coveralls.

They probably are new, Renie thought. *Just switched back to default setting.* Even someone who had spent as much time in simulation as she had was finding it hard to reconcile herself to this amazingly realistic new world—no, new *universe,* for all intents and purposes, with different rules for every piece of it.

"I'm really sorry," Lenore said, "but I still don't have anybody to help you with your gear. A lot of people aren't on the Hive today—I think it's some kind of system problem. Things are pretty crazy. So what you've got is those of us who are at the end of shift, and mostly we're all in the middle of something." She made an appropriately sad face. "But I thought I'd give you a quick tour of the place anyway. Then, if you want, you can come along with me and Cullen to look at the *Eciton burchelli* bivouac. It's spectacular major, and you'd probably like it better than sitting around here."

!Xabbu clambered up onto Renie's shoulder to gain a better conversational position. "What is this thing you are going to see?"

"Ants. Come along—you've never seen anything like it. By the time we get back, they should have the system problems ironed out, and someone will be able to help you."

Renie looked at !Xabbu, who shrugged his narrow simian shoulders. "Okay. But we really need to get out of here, and not just for your sake."

"I utterly understand." Lenore nodded earnestly. "You probably have things to do at home. It must be big slow being stuck online."

"Yes. Big slow."

Lenore wiggled her fingers and the conference room disappeared, replaced instantly by a huge, domed auditorium. Only a few of the seats were filled, and tiny spots of light gleamed above a dozen or so others, but the vast room was mostly deserted. On the stage—or rather above the stage—floated the largest insect Renie had ever seen, a grasshopper the size of a jet plane.

"... *The exoskeleton,*" a cultivated, disembodied voice was saying, "*has many survival advantages. Evaporation of fluids can be reduced, a definite plus for small animals whose surface-area-to-volume ratio makes them prone to fluid loss, and the skeletal structure also provides a great deal of internal surface area for muscle attachment. . . .*"

The grasshopper continued to pivot slowly in midair, but one of its sides detached and lifted away from its body, an animated cutaway.

"Normally this would be for the first-year students," Lenore explained, "the lucky ones who get to come to the Hive at all. But there's almost nobody here today, like I told you."

As various bits of the grasshopper drifted loose, some vanishing to provide a better view of the section they had covered, other parts were highlighted briefly, lit from within.

"*The exoskeleton itself is largely made up of cuticle, which is secreted by the epidermis directly beneath, a layer of epithelial cells which rest on a granular layer called the 'basement membrane.'*" Various strata in the exposed armor glimmered into life and then faded. *"The cuticle itself is not only extremely efficient at controlling fluid loss, it serves as protection for the animal as well. Insect cuticle has a tensile strength as great as aluminum with only half the weight. . . ."*

!Xabbu was staring solemnly up at the revolving grasshopper. "Like gods," he murmured. "Do you remember when I said that, Renie? With these machines, people can behave as though they were gods."

"Pretty chizz, huh?" said Lenore. "I'll show you some more of the place."

With another finger flick they left the auditorium. Lenore's tour of the Hive took them to the cafeteria—although, she quickly explained, no one really ate there; it was more of a gathering place. High windows made one wall of the beautiful room entirely transparent, looking out onto a grass-forested hillside and the edge of a massive tree root. The difference in perspective between the human-sized objects in the room and the insect's-eye view made Renie faintly uneasy, like staring down a very steep angle.

Their guide whisked them through a variety of other spaces—mostly lab rooms, which were smaller versions of the auditorium, where virtual specimens and data could be manipulated in at least three dimensions and a rainbow of colors. They were also shown some "quiet spots" designed just for relaxation and deep pondering, created with the same care that might be lavished on *haiku* poems. There was even a museum of sorts, with small representations of various anomalies discovered in the living laboratory outside the Hive's walls.

"One of the most amazing things," Lenore said, gesturing at a many-legged creature hovering in midair and lit by invisible light sources, "is that some of these aren't like anything in the real world at all. We wonder sometimes if Kunohara's playing games with us—Cullen's sure of it—but our charter is predicated on an accurate simulation of a ten-thousand-meter-square cross-section of real terrain, with real life-forms, so I'm not sure I believe that. I mean, Kunohara's pretty serious about the field himself. I can't see him just inventing imaginary insects and throwing them into an environment he's been so careful to maintain."

"Are there other things that are strange in this simulation world?" asked !Xabbu.

"Well, reports sometimes of objects that don't belong in any real-world simulation at all, and some weird effects—ripples in the base media, funny lights, local distortions. But of course, entomologists are just as likely as anyone else to get tired and see things, especially in a place like this, which is already pretty overwhelming."

"Why did this Kunohara person make all this?" Renie wondered.

"Your guess is as good as mine." Lenore flipped her hand through her hair, and this very human gesture paradoxically reminded Renie that she was watching a simulation, that the real Lenore might look nothing like this creature before her, and was certainly physically somewhere else entirely. "I read somewhere that he was one of those kids that was obsessed by bugs when he was little—of course, that's true for most of us here. But the difference was, he made money at it. Secured some crucial biomedical patents when he was in his early twenties—that Cimbexin stuff they're trying to use as a cellular-growth on-off switch was one of his, and that self-fitting tile, Informica—and made millions. Billions, eventually."

"And so he built this with the money?" !Xabbu was examining a caddisfly larva with what seemed too many legs as it emerged from its chrysalis over and over in a looped display.

"No, we built this, if you mean the Hive—well, a consortium of universities and agribusinesses did. But Kunohara built the world out-side—the simulation we're studying. And it's really pretty amazing. Come on, I'll show you."

The transition from the Hive museum to the cabin of the dragonfly-plane was instantaneous. Cullen was already in his pilot's seat. He nodded in greeting, then returned to his instruments.

"Sorry to jump you around like that," said Lenore, "but we take advantage of our sovereignty in the Hive and don't waste much time imitating normality. As soon as we go through the hangar doors, ev-erything happens in real time and like real life, even if it *is* happening in Giant Bug World. Kunohara's rules."

"He'd make us walk if he could," Cullen said. "Every now and then one of our sims gets munched—a migration specialist named Traynor got cornered by a whip scorpion the other day. Turned him into bug-food faster than I can say it. I bet Kunohara thought that was pretty funny."

"What happened to him?" !Xabbu asked worriedly, clearly picturing what a scorpion would look like at this scale.

"To Traynor? Just a rude shock, then he got bounced out of the system." Cullen rolled his eyes. "That's what always happens. But then we had to reapply to get him another licensed sim. That's why Angela wasn't exactly pleased to see you. The celebrated Mr. K. is pretty tight-sphinctered about what goes in and out of his simworld."

"Thanks for that vivid image, Cullen," said Lenore.

"Belt up," he responded. "I'm talking to you two rookies in particu-lar. I've got clearance, and we're ready to fly. You don't want to get tactor-bounced any more than necessary."

As Renie and !Xabbu scrambled to secure themselves, the hangar door slid open, revealing a wall of shadowy plant shapes and a light gray sky.

"What time is it?" Renie asked.

"Where you are? You'd know better than me." Lenore shook her head. "This simworld's on GMT. It's a little after five AM here. The best time to see the *Eciton* is when they start moving around dawn."

"We're cutting it fine, though." Cullen frowned. "If you'd been here on time, Kwok, we'd be there by now."

"Shut up and fly this old crate, bug-boy."

!Xabbu sat quietly, staring out the window as the mountainous trees loomed and then slid past on either side. Renie could not help but be impressed herself: It was daunting, seeing things from this perspective. A lifetime of ecological catastrophes being pumped through her consciousness by the newsnets had left her with a feeling of the environment as a fragile thing, an ever-thinning web of greenery and clean water. In the real world that might be so, but to be brought down to this size was to see nature in its former terrifying and dictatorial splendor. She could at last truly imagine the Earth as Gaea, as a single living thing, and herself as a part of a complicated system rather than a something perched atop the ladder of Creation. So much of that sense of mastery was perspective, she realized— simply a product of being one of the larger animals. At her current size, every leaf was a marvel of complexity. Beneath every stone, on every lump of dirt, lived whole thriving villages of tiny creatures, and on those animals lived even more minute creatures. For the first time, she could imagine the chain of life down to molecules, and even smaller.

And has someone built that here as well? she wondered. *As !Xabbu said, are we becoming gods, that we can grow ourselves as big as a universe, or walk inside an atom?*

It was hard not to be impressed by Atasco and Kunohara and the rest—at least those who had not knowingly built their wonderlands with the suffering of others. What she had seen so far was truly stunning.

"God *damn*." Cullen slapped his hand against the steering wheel. "We're late."

Renie leaned so that she could look past him, but all she could see through the windshield was more of the giant forest. "What is it?"

"The troop's already on the move," said Lenore. "See those?" She pointed to several dark shapes fitting above them in the branches.

"Those are antbirds and woodcreepers. They follow the *Eciton* swarm when it travels, and feed on the creatures driven ahead of it."

"I'm going to have to put on the autopilot," Cullen said crossly. "It's going to be bumpy, but don't blame me—*I* was on time."

"Human pilots aren't fast enough to avoid all the bird strikes," Lenore explained. "Don't take Cullen's charming manners too personally. He's always like this before breakfast, aren't you, Cully?"

"Get locked."

"It is too bad, though," she went on. "One of the most interesting things about the *Eciton* is how they make their camp—their 'bivouac' as it's called. They have tarsal claws, these hooks on their feet, and when the troop stops, they grab each other and link up into long hanging vertical chains. Other ants hook on, until eventually there's a kind of net many layers deep, made entirely of ants, that covers the queen and her larvae."

Renie was fairly certain she'd heard of more disgusting things in her life but she couldn't think of any offhand. "These are army ants?"

"One type," agreed Lenore. "If you're from Africa, you may have seen driver ants . . ."

Her disquisition on Renie's domestic insects was cut short as the dragonfly plane abruptly dropped like a stone, then tumbled in midair before pulling out of its dive and into a long, flat skim above the grass forest. Cullen whooped. "Damn, we're quick!"

Renie was struggling not to throw up. Even !Xabbu, despite the mask of baboon features, looked more than a little unsettled.

Lenore's naturalist lecture was kept on hold over the next few minutes by a further succession of evasive procedures. Passing through an almost continuous serious of dives, banks, and loop-the-loops to avoid birds that Renie seldom even saw before the autopilot reacted, the dragonfly seemed to travel ten times as far vertically and horizontally as it did forward. In fact, Lenore explained, they really weren't even trying to go forward; instead, they were waiting in place for the swarm to approach.

Between being rattled against !Xabbu in the passenger alcove and bouts of severe queasiness, Renie managed to wonder at how realistic these sensations of weightlessness and g-force were. It seemed hard to believe that they could be generated solely by the V-tanks in which their bodies were currently floating.

A vast feathered shadow suddenly loomed in the windshield. Another thought-swift jerk in direction, this one an unadvertised columnar rise that seemed to slam her guts down into her shoes, finally proved too much. Renie tasted vomit at the back of her mouth, then felt her stomach convulse. There were no visible results of sickness within the simulation; a moment later, except for the slowing contractions in her midsection, even Renie felt as though it had never happened.

Must be the waste hoses in my mask pumping it away, she thought weakly. *That mask that I can't feel anymore.* Aloud, she said, "I can't take much more of this."

"Problem not." Cullen, body language suggesting he wasn't too thrilled with having passengers at all, reached out to the wheel and dropped the dragonfly into a sharp spiral. "It will only get worse when the swarm shows up, when we're trying to take readings *and* avoid those damn birds."

"It's too bad," Lenore said. "You won't have quite as close a view. But we'll try to set you down somewhere you can still see." She pointed at the viewscreen. "Look, there's the prey wave-front! The *Eciton* are almost here."

Hurrying through the matted foliage, dawn light winking dully on wing and carapace, came a seething rout of insects—madly-stilting beetles, skimming flies, large creatures like spiders and scorpions treading the slower, smaller prey underfoot in their hurry to escape the great enemy: Renie thought it looked like some bizarre insectoid prison break. As moments passed, and as the dragonfly spiraled down, the wave of prey insects grew denser and more chaotic. The blankly inhuman heads and jointed limbs jerking in heedless flight upset her. They looked like an army of the damned, hopelessly fleeing the trumpets of the Last Judgment.

"See those?" Lenore pointed out a group of slender-winged insects that flew above the panicked herd, but seemed far more purposeful than those below. "Those are *ithomiines*—ant butterflies, so-called. They follow the *Eciton* everywhere, just like the antbirds do—in fact, they feed on the birds' droppings."

The dragonfly's hatch hissed open. Overcome by a little too much of Nature at her most cloacal extremes, Renie struggled down the ladder and onto the top of a mossy stone, then bent double to coax the blood back into her head. !Xabbu clambered down and stood beside her.

"Just stay fairly still," Lenore called down through the hatchway. "The birds and others have plenty to feed on, but you don't want to call attention to yourselves unnecessarily. We'll be back to pick you up in about half an hour."

"What if something gets us?"

"Then I guess you'll be offline sooner than we thought," was Lenore's cheerful rejoinder. "Enjoy the show!"

"Well, thank you so much," Renie growled, but the dragonfly wings had beat into life again, pressing her down by the force of their wind, and she doubted the woman had heard. A moment later the dragonfly leaped upward with the force of a brief and localized hurricane, then zigzagged forward over the oncoming insect stampede and disappeared into the forest.

Now that they were out in the open, Renie could hear the sounds properly, and realized that she had never thought of Nature as being noisy. In fact, she realized, most of the nature she'd seen had possessed a classical sound track and voice-over narration. Here, the twittering of the hunting birds alone was almost deafening, and with the clicking and rasping of prey in full flight, coupled with the swarms of flies that buzzed above the hurrying mass, she and !Xabbu might have been listening to some kind of bizarre factory floor working at a nightmarish level of production.

She lowered herself to a tuft of moss; when she sank in and found herself surrounded by stiff tubular stems, she realized the moss was almost as deep as she was tall. She moved to a bare section of rock and sat down.

"So what do you think?" she said to !Xabbu at last. "This must make you feel very excited about your own hopes. I mean, if they can build this, then surely you can build the place you want to."

He squatted beside her. "I must confess that I have not been thinking about my project in the last hours. I am amazed by all this. I am amazed. I could never have dreamed such things were possible."

"Neither could I."

He shook his head, his tiny monkey brow crinkling. "It is a level of realism that actually frightens me, Renie. I think I know now how my ancestors and tribesmen must have felt when they saw an airplane for the first time, or the lights of a big city."

Renie squinted into the distance. "The grass is moving. I mean *really* moving."

!Xabbu narrowed his own deep-sunken eyes. "It is the ants. Grandfather Mantis!" he gasped, then murmured something unintelligible in his own language. "Look at them!"

Renie could have chosen to do nothing else. The leading edge of the ant swarm was pouring into the comparatively clear space before them in relentless, viscous waves like lava, smothering grass, leaves, and everything else. The ants were mostly dark brown, with reddish abdomens. Each slender insect was almost twice as long as Renie was tall, not counting the segmented antennae which seemed to move a dozen times for every other motion the ants made. But it was not as individuals that they exercised their profound, horrifying magic.

As the main body of the swarm surged into view, Renie gaped, unable to speak. The front stretched away out of sight in a line that was miles across by her perspective, and it was not a thin front. The swarming, seething mass of ants streamed back into the vegetation in such thickly clotted thousands that it seemed the entire edge of the world had grown legs and was marching toward them.

Despite the first appearance of inexorable progress, the *Eciton* did not simply march. The outriders scurried forward, then turned and hurried back to the nearest pseudopod of the writhing mass; in the meantime, others followed the path they had just blazed, and then explored farther before hurrying back themselves, until the entire living clot had moved into the area the outriders had just visited. Thus the army crawled forward like some huge amoeba, a vast seething lump that was nevertheless questingly alive down to its last particle, an army that to Renie's vastly shrunken gaze might have covered all of Durban beneath its hurrying bodies.

"Jesus Mercy," Renie whispered. "I've never . . ." She fell back into silence.

The dragonfly appeared from out of the trees farther back in the swarm, and moved over the front of the column, darting and then hovering while its human pilots made their observations. It swerved with reflexive suddenness to avoid a brown-and-white bird, which continued in its downward plummet and snatched up a struggling cockroach instead.

Seeing the dragonfly plane made Renie feel a little less overwhelmed. It was a simulation, after all, and even if within this simulation she were no more than a tiny fleck in the path of an ant swarm, nevertheless humans had built it, and humans could bring her back out of it safely.

The ant mass had surged to within what by her terms was only a quarter of a mile from the base of the rock on which she and !Xabbu sat, but their vantage point seemed to stand outside the main thrust of the swarm's pulsing forward movement, so she was able to relax a little and even enjoy the sheer spectacle. Lenore had been right—it was an amazing show.

"They are very fast, especially when we are so small," said a voice behind her. "The leading edges of an *Eciton burchelli* raid move at about twenty meters per hour."

Renie jumped in shock. For half a moment, she thought that Cullen had landed the plane and that he and Lenore had snuck up on them, that she had been watching a real dragonfly instead of the Hive aircraft, but the white-robed sim standing a few paces away up the hill was clearly someone entirely new.

"They are hypnotic to watch, are they not?" the stranger asked. He smiled within the shadow of his hood.

"Who are you?"

The stranger brushed the hood back just casually enough to avoid melodrama, revealing close-cropped black hair and a heavily lined, Asian face. "I am Kunohara. But you have probably guessed that, haven't you? They do still mention my name at the Hive, I presume." His diction was careful, his English overprecise but otherwise flawless. Renie did not think he was using any translation gear.

"They mentioned you, yes."

"This is your world, is it not?" !Xabbu asked the newcomer. Renie could see subtle signs of her friend's nervousness, and she was not tremendously comfortable with the stranger herself. "It is very, very impressive."

"The Hive people have certainly brought you to see one of its most spectacular manifestations," Kunohara said. "The swarm looks full of confusion, but it is not. Do you see the spider, there?" He pointed down to the nearest edge of the boiling mass. A long-legged green spider had failed to outrun one of the pseudopods, and now was clinched in doomed combat with a trio of large-headed ants. "She has encountered the true soldiers of the *Eciton* swarm. They 'walk point,' as the military people would put it. They only fight to defend the swarm—most prey is killed by the minor and media workers. But see what happens!"

The spider had been turned onto its back; its struggles were slowing. Even as its legs kicked feebly, a group of smaller ants rushed over it. Two of them severed its head with jaws as sharp and competent as gardener's shears; others began to bite through other parts and carry them away, back to the body of the swarm. Within moments, all that was left was the heavy, smooth abdomen and attached bits of the thorax.

"They will bring up a submajor," said Kunohara, with as much satisfaction as if he watched the last act of a favorite opera. "See, the soldiers have already gone back to their patrol. They do not carry things, but a submajor does."

A larger ant indeed appeared as if summoned, straddled the remaining piece of the spider, which was larger than the ant itself, and grasped the edge of the ragged thorax in its jaws. Several of the smaller ants came up to help, and together they trundled it back into the foraging mass.

"You see?" Kunohara began to walk slowly down the hill, still watching the *Eciton* swarm. "It seems to be chaotic, but only to the uninformed eye. In reality, a finite but flexible series of behaviors, when multiplied by thousands or millions of individuals, creates extreme complexity and extreme efficiency. Ants have lived for ten million generations, where we have only thousands. They are perfect, and they care nothing about us—one writer, I remember, said they were 'pitiless and elegant.' Of course, one could possibly say the same of high-level simulations as well. But we have only begun to discover the complexity of our own artificial life." He stopped and gave a curious smile, shy and yet not very winning. "I am lecturing again. My family always told me that I loved the sound of my own voice. Perhaps that is why I spend so much time alone now."

Renie didn't quite know what to say. "As my friend said, this is very impressive."

"Thank you. But now it is perhaps time for *you* to talk." He took a few steps down the stone toward them. Beneath the white robe and white baggy trousers, Kunohara was barefooted. Now that he was closer, she could see he was not a great deal taller than !Xabbu—or at least his sim was only a little larger than !Xabbu would have been in his own body. She gave up. It was too much like a problem in Einsteinian relativity. "What brings you here?" Kunohara asked. "You have come from Atasco's simulation world, have you not?"

He knew. Renie wondered how that could be. Then again, he had access to all the machineries of the simulation, while she and !Xabbu were no more free here than lab rats.

"Yes," she admitted. "Yes, we have, as a matter of fact. Something was going wrong there, so we came through. . . ."

"A back door into my world, of course. There are several of those. And there was more than something merely going wrong, as I think you probably know. Bolivar Atasco has been killed. In real life."

!Xabbu's small fingers tightened again on her arm, but something about Kunohara's bright eyes made her think lying would be a mistake. "Yes, we knew that. Did you know Atasco?"

"As a colleague, yes. We shared resources—programming on this level is almost incomprehensibly expensive. That is why I have a microscopic version of one of the forests in Atasco's version of Colombia. It allowed us to share raw materials at the earliest stages, although we differed in our focus. Now, despite being representations of the same geographical area, they are completely different in effect. Bolivar Atasco's interest was at the human scale. Mine, as you have noticed, is not."

Renie felt obscurely as though she were playing for time, although nothing Kunohara had done suggested any ill will. "What is it about insects that interests you so much?"

He laughed, a strange, breathy giggle. Renie had the impression she had done something expected but still disappointing. "It is not that I am so interested in insects, it is that everyone else is so interested in humans. Atasco and his Grail Brotherhood friends are an excellent example. All that money, all that power, and their concerns still so restrictedly human."

Beside her, !Xabbu had gone as still as stone. "The Grail Brotherhood? You know about them?" Renie asked, then paused before deciding to push forward. "Are you a member?"

He giggled again. "Oh, no, no. Not my cup of tea at all, as the expression goes. Nor am I interested in the opposite side of the coin, those deadly earnest folk from the Circle."

"The Circle?" !Xabbu almost squeaked. "What do they have to do with this?"

Kunohara ignored him. "Always these dualisms—mechanists or spiritualists." He extended both hands as though waiting to catch something that might fall from the air. "Always choosing one side of the coin, instead of simply choosing the coin itself. Both have so strongly rejected the other's side that they will regret it one day." He clapped his palms together, then extended a closed hand toward !Xabbu. It was a clear invitation. The Bushman hesitated for a moment, then reached out with a thin monkey finger and touched Kunohara's fist. It opened to reveal two butterflies sitting on his palm, one black, one white—insects built to their human scale rather than the titan forms of the simulation. Their wings fluttered gently in the breeze.

Renie and !Xabbu were both very quiet, watching Kunohara and his butterflies.

"Speaking of the dualistic approach, there are a pair of ideas you might find useful," Kunohara said, "if any of this matters to you, that is. On the mechanistic side, may I point out Dollo's Law, beloved of the early A-life theorists, although strangely ignored by the Grail engineers. Turning to spiritual iconology, you might find the Buddhist figure *Kishimo-jin* of interest—and also because as a parable it suggests reasons for tentative optimism. However, Buddhists tend to think in longer terms than is strictly comfortable for the rest of us, so perhaps you won't find it personally very soothing." He closed his hand and then swiftly opened it again. The two butterflies had been replaced by a single gray one. Kunohara flung it upward. It beat its wings a few times, then popped out of existence.

"What is this about?" Renie demanded. "These riddles? Why can't you just tell us whatever it is you think we should know?"

"Oh, no, that is not the way of true learning." Kunohara abruptly giggled again; Renie was beginning to find it a very irritating sound. "Any Zen master worth his certificate will tell you that beggars truly cannot be choosers."

"Who are you? Why are you even talking to us?"

Kunohara turned. His gaze, though still bright and steady, was opaque, as though whatever lived behind the simulated face was losing interest. "Why talk to you? Well, the precise entomological term for my interest would be 'gadfly,' I believe. And my simulation should tell who I am, and why I have only passing interest in the conflicts of gods." He pointed to the teeming throng of ants below, an ocean of chewing, crawling monsters. "By the way, speaking as I was of mechanists, I believe your friends from the Hive are soon to understand the fallacy of control a little more clearly." He brought his hand to his white-robed chest. "As for me—well, as I said, my simulation should reveal all. You see . . . I am only a *little* man."

The next moment Renie and !Xabbu were alone on the rock outcropping.

She was the one to break the long silence. "What was that about? I mean, what did he want—could you make any sense of that?"

"He said 'the Circle'—spoke of them as though they were in some way like the Grail Brotherhood." !Xabbu seemed dumbfounded, his hand clapped flat on his sloping skull.

"So? I've never heard of them. Who are they?"

!Xabbu's monkey face was so mournful she felt she might cry just looking at him. "They are the people who sent me to school, Renie. This I told you. At least, that is what the group who paid for my schooling were named—the Circle. Could it be coincidence?"

Renie couldn't think anymore. Kunohara's words rolled around in her mind, beginning to jumble together. She needed to remember. There were things he had said that she would want to consider later. All she could do in way of response to !Xabbu was shake her head.

They were still sitting silently when the dragonfly returned and lowered its ladder.

"This is like being in the frigging Stone Age!" Cullen raged as she and !Xabbu strapped themselves in. "I mean, just unbelievable!"

"The system's doing all kinds of weird things," Lenore explained. "We can't communicate with the Hive properly."

"Can't communicate at all," snarled Cullen. "Can't go offline, can't do anything."

"You can't go offline either?" Renie could almost hear a distant drumbeat again, a rising signal of apprehension direct from her animal hindbrain.

Lenore shrugged. "Yeah, you're not the only ones, it seems. Ordinarily it wouldn't make much difference, but the *Eciton* swarm has turned. It's heading toward the Hive."

"Right," said Cullen bitterly, "and if they get there without us warning anyone so they can seal it off, the damn make-believe ants will just wipe it out. Playing by Kunohara's stupid rules, we'll have to rebuild and reprogram almost from scratch."

Renie had been about to mention their encounter with the sim-world's master, but suddenly decided not to. She gave !Xabbu a significant look, hoping he would understand and keep quiet about their experience.

Something was definitely going on, and Renie had a distinct and depressing feeling it was a lot more complicated than these two young entomologists dreamed. The Otherland network was changing—Sellars had said something about that. It had reached some kind of critical mass. But these two only knew it as a wonderful site to do academic simulations, an excellent toy, a kind of scientist's theme park; they didn't realize that the place was an ogre's castle built with bones and blood.

The silence stretched. The plane skimmed on, passing great curved walls of bark, shooting between leaves that stretched like vast green sails.

"I have a question," !Xabbu said at last. "You say that like us, you cannot leave the simulation, and that you cannot communicate with your home, the Hive."

"It's not my home," the pilot snapped. "Jesus, monkey-man, I do have a *life,* you know."

"Don't be a grump, Cully," Lenore said gently.

"What I do not understand," said !Xabbu, "is why you do not simply unplug yourself." His small eyes stared intently at the pilot. "Why do you not do that?"

"Because someone has to pass the message about the *Eciton* swarm," Cullen said.

"But could you not do that better from offline, if normal communication within this simulation world is not working?"

Renie was impressed by the way the little man had thought things through; clearly, he was using the Hive people's dilemma to explore their own problem.

"Well," said Cullen with sudden and surprising fury, "if you really want to know, I can't *find* my goddamn jack. It's like it isn't even there. Something's gone utterly, utterly scanned with the whole thing. So unless someone comes into my lab and pulls my plug, I'm going to have to wait until the system resets, or whatever locking else is wrong gets fixed."

Now Renie heard the fear beneath the anger, and knew her own forebodings had been all too well-founded.

Before anyone could say anything else, something knocked the plane sideways.

"Christ!" shouted Cullen. He dragged himself upright, fighting gravity. "Christ! We've lost half the instrument lights!" He struggled to pull the wheel back. The dragonfly-plane wobbled badly, stalled for a moment, then surged into life again. It leveled itself, but something was clearly very wrong. "What was *that?*" he demanded.

"Bird, I think." Lenore was leaning forward, touching lights on the control panel, of which more was now dark than illuminated. "Two of the wings are damaged, and we're missing a leg or two as well."

"I can't keep this thing up in the air," Cullen said through gritted teeth. "Shit! That's about a year's worth of my salary shot to hell if this thing's ruined."

"They're not going to make you pay for it." Lenore sounded like she was talking to a frustrated child, but she herself had an air of barely-controlled panic. "Can we make it back okay?"

Cullen considered for a moment. "No. We could never evade another bird, and if we lose one more wing, I won't even have a half-assed chance of landing."

He was worrying about losing a major chunk of programming in some weird reality-swap with Kunohara, Renie realized, but she could no longer think about the perils of Otherland in such a distanced way. They were in immediate danger of crashing to the ground, with everything the simulation could make of that—including, perhaps, the ultimate reality.

"Land," she said. "Don't mess about. We'll walk back."

Cullen darted a look at her, momentarily calm with a kind of amused rage. "Jesus, we really are back to the Stone Age. On foot in Bugland." He pushed the wheel forward and started working the pedals. The dragonfly lurched downward, threatened to tip over on its nose, then leveled again and began a slow, juddering spiral toward the forest floor.

Something dark momentarily blotted the window.

"Cullen, the autopilot's gone," Lenore warned him.

Cullen jerked the plane to one side. The bird missed them, rocketing past like a surface-to-air missile and buffeting them with the wind of its passing. Cullen fought to drag the plane upright once more, but now something was definitely wrong, and the downward spiral took on a deeper, swifter angle.

"Brace yourselves!" he shouted. "I don't think the tactor settings will let anything too painful happen, but—"

He didn't get a chance to finish. The dragonfly caught a wing on a low-hanging branch. After a grinding crunch, the plane flipped over and plummeted toward the ground. Renie had only about a second to prepare, two or three heartbeats, then something flung her against the cabin wall and her head exploded with light, which drained away a moment later into darkness.

CHAPTER 6

Man from the Dead Lands

THE man named Birdcatcher had pressed his stone spear so tight against Paul Jonas' guts that the point had pierced the skin. Paul took a shallow breath and felt the pain expand like a tiny star as his stomach pressed against the spearhead. He was trapped, pinned on his back with the other man standing over him.

"What do you want?" he asked, struggling to keep his voice quiet and calm.

Birdcatcher had the wild look of a first-time bank robber. "If I kill you, you will go back to the Land of the Dead and leave us alone."

"I'm not from the Land of the Dead."

Birdcatcher's brow jerked in confusion. "You said that you were."

"No, I didn't. *You* said that when you pulled me out of the river. I just didn't argue with you."

Birdcatcher squinted fiercely but did nothing, puzzling over Paul's words but not discounting them completely. Deceit was apparently not common among the People, something that at another time Paul would have found fascinating.

"No," Birdcatcher said at last, slow and deliberate as a judge delivering sentence. He appeared to have reached the limit of his reasoning ability and given up. "No, you are from the Land of the Dead. I will kill you, and you will go back."

Paul brought up his hands to clasp the barrel of Birdcatcher's spear and twisted it hard, but the Neandertal held it braced between his chest and arm and would not let go. Paul hung on and pushed back with all his power as Birdcatcher leaned forward to dig it in deeper. Paul thought he could feel the tissues of his belly stretching before the stone point. His arms trembled with the strain of holding it away.

"Stop!"

Keeping his weight on the spear, Birdcatcher turned to look for the voice. Runs Far was walking quickly toward them, hands extended as though Birdcatcher's anger was a living thing that might suddenly attack. "Stop," he said again. "What are you doing?"

"He has come from the Land of the Dead," Birdcatcher declared. "He has come for my boy child."

"Boy child?" Paul shook his head. "I don't know anything about any child."

Others of the People had begun to wake and move toward them, a tatty horde of shadows that appeared barely human in the weak light from the coals.

"He is a ghost," Birdcatcher said stubbornly. "He came from the river to take my boy child."

Paul felt sure Runs Far would now say something wise and chieflike, but instead the other man only grunted and stepped back into the dark.

This isn't how it's supposed to be, Paul thought desperately. *If this were a story, I would have saved his life or something, and he'd have to help me.* He pushed on the spear again, but he had no leverage. For long moments he and Birdcatcher remained locked in silent tension, but Paul knew he could not hold the sharp point away much longer.

"Let me see the child," he pleaded, his voice thin because he could not take a deep breath. "Let me help him if I can."

"No." Fear streaked the rage in his voice, but there was not an ounce of give.

"Why is Birdcatcher trying to spill blood in our home?"

Dark Moon's quavering voice hit them like a splash of cold water. Birdcatcher had not flinched at Runs Far's appearance, but now he pulled the spearpoint from Paul's belly and took a step back. The ancient woman shuffled toward them, leaning on Runs Far's arm. She had evidently just awakened; her wispy hair stood up in tangles like smoke.

"Please," Paul said to her, "I am not a ghost. I do not mean the People any harm. If you want me to go away, I will go away." But even as he said it, he thought of the freezing darkness outside, peopled with monsters he could only dimly picture from half-forgotten books. Sabertooth tigers? Didn't horrors like that live side by side with the cave dwellers? But what was the alternative—a fight to the death against a Stone Age savage?

I'm not Tarzan! Helpless fury filled him. *What is the point of all this? I work in a bloody museum, for Christ's sake!*

"You say you will help the child." Dark Moon bent over him, her eyes wide, her face mostly in shadow.

"No." Paul fought despair and frustration. "No, I said I will help him if I can." He paused, still short of breath. Trying to communicate with these people was maddening, despite the common language.

Dark Moon reached her hand out to Birdcatcher, who shied away as though he feared being burned. She shuffled a few steps closer and reached out once more. This time he permitted her to touch his arm, which she encircled with her birdlike claws.

"He will go to the child," she said.

"No." Birdcatcher almost whispered, as though he spoke through great pain. "He will take my boy child away."

"If the dead call to your child, they call," said Dark Moon. "If they do not, they do not. You cannot keep away death with a spear. Not this kind of death."

Birdcatcher darted a glance at Paul, as if to remind her that he had been doing just that, but her hand tightened on his arm, and he dropped his head like a sullen adolescent.

Dark Moon turned to Paul. "Come to the child, Riverghost."

No one in the tribe offered to help him up, so Paul struggled to his feet alone. The place where Birdcatcher had jabbed him throbbed painfully, and when he put his hand to the spot he felt wetness on his fingers. The old woman and Runs Far turned and began a slow progress across the cave. Paul stepped in behind them, his reluctance increased when Birdcatcher followed him and rested the spearpoint lightly but eloquently against his back.

I have to get out of here, he thought. *These are not my people, and whatever this place is, it's not my place. I don't understand the rules.*

They led him toward a tent, one of the last in the line, so far from the fire that it had a small blaze of its own burning in a stone circle before it. Paul could imagine Birdcatcher sitting before the flames, brooding, working up his courage. If his grudge was over a sick child, it was hard to hate the man.

A swift shallow jab at his back when he hesitated at the camp's edge restored a little of his earlier dislike.

Birdcatcher's tent was smaller than some of the others; Paul had to stoop to make his way through the door flap. Three children waited in the tent, but only two looked up at his entrance, a goggle-eyed infant wrapped in furs and the little girl he had seen earlier. Mouths open, both had gone completely still, like startled squirrels. Between them lay a small boy, apparently being tended by the older girl, wrapped in hides so that only his head was exposed. His dark hair was matted on his forehead, and his eyes had rolled back beneath the trembling lids, so that the firelight spilling through the tent flap exposed two slightly pulsing slivers of white.

Paul knelt and gently touched his hand to the boy's forehead. He ignored Birdcatcher's angry murmur and kept his hand in place as the child weakly tried to turn his head away; the flesh seemed as hot as one of the stones on which the People cooked their food. When the boy, who looked to be nine or ten years old, brought up a feeble hand to push at Paul's wrist, he let go and sat up.

He stared at the small, pale face. This was another way in which this entire mad dream was disastrously unlike a good old-fashioned story. In flicks, in science fiction tales, one of the visitors from the future always knew modern medicine, and could make a jury-rigged defibrillator out of palm fronds, or whip up a quick dose of penicillin to save the ailing chief. Paul knew less about doctoring a child than had his own mother and grandmother, who at least had been raised in the fading tradition of women's special wisdom. Penicillin? Didn't it grow on moldy bread, somehow? And who was to say the child had an infection anyway, and not something far more difficult to cure, like a heart murmur or kidney failure?

Paul shook his head in frustration. He had been a fool even to offer to see the child, although he doubted that he had given the boy's father any false hope. He could feel Birdcatcher breathing on the back of his neck, could sense the man's tension as though the air in the immediate vicinity threatened a sudden storm.

"I don't think . . ." Paul began, and then the ill child began to speak.

It was little more than a whisper at first, the barest scratchings of breath across dry lips. Paul leaned toward him. The boy twitched and threw back his head, as though fighting to shake loose some invisible thing that clung to his neck, and his rasping voice grew louder.

". . . So dark . . . so cold . . . and all gone, all gathered, gone through the windows and doors and across the Black Ocean . . ."

Some of the People gasped and whispered. Paul felt a shudder run up his spine that had nothing to do with the spear pressed against his back. The Black Ocean . . . he had heard that phrase before. . . .

". . . Where are they?" The boy's grimy fingers scraped at the tent floor, snatching at nothing. "All I have is the dark. The voice, the One . . . took them all away through the windows. . . ."

His voice dropped back to a whisper. Paul leaned closer, but could make out nothing more in the fading, rustling speech which eventually became too quiet to hear. The fretful movements subsided. He stared down at the boy's pale features. The sagging mouth again seemed nothing but a conduit for wheezing breath. Paul had just lifted his hand to touch the child's forehead again when the boy suddenly opened his eyes.

Black. Black like holes, black like space, black like the inside of a closet door after it swings shut. The gaze roved a moment, unfocused, and someone behind him cried out in fear. Then the two pupils fixed on him and held him.

"*Paul? Where are you?*" It was *her* voice, the painful music of so many dreams. Hearing it here, in this shadowed place, he thought his heart would stop from the shock. For a long moment he could not breathe. "*You said you would come to me—you promised.*" Trembling, the boy reached up and caught at his hand with a grasp stronger than he ever could have imagined from such small fingers. "*Before you can find the mountain, you must find the wanderer's house. You must come to the wanderer's house and release the weaver.*"

Catching his breath at last, gasping it in like a man surfacing from ocean depths, he pulled away, struggling to fight free of the child's grip. For a moment the boy half-rose from the bed, hanging onto Paul like a fish on a line, but then his hold slipped and he fell back, silent and limp, his eyes shuttered once more. He had left something in Paul's hand.

After he uncurled his fingers, Paul had only a shivering moment to stare at the feather lying on his palm before something struck him explosively on the side of his head, tumbling him to his knees. There was a noise and stir at his back that seemed as distant as an old rumor, then something heavy collapsed onto him and fingers curled around his throat.

He could not see who he was fighting and did not care. He thrashed, trying to shake free of the vicious, unfair weight on top of him. Everything was stripes of light and dark and a wash of incomprehensible noise, but the roaring blackness in his head was fast blotting out all of it. He struggled with a force he did not know he had, and one of the strangling hands slipped from his neck. When it could not find its hold again, it gripped and gouged at his face instead. He tried to claw it away, then threw himself forward, struggling toward air as though he were in deep water—but his breathlessness went with him and could not be shaken loose. Something sharp scraped along his side, leaving a cold trail, and a little of his madness went away at the painful touch.

He rolled until he felt something stop him, then tried to get to his feet. The thing that clutched his face lifted away again, and once more something cold and sharp jabbed at his side. Paul threw himself forward and the thing restraining him gave way. The light changed as he fell forward, and the noises around him now came with echoes.

Something bright was right beside his head. He was filled with a fury, a frustrated rage that he somehow knew had long been trapped inside him, and had only now escaped. When he understood that the bright something was the blaze of the small campfire, that he had smashed his way out of the tent, he rolled toward it and tipped the murderous shape clinging to his back into the stone ring. Screaming as the elk in the hunters' pit had screamed, it let go of him and scrambled up and away, beating at the places where the fire had caught. But Paul was no longer interested in mere survival: he leaped across the campfire and pulled his enemy down, caring nothing for the flames that scorched his own skin. For a brief moment he saw Birdcatcher's terrified face beneath him. Something round and heavy and hot was in his hand—a stone from the firepit, a part of him realized, a cold, remorseless part. He raised it up so he could smash Birdcatcher and everything else back into darkness, but instead he himself was struck, a sudden and surprising blow to the back of his head that sent a jolt like an ungrounded electrical wire along his backbone and threw him down into nothing.

THE voices seemed to be arguing. They were small voices, and far away, and they did not seem terribly important.

Was it his mother and father? They did not argue much—usually the older Jonas treated Paul's mother with deference bordering on contempt, as though she were a poorly-made object that could not stand even ordinary handling. But every now and then his father's air of benign disinterest would vanish, usually when someone outside the house had rejected one of his ideas, and then there would be a brief flurry of shouting followed by silences that lasted hours—silences which had made the younger version of Paul feel that everyone in the house was listening for him to make a noise and thereby spoil something.

On those very few occasions when his mother stood up for herself and argued back, still in her fumbling, apologetic way, the shouting would not last any longer, but the silences might stretch for a day or more. During those long, deadly days, Paul stayed in his room, unwilling even to go out into the silence, calling up maps of faraway places on his screen instead, making plans for escape. In the endless middle hours of a still afternoon, he sometimes imagined that the house was a toy snow globe—that outside his room the corridors were slowly filling with clouds of settling, silent white.

The voices went on arguing, still distant, still unimportant, but he had noticed in an offhand way that they were both male. If one was his father, then perhaps the other was Uncle Lester, his mother's brother, a man who did something to help banks make contacts overseas. He and Paul's father disagreed famously about politics—Uncle Lester thought that anyone who voted Labour understood nothing about the way the world *really* worked—and sometimes would argue semicordially for hours, while Paul's mother nodded and occasionally smiled or made a face of mock-disapproval, pretending to be interested in their extravagant assertions, and while Paul himself sat cross-legged on the floor in the corner looking at one of his mother's precious books of reproductions, old-fashioned books on paper that her own father had given to her.

There was one in particular Paul had always liked, and listening now to his father and Uncle Lester argue, he saw it again. It was by Bruegel the Elder, or at least he thought it was—for some reason he was having trouble summoning names just now—and showed a group of hunters marching down a snowy hillside, returning to a feast in the town below. The painting had moved him in ways he could not quite describe, and when he had gone to university, he had used it as the default on his wallscreen; on nights when his roommate had gone home to his family, Paul would leave it on all night, so that the white snow and the colorful scarves had been the last thing he saw before falling asleep. He did not know why it had become such a favorite—just that something about the conviviality of it, the shared life of the villagers in the picture, had moved him. An only-child thing, he had always supposed.

Thinking of that picture now, as the argument grew louder and then softer in slow waves, he could almost feel the sharp cold of

Bruegel's snow. White, all white, sifting and settling, turning all the world uniform, covering up all that would otherwise cause pain or shame. . . .

Paul's head hurt. Was it thinking about the cold that had done it, or the continuing prattle of those people arguing? In fact, who were those people? He had thought one of them might be his father, but the other certainly could not be Uncle Lester, who had died of a heart attack while on vacation in Java almost ten years back.

In fact, Paul realized, more than his head hurt. His entire body was being bounced, and every bump was painful. And the pain itself was touched with frost.

Even as he thought this, he dropped for half an instant straight down and thumped onto something uncomfortably solid. Solid and cold. Even through the dizziness, the heavy-headedness, he was sure of that. The ground was very, very cold.

". . . With his blood," one of the voices was saying. "That brings a curse. Do you want the curse of a man from the dead lands?"

"But that is Birdcatcher's spear," another said. "Why do we give it to this one?"

"Not give, leave. Because Riverghost's blood is upon it, and we do not want him drawn back to our place by his blood. Mother Dark Moon said so. You heard her speak."

The cold was growing worse. Paul began to shiver, but the motion made his bones feel as though they were grinding together on their raw ends, and he let out a whimper of discomfort.

"He wakes. Now we go back."

"Runs Far, we leave him too close to our place," the second voice said. "It would be better to kill him."

"No. Mother Dark Moon said his blood would curse us. Did you not see how just a little of it made Birdcatcher ill? How it called out to the bad thing in Birdcatcher's child? He will not come back."

Paul, his head pulsing, aching like one great bruise, still could not decide how exactly he should go about opening his eyes, so he felt rather than saw someone bending down and bringing a face close to his.

"He will not come back," Runs Far said next to his ear, speaking almost as though for Paul's benefit, "because Mother Dark Moon has said that if he comes back, then it is he who will be cursed, not us. That the People will kill him then without fear of his blood."

The nearness of the man grew less, then something thumped down beside Paul. He heard a rhythmic noise that, after a few moments, he realized was the People's footsteps crunching away.

Some idea of what had happened was beginning to come back, but what was coming even more swiftly was the freezing cold. A vibrato of shivers ran through him, and he doubled up like a blind worm, huddling into his own body for warmth. It did no good—the cold was still touching him all the way down one side, sucking the life out of him. He rolled over so that he was facedown, then struggled until his knees were under his belly. He set his hands flat and tried to lift himself up. A wave of nausea and dizziness ran through him, and for an instant blackness came and drove even the cold away—but only for an instant.

As the inner darkness receded, Paul opened his eyes. At first nothing changed. The night sky stretched above him, an unimaginable, velvet black, but as his vision returned, he saw that this black was pierced with merciless, glittering stars. The uppermost edge of a wide yellow moon peered from behind the trees on one side of the hilltop. Beneath the sky lay a hillside, all whiteness, so that the world seemed to have been reduced to the simplest of dichotomies. And Paul himself was the only other thing in the world, trapped between black and white.

Why me? he wondered sorrowfully. *What did I do, God?*

A wind came down on him. It only lasted a moment, but that moment was like knives. Paul shuddered violently and dragged himself to his feet. He swayed, but managed at last to find balance. His head was throbbing, his bones felt broken. He tasted metal, and spat out a dark glob of blood that made a tiny hole in the white hillside. A sob hitched his breathing. A distant howl—like a wolf's, but much deeper—rose and fell, echoing across the white moonscape, a terrifying, primordial sound that seemed to mark out his hopeless loneliness.

They've left me to die. He sobbed again, furious and helpless, but swallowed it down. He was afraid to cry in case it might knock him to his knees. He didn't know whether he'd be able to get up a second time.

Something long and dark lay in the snow by his feet, bringing back Runs Far's words. *Birdcatcher's spear.* He stared, but could only make sense of it at the moment as something to lean on. He wrapped the fur cloak more tightly—what kind of death sentence had they passed, that he had been left his clothing?—then bent carefully. He almost overbalanced, but steadied and began the intricate process of picking up the spear while his legs threatened to buckle and his head suggested that it might explode. At last he wrapped his hand around it, then used it to push himself back upright.

The wind freshened. It stabbed and scraped.

Where do I go? For a moment he considered following the footsteps back to the cave. If he could not persuade them to let him back in, perhaps at least he could steal their fire, like the story Dark Moon had told. But even with his head full of blood and broken crockery, he knew that was foolishness.

Where should he go? Shelter was the answer. He must find some place where the wind could not reach him. Then he would wait until it got warmer again.

Until it gets warmer. It struck him as so blackly funny that he tried to laugh, but could only summon a wheezing cough. *And how long will that be? How long is an Ice Age, anyway?*

He began to trudge down the hillside, each step through the deep snow a small, exhausting battle in a war he had no real hope of winning.

The moon had climbed above the tree line, and now it hung full and fat before him, dominating the sky. He did not, could not, think of what he would have done had the night been moonless. As it was, he still failed to recognize many of the treacherous deep spots in the silvery snow in time to avoid them, and each time he fell into a hole it took longer to extricate himself. He was shod in some kind of thick hide turned fur-side-in, but his feet were so cold anyway that he had begun to lose track of them some time ago. Now it seemed his legs ended several inches above his ankles. It didn't take a university education to tell him that was a bad sign.

Snow, he thought, stumbling hip-deep in the stuff. *Too much snow.* This and other maddeningly obvious thoughts had been his companions for the last hour. It took strength to chase them away, to stay focused, and he did not have enough strength left to spare.

Snow—snow-white, snow-drop, snow-drift. He picked up a foot—he wasn't quite sure which one—and put it down again, sinking through the crust. The wind bit at his face where the cloak sagged away from his cheeks. *Snowdrift.*

Drift was the world, all right. That was all he'd ever done. Drifted through life, drifted through school, drifted through his job at the Tate Gallery, making the same tired jokes over and over for ladies' luncheon parties. He had thought once that he would become something, be a person who made a difference. As a child, he had wrestled with the idea without even realizing it, unable to envision what that someday person would do, who that person would actually be. Now, as if some God of Underachievers had noticed his directionlessness and mandated a punishment to fit his crime, he had apparently been condemned to drift through time and space as well, like a man lost after closing time in an endless museum.

Yes, that was exactly what he had done—drifted. Even here in this cold, primitive place, with his memory returned—or most of it—he had allowed others to choose his directions. The People had dragged him from the river when he could not free himself, and had decided that he was . . . what had Runs Far said? . . . a man from the dead lands. And he had acceded, just as ineffectually full of self-pity as if someone had set down a briefcase on the last empty seat in the Underground, forcing him to stand.

Riverghost, they called him. They were more right than they knew. Certainly everywhere he had been since this mad ride began, he had floated like a homeless spirit. And everywhere he had been, he had found himself at one point or another adrift in a river, as if it were all the same river, a perfect metaphor for his unguided life, the same river over and over. . . .

A sudden memory cut through Paul's wandering thoughts. *"They will look for you on the river."* Someone had said that to him. Had it been a dream, one of his strange, strange dreams? No, it had been the voice from the golden crystal—in his dream it had been a singing harp, but the crystal had spoken to him here in the Ice Age. *"They will look for you on the river,"* the crystal had told him. So it was true—the river did mean something. Perhaps that was why he could not escape it.

Paul paused. Through the pain and confusion something else struck him, not a memory, but an idea. It filled him with a painful clarity that for that instant pushed everything else away. He had drifted and drifted, but no longer. If he were not to float and tumble forever like a leaf in the wind, he must take some control.

The river is where I pass from place to place. He knew it with certainty, though the thought had not come to him until just this second. *The Looking Glass land, Mars, here—I came in from the river each time. So if I look for it . . .*

If he looked for it, he had a direction. If he found it, things would change, and he would come closer to some sort of understanding.

He struggled to remember how the People's hunting party had traveled, tried to make sense of the moon's position, but he had never learned to do such things in his other life and felt a fraud even trying here. But he did know that water found the lowest places. He would continue downhill. He would go down, and he would get out. He would not drift. He would not drift any more.

The moon had passed most of the way across the black reaches above him, but still not far enough to suggest that dawn would be

coming soon. Every step was an agony now, each surge forward coming only after he made promises to his body he doubted he could ever
keep. The only solace was that he had traversed the steepest part of
the hillside; as he tottered through the shrubby, snow-covered trees,
the ground before him was almost level.

But even such a small slope was difficult in these conditions. Paul
stopped, leaning on the spear, and thanked Birdcatcher for having
stuck him with it, thereby rendering it taboo with Paul's own blood.
Then he wondered if that were really so. Runs Far and Dark Moon's
interpretation of what might be dangerous had resulted in Paul not
being killed in the first place, and then being dumped with warm
clothes and a spear. Perhaps in their own way the two of them had
been trying to give him a chance.

No sense in wasting it. He took a deep breath and limped forward.

Strange to think that he might well owe his life to a pair of Neandertals, contemporaries of his own incredibly distant ancestors.
Stranger still to think of these people—of *the* People—living their lives
in something like normality until he had stumbled onto them. Who
were they, really? Where was he?

Paul Jonas was still considering this when the wind shifted and the
smell of death washed down the hillside onto him.

His skin tightened with the sudden thrill of fear, and every hair on
his head stood on end. The stink was more than rotting flesh, it was
laced with animal musk and urine and dirt and blood, too. It was
despair. It was the end of the road. He twisted to look behind him,
and a dark shape on the hillside behind him abruptly froze, so that
for half an instant he thought his own dark-hindered eyes had fooled
him, that the shape was only a rock. But then another shadow moved
farther up on the slope; as it turned its head, muzzle sniffing at the
shifted wind and the new smells it brought, Paul saw eyes glint yel-
low-green with reflected moonlight.

The wind became brisker, blowing the horrid tang past him again,
and all his muscles tensed as his hindbrain sent out the most primitive
of alarms. Even in the grip of mounting panic, he knew that it would
do no good to run. Another heavy four-legged shape was coming
slantways across the hillside. If they had not attacked him yet, these
nameless beasts, it was because they weren't sure what kind of thing
he was either, how dangerous he might be. But if he fled . . . Even
Paul, who had seen fewer wild animals growing up than most suburban children, felt certain that would be the universal signal for *dinner
is served.*

Turning then and taking a careful step forward, then another, continuing to walk despite the knowledge that those huge dark shapes were behind him and drawing closer, was perhaps the bravest thing he had ever done. He felt an absurd urge to whistle, like someone in a cartoon keeping up a brave front. He wished he *were* a cartoon, an unreal creation that could survive the most terrible damage and then pop back into shape, whole and ready for another adventure.

The wind changed direction once more, blowing into his face, and Paul fancied he could hear a deep growl of approval from the hillside as the things caught his scent again. He had only one chance, and that was to find a place where he could make some kind of stand—a cave, a tall boulder, a high tree to climb. No wonder the People made their home in holes in the mountainside. His vacations limited to sunny places with beaches, and an occasional trip to the Scottish Highlands or the Cotswolds, he had never truly understood the horrible, helpless solitude of Outside. But now he was as Outside as he could imagine being.

The snow was shallower here, and although he could now walk a little faster, the footing had grown even more treacherous, as though a sheet of ice lay beneath the snow. Paul cursed silently, but kept this legs moving. He could not afford to slip. As far as the creatures behind him were concerned, Falling Down would undoubtedly come under the same heading as Running Away.

Something moved on the right side of his field of vision. As carefully as he could, he tilted his head to look. The shadow was padding along the snowfield, pacing him, only a long stone's throw away. Its shaggy head and back were doglike, but it seemed wrong somehow, distorted. Steam drifted up from its jaws in little clouds.

The ground beneath him was almost entirely flat now, but even the stunted trees were becoming scarce. He could see nothing before him but unfigured whiteness—no stones, no shelter. He looked back over his shoulder, wondering if he could circle around and move back up the hillside to some of the rocks he'd passed earlier, but the pair of shapes crisscrossing on the slope behind him killed that idea in an instant. There were three of them, all somehow the wrong shape or size, a hunting pack.

Trying to look back while walking forward was a mistake. Paul stumbled, then skidded. For a horrible moment he thought he was going to go completely over, but a scrabbling lunge with the butt of Birdcatcher's spear kept him partially upright, although he banged one knee down on the surprisingly hard ground. It would have been terribly painful if he had not been almost frozen through; instead, he felt nothing but a new weakness in the joint. The three shapes, now close together again, stopped to observe his struggles, eyes pale gems hanging in the darkness, winking on and off behind the curtain of their smoking breath.

Even with his hand, it was hard to find purchase on the slick ground beneath the dusting of snow. As he labored to push himself up, he realized that it *was* ice, an entire sheet of ice, onto which he had fallen. The initial outrage at this further indignity was pushed aside by a burst of unexpected hope.

The river. . . ?

As if sensing his tiny revival of spirit and wanting to put a quick end to it, the nearest of the three shapes abruptly loped toward him, covering the distance effortlessly. It moved so much more quickly than he had expected that it was only a dozen meters away when Paul suddenly realized what was happening and raised his spear.

"Hey! Get back!" He waved his free arm violently, then jabbed at the dark shape with the spear, hoping that it did not recognize the sheer terror in his shrill tones.

The beast stopped, but did not retreat. It regarded him with lowered head, and a deep, pulsating growl shook the air between them. It was then, with a shock like a physical blow, that Paul realized what had seemed so very wrong about these things. The creature was some kind of hyena, but far, far too big—as tall at the shoulders as a small horse, its body broad and thick-boned. The steaming jaws were wide enough to close around his whole torso.

The beast growled again, a powerful rumble he could feel in the center of his bones. The sound jellied his legs, and Paul had to fight to remain upright. The wind brought the stench of dead meat and musk back down on him. His heart, already beating too fast, seemed to be running downhill, in danger any moment of a fatal tumble.

Cave hyena. The name came back to him abruptly, something he had seen in a documentary, or in a natural history exhibition—as if it mattered what this horrible monster was called. Cave hyena, the stalker of the Ice Age plains, a walking death machine that no man had faced for five hundred centuries.

Paul took a shaky step backward. The hyena moved a matching pace toward him, head still low, eyes glowing will-o'-the-wisp green. Its two companions paw-crunched down the hillside and fanned out on either side with the unhurried nonchalance of contract assassins. Paul lifted the spear and waved it again. He tried to shout, but could make no sound except a choking gasp.

The river! he thought wildly. *I'm on the river!* But what good would it do him now? He had no idea how to use it to travel from one place to another, and he knew he could no more outrun these monsters than he could saddle one of them and ride it at Ascot.

The nearest hyena growled again, then lunged forward. As the creature came toward him at a slow trot, he dropped to his knees and did his best to brace the spear against the slick ground. The thing shambled down on him, picking up speed, slower than a normal hyena, but far faster on snow than Paul was.

Perhaps it did not see the spear against Paul's tattered clothes, or perhaps it did not know what a spear was. Mouth so wide he could feel its breath like the heat from a furnace vent a full second before it reached him, the hyena drove onto the spearhead with a shock that almost tore Paul's arms from their sockets. He grunted with pain and hung onto the shaft as he felt the spear crunch through muscle and gristle. The thing let out a howl of pain and crashed into him. He was flung sideways, as though he had been hit by a car, and the spear was almost torn from his frozen grasp as the hyena stumbled past. Paul was jerked straight out onto his belly and dragged an agonizing distance across the ice before the spear worked loose from the animal's flesh.

Stunned, Paul lay on his face for a second, trying to remember which were his arms and which were his legs. He heard a noise like a pistol shot, and for a mad moment thought that, as in *Peter and the Wolf,* a huntsman had come to save him with a big gun. Then he lifted his head and saw the wounded hyena suddenly slide backward into a black hole in the white ground.

A snarl from behind spun Paul around. The other two beasts were loping forward on their thickly muscular legs. He staggered to his feet, slipping and skidding, and in hopeless despair raised the spear above his head to swipe at them. There was another explosive *pop,* then another, and the very ground beneath him shot out radiating crooked black lines, so that for a moment it seemed he stood at the center of a spiderweb. The ice shuddered and settled. He had a moment to wonder why one of his legs seemed shorter than the other, and was also suddenly even colder than it had been—or hotter, perhaps; it was hard to tell—and then the ice beneath him collapsed and the hungry black water sucked him down.

CHAPTER 7

Grandfather's Visit

NETFEED/BUSINESS: Krellor Dumps MedFX
(visual: Krellor with Vice President Von Strassburg)
VO: Uberto Krellor has sold his multimillion dollar MedFX medical supply
company, one of the last remaining members of his Black Shield family of
companies, to the Clinsor Group, which now becomes the world's largest
supplier of medical equipment to clinics and hospitals. Krellor, who lost
billions when the nanotechnology industry suffered customer confidence
setbacks, has now sold off most of his holdings to satisfy his creditors.
(visual: Krellor and Hagen at Swiss Olympic pavilion in Bucharest)
But though his fortunes are down in other ways, Krellor has recently
remarried his former wife Vila Hagen. Their troubled first marriage made
them almost permanent fixtures in the tabnets.
KRELLOR: "It's not a sell-off, it's a reorganization—do you understand
nothing? Now please leave us alone, we are trying to enjoy our honeymoon."

FOR all the time they had spent in the simulation together, it was still a shock when Renie opened her eyes to find the baboon's face only inches from her own.

"Are you well?" !Xabbu stroked her arm solicitously. "We have crash-landed. Like in a film."

Renie was not entirely sure that she *was* well: Her head hurt, the world seemed badly off-kilter, and she was having terrible problems moving her limbs. The last of those problems was solved when she managed to unhook the safety harness that was holding her against the crumpled wall of the dragonfly-plane; the second became more comprehensible when she then rolled down into the cockpit—the dragonfly was apparently standing on its nose.

"We're alive," she decided.

"Just barely." Beneath her, half-wedged into the wreck of the instrument panel, Cullen was struggling furiously to free himself. "I mean, just barely by the simulation's standards. *Christ!* Look at this!" He slammed the shattered panel with his fist. "Ruined."

"Will you forget about your stupid toy plane?" Lenore was in a worse position than Cullen—the copilot's seat had crumpled forward, along with a good piece of the plane's floor, pinning her against the panel. She also sounded far more frightened than her colleague; the unsteady edge to her voice made Renie's headache worse. "Get me out. *Now!*"

"Come give me a hand," Renie called to !Xabbu. She turned to find that he had vanished from the plane's ruined cabin. "!Xabbu?"

"Get me out of here!" demanded Lenore.

Renie hesitated. The two scientists needed help, but she was suddenly terrified that she might lose the little man, her friend, and be truly alone in this place.

"God damn you, bitch!—you help me!" Lenore shrieked.

Renie whirled, shocked, but the look on the woman's well-simulated face blew her anger out like a candle: Lenore Kwok was in the grip of real, twitching panic.

"We'll get you out," Cullen said, despite still being trapped himself. "Calm down, Lenore."

"Shut up!" She scrabbled frantically at the wreckage that restrained her.

Renie hurriedly began shifting the bits of cabin that had settled around Cullen, marveling again at the complexity and realism of the simulation. Even the broken things broke in convincing ways.

"What are you doing?" Lenore shouted.

"You've got more things on top of you than he does," Renie explained as gently as she could. "If I can get him loose, he can help me. I don't think I can do it myself."

"Where's that goddamn monkey?" The woman's eyes roved wildly around the cabin, as though !Xabbu might be hiding from her.

"I don't know. Just try to be calm, like Cullen said."

"You don't understand!" Lenore was wild-eyed, breathing harshly. "I can't feel my legs! They won't move!"

"Oh, for God's sake," said Cullen. "That's just panic, Lenore—power of suggestion. It's a simulation, and right now it's holding you in one position. Nothing's happened to your legs. Don't be stupid."

Renie gave him a hard look. "Cullen, please shut up."

"Here, see!" !Xabbu had appeared in the hatchway, originally a respectable opening in the belly of a simulated plane, now occupying a tower-window position several yards above them. "It is a thorn from a plant." He dropped something down to Renie, who caught it as much in self-defense as anything else. It looked a bit like a smooth antelope horn, as long as her outstretched arm and nearly as wide, tapering to a point at one end. She tried to bend it, but could not. "This might work," she told !Xabbu as he clambered in beside her.

With the thorn as a lever, she was able to bend back a large enough portion of the instrument panel to allow Cullen to slide free. As he stretched and rubbed his sore joints, his partner's panicked demands began again.

"All right, all right," he said. "You're really scanbound, Kwok, you know that?"

"Let's just try to help her." Renie found what seemed a good fulcrum-point for the lever and began to work at pulling back the copilot's chair.

"Don't waste your energy. There's an easier way." Cullen clambered up the floor until he located a panel door. Taking the thorn from Renie, he pried open the door and pulled out a metal box with a handle. "See? Because of Kunohara's stupid rules, we have to have damn virtual repair kits in our damn virtual planes. Is that insane, or what?" He climbed back down the upraised floor and took a wrench from the tool kit, then removed the nuts that held the copilot seat to the floor. The crash had crumpled the dragonfly's framework; it took several kicks before he could knock the seat off its tracks.

A few more minutes of surprisingly hard work permitted them to pull Lenore free.

"I . . . I still can't move my legs," she said in a quiet little ghost-voice. Renie liked this new tone even less.

With help from !Xabbu's agile feet and hands, they managed to haul her up to the hatchway and then carefully lower her three body-lengths down to the ground. The dragonfly had crashed headfirst, auguring into the forest floor like a World War I biplane; the delicate wings had fallen forward over the buried nose and its shiny, cylindrical tail pointed toward the sky.

"I can't walk," Lenore murmured. "My legs won't work."

"That's shit, utterly," Cullen snapped. "Look, in case you've forgotten, we were about, oh, I'd guess thirty minutes ahead of that *Eciton* swarm, and it's going to raise hell at the Hive if we don't warn them." He paused. A more uncertain look moved swiftly across his long face. "Not to mention that we're in front of it ourselves."

"Oh, my God." Renie, immersed in the problem of getting Lenore out of the broken plane, had completely forgotten the army ants. "Oh, Jesus Mercy, they'll eat us. Oh, God, how horrible."

"They won't *eat* us," said Cullen disgustedly. "They'll just keep us from warning the Hive, and we'll lose more money than I can imagine having to reprogram and rebuild. This *is* a simulation—you seem to keep forgetting."

Renie looked at him, then at !Xabbu, who arched his eyebrows, an odd expression of simian fatalism. She agreed; there was no point wasting time on argument. "Right, it's a simulation. But let's get going, okay?"

With Renie and !Xabbu's help, Cullen hauled Lenore into a piggy-back position. "How are your legs?" he asked. "Is there pain?"

"I can't feel them now . . . I just can't make them work." Lenore closed her eyes and clung tightly to Cullen's neck. "I don't want to talk. I want to go home."

"We're working on it," said Renie. "But any information might . . ."

"No." Lenore's surliness had become childlike. "I'm not going to talk about it anymore. This is so stupid. None of this is happening."

Which, Renie reflected as they began making their way through the forest of grass, was as unhelpful a comment as anything she could remember hearing recently.

Cullen, despite carrying Lenore's extra weight, was at first determined to lead their small party as well. Renie was reluctant to surrender control, but before she and the entomologist could battle it out, !Xabbu pointed out that he was undoubtedly best suited to go first. After Cullen had been assured that !Xabbu had long experience with hunting and tracking, and thus that it made *scientific sense,* he told the Bushman in which direction the Hive lay and !Xabbu got down to the business of finding a way through the ground-jungle.

It was one of the strangest and most surreal journeys Renie had ever taken—which, considering the nature of what she had experienced in the last few months, was saying a great deal. The world from insect height was an astonishing place, full of frightening yet fascinating things. A caterpillar that she would not have looked at twice in the real world was now a shining, living psychedelic object the size of a bus. As she and the others filed carefully past it, the caterpillar moved a pace forward along the leaf it had been stripping and the step rippled through all its legs, stem to stern, like a chorus-line kick. When the long lockstep was over, the vertical jaws began working the leaf again, making a racket much like the box-cutting machine in a factory where Renie had held a summer job.

As they hurried toward the Hive, they passed through an entire safari park worth of chitinous wonders—aphids clinging to plant stems like zero-gravity sheep grazing in an upside-down meadow, mites burrowing in decaying plants with the single-mindedness of dogs searching for buried bones, even a leafhopper that jumped away as they approached, catapulting nearly into orbit with an audible twang of exoskeletal flexing. If it had been the same proportional size to her in real life, Renie marveled, it could have leaped directly to the top of the tallest building in downtown Durban.

At one point, !Xabbu carefully led them around a spiderweb—an incredible work of engineering when seen from this perspective, but the thought of stumbling into it gave Renie the shivers. She looked back at it nervously several times but never saw any sign of its manufacturer.

The vegetation was fascinating, too, each plant a revelation of complexity. Even the mold, whose surface was a riot of shapes disguised in ordinary life by its tiny size, was worth marveling over. The very earth had to be looked at anew, since what seemed the flattest trail to a normal human eye could contain deep, slippery-sided pits and uncountable other obstructions to travelers of insect size.

But despite the unceasing spectacle, the memory of what was behind them was never out of Renie's thoughts. !Xabbu picked his way through the microjungle with great skill, finding pathways where she knew that she would have been completely stymied, but she still feared that they were not traveling fast enough. Cullen could not move easily with Lenore on his back; watching his pace grow ever slower, Renie struggled to beat down irritation and fear. Even !Xabbu's patient expertise frustrated her, since his manner was so calm that he did not seem to be hurrying, although she knew he was.

They halted, instinct freezing them in place, as a shadow thrown by a bird high above them momentarily eclipsed the sun.

"I can't go on like this," Cullen gasped when the shadow had gone. He let Lenore slide to the ground and stood over her, sucking air. "You're too heavy, Kwok."

"I'll carry her for a little while." Renie did not want an argument between Cullen and Lenore, or any delay at all that could be avoided.

"We can't stop. Those bloody ants will kill us, virtually or otherwise."
She bent and tried to coax Lenore to climb onto her back, but the
sullen, silent entomologist was no more use than an infant. Renie
swore, then grabbed her and flung her over her shoulder like a sack
of meal.

"Come on, while I can stand it," she said, voice tight with effort.

As they stumbled on, Renie found herself wishing, not for the last
time, that the simulation were not quite so amazingly realistic. Lenore's weight hung in exactly the same awkward way it would have
in RL: just keeping the scientist balanced on her shoulder and putting
one foot in front of the other was an exhausting job.

Winged insects in flight for their lives began to hum past overhead,
the first tangible evidence of the *Eciton* swarm. It was horribly frustrating to watch them zooming by, going in the same direction, but at
ten or twenty times the human's walking speed. Renie's back was
aching. She contemplated, then regretfully discarded, the idea of just
dropping the Kwok woman on the ground and legging it as fast as
she could, unencumbered. Lenore appeared to be in shock, and Renie
knew that if the simulation itself was frighteningly realistic, its effects
had to be treated with the same degree of seriousness: This woman's
affliction was just as crippling as if they were fleeing for their lives in
a real jungle.

"There!" shouted Cullen. "I can see it!"

Renie stepped up beside him. They had reached the summit of the
center spine of a fallen palm frond. From this comparatively high
place, lifted above the leaf mold of the forest floor, they could at last
see the Hive's windows glinting from the distant hillside. "How far is
that, in RL distance?" she panted. "If we were normal size? A few
meters? If only . . ."

"Yeah," Cullen said, "if only." He began to trot down the other
side of the leaf, leaving Renie to stagger forward again, still balancing
Lenore.

They were crossing a relatively clear patch of ground at the base of
the rise on which the Hive was situated when the first ground-level
refugees from the swarm began to spill out of the vegetation behind
them. A long-legged spider stilted past, tall as a house. Smaller but
even less pleasant animals followed, boiling out of the jungle in a
wash of agitated noise.

"We can't outrun them." Renie staggered even as she spoke and
almost fell, then lowered Lenore to the ground. A fly skimmed over
their heads, making a noise like a small jet helicopter. "We have to
find someplace safe. High ground."

"Are you crazy?" Cullen demanded, then pointed at the Hive. "That's millions worth of code standing there."

"Jesus Mercy! You don't *get* it, do you?" A part of Renie knew screaming was not good strategy, but she didn't care. "This is not about gear, this is about staying alive!"

!Xabbu had noticed their absence and was hurrying back toward them. A centipede, a shiny, sinuous thing which a moment before had been in full flight, suddenly side-wound toward him and struck, but the small man in the baboon body jumped to safety, narrowly eluding the rounded, fanged head. His baboon sim bared its fangs and dropped into defensive posture. The centipede hesitated, then turned and paddled on, its instinctive desire to hunt muted by the swarming death behind it.

"We have to climb something," Renie shouted to !Xabbu. "We'll never make it back in time."

"That's . . . that's irresponsible." Cullen sounded uncertain now. Another shadow wheeled overhead, yet another antbird preying on the scurrying refugees.

"Here." !Xabbu stood at the base of a fern, beckoning. "If we climb this plant, we can reach a place they will not go, I think."

Renie bent and heaved Lenore up onto her shoulder. She had taken a few steps when something smacked hard against her back and knocked her off balance. As she struggled to regain her footing, Lenore thrashed in her arms, pummeling Renie's back with her fists.

"Put me down! *Put me down!*"

Renie let her slide to the ground, but took care not to let her tumble helplessly, and received a flailing fist against her ear for her trouble. "What the hell are you playing at?" she growled.

Lenore had curled up like a woodlouse. Cullen strode over. The racket of fleeing insects was growing louder, and the flood of refugees was beginning to widen, threatening the place they stood. "God damn it, Kwok, what are you doing?"

"Leave me alone." Lenore did not look up at him. "I don't want to do this anymore."

Cullen reached down to grab her. Her legs still did not move, but she thrashed furiously from the waist up and managed to land a hard blow on his face. Swearing, he let her drop. "You're scanned! What is this?"

"You must hurry!" !Xabbu called from a position high up the fern stem. "I can see the ants!"

"We're not going without Lenore!" Cullen looked like someone who was watching his house burn down. "I mean, I can't just leave her here." He took the woman's arm, but she shook him off. "What's wrong with you?" he demanded.

"This is just so . . . stupid!" she wailed. "It's stupid, and it hurts! And I'm not going to do it anymore." She opened her eyes wide, staring with an almost mad intensity. "It's not real, Cullen—none of this is real. It's a game, and I'm not going to play this stupid game anymore." She slapped hard at his hand. He withdrew it.

"Right," said Renie. "You deal with her if you want." She turned and hurried across the open space toward !Xabbu and the sanctuary of the fern. A beetle veered from the leading edge of the oncoming throng and ratcheted past in front of her, creaking like a sloop in full sail. She paused, bouncing in place until it had passed, then sprinted forward.

"I can't just leave her!" Cullen shouted after Renie.

"Then don't! Stay!" Renie reached the bottom of the stalk and grabbed at the thick fibers that covered it like a pelt, scrabbling with her boots until she had pulled herself off the ground. When she reached the first place where she could stand, she turned to look back. Cullen was shouting something at Lenore—impossible to hear above the mounting din—but she had curled back into a fetal ball and was paying no attention. Again he tried to lift her, which brought her to life, gouging and elbowing. Renie shook her head and resumed climbing.

"Up here." !Xabbu shinnied down the stalk toward her, moving as easily in his baboon form as Renie would on a broad staircase. "Put your foot on this place—yes, there. Why will that Lenore woman not come?"

"Shock, I guess—I don't know." Renie's foot slipped and she dangled by one arm for a moment, kicking in heart-freezingly empty air, but !Xabbu reached down with both hands and clutched her wrist, giving her the courage to look for a foothold. When she had found one, and was again firmly set, she saw Cullen reach the base of the stalk and begin to climb.

The noise grew louder, rising until it was like the roar of the ocean in a narrow cove. The sky was filling with hopping and flying insects of all sizes. Some skimmed so close that their wingtips scraped the outer fronds of the fern, making the leaves dance. The horde on the ground grew even more numerous. Diving antbirds snatched some of them, but nothing slowed the exodus.

Renie and !Xabbu reached a point midway up the fern where the distance to the next jutting stem was too great for Renie to climb without exceptional difficulty, so they moved away from the central stalk and into the folded gully of a leaf. As they stepped onto it, the curling frond swayed alarmingly, bounced by the breeze rather than by the inconsequential weight of the tiny humans.

Cullen appeared behind them, talking to himself. "She'll be all right. It's just . . . she'll be pushed offline. The system's locked, anyway."

Looking at his pale, worried face, Renie no longer felt any urge to argue with him.

They made their way across the leaf's hairy surface until they were near its outer edge and could see Lenore in her white jumpsuit curled on the ground far below, like a discarded grain of rice. Staring, Renie felt !Xabbu's hand close on her arm. She looked up to follow his pointing finger.

A short distance from them lay a small tree which had fallen some time in the past and been partly subsumed by the forest floor, so that the gray-brown of its bark showed in only a few places through the moss and the grasses that had grown over it. From Renie's and !Xabbu's perspective, it was as tall and long as a line of hills.

The *Eciton* army had reached the top of the log, and swarmed along its summit like soldiers on a captured ridgetop. The first few scouts were even now climbing back up from their forays to the ground, and as Renie watched, the first pseudopod of ant bodies boiled down and made contact with the forest floor again. The entire log disappeared beneath a living carpet of ants; moments later, the swarm was extruding tendrils of troops out across the open space Renie and the others had just vacated.

"It's not real," Cullen said hoarsely. "Remember that. Those are numbers, little groups of numbers. We're watching algorithms."

Renie could only stare with horrified fascination as the ants flowed forward. One of the leading scouts approached Lenore's unmoving form and stood over her, probing with his antennae like a dog sniffing a sleeping cat, then turned and hurried back to the nearest arm of the swarm.

"The simulation kicks us out when something happens." Cullen was almost whispering now. "That's all. It's a game, like she said. Kunohara's goddamn game." He swallowed. "How can she just *lie* there?"

!Xabbu's grip on Renie's arm tightened as Lenore was surrounded by antenna-waggling workers.

"Use the defense spray!" Cullen shouted. The tiny figure did not respond. "Damn it, Kwok, use the *Solenopsis* spray!"

Then, suddenly, she did move, struggling to crawl away on elbows and useless legs, but it was too late.

From the corner of her eye, Renie saw Cullen flinch. "Oh, my God," he said, "she's screaming. Oh, Christ. Why is she screaming? It's just a simulation—there's no pain function . . ." He trailed off, gape-jawed and ashen.

"She's just frightened," Renie said. "It must be . . . it must be horrible to be down there, even if it's only a simulation." She found herself praying that her own instincts were wrong. "That's all."

"Oh, God, they're killing her!" Cullen leaped up and almost overbalanced. !Xabbu grabbed his jumpsuit leg, but the baboon's mass was too small to do much good. Renie grabbed the scientist's flight-suit belt and pulled him away from the edge. "We have to," he babbled, "we can't . . ." Cullen fell silent, still staring.

Below, the worker ants had finished. Lenore's sim had been small; they did not have to call one of the large submajors to carry the pieces back to the swarm.

Cullen put his face in his hands and wept. Renie and !Xabbu watched silently as the rest of the swarm eddied past.

It took the better part of an hour before the last stragglers vanished. The flow of ants had gone on so long that Renie could not sustain either horror or fascination. She felt numbed.

"It was a shock, that's all." Cullen had apparently recovered his self-possession. "Lenore's gone offline, of course—it was just so dreadful to watch." He peered over the edge of the leaf at the arid field of destruction. "I hadn't expected it to be . . . to be that bad."

"What were you shouting about?" Renie asked. "Some kind of spray?"

Cullen pulled a silvery wand from the pocket. "Chemical defense spray from *Solenopsis fugax*—robber ants. We imported it, so to speak, to give us a little protection in the field. Everyone at the Hive carries one when they're doing fieldwork." He dropped the tube into his pocket and turned away from the rim of the leaf. "*Solenopsis* is a European ant, really, so I guess in a way it's cheating."

Renie stared at him, momentarily speechless. Only someone living in a fantasy world—or, she supposed, someone who was a scientist to the core—could watch what had just happened to his colleague and still be talking as though the whole thing were only an experiment gone slightly sour. But there seemed no point in arguing—she could prove nothing. "We'd better get moving again," she said instead. "The swarm must be far away by now."

Cullen looked at her, expression blank. "Get moving where?"

"To the Hive, I suppose. See if we can salvage something so we can get out of here."

!Xabbu looked up. "We should go back to the river."

"I don't know what either of you are talking about," Cullen said. "The simulation's wrecked. I don't understand you people anyway—you act like this was all real. There's no point in going anywhere. There's nowhere to *go*."

"You're the one who doesn't understand." She began walking toward the stem of the leaf, their route down. "In fact, there's a *lot* you don't understand, and I really don't have the time or strength to explain now, but even you must have noticed that things have gone pretty seriously wrong. So if you want to survive to see RL again, I strongly suggest you shut up and get moving."

It was like walking across a battlefield, Renie thought, far worse than it had looked from atop the leaf. Where the *Eciton* swarm had traveled, the microjungle was absolutely empty of any living thing but plants, and only the largest of those had survived undamaged: At ground level the ants had left behind only skeletonized stems and a scattering of tiny, unrecognizable fragments of matter.

Cullen, who was leading them up the hillside toward the Hive, had been silent since Renie's explosion—more likely because he believed she was dangerously crazy, Renie suspected, than because he trusted her judgment about what was going on.

She didn't even know exactly what to believe herself. Had they really seen a woman brutally killed by giant ants, or had they only watched the playing out of a simulation, an imaginary human form dismembered by imaginary insects, with the human dropping out of the puppet body like Stephen or one of his friends when they lost a combat game?

But of course, the last time Stephen had played an online game, something had changed, and he had never come back. Who could say for certain that Lenore had made it back to RL either, or that Renie or !Xabbu or the young entomologist stalking tight-lipped in front of them would survive a similar piece of bad luck?

!Xabbu descended from a quick foray up the curling length of a creeper. "The ants have passed on. I cannot see any of them near the Hive building."

Renie nodded. "That's one less thing to worry about. I hope we can fly one of those planes—it's a long, long walk back to the river, and even if we don't run into the ants again, I don't fancy our chances."

!Xabbu looked thoughtful. "We know that something is wrong with this network, Renie. And now it seems that it has gone wrong for others besides just us."

"It does seem that way."

"But what could make this happen? Our friends could not go out of this Otherland place—could not go offline, I mean—and now these people cannot either, and they have nothing to do with our search, as far as I can see."

"There's something gone seriously weird with the whole system." Renie shrugged. "I can't even guess. We don't have enough information. We might *never* have enough information, because from what Sellars said, there's never been a system like this."

"Oh, *shit*." Cullen had paused at the crest of the lower hill. Before him, the Hive lay open and plundered.

The great windows across the front had been smashed inward, likely by the sheer weight of the ant swarm. The ants had carried out all kinds of objects, but seemed to have rejected many of them, seemingly at random: The promontory in front of the building was littered with virtual objects from inside, sections of walls and bits of furniture and specimens from the museum being among the more recognizable. There were less pleasant remnants as well, bloodless bits of the simulated bodies the Hive's human inhabitants had once worn, strewn all across the landscape. Torn or snipped from the original owners, they looked less real than they had when part of a sim, like a scattering of doll parts, but it was still horrible. Cullen stared at it so bleakly that it seemed he might never move again.

Renie took his arm and urged him forward. They passed through one of the sliding hangar doors, which had been pried upward until it had crumpled, and thus allowed them more than ample headroom. Now it was Renie who felt her insides go cold and heavy. The Hive's small air force, perhaps because of the planes' resemblance to insects, had been shredded by the *Eciton* army. Only a few recognizable pieces remained, and these were not enough to cobble together a patio chair, let alone a flying machine.

Renie wanted to cry, but would not indulge herself. "Are there any other planes?"

"I don't know," Cullen said bleakly. "Angela's hopper, maybe."

"What's that? Where is it?"

"Renie?" !Xabbu stood at the hangar door, looking out over the debris-carpeted hillside. His voice was strangely pitched. "Renie, help me."

Alarmed, she turned and sprinted to his side. Something very large was making its way steadily up the slope toward them, a bright green thing the size of a construction crane. It swiveled its triangular head from side to side as though searching aimlessly, but it was stalking steadily toward them.

"It is him." !Xabbu spoke in a hushed, clench-throated whisper. "It is Grandfather Mantis."

"No, it's not." She wrapped her hand around his slender baboon fore-leg, trying to stay calm despite the terror spiking sharply inside her, rattling her heart in her rib cage and squeezing out her breath. "It's . . . it's another simulation, !Xabbu. It's just a regular praying mantis." If something the relative size of a Tyrannosaurus could be in any way regular, she thought wildly. "It's another one of Kunohara's bugs."

"That's not fair." Cullen's voice was flat. "That's a *Sphodromantis Centralis*. They're not indigenous to this environment—they're from Africa."

Renie thought this was pretty rich coming from the man who'd brought in European robber-ant spray, but with the mantis a few dozen paces away and closing, it didn't seem like a good time to dis-cuss VR ethics. She tugged at !Xabbu's furry arm. "Let's get out of here."

"Unless it's supposed to have come in on a ship," Cullen murmured. "That's how they got to the Americas in the first place."

"Jesus Mercy, will you shut up? Let's—" She broke off. The mantis had turned its head toward them, and now began striding faster up the hillside, scythelike forearms extended, a vast machine of razoring clockwork. "What do those things eat?" Renie asked faintly.

"Anything that moves," said Cullen.

She let go of !Xabbu and shoved Cullen several steps back into the depths of the hangar. "Let's go! You said there was a plane or some-thing—Angela's plane, you said. Where?"

"Her hopper. On the roof, I think. Unless she took it."

"Right. Come on!" She looked back. "!Xabbu!" she shrieked. "What are you doing?" The baboon was still crouching beneath the crumpled hangar door as if waiting for death. She sprinted back and picked him up, a not inconsiderable effort after the long day carrying Lenore.

"It is him, and I have seen him," he said into her ear. "I cannot believe this day has come."

"It is not a 'him,' and it certainly isn't God, it's a giant monkey-eating bug. Cullen, will you get goddamn going? I don't know how to get to the roof—you do."

As if suddenly waking from a dream, the entomologist turned and ran toward the back wall of the hangar with Renie a step behind him. As they reached the door that led inside, the simulated metal of the hangar door gave a protesting screech. Renie looked back. The mantis had almost entirely forced its way in, and was pulling its long abdo-men and back legs through the gap. The head pivoted in a horrible, robotic fashion as the blank green domes of its eyes tracked their flight.

The door into the complex was unlocked, and slid open at a touch, but there was no way to bar it behind them. !Xabbu stirred in her arms. "I am all right, Renie," he promised. "Put me down!"

She let him clamber down, and they all sprinted toward the door at the far end of the corridor.

"Why don't we just . . . go there?" Renie asked Cullen as she dodged bits of simulated debris. "You don't have to do things like walk and run here, do you?"

"Because it's not working, damn it!" he shouted. "I tried. Kunohara turned off the protocol or something. Just be glad we had elevators made for this thing in case he ever changed his mind about how many corners we could cut in here."

The elevator was on their floor, its doors partially open, but Renie's moment of hope was quickly ended: the doors themselves were bowed outward, as though something inside had tried to smash its way free. As they stared, something large and dark heaved and the parted doors clanked and quivered. One of the ant soldiers had been trapped inside, and was battering the elevator to pieces.

Cullen shouted with frustration and fear as he slid to a halt. They all turned at a loud grinding noise in the corridor behind them. The wedge-shaped head of the mantis had pushed open the door from the hangar, and the doorframe itself was crumpling as the creature forced the rest of its massive body through the opening.

"Stairs! Back there!" Cullen pointed at a branching hallway back down the corridor.

"Let's go, then!" Renie grabbed at !Xabbu's furry arm in case he was struck by another bout of religious devotion. The mantis tore away the last pieces of the doorframe; as they ran toward it, the huge green thing stepped into the corridor and rose until its antennae brushed the high ceiling, a giant museum display come to murderous life. Renie and the others reached the cross-corridor and turned the corner so fast they skidded and almost fell on the slippery floor, but Renie knew the monster could cover the distance to them in only a few strides. She let go of !Xabbu and began to sprint.

"Hurry!" she screamed.

Her friend was on all fours, matching her pace, Cullen a few steps behind as they slammed through the doors and into the stairwell. Renie cursed when she saw that the staircase was too wide to be a deterrent to the pursuing monster, but she prayed that steps might slow it down. She eased her own pace a little and shoved Cullen ahead of her in case he might suddenly remember a better route.

They had only reached the second landing when the mantis knocked the doors spinning off their hinges below them. Renie looked down as she leaped up onto the next set of stairs, but wished she hadn't. The creature had begun climbing straight up the middle of the stairwell, bracing itself with long, jointed legs against both stairs and walls. Its blank, headlight eyes watched her hungrily, so close it seemed she could reach down and touch the armored head.

"Try the doors!" she screamed up to her companions. !Xabbu rattled the latch of the third landing door as they dashed past, but it was firmly locked.

"It's only a few more floors to the roof," Cullen shouted.

Renie shifted herself into a more careful gear, struggling to avoid slipping. She doubted that any one of them would survive a tumble— their pursuer was only a couple of meters beneath them, filling the stairwell like a demon rising from the infernal pit.

Then, for a moment, the creature actually reached *past* her—the end of a vast green leg rose and touched the staircase wall above her head. Terrified, Renie could only throw herself down against the stairs and crawl underneath it, positive that at any moment one of the forearms would close on her like a giant pair of pliers, but the mantis slipped its hold and sagged, then fell back half a floor before it got a grip against the stairwell again, and she began to feel they might actually outrace it to the roof.

Jesus Mercy, she thought suddenly. *What if the way onto the roof's locked, too?*

As she staggered onto the last landing. Cullen was rattling the bar of the door with no effect. She could hear the creature clambering toward them again, a leathery creaking and popping like the world's largest umbrella being unfurled.

"It's locked!" Cullen screamed.

Renie threw herself against the door, slamming the bar. It popped open, revealing a broad vista of late afternoon sky. *Not locked, just jammed.* It was a prayer of thanksgiving. She stepped to the side as Cullen stumbled backward through the doorway, !Xabbu at his feet and tugging him. The great green head of the mantis rose up out of the shadows of the stairwell behind him like a tricornered moon. A leg scraped across the stairwell landing as it sought a firm foothold.

"Where's the bloody plane?" she shouted at Cullen.

The scientist regained his equilibrium and looked around, his eyes panicky-wide. "Over there!"

Renie slammed the door closed behind him and took the thorn from her belt. She jammed it through the handle, knowing as she did so that it was a straw in a hurricane, then sprinted after the others toward a wind-wall that ran halfway across the gray roof, hiding whatever might be on the far side. "Are you sure it's there?" she shouted. Cullen said nothing, running flat out. As if in answer, something went *pop* behind her. The thorn shot past, skipping along the rooftop, followed by the grating sound of another doorframe being wrenched loose.

As they reached the edge of the wind-wall, she heard the door burst outward. Despite the overwhelming fear, Renie was also furious. How could an insect be so single-minded? Why hadn't it given up long ago? Surely a real mantis in the real world wouldn't behave in this monster-movie fashion? She half-suspected Kunohara—some kind of horrible payback he had built into his simulation for those who ignored Nature's power.

On the far side of the wall, with the panorama of the oversized forest looming above and beyond, Cullen was already dragging the tarp from a lumpy object not much larger than a minibus. Renie and !Xabbu each snatched at a corner and pulled; the covering slid away to reveal an expanse of brown, yellow, and black enameling—a six-legged monstrosity shaped like a sunflower seed.

"It's another damn bug!"

"A *Semiotus*. All our vehicles look like bugs." Cullen shook his head sadly. "Angela didn't get out, I guess." He thumbed the latch panel and the doors swung upward. The entomologist pulled down the steps and Renie clambered into the snug cockpit.

As !Xabbu swung up behind her, a shadow fell across them. Renie whirled to see the mantis step around the edge of the wind-wall, massive legs lifting and falling with the terrible precision of sewing machine needles, head swiveling high above the hopper. Cullen stood frozen at the base of the ladder as the great head descended toward him. In the stark, timeless moment, Renie could hear air hissing through the spirucules along the creature's side.

"That spray," she tried to call, but only huffed a little air through a throat clenched shut by terror. She found her voice. *"Cullen, the spray!"*

He took a stiff pace backward, fumbling in his pocket. The head tilted as it followed him, smooth as if on oiled bearings. The great scythelike arms came up and extended past him on either side with terrible deliberation, until the tip of one touched the side of the ship with a faint metallic *ping*. Cullen held up the cylinder in a trembling hand, then blasted a spattering stream into the blank triangular face.

The moment exploded.

The mantis juddered back, hissing like a steam compressor. The arms snapped down as they retracted, smacking Cullen to the ground, then the creature crabbed backward several steps, sawing at the air and its blinded eyes. Renie saw !Xabbu swing back down to the ground and grab Cullen by the collar; the entomologist's arm remained behind, lying on the roof as if discarded in a forgetful moment, still swaddled in a jumpsuit sleeve that now gaped raggedly at one end.

"You are not Grandfather Mantis!" !Xabbu shrilled at the monster as he struggled to drag the scientist away. "You are only a thing!"

In the depths of the nightmare, operating on pure instinct, Renie scrambled down to help; as the mantis convulsed above them they heaved Cullen into the plane and pulled down the door. Renie could see their pursuer through the side window, still ratcheting in place like a broken toy, but becoming less manic and more purposeful by the second.

There was no blood where Cullen's arm had been. She grabbed and squeezed anyway, not sure what the rules were for near-mortal virtual injuries, and screamed, "How do we make this hopper fly?"

Cullen's eyes fluttered open. "It . . . hurts," he said breathlessly. "Why should it hurt. . . ?"

"How do we fly the damn plane? That thing's coming back!"

In wheezing monosyllables, Cullen told her, then passed out. She left !Xabbu looking for something to bind his wound, then thumbed the buttons he had mentioned in what she hoped was the right order. The vehicle shuddered as its wings rotated out from under the wingcase, then vibrated into swift-beating life. Renie managed to get the legs moving to turn the head of the vehicle away from the wall and out toward the edge of the building. As the hopper swiveled, the scarecrow form of the mantis heaved into view before the viewscreen, groping toward them.

Renie said a silent prayer, pulled back on the wheel, and gave the hopper all the throttle she could. It jumped, slamming !Xabbu and Cullen back against the padded cabin wall and rattling Renie in her pilot's seat, then skimmed upward just out of reach of the mantis' last, stabbing clutch.

Within moments the wreckage of the Hive was far below. Renie tugged the wheel a few times, once beginning an alarming dive, then at last found what she wanted. They banked and then flew on into the towering forest, toward the setting sun.

"That was not Grandfather Mantis," !Xabbu said solemnly behind her. "I forgot myself—I am ashamed."

Renie began to shiver, and for a moment feared she might never stop. "Bugs," she said, still shuddering. "Jesus Mercy."

CHAPTER 8

Fighting Monsters

NETFEED/PEOPLE: "One Angry Man" Dies
(visual: Gomez answering reporters' questions in front of courthouse)
VO: Nestor Gomez, who referred to himself in court as "just one angry man,"
died in a hospice in Mexico City, aged 98. Already in his sixties and retired
from his factory job at the time he first came to fame, Gomez was celebrated
as a hero by many after he machine-gunned a car full of young men in a
rest stop outside Juarez, Mexico. He claimed that the youths had been
harrassing him.
(visual: charred wreckage of car)
Even more controversial than the killings was an eyewitness claim that
Gomez set fire to the car while some of the wounded victims were still alive.
His Mexico City trial ended in a hung jury. Two subsequent trials also failed
to reach a verdict. Gomez was never tried in America, even though all five
victims were Americans.
(visual: Gomez being greeted at airport in Buenos Aires)
For years after the incident, he was a featured speaker at meetings of anti-
crime groups in many countries, and the expression "to Gomez" became
synonymous with violent and even excessive retribution . . .

"IT seems scanny," Fredericks said, enjoying the shade of a grass
stem. "I mean, I know we don't need to eat or anything, but it
just doesn't seem like morning without breakfast."

Orlando, feeling vastly more comfortable than he had during the worst of the fever, shrugged. "Maybe there's a coffee bar down the river someplace. Or a puffed rice plantation."

"Don't even talk about it," Sweet William grumbled. "No coffee, no fags—that means ciggies, just so you nice Yank boys don't get confused—this is hell, as some Shakespeare bloke said, nor am I out of it."

Orlando grinned, wondering what William would think if he knew one of the Yank boys was really a girl. But for that matter, how did they know Sweet William wasn't a girl himself? Or that Florimel wasn't a boy?

"So what do we do?" Quan Li asked. "Where do we go? Should we not look for the others?"

"We can do anything that we want." Florimel was just returning from a scouting trip up the riverbank, with T4b hissing and clanking at her side. "But we had better stay off the water for a while. The fish are feeding."

Even the stories the others had told him about the splashing frenzy that had sunk their leaf-boat could not dim Orlando's good mood. He clambered to his feet, still a little weak, but better than he'd been in days, and brushed the dust from Thargor's coarse-woven loincloth. It was funny how when you looked close enough—or got small enough—even dirt had its own dusty residue. Dirt particles so small he couldn't even have seen them when he had been his normal size bumped together and were ground down finer still. He supposed it would go on, smaller and smaller, until you got down to the size of molecules, and even there you would find bits of micro-lint in the molecular wrinkles. Utterly scanbark, as Fredericks liked to say . . . "Do we have any idea of where Renie and her friend—Kobbu, whatever his name was—where they might be?" Orlando asked. "I mean, did anyone see them after they went in the water?"

"They are still alive."

Everyone turned to look at Martine, who was huddled against the stones—grains of beach sand if Orlando and the others had been normal size—that the travelers had piled to make a windbreak for their night's shelter. Her sim looked a little less ragged and careworn today, although Orlando wondered if he might be projecting some of his own heightened spirits. "What do you mean?" he asked.

"I . . . can just tell. I can . . . feel them, I suppose." Martine rubbed at her face so hard it seemed to change shape, and for the first time Orlando saw what seemed like a true measure of her blindness: he didn't think a sighted person would make a gesture that seemed so private. "There are not words for these things, but I have always used nonvisual methods to work with information, yes? You understand? That is how my system is designed. Now I am getting things I never have before, new and very strange information. But slowly—too slowly, because it is a painful process—it is starting to make some sense." She turned toward Orlando. "You, for example. You are sounds, yes—I can hear your clothes rubbing skin, and your heart beating, and you breathing, with a little, how would you say, bubbling in your lungs from your sickness. I can smell the leather belt you are wearing, and your own person-scent, and the iron of the sword. It is rusting just a bit, by the way."

Orlando looked down, embarrassed. Thargor would never have let his sword go untreated after a prolonged immersion. He scooped up a handful of fine micro-sand and began rasping the blade clean.

"But that is only part," Martine continued. "Now I have other information coming to me, and there are not names for it. Not yet, anyway."

"What do you mean?" asked Quan Li worriedly. "What is coming?"

"I mean that what I experience, I cannot put into words yet. It is as if you tried to describe color to someone blind like me." She frowned. "No, that is not correct, because there was a time when I could see, and so I remember colors. But if you tried to describe 'red' or 'green' to someone who had never seen any colors at all—how would you do that?

"You, Orlando, I can feel also as a set of ripples in the air, but they are not ripples, and it is not air. They are things that tell me an Orlando-shaped thing *has* to be somewhere nearby. And I feel this forest as . . . numbers, in a way. Little hard things, millions of them, pulsing, talking to one another. It is so hard to say." She shook her head, pressing fingers against temples. "The whole of this network—it is for me like being in a river of information. It tosses me, and spins me, and it almost drowned me. But I am beginning to understand a little of how to swim."

"*Ho dzang!*" said Fredericks, a drawn-out exhalation. "But far scanny, too."

"So you're sure that Renie and the baboon-man are still alive?" Orlando asked.

"I can . . . yes, feel them. Faint, like a very distant sound. I do not think they are close, or perhaps I am only sensing some . . . residue." Her face went slack in sadness. "Maybe I have spoken too soon. Perhaps they are gone, and I sense only where they once were."

"So you can tell us all apart with . . . what, sonar?" Florimel sounded angry, perhaps a little frightened, too. "What else do you know about us? Can you read our minds, Martine?"

The blind woman spread her hands as if to ward off a blow. "Please! I know only what I sense, and that has no more to do with what truly goes on in your thoughts than someone who looked at your face would see, or someone who heard your voice."

"So calm down, Flossie," Sweet William said, grinning.

"My name is not 'Flossie,' " The look on her virtual face would have curdled milk. "It is a bad joke, if it is a joke."

"But who are you?" Orlando asked. "Who are any of you?" The others turned toward him. "I mean, I still don't know who any of you are. We have to trust each other, but we don't know anything about the people we're supposed to trust."

Now it was William's turn to be sour. "We don't *have* to do anything. I, for one, am not planning on making a career out of this lark, and I don't care what dreary, dreadful things you all used to do with your spare time."

"That's not good enough," Orlando said. "Look, I'll tell you the real truth. My name is Orlando Gardiner. I'm fifteen years old."

"Not for another three months," said Fredericks.

"Just a teenager? What a surprise." William rolled his eyes.

"Shut up. I'm trying to do something." Orlando took a breath, getting ready. "I'm almost fifteen years old. I have progeria. It's a disease, and it's going to kill me pretty soon." As when he had confessed to Fredericks, he felt a certain exhilaration, the cold splash of a long-dreaded jump from the high board. "Don't say you're sorry, because that's not what's important." William arched an eyebrow, but remained silent; Orlando hurried on. "And I've spent years on the net, doing gaming, and I'm really good at it. And for some reason I stumbled onto this whole thing, and I don't know anyone who's sick because of it, but it's what I'm going to do now, and . . . and it's more important to me than anything else has ever been."

Finished, he felt a flush heating his real skin, and hoped that it would not call forth a twin on his virtual face. No one spoke.

"My name's Sam Fredericks," his friend said at last into the uncomfortable silence. "And I'm fifteen, too—but I really am fifteen." Fredericks smiled almost shyly at Orlando. "I'm here because Gardiner brought me here. But I'm just as trapped as if I were here to save somebody. *Fenfen,* I guess I *am* here to save somebody. Me. Us."

Orlando, despite the embarrassment of having his age corrected, did not point out Fredericks' omissions. He—or she—would wear the face he wanted, as would all the others.

"And I am Martine Desroubins," the blind woman said. "I am a researcher. I have been blind since I was eight. An accident. I live by myself, in the Haut-Languedoc in the southern part of France, near Toulouse. I came with Renie and !Xabbu and Murat Shagar Singh, who was killed when we entered the Otherland network." She nodded her head as if to punctuate the dry recitation. Orlando heard the empty places in what she said, but again did not question.

"Far scanning, this." T4b had his arms crossed across his spiky chest. "You wanna know my ID for what? You with netnews?"

"Good God. *I* can speak clearer English than that," Florimel said, "and it is not my native language."

"Just tell us what you're doing here," Orlando pleaded. "What's your real name?"

"Ain't telling no names." He glowered, insofar as a cartoonish chrome battle-mask could be made to glower. "Here for my shadow, me—my zizz."

"What does that mean?" asked Quan Li.

"A friend he hangs around with," translated Orlando, who had a young suburbanite's fascination with Goggleboy-speak.

"Not no friend," T4b said indignantly. "He my shadow—we from the box together!"

"They're, um, sort of in the same gang," Orlando explained to the group's only certified grandmother. "So, T4b, what happened to your friend?"

"Came to this scan palace to find out, didn't I?" the robot said. "My zizzy's in the hospital. Found him almost sixed on the floor at his cot. Thought it was charge-burn, but he was togged into like the mama-papa net."

Orlando was feeling increasingly ludicrous, but he soldiered gamely on with his translation. "He says his friend is in the hospital, just like Renie's brother. At first when they found him, they thought it was charge damage, but he was connected to the regular net."

"In fact, isn't 'T4b' a kind of charge, my dear BangBang?" asked Sweet William.

"You ain't dupping." The robot's voice took on a kind of sullen rapture. "Far tasty jolt, T4b. Go to heaven, straight. My name, my fame, see?"

"Lord help us," William said. "He's a chargehead. That's just brilliant, isn't it?"

T4b brandished a spiny fist. "Brilliant *this,* funny-boy."

"Oh, stop it." The high spirits with which Orlando had begun the morning were beginning to fade, and the sun was not all the way into the sky. "Quan Li?"

"Hasn't everyone heard my poor story already?" She looked around, but no one spoke. "It was my granddaughter." Quan Li fell silent for a long moment. "Jing, my pretty little kitten, my dear one. She, too, fell into . . . into a sleep, like Renie's brother, like . . . like this man's friend. I have tried long and hard to discover the reason." She seemed uncomfortable to have everyone listening to her. "I live in New Kowloon, in Hong Kong," she added. "Is that not enough to say about someone like me? I am very, very old."

Orlando smiled, but he doubted she could be as shy and polite as she acted—it could not have been easy to push forward until she found this place, with her whole family telling her it was pointless and foolish. "Who else?"

"I am only doing this because the river is not yet safe," said Florimel. "At other times, I will not be convinced to talk when there are things to do, and I do not think it is particularly important who we *are*." She said the word with mocking emphasis. "You know my name. My last name is not important. I am originally from Baden-Württemberg. My home now is outside Stuttgart."

Orlando waited, but there was no more forthcoming. "Is that all?"

"What else do you need to know?"

"Why are you here?" It was Fredericks who asked this time. "And where did you learn to do those things you did to Orlando? Are you a doctor or something?"

"I have some medical training, but I am not a doctor. It is enough to say."

"But why are you here?" Orlando prompted.

"All these questions!" Florimel's sim face drew its eyebrows together in a fierce frown. "I am here because a friend became ill. You may ask more questions, but you will get no more answers."

Orlando turned to the man in black. "And you?"

"You know all you need to about me, chuck. How did BangBang, in his infinite wisdom, put it—'My name, my fame?' Well, this is what you get—this name, this face. And just because you've contracted some exotic, soap-opera illness and we're all sorry for you doesn't get you any more than that." The teasing edge of Sweet William's normal tone was gone. He and Florimel both appeared ready to fight rather than to divulge more about themselves.

"Well, it's better than nothing, I guess. So now what do we do?" Orlando turned his gaze out to the roiling green river. "Go downstream? And if we're going back on the river, how? Our boat, the leaf—it sank."

"Perhaps we should try to find Renie and her friend," said Quan Li. "They may need our help."

"I hardly think that a bunch of people the size of orange pips should waste too much time wandering around searching for *other* tiny people who may or may not be there in the first place," declared William. "You lot might enjoy being eaten by something, but I like my pleasures, especially the masochistic sort, more refined."

"We need to stay close to the river, don't we?" Fredericks asked. "That's how we get out of this place and into another simulation."

"Well, I'm all in favor of getting out of this place, as fast as frigging possible," William said.

"First smart thing, you." T4b nodded vigorously. "Let's get flyin'. Don't want no more *sayee lo* fish-swallowing, me."

"Just like that?" demanded Orlando, outraged. His own vulnerability had made him sensitive. "We just take off, and maybe leave Renie and her friend hurt, or lost?"

"Look, sweetness," William growled, "first off, you are going to have to learn the difference between real life and one of your action-adventures. For all we know, they're dead. For all we know, some horrible earwig the size of a bus may come around the corner any second and pinch all our heads off, and *we'll* be dead, too. Really dead. This is not a hooray-for-elves! story."

"I *know* it's not a story!" But even as he spoke, Orlando regretted that it wasn't. If he were really Thargor, and this were the Middle Country, it would be time for some serious smiting. "That's the point. We're in trouble. Renie and her friend are in this with us. And in case you didn't notice, there aren't a whole lot of us to spare."

"I think what Orlando says makes sense," Quan Li offered.

Fredericks and T4b now joined the argument, although it was hard to hear what either was saying in the general din. Orlando fought an urge to stick his fingers in his ears—were *any* of these people grown-ups?

"Stop!" Martine's voice was hoarse. The others paused, halted as much by the evident pain beneath her words as what she was saying. "Perhaps we can find some sort of compromise. We will need a boat, as Orlando has said. Perhaps some could begin building such a boat, while others looked for our two missing friends."

"*Dzang*, yeah. I can work on a boat," said Fredericks. "I did it when we were on the island. It worked, too, didn't it, Orlando?"

"Oh, sure. It stayed above water for nearly half the trip."

Fredericks rewarded him with a punch on the shoulder.

"That is fine," said Martine. "For me, I feel that I should be among those searching for the others. I would be little help with building."

Quan Li volunteered to accompany her, as did Florimel. After much

argument, Sweet William and T4b decided to help gather material to
build the boat. "After all," William pointed out, "there's not a lot of
difference between getting eaten up while searching or getting eaten
up while doing construction."

"We will return before the sun goes down," Martine promised.

"Yes, but if you do come back after dark," William said, "try not to
make noises like a giant bug or we might stick you with something
sharp by accident."

Building the raft of reeds with Fredericks had been one thing—
Orlando had been deathly ill through most of that process, and what
little work he had done, Fredericks had directed. Now he felt himself
again, and found he was part of a very fractious four-person commit-
tee. Fredericks wanted to build another raft, but William pointed
out—quite correctly, Orlando had to admit—that even a large raft was
not going to be heavy enough or deep-bottomed enough to keep them
afloat on the river. At their size, even the river's milder moments of
choppiness would be like a terrible storm at sea. But Fredericks proved
stubborn, as he often did. He felt that the raft experiment had worked
once—although, as Orlando had earlier pointed out, even that conclusion depended on how you read the data—and that they did not have
the equipment or materials to build anything more complicated. Orlando had to agree with him on the latter point.

The disagreement rapidly degenerated into a bout of mutal recrimi-
nations until T4b accidentally made the best suggestion of the afternoon and a plan began to develop. During the course of one short-
lived moment of calm discussion, the robot Goggleboy said that what
they really needed was their old leaf back. A few minutes later, when
Orlando had given up for a bit on mediating between Fredericks and
Sweet William, and was staring up at the vast trunk of a tree looming
over the riverbank like a cylindrical cliff-face, T4b's words came back
to him.

"Hold on," he said. "Maybe we *do* need our leaf back. Or another
leaf."

"Sure we do," William said, rolling his eyes. "And at the first
thumping it will go over, just like the last one, and we'll all swim the
rest of the way back to the real world. Won't that be fun?"

"Just listen. We could make a raft, like Fredericks said, but put it
inside a leaf—like a deck. That would give it some . . . what do you call
it?"

"Kitsch value?" suggested William.

"Structural integrity. You know, it would brace it. And then we could make some outriggers, like they have on Hawaiian canoes. Pontoons, is that the word? That would keep it from tipping over."

"Hawaiian canoes?" William smiled despite himself, Pierrot lips quirking at the edges. "You truly are a mad boy, aren't you? What, do you spend all your time living in fantasy worlds?"

"Think it's good, me," said T4b suddenly. "Make one sixing boat, no dupping."

"Well, maybe." William raised an eyebrow. "Pontoons, is it? Suppose there's no harm trying it. No harm till we drown, that is."

The sun was high overhead, already past the meridian and heading for its setting point somewhere on the far side of the river. Orlando was discovering how far he still had to go before he'd be at even his normal level of fitness. The tactor settings were either simply lower here, or some of Thargor's more superhuman characteristics didn't translate into the Otherland network. Certainly the barbarian's famous indefatigability was absent: Orlando was dripping with virtual sweat and exhausted by very real aches in every joint and muscle.

Fredericks was not any more cheerful, or at least his sim face looked red and uncomfortable. He stood up from where he was forcing in the last crossbeam, wedging it into the leaf by using a piece of sand big as his two fists as a hammer-stone. "We're ready for the mat, now."

Orlando gestured to T4b, then climbed gingerly over the edge of the leaf and down onto the beach. They had chosen a smaller leaf than the one that had brought them here, but even so it had taken them a large part of the morning just to drag it down to the river's edge, and Orlando felt as if he had been chopping with his sword for days to cut enough of the bamboolike grass shoots to weave the frame.

William, piecing together the last fibers of the coarse mat, had been forced to saw the tiny shoots used in its manufacture with a jagged stone, and did not seem to have enjoyed his task, either. "Whose bloody idea was this?" he asked as Orlando and T4b trudged up. "If it was mine, take this heavy thing and hit me with it."

Orlando no longer had the strength or breath for jokes, even the stupid ones that had helped him through the hard work earlier. He grunted, then bent and grabbed one edge of the mat. After a moment, T4b leaned over with an answering groan and found a handhold of his own.

"Oh, for God's sake, you sound like a couple of Tasmanian washerwomen." William struggled up from his seated position and walked to the far side. "You pull, I'll push."

Together they wrestled the mat over the curled edge of the leaf; then, with a great deal of swearing, shoved it more or less into place.

"Finished, true?" asked T4b hopefully.

"No." Fredericks sucked his lower lip thoughtfully. "We need to tie this down. Then we need to cut something long enough to make Orlando's pontoons."

"They're not *my* pontoons," Orlando growled. "*I* don't need any damn pontoons. They're for the boat."

William rose, a pitch-black scarecrow, his tassels and fringes fluttering in the breeze off the river. "You two tie the mat down. I'll go look for some more bloody reeds to make the outrigger thingies. But when you get done resting, Orlando my chuck, *you* can come cut them down. You're the one who brought a sword to the picnic, after all."

Orlando nodded a weary assent.

"And why don't you come with me, BangBang," William continued. "That way if something with too many legs comes sneaking up on me, you can bash it with your big metal fists."

The robot shook its head, but rose unsteadily and limped after the departing death-clown.

Orlando watched them go with something less than complete satisfaction. Sweet William was right about one thing, anyway: if this were an adventure game, Orlando could have relied on allies with definable and helpful powers—swiftness, agility, strength, magical abilities. As it was, except for Martine's new input, the group's only real skills seemed to be at dressing funny.

He slumped, waiting for the inevitable summons from Fredericks, but in no condition to anticipate it. A pair of giant flies swooped and barrel-rolled like vintage planes above a bit of drying something-or-other a short way up the beach. The noise of their wings made the air vibrate until it was almost impossible to think, but there was a kind of beauty in them, too, their glossy bodies rainbowing as they caught the sun, their swift-beating wings an almost invisible iridescence.

Orlando sighed. This whole Otherland thing locked, basically. If it were a game, the rules would be defined, the moves to victory comprehensible. Games made sense. How had little Zunni from the Wicked Tribe put it? "*Kill monster, find jewel, earn bonus points. Wibble-wobble-wubble.*" Not much like real life, maybe, but who wanted real life? Or even this bizarre variation? No rules, no goals, and no idea even of where to begin.

"Hey, Gardino, are you going to sit there working on your tan, or are you going to help me finish this?"

He stood, sighing again. And what had they learned so far, that would take them any closer toward their objectives? That they were trapped in the Otherland network, somehow. That they needed to stay alive until Sellars could get them out again. That somewhere, in one of who could guess how many simulations, a guy named Jonas was running around, and Sellars wanted them to find him.

"A needle in a haystack the size of a locking galaxy," Orlando muttered as he clambered onto the leaf.

Fredericks frowned at him. "You shouldn't sit in the sun so long. You're getting woofie in the head."

Another hour had passed, and none of the others had returned. The sun had sunk behind the pinnacles of the trees, throwing vast fields of early night across the riverbank. The leaf-boat lay in one of them, and the local weather was almost chilly. Orlando, grateful for the relief, was dragging another long reed back toward the boat, for use as a barge pole in shallower waters, when something big came hissing out from under a pile of stones. Fredericks shouted a horrified warning, but Orlando had already seen the dark blur at the corner of his vision. He threw himself sideways, rolled, and came up without the reed, but with his sword in his hand and his heart hammering.

The centipede was at least a half-dozen times as long as Orlando was tall, dusty brown and covered with bits of crumbling earth. It came toward him in strange, sidewinding fashion, forcing him to give ground. Except for movement, it was hard to distinguish the creature from the background; Orlando was grateful there was still a little daylight left.

A shudder ran through the creature, a ripple of its armor plates, and for a moment the centipede's entire front end lifted from the ground. Orlando thought he could see pistoning spikes just below its mouth, and had a sudden, maddeningly distant memory that these creatures were poisonous. The front limbs dropped and the beast rushed forward on dozens of segmented legs, bearing down on him like a fanged monorail. Orlando could hear Fredericks shouting something, but he had no attention to spare. Years of Thargor-experience rolled through him in half a second. This was not the kind of high-bellied creature you could get under, like a gryphon or most dragons. But with all those legs, it would strike sideways very quickly, perhaps faster than he could matador out of the way.

With a noise like a small stampede, the centipede was on him. Orlando sprang from a crouch even as the thing's front legs tried to hook him toward its mouth. He clambered up onto the head, then had time enough for one stabbing blow to what he hoped was the creature's eye before it kinked in fury and threw him to the side. He landed heavily and scrambled back onto his feet as quickly as his throbbing

muscles could manage. Fredericks was atop the leaf, watching in
agony, but Orlando could think of no way his friend could help him
without weapons.

As he backed away, the huge bug bent itself in a semicircle, following him with its front end even as the rest of its body held in place.
Unlike the mostly anthropomorphic creatures of the Middle Country,
it gave off no suggestion of feeling or thought at all. It was simply a
hunter, a killing machine, and he had walked too near its hiding place
at sundown.

Orlando reached down and grabbed the barge pole he had dropped,
a rigid stem of grass twice his own length. He doubted it was strong
enough to pierce the centipede's armor plating, but it might help to
keep the creature at bay until he could think of something else to do.
The only problem, he quickly discovered, was that he could not support the pole and hold his sword, too. He let the stem droop as the
centipede began another sidewinding charge, and shoved the blade
through his belt.

He managed to raise the pole just enough to jab it at the centipede's
head. It lodged so hard against the creature's mouth parts that if Orlando had not dug the butt-end into the earth behind him, he would
have slid right up the stem into the poison fangs. It bent, but did not
snap. The centipede, arrested by something it could not see, rose clawing toward the sky until its first three pairs of legs were off the ground.
The reed straightened and popped free. Released, the beast thumped
heavily back to the ground, hissing even louder.

Orlando dragged the stem backward, looking for a new position to
defend. The far end of the reed had been chewed to pulpy splinters.
The centipede lockstepped toward him again, more cautiously this
time, but showing no signs of going away to look for a more compliant
meal. Orlando cursed weakly.

"I see the others!" Fredericks was shouting. "They're coming back!"

Orlando shook his head, trying to get his breath back. Unless their
companions had kept some big secrets, he couldn't imagine any of
them making much difference. This was pure monster-killer work,
and Orlando was one of the best. Or was it Thargor who was one of
the best. . . ?

Jeez, listen to me, he thought blurrily, dragging the pole up into a
protective posture again. Sharp things clashed in the shadows of the
centipede's mouth. *Can't tell the difference between one kind of not-real and
another. . . .*

He jabbed at its head, but this time he could not get the reed seated
against the ground. The bug shoved forward and the long stem slid to

one side off the dirty-brown carapace, catching between two of the driving legs like a stick in bicycle spokes. Orlando hung onto the pole as it jerked and flung him through the air to one side; he landed hard enough to squeeze the breath from his body. The great multilegged shape swiveled into a tight turn, rippled forward a half-dozen steps, then reared over him, legs hooking inward like two hands' worth of giant, snatching fingers. Orlando scrabbled backward, but it was a hopeless attempt at escape.

The centipede lifted and stretched farther, its killing parts locked in place above him like some horrible industrial punch-press. Fredericks' distant voice was now a meaningless shrill, fast disappearing in a rising wash of pure sound, a great storm, a slow explosion, but all somewhere far away and meaningless as Orlando struggled to lift the heavy stem one last time. In this moment of slow time, Death was upon him. The universe had nearly stopped, waiting for that ultimate second to tick over.

Then the second crashed upon him with blackness and wind. A cold thunder blasted down from above, a vertical hurricane that blew him flat and filled the air with stinging, blinding dust. Orlando screamed into dirt, knowing that any moment he would feel poison spines hammer down into his body. Something struck his head, throwing stars into his eyes, too.

The wind lessened. The darkness grew a little less. Fredericks was still shrieking.

Orlando opened his eyes. He squinted against the swirling dust, astonished to discover himself still alive in this world. Stones as big around as his thigh rolled past him as an impossibly vast black shape, like a negative angel, rose into the sky overhead. Something slender and frenetic and comparatively tiny writhed in its talons.

Talons. It was a bird, a bird as big as a passenger jet, as a shuttle rocket—bigger! The explosive force of its wings, which had pinned him at the base of an invisible column of air, suddenly shifted as the bird tilted and vaulted away, the centipede still struggling helplessly in its claws, on its way to feed a nest full of fledglings.

"Orlando! Orlando, hey!" Fredericks was keening softly, far away, unimportant compared to the awesome sight of a certain, inescapable death being sucked away into the evening sky. *"Gardiner!"*

He looked up to the bluffs above the beach, where Sweet William and T4b had dropped their bundles of reeds to stare in astonishment after the swift-rising bird. He turned to Fredericks, and the boat, but they were gone.

A heart-stopping instant later he saw that they were only displaced, that the new leaf-boat they had so laboriously built in one place was now quite a way distant. It took a moment for his dazed mind to put together the information and realize that the leaf was on the river, blown into the water by the bird's flapping wings, and was drifting slowly out toward the strong current. Fredericks, alone on board, was leaping up and down, waving his arms and shouting, but already his voice was growing too faint to understand.

Befuddled, Orlando looked up to the bluffs. The two figures there had finally seen Frederick's situation, and were making their way down the mossy bank as swiftly as they could, but they were a minute's run away at least, and Fredericks was only a score of seconds from the current that would sweep him away forever.

Orlando picked up the barge pole like a javelin and dashed along the beach. He sprinted toward a headland, hoping he might be able to extend the long stem to Fredericks, but when he got there, it was clear that even with three such poles he would not be able to reach his friend. The leaf caught for a moment in an eddy, buffeted between the faster current and the small backwater below the headland. Orlando looked at his friend, then back at T4b and Sweet William, still distant and small as they ran toward him across the strand. He turned and scrambled down the headland, got a running start, and flung himself off into the backwater.

It was a near thing, even in reasonably warm water. Orlando had almost run out of strength, and was wondering what had happened to his legs (which he could no longer feel) when Fredericks reached down and plucked the floating barge pole from the water. Orlando was just deciding that traveling to a virtual universe to drown seemed a long way around for a person with a terminal illness, when the centipede-chewed end of the pole slapped down next to him, nearly braining him.

"Grab it!" Fredericks shouted.

He did, then his friend helped him struggle over the edge of the leaf onto the mat they had spent much of the afternoon weaving. Orlando had strength only to huddle down out of the evening wind, shivering, as water drizzled off him and the river swept them away from the beach and their two astounded companions.

*   *   *

"It's yours, Skouros," the captain said. "It's *Merapanui*. On your system even as we speak."

"Thanks. You're a mate." Calliope Skouros did not say it like she meant it, and to avoid any accusations of subtlety, she curled her lip as well. "That case has been history so long that it smells."

"You wanted one, you got one." The sergeant made a wiping-her-hands gesture. "Don't blame me for your own ambition. Make a last pass, call the witnesses. . . ."

"If any of them are still alive."

". . . Call the witnesses and see if anyone's remembered anything new. Then dump it back in the 'Unsolved' list if you want. Whatever." She leaned forward, narrowing her eyes. Skouros wondered if the sergeant's cornea-reshaping had been less than she'd hoped for. "And, speaking on behalf of the entire police force of Greater Sydney, don't say we never give you anything."

Detective Skouros stood up. "Thank you for this rubber bone, O glorious mistress. I wag my tail in your general direction."

"Get out of my office, will you?"

"It's ours and it's impacted," she announced. The pressure vents on her chair hissed as she dropped her muscular body onto the seat.

"Meaning?" Stan peered at her over the top of his old-fashioned framed lenses. Everything about Stan Chan was old-fashioned, even his name. Calliope still could not understand what parents in their right minds would name a child "Stanley" in the twenty-first century.

"Impacted. Suctioning. Locked up. It's a rotten case."

"This must be that Merapanui thing."

"None other. They've finally kicked it loose from the Real Killer investigation, but it's not like they were doing anything with it over there. It's already five years old, and I don't think they did anything but look it over, run the parameters through their model, then throw it out again."

Her partner steepled his fingers. "Well, did you solve it already, or can I have a look at it, too?"

"Sarcasm does not become you, Stan Chan." She kicked the wallscreen on, then brought up a set of branching box files. The case file popped to the top of the activity log, and she spread it out on the screen. "Merapanui, Polly. Fifteen years old. Living in Kogarah when she was killed, but originally from up north. A Tiwi, I think."

He thought for a moment. "Melville Island—those people?"

"Yep. Homeless since she ran away from a foster home at thirteen. Not much of an arrest record, other than vagrancy-related. A few times for shoplifting, two offensive conducts. Locked up a couple of days once for soliciting, but the case notes suggest she might actually have been innocent of that."

Stan raised an eyebrow.

"I know, astonishing to contemplate." Calliope brought up a picture. The girl in the stained shirt who stared back had a round face that seemed too large on her thin neck, frightened wide eyes, and dark, curly hair pulled to one side in a simple knot. "When she was booked."

"She seems pretty light-skinned for a Tiwi."

"I don't think there *are* any full-blooded Tiwi any more. There's damn few of us full-blooded Greeks."

"I thought your grandfather was Irish."

"We made him honorary."

Stan leaned back and brought his fingertips together again. "So why did it get pulled out of the dormant file by the Real Killer crew?"

Calliope flicked her fingers and brought up the scene photos. They were not pretty. "Just be glad we can't afford full wrap-around," Calliope said. "Apparently the type and number of wounds—a big hunter's knife like a Zeissing, they think—were similar in some respects to Mr. Real's work. But it predates the first known Real murder by three years."

"Any other reasons they gave up on it?"

"No similarities besides the wound patterns. All the Real victims have been whites of European descent, middle-class or upper-middle. They've all been killed in public places, where there was at least theoretical electronic security of some sort, but the security's always failed in some way. Put that damn eyebrow down—of *course* it's weird, but it's not our case. This one is."

"Speaking of, why did you ask for this Merapanui thing in the first place? I mean, if it isn't a prostitute getting offed by a client, it's a crime of passion, a one-shot. If we want casual murders, we got streets full of them every day."

"Yeah?" Calliope raised a finger and flicked forward to another set of crime scene snaps, these from an angle that showed all of the victim's face.

"What's wrong with her eyes?" Stan asked at last, rather quietly.

"Couldn't say, but those aren't them. Those are stones. The killer put them in the sockets."

Stan Chan took the squeezers from her and enlarged the image. He stared at it for a dozen silent seconds. "Okay, so it's not your usual assault-whoops-homicide," he said. "But what we still have here is a five-year-old murder which had a brief moment of erroneous fame when it seemed like the perp might be an important killer who's been splashed all over the newsnets. However, what it really is, Skouros, is some other cop's leftovers."

"Succinct, and yet gloriously descriptive. I like your style, big boy. You looking for a partner?"

Stan frowned. "I suppose it beats cleaning up after cake dealers and chargeheads."

"No it doesn't. It's a shit case. But it's ours."

"My joy, Skouros, is unbounded."

It was never an easy choice on office days between taking the light rail or driving the underpowered e-car the department leased for her, but though urban traffic insured that driving was slower, it was also quieter.

The auto-reader was picking its way through the case notes, making bizarre phonetic hash out of some of the Aboriginal and Asian names of the witnesses—not that there were many witnesses to anything. The murder had happened near a honeycomb beneath one of the main sections of the Great Western Highway, but if the squat had been occupied before the murder, it was empty by the time the body was discovered. The people who lived in such places knew that there was little benefit in being noticed by the police.

As the details washed over her again, Calliope tried to push all the preconceptions from her mind and just listen to the data. It was almost impossible, of course, especially with all the distractions that came from the tangled traffic streams humping along in fits and starts beneath the bright orange sunset.

First off, she was already thinking of the killer as "he." But did it have to be a man? Even in her comparatively brief career, Calliope had worked homicide in Sydney long enough to know that women, too, could end another's life, sometimes with surprising violence. But this bizarre, iron-nerved, obsessive play with the body—surely only a man would be capable of such a thing. Or was she sliding into prejudice?

There had been a time only a few years back when some group in the United States—in the Pacific Northwest, if she remembered correctly—had claimed that since the majority of social violence was caused by men, and because there were certain genetic indicators in some males that might indicate predisposition to aggression, male children bearing those indicators should be forced to undergo gene therapy *in utero*. The opposition groups had shouted long and loud about the proposed law being a kind of genetic castration, a punishment for the crime of simply being male, and the whole debate had degenerated into name-calling. Calliope thought that was too bad, actually. She had seen enough of the horrifyingly casual bloodshed caused almost entirely by young males to wonder if there wasn't something to what the bill's proponents had to say.

When she mentioned it to him, Stan Chan had called her a fascist lesbian man-hater. But he had said it in a nice way.

It was certainly true that she had to avoid making assumptions without the facts, but she also needed to try to wrap her mind around the person, needed to *find* the perp before she could find him—or her. For now she would have to trust her instincts. It felt like man's work, of the most twisted sort, so unless she stumbled on overwhelming evidence to the contrary, the person they were seeking would remain a *him*.

But beyond the assumption of a male perp, not a lot stood out, at least in the way of unifying themes. There had been no trace of sexual assault, and even the violence-as-sex aspect seemed oddly muted. In many ways it appeared to be more ritual than rape.

Ritual. The word had a vibration, and she had learned to trust the part of her that felt those kinds of resonance. Ritual. She would file that away.

Other than that, there was little to go on. The murderer was not as thorough in his avoidance of physical evidence as the Real Killer, but Polly Merapanui's death had found her effectively out-of-doors, the only shelter being the concrete overpass, an area scoured by wind so that no useful traces remained, even to the department's hideously expensive ForVac particle-sucker. The perp had worn gloves, and if Polly had fought, she had not carried away any trace of her murderer beneath fingernails.

If only the old superstition were true, Calliope thought, not for the first time in her homicide career—if only dying eyes actually retained an image of what they last saw.

Perhaps the killer believed that ancient superstition. Perhaps that explained the stones.

The voice of the auto-reader droned on, emotionless as a clock. The sign indicating her exit swam into view, a distant smear above the river of taillights. Calliope edged toward the left lane. No physical evidence, a victim that most would agree was as inconsequential as a human being could be, a handful of useless witnesses (mostly itinerants and uncooperative relatives) and a truly disturbing *modus operandi* that had never been seen again—Stan was right. They had someone else's bad case, with what little juice it had once possessed sucked out of it.

But the girl, who had possessed nothing in life *except* life, was not entirely inconsequential. To declare that would be to declare that Calliope Skouros herself was inconsequential, for what had she chosen to do with her own days and nights except defend the resentful and avenge the unwanted?

That's inspiring, Skouros, she told herself, leaning on her horn as some idiot on his way home from four or five after-work beers cut her off. *But it's still a shit case.*

FREDERICKS was crouching in what would have been the prow if the leaf were a proper boat, staring out over the rapidly darkening water. The river had carried them to this point without too much violence, but Fredericks had a firm grip on the fibers of the mat anyway. Watching his friend's head waggle from side to side with the motion of the water had begun to make Orlando feel queasy, so he was lying flat on his back, looking up at the first prickling of stars in the sky.

"We've lost them all," Fredericks said dully. This was not the first time since they had been swept away that he had made this doomful remark. Orlando ignored him, concentrating instead on convincing himself that his scanty clothes were drying, and that the air was actually warm. "Don't you care?"

"Of *course* I care. But what can we do about it? It wasn't me who got stuck on this stupid boat."

Fredericks fell silent. Orlando regretted his words, but not to the point of retracting them. "Look, they know which way we're going," he said at last by way of apology. "If we . . . whatever you call it, *go through,* we'll just wait for them on the other side. They'll find a way to get down the river, and then we'll all be in the next simulation together."

"Yeah. I guess so." Fredericks turned to face Orlando. "Hey, Gardiner?"

Orlando waited a few seconds for Fredericks to finish the sentence, then realized his friend wanted conversation. "Yeah?"

"Do you . . . do you think we're going to get killed?"

"Not in the next few minutes, if we're lucky."

"Shut up. I'm not spanking around, I mean it. What's going to happen to us?" Fredericks scowled. "I mean . . . I don't know, I miss my parents, kind of. I'm scared, Orlando."

"I am, too."

As the darkness thickened, the immense trees sliding past on either side became an unbroken wall of shadow, like the cliffs surrounding a deep valley.

"Valley of the Shadow of Death," Orlando murmured.

"What?"

"Nothing." He dragged himself upright. "Look, we can only do what we're doing. If there were a simple way to get out of this, one of us would have found it already. Remember, Sellars made it hard to get here, so even if they seem like the Scanmaster Club sometimes, Renie and the others must be pretty smart. So we just have to hang on until we solve it. Pretend it's one of the Middle Country adventures."

"Nothing in the Middle Country ever really hurt. And you couldn't get killed. Not for real."

Orlando forced a smile. "Well, then I guess it's about time old Thargor and Pithlit had a serious challenge."

Fredericks tried to return the smile, but his was even less convincing.

"Hey, what do you look like?" Orlando asked suddenly. "In RL?"

"Why do you want to know?"

"I just wondered. I mean, are you tall, short, what?"

"I don't want to talk about it, Orlando. Ordinary-looking, I guess. Talk about something else." Fredericks looked away.

"Okay. You still haven't ever told me where 'Pithlit' comes from. The name."

"I said I don't remember."

"*Fenfen.* I don't believe you. So tell me."

"I . . . well . . ." Fredericks met his eyes defiantly. "If you laugh, even a little, you're impacted to the utmost."

"I won't laugh."

"After a character in a book. A kid's book. A stuffed animal, sort of, named Piglet. When I was little I couldn't say it right, so that's what my parents called me. When I started doing the net—well, it was sort of my nickname. Are you laughing?"

Orlando shook his head, teeth firmly clamped. "No. Not . . ." He broke off. A noise which had been rising for many seconds was now clearly audible above the rush and roar of the water. "What's that?"

Fredericks stared. "Another bug. It's hard to tell. It's flying really low."

The winged thing, coming rapidly after them from upstream, had dropped so close to the river's surface that one of its feet broke a wavelet into white foam. The insect tipped and wobbled, then seesawed up to a higher level before regaining its course. It skimmed past them at an angle, showing itself to be almost half the size of their boat, then banked steeply a long distance downstream and began to fly back toward them.

"It's going to attack us," Fredericks said, fumbling for the barge pole.

"I don't know. It seems injured or something. Maybe sick . . ." Orlando's attention was captured by something in the waters beneath the veering insect. "Look! It's that blue sparkly stuff!" Fredericks stood and balanced unsteadily, intent on the low-flying bug. He raised the pole up above his head as it approached, as though to knock it out of the sky. "Jeez, are you scanned to the utmost?" Orlando dragged him down. Fredericks had to let go of the pole to keep from falling, but saved it from bouncing overboard after he had fallen to his knees. "That thing's ten times your size." Orlando chided him. "You hit it with that, you'll just get knocked into the water."

The insect hummed closer. As it neared, already banking, Orlando crouched on all fours, ready to drop to his belly if it flew too low. The creature was some kind of tropical beetle, he saw, its rounded brown shell touched with yellow. As it swept past, Orlando saw that the forward part of the wingcase had lifted, and that something was moving there, wiggling . . .

". . . *Waving?*" he said in astonishment. "There's a person in there!"

"It's Renie!" shouted Fredericks as the insect buzzed past. "I'm sure it's her!"

The glimmer was all around them now. The waters seemed to froth with glowing sky-blue. Upstream, the flying insect was making a wide turn, but Orlando could hardly see it. The very air was full of dancing light.

"They found us!" Fredericks bounced up and down. "They're flying in a bug! How can they do that?"

"I don't know," Orlando shouted. The noise of the river had grown to an endless wash, and blue light was leaping from his skin. The dark shadow of the flying insect was overhead now, pacing them, and it also flew through sprays of blue tracer-fire. "We'll ask them on the other side—"

And then the roaring overwhelmed them, and the light filled everything, and they passed through into another place.

CHAPTER 9

The Hollow Man

NETFEED/ENTERTAINMENT: I Loved The "Papa Diabla," Could Have
Done Without The Warm Gazpacho.
(Restaurant review of Efulgencia's World Choir, Oklahoma City, USA.)
(visual: "Iguana con Bayas" on a serving platter)
VO: ". . . My other major complaint with EWC would not perhaps be a
problem for other diners. EWC is one of the last to get on the "random
restaurant" dining loop, and their use of it is aggressive—there must have
been six changes of connection during our meal, which hardly leaves enough
time to ask the new arrivals what restaurant they're in, let alone what they're
eating, what they think of it, or anything else, before they've vanished and
the next party has popped in. Now, I never enjoyed this sort of thing even
when it was a novelty, but clearly EWC is looking for a younger, crunchier,
scorchier type of customer than yours truly—the pop-eyed, batter-fried
iguana is another giveaway . . ."

THE light was going fast. Renie, who had not felt confident for a
single moment since the hopper had lifted into the air, began
fumbling on the instrument panel for the insect-plane equivalent of
headlights. Realizing how many switches she could flick which would
not be in her best interest to flick, she gave up and concentrated on
maneuvering the little flyer through the overwhelming, monstrous
forest.

"He still seems to be alive," !Xabbu said from his crouch at Cullen's side. "Since there is no blood, it is hard to tell how much damage he sustained when that creature pulled his arm off. I have knotted his coat around the wound, in any case, and he is sleeping again now."

Renie nodded, mostly intent on avoiding a fatal piloting error. It would be easy to mistake a shadowy tree limb for part of the greater darkness, and from the perspective of their own skewed measurements, the ground was several hundred feet below them. She had contemplated trying to fly higher, to reach a place above the treetops, but she didn't know whether this plane could be expected to fly safely at an altitude of what would be equivalent to thousands of feet, and in any case she liked her chances of not hitting anything better down here, where the trees were mostly trunk.

"Are you sure he said the river was in this direction?" she asked.

"He said west. You heard him, Renie."

She nodded, and realized her teeth were locked so tight her jaw hurt. She unclenched. She had received enough glimpses of the sunset through the trees until just a little while ago that she actually felt confident that they were flying west, but she needed something to worry about, and whether they were headed in the right direction was—in total contrast to all their other difficulties—a problem of almost manageable size.

As they sped on through the evening, she gained enough confidence that she could almost enjoy the spectacle. Once they skimmed past a squirrel big as an office building, which turned a vast, liquid brown eye to watch them. Other insects, a large moth and a few mosquitos, fluttering along on errands of their own, passed the hopper without a second glance, like bored commuters pacing on a station platform. The moth was beautiful at this size, covered with a feathery gray pelt, each faceted eye a cluster of dark mirrors.

The distance between trees had grown wider, as much as a quarter-minute or more now separating each gargantuan trunk. Tendrils of mist drifted upward from the ground, twining among the branches and obscuring vision, but before Renie could add this to her catalogue of worries, the forest finally dropped away behind them. A strip of beach flashed past, then nothing lay below but gray-green water.

"The river! We're there!" She didn't dare take her hands off the wheel to clap, so she bounced in her padded seat.

"You have done well, Renie," !Xabbu said. "Shall we look for the others?"

"We can try. I don't know that we'll find them, though. They might have got back on the boat and headed on downstream." She tipped the hopper into a long, gradual turn. It was much less smooth in flight than the dragonfly, which had a wider wingspan, and it juddered as the wind shifted, but she had not hurried the turn, so she was able to straighten the little craft out again and head it along the river's flow. It was true that these virtual planes were made for scientists to use, not professional flyers, but she was still proud of herself.

She flew on for a few minutes, but it quickly became obvious that she would not be able to spot the others unless they were on the water or very well exposed on the beach. She was looking for a place to land, with the idea of continuing the search in full daylight, when !Xabbu sat up and pointed.

"What is that? I see a leaf, but I think I see something pale moving on it."

Renie could not make out much more than a dark shape bobbing on the water. "Are you sure?"

"No, but I think so. Can you fly this airplane closer to the river?"

She was surprised by how quickly the little craft hopped forward when she gave it some throttle. They dipped down, almost too low, and Renie cursed as they clipped the top of one of the river swells. It took her a few moments to fight the hopper back into submission. She skimmed past the leaf, not quite so low this time.

"It is them!" !Xabbu said, excited. "Or at least some of them. But they looked frightened."

"We must look like a real bug."

As she began her turn, !Xabbu said, "The water is strange here. The blue lights, as we had before."

"We should get them to the beach if we can." Renie started back upstream. With !Xabbu's help she managed to get the door open. Air rushed in, wild as an animal, bouncing them in their harnesses. Cullen groaned from behind his straps. Renie got her hand out the window and waved as they swooped past the startled faces on the boat.

"Turn back!" she shouted into the wind.

Whether they did not hear her, or had no way to steer, the leaf-boat did not change course. The current bore it on, and by the time Renie had completed another turn upstream and was heading back toward them, they had already reached the onset of the glimmering waters.

Renie pulled the door shut. "How many of them are there?"

"I could only see two."

She considered for only a moment. "If they can't stop, we have to go through with them. Otherwise, we might never find them again."

"Of course," said !Xabbu. "They are our friends."

Renie wasn't sure she was quite ready to call their fellow refugees friends, but she understood !Xabbu's impulse. Being lost was a lonely thing even in a world that made sense. "Right. Here we go."

They were almost level with the boat when snakes of neon-blue light began to arc along the windshield. As a flurry of sparks streamed from the wing, Renie had a frightening memory of the last Ares space mission, the one with the faulty shielding that had burned up on reentry. But this was cold fire, it seemed—foxfire, will-o'-the-wisp.

The world beyond the windshield went completely blue, then completely white. She felt a moment of still, weightless peace . . . then everything went abruptly and horribly upside down. The windows blew out and they were whirling in blackness, flipping end over end through a roaring tumult so loud that Renie could not hear her own scream.

End over end became a centrifugal blur. The roar increased, and for a few merciful instants, Renie lost consciousness. She floated back toward awareness, touched it, but did not take a firm grasp as she felt the spinning slow. The plane shuddered, then they struck down with a grinding rasp and a series of violent impacts that ended in a thump like a small explosion.

Black and cold were all around her. For long moments, she was too stunned to speak.

"Renie?"

"I'm . . . I'm here." She struggled upright. She could see nothing but a faint gleam of stars. The shape of the plane was all wrong, somehow, but she could not think about it. Things were pressing painfully against her, and something cold was creeping up her legs. "We're in water!" she shouted.

"I have Cullen. Help me to pull him out." !Xabbu's slender baboon fingers touched hers in the dark. She followed his arm to Cullen's clothing, then together they pulled the injured man up the sloping floor toward the opening and the wide night sky. The water was thigh-high and rising.

Renie dragged herself out through the crooked doorway, then leaned back and got a firm hold on Cullen before pulling him out into the waist-deep water. The air was strangely charged, tingly as in a storm, but the black sky seemed clear. The current tugged at her so that she had to brace herself as !Xabbu scrambled out, but the river was surprisingly shallow; Renie decided they had crashed on the edge of a sandbar or some other kind of underwater shelf. Whatever it was, the river remained shallow all the way to the shadowy bank. Stumbling, they carried Cullen onto land, then dropped into a heap.

Renie heard a creaking noise and looked back toward the plane, but could make out only a shapeless darkness protruding above the waters. The shadow lurched with the current, groaning with a sound more wooden than metallic, then slid off the bar and down into the waters.

"It's gone," she said quietly. She was beginning to shiver. "The plane just sank."

"But we are through into another place," !Xabbu pointed out. "Look, the big trees are gone. The river is a true size again."

"The others!" Renie suddenly remembered. *"Hello! Hello! Orlando? Are you out there? It's us!"*

The land all around seemed flat and empty. No answer came back except the liquid murmur of the river and a lone cricket who seemed to have been on hold until just this moment, and now began sawing determinedly at his two-note song.

Renie called again, !Xabbu joining her, but their only reply came from Cullen, who began to mumble and thrash weakly on the bank. They helped him sit up, but he did not answer their questions. In the darkness, it was hard to tell if he were truly conscious or not.

"We have to get him some help," she said. "If this is another simulation, maybe things are different here—maybe he can get offline." But she did not feel hopeful even as she said it, and wondered for whose benefit she was speaking. She and !Xabbu got Cullen to his feet, then guided him up the riverbank. At the top of the rise they found an open field, and in the distance, much to Renie's joy, a vast array of orange lights.

"A city! Maybe that's where Orlando and the rest have headed. Maybe they didn't know we were coming through with them." She got an arm around Cullen. !Xabbu took the point, a few paces ahead as they stumbled through tangled growth toward the lights. He stopped to riffle in the vegetation at their feet.

"Look, this is corn." He waved an ear in front of her face. "But all the stalks have been smashed to the ground, like an elephant or a herd of antelope have passed through here."

"Maybe it was," she said, trying to keep her teeth from chattering. "And you know something? As long as it wasn't giant bugs, I don't care *what* did it." She looked around. The flat fields extended away on all sides into the darkness. "But it would be nice to know where we're supposed to be, I guess."

!Xabbu, now a few dozen yards ahead, had stopped. "Whatever knocked this corn down has knocked over the fence as well," he said. "See."

Renie reached his side and let Cullen sit, which the entomologist did in swaying silence. Before them a heavy chain-link fence that looked to have been a dozen feet high now lay stretched across the broken corn like a snapped ribbon. "Well, at least we won't have to go looking for a gate." She bent to grab a rectangular metal sign, still held to the fence by one bent bolt. When she had twisted it free, she tilted it until it caught the light of the prairie moon.

"*TRESPASSERS WILL BE EXECUTED*" it proclaimed in huge black letters. At the bottom, in smaller print, was written: "*By Orders of His Wise Majesty, the Only King of Kansas.*"

"YOUR turn now," said Long Joseph. He stared out over Jeremiah's shoulder, eyes roving. "All them signs, no problem."

Jeremiah Dako put down his book. "Signs?"

"Yeah, those what-are-they—vital signs. Still the same. Heart going fast sometime, then slow, but everything else the same. If I watch anymore, I'm going crazy."

Despite having just been on watch for six hours, Long Joseph Sulaweyo followed Jeremiah back into the lab. As Jeremiah confirmed that all the various monitors—body temperature, respiration, filters, hydration, and nutrition—were as Long Joseph had said, Renie's father paced along the gallery, looking down on the silent V-tanks. His footsteps sent dry echoes scurrying through the cavernous room.

As Long Joseph crossed in front of him for the dozenth time, Jeremiah pulled off the headset and slapped it down on the console. "Good God, man, would you go do that somewhere else? It's bad enough I have to listen to you going pad, pad, pad around the place all night, but not here, too. Believe me, no one wishes more than I do that there was something here for you to drink."

Long Joseph turned, but more slowly than usual. His growl was a ghost of its former self. "What you doing, watching me sleep? Following me around at night? You come after me, try to get mannish, I'll whip you. That's the truth."

Jeremiah smiled despite himself. "Why is it that people like you always think that every homosexual you meet is dying to get you into bed? Believe me, old man, you are not my type."

The other glowered. "Well, that pretty damn sad for you then, because I the only one here."

Jeremiah laughed. "I promise I'll let you know if you start to look good."

"What, something wrong with me?" He seemed genuinely insulted. "You like those little soft fellows? Pretty-boys?"

"Oh, Joseph . . ." Jeremiah shook his head. "Just go do something. Go read a book. The selection is not very good, but there are some interesting ones."

"Read books? That's like eating *mielie pap*—it start out bad, then it get no better." Joseph took a deep breath and let it out slowly, over-burdened by the mere thought of literature. "Thank God there is some net, that's all I say. If we had no net, I would have to kill myself right now."

"You should not watch it so much. We are not supposed to use any more power than we have to—that Martine woman said it made it easier to disguise the power we were stealing if we kept it to a minimum."

"What are you talking about?" Long Joseph had found his outrage again. "We running those . . . those big tank things there," he waved at the wire-festooned sarcophagi, "and all this nonsense 'round here," his irritated swipe took in the computers, the lights, and Jeremiah himself, "and you worrying about me getting a few drops off the net?"

"I suppose you're right." Jeremiah picked up the headphones again. "Well, why don't you go watch some, then. Let me do my tests."

A minute later, Long Joseph's spare shadow fell across him again. Jeremiah waited for the other man to say something. When he did not, Jeremiah pulled off the headphones; it had been days since they had heard Renie or !Xabbu speak, in any case. "Yes? Come back for a recommendation on some reading material?"

Long Joseph scowled. "No." He was not looking at his companion, but rather at everything else, as though he tracked something which had both the power of flight and the wandering indirection of a gold-fish.

"Well, what is it?"

"I don't know." Long Joseph leaned on the railing, still staring up into the four-story expanse overhead. When he spoke again, his voice had risen in pitch. "I am just . . . I don't know, man. I think I am about gone crazy."

Jeremiah slowly put the headphones down. "What do you mean?"

"It just . . . I don't know. I can't stop thinking about Renie, thinking about my boy Stephen. And how there's nothing I can do. Just wait while all this foolishness go on."

"It's not foolishness. Your daughter's trying to help her brother. Someone killed my Doctor Van Bleeck over this. It's *not* foolishness."

"Don't get angry. I didn't mean . . ." Long Joseph turned to look at Jeremiah for the first time. His eyes were red-rimmed. "But me, I doing *nothing*. Just sit in this place all day, every day. No sun, no air."

He raised his fingers to clutch his own throat. "Can't breathe, hardly. And what if my Stephen needs me? Can't do him no good in this place."

Jeremiah sighed. This was not the first time this had happened, although Long Joseph sounded more distressed than usual. "You know this is the best thing you can do for Renie *and* for Stephen. Don't you think I'm worried, too? My mother doesn't know where I am, I haven't visited her for two weeks. I am her only child. But this is what we have to do, Joseph."

Long Joseph turned away again. "I dream about him, you know. Dreams all strange. See him in water, drowning, I can't reach him. See him going away, up one of those escalators, don't even see his face, but I'm going down, too many people and I can't get after him." His broad hands spread, then gripped the railing. The knuckles stood up like tiny hills. "He always going away. I think he is dying."

Jeremiah could think of nothing to say.

Long Joseph sniffed, then straightened. "I only wanted a drink so I don't have to *think* so damn much. Think about him, think about his mother—all burned up, cryin', but her mouth wouldn't work right, so she just made this little sound, *hoo, hoo.* . . ." He wiped angrily at one eye. "I don't want to think about that no more. *No more.* That's why I wanted a drink. Because it is better than killing myself."

Jeremiah stared intently at the displays on the console in front of him, as if to look up, to turn his gaze onto the other man, would be to risk everything. At last Long Joseph turned and walked away. Jeremiah listened to his steps receding around the gallery, slow as an old-fashioned clock striking the hour, followed by a hiss and muffled thump as the elevator door closed behind him.

"THERE are people coming, Renie." !Xabbu touched her hand. "More than a few. The voices I hear are women's voices."

Renie held her place, breathless, but the only sound in her hearplugs was the wind soughing through broken cornstalks. Cullen staggered to a stop beside her, as volitionless as an electronic toy separated from its controlling signal.

"We have no idea who they are," she said in a whisper. "Or what this place is, except that it's some kind of imaginary United States." She wondered if they had somehow wandered back into the Atascos' alternate America. Would that be bad or good? They knew the place already, which would be a definite advantage, but the Grail Brotherhood would be scouring its every virtual nook and cranny looking for the people who had fled Temilún.

Now she could hear what !Xabbu had detected almost a minute earlier—voices approaching, and the sound of many feet tramping through the devastated cornfield.

"Get down," she whispered, and pulled Cullen onto his knees among the shielding stalks, then eased him onto his stomach with !Xabbu's help. She hoped the wounded entomologist had enough sense left to keep quiet.

The sounds grew nearer. A good-sized party was passing them, perhaps headed for the damaged fence. Renie strained to hear their conversation, but caught only a few disjointed fragments that seemed to be about the merits of treacle pudding. She also heard several references to someone named Emily.

Something rustled beside her, an almost inaudible scrape among the leaves near her head. She turned to see that !Xabbu had disappeared. Frightened, she could only lie as silently as possible while the invisible group crunched past a few meters away. Her hand rested on Cullen's back, and she did not notice for long moments that she was rubbing in circles the same way she had done many times to soothe a frightened Stephen.

The voices had just stopped two dozen meters away when !Xabbu appeared again beside her, popping out of the cornstalks so suddenly that she almost shouted in surprise.

"There are a dozen women fixing the fence," he said quietly. "And a strange thing, a mechanical man, that tells them what to do. I think they will be working there a good time, though—the section of fence they must lift is very large."

Renie tried to make sense of this. "A mechanical man? A robot, you mean?"

!Xabbu shrugged. "If robots are the things I have seen on the net, like our friend T4b, no. It is hard to explain."

Renie gave up. "It doesn't matter, I guess. Do you think we should . . ."

!Xabbu's small hand abruptly flicked out and lightly touched her lips. By moonlight she could see little more than his silhouette, but he was frozen in a posture of alarm and attention. A moment later she heard it: something was moving toward them, swishing through the trampled vegetation with little regard for stealth.

Although they had no reason yet to suppose the inhabitants of this simulation to be hostile, Renie still felt her heart speed. A thin shape pushed through into a small clear space nearby, separated from them only by a single row of bent stalks. Moonlight revealed a very young Caucasian woman with wide dark eyes and a ragged short haircut, dressed in a crude smock.

As Renie and !Xabbu watched, she dropped into a crouch, lifted the hem of her garment, and began to urinate. As she did so, she sang tunelessly to herself. When she was certain that the puddle forming was moving away rather than toward her feet, the girl reached into the breast pocket of her smock, still humming and murmuring, and pulled out something no bigger than a grape which she lifted up above her upturned face until it caught the moonlight, then inspected with the ritualistic air of someone doing something important for the hundredth or perhaps even thousandth time.

The moon's soft light glinted for a moment on the facets. Renie gasped—a strangled little noise, but enough to startle the young woman, who hurriedly thrust the tiny golden gem back into her pocket and looked around wildly. *"Who's there?"* She stood up, but did not immediately retreat. "Who's there? Emily?"

Renie held her breath, trying not to make the damage any worse, but the young woman was more curious than fearful. As she scanned the surrounding vegetation, something caught her eye. She moved toward them with the caution of a cat approaching a new household appliance, then abruptly leaned forward and pulled the corn to one side, revealing Renie and the others. The girl gave a squeak of surprise and jumped back.

"Don't scream!" Renie said hurriedly. She scrambled up onto her knees and held her hands out placatingly. "We won't hurt you. We're strangers here, but we won't hurt you."

The girl hesitated, poised for flight and yet with curiosity again taking the upper hand. "Why . . . why do you have *that* with you," she said, jutting her chin at !Xabbu. "Is it from Forest?"

Renie didn't know what would be the proper thing to say, "He's . . . he travels with me. He's friendly." She took a risk, since the girl did not seem to mean them immediate harm. "I don't know what forest you're talking about. We're strangers here—all of us." She pointed to Cullen, who was still lying on the ground, almost oblivious to what was going on. "Our friend has been hurt. Can you help us? We don't want to make any trouble."

The girl stared at Cullen, then darted a worried glance at !Xabbu before returning to Renie. "You don't live here? And you're not from Forest? Not from the Works either?" She shook her head at the wonder of it all. "More strangers—that's two times just during Darkancold!"

Renie spread her hands. "I don't understand any of that. We are from somewhere else entirely, I'm pretty sure. Can you help us?"

The girl started to say something, then tilted her head. In the distance, voices were calling. "They're looking for me." She wrinkled her forehead, pondering. "Follow us back. Don't let anyone else see you. You're *my* secret." A sly look stole over her face, and she suddenly looked far more a child than an adult. "Wait at the edge of the corn when we get there. I'll come back and find you." She took a step away down the row, then turned back to stare in gleeful fascination. "More strangers! I'll come find you."

"What's your name?" Renie asked.

"Emily, of course." The young woman made a clumsy mock-curtsey, then laughed, mischievous, strangely febrile.

"But you were calling for Emily when you heard us—your friend, someone." The voices were getting louder. Renie stepped back into the shadows and raised her whispering voice so it would carry. "Is your friend named Emily, too?

"Of *course*." Confused, the girl narrowed her eyes as she backed toward those who were searching for her. "Silly. *Everyone* is named Emily."

They did not wait long at the edge of the cornfield. Renie had scarcely had sufficient time to note the huge factory silos and jerry-built buildings, like a township on the industrial outskirts of Johannesburg, and to worry again about Cullen's condition, when Emily's slender shadow crept back across the open dirt toward them.

!Xabbu reappeared at Renie's side at just that moment, but had no time to tell her what he had seen on his brief scouting expedition before the girl reached them, talking in a quiet but nonstop babble of excitement.

"I knew it would be a day for things to happen today, I *knew* it! Come on now, follow me. We had treacle pudding, see, two days in a row! And it wasn't Crismustreat, because we had that already, just a few days ago—we always count the days in Darkancold until Crismustreat, of course, but I can't remember how many days it's been since." The girl, showing little more than basic concern for stealth, led them across a vast yard littered with the angular shapes of parked machinery. She took only a short breath before continuing. "But there it was, treacle pudding again! And the happymusic wasn't that *falalala,* so I knew it wasn't Crismustreat come around again, and anyway it would have been much too early. And then we had that incoming—terrible bad, that one was—and I thought maybe that was the strange thing that was going to happen today, but it was you! Think of that!"

Renie was able to understand very little, but knew there was probably vital information to be had. "Where did you get that thing from?
That little . . . gem or jewel?"

Emily turned and looked at her, eyes squinty with suspicion. A moment later, as if the wind had changed, she seemed to decide the
newcomers were trustworthy. "My pretty thing. *He* gave it to me. He
was my other surprise, but he was the first one. You're the second one.
And treacle pudding twice this month!"

"Who was . . . he?"

"The other stranger, silly. I told you. The strange henry."

"Henry? That was his name?"

Their guide sighed, full of theatrical suffering. "They're *all* named
Henry."

Emily, it became clear at last, was actually Emily 22813. All the
women who lived and worked in this place were called Emily—or
"emily," since it was used as a descriptive term for a woman as well.
And all the men were henrys. Emily 22813 and her workmates—Renie
guessed from the size of this factory farm that there must be hundreds
here—spent their days planting and tending beans and corn and tomatoes.

"Because that's what the king wants us to do," was Emily's only
explanation of why she and her fellows were working in what seemed
to Renie to be slave-labor conditions.

The place itself, as far as Renie could decipher, was named "Em
Rell," which she guessed was derived in some way from the name for
the women: She could not come up with any other associations with
the United States in general or to Kansas, a place she knew of only as
being part of the farming heartland of North America.

Em Rell, or whatever it was, seemed strangely deserted. None of
Emily's coworkers were to be seen, no sentries moved among the stationary tractors and haphazard stacks of empty crates. Unimpeded,
Renie and the others passed into the glow of the orange lights that
were strung on every pole and wire, and across the great yard, until
Emily stopped them in front of a barn, a huge structure that dwarfed
even Renie's outsized former home, the Durban civic shelter. It looked
like a jet hangar surrounded by drifts of grain dust. "There's a place
in here where you can sleep." Emily pointed them to iron stairs which
clung to one outside wall. "Up there, in the loft. No one ever looks."

!Xabbu scampered up the ladder, popped in and out of the un-
screened window, then swiftly descended. "It is full of equipment,"
he said. "It should be a good place to hide."

With Emily's help, they boosted the sagging Cullen up the steps. As they maneuvered him through the wide loading window, Emily said "I have to go now. We have a little sleep-extra tomorrow, because of the fence. If I can, I'll come back to see you in the morning. Good-bye, strangers!"

Renie watched the lithe form quickstep down the stairs and vanish into the shadows beside one of the long, low barracks. A side door opened and closed as Emily slid back inside. A moment later a strange, rounded shape appeared at the far end of the barracks. Renie ducked back into the windowframe, where the moonlight could not reach her, and watched the figure totter past. It made a faint whirring noise, but she could see little more of it than a pale glow of eyes before it rounded the corner of the barracks and was gone.

The loft itself, although it stretched across only the shorter span of the barn, was longer than the street on which Renie lived in Pinetown and full of potential sleeping places. They settled in a protected niche close to the window and the stairs. !Xabbu found long burlap sacks stuffed with heavy aprons; a few of these sacks, laid out behind a pile of anonymous boxes which provided a fence between their resting place and the window, made a good bed for Cullen; the young scientist's eyes were already closed as they dragged him onto it. They pulled out more sacks and made themselves as comfortable as they could. Renie would have loved to puzzle over the day's happenings with !Xabbu, but sleep was tugging hard at her, so she let it drag her down.

Emily came as promised, earlier in the morning than Renie would have preferred. As she sat listening to the young woman's chatter, Renie decided that she understood what people meant when they said they would be willing to sell their souls: she would have traded that article away in a heartbeat for one cup of decent coffee and a couple of cigarettes.

I should have had Jeremiah put caffeine into the dripline at decent intervals, she thought sourly. *Well, next time . . .*

The cup of liquid Emily had smuggled out of the workers' cafeteria—"brekfusdrink" she called it, apparently all one word—was gaggingly and most definitely *not* coffee. It had an odd chemical taste, like unsweetened cough syrup, and even the small sip Renie took before hurriedly handing it back made her heart race. She reminded herself that the girl meant it as an act of kindness.

After Emily had breathlessly recounted all the events of their discovery and rescue the night before, with just as much guileless enthusiasm as if Renie and !Xabbu had not experienced them firsthand, she told them she would be released from her work detail early today to see the "medical henrys"—a regular checkup that from her brief description sounded more like veterinary medicine than the sort Renie was used to—and that she would try then to slip in and visit them. Outside, the grating, scratchy recordings of what Emily called "happy-music" had begun booming from the compound's loudspeakers. Already chafing at the idea of spending an entire day stuck in the loft and subjected to that din, Renie questioned the girl about this place to which the river had delivered them, but Emily's vocabulary was very basic and her viewpoint narrow. Renie garnered little new information.

"We don't even know if Orlando and the others made it through," Renie said crossly after the young woman had left. "We don't know anything. We're just flying blind." This brought Martine to mind, and gave her such a sharp and surprising sense of regret at having lost contact—after all, she hardly even *knew* the French woman—that she missed part of what !Xabbu was saying.

". . . look for this Jonas man. And we must believe that Sellars will find us again. He is without doubt very clever."

"Without doubt. But what *is* his angle, anyway? He seems to have gone to a lot of trouble just to save the world."

!Xabbu frowned for a moment, puzzled, then saw the irritated joke in her words. He smiled. "Is that what all city-people would think, Renie? That someone would never do something unless for himself or herself to profit?"

"No, of course not. But this whole thing is so strange, so complicated. I just don't think we can afford to take anyone's motives for granted."

"Just so. And perhaps Sellars is close to someone who has been harmed by the Grail Brotherhood. No person who is traveling with us has explained all the reasons they are here."

"Except you and me." She took a deep breath. "Well, actually, I'm not entirely sure about you. I'm here for my brother. But you never even met him, not really." She realized it sounded like she was questioning his motives. "You've done far more than any friend should have to, !Xabbu. And I am grateful. I'm sorry I'm in such a foul mood this morning."

He shrugged gracefully. "There is no fence around friendship, I do not think."

The moment hung. !Xabbu at last turned to see to Cullen, who had not yet shown any sign of waking. Renie moved to the window to wrestle her demons in silence.

When she had arranged a few of the boxes nearby so she could look out with little chance of being seen, she settled in, chin propped on fists. Below her, the vast compound had swung into its working day. The happymusic gurgled on, so limpingly out of time it made it difficult to think clearly; Renie wondered if that were one of its purposes. No men were in sight, but herds of slow-walking women, all in near-identical smocks, were being led back and forth across the compound's open space at regular intervals, each band under the guardianship of one of the strange mechanical men. !Xabbu had been right—they did not resemble any of the robots she had seen on the net, either the real-world industrial automata or the gleaming human duplicates on display in science fiction dramas. These seemed more like something from two centuries earlier, roly-poly little metal men with windup keys in their backs and rakish tin mustachios anchored to their permanently puzzled, infantile faces.

The novelty value of what was going on below soon waned. The fat white sun rose higher. The loft began to grow uncomfortably warm, and the air outside turned hazy and as refractive as water. In the distance, shimmering now only because of the scorching sun, was the city whose lights they had seen the night before. It was hard to make out details, but it seemed flatter than it should for such a size, as though some plains-striding giant had topped it as offhandedly as a boy decapitating a row of dandelions. But even so, it was the only thing that gave the horizon any shape; except for a suburb-wide patch of pipes and scaffolding nestled against the city's outskirts, apparently a gargantuan gasworks, the flatlands stretched away on all other sides, a quilt of yellow-gray dirt and green fields, devoid of verticality. It was fully as depressing as the worst squalor to be found in South Africa.

What's the point of all that amazing technology if you build something like this? She was doomed this morning, it seemed, to a succession of miserable thoughts.

Renie wondered if they should head for the city, depressing as it looked. There was little to be learned on this vegetable plantation, or at least Emily did not seem capable of telling them much—surely they could get better information in the distant metropolis. The only duties they could remotely claim were to find their companions and look for Sellars' escaped Grail prisoner, and they were doing neither at this moment, stuck in a loft which was rapidly turning into an oven.

She scowled, bored and unhappy. She didn't want coffee anymore. She craved a cold beer. But she would *murder* for a cigarette. . . .

Despite the day's grim and monotonous start, two things happened in the afternoon, neither of them expected.

A little past noon, when the air seemed to have become so densely hot that inhaling it was like breathing soup, Cullen died.

Or at least that seemed to be what had happened. !Xabbu called her over from her perch by the window, his voice more confused than alarmed. The entomologist had responded very little all morning, sliding in and out of a deep doze, but now his sim was inert, curled in the same fetal position in which he had last been sleeping, but stiff as the exoskeletal corpse of a spider.

"He's dropped offline at last," Renie said flatly. She wasn't certain she believed it. The rigidity of the sim was disturbing: propped on its back, unnaturally bowed, it looked like the remains of some creature dead and dried by the roadside. Their fruitless examination over, she eased the sim back into the position in which it and the real Cullen had finally ceased working in tandem.

!Xabbu shook his head, but said nothing. He seemed far more disturbed by the loss of Cullen than she was, and sat for a long time with one baboon hand resting on the sim's rigid chest, singing quietly.

Well, we don't know, she told herself. *We don't know for sure. He could be offline now, having a cool drink and wondering about the whole strange experience.* In a way, it wasn't that different from RL, really. When you were gone, you left no certainty for those who stayed behind, only an unsatisfactory choice between blind faith or finality.

Or he could have just lain here next to us while his real body wasted away from shock and thirst—until it killed him. He said that he was going to be stuck in his lab until someone came in, didn't he?

It was too much to think about just now—in fact, it was getting harder to think every moment. The oppressive heat had continued to mount, but now there was suddenly a new, stranger heaviness to the steamy air, with an electrical tingling quality—almost a sea-smell, but as if from an ocean that just happened to be boiling.

Renie left !Xabbu still keening quietly over Cullen's sim. As she reached the window, a curtain of shadow fell on it, as though someone had put a hand over the sun. The sky, a withering flat blue only moments before, had just turned several shades darker. A stiff wind was stirring the dust of the compound into erratic swirls.

The four or five convoys of emilys down below stopped as one, and stood staring open-mouthed at the sky while their mechanical overseers whirred and ratcheted at them to move. Renie was momentarily revolted by the women's passive, bovine faces, then reminded herself that these were slaves, as many of her own people had once been. They were not to blame for what had been done to them.

Then one of the emilys suddenly shrieked "Incoming!" and broke from her flock, hurrying toward the apparent security of the barracks. At least half the others began to run also, scattering in all directions, screaming, some knocking each other down in panicked flight. Puzzled, Renie looked up.

The sky was suddenly darker, and horribly alive.

At the center of the mass of thunderheads which had sprung from nowhere and now clustered almost directly above the compound, a vast black snake of cloud began to writhe. As Renie gaped, it jerked back like a tugged string, then stretched down again for a moment until it almost touched the top of one of the silos. The wind was swiftly growing stronger; smocks drying on the long clotheslines began to whip and snap with a noise like gunshots. Some of the garments tore free of the line and flew, as though by snatched by invisible hands. The very air shifted, all within seconds, hissing at first before deepening into a roar: Renie's ears spiked with pain and then popped as the pressure changed. All around her the light turned a faint, putrid green. Wind howled even faster across the yard, bringing a horizontal blizzard of grain dust.

"Renie!" !Xabbu called from behind her, surprised and fearful, barely audible above the growing roar. "What is happening. . . ?"

Lightning shimmered along the thunderheads as the black snake contorted again, an idiot dance between earth and cloud that looked like ecstasy or pain. The word that had been at the back of Renie's head for half a minute suddenly leaped forward.

Tornado.

The funnel of air writhed once more, then reached down, plunging earthward like the dark finger of God. One of the silos exploded.

Renie flung herself back from the window as a hailstorm of debris clattered along the side of the barn. Bits of roof tile skimmed past her head and shattered against the packing crates. The sound of the wind was dense and deafening. Renie crawled until she felt !Xabbu's hand touch hers. He was shouting, but she could not hear him. They scrambled on their hands and knees toward the rear of the loft, looking for shelter, but all the while something was trying to suck them back toward the open window. Stacks of boxes were vibrating, walking toward the window in tiny, waddling steps. Outside, there was blackness and blur. One of the piles of crates tottered, then tipped over. The boxes bounced once, then were lifted invisibly and yanked through the open window.

"Downstairs!" Renie screamed into the baboon's ear.

She could not tell if !Xabbu heard her above the jet-turbine wail of the tornado, but he tugged her toward the stairwell leading down to the barn floor. The crates had been pulled to the window and were being sucked out. For long instants a cluster of them would stick and the wind in the loft would drop; then the clot would shift loose and spring out into the howling darkness and the wind would do its best to suck Renie and !Xabbu back again.

Grain sacks and tarpaulins flapped toward them like angry ghosts as they half-crawled, half-tumbled down the stairs. The suction was less on the barn floor, but static electricity sparked from the tractors and other equipment, and the great doors leading to the fields were pulsing in and out like lungs. The building shuddered down to its very foundation.

Renie did not remember afterward how they made it across the floor, through the multi-ton pieces of farm equipment shifting like nervous cattle, through the blizzard of loose paper and burlap and dust. They found an open space in the floor, a mechanic's bay for the tractors, and slid over the edge to drop to the oily concrete a few feet below. They huddled against the inner wall and listened as something monstrously powerful and dark and angry did its best to uproot the massive barn and break it to pieces.

It might have been an hour or ten minutes.

"It's getting quieter," Renie called, and realized she was barely shouting. "I think it's going past."

!Xabbu cocked his head. "I will know that smell, next time, and we will run to a hiding place. I have never seen such a thing." The winds were now merely loud. "But it happened so fast. 'Storm,' I thought, and then it was upon us. I have never seen weather change so swiftly."

"It did happen fast." Renie sat up a little straighter, easing her back. She was, she was only now realizing, bruised and sore all over. "It wasn't natural. One moment, clear skies, then—whoosh!"

They waited until the sound of the winds had died completely, then climbed out of the bay. Even in the protected ground floor of the barn, there had been damage: the huge loading doors had been knocked askew, so that a triangle of sky—now blue again—gleamed through the gap. One huge earth grader, in a space nearest to the loft, had been tumbled onto its side like a discarded toy; others had been dragged several yards toward the upstairs window, and lighter debris was strewn everywhere.

Renie was surveying the damage in wonder when a shape slipped in through the damaged loading doors.

"You're here!" Emily shrieked. She ran to Renie and began patting her arms and shoulders. "I was so frightened!"

"It's all right . . ." was all Renie had time to say before Emily interrupted.

"We have to run! Run away! Braincrime! Bodycrime!" She grabbed Renie's wrist and began tugging her toward the doors.

"What are you talking about? !Xabbu!"

!Xabbu loped forward and for a moment there was a strange tug-of-war between the baboon and the young woman, with Renie the thing being tugged. Emily let go and began patting at Renie again, bouncing up and down with anxiety. "But we have to run away!"

"Are you joking? It must be chaos out there. You're safe with us. . . ."

"No, they're after me!"

"Who?"

As if in answer, a line of wide, dark shapes appeared in the doorway. One mechanical man after another stumped through the door, all surprisingly swift, and all buzzing like beehives, until half a dozen had fanned out into a wide circle.

"Them," said Emily redundantly. "The tiktoks."

Renie and !Xabbu both thought of the stairs to the loft window, but when they turned they found that mechanical men entering from another part of the barn had already flanked them. Renie feinted back toward the loading doors, but another one of the clockwork creatures stood wedged in the gap there, cutting off escape.

Renie fought down her fury. The stupid girl had led her pursuers right to them, and now they were all trapped. Any one of the mechanical guards had to weigh at least three or four times as much as Renie did, and they also had the advantage of numbers and position. There was nothing to do except hope that whatever happened next would be better. She stood and waited as the buzzing shapes closed in. A foam-lined claw closed on her wrist with surprising delicacy.

"*Bodycrime,*" it said with a voice like an ancient scratched recording. The black glass eyes were even emptier than those of the praying mantis had been. "*Accompany us, please.*"

The tiktoks led them out of the barn into a scene like a medieval painting of hell. The skies had cleared, and once more the sun beat down. Bodies of dead and injured humans, mostly women, lay everywhere in the harsh light. Walls had collapsed, smashing those huddling against them under rubble. Roofs had torn free and swept down the street like mile-a-minute glaciers, grinding everything in their path to jelly and dust.

Several of the tiktoks had been destroyed as well. One seemed to have been dropped from a great height; its remains lay just outside the barn, a sunburst of shattered metal plates and clocksprings thirty feet wide. At the point of impact, part of its torso still held together, including one arm; the hand opened and closed erratically, like the pincer of a dying lobster, as they were marched past.

It did not matter that Renie believed most if not all of the human victims to be animated puppets. The destruction was heart-rending. She hung her head and watched her own feet tramping through the settling dust.

The tornado had missed the farming camp's railyard, although Renie could see the track of its destruction only a few hundred yards away. She and !Xabbu and Emily 22813 were herded onto a boxcar. Their captors stayed with them, which gave Renie pause. Clearly there were fewer functioning tiktoks, or whatever they were called, than there had been half an hour earlier: that six of them should be delegated to guard the two of them—and Emily, too, although Renie doubted that the girl meant much in the larger scheme of things—must mean their crime was considered serious indeed.

Or perhaps just strange, she hoped. The mechanical men were clearly not great thinkers. Perhaps the presence of strangers was so unusual in their simulation that they were having a bit of organizational panic.

The train pulled out of the railyard, rattling and chugging. Renie and !Xabbu sat on the slatted wood floor of the boxcar, waiting for whatever would happen next. Emily at first would only pace back and forth under the dull black eyes of the tiktoks, wringing her hands and weeping, but Renie persuaded her at last to sit down beside them. The girl was distraught, and made almost no sense, mixing bits of babble about the tornado, which she seemed hardly to have noticed, with mysterious ramblings about her medical examination, which she seemed to think was the reason she was in trouble.

She probably said something about us while she was being checked, Renie decided. *She said the doctors were "henrys"—human men. They're probably a bit more observant than these metal thugs.*

The train clacked along. Light flickered on the boxcar's inner wall. Despite her apprehension, Renie found herself nodding. !Xabbu sat beside her, doing something strange with his fingers that at first completely puzzled her. It was only when she woke from a brief doze, and for a moment could not focus her eyes correctly, that she realized he was making string figures with no string.

The trip lasted only a little more than an hour, then they were hauled out of the car by their captors and into a bustling and far bigger railyard. The large buildings of the city Renie had seen earlier loomed directly overhead, and now she could see that they had seemed strange because many of the tallest were only stumps, scorched and shattered by something that must have been even more powerful than the tornado she and !Xabbu had experienced.

The tiktoks led them across the yard, through the gawking throng of worker-henrys in overalls, then loaded Renie and her companions onto the back of a truck. The flatbed took them not into the heart of the blasted city, but along its outskirts to a huge two-story building which seemed entirely made from concrete. They were taken from the truck and into a loading bay, then led into a wide industrial elevator. When they were all inside, the elevator started down without a button being pushed.

The elevator descended for what seemed like minutes, until the soft buzzing of the tiktoks in the elevator car began to make Renie claustrophobic. Emily had been weeping again since they had reached the loading dock, and Renie feared that if it went on much longer she would start screaming at the girl and not be able to stop. As if sensing her distress, !Xabbu reached up and wrapped his long fingers around hers.

The doors opened into blackness, unclarified by the elevator's dim light. Renie's neck prickled. When she and the others did not move, the tiktoks prodded them forward. Renie went slowly, testing the ground with a leading toe, certain that at any moment she would find herself standing at the edge of some terrible pit. Then, when they had taken perhaps two dozen paces, the sound of the tiktoks suddenly changed. Renie whirled in panic. The mechanical men, round shadows with glowing eyes, were backing toward the elevator in unison. As they stepped in and the doors closed, all light went with them.

Emily was sobbing louder now, just beside Renie's left ear.

"Oh, shut *up!*" she snapped. "!Xabbu, where are you?"

As she felt the reassuring touch of his hand again, she became aware for the first time of the background noise, a rhythmic wet squelching. Before she could do more than register this oddity, a light bloomed in the darkness ahead of them. She began to say something, then stopped in astonishment.

The figure before them lolled in a huge chair, which Renie at first thought was carved like an ornate papal throne; it was only as the greenish light grew stronger, pooled on the seated figure, that she could see the chair was festooned with all kinds of tubes, bladders, bottles, pulsing bellows, and clear pipes full of bubbling liquids. Most of these pipes and tubes seemed to be connected to the figure on the chair, but if they were meant to give it strength, they were not doing their job very well: the thing with the misshapen head seemed barely capable of movement. It turned toward them slowly, rolling its head on the back of the chair. One of the eyes on its masklike face was fixed open as if in surprise; the other gleamed with sharp and cynical interest. A shock of what looked like straw protruded from the top of the head and hung limply down onto the pale, doughy face.

"So you are the strangers." The voice squelched like rubber boots in mud. It took a deep breath; bellows flapped and farted as it filled its lungs. "It is a pity you have been caught up in all this."

"Who are you?" Renie demanded. "Why have you kidnapped us? We are just . . ."

"You are just in the way, I am afraid," the thing said. "But I suppose I'm being impolite. Welcome to Emerald, formerly New Emerald City. I am Scarecrow—the king, for my sins." It made a liquid noise of disgust. Something appeared from the shadows near its feet and scampered back and forth, changing tubes. For a moment, in her numbed astonishment, Renie thought it was !Xabbu, then she noticed that this monkey had tiny wings. "And now I have to deal with this wretched young creature," the shape on the chair went on, extending a quivering gloved finger at Emily, "who has committed the worst of all bodycrimes—and at a very inconvenient time, too. I'm very disappointed in you, child."

Emily burst into fresh sobs.

"It *was* her you were after?" Renie was trying to make sense of this. Emerald City—Scarecrow—Oz! That old movie! "What are you going to do with *us,* then?"

"Oh, I'll have to execute you, I'm afraid." The Scarecrow's sagging face curled in a look of mock-sadness. "Terrible, I suppose, but I can't have you running around causing trouble. You see, you've showed up in the middle of a war." He looked down and flicked the winged monkey with a finger. "Weedle, be a good boy and change my filters, too, will you?"

CHAPTER 10

Small Ghosts

NETFEED/SPORTS: *Tiger on a Leash*
(visual: Castro practicing with other Tiger players)
VO: Elbatross Castro is only the latest player with a troubled offcourt history
to agree to a tracking implant as part of the terms of his huge contract—a
device that lets his team know where Castro is at any moment and even what
he's eating, drinking, smoking, or inhaling—but he may be the first to have
used jamming equipment on the implant, thus raising a difficult legal issue
for the IBA and his team, the Baton Rouge GenFoods Bayou Tigers, last
year's North American Conference champions . . .

WHILE her mother was looking at some kind of fake person, Christabel turned away from her and scrunched up against the mirror. Wearing her dark glasses indoors, she thought she looked sort of like Hannah Mankiller from the *Inner Spies* show. "Rumpelstiltskin," she said as loud as she dared. "Rumpelstiltskin!"

"Christabel, what are you doing, mumbling into the mirror? I can't understand a word you're saying." Her mother looked at her as the fake person continued to talk. Another person in a hurry walked right through the fake woman, who went all wobbly for a moment, like a puddle when you stepped in it, but still did not stop talking.

"Nothing." Christabel stuck out her lower lip. Her mother made a face back at her and turned to listen to the hollowgran some more.

"I don't like you wearing those indoors," Mommy said over her shoulder. "Those dark glasses. You'll bump into something."

"No, I won't."

"All right, all right." Her mother took her hand and led her farther into the store. "You must be having one of those difficult phases."

Christabel guessed that Difficult Faces meant sticking out your lip, but it might also mean not taking off your Storybook Sunglasses. Mister Sellars had said her parents mustn't find out about the special glasses. "My face isn't difficult," she said, trying to make things better. "I'm just listening to *The Frog Prince*."

Mommy laughed. "Okay. You win."

Normally, Christabel loved to go to Seawall Center. It was always fun just to get in the car and go out of the base, but the Seawall Center was almost her favorite place in the world. Only the first time, when she had been *really* little, had she ever not loved it. That time she had thought they were going to the "See Wol Center." "Wol" was the name Owl called himself in Winnie-the-Pooh, Christabel's favorite stories, and she had waited all day to see Owl. It was only when she started crying on the way back about not seeing him that Mommy told her what the name really was.

The next time it was much better, and all the other times. Daddy always thought it was dumb to drive all the way there, three quarters of an hour each way—he always said that, too, "It's three quarters of an hour each way!"—when you could get anything you wanted either at the PX or just by ordering, but Mommy said he was wrong. "Only a man would want to go through life without ever feeling a piece of fabric or looking at stitches before buying something," she told him. And every time she said that, Daddy would make a Difficult Face of his own.

Christabel loved her Daddy, but she knew that her mother was right. It was better than the PX or even the net. The Seawall Center was almost like an amusement park—in fact, there was an amusement park right inside it. And a round theater where you could see net shows made bigger than her whole house. And cartoon characters that walked or flew along next to you, telling jokes and singing songs, and fake people that appeared and disappeared, and exciting shows happening in the store windows, and all kinds of other things. And there were more stores in the Seawall Center than Christabel could ever have believed there were in the whole world. There were stores that only sold lipstick, and stores that only sold Nanoo Dresses like Ophelia Weiner had, and even one store that sold nothing but old-fashioned dolls. Those dolls didn't move, or talk, or anything, but they were beautiful in a special way. In fact, the store with the dolls was Christabel's favorite, although in a way it was kind of scary, too—all those eyes that watched you as you came in through the door, all those quiet faces. For her next birthday her mother had even told her she could pick out one of the old-fashioned dolls to be her very own, and even though it was still a long time until her birthday, just coming to Seawall Center to look and wonder which doll she should pick would normally have been the definite best part of the week, so good that she wouldn't have been able to get to sleep last night. But today she was very unhappy, and Mister Sellars wouldn't answer her, and she was really afraid of that strange boy, whom she had seen again last night outside her window.

Christabel and her mother were in a store that sold nothing but things for barbecues when the Frog Prince stopped talking and Mister Sellars' voice took his place. Mommy was looking for something for Daddy. Christabel walked a little way into the store, where her mother could still see her, and pretended to be looking at a big metal thing that looked more like a rocketship from a cartoon than a barbecue.

"Christabel? Can you hear me?"

"Uh-huh. I'm in a store."

"Can you talk to me now?"

"Uh-uh. Kind of."

"Well, I see you've tried to reach me a couple of times. Is it important?"

"Yes." She wanted to tell him everything. The words felt like crawly ants in her mouth, and she wanted to spit them all out, about how the boy had watched her, about why she hadn't told Mister Sellars, because it was her fault she couldn't cut the fence by herslf. She wanted to tell him everything, but a man from the store was walking toward her. "Yes, important."

"Very well. Can it be tomorrow? I am very busy with something right now, little Christabel."

"Okay."

"How about 1500 hours? You can come after school. Is that a good time?"

"Yeah. I have to go." She pulled off the Storybook Sunglasses just as the Frog Prince got his voice back.

The store man, who was pudgy and had a mustache, and looked like Daddy's friend Captain Perkins except not so old, showed her a big smile. "Hello, little girl. That's a pretty good-looking machine, isn't it? The Magna-Jet Admiral, that's state of the art. Food never touches the barbecue. Going to get that for your Daddy?"

"I have to go," she said, and turned and walked back toward her mother.

"You have a nice day, now," said the man.

Christabel pedaled as fast as she could. She didn't have much time, she knew. She had told her mother that she had to water her tree after school, and Mommy had said she could, but she had to be home by fifteen-thirty.

All of Miss Karman's class had planted trees in the China Friendship Garden. They weren't trees really, not yet, just little green plants, but Miss Karman said that if they watered them, they would definitely be trees some day. Christabel had given hers extra water on the way to school today so that she could go see Mister Sellars.

She pedaled so hard the tires of her bicycle hummed. She looked both ways at every corner, not because she was checking for cars, like her parents had taught her (although she did look for cars) but because she was making sure that the terrible boy wasn't anywhere around. He had told her to bring him food, and she had brought some fruit or some cookies a couple of times and left it, and twice she had saved her lunch from school, but she couldn't go all the way to the little cement houses every day without Mommy asking a lot of questions, so she was sure he was going to come through her window some night and hurt her. She even had nightmares about him rubbing dirt on her, and when he was done, Mommy and Daddy didn't know who she was any more and wouldn't let her in the house, and she had to live outside in the dark and the cold.

When she reached the place where the little cement houses were, it was already three minutes after 15:00 on her Otterland watch. She parked her bike in a different place, by a wall far away from the little houses, then walked really quiet through the trees so she could come in on a different side. Even though Prince Pikapik was holding 15:09 between his paws when she looked at her watch again, she stopped every few steps to look around and listen. She hoped that since she hadn't brought that Cho-Cho boy any food for three days, he would be somewhere else, trying to find something to eat, but she still looked everywhere in case he was hiding in the trees.

Since she didn't see him or hear anything except some birds, she went to the door of the eighth little cement house, counting carefully as she did every time. She unlocked the door and then pulled it closed behind her, although the dark was as scary as her dreams about the dirty boy. It took so long for her hands to find the other door that she was almost crying, then suddenly it pulled open and red light came out.

"Christabel? There you are, my dear. You're late—I was beginning to worry about you."

Mister Sellars was sitting in his chair at the bottom of the metal ladder, a small square red flashlight in his hand. He looked just the same as always, long thin neck, burned-up skin, big kind eyes. She started to cry.

"Little Christabel, what's this? Why are you crying, my dear? Here, come down and talk to me." He reached up his trembly hands to help her down the ladder. She hugged him. Feeling his thin body like a skeleton under his clothes made her cry harder. He patted her head and said "Now then, now then," over and over.

When she could get her breath, she wiped her nose. "I'm sorry," she said. "It's all my fault."

His voice was very soft. "What's all your fault, my young friend? What could you possibly have done that should be worth such suffering?"

"Oye, weenit, what you got here?"

Christabel jumped and let out a little scream. She turned and saw the dirty boy kneeling at the top of the ladder, and it scared her so much she wet her pants like a baby.

"Quien es, this old freak?" he asked. "Tell, *mija*—who this?"

Christabel could not talk. Her bad dreams were happening in the real world. She felt pee running down her legs and began to cry again. The boy had a flashlight, too, and he shined it up and down Mister Sellars, who was staring back at him with his mouth hanging open and moving it up and down a little, but with no words coming out."

"Well, don't matter, *mu'chita*," the boy said. He had something in his other hand, something sharp. *"No importa,* seen? I got you now. I got you now."

"**O**F course I understand being careful," said Mr. Fredericks. He held out his arms, staring at the green surgical scrubs he had been forced to don. "But I still think it's all a bit much." Jaleel Fredericks was a large man, and when a frown moved across his dark-skinned face it looked like a front of bad weather.

Catur Ramsey put on a counterpoint expression of solicitude. The Frederickses were not his most important clients, but they were close to it, and young enough to be worth years of good business. "It's not really that different from what we have to go through to visit Salome. The hospital's just being careful."

Fredericks frowned again, perhaps at the use of his daughter's full name. Seeing the frown, his wife Enrica smiled and shook her head, as though someone's wayward child had just spilled food. "Well," she said, and then seemed to reach the end of her inspiration.

"Where the hell are they, anyway?"

"They phoned and said they'd be a few minutes late," Ramsey said quickly, and wondered why he was acting as though he were mediating a summit. "I'm sure . . ."

The door to the meeting room swung open, admitting two people, also dressed in hospital scrubs. "I'm sorry we're late," the woman said. Ramsey thought she was pretty, but he also thought that, with her dark-ringed eyes and hesitant manner, she looked like she'd been through hell. Her slight, bearded husband did not have the genetic good start his wife enjoyed; he just looked exhausted and miserable.

"I'm Vivien Fennis," the woman said, brushing her long hair back from her face before reaching a hand out to Mrs. Fredericks. "This is my husband, Conrad Gardiner. We really appreciate you coming."

After everyone, including Ramsey, had shaken hands, and the Gardiners—as Vivien insisted they be called for the sake of brevity—had sat down, Jaleel Fredericks remained standing. "I'm still not sure why we're actually here." He waved an impatient hand at his wife before she could say anything. "I know your son and my daughter were friends, and I know that something similar has happened to him, to . . . Orlando. But what I don't understand is why we're here. What couldn't we have accomplished over the net?"

"We'll get to that." Conrad Gardiner spoke a little sharply, as though he felt a need to establish his own place in the hierarchy. Fredericks had that effect on people, Ramsey had noticed. "But not here. That's part of why we wanted to see you in person. We'll go outside somewhere."

"We'll go to a restaurant. We don't want to say anything about it here," Vivien added.

"What on earth are you talking about?" Fredericks' thunderhead frown had returned. "You have lost me completely."

Ramsey, who was practicing the silence that he generally found useful, was intrigued but also worried. The Gardiners had seemed quite level-headed in the few conversations he'd had with them, deadly serious in their desire to talk to Mr. and Mrs. Fredericks in person, but also secretive. He had trusted them on gut instinct. If they turned out to be conspiracy-mongers of some kind, UFO cultists or Social Harmonists, he would quickly begin to regret his own role in persuading his clients to fly out from Virginia.

"I know we sound mad," said Vivien, and laughed. "We wouldn't blame you for thinking it. But just wait until we've all had a chance to talk, please. If you still think so, we'll pay for your trip here."

Mr. Fredericks bristled. "Money is not the issue . . ."

"Jaleel, honey," his wife said. "Don't be stuffy."

"But first," Vivien continued as though the tiny sitcom had not happened, "we'd like you to come see Orlando."

"But . . ." Enrica Fredericks was taken aback. "But isn't he . . . in a coma?"

"If that's what it is." Conrad's grin was bitter. "We've been . . ." He broke off to stare at something in the corner, where the coats had been piled in a heap on the one unused chair. The stare went on too long; the others turned, too. Ramsey couldn't see anything there. Gardiner rubbed at his forehead with the heel of his hand. "Sorry, I just thought . . ." He let out a long breath. "It's a long story. I thought I saw a bug. A very particular bug. Don't ask—it will take too much time, and I'd rather explain later. It'll be easier if you just go on thinking we're crazy for now."

Ramsey was amused. His clients exchanged a covert look between themselves, then Mrs. Fredericks stole a glance in Ramsey's direction. He gave a little head-shake, silently saying *don't worry about it*. In his not-inconsiderable experience with the deranged, the genuine loonies were not usually the ones who suggested that what they were doing must seem insane.

"You don't have to come with us when we go see Orlando," said Vivien, rising. "But we'd like you to. We'll only stay a minute—I'm going to be spending the evening with him after we've all finished."

As they moved out into the hospital corridor, the women fell in beside one another, the men paired up behind them, and Ramsey took up the rear, this shielded position enabling him to forget his dignity long enough to try a subtle skating motion on the paper hospital shoes.

He hadn't been getting out enough, there was no question about it. Ramsey knew that if he didn't make a point of doing a little less work, he would wind up at the least shocking some client by bursting into inappropriate laughter in a serious meeting, as he'd almost done a few times in the last weeks, or at worst pitching over dead at his desk some day, as his father had done. Another decade—less, now—and he'd be in his fifties. Men still died from heart attacks in their fifties, no matter how many modern medications and cellular retrainers and cardiotherapies there might be.

But that was the thing about work, wasn't it? It always seemed like something you could just put down, or trim the excess from, or ignore if things got bad enough. But when you got up close to it, things were different. It wasn't simply work, it was the tortuous mess of the DeClane Estate, which had become a dreadful gallows soap-opera that had paralyzed three generations. Or it was old Perlmutter trying to win back the company he had built and then lost in a boardroom mugging. Or Gentian Tsujimoto, a widow trying to win compensation for her husband's poorly-treated illness. Or, as in the case of the Frederickses, it was an attempt to make some kind of legal sense out of their daughter's stunningly mysterious illness, if only because *some* sense was better than no sense at all.

So, when he told himself he had to cut back on work, which people was he going to say "I'm sorry" to? Which trust for which he had labored to be worthy all his working life, which important connection or fascinating puzzle or heart-rending challenge, would he give up?

It was all very well to say it, and he certainly didn't want to follow his father into the first-class section of the Coronary Express, but how did you start throwing away the most important parts of your life, even to *save* that life? It would be different if he had anything much outside the office worth saving himself for . . .

Half of Decatur "please-call-me-'Catur-it's-what-my-mom-called-me" Ramsey was hoping that the Gardiners' portentous hints would lead to something as intriguing as the California couple had made it sound. A career case. The kind of thing that put you not just into the law books, but wove you into the fabric of popular culture like Ku-melos or Darrow. But the part of him that had spent way too many nights staring at a wallscreen so cluttered with documents his eyes ached, dictating until he was hoarse while trying not to choke on the occasional hasty mouthful of take-out Burmese, could not help but hope that the Gardiners were in fact, and against his own estimation, complete and utter loons.

When they had donned the head-coverings and stepped through the sonic disinfectant, Mr. Fredericks had another attack of irritation. "If your son is suffering from the same thing that's affected Sam, why is all this necessary?"

"Jaleel, don't be difficult." His wife was finding it hard to conceal her anxiousness. Ramsey had seen her at her daughter's bedside, and knew that underneath the smart clothes and composed features she was clinging to normality like a shipwreck victim to a spar.

"It's okay," Vivien said. "I don't blame you for wondering. Your Salome is in a slightly different situation."

"What does that mean?" asked Mrs. Fredericks.

"Sam, not Salome." Her husband did not wait for her question to be answered. "I don't know why I ever let Enrica talk me into that name. She was a bad woman. In the Bible, I mean. What kind of thing, to name a child?"

"Oh, now, honey." His wife smiled brightly and rolled her eyes. "The Gardiners want to see their boy."

Fredericks allowed himself to be led through the air lock corridor and into the private room where Orlando Gardiner lay under a plastic oxygen tent like a long-dead pharaoh in a museum case.

Enrica Fredericks gasped. "Oh! Oh, my God. What's . . ." She put a hand to her mouth, eyes wide in horror. "Is that . . . going to happen to Sam?"

Conrad, who had moved to stand at the foot of Orlando's bed, shook his head, but said nothing.

"Orlando has a disease," his mother said. "He had it long before any of this happened. That's why he's here in the aseptic wing. He's very susceptible to infection at the best of times."

Jaleel Fredericks' frown now had a different character, that of someone watching a terrible wrong at one remove, a netfeed/news report of a famine or terrorist bombing. "An immune system problem?"

"In part." Vivien reached her hand into the glove built into the tent and caressed Orlando's almost skeletally thin arm. His eyes were only white crescents between the lids. "He has progeria. It's an aging disease. Someone slipped up in the genetic testing—they must have. But we could never prove it. We knew it had been in my side of the family a few generations back, but the chances were so small it would be in Conrad's, too—well, when his tests came back negative, we never thought about it again." Her eyes returned to her son. "If I had known, I would have had an abortion." Her voice tightened. "And I love my son. I hope you understand that. But if I went back in time and had the choice again, I would have ended the pregnancy."

A long silence was broken by Jaleel Fredericks, his deep voice softer now. "We're very sorry."

Orlando's father actually laughed, short and harsh, a strangled sound that was clearly not meant to have come out. "Yeah, so are we."

"We know you've been suffering, too," Vivien said. "And we know how hard it must have been for you to leave Sam, even for a day, to come out here." She removed her hand from the glove and straightened up. "But we wanted you to see Orlando before we all talked."

Mrs. Fredericks still had one hand over her mouth; her mascara, fashionably exaggerated, was beginning to run a little at the corner of her eyes. "Oh, the poor boy."

"He's a *wonderful* kid." Vivien was having trouble speaking. "I can't tell you how brave he's been. He's been . . . different all his life. Stared at when he goes out. And he's known since he was little that the chances of him living . . . even long enough to be a teenager . . ." She had to stop. Conrad looked at her from the foot of the bed, but did not move to comfort her. It was Enrica Fredericks who at last stepped forward and put a hand on her arm. Orlando's mother made a visible effort to gather herself. "He hasn't deserved any of this, and he's dealt with it so well that . . . that it would break your heart just to see it. It's all been so *unfair*. And now this! So I . . . so we wanted you to understand about Orlando, and about what a rotten deal he got. When we explain why we called you."

Catur Ramsey took it upon himself to break this silence.

"Sounds like it's time for us all to go somewhere and talk."

"So," Enrica Fredericks said, "this menu looks lovely." Her good cheer was as brittle as old glass. "What do you recommend, Vivien?"

"We've never been here before. We picked it at random out of a directory. I hope it's okay."

In the silence, the snapping of the awning overhead was quite loud. Ramsey used his wineglass to pin down his napkin, which was threatening to blow away, and cleared his throat. "Perhaps we should jump right in, so to speak."

"That's why we're sitting outside, too," Conrad said suddenly.

"You've lost me again," Fredericks replied. He squinted at the menu. "I think I'm going to have the sea bass." He called the skulking waiter over from where he was huddling out of the wind. "Are you sure this is Pacific sea bass?"

When they had ordered, and the waiter had hurried back to the warmth of the indoor portion of the restaurant, Vivien began to speak.

"The problem," she said, tracing a near-transparent circle of white wine on the tabletop, "is that kids today don't write anything down. They talk—God knows, they talk—and they go places together on the net, but they don't write anything down."

"Yes?" said Fredericks.

"We've had a really hard time figuring out what Orlando's been up to," Conrad Gardiner said. "On the net. But we think that's what's wrong with them both."

"That's not possible." Enrica Fredericks' voice was flat. "It doesn't work that way. Our doctor told us. Unless someone . . . someone ran some charge on them." Her face was pinched and angry. "That's what they say, isn't it? 'Ran some charge'?"

"That may be it," Vivien said. "But if so, it's some kind of charge the doctors haven't heard of. Anyway, you'd have to abuse it seriously for years to have that effect—no, even then it wouldn't be the same. Look, you said it yourself—you can't unplug Sam. She screams, she fights, you have to plug her back in. The same thing's true with Orlando, except that he's been so sick we can only tell the reaction by what happens to his vital signs. We've checked with neurologists, neuropsychologists, charge-addiction treatment centers, everything. No one's ever heard of anything like this. That's why we contacted you."

The salads and hors-d'oeuvres arrived. Ramsey frowned at his bruschetta. Maybe it was time to start taking this health stuff seriously. There was a list a mile long for heart transplants, even with the new generation of clonal replacements. He would have been better off ordering a green salad.

He pushed away the bruschetta.

"Forgive me for being impatient," said Jaleel Fredericks, "but it seems to be my role in this particular gathering. What is the point? We know all this, although not the details."

"Because we all know that something has happened to your Sam and our Orlando, but we don't think it's an accident."

Fredericks raised an eyebrow. "Go on."

"We've done our best to open up all Orlando's files on his system. That's why it's so frustrating that kids don't even use mail any more, like we did. There are pathways, but no records to speak of. And to make things more difficult, his agent has been removing files. In fact, that's one of the things we're worried about."

Ramsey sat forward, intrigued. "Why is that?"

"Because it's not supposed to happen," Conrad said. He was drinking only water, and he stopped to take a long swallow. "We froze the house system when this happened—well, all of Orlando's part of it, anyway. The only way his agent could be moving files against our wishes is with Orlando's permission, and . . . well, you saw him. So why is it that the thing is still removing files and destroying others? It's even hidden itself, so we can't turn it off without killing the whole system and losing any evidence we've got of what happened to Orlando. In fact, the thing's gone AWOL entirely. The robot body it uses around the house is gone, too. That's what I thought I saw in the hospital." He shook his head. "The whole thing is creepy."

"But I don't understand," Enrica said plaintively. "Why would any of this happen? If someone's hiding files, or destroying them, or whatever, what reason could there be?"

"We don't know." Vivien toyed with a celery stick. "But we saw enough before the files disappeared to know that Orlando was in touch with some strange people. He was . . . he *is* a very, very smart kid. Spent all his time on the net. So we want to find out where on the net he's been, what he's been doing, and who he's been doing it with. And we don't want anyone to know that we're trying to find out, which is why we're sitting outdoors at an unfamiliar restaurant."

"And from us. . . ?" Fredericks asked slowly.

"We want your files. Sam and our son were doing something together. Someone or something has corrupted our system, against our express orders. Yours may still be untouched—and in any case, you owe it to yourselves to find out, even if you think we're nuts. But we want your files. Or Sam's, to be perfectly accurate." Vivien fixed him with a surprisingly fierce gaze. "We want to find out who did this to our son."

Vivien and Jaleel stared at each other. Their partners looked on, waiting for the outcome, but Ramsey already knew what it would be. He sat back, caught in a mix of elation and despair. Not loonies, then. And with a really interesting puzzle that might turn out to be nothing, but certainly could not be ignored. It would, of course, mean a lot of research, a ton of detail, and a variety of very difficult problems to solve.

It seemed he was going to be spending a lot more time at work.

OLGA Pirofsky put the last melon in the bag, then took her groceries up to the express counter. You could have anything and everything delivered, but there was still something to be said for actually handling a piece of fruit before you bought it. It kept you in touch with something from human history that was now almost lost.

She walked home down Kinmount Street, as she always did, making her way under the great elevated tracks that carried the maglev commute train south to Toronto. Juniper Bay was basking in sunshine today, and the warmth felt good on the back of her neck.

She stopped, as she had told herself she wouldn't, (but knew that she would) in front of the children's store. An array of holographic youngsters played decorously in the window, and handsome phantom babies modeled handsome baby outfits. It was early in the afternoon, so most of the real children were in school somewhere; only a handful of mothers and fathers with strollers were inside the store.

Olga watched them through the window as they moved with perfect assurance from display to display, stopping occasionally to soothe a cranky infant, or to share a joke or a question with each other, living completely in the now—a now in which happy parenthood would go on forever, with the small provision that anything bought last month would already be too small. She wanted to hammer on the window and warn them not to take anything for granted. She had thought once that she would be one of those people, one of those frighteningly blithe people, but instead she felt like a homeless spirit, watching in envy from the cold.

A floater—a toy that constantly changed its magnetization, making it hard to keep it between two accompanying paddles—bumbled past, being tossed between two of the holographic tykes. *But I'm not a ghost,* she realized. *Not really. These imaginary window-children are ghosts. Uncle Jingle and his friends are ghosts. I'm a real person, and I've just bought some melons and tea and twelve packs of dog food. I have things to do.*

Not entirely convinced, but at least having manufactured the strength to pull herself away from the children's store, she continued her walk home.

Someday I won't be able to leave, she thought. *I'll just stand and stare through that window until winter comes. Like the Little Match Girl.*

She wondered if that would be a bad way to go.

"We'll come back and help Princess Ape-i-cat later, kids. But first, Uncle Jingle needs you to take a walk with him over to Toyworld!"

The Pavlovian cheers came back, filling her hearplugs. Uncle Jingle dismissed a quick mental image of leading her charges through a snowy railyard onto windowless boxcars. It was silly, thinking that way—these were just commercials, just harmless capitalist greed. And if it wasn't harmless, it certainly was part of the world they lived in. It was *most* of the world they lived in, or at least it felt like that sometimes.

"We're going to sing the 'Let's Go Shopping' song," she said, spreading her arms in a gesture of excitement, "but first I want you to meet someone. Her name is Turnie Kitt, and she's the newest member of The Kasualty Klub! She's very educational, and she'll show you why!"

The kids—or their online avatars—jumped up and down, whooping. The Kasualty Klub was a favorite toy series, and all its grisly members, Compound Ken, Decapitate Kate, and others even less savory, were a serious hit. The new tie-in episodes would begin soon, and Uncle Jingle was not looking forward to them at all. As Turnie Kitt began to explain how after her limbs had been twisted off, she would fountain lifelike blood until pressure was applied, Uncle Jingle hit the four-hour wall and ceased to be Olga Pirofsky.

*   *   *

. . . Or rather I stop being Uncle Jingle, she thought. *It's hard to remember where the line is, sometimes.*

A voice buzzed in her hearplugs. *"Nice show, Miz P. McDaniel'll take 'em from here."*

"Tell Roland I said 'break a leg.' But tell him not to do it in front of *that* group, or they may pull it off to watch his lifelike blood fountaining."

The technician laughed and clicked off. Olga unplugged. Misha was sitting across the room from her, head cocked on one side. She wiggled her fingers near the floor, and he came forward to be scratched on the white spot beneath his chin.

She hadn't had any recurrences of the headaches lately. That was something to be grateful for. But as though they had been the first thin end of a wedge driven into the core of her being, the mysterious pains had split her open. More and more often in these last weeks, she found that the show upset her, its flashier and more commercial aspects seeming little different than the slaughters of animals and slaves the ancient Romans had used to spice up their entertainments. But the show had not changed any, Olga had: the bargain she had once struck with herself, where her disapproval about content would take second place to the joy of working with kids, was beginning to come apart.

And even though the head pains had been absent, she could not forget them, or the revelation that had struck her on that day. She had talked to her new doctor about it, and to the show's medical people, and they had all reassured her that online headaches were not unusual. They seemed to have forgotten that just weeks before they had been testing her for brain tumors. She had found the common link, they told her, and should be happy it was so easy to remedy. She was spending too much time online. She should seriously think about some time off.

Of course, the undercurrent was plain: *You're getting a bit old for this anyway, aren't you, Olga? The Uncle Jingle gig is a young person's job, all that bouncing and singing and strenuous, cartoony overacting. Wouldn't you be happier leaving it to someone else?*

Under other circumstances, she would have wondered whether they might not be right. But these were not normal headaches, any more than Compound Ken's little specialty was a bumped shin.

Olga got up and wandered to the kitchen, ignoring the pins and needles of four hours in the chair. The groceries still sat in the bag on the counter. Misha, who was very firm about routine, stood by her feet, waiting. She sighed and emptied a pack of food into his bowl.

If your doctors didn't believe you, what then? She had begun calling around, of course, checking with various other medical (and sort-of-medical) people, and with the Interactive Performer's Guild. She had asked Roland McDaniel to ask retired performer friends if they had ever experienced something similar. She had even broken her own rule about using the net in her free time to begin to examine articles and monographs on net-related disabilities. A nice young man in neurobiology at McGill University had responded to her questions by giving her a list of a whole new series of possibilities, apparently unrelated specialty disciplines that might have some bearing on her problem. So far, not a single thing had proved useful.

She left Misha making little *snarfle* noises over his bowl and went to lie down on the couch. Her special chair, as festooned with wires as an execution device, stood in silent reproach. There was more research to be done—far more. But she was so tired.

Maybe they all were right. Maybe it was her work. Perhaps a long vacation was just what she needed.

She grunted, then swung her legs off the couch onto the floor and stood up. On days like these, she felt every year of her age. She walked slowly to the chair and climbed in, then hooked herself up. Instantaneously, she was in the top level of her system. The company supplied her with the very best equipment—it was a pity, really, that they had to waste it on someone who cared so little about modern machinery.

Chloe Afsani took a while to answer; when she did, she was wiping cream cheese off her upper lip.

"Oh, I'm sorry, dear. I've interrupted your lunch."

"Problem not, Olga. I had a late breakfast—I'll survive a little while longer."

"Are you sure? I hope I'm not adding to your work load too much." Chloe was now a manager in the network's fact checking department, a hive of plugged-in people in sightless rows that had made Olga more than a little nervous when she had gone to ask her favor. Chloe had been a production assistant on the Uncle Jingle show when she first broke in to the business—a "junior blip," as she termed it—and Olga had been a confidante during the breakdown of the younger woman's first marriage. Even so, Olga had hated to ask the favor—it always made friendship seem like a trade agreement.

"Don't worry about it. In fact, I've got some good news for you."

"Really?" Olga jumped a little at an odd sensation, then realized it was only Misha climbing into her lap.

"Really. Look, I'm sending you everything, but I can give you the basics now. It was a pretty broad subject area, because there have been so many vaguely health-related things written about net use. Ergonomics alone, thousands of hits. But the more you narrow it down, the easier it gets.

"I'll cut to the chase. There have been a ton of supposedly net-related illnesses, chronic stress, disorientation, eyestrain, pseudo-PTSS—I've forgotten what they actually call it—but the only thing that would be what you're talking about—in other words, the only thing that might be other than just you working too hard—is something called Tandagore's Syndrome."

"What's a Tandagore, Chloe?"

"The person who discovered it. Some guy in Trinidad, if I remember right. Anyway, it's kind of controversial—not fully accepted yet as a distinct thing, but they're talking about it in a few researcher SIGs. In fact, most doctors and hospitals don't use the term. That's in part because there are so many different variations, from headaches to seizures, all the way up to comas and one or two deaths." Chloe Afsani saw the look on the other woman's face. "Don't worry, Olga. It's not progressive."

"I don't understand what you mean." Misha was nudging her stomach in a very distracting way, but Chloe's words had struck a chill into her. She stroked the little dog, trying to quiet him.

"You don't go from one symptom to a worse one. If you have this—and no one's saying you do, sweetie, in fact I'll explain why I doubt it—and you're getting headaches, then that's probably as bad as it's going to get for you."

The thought of spending the rest of her life going from one of those bolts of brilliant, sickening pain to the next was more frightening in some ways than the possibility of just dying. "Is that the good news?" she asked weakly. "Is there a cure?"

"No cure, but that wasn't the good news." Chloe smiled a sad smile. Her teeth seemed to have gotten whiter since she had gone into management. "Oh, Olga sweetie, am I making things worse? Just hear me out. You probably don't have this in the first place, because something like ninety-five percent of the sufferers are children. And, what makes it even more likely that you don't have this, and that what you've got instead is just a bad, bad case of need-a-vacation, is the fact of where you work."

"What does that mean?"

"Here's the good news at last. Tandagore's Syndrome appears to be net-related, right? That is, the one common element, not counting the mostly-children angle, is heavy net usage."

"But I use net equipment all the time, Chloe! It's my job, you know that!"

"Let me finish, sweetie." She said it as she might to a cranky child. "Out of all the cases of all the kids that the research engines could find, not a single one of them had ever been a participant on the Uncle Jingle show, or any of the spin-offs. I cross-collated the WorldReach medical files with the network's, so I know. Think about that. There have been *millions* of kids over the years who've participated, and not a single one has ever become sick in this particular way."

"So you're saying . . ."

"That when they figure out what it is, it'll probably be some kind of glitch in transmission signals, maybe, or something like that— something that interferes with brainwaves, maybe. That's what Tandagore thinks, according to the articles. But whatever it is, it sure isn't in *our* transmission signals, is it? *Ipso facto*—an important term for someone in my department to know, don't you think?—you don't have Tandagore's Syndrome."

Olga petted Misha and tried to make sense of it all. "So you're saying that I don't have something I never heard about until today?"

Chloe laughed, but there was a little frustration beneath it. "I'm saying that this Tandagore thing is the only possibility other than plain old stress, or things your doctor already looked for. Your doctor says you're fine. You can't have Tandagore because no one connected even remotely with the show ever has, so it must be simply overwork and too much worrying." Chloe smiled brightly. "So stop worrying!"

Olga thanked her with more heartiness than she felt and clicked off. Misha had fallen asleep, so even when she unplugged, she remained in the chair. The sun had gone down behind the train tracks, and the living room had fallen into shadow. Olga listened to the sounds of the birds, one of the reasons she lived in Juniper Bay. Big enough to have link stations that could handle major throughput, small enough still to have birds. There were none left in Toronto except pigeons and seagulls, and someone on the newsnets had said all the surviving pigeons were a mutant strain anyway.

So it was either simple stress, or it was a Whatsit Syndrome she couldn't have. Chloe was young and smart and had the best commercial research engines at her disposal, and she said so. Which meant the rest of Olga's own research could be avoided. Why didn't she feel better?

From the far side of the room, the Uncle Jingle figure looked back at her, black button eyes and xylophone teeth. His huge smile was really a kind of smirk, wasn't it? If you really studied it.

It's strange, she thought. *If there have been a million cases of this stuff and not a single one was someone who had hooked into the show. I mean, it's hard to find a kid out there who hasn't been plugged into Uncle Jingle at some time or other.*

The room felt cold. Olga suddenly wished the sun would come back.

In fact, that seems more than a little strange. That seems . . . very unlikely.

But what could it mean except coincidence, that lots of kids were having problems from being on the net, but no one who'd ever been involved with her own show? That there was something extra-good about their equipment? Extra-healthy?

Or . . . She pulled Misha closer. The dog whimpered and flailed his paws, as though dogpaddling in some dream-river, then settled again. The room was getting quite dark now.

Or the other way around? So bad that someone didn't want anyone to make a connection between the two?

That's silly, Olga. Stupid. Someone would have to be doing it on purpose, then. You've gone from headaches to paranoia.

But the monstrous idea would not go away.

CHAPTER 11

Utensils

NETFEED/NEWS: Plug or Play, Charge Addicts Told
(visual: waiting room in Great Ormond Street Hospital)
VO: England's first-ever Liberal Democrat government has given that
country's charge addicts a choice: either have their neurocannulas—"cans"
as the addicts, or "heads," call them—permanently sealed with a polymer
glue, or accept a software device known as a "gear filter," which will block
any unacceptable programming, and can also be set to dispense helpful
subliminals. Under new law, all registered addicts must agree to one of these
two options if they wish to keep their benefits. Citizens' rights groups are
furious . . .

AS the blue light died, water was suddenly everywhere around them. In some incomprehensible fashion they were in the middle of it but still dry, rushing forward through damp air as though the river had curled into a tube around them. The noise was so loud that when Orlando shouted, not only could Fredericks not hear him, he could not hear himself.

They rocketed through a curve at high speed, then the front of the leaf-boat plunged downward. Orlando grabbed desperately for a handhold, but could feel himself lifting free of the boat, floating backward even as they fell.

The light changed. An instant later they slammed down into something that shook them so hard that it was only a few dazed moments later, when he felt himself beginning to sink, that Orlando realized they had landed in more water. Within moments he had lost the leaf-boat completely. The river or waterfall or whatever it had become was pounding down almost on top of him, roiling the surface so badly that he could not understand which way was up. He finally caught a glimpse of Fredericks floating face-down a short distance away, but even as he tried to call to him, his friend was caught up by the surging waters and pulled beneath the surface.

Orlando took a deep breath and dove after him, then turned until he saw Fredericks' motionless form drifting down. The water was brilliantly clear, and all the lake bottom he could see was a bright and featureless white. Orlando kicked hard, thrusting himself toward his friend. He managed to get one hand wrapped in the cowl of Fredericks' Pithlit robe, then struggled toward what he guessed was the surface, a darker spot in the middle of a leaning ring of whiteness.

It seemed to take days. Fredericks' limp weight was the single heaviest thing he had ever lifted. At last, with his breath turning to fire in his chest, he broke the surface and heaved Fredericks' head above water. His friend took a racking breath, then coughed out what seemed like gallons. He appeared strange in some way Orlando could not immediately define, but it was impossible to look too carefully with waves slapping at both their faces. Orlando kicked to keep them above the surface, but the cataract was still thundering down only a few meters away and he was losing strength rapidly. A brief but depressing glimpse between waves showed him that the white walls or shore above the waterline appeared smooth as glass.

"Can you swim?" he gasped. "I don't think I can hold you up."

Fredericks nodded miserably. "Where's the boat?"

Orlando shook his head.

Fredericks began a weary crawl-stroke toward the nearest wall. Orlando did his best to follow, and regretted once again that he had never had swimming lessons. Swimming in Otherland was nothing like when Thargor stroked his way across a deep tarn or castle moat in the Middle Country. For one thing, Thargor didn't get tired this easily.

He caught up to Fredericks, who was pawing hopelessly at the smooth white wall. "What is this?" his friend moaned. "There aren't any handholds."

Orlando looked up. Above them, the sheer wall rose for several more meters, and above that . . . "Oh, *fenfen*," Orlando said, then a wave slapped him in the face and he drank more water. It was fresh, not salt, which made sense. "Not again!" he said when he could breathe. "What?"

Orlando pointed. The cataract was pouring down from a long silver pipe connected to the white wall, with two odd crenellated circles flanking it. Faucet. Taps. They were in a sink. Hanging in the air far overhead, glowing like the moon, and seemingly only slightly smaller, was a vast lightbulb.

"No!" Fredericks moaned. "This is *so impacted.*"

The bad news was that their boat, or something dark that seemed to be their boat, was trapped at the bottom of the sink, battered beneath the stream of water sluicing down from the titan faucet. The good news, as they discovered a few moments later, was that it seemed to have blocked the drain and the water in the sink was rising.

"If we just stay afloat, it'll lift us over the top." Fredericks swung sopping hair off his face and turned to Orlando. "Are you okay? Can you make it?"

"I don't know. I guess so. I'm really tired." His friend still looked odd—simplified somehow—but Orlando could not summon the energy to try to figure out what was wrong.

"I'll help when you need it." Fredericks felt the porcelain. "This is so barking. It's like being stuck in the deep end of the pool forever."

Orlando had no more breath to waste.

Slowly, the water inched up the walls of the sink. When he felt his rhythm working properly for a moment, his legs moving without too much pain, Orlando looked up. The angle of the sink walls made it hard to see anything much below the ceiling, but there was still something decidedly strange about the place, and it was nothing as straightforward as the disproportionate size. The shadows fell oddly, and both the lightbulb and sink seemed inexplicably unreal, although there was nothing ghostly or insubstantial about either of them. Even the water seemed to move too slowly, and with none of the absolute realism it had possessed in other parts of the network.

He looked at Fredericks, and finally realized what had been bothering him. His friend's features, while still three-dimensional, had become somehow flatter, as though rendered with much less sophisticated animation gear than they had encountered elsewhere in the Otherland network. But what did it mean?

It was only when the Indian brave—a comic savage with an impossibly red face, a nose like a sausage, and rolling eyes—climbed up onto the edge of the sink and peered down at them that Orlando realized they were stranded in some kind of cartoon.

"Ugh," the Indian said. "You seen papoose?"

Fredericks goggled at the stranger. "This can't be happening."

"Can you help us out?" Orlando shouted. "We're drowning!"

The Indian stared at them for a moment, his fierce but simple expression absolutely unreadable, then reached into his buckskin vest and produced, from nowhere, a length of rope. His arms bending in ways that jointed appendages did not bend, he quickly threw a loop around one of the faucets, then tossed the other end down to them.

It was not a swift process, but with the Indian pulling and Orlando and Fredericks keeping their feet flat against the slippery porcelain wall, they managed to climb the last few meters to safety. Orlando clung to the chilly faucet in gratitude.

"So? Palefaces seen papoose?" The Indian had stowed the rope, and now stood with arms folded across his chest. Orlando couldn't remember exactly what a papoose was, but he was not going to let a potentially friendly contact go to waste.

"No. But we owe you our lives. We'll help you look." Fredericks shot him a look, but Orlando ignored him. "What can we do?"

The Indian looked down into the sink. "Better come back to teepee. Soon water reach top, spill over, make big lake on floor."

Fredericks was looking Orlando up and down. "You look really weird, Orlando. Like a Captain Comet play figure or something."

Orlando looked down. His torso was indeed an exaggerated, upside-down triangle. He could only imagine what Thargor's features must look like in this shorthand form. "Yeah, well, you look pretty scanny, too," he pointed out. "Like some kind of Uncle Jingle reject. Your feet don't even have toes."

The Indian seemed to find their conversation either unintelligible or irrelevant. He turned and began walking along the edge of the sink, then suddenly leaped down into apparent nothingness.

"Jee-zus!" Fredericks stared. "He just jumped!"

"Come on." Orlando limped after their rescuer.

"Are you. . . ? What, you're going to jump off, just because he did? He's some kind of construct, Orlando!"

"I know. He's an old-fashioned cartoon. Just look at this place. It's all a cartoon, Fredericks, an animated drawing. Like from the last century."

"I don't care. We could go that way instead." Fredericks pointed. On the far side of the sink, a long smooth wooden counter led away, a clutter of shelves at the back hidden by shadow. "At least we can see where we'd be going."

"Yeah, but he went *that* way."

"So?"

"So we don't know our way around. So let's get going, before we lose the only person since we've been in this impacted network who's done anything nice for us."

Fredericks clambered to his feet, streaming water. "I will never, never let you talk me into anything again. Ever."

Orlando turned and limped toward the place where the Indian had disappeared. "Fair enough."

The cartoon brave had not, as it turned out, jumped to his doom. Below the edge of the sink, only a body-length down, stood a small table—small by the standards of the environment, although to Orlando and Fredericks it was at least an acre wide—cluttered with an array of boxes and bottles. Beyond the table, squatting in the corner like a particularly fat black dog, stood some kind of impossibly antique-looking stove. Red light showed through the slits in its grille.

The Indian was standing in front of one of the boxes, a rectangular cardboard shape that loomed twice his own height. Painted on its cover was a stylized tent, and above it the words "Pawnee Brand Matches."

"Come to my teepee," he said, gesturing toward the box. "We smoke peace pipe."

Fredericks shook his head in disgust, but followed Orlando. The Indian reached the box and stepped *into* it, right through the surface, as though the heavy cardboard were permeable as air. Orlando shrugged and did the same, half-expecting to bump his face against the flat picture of the tent, but instead suddenly found himself inside a three-dimensional and surprisingly spacious version of the painted teepee. Fredericks followed a moment later, eyes wide. A campfire burned at the center of the conical space, the smoke twining upward to the hole at the top where the tentpoles came together.

The Indian turned and gestured for them to sit, then lowered himself to face them. A woman came forward from the shadows, equally bright red and exaggerated of feature, and stood beside him. She wore a deerskin blanket and a single feather in her hair.

"Me named Chief Strike Anywhere," the Indian said. "This my squaw, Dispose Carefully. Who you, palefaces?"

As the squaw brought them blankets to wrap around their wet, cold virtual bodies, Orlando introduced himself and Fredericks. Strike Anywhere grunted his satisfaction, then called for his wife to bring the peace pipe. As he filled it with something from a pouch—also produced from nowhere—Orlando began to wonder how he would light it, since the Chief himself, judging by his pale wooden neck and round crimson head, seemed to be an old-fashioned match. A bemused vision of the chief rubbing his head against the floor and bursting into flame was proved wrong when the pipe began to smoke without introduction of any visible incendiary.

The smoke was hot and foul, but Orlando did his best to hold it in. As Fredericks struggled to do the same, Orlando wondered again about the strange capacities of the Otherland network. How sophisticated would it have to be to reproduce the sensation of inhaling heated smoke? Would that be easier than simulating the gravity of being spurted out of a giant faucet, or more difficult?

When they had all sucked on the pipe, Strike Anywhere handed it back to his wife, who performed a sleight of hand to make it vanish again. The chief nodded. "Now us friends. I help you. You help me."

Fredericks was distracted by the bowl full of berries that Dispose Carefully was setting in front of him, so Orlando took it on himself to continue the conversation. "What can we do to help you?"

"Bad men take my papoose, Little Spark. I hunt for him. You come with me, help find papoose."

"Certainly."

"Help kill bad men."

"Uh . . . certainly." He ignored Fredericks' look. They were only cartoons, after all. It wouldn't be like helping to kill real people.

"That good." Strike Anywhere folded his arms on his chest and nodded again. "You eat. Then you sleep little. Then, when midnight come, we go hunting."

"Midnight?" Fredericks asked around a mouthful of berries.

"Midnight." The cartoon Indian smiled a hard smile. "When all of Kitchen awake."

IT was the same nightmare; as always, he was powerless before it. The glass broke, showering outward into the sunlight like a spray of water, each piece spinning like a separate planet, the cloud of iridescence a universe that had lost its equilibrium and was now flying apart in high-speed entropic expansion.

The cries echoed and echoed, as they always did.

He woke, shuddering, and brought his hand to his face, expecting to feel tears, or at least the sweat of terror, but his own features were hard and cold beneath his fingers. He was in his throne room in the lamplit great hall of Abydos-That-Was. He had fallen asleep and the old nightmare had returned. Had he cried out? The eyes of a thousand kneeling priests were on him, startled stares in frozen faces, like mice caught in the pantry when the light is switched on.

He rubbed his mask of a face again, half-believing that when he took his hands away he would see something else—but what? His American fortress on the shore of Lake Borgne? The inside of the tank that kept his failing body alive? Or the house of his childhood, the chateau in Limoux, where so much had begun?

The thought of it brought him a sudden picture, the reproduction of David's drawing that had hung on the back of his bedroom door, Napoleon the First crowning himself emperor while a disconsolate pope looked on. What an odd picture to have in a child's room! But he had been an odd child, of course, and something in the grandeur of the Corsican's unstoppable self-belief had caught his imagination.

It was strange to think of the old house again, to see so clearly his mother's heavy curtains and thick Savonnerie carpets, when all of it—and all of the people except him—were so many, many years gone.

Felix Jongleur was the oldest human being on Earth. Of that he felt certain. He had lived through both World Wars of the previous century, had watched the foundation and decay of the Communist nations of the east and seen the rise of the city-states along the Pacific Rim. His fortune, established first in West Africa, in bauxite and nickel and sisal, had grown with the years, spreading into industries of which his *hommes des affaires* father, Jean-Loup, could never have even dreamed. But though his fortune was self-renewing, Jongleur himself was not, and as the century and the millennium waned, the bolder news agencies readied their obituaries, with the emphasis on the mysteries and unfounded assertions that had clouded his long career. But the obituaries remained unused. In the decades after the turn of the new century, he had abandoned day-to-day use of his dying body in favor of an existence in virtual space. He had slowed his physical aging by, among other things, experimental cryogenic techniques, and as the facilities of virtuality had improved—in large part because of research funded out of his own fortune, and the fortunes of like-minded folk he had gathered around him—he had found himself reborn into a second life.

Like Osiris in truth, he thought. *The Lord of the Western Horizon, slain by his brother, then resurrected by his wife to live forever. The master of life and death.*

But even in the sleep of gods, there could be bad dreams.

"Great is he who brings life to the grain, and to green things," someone was singing nearby. *"O, Lord of the Two Lands, he who is mighty in worship and infinite in wisdom, I beg that you hear me."*

He took his hands away from his face—how long had he been sitting this way?—and frowned at the priest who writhed on his belly at the bottom of the steps. Sometimes the rituals he had designed annoyed even him. "You may speak."

"O, Divine One, we have received a communication from our brethren in the temple of your dark brother, the burned one, the red, raw one." The priest bumped his face against the floor, as though even to speak of that entity pained him. "They wish most urgently to drink of your wisdom, O Great House."

Set. The Other. Jongleur—no, he was fully Osiris again; he needed the armor of godhood—straightened on his throne. "Why was I not told at once?"

"They have only now spoken to us, Lord. They await your divine breath."

No one would interrupt his meditations for a problem germane only to the simulation—it was unthinkable—so he knew it must be the engineers.

Osiris gestured, and a window opened before him in the air. For half an instant, he could see the anxious face of one of the technicians from the Temple of Set, then the image froze. The technician's voice fizzed and died, then crackled into life again, like a radio signal during sunspot activity.

"*. . . Need a greater . . . readings are . . . please give us . . .*" The voice did not come back.

The god was perturbed. He would have to go to them. He would have none of his usual time to prepare. But it was not to be helped. The Grail—everything—depended on the Other. And only he, of all the Brotherhood, realized how precarious a foundation that was.

He gestured again. The window disappeared. A score of priests carrying something huge and flat came hurrying forward from the shadows at the back of the great hall. The other priests struggled to get out of the way, but some could not and were knocked down and then trampled by those carrying the ponderous burden. Osiris took a breath to calm himself, to find the peaceful center where problems were solved and death itself had been so often outwitted, as two score of priests raised the polished bronze mirror before him, groaning beneath its immense weight.

Osiris rose, and watched himself rise, observing with a little satisfaction even in this moment the majesty of the Lord of the West standing before his throne. He walked forward until he could see nothing but his own brazen reflection, paused for one last moment, then stepped through.

* * *

The temple was deserted except for half a dozen men in desert-pale robes. The priest-technicians were so upset that none of them remembered to kneel as Osiris appeared, but the god put aside his displeasure for the moment. "I could not understand your message. What is wrong?"

The chief engineer pointed to the door of the tomb chamber. "We can't get through. It . . . *he* . . . won't let us."

Osiris thought the man seemed curiously intense, his energy almost feverish. "Are you speaking metaphorically?"

The priest shook his head. "He's resisting communication, but his readings are very, very low. Frighteningly low." He took a breath, and ran his hands through hair that did not grace the shaven-headed sim. "It started about an hour ago, a real fast downturn. That's why Freimann was trying to communicate—just to see if he was capable of it, or if he was . . . I don't know what you'd call it. Sick." Again the quaver in the priest's voice, as though at any moment he might burst out laughing or weeping.

"Someone other than me spoke to him?"

The head shake was more emphatic now. "Freimann tried. I told him we should wait until you got here. But he was top of the onsite CoC and he overruled me. He got on the direct line and tried voice communication."

"And nothing happened."

"Nothing? No, something definitely happened. Freimann's dead."

The god shut his eyes for a brief moment. So this was the reason for the technician's overexcited state. Would he have to deal with two emergencies at the same time, a tantrum by the Other and a mutiny among his hired lackeys? "Tell me."

"Not much to tell. Just . . . he opened the line. Asked if . . . if the Other was there. Did it . . . did *he,* sorry . . . did he want something. Then Freimann made a funny noise and just . . . stopped. His sim went rigid. Kenzo dropped offline and found him on his office floor, bleeding from the nose and the corners of his eyes. Profound cerebral hemorrhage, as far as we can tell."

Osiris swallowed an involuntary curse; it seemed inappropriate to bring other deities into his own godworld, even in name only. "Is someone taking care of it?"

"It?" A strangled laugh escaped the technician. "You mean Freimann? Yes, security has been called in. If you mean the other 'it,' none of us are going near him. We've been convinced. He doesn't want to talk to us, we don't want to talk to him." The laugh again, threatening to turn into something else. "This wasn't in the job description, you know."

"Oh, pull yourself together. What is your name?"

The priest seemed taken aback—as if a god had time to memorize every one of his worshiper's names. "My real name?"

Behind the mask of the deity, Osiris rolled his eyes. Discipline was breaking down entirely. He would have to think of a way to stiffen this whole department. He had believed he had hired tough-minded types. Obviously, he had underestimated the effect of daily contact with the Other. "Your Eyptian name. And make it quick, or security will have to drop by your office, too."

"Oh. *Oh.* It's Seneb, sir. Lord."

"Seneb, my servant, there is nothing to fear. You and the others will remain at your positions." He had been tempted to give them all the afternoon off while he dealt with the Other's latest bit of bad behavior, but he didn't want them talking to each other, reinforcing their fears and comparing notes. "I will speak with him myself. Open the connection."

"He's closed it, sir—Lord."

"I realize that. But I want it open, at least on our end. Do I make myself clear?"

The priest made a shaky obeisance and scuttled off. Osiris drifted forward until he hung before the great doors to the tomb chamber. The hieroglyphs incised in the dark stone glowed, as if aroused by his presence. The doors swung open.

Inside, the subtle cues of a throughputting connection were gone. The black basalt sarcophagus lay as cold and inert as a lump of coal. There was none of the usual charged air, none of the feelings of standing before a portal into a not-quite-comprehensible elsewhere. The god spread his bandaged arms before the great casket.

"My brother, will you talk to me? Will you tell me what is paining you?"

The sarcophagus remained a mute lump of black stone.

"If you need help, we will give it to you. If something is hurting you, we can make it stop."

Nothing.

"Very well." The god floated closer. "Let me remind you that I can also *give* pain. Do you wish us to make it more difficult for you? You must speak to me. You must speak to me, or I will cause you even greater unhappiness."

There was a subtle change in the room, a tiny adjustment of angles or light. As Osiris learned forward, he heard the voice of Seneb, the priest, in his ear.

"Lord, he's opened . . ."

"Shut up." *Idiot. If these were not such difficult positions to fill properly, I would have him killed this instant.* The god waited expectantly.

It rose up as if from some unimaginable distance, a shred of voice from the bottom of a deep, deep well. At first Osiris could hear it only as a sussuration, and for a moment he feared he had been mistaken, that he was listening to the movement of the sands of the endless desert outside. Then he began to hear words.

". . . an angel touched me . . . an angel . . . touched me . . . an angel . . . touched . . . me . . ."

Over and over, the refrain went on, as scratchy and remote as something played on a gramophone back in Felix Jongleur's childhood. Only the bizarre lilt to the painfully inhuman voice demonstrated that the words were supposed to have a melody. The god stood listening in amazement and confusion and more than a little fear.

The Other was singing.

IN his dream he thought it was an airplane, something from a history-of-flight documentary, all struts and guywires and canvas. It passed him, and someone in the cockpit waved, and there was a smiling monkey painted on the plane's side, and even though it was flying away now, the sputtering noise of the engine got louder and louder. . . .

Orlando opened his eyes to darkness. The noise was right next to him, and for a moment he thought the dream had followed him, that Renie and !Xabbu were flying toward him and would take him back to the real world. He rolled over, blinking blearily. Chief Strike Anywhere was snoring, and it did indeed seem as loud as a small plane. The Indian's outsized nose was bouncing like a balloon in the stream of his exhaled breath. His squaw lay curled beside him, snoring in coloratura counterpoint.

It's a cartoon. It still hadn't quite sunk in. *I'm living in a cartoon.* Then the dream came back to him.

"Fredericks," he whispered. "Where's Renie and !Xabbu? They came through with us, but where are they?"

There was no reply. He turned to shake his friend awake, but Fredericks was gone. Beyond the empty bedroll, the flap of the teepee fluttered in the wind of the chief's noisy slumbers.

Orlando clambered to his knees and crawled toward the flap, heart suddenly pounding. Outside, he found himself surrounded by boxes and bottles, and although he could not easily make out the labels in the near-dark (the lightbulb had been dimmed so that it barely shone) he could hear the sound of loud snores coming from some of them as well. To his left, the facing wall of the kitchen cabinets led up to the sink, as invisible from his position as the top of a tall plateau. There was no sign of Fredericks there, and no visible way for him to have climbed it. Containers of various kinds blocked Orlando's view to the other side of the table. He walked forward, stepping carefully past a wrapped bar of something called Blue Jaguar Hand Soap, which rumbled rather than snored.

He saw the glow first, a faint red light outlining the edge of the table like a miniature sunset. It took him a moment to make out the dark silhouette. Was it Fredericks? What was he doing standing so close to the edge?

Orlando was suddenly very frightened for Fredericks. He hurried forward. As he sprinted past a jar of Captain Carvey's Salts of Magnesia, a groggy voice demanded, "Hark at that! Who goes there? What bell is it?"

There was something odd in his friend's posture, a slump in the shoulders, a rubberiness to the neck, but it *was* Fredericks, or at least the current cartoon version of him. As Orlando drew nearer, slowing because he was afraid he might stumble over something so near to the edge of the dark tabletop, he could hear a faint voice that at first he thought was Fredericks talking to himself. It was barely audible, a murmur that rose and fell, but within a few steps Orlando knew that such a sound could not be coming from Sam Fredericks. It was a deep, harsh voice that hissed its sibilants like a snake.

"Fredericks! Get back from there!" He approached very slowly now, not wanting to startle his friend, but Fredericks did not turn. Orlando put a hand on his shoulder, but there was still no response.

". . . You're going to die here, you know," the hissing voice said, now quite clear, although still pitched very low. *"You should never have come. It's all quite hopeless, and there's nothing you can do about it, but I'm going to tell you anyway."* The laugh that welled up was as ludicrously melodramatic as the chief's snores, but it still set Orlando's heart pattering again.

Fredericks was staring down into the red glow beyond the tabletop, simplified Pithlit-face slack, eyes open but unseeing. Scarlet light glimmered in the depths of the black iron stove, and flames licked at its grille like the hands of prisoners clutching prison bars. But something more substantial than the flames was moving within the stove.

"Hey, wake up!" Orlando grabbed Fredericks' arm and pinched. His friend moaned, but still gazed slackly at the stove and the dancing flames.

"And there you are," the voice crackled up from the stove. *"Come to save your friend, have you? But it won't do any good. You're both going to die here."*

"Who the hell are you?" Orlando demanded, trying to pull Fredericks away from the brink.

"Hell, indeed!" said the voice, and laughed again. Suddenly Orlando could see the shape that had been camouflaged by the flames, a red devil from some ancient book or opera, with horns and a tail and a pitchfork. The devil's eyes widened, and he flashed his teeth in an immense, insane grin. *"You're both going to die here!"* He was dancing in the heart of the stove, stomping up the tongues of fire like he was splashing in a puddle, and although Orlando knew that it was all a simulation, and a particularly silly one at that, it did not stop the rush of fear that ran through him. He grabbed Fredericks firmly and dragged him away from the edge, and did not let go until they were stumbling back toward the teepee.

"I'll be seeing you again!" the devil shouted gleefully. *"You can bet your soul on that!"*

Fredericks pulled away from him as they reached the tent door, rubbing his eyes with his balled fists. "Orlando? What's . . . what's going on? What are we doing out here?" He swiveled to examine the now-silent tabletop. "Was I sleepwalking?"

"Yeah," Orlando said. "Sleepwalking."

"Scanny."

The chief was awake, sharpening a huge tomahawk on a stone wheel that had apparently come out of thin air, like so many other things, since it had certainly not been in the teepee before. He looked up from the hail of sparks as they entered. "You awake. That good. Midnight soon."

Orlando wouldn't have minded a bit more sleep, but each bit of Otherland seemed to have its own cycles of time. He and Fredericks would have to catch up whenever they found a chance.

"I just realized Renie and the rest didn't come through," he said quietly to Fredericks as the chief and his squaw began packing things into a deerskin bag. "I mean, we would have seen them in the sink, right?"

"I guess so." Fredericks' expression was morose. "But how could that be? They went through like the same time we did."

"Maybe there are different levels on the river. Maybe flying through sends you somewhere different than sailing through."

"But then we'll never find them! They could be anywhere!"

Chief Strike Anywhere stepped toward them and pointed to Orlando's sword. "You have big knife. That good. But you," he said to Fredericks, "no knife. That bad." He handed Fredericks a bow and a quiver of arrows.

"Pithlit never uses a bow," Fredericks whispered. "What am I supposed to do with these?"

"Try to shoot only people that aren't named Orlando."

"Thanks a lot."

The chief led them to the tent flap. His wife stepped forward to hold it open. "Find Little Spark," she said. "Please find."

She was not in the least like an actual person, but the tremor in her ridiculous pidgin English was real, and Orlando's chill abruptly returned. These people thought they were alive. Even the cartoons! What kind of madhouse were they stuck in?

"We'll . . . we'll do our best, ma'am," he said, and followed the others out onto the tabletop.

"Jeez," he gasped. "This is *hard.* I never realized how strong Thargor was."

Fredericks started to say something, then clamped his jaw shut as the rope swung them out from the table leg, so that for a moment they were spinning over empty darkness. Strike Anywhere had long before outsped them in the downward climb, and they had no idea if he was even still on the rope.

The rope swung back, and after a few unpleasant thumps against the table leg they resumed their careful descent. "I still feel like Pithlit," Fredericks said, "but he was never that strong to begin with."

"I took this stuff for granted," Orlando said between deep breaths. "Can you see the ground yet?"

Fredericks looked down. "Yeah. Maybe."

"Tell me you do even if you don't."

"Okay. Almost there, Gardino."

A few more minutes did in fact bring them into safe dropping distance. The shadows beneath the table were deep and dark, and they could see the Indian only by the gleam of his eyes and teeth. "Have canoe here," he said. "We go on river. Plenty faster."

"River?" Orlando squinted. A curving line of water stretched before them, curiously circumscribed when logic suggested it should have spread into a flat puddle. Instead, it held its shape and flowed merrily by along the floor, past the battlements of the kitchen counter on one side, coiling away past the iron stove in the other direction. Where it passed the red-gleaming stove, the water seemed to steam faintly.

Orlando hoped they weren't going in that direction. "Why is there a river here?"

Strike Anywhere was wrestling a birchbark canoe out of the shadows. He emerged from beneath the table, turned the canoe over and put it on his head, then began to carry it toward the gleaming river as Orlando and Fredericks scrambled after him. "Why river?" His voice echoed inside the canoe. He seemed confused by the question. "Sink overflow." He gestured to where a cataract of water was pouring down the front of the cabinet, pooling at its base, and extending a tongue of river in each direction. For water that was falling such a distance, it did not splash very much. "Sink *always* overflow."

Orlando decided he was not going to figure out the whys and wherefores of this place so easily; it would be better just to concentrate on what happened next. Still, his Thargor-training made him very uncomfortable with not knowing the ground rules.

Strike Anywhere helped them into the canoe, prestidigitally produced a paddle, and edged the craft out onto the river.

"And who are we following?" Orlando asked.

"Bad men," the Indian said, then brought a long, unjointed finger to his lips. "Talk quiet. Kitchen waking up."

It was hard to see anything by the lunar light of the bulb far overhead. Orlando settled back, watching the shadows of counter and cabinets slide past.

"What are we doing this for?" Fredericks whispered.

"Because he helped us. Someone stole his kid." The memory of Dispose Carefully's tragic eyes seemed an unanswerable argument.

Fredericks apparently did not feel the same way. "This is stupid, Orlando. They're just Puppets!" He lowered his head and spoke into Orlando's ear, unwilling to state this harsh fact loud enough for the Puppet nearest them to hear. "We've lost the only real people, maybe, in this whole impacted place, and instead of looking for them, we're risking our lives for . . . for code!"

Orlando's rebuttal died on his tongue. His friend was right. "It just . . . it just seems like we should do this."

"It's not a game, Gardiner. This isn't the Middle Country. It's a *whole* lot weirder, for one thing."

Orlando could only shake his head. His faint and entirely inexplicable belief that they were doing the right thing did not lend itself well to argument. And in fact, he thought, maybe he was just kidding himself. The simple fact of being able to move around without feeling like it would kill him had obscured some of the harsher facts, and he had quickly fallen into the gaming mode of taking any challenge, of building sudden and apparently pointless allegiances. But that was game logic—this, their situation, was not a game. Actual lives were at stake. The people they were contending against were not the Table of Judgment, a claque of moonlighting engineers and role-playing idiot savants. Instead, unless Sellars had made the whole thing up, the masters of Otherland were incredibly rich, powerful, and ruthless. In fact, they were murderers.

And what was Orlando's response to this threat, and to being separated from the only other people who understood the danger? Getting sidetracked into a search for a lost cartoon baby with a cartoon Indian through an animated kitchen. Fredericks was right. It didn't make a lot of sense.

He opened his mouth to admit his own stupidity, but at that moment the chief turned and brought finger to lips once more. "Sssshhhhh."

Something was bobbing on the water just in front of them. The Indian did not give it a look as he steered the canoe silently past it; his attention was fixed farther ahead. Orlando had time only to notice that the floating object was a waterlogged box, sinking rapidly, and that the faint smudge of words painted on it advertised some kind of floor wax, then his attention was diverted by the sound of slow, labored breathing.

"What's that?" Fredericks asked nervously.

A shape gradually materialized on the river before them—an extremely odd shape. Strike Anywhere paddled forward until they were within a few feet of it, but Orlando still could not make out exactly what was floating on the water beside them. It was a hinged object, like an open oyster shell, but another shape, scrawny and bent, stood inside it, like the famous Venus Orlando had seen in so many advertisements and on so many nodes.

It was some kind of turtle, he realized finally, but it was naked, and standing in its own open shell. Even more ludicrously, it was blowing against the raised half-shell, as though to force itself forward.

"That is so *tchi seen*," Fredericks murmured. "It's . . . it's a turtle."

The scrawny figure turned toward them. "I am not," it said in a dignified but very nasal voice. It produced a pair of spectacles from somewhere and balanced them on the end of its beaklike nose, then examined the newcomers carefully before speaking again. "I am a tortoise. If I were a turtle, I would be able to swim, wouldn't I?" It turned back and blew out another great shuddering breath, but the shell did not move forward even a centimeter. Instead, the canoe slid alongside, and Chief Strike Anywhere backed water to hold them there.

"That not work," he observed evenly.

"I've noticed," said the tortoise. "Any other useful comments?" His dignity was more than a little pathetic. Wearing nothing but his baggy bare skin, and with his head wobbling slightly at the end of his wrinkled neck, he gave the impression of an old bachelor caught outside in his pajamas.

"Where you going?" Strike Anywhere asked.

"Back to shore, as quickly as possible." The tortoise frowned. "Although I would have thought I'd be closer by now. My shell, though water-repellent, does not appear well-suited for river travel."

"Get in boat." The chief paddled a little closer. "We take you."

"Very kind!" The tortoise nevertheless examined him a moment longer. "Back to the land, you mean?"

"Back to land," the Indian affirmed.

"Thank you. You can't be too careful. A large jar of Great White scouring powder offered me a ride on its back a little earlier. 'Just grab my fin,' it insisted. But the whole thing didn't feel . . . right, if you know what I mean." The tortoise stepped from the velvety interior of its shell into the canoe, then leaned back and recaptured the floating carapace. The chief angled the canoe toward the shore at the base of the cabinet.

The tortoise began to step into its shell, then noticed Orlando and Fredericks watching. "It would be a little more polite," it said carefully, "if you would turn your backs while I dressed. Failing room to do that, you might at least avert your eyes."

Orlando and Fredericks stared at each other instead, and as the tortoise pulled his outer covering back on, making fussy little noises as he adjusted it, they fought mightily against the laugh that immediately began to bubble between them. Orlando bit his lip hard, and as he felt it sting, suddenly wondered how much of his virtual behavior the suppressor circuits in his neurocannular implant were actually suppressing in RL. Was he biting his real lip right now? What if his family, or the hospital people, were actually listening to all the things he was saying, watching all the things he was doing? They would really wonder what was going on. Or they would think he had scanned out utterly.

This, which started out as an unhappy thought, suddenly struck him with its absurd side as well, and the long-withheld laugh burst out of him.

"I hope you are enjoying yourself," the tortoise said in a frosty tone.

"It's not you," Orlando said, gaining control again. "I just thought of something. . . ." He shrugged. There was no way to explain.

As they neared the bank of the river, they could see something sparkling on the shore and hear faint but lively music. A large dome stood on the floor just at the water's edge. Light streamed out of it through hundreds of small holes and a variety of odd silhouettes were passing in and out of a larger hole in the side. The music was louder now, something rhythmic but old-fashioned. The strange shapes seemed to be dancing—a group of them had even formed a line in front of the dome, laughing and bumping against each other, throwing their tiny wiggling arms in the air. It was only as the canoe drew within a stone's throw of the bank that its crew could finally see the merrymakers properly.

"Scanbark!" Fredericks whistled. "They're vegetables!"

Produce of all types staggered in and out of the main door of the dome beneath a large illuminated sign which read *"The Colander Club."* Stalks of leek and fennel in diaphanous flapper dresses, zucchini in zoot suits, and other revelers of a dozen well-dressed vegetal varieties packed the club to overflowing; the throng had spilled out onto the darkened linoleum beach in cornucopiate profusion, partying furiously.

"Hmmph," the tortoise grunted disapprovingly. "I hear it's a very seedy crowd." There was not the slightest suggestion of humor.

As Orlando and Fredericks stared in amazed delight, a sudden, hard impact shivered the canoe and tipped it sideways, almost tumbling Orlando overboard. The tortoise fell against the railing, but Fredericks shot out a hand and dragged him down into the bottom of the boat where he lay, waggling his legs violently in the air.

Something struck the boat again, a jarring thump that made the wood literally groan. Strike Anywhere was fighting to keep the canoe afloat in the suddenly hostile waters, his big hands whipping the paddle from one side of the canoe to the other as it threatened to overturn.

As Orlando struggled for balance in the bottom of the canoe, he felt something scrape all the way down the keel beneath him. He scrambled onto his hands and knees to see what had happened.

A sandbar, he thought, but then: *A sandbar in the middle of a kitchen floor?*

He peered over the side of the pitching canoe. In the first brief moment he could see only the agitated waters splashing high, glowing in the lights from the riverside club, then something huge and toothy exploded up out of the water toward him. Orlando squealed and dropped flat. Huge jaws gnashed with a loud *clack* just where his head had been, then banged against the edge of the canoe hard enough to rattle his bones as the predatory shape fell back into the water.

"There's something . . . something tried to bite me!" he shouted. As he lay, shivering, he saw another vast pair of jaws rise on the far side of the canoe, streaming water. They opened and then clashed their blunt teeth together, then the thing slid back down out of sight. Orlando groped at his belt for his sword, but it was gone, perhaps overboard.

"Very bad!" Strike Anywhere shouted above the splashing. The canoe sustained yet another heavy blow, and the Indian fought for balance. "*Salad tongs!* And them heap angry!"

Orlando lay beside Fredericks and the feebly thrashing tortoise in the bottom of the canoe, which was rapidly filling with water, and tried to wrap his mind around the idea of being devoured by kitchen utensils.

DREAD was reviewing the first batch of data from Klekker and Associates on his southern Africa queries, and enjoying the solid bodily hum of his most recent hit of Adrenax, when one of his outside lines began blinking at the corner of his vision. He turned down the loping, percussive beat in his head a little.

The incoming call overrode his voice-only default, opening a window. The new window framed an ascetic brown face surmounted by a wig of black hemp laced with gold thread. Dread groaned inwardly. One of the Old Man's lackeys—and not even a real person. It was the strangest kind of insult. Of course, Dread considered, with someone as rich and isolated as the Old Man, maybe he didn't even realize it was an insult.

"The Lord of Life and Death desires to speak with you."

"So he wants me to come visit the film set?" It was a reflexive remark, but Dread was irritated with himself for wasting sarcasm on a puppet. "A trip to V-Egypt? To whatever it is, Abydos?"

"No." The puppet's expression did not change, but there was a greater primness in its speech, a tiny hint of disapproval at its levity. Maybe it wasn't a Puppet after all. "He will speak to you now."

Before Dread had more than an instant to be surprised, the priest winked out and was replaced by the Old Man's green-tinged death-mask. "Greetings, my Messenger."

"And to you." He was taken aback, both by the God of Death's willingness to dispense with formalities, and by the knowledge of his own double game, emblemized by the documents even now sitting on the top level of his own system. The Old Man couldn't just pop in past the security and read them while the line was open, could he? Dread felt a sudden chill: it was very hard to guess what the Old Man could or couldn't accomplish. "What can I do for you?"

The strange face peered at him for a long moment, and Dread suddenly very much wished he had not answered the call. Had he been found out? Was this the lead-up to the horrible and only eventually fatal punishment that his treachery would earn?

"I . . . I have a job for you."

Despite the odd tone in his employer's voice, Dread felt better. The old man didn't need to be subtle with someone as comparatively powerless as he, so it seemed unlikely he knew or even suspected anything.

And I won't be powerless forever. . . .

"Sounds interesting. I've pretty much tied up all the loose ends from Sky God."

The Old Man continued as though Dread hadn't spoken. "It's not in your usual . . . field of expertise. But I've tried other resources, and haven't . . . haven't found any answers."

Everything about the conversation was strange. For the first time, the Old Man actually sounded . . . old. Although the bandit adrenals were racing through his blood, urging him either to flee or fight, Dread began to feel a little more like his normal, cocky self. "I'd be glad to help, Grandfather. Will you send it to me?"

As if this use of the disliked nickname had woken up his more regular persona, the mask-face abruptly frowned. "Have you got that music playing? In your head?"

"Just a bit, at the moment . . ."

"Turn it off."

"It's not very loud. . . ."

"Turn it *off*." The tone, though still a bit distracted, was such that Dread complied instantly. Silence echoed in his skull.

"Now, I want you to listen to this," the Old Man said. "Listen very carefully. And make sure you record it."

And then, bizarrely, unbelievably, the Old Man began to sing.

It was all Dread could do not to laugh out loud at the sheer unlikeliness of it all. As his employer's thin, scratchy voice wound through a few words set to an almost childishly basic tune, a thousand thoughts flitted through Dread's mind. Had the old bastard finally lost it, then? Was this the first true evidence of senile dementia? Why should one of the most powerful men in the world—in all of *history*—care about some ridiculous folk song, some nursery rhyme?

"I want you to find out where that song comes from, what it means, anything you can discover," the Old Man said when he had finished his creaky recital. "But I don't want it known that you're doing the research, and I *particularly* don't want it to come to the attention of any of the other Brotherhood members. If it seems to lead to one of them, come back to me immediately. Do I make myself understood?"

"Of course. As you said, it's not in my normal line. . . ."

"It is now. This is *very important.*"

Dread sat bewildered for long moments after the Old Man had clicked off. The unaccustomed quiet in his head had been replaced now with the memory of that quavering voice singing over and over, *"an angel touched me . . . an angel touched me."*

It was too much. Too much.

Dread lay back on the floor of his white room and laughed until his stomach hurt.

CHAPTER 12

The Center of the Maze

HIS first thought, as he struggled toward the surface of yet another river, was; *I could get tired of this very quickly.*

His second, just after his head broke water, was: *At least it's warmer here.*

Paul kicked, struggling to keep afloat, and found himself beneath a heavy gray sky. The distant riverbank was shrouded in fog, but only a few yards away, as if placed there by the scriptwriter of a children's adventure serial, bobbed an empty rowboat. He swam to it, fighting a current that although gentle was still almost too much for his exhausted muscles. When he reached the boat, he clung to its side until he had caught his breath, then clambered in, nearly turning it over twice. Once safely aboard, he lay down in the inch of water at the bottom and dropped helplessly into sleep.

He dreamed of a feather that glittered in the mud, deep beneath the water. He swam down toward it, but the bottom receded, so that the feather remained always tantalizingly out of reach. The pressure began to increase, squeezing his chest like giant hands, and now he was aware also that just as he sought the feather, something was seeking him—a pair of somethings, eyes aglitter even in the murky depths, sharking behind him as the feather dropped farther from his grasp and the waters grew darker and thicker. . . .

Paul woke, moaning. His head hurt. Not surprising, really, when he considered that he had just made his way across a freezing Ice Age forest and fought off a hyena the size of a young shire horse. He examined his hands for signs of frostbite, but found none. More surprisingly, he found no sign of his Ice Age clothes either. He was dressed in modern clothing, although it was hard to tell quite how modern, since his dark pants, waistcoat, and collarless white shirt were all still dripping wet.

Paul dragged his aching body upright, and as he did so put his hand on an oar. He lifted it and hunted for a second so that he could fill both of the empty oarlocks, but there was only the one. He shrugged. It was better than no oar at all. . . .

The sun had cleared away a bit of the fog, but was itself still only directionless light somewhere behind the haze. Paul could make out the faint outlines of buildings on either side now, and more importantly, the shadowy shape of a bridge spanning the river a short distance ahead of him. As he stared his heart began to beat faster, but this time not from fear.

It can't be . . . He squinted, then put his hands on the boat's prow and leaned as far forward as he dared. *It is . . . but it can't be. . . .* He began to paddle with his single oar, awkwardly at first, then with more skill, so that after a few moments the boat stopped swinging from side to side.

Oh, my sweet God. Paul almost could not bear to look at the shape, afraid that it would ripple and change before his eyes, become something else. *But it really is. It's Westminster Bridge!*

I'm home!

*   *   *

He still remembered the incident with a burn of embarrassment. He and Niles and Niles' then-girlfriend Portia, a thin young woman with a sharp laugh and bright eyes who was studying for the Bar, had been having a drink in one of the pubs near the college. They had been joined by someone else, one of Niles' uncountable army of friends. (Niles collected chums the way other people kept rubber bands or extra postage stamps, on the theory that you never knew when you might need one.) The newcomer, whose face and name Paul had long since forgotten, had just come back from a trip to India, and went on at length about the scandalous beauty of the Taj Mahal by night, how it was the most perfect building ever created, and that in fact its architectural perfection could now be scientifically proved.

Portia suggested in turn that the most beautiful place in the world was without question the Dordogne in France, and if it hadn't become so popular with horrible families in electric camping wagons with PSATs on the roof, no one would dare question that fact.

Niles, whose own family traveled extensively—so extensively that they never even used the word "travel," any more than a fish would need to use the word "swim"—opined that until all those present had seen the stark highlands of Yemen and experienced the frightening, harsh beauty of the place, there was no real reason to continue the conversation.

Paul had been nursing a gin and tonic, not his first, trying to figure out why sometimes the lime stayed up and sometimes it went to the bottom, and trying equally hard to figure out why spending time around Niles, who was one of the nicest people he knew, always made him feel like an impostor, when the stranger (who had presumably had a name at that time) asked him what he thought.

Paul had swallowed a sip of the faintly blue liquid, then said: "I think the most beautiful place in the world is the Westminster Bridge at sunset."

After the explosion of incredulous laughter, Niles, perhaps hoping to soften his friend's embarrassment, had done his best to intimate that Paul was having a brilliant jape at the expense of them all. And it *had* been embarrassing, of course: Portia and the other young man clearly thought he was a fool. He might as well have worn a tattoo on his forehead that said "Provincial Lout." But he had meant it, and instead of smiling mysteriously and keeping his mouth shut, he had done his best to explain why, which had of course made it worse.

Niles could have said the same thing and either made it a brilliant joke or defended it so cleverly that the others would have wound up weeping into their glasses of merlot and promising to Buy British, but Paul had never been good with words in that way—never when something was important to him. He had first stammered, then muddled what he was trying to say, and at last became so angry that he stood up, accidentally knocking over his drink, and fled the pub, leaving the others shocked and staring.

Niles still tweaked him about the incident from time to time, but his jokes were gentle, as though he sensed, although he could never really understand, how painful it had been for Paul.

But it had been true—he thought then, and still did, that it was the most beautiful thing he knew. When the sun was low, the buildings along the north bank of the Thames seemed fired with an inner light, and even those thrown up during the intermittent cycles of poor taste that characterized so much of London's latter-day additions took on a glow of permanence. That was England, right there, everything it ever was, everything it ever could have been. The bridge, the Halls of Parliament, the just-visible abbey, even Cleopatra's Needle and the droll Victorian lamps of the Embankment—all were as ridiculous as could be, as replete with empty puffery as human imagination could contrive to make them, but they were also the center of something Paul admired deeply but could never quite define. Even the famous tower that contained Big Ben, as cheapened by sentiment and jingoism as its image was, had a beauty that was at once ornate and yet breathtakingly stark.

But it was not the kind of thing you could describe after your third gin and tonic to people like Niles' friends, who ran unrestrained through an adult world that had not yet slowed them down with responsibility, armed with the invincible irony of a public-school upbringing.

But if Niles had been where Paul had just been, had experienced what Paul had experienced, and could see the bridge now—the dear old thing, appearing out of the fog beyond all hope—then surely even Niles (son of an MP and now himself a rising star in the diplomatic service, the very definition of urbane) would get on his knees and kiss her stony abutments.

Fate turned out to be not quite as generous a granter-of-wishes as it might have been. The first disappointment—and as it turned out, the smallest—was that it was not, in fact, sunset. As Paul paddled on, almost obsessed with the idea of docking at the Embankment itself, instead of heading immediately to shore in some less auspicious place, the sun finally became visible, or at least its location became less general: it was in the east, and rising.

Morning, then. No matter. He would climb ashore at the Embank-ment as planned, surrounded no doubt by staring tourists, and walk to Charing Cross. There was no money in his pockets, so he would become a beggar, one of those people with a perfunctory tale of hard-ship that the begged-of barely acknowledged, preferring to tithe and escape as quickly as possible. When he had raised money for tube fare, he would head back to Canonbury. A shower at his flat, several hours of well-deserved sleep, and then he could return to Westminster Bridge and watch the sunset properly, giving thanks that he had made his way back across the chaotic universe to sublime, sensible London.

The sun lifted a little higher. A wind came out of the east behind it, bearing a most unpleasant smell. Paul wrinkled his nose. For two thousand years this river had been the lifeblood of London, and people still treated it with the same ignorant unconcern as had their most primitive ancestors. He smelled sewage, industrial wastes—even some kind of food-processing outflow, to judge by the sour, meaty stench—but even the foulest odors could not touch his immense relief. There on the right was Cleopatra's Needle, a black line in the fogs that still clung to the riverbank, backdropped by a bed of bright red flowers fluttering in the breeze. Gardeners had been hard at work on the Em-bankment, to judge by the yards and yards of brilliant scarlet. Paul was reassured. Perhaps there was some civic ceremony going on today, something in Trafalgar Square or at the Cenotaph—after all, he had no idea how long he'd been gone. Perhaps they had closed the area around Parliament, it did seem that the riverbank was very quiet.

Growing out of this idea, which even as it formed in his mind quickly began to take on a dark edge, was a secondary realization. Where was the river traffic? Even on Remembrance Sunday, or some-thing equally important, there would be commercial boats on the river, wouldn't there?

He looked ahead to the distant but growing shape of Westminster Bridge, unmistakable despite the shroud of mist, and an even more frightening thought suddenly came to him. Where was the Hunger-ford Bridge? If this was the Embankment coming up on the right, then the old railroad bridge should be right in front of him. He should be staring up at it right now.

He steered the rowboat toward the north bank, squinting. He could see the shape of one of the famous dolphin lampposts appear from the fog, and relief flooded through him: it was the Embankment, no question.

The next lamppost was bent in half, like a hairpin. All the rest were gone.

Twenty meters before him, the remains of this end of the Hunger-
ford Bridge jutted from a shattered jumble of concrete. The girders
had been twisted until they had stretched like licorice, then snapped.
A ragged strip of railroad track protruded from the heights above,
crimped like the foil from a candy wrapper.

As Paul stared, his mind a dark whirlpool in which no thought
would remain stationary for more than an instant, the first large wave
lifted the rowboat up, then set it down again. It was only as the second
and third and fourth waves came, each greater than the one before,
that Paul finally tore his eyes from the pathetic northern stub of the
bridge and looked down the river. Something had just passed under
Westminster Bridge, something as big as a building, but which nevertheless moved, and which was even now stretching back up to its full
height, on a level with the upper stanchions of the bridge itself.

Paul could make no sense of the immense vision. It was like some
absurd piece of modernist furniture, like a mobile version of the
Lloyds Building. As it splashed closer, moving eastward along the
Thames, he could see that it had three titanic legs which held up a
vast complexity of struts and platforms. Above them curved a broad
metal hood.

As he stared, dumbfounded, the thing stopped its progress for a
moment and stood in the middle of the Thames like some horrible
parody of a Seurat bather. With a hiss of hydraulics that Paul could
hear clearly even at this distance, the mechanical thing lowered itself
a little, almost crouching, then the great hood swiveled from side to
side as though it were a head and the immense construct was looking
for something. Steel cables which hung from the structures above the
legs bunched and then dangled again, making whitecaps on the river's
surface. Moments later, the thing rose back to full height and began
stilting up the river once more, hissing and whirring as it moved
toward him. Its passage, each stride eating dozens of meters, was
astoundingly swift: while Paul was still locked in a kind of paralysis,
his joy turned to nightmare in mere seconds, the thing sloshed past
him, going upstream. The waves of its passage bounced the little boat
roughly, thumping it so hard against the riverwall that Paul had the
breath smashed out of him, but the great mechanical thing paid no
more attention to Paul and his craft as it passed than he himself
would have given to a wood chip floating in a puddle.

Paul lay across the rowing bench, stunned. The mists were thinning
as the day grew brighter. He could see Big Ben clearly for the first
time, just beyond the bridge. He had thought its top was shrouded in
fog, but it was gone. Only a scorched stump protruded above the shattered rooftops of Parliament.

The waves subsided. He clung to the railing and watched the metal monstrosity stalk away down the river. It stopped briefly to uproot some wreckage where the stanchions of Waterloo Bridge had once stood, pulling the great muddy mass of cement and iron from the depths with its steel tentacles, then dropped it again like a bored child and disappeared into the fog, heading toward Greenwich and the sea.

THERE were other mechanical monsters, as Paul learned in the days ahead, but he also learned he did not have to work much to avoid them. They did not bother with individual humans, any more than an exterminator who had finished his job would waste time crushing a lone ant on the walkway. But in the immediate hours afterward, he expected to be seized and smashed by one of the gigantic machines at any moment.

Certainly, they had already proved their capacity for destruction. London, or what he could see of it from the river, was a wasteland, the damage far worse than anything it had suffered since the days of Boudicca. The giant machines had smashed and burned whole blocks of streets, even leveled entire boroughs, in what seemed purely wanton destruction. And he knew that the worst was hidden from him. He could see a few bodies scattered in open spaces on the riverbanks, and many more bobbed past him on the river current in the days that followed, but when the wind suddenly turned toward him the smell of death became truly dreadful, and he knew that there must be thousands and thousands more corpses than he could see, trapped in underground stations that had become vast tombs or crushed in the rubble of fallen buildings.

Other incursions had been more subtle. What he had thought in the first hour were red flowers on the Victoria Embankment instead proved to be an alien vegetation. It was everywhere, waving scarlet stems filling up the verges and the traffic islands, swarming over deserted gardens, festooning the remaining bridges and lampposts; for miles at a stretch, the only things moving other than Paul and the river were fronds of the red weed swaying in the rotten wind.

But as shocking as it was to see London in its death throes, other and even stranger surprises awaited him.

Within hours of his encounter with the first metal giant, Paul began to understand that this was not *his* London, but the city as it might have been generations before his birth. The shop signs he could see from his boat were written in funny, curling script, and advertised services that seemed hopelessly quaint: "millinery," "dry goods," "hosiery." The few cars still recognizable as such were ridiculously old-fashioned, and even the human corpses putrefying in the street seemed oddly antique—most noticeably those of the women, who were dressed in shawls and ankle-length skirts. Some of these nameless dead even wore hats and gloves, as though death itself were an occasion that must be met in formal dress.

Hours passed after the shock of seeing the first invader before Paul realized what place he had actually found.

He had steered the boat to a deserted jetty across from Battersea in order to rest his aching arms. In another London—in *his* London—the famous power station that had dominated this part of the riverfront was long gone, and the municipal authorities were building cloud-piercing fibramic office towers on the spot, but in this London the station itself apparently would not be built for decades yet. But since some terrible conflict seemed to have slaughtered almost everyone, the power station would probably *never* be built. It was all so confusing!

The sun was dipping low in the west, which softened the ragged skyline and made the destruction a tiny bit more tolerable, and for a long moment Paul just sat in as much personal stillness as he could muster, trying not to think about what lay all around him. He shut his eyes to further the process, but the feeling of imminent doom was so strong he could not keep them closed. At any moment, one of those grotesque, skyscraping machines might appear on the horizon, a tripod remorseless as a hunting beast, hood swiveling until it caught sight of him. . . .

Tripods. Paul stared at the brown water of the Thames swirling around the jetty, but he was no longer seeing it. Tripods, giant war machines, red weeds growing everywhere. There was a story like that, wasn't there. . . ?

It came to him like a blast of cold air, not as the satisfying answer to a question, but as the unwelcome beginning of an even more frightening problem.

Oh, God. H. G. Wells, isn't it? War of the Worlds, *whatever that thing is called. . . .*

It was one of those works he felt he knew quite well, even though he hadn't actually read the book or seen any of the numerous adaptations (several versions of which, both interactive and straight, were available on the net.) But there was, he felt quite sure, no version like this. Because this was not a version. This was horribly real.

But how can I be somewhere that's also a made-up story?

Even a moment's contemplation of this made his head hurt. There were far too many possibilities, all of them utterly mad. Was it a make-believe place, based on a famous story, but constructed just for him? But that was impossible—he had already decided it was ridiculous to imagine someone building an entire Ice Age set, and how much more mind-numbingly expensive would this London be? And when he considered how many different places he had seen already . . . no. It was impossible. But what other answers were there? Could this be some real place, some London in another dimension that had been invaded by space aliens, and which Wells had somehow tapped into? Was that old author's device, the alternate universe, really true?

Or was it something even stranger—one of those quantum things that Muckler at the gallery was always raving about? Had the fact of Wells' invention caused this place to come into being, a branching of reality that did not exist until the man from Bromley first set pen to paper?

That only led to more questions, each more boggling than the last. Did every made-up story have its own universe? Or just the good ones? And who got to decide?

And was he himself, already missing part of his past, now caught in some ever-ramifying journey, into dimensions farther and farther from his own?

At another time he might have laughed at the idea of a multiple universe run on the basis of editing decisions, but nothing about his situation was in the least bit funny. He was lost in a mad universe, he was impossibly far from home, and he was alone.

He slept that evening in a deserted restaurant near Cheyne Walk. It had been looted of everything remotely resembling food, but he was not feeling particularly hungry, especially when every change of wind brought the smell of putrefaction from some new quarter. In fact, he could not remember the last time he had felt truly hungry, and could but dimly remember the last time he had eaten, but the thought only raised more questions, and he was very tired of questions. He pulled drapes from the windows and wrapped himself in them against the cold from the river, then slid down into a heavy, dreamless sleep.

As he made his way up the Thames the next day, moving faster because of a pair of oars he had salvaged from another abandoned boat, he found that he was not the only human being in this ruined London. From the river, and during the course of a few cautious landings before the sun began to set again, he saw nearly a dozen other people, but they were as wary of contact as rats: all of them either ignored his cry of greeting or actually fled on seeing him. Thinking of how everything edible had been taken from the restaurant and the shops he had explored on either side of it, he wondered if these people did not have good reason to shun other survivors. And survivors they clearly were, all of them ragged and blackened with dust and soot, so that at a distance he could not have guessed the ethnicity of any of them.

He found an entire community at Kew the next day, several dozen people in tattered clothes, living in the royal gardens. Paul did not come ashore, but hailed them from the river and asked for news. A small deputation came down to the water's edge and told him that the aliens—the "machine creatures" as these survivors called them, had largely moved away from London, pursuing their inscrutable aims northward, but there were still enough left behind to make life in the city a very hazardous thing. They had themselves come to Kew Gardens only a week ago from Lambeth, which had been almost completely destroyed, and had already lost a few of their party who had been caught on the open green when a tripod had appeared and stepped on them, apparently by accident. When the Kew survivors had finished trapping and eating the last of the squirrels and birds, they told Paul, they planned to move on.

It was good to talk to other people, but there was something in the way they inspected him that made Paul uncomfortable. One of the men invited him to join them, but he only thanked them and rowed on.

The oddest thing, he thought as he made his way up the river toward Richmond, was that his memory of *War of the Worlds* was that the Martians had proved susceptible to Earth diseases, and had died within a few weeks of beginning their campaign of devastation. But the survivors at Kew had said the first Martian ships had arrived in Surrey over half a year ago. Paul was curious about this variance from the Wells story, and picked up scraps of newspaper dated in the last days before the Martian invasion when he came across them, but of course there was nothing available to tell him the current date. Civilization had come to a halt on the day the Martians came.

In fact, that was the strange thing about the whole situation. Unlike the other stops on his involuntary pilgrimage, this post-invasion England seemed to have reached a kind of stasis, as though someone had played an endgame, then left without removing the pieces from the board. If London was any example, the country, perhaps the world, was completely in the hands of the invaders. The creatures themselves had left only a token force. The tiny residue of human survivors were scrabbling just to survive. It all felt so . . . empty.

This spawned another thought, which began to grow as the day went on, as Paul passed and called out to a handful of other scavenging humans with no result. All of the places he had been since he had somehow lost his normal life were so . . . so *old*. They were situations and scenarios that suggested a different era entirely—the turn of the century H. G. Wells novel, the strange *Boy's Own Paper* version of Mars—another and quite different Mars than the one which had spawned these invaders, which was an interesting thought in itself— and the Looking Glass place where he had met Gally. Even his dimmest memories seemed to be of an antique and long-concluded war. And the Ice Age, that was just plain ancient. But there seemed another common element as well, something that troubled him but that he could not quite name.

It was the fourth day, and he was just east of Twickenham, when he met them.

He had just passed a small midstream island, and was working his way alongside an open green space on the north side of the river, a park of some kind, when he saw a man walking aimlessly back and forth on the bank. Paul thought he might be another of those whose minds had been permanently deranged by the invasion, because when he hailed him, the man looked up, then stared at him as though Paul were a ghost. A moment later the man began to leap up and down, waving his arms like a spastic flagman, shouting over and over again: "Thank goodness! Oh, heavens! Thank goodness!"

Paul steered closer to the riverbank as the stranger ran down toward him. Caution long since having gained the upper hand over his desire to commune with living humans, Paul stayed a little way out into the water while he made a hasty examination. The middle-aged man was thin and very short, perhaps not much more than five feet in height. He wore spectacles and a small mustache of the sort a later generation would identify with German dictators. But for the ragged state of his black suit, and the tears of apparent gratitude in his eyes, he might have just walked away from his desk in a small, stuffy assurance firm.

"Oh, thank the good Lord. Please come help me." The man pulled a kerchief from his waistcoat pocket and used it to mop his face. It was impossible to tell what color the cloth had once been. "My sister. My poor sister has fallen down and she cannot get up. Please."

Paul stared at him hard. If he was a robber, he was a very unlikely-looking one. If he was the front man for a gang of thieves and murderers, they must be very patient to set bait for the infrequent river travelers. Still, it did not pay to be hasty these days. "What happened to her?"

"She has fallen and hurt herself. Oh, please, sir, do a Christian good deed and help me. I would pay you if I could." His smile was sickly. "If it meant anything. But we will share what we have with you."

The man's sincerity was hard to doubt, and it would take a gun to equalize the difference in their sizes. He had not showed one yet, and Paul had been in range for quite some time. "All right. Let me just tie up my boat."

"God bless you, sir."

The small man bounced from foot to foot like a child waiting to use the toilet as Paul waded ashore, then made his rowboat fast. The man beckoned to him to follow, and set out up the bank toward the trees in a strange, awkward trot. Paul doubted that before the invasion the man had ever gone faster than a walk since he had been a child at school.

As if the memory of former dignity suddenly returned with the presence of a stranger, the man in the black suit abruptly slowed and turned around. "This is so very kind of you. My name is Sefton Pankie." Walking backward now, and in imminent danger at any moment of tripping over a root, he extended a hand.

Paul, who had decided some time back that since he couldn't trust his own mind, he certainly couldn't trust anything else he encountered, shook the man's hand and gave a false name. "I'm . . . Peter Johnson."

"A pleasure, Mr. Johnson. Then if we've done that properly, do let us hurry."

Pankie led him up the hill, through a patch of the ubiquitous red Martian grass that held the hilltop like a conqueror's flag, and down the other side into a copse of beech trees. Just when Paul was beginning to wonder again if the stranger might be leading him into some sort of ambush, the small man stopped at the edge of a deep gulley and leaned over.

"I'm back, my dear. Are you all right? Oh, I hope that you are!"

"Sefton?" The voice was a strong alto, and more strident than melodious. "I thought certain you had run off and left me."

"Never, my dear." Pankie began to make his way down into the gulley, using tree roots for handholds, his lack of coordination again apparent. Paul saw a single figure huddled at the bottom and swung down to follow him.

The woman wedged in a crevice at the bottom of the gulley had lodged in a difficult and embarrassing position, legs in the air, dark lacquered hair and straw hat caught in a tangle of loose branches. She was also extremely large. As Paul made his way down to where he could see her reddened, sweat-gleaming face, he guessed that she was at least Pankie's age, if not older.

"Oh, goodness, who is this?" she said in unfeigned horror as Paul reached the bottom of the gulley. "What must you think of me, sir? This is so dreadful, so humiliating!"

"He's Mr. Johnson, my dear, and he is here to help." Pankie squatted beside her, stroking the expanse of her voluminous gray dress like the hide of a prize cow.

"No need to be embarrassed, Ma'am." Paul could see the problem clearly—Pankie's sister weighed perhaps three times as much as he did. It would be hell just getting her shifted loose, let alone helping her back up the steep slope. Nevertheless, he felt sorry for the woman and her embarrassment, doubly worse because of its indelicacy—already he was beginning to absorb the Edwardian mores of this place, despite their irrelevance in the face of what the Martians had done—and bent himself to the task.

It took almost half an hour to get the woman disentangled from the branches at the bottom of the gulley, since she shrieked with pain every time her hair was tugged, no matter how gently. When she had finally been freed, Paul and Sefton Pankie began the formidable job of helping her up the hill to safety. It was nearly dark when, all extremely disheveled, dirty, and soaked in sweat, they finally stumbled onto the level area at the top.

The woman sank to the ground like a collapsing tent, and had to be persuaded over some minutes to sit up again. Paul built a fire with dry branches while Pankie hovered around her like a tickbird servicing a rhino, trying to clean the worst of the dirt from her with his kerchief (which Paul thought must be a record for pointless exercises.) When Paul had finished, Pankie produced some matches, clearly a treasured possession at this point. They put one into service with lip-biting caution, and by the time the sun had disappeared behind the damaged skyline on the far side of the river, the flames were climbing high into the air and spirits were generally restored.

"I cannot thank you enough," the woman said. Her round face was scratched and smeared with dirt, but she gave him a smile clearly intended to be winsome. "Now it may seem silly, after all that, but I believe in proper introductions. My name is Undine Pankie." She extended a hand as though it were a dainty sweetmeat for him to savor. Paul thought she might be expecting him to kiss it, but decided that a line had to be drawn somewhere. He shook it and reintroduced himself under his hastily-assumed name.

"Words cannot express my gratitude," she said. "When my husband was gone so long, I feared he had been set upon by looters. You can imagine my horror, trapped and alone in that terrible, terrible place."

Paul frowned. "I'm sorry—your husband?" He turned to Pankie. "You said you needed help to save your sister." He glanced back to the woman, but her look was one of perfect innocence, although there was some poorly-hidden irritation to be seen.

"Sister? Sefton, what a curious thing to say."

The small man, who had been busy with a futile attempt to reorder her hair, gave an embarrassed chuckle. "Is, isn't it? I can't imagine what got into me. It's this invasion thing, don't you know. It has quite rattled my wits."

Paul accepted their explanation—certainly Undine Pankie showed no signs of guilt or duplicity—but he was obscurely troubled.

Mrs. Pankie recovered herself quite rapidly after that, and spent the rest of the evening holding forth about the terror of the Martian invasion and the horrors of living rough in the park. She seemed to give these burdens about equal weight.

Undine Pankie was a garrulous woman, and before Paul finally begged leave to lie down and sleep, she had told him more than he had ever wanted to know about life among the *petit bourgeois* of Shepperton, both pre- and post-invasion. Mr. Pankie, it turned out, was a chief clerk in the county surveyor's office—a position his wife clearly deemed beneath his due. Paul could not help feeling that she thought that, with diligence and artful politicking, this might one day be remedied—which, unless the Martians reopened the surveyor's office, he thought was unlikely. But he understood the need to cling to normality in abnormal situations, so as Mrs. P. described the perfidy of her husband's unappreciative supervisor, he tried to look properly saddened, yet optimistic on Mr. Pankie's behalf.

Mrs. Pankie herself was a homemaker, and she mentioned more than once that she was not alone in thinking it the highest position a woman could or should aspire to. And, she said, she ran her house as a tight ship: even her dear Sefton, she made very clear, knew "where to toe the line."

Paul could not miss Mr. P.'s reflexive flinch.

But there was one great sorrow of Undine Pankie's life, which was that the Lord had seen fit to deny her the joy of motherhood, that most sublime of gifts a woman could give to her husband. They had a fox terrier named Dandy—and here for a moment she became muddled, as she remembered that they did *not* have a fox terrier, any more than they had a house, both of them having been incinerated by a sweeping blast from a Martian heat-ray that had devastated their entire block, and which the Pankies had escaped themselves only because they had been at a neighbor's, trying to get news.

Mrs. Pankie halted her account to weep a few tears for brave little Dandy. Paul felt the tug of the grotesque, to have seen so much ruin, and then to see this huge, soft woman crying over a dog while peering at him from the corner of her eye to make sure he saw how helplessly sentimental she was. But he, who had no home or even idea of how to reach it—how was he to judge others and their losses?

"Dandy was just like a child to us, Mr. Johnson. He was! Wasn't he, Sefton?"

Mr. Pankie had started nodding even before her appeal. Paul didn't think he had been listening very closely—he had been poking the fire and staring up at the red-washed tree limbs—but clearly the man was an old hand at recognizing the conversational cues that led up to his own expected bits.

"We wanted nothing more in this world than a child, Mr. Johnson. But God has denied us. Still, I expect it is all for the best. We must rejoice in His wisdom, even when we do not understand His plan."

Later, as Paul lay waiting for sleep, with the twinned snores of the Pankies beside him—hers hoarsely deep, his flutingly high—he thought she had sounded like she might very well be a little less tolerant if she ever met God face-to-face. In fact, Undine Pankie sounded like the kind of woman who might give Him a rather unpleasant time.

She scared Paul badly.

It was strange, he thought the next morning as the boat floated up the Thames, how the tiniest hint of normality could push away the worst and most unfathomable horrors and fill up the day with trivia. The human mind did not want to work too long on vapors—it needed hard fuel, the simple simian things, catching, grasping, manipulating.

It had been less than a day since he had met the Pankies, and already they had turned his solitary odyssey into a kind of punter's day trip. Just this moment they were wrangling over whether Mr. Pankie could catch a fish with a thread and a safety pin. His wife was of the strong opinion that he was far too clumsy, and that such tricks should be left to "clever Mr. Johnson"—the last said with a winning smile that Paul thought had more in common with the lure of a flesh-eating plant than with a normal human facial expression.

But the fact was, they were here, and he had been so subsumed in their relentless, small-minded normality that he had not thought about his own predicament at all. Which was both good and bad.

When he had arisen that morning, it was with more than a little distress to find the Pankies spruced up to the limits of their meager abilities and, as they put it, "set to go." Somehow the idea had developed, with no help from Paul, that he had offered to take them upriver, in search of something more closely resembling civilization than this park on the outskirts of Twickenham.

Mrs. Pankie's attempts to convince him of the benefits of company—"it will be almost like a holiday, won't it, like a jolly children's adventure?"—were almost enough in themselves to send him fleeing, but the couple's need was so naked that he could not turn them down.

But as they had made their way down the riverbank to his boat, which happily was still where he had left it, an odd thing happened. He had gone ahead to pull it all the way onto the shore—the idea of wrestling Undine through the water and trying to boost her into a rocking boat being more than he could bear—and when he turned to watch them coming down the bank, the two shapes, one massive and one small, sent a bolt of terror through him, a rush of fear so sudden and so powerful that for a moment he thought he was having a heart attack.

The things in the castle! He saw them clearly in those shapes on the riverbank, the two dreadful creatures that had been following him so long, the large hunter and the small, both heartless, both remorseless, both more terrifying than any mere human pursuers should be. And now they had caught him—no, he had delivered himself to them.

Then he blinked, and the Pankies were again just what they appeared: two unfortunate denizens of this unfortunate world. He squinted, steadying himself on the railing of the boat. Now that the panic had subsided, the situation did not *feel* the same as when his two stalkers had come close before: on those occasions he had felt naked fear from their mere proximity—a sensation as tangible as chill or nausea. But here, until he had seen the resemblance in the silhouettes, he had felt no alarm at anything except the possibility that Undine Pankie might talk all night.

And surely, if these people *were* his enemies, they could easily have taken him when he slept. . . .

Mrs. Pankie leaned on her hardworking little husband and waved, holding her crushed hat firmly on her head as the wind freshened. "Oh, look at the boat, Sefton. What a noble little craft!"

It was coincidence, he decided, that was all. One that had struck him on a very tender place, but a coincidence all the same.

* * *

But if the Pankies were not his enemies, he thought as the greenery of Hampton Wick slid past on the north bank, they had certainly managed to distract him, and that might be harmful in the long run. The fact was, he had a goal of sorts, and he had not come a whit closer to it as far as he could tell since crossing into this other England.

Her voice—the voice of the bird-woman in his dreams—had spoken to him through the Neandertal child and told him what to do. *"You said you would come to me,"* she had chided him. *"The wanderer's house. You must find it, and release the weaver."*

But who or what was the weaver? And where in this or any other world could he find something as vague as "the wanderer's house"? It was like being sent on the most obscure scavenger hunt imaginable.

Maybe I'm the wanderer, he thought suddenly. *But if so, and I found my house, then I wouldn't need anything else, would I? I'd be home.*

Unless I'm supposed to find my house, but find it here in this other London?

The prospect of actually doing something was intriguing. For a moment he was tempted to turn the boat and begin rowing back toward the crippled heart of London. Certainly the house in Canonbury that contained his flat would have been built by this time—most of his street was Georgian—but it was an open question as to whether there was anything of it left. And according to all accounts, the dead were much more numerous in the center of the city.

It seemed, the more he thought about it, a rather long chance— "wanderer" could mean so many things. But what other ideas did he have. . . ?

"He's muddled it again, Mr. Johnson. Stop it, dear, you'll just break the thread! Really, Mr. Johnson, you must come and help my Sefton."

Paul sighed quietly, his thoughts again scattered like the flotsam bobbing on the brown river.

The Thames narrowed as they approached Hampton Court, and for the first time Paul saw something almost like normal English life. As he soon discovered, the people here had followed in the wake of the tripods' original march, and a community of the dispossessed had begun to form a few months after the invasion. These refugee villages were even heralded by the unusual sight of smoke; the residents boldly tended their campfires and transacted their barter in the open, protected by a mile-wide perimeter of sentries with signal mirrors and a few precious guns. But Paul guessed that they had hiding places prepared—that, like rabbits grazing on a hillside, they would be gone to cover at the first hint of danger.

Mrs. Pankie was delighted to see a few small settlements at last, and when they made their first stop at one of them, she climbed out of the boat so quickly that she almost turned it over.

A man with a snarling dog on a rope leash traded them a heel of bread for news from the east. When Paul told him what he had seen only days before in the middle of London, the man shook his head sadly. "Our vicar in Chiswick said the city'd burn for its wickedness. But I can't see where any city could be *that* wicked."

The man went on to tell him there was actually a market of sorts at Hampton Court itself, which would be the best place to go for news and a chance for the Pankies to hook on with one of the local communities. " 'Course, no one takes in any what can't pull their weight," the man said, casting a dubious eye at Undine Pankie. "Times are too hard, they are."

Mrs. Pankie, rapturous at the mere thought of being able to set up housekeeping once more, ignored him. Sefton gave a curt little nod as they parted from the man, as though he realized his wife had been insulted, but was too much of a gentleman himself to acknowledge it.

The palace appeared shortly past a sharp bend in the river, its forest of turrets crowding up into the thin sunlight. There were a disappointingly small number of people ranged on the lawns above the Thames, but when Paul brought the boat in and helped hand Mrs. Pankie ashore, he was told by a woman sitting on a wagon that the market itself was in the Wilderness behind the palace.

"For that's what happened when we were in sight of the river before, and one of them Martian dreadnoughts came sailing past," she said, pointing to the Great Gatehouse, which had been smashed to blackened rubble. For yards in front of the fallen walls, the ground was as smooth and shiny as a glazed pot.

Mrs. Pankie hurried ahead through the grounds. Her husband struggled to keep up with her—like the bear her shape resembled, she was deceptively quick—but Paul decided on a more leisurely stroll. He passed several dozen people, some with what seemed their entire families loaded onto haywains. Others drove racy little traps and gigs that might once have been evidence of prosperity, but were now only flimsier methods of transportation than the farm wagons. No one smiled or did more than nod in return to his greetings, but these market-goers seemed far more ordinary than any of the other survivors he had met. Just the fact of having a market to go to, after so many black months, was enough to lift spirits. The Martians had come, and humanity was a conquered race, but life continued.

As he made his way across the cobbled parking lot toward the Tiltyard Gardens and the crowd of people he could see there, he reflected that whether this was the place the dream-woman had spoken of or not, it was at least an England, and he missed England. A terrible fate still hung over the heads of these people, and those who were here had already suffered terribly—whenever he began to forget the abnormal conditions, he saw another market-goer with missing limbs or terrible burn scars—but building a life out of the destruction he had seen at least had a purpose. He could not say as much for the rest of his journey to this point.

In fact, he realized, he was tired—tired of thinking, tired of traveling, tired of almost everything.

Leaving the red brick walls behind and crossing through into the greenery of the so-called Wilderness, actually a precise garden of hedges and yew trees, raised his spirits a little, even though here, too, patches of the scarlet alien grass had taken root. The market was in full swing. Piles of produce filled the backs of wagons, and barter was brisk. Everywhere he looked someone was vigorously denying the obvious truth someone else was promoting. If he squinted his eyes, it looked almost like a country fair from an old print. He could not see the Pankies anywhere, which was not entirely a tragedy.

As he stood surveying the crowd, which might have contained as many as two or three hundred people, he noticed a dark-haired, dark-complected man who seemed to be looking back at him with more than idle interest. When Paul's gaze met his, the newcomer dropped his eyes and turned away, but Paul could not shake the idea that the man had been watching him for some time. The dark-skinned man stepped past a pair of women haggling over a dog in a basket—Paul was not positive for what the animal was being sold, but he had a notion, and hoped Undine Pankie did not see—and vanished into the crowd.

Paul shrugged and wandered on. Other than his Asiatic features, which even in this earlier time were not impossibly rare, the man had seemed no different than anyone else, and he certainly had not triggered the kind of response Paul had come to associate with danger from his pursuers.

His thoughts were interrupted by the sudden appearance of the Pankies. Mrs. P. was in tears, and her husband was trying, rather ineffectually, to soothe her. For a moment, Paul thought she had seen the dog transaction and been reminded of poor cooked Dandy.

"Oh, Mr. Johnson, it's too cruel!" She clutched at his sleeve and turned her wide face up to him imploringly.

"Perhaps they only want to raise it as a guard dog . . ." he began, but the woman was not listening.

"I've just seen her—just the age our Viola would have been, if she hadn't . . . Oh, it's cruel, it's cruel."

"Here, now, Mrs. Pankie." Sefton looked around nervously. "You're making a scene."

"Viola?"

"Our little girl. She was just the *image*! I wanted to go speak to her, but Mr. Pankie wouldn't let me. Oh, my poor little girl!"

Paul shook his head. "Your little girl? But you said you had no . . ."

"Made up," said Sefton Pankie firmly, but Paul thought he heard panic in the man's voice. "A lark, really. We made up a child, you see—named her Viola. Isn't that right, Mrs. Pankie?"

Undine was sniffling and wiping at her nose with her sleeves. "My dear Viola."

". . . And this girl over by the hedges, well, she looked like we'd imagined . . . imagined this daughter might look. You see?" He produced a smile so sickly that Paul wanted to look away. Whatever this was, madness or duplicity, it felt like a glimpse into something he should not see.

Mrs. Pankie had stopped crying, and seemed to have realized she had overstepped herself. "I'm so sorry, Mr. Johnson." Her smile was no more reassuring than her husband's. "You must think me a fool. And I am—I'm an old fool."

"Not at all . . ." Paul began, but Sefton Pankie was already hustling his wife away.

"She just needs some air," he said over his shoulder, ignoring the fact that in the open gardens there was nothing but. "This has all been terribly hard on her . . . terribly hard."

Paul could only watch them stagger off into the crowd, the large leaning on the small.

He was standing by the tall hedges that marked the outside of the famous maze, chewing on some skewered meat that the man selling it had sworn up and down was goat. The vendor had exchanged these viands and a mug of beer for Paul's waistcoat, a price that though high did not seem at the moment out of line. Paul had drained off the beer in one swallow. A little comfort seemed very important just now.

His thoughts were whirling about, and he could not bring them to any order. Could it be as simple as it seemed—that the Pankies, in their insularity, had invented a story-child to fill their childless years? But what had they meant when they said the girl was just the age their Viola would have been, *if she hadn't. . .* ? Hadn't what? How could you lose—presumably to death—a child you had made up in the first place?

"You are a stranger here."

Paul jumped. The dark-skinned man was standing in the archway that formed the entrance to the maze, a serious expression on his face, his brown eyes wide.

"I . . . I am. I'm sure a lot of folk are. There isn't a market like this for miles and miles."

"No, there is not." The stranger gave a brief, perfunctory smile. "I would like very much to speak with you, Mr. . . ?"

"Johnson. Why? And who are you?"

The man answered only the first question. "Let us say that I have some information that might be of use to you, sir. To someone in . . . special circumstances, at any rate."

Paul's pulse had not returned to normal since the stranger had first spoken, and the careful words the man chose did not slow it any. "Then talk."

"Not here." The stranger looked grave. "But we will not go far." He turned and indicated the maze. "Come with me."

Paul had to make a decision. He did not trust the man at all, but as he had noticed earlier, he had no visceral fear-reaction to him, either. And, like Mr. Pankie, although not to the same degree, the stranger was not of a size to be very threatening. "Very well. But you still haven't told me your name."

"No," said the stranger, gesturing him through the turnstiles, "I have not."

As if to allay Paul's worries, the stranger kept at least a yard of physical distance between them at all times as he led him between the hedge-walls of the maze. Instead of offering revelations, though, he made small talk, asking Paul the state of affairs elsewhere—he did not know, or pretended not to know, where in England Paul had come from—and telling him in turn about the post-invasion rebuilding in the area around Hampton Court.

"Human beings, always they build again," the stranger said. "It is admirable, is it not?"

"I suppose." Paul stopped. "Listen, are you going to tell me anything real? Or were you just trying to get me in here so you can rob me or something?"

"If I were only robbing people, would I speak to them of special circumstances?" the man asked. "Because very few can have such understanding of those words as you, I am thinking."

Even as a premonitory chill ran down his spine, Paul finally realized what the very faint touch of accent was: the stranger, despite flawless English, was Indian or Pakistani. Paul decided the time had come to brazen it out.

"Suppose you're right. So what?"

Instead of rising to the bait, the stranger turned and walked on. After a moment, Paul hurried to catch up. "Just a little farther now," the man said. "Then we can talk."

"Start now."

The stranger smiled. "Very well. I will tell you first that your traveling companions are not what they seem."

"Really? What are they, then? Satan cultists? Vampires?"

The dark man pursed his lips. "I cannot tell you, exactly. But I know they are something other than a very nice, jolly couple from England." He spread his hands as they turned the hedge-corner and found themselves at the heart of the maze. "Here we are."

"This is ridiculous." Paul's anger fought hard to overcome a sickly, growing fear. "You haven't told me anything. You've dragged me all this way, and for what?"

"For this, I am afraid." The stranger lunged forward and grabbed Paul around the waist, imprisoning both his arms. Paul struggled, but the man was surprisingly strong. The light at the center of the maze abruptly began to change, as though the sun had suddenly changed direction.

"Halloo!" Mrs. Pankie's shrill cry came from a few passages away. "Halloo, Mr. Johnson? Are you there? Have you found the middle, you clever man?"

Paul could not get enough air to call for help. All around him, a yellow glow was spreading, making the benches and hedges and gravel path dim into buttery transparency. Recognizing the golden light, Paul intensified his struggles. For a moment he got a hand loose and grabbed at the dark man's thick black hair, then the other got a leg behind his, pushed him off balance, and forced him stumbling backward through the light and into sudden nothingness.

Second:

VOICES IN THE DARK

May she flow away—she who comes in the darkness,
Who enters in furtively
With her nose behind her, her face turned backward—
Failing in that for which she came!

Have you come to kiss this child?
  I will not let you kiss him!

Have you come to injure him?
  I will not let you injure him!

Have you come to take him away?
  I will not let you take him away from me!

—Ancient Egyptian Protective Charm

CHAPTER 13

The Dreams of Numbers

NETFEED/DOCUMENTARY: "Otherworld"—The Ultimate Network?
(visual: Neuschwanstein Castle, with fog rising from the Rhine)
VO: What kind of world would the richest people on Earth build for
themselves? BBN has announced that they are preparing documentary on
the "Otherworld" project, a simulation-world much whispered about in
virtual engineering circles. Does it exist? Many say that it is no more real
than Never Never Land or Shangri-La, but others claim that even if it has
been decommissioned, it did exist at one time, and was the single greatest
work of its type . . .

IT did not think. It did not live.

In fact, it possessed no faculty that had not been given to it by its creators, and at no point had it approached the crucial nexus at which it might—in the classic science-fictional trope—become more than the sum of its parts, more than simply an amalgam of time and effort and the best linear thinking of which its makers were capable.

And yet, in its growing complexity and unexpected, yet necessary, idiosyncrasy, and with no regard for the distinctions made by the meat intelligences which had created it, the Nemesis program *had* discovered a certain autonomy.

* * *

The program had been created by some of the best minds on the planet, the J-Team at Telemorphix. The full name of the group was Team Jericho, and although their patron and mentor Robert Wells had never made entirely clear what walls they were meant to bring tumbling down with this or any of their other projects, they nevertheless went at their assigned tasks with a certain *esprit de corps* common to those who considered themselves the very best and brightest. Wells' chosen were all gifted, intense, and frighteningly focused: there were stretches, in the searing heat of deadline, when they felt themselves to be nothing more than incorporeal minds—or, for brief moments, not even full mentalities, but only The Problem itself, in all its permutations and possible solutions.

Just as its creators were largely unconcerned with their own bodies—being content even at the best of times to dress them carelessly and feed them negligently, but when a project due date loomed, likely to ignore the demands of sleep and hygiene almost entirely—the Nemesis program was largely detached from the matrix in which it operated, the Grail Project (or, as those few who knew the whole truth called it, Otherland). Unlike the majority of inhabitants of that particular binary universe, which had been grown from artificial life templates to mimic the actions of living creatures, Nemesis was designed to mimic real-world organisms only insofar as it was necessary for smooth movement and inconspicuous surveillance, but it did not consider itself a part of the environment any more than a bird of prey considered itself part of the branches on which it occasionally came to rest.

Moreover, a hardwired obsession with the *being* of things rather than their *seeming* directed it, an impulse quite different from that which had been built into the other aggregations of code that imitated life throughout the network. Nemesis was a hunter, and although lately its need to hunt in the most efficient manner had brought it to contemplate certain changes in its mode of operation, it still could no more act as the normal artificial life objects within the Grail Project could act than it could spring free into the open air beyond the electronic universe.

Nemesis occupied its own reality. It had no body, and hence no bodily concerns, even when the cloud of values that accompanied it changed to create a new and convincing organism-imitation inside a simulation. But the mimicry of life was only for the benefit of observers—Nemesis itself was not *in* or *of* the simulations. It moved through them, above them, over them. It propagated through numerical space like a coherent fog, and was no more aware that it was simulating an endless array of bodies that would appear realistic to VR-abetted human sensory organs than rain could be aware it was wet.

Since the code-switch had been thrown, since the first command had, like lightning above Castle Frankenstein, brought it to its approximation of life, Nemesis had pursued its intractable needs in the linear fashion its creators had designed—search for anomalies, determine greatest/nearest anomaly, move toward it and examine for points of comparison, then, inevitably, move on, the quest still unsatisfied. But the whirling chaos of information that was the Otherland network, the sea of shifting values that humans, although they had created it, could scarcely comprehend, was not entirely what Nemesis had been programmed for. In fact, the difference between the conceptual map of Otherland which Nemesis had been given and the Otherland through which it moved were so different that the program had come close to being paralyzed in its very first moments by this simple and most basic paradox: *If the search is for anomalies, and everything is anomalous, then the starting point is also the ending point.*

But without knowing it, the fallible meat intelligences of the Telemorphix J-Team had given their creation more flexibility than they intended. In the ganglionic mesh of subroutines, the drive to hunt, to move forward, found the necessary distinctions that would allow it to treat Otherland as an undiscovered country, which thus freed it from its reliance on the original conception. It would find the pattern of this new, anomalous version of the matrix, and then look for anomalies to that pattern.

With this flexibility, however, came newer and greater complexity, and the realization that even after bypassing the initial problem, the task as constituted could not be completed. The smaller anomalies of the system, the kind which Nemesis had been created to examine, were too many: Nemesis as originally constituted could not inspect and consider them all as fast as new ones arose.

But it was not an impossible disparity. The J-Team, those deities that Nemesis could not imagine, and hence could not worship or even fear, had only failed in their estimates by a smallish factor. Thus, if some degradation of perception could be allowed without spoiling the ultimate success of its hunt, Nemesis could divide itself for greater coverage. Although the program had no perception of an "I," a controlling intelligence at the center of itself—a convenient illusion that its creators universally shared—it nevertheless operated as a central control point, a processing nexus. Subdividing that control point would reduce its capacities in each subordinate unit, but would allow faster processing of the gross inspections.

There was another factor arguing for subdivision as well, a strange thing which had come to the Nemesis program's notice and sparked its cold interest. During its timeless hours of movement and inspection, as it floated on the number-winds and learned from their shape and force, it had become aware of something else, something so far from the conceptual map of the environment it had originally been given as to briefly constitute a new danger to the Nemesis program's logical integrity.

Somewhere—another metaphor that meant nothing to the program, since information space had no recourse to physical distance or direction, except to simulate them for humans—somewhere on the distant edge of Otherland, things were . . . *different.*

Nemesis did not know how they were different, any more than it knew how something in a universe without spatial distance could be far away, but it knew that both things were true. And, for the first time, Nemesis felt a pull that could not entirely be explained by its programming. It was another anomaly, of course, something the human creators had not known of or even suspected, but this anomaly was of such a different order to those which drew the program's hunting attention that it should most likely have gone unnoticed, as something which does not move at all is invisible to certain predators. But something about this distant "place," where things were different, where the currents of numerate existence moved in a new and—to Nemesis—incomprehensible way, had caught its attention, and now had become the closest thing to an obsession that a soulless, lifeless piece of code could entertain.

So, of the many subordinate versions of itself it would create, while committing a kind of suicide-by-diminishment of its central self, Nemesis had decided it would designate one carefully-constructed subself to go in search of this Greater Anomaly, to fare outward on the currents of information toward that unimaginably distant no-place, and—if it could—to bring back something resembling Truth.

Nemesis did not think. It did not live. And only someone who did not understand the limits of simple code, the chill purity of numbers, would dare to suggest that it might dream.

CHAPTER 14

Games In The Shadows

"**C**ODE *Delphi. Start here.*
    "I used to love the rain. If there is anything I miss because
I have lived so long in my home beneath the ground, it is the feeling
of rain on my skin.

"Lightning, too—that bright slash in the sky, as though for a moment the universe of matter had been torn open to reveal the transcendent light of eternity. If there is anything I miss because of the way I am, it is the sight of God's magnificent face peering through a crack in the universe."

"My name is Martine Desroubins. I can no longer continue my journal by normal methods, as I will explain, so I am subvocalizing these entries into . . . into nothingness, for all I know . . . in the hope that someday, somehow, I will be able to retrieve them. I have no idea what sort of system underlies the Otherland network, or the extent of its memory—it may be that these words will indeed be lost forever, just as if I had shouted them into a high wind. But I have made a ritual of these summations, these self-reflections, for too many years to stop now.

"Perhaps someone else will pull these words out of the matrix someday, years from now, when all the things that concern me now, that frighten me so, will be past history. What will you think, person from the future? Will the things I say even make sense? You do not know me. In fact, even though I have kept this journal all my adult life, sometimes I still find myself listening to the thoughts of a stranger.

"Am I speaking to the future, then, or like all the madwomen of history, am I only mumbling to myself, alone in a vast personal darkness?

"There is no answer, of course."

"There have been times before this when I have gone days without keeping this journal—weeks even, during illnesses—but never has the empty time hidden changes as astonishing as what I have experienced since I last set out my thoughts. I do not know where to begin. I simply do not know. Everything is different now.

"In a way, it is wonderful that I can even take up my journal once more. For a time, I feared I would not think coherently again, but as the days—or the illusion of days—go by in this place, I am finding it a little easier to suffer the stunning wash of input that is Otherland, or as its creators call it, the Grail Project. My physical skills, too, have improved somewhat, but I am still childishly clumsy and confused by the world around me, still almost as helpless as when I first lost my sight twenty-eight years ago. That was a terrible time, and I had sworn never to be so helpless again. God makes a point of calling one's bluff, it seems. I cannot say that I approve of His sense of humor.

"But I am not a child any more. I wept then, wept every night, and begged Him to give me back my sight—give me back the world, for that is what it seemed I had lost. He did not help me, and neither did my fretting, ineffectual parents. Helping was beyond their power. I do not know whether it was beyond His."

"It is strange to think of my mother and father, after so long. It is stranger still to think that they are still alive, and at this moment are living perhaps less than a hundred kilometers from my physical body. The distance between us was already so great, even before I crossed over into this inexplicable Otherland—this imaginary universe, this toy of monstrous children.

"My parents meant no harm. There are worse summations you can make of people's lives, but that is small comfort. They loved me—they still do, I am sure, and my separation from them probably causes them great pain—but they did not protect me. That is hard to forgive, especially when the damage was so great.

"My mother Genevieve was an engineer. So was my father Marc. Neither of them got on well with other people; both felt more comfortable with the certainties of numbers and schematics. They found each other like two timid forest creatures and, recognizing a shared outlook, decided to hide from the darkness together. But you cannot hide from darkness—the more lights, the more shadows they make. I remember this well from the time when there was still light for me.

"We scarcely went out. What I remember is sitting in front of the wallscreen every evening, watching one of the science fiction shows they loved so much. Always linear dramas—interactives did not interest them. They interacted with their work and each other and, marginally, with me. That was quite enough commitment to the world outside their own heads. As the wallscreen flickered, I colored in coloring books, or read, or played with building toys, and my parents sat on the overstuffed couch behind me smoking hashish—'discreetly' is how they once phrased it—and chattering to each other about some silly scientific mistake or piece of illogic in one of their beloved shows. If it was one they had seen before, they would discuss the mistake again just as cheerfully and exhaustively as they had the first time they had spotted it. Sometimes I wanted to scream at them to be quiet, to stop talking nonsense.

"They both worked at home, of course, most of their contact with colleagues coming through the net. That had undoubtedly been one of the most important things for them about their chosen profession. If it had not been for my school, I might never have left the house at all.

"My parents' lack of engagement with the outside world, at first largely a bemused disinterest, began to sour over the years. My mother in particular became more and more fearful of all the hours when I was out of her sight, as though I were some daring child astronaut who had left our safe spaceship home, and the quiet streets of the Toulouse suburbs were an alien landscape full of monsters. She wanted me back on board as soon as school was over. By the time I was seven years old, if there had really been such a science-fiction thing as a teleport machine to bring me instantaneously from my classroom back to the living room, she would have bought one, no matter how expensive.

"In the early part of my childhood, when they were both working, they might even have been able to afford such a device if it had existed . . . but things went wrong. My father's casual cheeriness was a mask over a kind of stunned helplessness in the face of any complication. One unpleasant executive hired in above him eventually drove him from a company he had helped found, and he was forced to settle for a lower-paying job. My mother's job vanished through no fault of her own—the company lost its contract with AEE, the European Space Agency, and her entire division was eliminated—but she found it almost impossible to go out and look for a new one. She made excuses and stayed home, living more and more on the net. My parents clung to their house in the quiet suburbs, but as months went by, they found it very expensive. The stoned discussions sometimes grew tense and accusatory. They sold their expensive processing station to a friend and replaced it with a cheap, second-hand model made somewhere in West Africa. They stopped buying new things. We ate cheaply, too—my mother made soup by the gallon, grumbling like a princess forced to be a scullery maid. Even now, I equate the scent of boiling vegetables with unhappiness and quiet rage.

"I was eight when the offer came—old enough to know that things were wrong at home without having the slightest ability to change anything. A friend of my father's suggested that my mother might be able to find work at a certain research company. She wasn't interested—nothing except a very bad fire would have driven her out of the house at that point, I think, and I am not sure even of that—but my father followed up, thinking perhaps he could find some extra part-time work there.

"That did not happen, although he went through several interviews and got to know one of the project managers fairly well. This woman, who I honestly think was trying to do my father a favor, mentioned that although they did not need any more engineers at present, they did need test subjects for a particular project, and the company funding the research paid very well.

"My father volunteered. She informed him that he did not fit their requirements, but from what she could see on his application form, his eight-year-old daughter did. It was an experiment in sensory development, funded by the Clinsor Group, Swiss-based specialists in medical technologies. Was he interested?

"To his credit, my father Marc did not instantly say yes, although the amount being offered was nearly as much as his wages for a year. He came home in a rather disturbed mood. He and my mother carried on whispered discussions all through the evening's linear dramas and louder ones after they had put me to bed. I discovered later that although neither of them were firmly for or against the idea, the shifting disagreement spawned by the offer brought them closer to separation than anything else in their marriage. How typical of them—even when they were having the worst argument of their lives, they did not know what they wanted.

"Three nights later, after a few calls for reassurance to the pseudo-academic organization being paid to perform the study—I do not exaggerate or insult here, since there were few universities left even then who did not owe their souls to corporate sponsorship—my parents had convinced themselves it would be all for the good. I think, in their strange and unsocialized way, they had even begun to believe that something important might come out of it for me personally, something more than simply money for the family—that some hidden aptitude of mine would emerge in the testing, and I would prove to be an even more exceptional child than they believed me to be.

"They were right in one sense—it did change my life forever.

"I remember my mother coming into my room. I had left early and gone to bed with a book because their strange, almost . . . somnambulistic, that is the word—their somnambulistic squabbling of the preceding days had made me nervous, and I looked up guiltily when she came in, as though I had been caught doing something wrong. The paint-thinner smell of hashish clung to her ragged jumper. She was a little dopey, as she often was by that time of the night, and for a moment, as she tried to think of how she wanted to explain the news to me, her slow inarticulacy frightened me. She seemed something not quite human—an animal, or some kind of alien doppelganger from one of the netshows that had run as background through my childhood.

"As she explained their decision I grew even more frightened. I was going to stay by myself for just a little while, she told me, and help some people with an experiment. Nice men and women—*strangers,* was what she really meant—were going to take care of me. It would help my family, and it would be interesting. All the other girls and boys in my school would be jealous of me when I came back.

"How could even a woman as self-absorbed as my mother have thought this would do anything but fill me with dread? I cried all night and for days afterward. My parents acted as though I were merely afraid of going off to summer camp or the first day of school, and told me that I was making a fuss over nothing, but even they must have realized there was something questionable about their parenting. They gave me my favorite desserts every night and went two weeks without smoking hash so they could save the money to buy me a new outfit.

"I wore the new coat and dress on the day I traveled to the institute. Only my father went with me on the plane to Zurich—at this point my mother could not even go down to drop a parcel in the corner letter box without hours of preparation. When we landed, on a day so gray that I have never forgot its dull metallic color through all the intervening darkness, I felt sure that my father was planning to abandon me, as the father of Hansel and Gretel had left his children in the forest. The people from the Pestalozzi Institute met us in a big black car, exactly the kind of vehicle little girls are instructed never to get into. It all seemed very secretive and ominous. What little I saw of Switzerland on the trip to the institute frightened me—the buildings were strange and there was snow on the ground already, although it had been pleasantly warm in Toulouse. When we got to the complex of low buildings, surrounded by gardens that must have been cheerful in a more cheerful season, they asked my father if he wished to spend the first night with me before the experiment began. He already had his ticket back that evening, more worried about leaving my mother alone than leaving me. I cried and would not kiss him good-bye.

"Strange, strange . . . the whole thing was strange. I asked my parents later—no, *demanded* that they tell me how they could send a young child away like that. They could offer no reason except that it seemed a good idea at the time. 'Who could ever imagine this would happen, dear?' is what my mother said. Who indeed? Perhaps someone who thought about things beyond the wallscreen and the living room.

"Oh, it makes me so angry even now.

"In their way, the workers at the Pestalozzi Institute were very kind. They worked with many children, and the Swiss do not love their sons and daughters less than other people do. There were several counselors on staff whose entire job was to help the subjects of research—for almost all the institute's work was with childhood development—feel comfortable. I remember a Mrs. Fuerstner who was particularly kind. I often wonder what happened to her. She was no older than my mother, so she is probably alive today, perhaps still in Zurich. I think it is safe to say she is not working for the institute, however.

"I was given a few days to become used to the idea of my new surroundings. I shared a dormitory-type room with many other children, most of whom spoke French, so I was not lonely in the ordinary sense of the word. We were well fed, and our keepers provided every kind of toy and game. I watched science fiction programs from the net, although they seemed curiously lifeless without my parents' running commentary.

"At last Mrs. Fuerstner introduced me to Doctor Beck, a golden-haired woman who I thought as pretty as a storybook princess. As the doctor explained in her sweet, patient voice about what I would be asked to do, I found it harder and harder to believe that anything bad would happen. Such a beautiful lady would never try to hurt me. And even if some mistake were made, I knew that Mrs. Fuerstner would not allow me to come to harm. You see, I had always been protected—although not in the most important ways, I later realized—and now these good people were assuring me that at least in that regard, nothing would change.

"I was to be part of an experiment in sensory deprivation. I am still not certain exactly what the institute thought it would learn from these exercises. At the hearings, they said they had been commissioned to study baseline biological rhythms, but also to examine how environmental factors affect learning and development. What use this would be to a medical and pharmaceutical multinational like the Clinsor Group was never made clear, but the Clinsor people had a huge research budget and many interests—the Pestalozzi Institute was only one of the many beneficiaries of their largess.

"It would be a sort of unusual holiday, Doctor Beck explained to me. I would be staying by myself in a very dark, very quiet room—like my room at home, but with its own bathroom. There would be plenty of toys and games and exercises to keep me occupied, but I would have to do them all in the dark. But I would not be alone, the doctor explained, not really, because she or Mrs. Fuerstner would always be listening over the speakers. I could call them any time and they would speak to me. It would only be for a few days, and when it was all over, I would get as much cake and ice cream as I could eat, and any toy I wanted.

"And my parents, she did not bother to add, would get paid.

"It seems silly to say this now, falsely significant, but as a child I had never been particularly afraid of the dark. In fact, if this were a story, I would begin my journal entry that way—'As a child, I was never afraid of the dark.' Of course, if I had known that I would be spending the rest of my life in darkness, I might have resisted that first descent.

"Much of the information the Pestalozzi Institute gathered from me and the other child subjects of their sensory-deprivation testing was essentially redundant. That is, it only confirmed that which had already been discovered in adult subjects, people who had been a long time underground, in caves or lightless cells. Child subjects displayed a few differences from adults—they adapted better in the long run, although they were also more likely to be adversely affected in their long-term development—but such obvious findings seem a very small result for such an expensive program. Years later, when I went back and read the company researchers' testimony from the lawsuit, I was furious to see how little wisdom the loss of my happiness had gained.

"At first, as Doctor Beck had said, it was very simple. I ate, played, and went about my days in the dark. I went to sleep in total darkness, and woke up in the same black nothing, often to the sound of one of the researchers' voices. I came to rely on those voices, and even, after a while, to *see* those voices. They had colors, shapes—things that I cannot easily describe, just as I cannot describe to my current traveling companions how my perceptions of this artificial world differ from theirs. I was getting my first taste of the synaesthesia brought on by narrowed sensory input, I suppose.

"The games and exercises were simple things at first, sound-identification puzzles, things that tested my time-sense and memory, physical routines to see how darkness affected my balance and general coordination. I'm sure that what I ate and drank and excreted were also being monitored.

"It was not long until I began to lose all grasp of time. I slept when I was tired, and if the researchers did not wake me, might sleep for twelve hours or more—or, just as likely, for forty-five minutes. And, not surprisingly, I awakened from these slumbers with no sense of how long I had been away. This in itself did not trouble me—it is only with age that we learn to fear loss of control over time—but other things did. I missed my parents, ineffectual though they were, and without being able to explain it, I think I had even begun to fear I would never be returned to the light.

"This fear proved prophetic, of course.

"From time to time Doctor Beck let me talk to one of the other children over the audio channel of the blanked wallscreen. Some of them were in isolated darkness as I was, others were in the light. I do not know what the researchers learned—we were children, after all, and although children can play together, they are not conversationalists. But one child was different. The first time I heard his voice, it frightened me. It hummed and quacked—in my mind's eye the sound had a hard, angular shape, like an ancient mechanical toy—and its accent was nothing I had ever heard. In retrospect I can say that the sounds came from a voice synthesizer, but at the time I created quite fearful mental pictures of what or who would have such a tongue in its head.

"The strange voice asked me my name, but did not offer its own. It sounded hesitant, and there were many long pauses. The whole matter seems strange to me now, and I wonder whether I might have spoken to some kind of artificial intelligence, or some autistic child whose deficits were being improved upon by technology, but at the time I remember being both fascinated and frustrated by this new playmate, who took so long to speak, and spoke so strangely when the words finally came.

"He was alone, he said. He was in darkness, too, as I was, or at least he did not seem to be able to see—he never spoke of vision, except in half-learned metaphor. Perhaps he was blind, as I am now blind. He did not know where he was, but he wanted to come out—he said that repeatedly.

"This new playmate was only with me a few minutes the first time, but on later occasions we spoke longer. I taught him some of the sound-only games the researchers had used on me, and I sang him songs and told him some of the nursery rhymes I knew. He was curiously slow to understand some things, and so quick with others as to be alarming—at times it seemed he was sitting with me in my pitch-black room, somehow watching everything I did.

"On our fifth or sixth 'visit,' as Doctor Beck called them, he told me that I was his friend. You cannot imagine a more heart-rending admission, and it will stay with me always.

"I have spent many days of my adult life trying to find that lost child—following the institute's records down every fruitless alley, tracking everyone who was ever involved with the Pestalozzi experiments—but I have had no luck. Now I wonder if it was a child at all. Were we perhaps the subjects of a Turing test of some kind? The training ground for a program that might someday be able to smoothly fool adults, but at this early stage could only flounder through conversations with eight-year-olds, and not very well?

"Whatever the case, I did not speak to him again. Because something else happened.

"I had been in darkness for many days—over three weeks. The institute's researchers were ready to bring my portion of the experiment to a close within another forty-eight hours. Thus, I was being given a particularly complex and thorough set of final diagnostic tests— delivered with pseudomaternal sweetness by Mrs. Fuerstner—when something went wrong.

"Depositions from the lawsuit are unclear, because the Pestalozzi people themselves are not certain, but something went gravely wrong in the institute's complex house system. I experienced it at first as the loss of Mrs. Fuerstner's soft, bewitching voice in mid-sentence. The hum of the air-conditioners, which had been a constant part of the environment, suddenly stopped as well, leaving behind a silence that was actually painful to my ears. Everything was gone—everything. All the friendly sounds which had made the darkness seem something less than infinite had ended.

"After a few minutes, I began to feel frightened. Perhaps there had been a robbery, I thought, and bad men had taken Doctor Beck and the others away. Or maybe some kind of big monster had got loose and killed them, and was now sniffing up and down the corridors, looking for me. I rushed to the thick, soundproofed door of my quarters, but of course with the system power gone, the door locks were frozen. I could not even lift up the hatch of the blackout slot where my meals were delivered. Terrified, I screamed for the doctor, for Mrs. Fuerstner, but no one came or answered. The darkness became dreadful to me in a way it had not in all the days before, a *thing,* thick and tangible. I felt it would take my breath, squeeze me until I choked, until I gasped in blackness itself and filled up with it, like someone drowning in a sea of ink. And still there was nothing—no noise, no voices, a silence like the tomb.

"I know now, from depositions, that it took nearly four hours for the institute's engineers to get the system up and running. To little Martine, the child I was, forgotten in the dark, it could have been four years.

"Then, at the last, as my mind wandered along the brink of an abyss, ready at any moment to tumble into a disassociation more permanent and total than any mere blindness, something joined me.

"Suddenly, and with no warning, I was no longer alone. I felt someone beside me, sharing the darkness with me, but it was not a relief to my terror. That someone, whoever or whatever it was, filled the emptiness in my apartment with the most dreadful, indescribable loneliness. Did I hear a child crying? Did I hear anything at all? I do not know. I do not know anything now, and at the time I was probably mad. But I felt something come and sit beside me, and felt it weeping bitterly in the smothering black night, a presence that was empty and cold and utterly alone, the single most terrible thing I have ever experienced. I was struck dumb and rigid with utter terror.

"And then the lights came on.

"Odd, the small things on which life hinges. Reaching an intersection just after the traffic light has changed, going back for a wallet and thus missing a plane, walking into the revealing glow of a streetlight when a stranger is watching—small happenstances, but they can change everything. The institute's system crash alone, massive and inexplicable as it was, should not have been enough. But one of the infrastructure subroutines had been incorrectly coded—the matter of a few misplaced digits—and the three apartments on my wing had been left out of the proper start-up procedures. Thus, when the system came up and the power went on, instead of the dull, slow-brightening glow of the transition lights, little more than a sliver of moon on a black night, our three apartments received the full thousand-watt nova of the emergency lights. The other two apartments were empty— one had not been used for weeks, the other's resident had been taken to the institute's infirmary a few days earlier because of chicken pox. I was the only one who saw the emergency lights come up like the blazing stare of God. Saw them for an instant, that is—the last thing I ever saw.

"It is not physical, they tell me, all of them—more specialists than I can remember. The trauma, bad as it was, should not have been permanent. There is no discernible damage to the optic nerve, and the tests indicate that I do actually 'see'—that the part of my brain that processes vision is still processing and responding to stimuli. But, of course, I *don't* see, no matter what any test may indicate.

" 'Hysterical blindness' is the old term—another way of saying that I could see if I wanted to. If that is true, it is only an academic truth. If I could see by wanting to, then I would not have spent all my years in blackness—could anyone believe anything else? But that one burning instant drove all memory of how to see from my mind, blasting me into permament blackness, creating in an instant the woman I am today as surely as Saul's new self was created on the Damascus road.

"I have lived in darkness ever since.

"The lawsuit was long—it took almost three years—but I remember little of it. I had been thrust into another world, as surely as if I had been enchanted by an evil fairy, and I had lost everything. It took a long time until I began to make a new world in which I could live. My parents won several million credits from Clinsor and the Pestalozzi Institute, and put almost half of it away for me. That money put me through special schools, and when I became an adult, it bought me my equipment, my home, and my privacy. In a way, it bought me my distance from my parents, too—there is nothing I need from them anymore.

"There is more to say, but the time has gone so fast. I do not know how long I have sat here whispering under my breath, but I can feel the sun beginning to rise in this strange place. In a way, I have started over here, just as I have started this new diary, spoken into nothingness with only the faintest hope that someday I can retrieve it. Was it the English poet Keats who called himself 'one whose name is written in water'? So. I will be Martine Desroubins, the blind witch of a new world, and I will write my name on air.

"Someone is calling me. I must go.

"Code Delphi. End here."

IT was a melodic sequence of chiming tones that spawned fractal sub-sequences even as the main theme repeated. The sub-sequences threw off subsidiary patterns of their own, creating layer after layer, until after a while the whole world became a mesh of sound so complex it was impossible to pick out one tone, let alone one sequence, from the whole. Eventually it became a single note with millions of harmonics moving in it, a streaming, shimmering, resonating F-sharp that was probably the sound of the universe beginning.

It was Dread's thinking music. Next to the chase, and the occasional adrenal boost, it was his only drug. He did not use it indiscriminately, hungrily, as a chargehead might canline a streamed pop of *2black,* but rather with the measured calm of a junkie doctor rigging up a hit of pure pharmaceutical heroin before going back to work. He had cleared the afternoon, hung a digital "Do Not Disturb" sign on his incoming lines, and now he was lying on his back in the middle of the carpet of his Cartagena office, a pillow behind his neck and a squeeze bottle of purified water at his side, listening to the chorus of the spheres.

As the single tone seemed to grow smoother and less complex—because, paradoxically, the iterations were growing exponentially, he felt himself rising up out of his body and into the empty silver space he sought. He was Dread, but he was also Johnny Wulgaru, and he was something else as well, something eerily close to the Old Man's Messenger of Death—but he was *more.* He was all those things, grown to the size of a star system . . . empty, full of blackness, and yet charged with light.

He felt the *twist* smolder up out of dormancy, a hot point at the very center of his being. Even as he floated in the silver nothingness of the music, he felt his own strength grow. He could reach out now, if he chose, and twist something far more complex and powerful than a security system. He had a glimpse of the earth lying below him, shrouded in darkness but for a spherical tracery of electronic pathways, a capillary array of tiny lights, and felt—in his silvery, music-maddened grandeur—that if he desired it, he could twist the whole world.

Somewhere, Dread felt himself laughing. It was worth laughing about. Too much, too much.

But was that how the Old Man felt? Was that what the Old Man's kind of power felt like, all the time? That the world was his, to do with as he wished? That people like Dread were just tiny spots of light, less significant than fireflies?

Even if so, Dread was not bothered. He was wrapped in his own silver smugness and did not need to envy or fear the Old Man. All would change, and very soon now.

No, he had other things to consider now, other dreams to dream. He let the single pulsing tone take him out of himself again. The twist warmed him as he returned to the cool, silvery place, the place where he could see far ahead and consider all the small things he needed to do along the way.

Dread lay on the bare office floor and listened to his thinking music.

She took an irritatingly long time to answer the call. He had already tapped in on the sim line and knew that the Otherland travelers were sleeping. What was she doing, taking another one of her showers? No wonder she was obsessed with her cat—she was practically one herself, constantly grooming. The bitch needed a little discipline . . . maybe the creative kind.

No, he reminded himself. *Remember the silver place.* He brought up a little music—not the thinking music (he had used his week's allotment, and he was very stern with himself about such things) but a faint echo, a quiet tonal splashing like water dripping in a pool. He would not let irritation spoil things. This was the thing he had been waiting for all his life.

Although the call carried his signature code, her voice came on without visuals. "Hello?"

Silver place, he told himself. *The big picture.* "It's me, Dulcie. What, did you just get out of the bath again?"

Dulcie Anwin's freckled face popped into view. She was indeed wearing a terrycloth robe, but her red hair was dry. "I just left the picture off when I answered the phone earlier, and forgot to turn it back on."

"Whatever. We've got a problem with our project."

"You mean because they've split up again?" She rolled her eyes. "If things go on this way, we'll be the only sim left. With the barbarian boys gone, we're down to four—five, counting ours."

"That's not the problem, although I'm not very happy about it." Dread saw a shadow move in the kitchen door behind her. "Is there someone there with you?"

Puzzled, she turned to look. "Oh, for God's sake. It's Jones. My cat. Do you honestly think I'd be having this conversation with you if someone else was here?"

"No, of course not." He turned the splashing music up a little louder, creating an annoyance-soothing calm for himself out of which he could produce a smile. "I'm sorry, Dulcie. A lot of work on this end."

"Too much work, is my bet. You must have been planning the . . . the project we just finished for months. When did you last take some time off?"

As if he were some poor, downtrodden middle-manager. Dread was inwardly amused. "Not for a while, but that's not what I want to talk about. We have a problem. Not only can't we bring in a third person to help drive the sim, we can't even use two people anymore."

She frowned. "What do you mean?"

"I guess you haven't been paying attention." He tried to make it sound light, but he was not happy to have to point out something so obvious, especially in light of what he was going to ask her. "This Martine—the blind woman. If she is telling the truth, and I see no reason to doubt it, then she's a real danger to us."

Dulcie, as though realizing she had been caught napping, now abruptly put on her professional face. "Go ahead."

"She processes information in ways we don't understand. She says she senses things in the virtual environment that you and I—or the rest of the Sky God refugees—can't feel. If she hasn't noticed yet that our sim is being inhabited by two different people, it's only a matter of time until she works through that white-noise problem of hers and it becomes clear to her."

"Ah." Dulcie nodded, then turned and walked back toward her couch. She sat down and lifted a cup to her lips and took a sip before speaking. "But I *did* think of that."

"You did?"

"I figured that the worst thing we could do would be to suddenly change whatever subliminal cues we're giving off." She took another sip, then stirred whatever was in the cup with a spoon. "She might already have developed a signature for us, and just accept it as what our sim gives off. But if we change again, then she'd notice something different. That's what I thought, anyway."

Some of Dread's early admiration for Dulcinea Anwin returned. Complete bullshit, but pretty good for something she'd thrown together on the spot. He couldn't help wondering if she'd sit there so calm and self-satisfied if she ever saw him in his true skin—was made witness to his true self, when all the masks were thrown aside. . . . He wrenched himself from the distracting line of thought. "Hmmm. I see what you mean. That makes sense, too, but I'm not sure I buy it entirely."

He could see her decide to try to consolidate what her quick thinking had bought her. "You're the boss. What do *you* think we should do? I mean, what are our options?"

"Whatever we're going to do, we should make a quick decision. And if we don't go on with things as they are, the only other option is for one of us to take over the sim full time."

"Full time?" She almost lost her hard-won composure. "That's . . ."

"Not a very appealing idea, I know. But we may have to do it—in fact, *you* may have to do it, since I've got so bloody much to do. But I'll think about what you said and call you back later. This evening, 2200 hours your time, right? The sim should be asleep then, or we can wander it off from the group to take a leak or something."

Her poorly-hidden irritation amused him. "Sure. 2200 hours."

"Thanks, Dulcie. Oh, a question. Do you know many old songs?"

"What? Old *songs?*"

"I'm just curious about something I heard. It goes . . ." He suddenly didn't want to sing to her—it would feel like he were surrendering a little of his edge to someone who was, after all, his subordinate. He chanted it instead: ". . . 'An angel touched me, an angel touched me . . .' Like that. Over and over."

Dulcie stared at him as though he might be engaged in some particularly devious trick. "Never heard it before. What got you so interested?"

He gave her his best smile—his *I'd be happy to give you a ride, sweetness* smile. "Nothing much. It sounded familiar, but I can't put my finger on it. 2200 hours, then." He clicked off.

*   *   *

*"C*ODE Delphi. Start here.

"It was only the river. Strange how even with ears as sharp as mine, ears augmented by the best sound-carrying equipment lawsuit money could buy—which are now processing information from what is apparently the best sound-generating equipment that Grail Brotherhood money can buy—I can still be fooled by the noise of running water.

"I have been thinking about this new journal, and I realize that I have begun it on a very pessimistic note. I am hoping that someday these entries can be retrieved, but to spend so much time talking about my own history seems to assume that someone other than myself will be the one to hear these thoughts. That may be pragmatic, but it is not the right spirit. I must pretend that I will one day rescue these thoughts myself. When I do, I will want to be reminded how I felt right at this moment.

"I cannot say much about coming through into this network, because I remember so little. The security system, whatever it was, seems to me of the same character as the program that captures children, the deep-hypnosis gear which Renie described so horrifyingly from her experience in the virtual nightclub. It seems to operate at a level below the subject's consciousness, and to cause involuntary physical effects. But I remember only a sense of something angry and vicious. Clearly it is a program or neural net whose sophistication and power dwarfs the things I know about.

"But since entering the network I have gradually found my way back through the awful, battering noise, both real and metaphorical, to a kind of sanity I feared I would never find again. And I can do things I never could do before. I have passed beyond the confusion into an entirely new realm of sensory input, like Siegfried splashed by the dragon's blood. I can hear a leaf fall, the grass grow. I can smell a drop of water trembling on a leaf. I can feel the very weather in its complicated, semi-improvisational dance, and guess which direction it will step next. In a way, it is all quite seductive—like a young eagle standing on a branch and spreading its wings against the open wind for the first time, I have the sensation of limitless possibility. It will be hard to give this up again, but of course I pray that we will succeed, and that I will live to do so. I suppose at such a time I would give it all up happily, but I cannot imagine such a thing convincingly.

"In fact, it is almost impossible to imagine success. Four of our number have been pulled away from us already. We have no way of knowing where Renie and !Xabbu have gone, and my sense of them being here, in this particular place, has sharply diminished. Orlando and his young friend have been swept away down the river. I do not doubt that the boys, at least, have passed through into one of the uncountable numbers of other simulations.

"And so we are five. The four who are lost are perhaps the four I would have preferred to stay with—Renie Sulaweyo in particular, despite her prickliness, has become almost a friend, and I find that I miss her very much—but, to be fair, perhaps that is only because I do not know the other four well yet. But they are a strange group, especially in contrast to the openness of !Xabbu and Renie, and I am not entirely easy with them.

"Sweet William is the strongest presence, but I would like to believe his sour irony hides that oldest of clichés, a kind heart. Certainly when we returned to the beach and found him and T4b, there was little question that William was devastated to have seen Orlando and Fredericks taken away. He feels, to my new and as yet not completely understood sensitivities, curiously incomplete. There is a hesitancy to him at times, despite his brash manner, like someone who is afraid of discovery. I wonder what his refusal to discuss his real life hides.

"The old woman, Quan Li, appears less complex, but perhaps she only wishes it to seem that way. She is solicitous and quiet, but she has made some surprisingly good suggestions, and she is certainly stronger underneath than she pretends. Several times during the afternoon, when even tough-minded Florimel was ready to quit the search for Renie and !Xabbu, Quan Li managed to find the resources to push on, and we could only be shamed into following her. Am I reading too much into things? It is not surprising that someone from her culture and generation might feel the need to hide her abilities behind a mask of diffidence. Still . . . I do not know.

"Florimel, who is as aggressively private as William, troubles me most of all. On the surface, she is all business, terse and almost contemptuous of the needs of others. But she herself seems at other times to be barely holding together, although I doubt anyone else would notice that but me. There are such strange fluctuations in her . . . what is the word? *Affect,* I think. There are such odd but subtle changes in her affect that at times it seems like she is a multiple personality. But I have never heard of a multiple personality pretending to be only one person. From what I understand, in true multiples each internal personage revels in its chance to become dominant.

"Still, my ability to understand all that I perceive is still limited, so perhaps I am mistaken, or am overinterpreting small oddities in her behavior. She is strong and brave. She has done no wrong and much good. I should judge her on that alone.

"Last of this small group, which may contain all that are left of

Sellars' desperate attempt to solve the Otherland enigma—after all, we can only hope that Renie and the others have survived—is the young man who calls himself T4b. That he *is* a man is also an assumption, of course. But certainly there are times when his energies and presentation feel decidedly *male* to me—he has a barely-hidden swagger sometimes that I have never seen on any woman. But he can be careful, too, in a curiously feminine way, which is why I assume he is younger than he pretends. It is impossible to discern age or anything else from his street dialect, which forces a few short words to serve a variety of meanings—he might be as young as ten or eleven for all I can tell.

"So here I am, with four people who are strangers, in a dangerous place surrounded by, I have no doubt, even *more* dangerous places. Our enemies must number in the thousands, with immense power and wealth on their side, and the controls to these pocket universes in their hands. We, in contrast, have already seen our number halved in just a few days.

"We are doomed, of course. If we even survive to reach the next simulation, it will be a miracle. There is danger everywhere. A spider the size of a truck caught an insect a few meters from me just yesterday afternoon—I could hear the fly's vibrations change as the life was sucked out of it, one of the most chilling things I have ever experienced in worlds real or virtual. I am so frightened.

"But from here on I will continue this journal as though that were not true, as though I believed that someday I might again move through the familiar spaces of my home and think about these moments as something in the past, as part of a heroic but diminishing time.

"I pray to God that may be true.

"Now someone *is* stirring. I must go, returning to this strange voyage. I will not say good-bye to you, my journal-of-the-air. I will only say, 'Until I see you again.'

"But I fear it is a lie.

"*Code Delphi. End here.*"

THE cat, with her usual queenly indifference to everything not directly Jones-related, was grooming herself in Dulcie Anwin's lap. Her mistress was psyching herself up for a confrontation. At least, that was what the first glass of that not-great Tangshan red had been about. The second glass—well, perhaps because the first had not made her ready *enough*.

She didn't want to do it. That was really what it came down to, and he would have to understand that. She was a specialist, had spent more than a dozen years refining her skills, had received on-the-job training that your average gear hack couldn't even imagine—the recent job in Cartagena had been perhaps the bloodiest, certainly for her personally, but by no means the oddest or most far-flung—and it was ridiculous for him to expect her just to shove that aside and become a full-time babysitter for a hijacked sim.

And for how long? Judging by the wandering way this whole thing was going, those people might be a year stuck in this network, if their life-support held up. She would have to give up even the pretense of a social life. She hadn't had a date in almost six weeks as it was, hadn't gotten laid in months, but this would be ridiculous. In fact, the whole thing was ridiculous. Dread would have to understand that. He wasn't even her boss, after all. She was a *contractor*—he was just one of the people she worked for, when she chose. She had *killed* a man, for Christ's sake! (A brief moment of worry squeezed her at this last thought. There was something rather jinxlike about that accidental juxtaposition.) She certainly didn't have to curry favor like some little mouse of a junior assistant.

Jones' increasingly energetic grooming was beginning to annoy her, so she dumped the cat off her lap. Jones shot her a look of reproach, then sauntered away toward the kitchen.

"Priority call," announced the wallscreen voice. *"You have a priority call."*

"Shit." Dulcie drained the last of her wine. She tucked her shirt into her pants—she wasn't going to be answering the phone in her robe any more; that was just *asking* not to be respected—and sat up straight. *"Answer."*

Dread's face popped onto the screen, a meter high. His brown skin had been scrubbed, his thick unruly hair pulled back in a knot behind his head. He also seemed more focused than he had earlier, when half the time he had seemed to be listening to some inner voice.

"Evening," he said, smiling. "You're looking well."

"Listen." She barely took a breath—no point in beating around the bush. "I don't want to do it. Not full-time. I know what you're going to say, and I'm certainly aware that you have lots of important things to do, but that still doesn't mean you can force me to take over the whole thing. It's not the money either. You've been very, very generous. But I don't want to do this full-time—it's been hard enough as it is. And although I will never say another word about it to anyone no matter what happens, if you insist, I'll have to resign." She took a deep breath. Her employer's face was almost entirely still. Then another smile began to grow, a strange one; his lips quirked up in a wide curve but never parted. His broad white teeth were entirely hidden.

"Dulcie, Dulcie," he said at last, shaking his head in a mockery of disappointment. "I called you back to say that I *don't* want you to take over the sim full-time."

"You don't?"

"No. I thought about what you said, and it makes sense. We risk making a more noticeable change. Whatever pattern we're showing by having two of us doing it, the blind woman may have already decided it's just the way our sim acts."

"So . . . so we're going to keep on splitting the job?" She snatched for something to help regain her emotional balance—she had leaned so far in anticipation of an argument that she was in danger of falling over. "But for how long? Is this just open-ended?"

"For the present." Dread's eyes seemed very bright. "We'll see what happens in the long run. And, in fact, you may have to take a little larger share of sim-time than you've been doing, especially in the next few days. The Old Man's put me onto something, and I have to get him some answers, keep him happy." The smile again, but smaller and more secretive. "But I'll still be taking over the puppet on a regular basis. I've got used to it, see? I kind of like it. And there's some . . . some things I'd like to try."

Dulcie was relieved, but also felt she was missing something. "So, then that's it, right? Things just kind of go on as they have. I do my job. You . . . you keep paying me the big credits." She knew her laugh didn't sound particularly convincing. "Like that."

"Like that." He nodded and his picture vanished.

Dulcie had several long seconds to feel herself relaxing, then his face popped on again without warning, forcing her to stifle a squeak. "Oh, and Dulcie?"

"Yes?"

"You won't resign. I just thought I should point that out. I'll treat you well, but you won't do *anything* unless I tell you to. If you even think about quitting, or telling anyone, or doing anything unusual with the sim without my permission, I will murder you."

Now he showed the teeth, and they seemed to spring out from his dark face and fill the wallscreen like a row of grave markers. "But first we'll dance, Dulcie." He spoke with the dreadful calm of the damned discussing the weather in hell. "Yes, we'll dance. My way."

Long after he had clicked off, she was still wide-eyed and shivering.

CHAPTER 15

A Late Crismustreat

NETFEED/DOC/GAME: IEN, Hr. 18 (Eu, NAm)—"TAKEDOWN!"
(visual: Raphael and Thelma Biaginni in front of burning house, crying.)
VO: The controversial contest/documentary continues with tonight's Part
Five. Contestant Sammo Edders follows up his successful (and ratings-
busting) arson on the Biaginni's house with an attempt to kidnap the three
Biaggini children. Smart money has the rapidly destabilizing Raphael B.
committing suicide long before the tenth and final episode . . .

RENIE stared at the hollow man, at his nodding head of straw, and her fear was washed away in a surge of indignation. "What do you mean, execute us?" She pulled herself free of the girl Emily's clinging grip. The idea that this lolling *thing*, this clownish figure from an old children's movie, should threaten them . . . "You're not even real!"

The Scarecrow's one mobile eye squinted quizzically and a weary smile twisted his sock-puppet mouth. "Whoa, there. Hurt my feelings, why don't you?" He raised his voice. "*Weedle!* I said change these wretched filters!" The rather nasty-looking little ape scampered forward, wings twitching, and began to pull at one of the mechanical devices attached to the throne. "No, I changed my mind," Scarecrow said, "get those damn tiktoks back in here first."

!Xabbu stood on his hind legs. "We will fight you. We have not come through so much just to lay down like dust."

"Oh, my God, another ape." The Scarecrow settled back in its throne, rattling the welter of pumps and tubes. "As if Weedle and his little flymonk pals weren't enough. I should never have saved them from Forest—it's not like they're grateful or anything."

A door hissed open and a half-dozen tiktoks stepped forward out of the darkness and into the light.

"Good," sighed the Scarecrow. "Take these outsiders away, will you? Put them in one of the holding cells—make sure the windows are too small for the baboon to get out."

The tiktoks did not move.

"Get on with it! What's your problem?" Scarecrow hoisted himself forward, sack head wobbling. "Oil dirty? Overwound? What?"

Something clicked, then a low whistle hummed through the small underground chamber. A new light flickered in the shadows, a shimmering rectangle that revealed itself to be a wallscreen in a frame of polished tubing, with dials and meters all along its lower edge. For a few seconds there was only static, then a dark, cylindrical shape began to form in the center of the screen.

"Hello, Squishy," it said to the Scarecrow.

Emily screamed.

The head on the screen was made entirely of gray, dully-gleaming metal, a brutal, pistonlike thing with a small slot for a mouth and no eyes at all. Renie felt herself drawing back with instinctive revulsion.

"What do you want, Tinman?" The studied boredom of Scarecrow's words did not completely mask a nervous undercurrent. "Given up on those little dust-devils of yours? Keep throwing 'em at me if you want. I eat 'em like candy."

"I'm rather proud of those tornadoes, now that you mention it." The metal thing had a voice like the buzz of an electric razor. "And you have to admit they're demoralizing to your meat-minions. But I called about something else, actually. Here, let me show you—it's cute." The bantering, inhuman voice took on a note of command. "Tiktoks, do a little dance!"

Horribly, all six of the windup men began to stumble through a series of clanking, elephantine steps, looking more than ever like broken toys.

"I located and usurped your frequency, my dear old friend." As Tinman laughed its grating laugh, the door inside its mouth slid up and down several times. "You must have known it was only a matter of time—the tiktoks were really supposed to be mine, after all. So, Uncle

Wiggly, I'm afraid we're in one of those *game over* situations which you player-types know so well." It indulged itself in another scraping chuckle. "I'm sure you'll be relieved to hear I'm not going to waste time on the standard 'now I have you at my mercy' speech. *Tiktoks, kill them now. All of them.*" The tiktoks abruptly ended their dance and took a juddering step into the center of the room, jackhammer arms raised. Emily waited with the stunned fatalism of a born slave; Renie grabbed her and dragged her back against the wall. Tinman swiveled the blank curvature of its head, following the movement. "Tiktoks, wait," he ordered. "And what are *these*, Scarecrow? Your charming guests, I mean."

"None of your business, fender-face," wheezed the Scarecrow. "Go ahead and make your play."

Renie stared at the goggling, idiot faces of the mechanical men and wondered whether she could dodge past them, but it was hard to weigh the chances of successful escape when the room's periphery was in darkness. Was the way they had come in still open? And how about Emily? Would she have to drag the girl with her, or could she leave her behind, gambling that she was only a sim? Could she do it even if she knew so for certain? The suffering in these simulation worlds seemed very real—could she condemn even a Puppet to torture and death?

Renie reached down for !Xabbu's hand but felt nothing. The baboon had disappeared into the shadows.

"Tiktok, examine that woman," Tinman ordered.

Renie straightened, hands raised to defend herself, but the mechanical man lumbered past her and lifted its clawlike hands toward Emily, who moaned and shrank back. It swept its pincers slowly up and down the length of her body, never closer than a few inches, like airport security running density-detectors over the pockets of a suspicious passenger. Emily turned her face away, weeping again. A few moments later the tiktok stepped back and its arms dropped to its rounded sides.

"Goodness," said Tinman, as though he had read the information directly from the tiktok's internal workings. "Goodness, gracious me. Could it be?" The buzzing voice had a peculiar cracked resonance— perhaps surprise. "My enemy, you astonish me. You have found . . . the Dorothy?"

Emily sank to the floor, limp with fright. Renie moved near her, the protective impulse the only thing that made sense in this entire, incomprehensible drama.

"Piss off," Scarecrow wheezed, clearly fighting for breath. "You can't have . . ."

"Oh, but I can. Tiktoks, kill them all except the emily," he rasped. "Bring her to me immediately."

The four clockwork men nearest the Scarecrow's throne turned and began to shuffle toward him, spreading into a crescent formation. The other two turned to face Renie and Emily where they stood in the shadows against the wall.

"Metal boy, you are so stupid that I'm beginning to get bored." Scarecrow shook his ponderous head, then hawked up something unpleasant and spat it into the corner. When the mechanical men reached the base of his throne, he raised his gloved hand and pulled a hanging cord.

With an immense, booming *clang,* as though an immense hammer had struck an appropriately sized anvil, the floor all around his throne abruptly fell away beneath the tiktoks. They dropped out of sight, but Renie could hear them pinballing downward for three or four long seconds, banging against the metal walls.

"Tiktoks, bring the emily to me!" Tinman ordered the two remaining mechanical men. "I may not be able to get you, Scarecrow, but you can't do anything to stop them either!"

Renie didn't know if that were true or not, but she did not wait to find out. She threw herself forward, hands extended, and thumped her palms against the nearest tiktok's chest. The creature was heavy, and only rocked, but one of its cylindrical legs swiveled in an unsteady step backward, protecting its balance.

"*Weedle!*" shouted the Scarecrow. "*Puzzle, Malinger, Blip!*"

Ignoring this nonsense, Renie bent her knees and wrapped her arms around the tiktok's barrel torso—she could feel the grinding vibration of the thing's gears right through to her bones—and shoved again, pushing with all the strength in her long legs. A foam-padded pincer found her arm, but she jerked her wrist free just before the claw could close, then heaved again, struggling to keep her weight low and her legs extended. The tiktok tilted, forced into another backward step to keep upright. The claw groped for her again, but she gave one last shove and jumped free. The thing took a rolling drunken step and its gear noises rose to the whine of an angry mosquito. It teetered at the edge of the pit that had opened around the Scarecrow's throne, then toppled and was gone.

Renie had only a heartbeat to savor her triumph before another pair of padded claws closed on her side and shoulder, pinching her so hard in both places that she yelped in shocked agony. The second tiktok did not hesitate, but shoved her across the concrete floor toward the open trench where the others had gone. Renie could only scream panicky curses and thrash at the thing behind her with useless backhand blows.

"!Xabbu?" she cried. "Emily! Help me!" She tried to dig in her heels but could not slow herself. The pit yawned.

Something surged past her and the pressure on her shoulder abruptly eased. She craned and saw that something small and simian had wrapped itself around the tiktok's face. The mechanical man was flailing at it, but its short arms were not able to do effective damage.

"Xabbu. . . !" she began, then suddenly several more monkey shapes dropped down out of the darkness overhead. The tiktok jerked its other arm free to flail at its attackers. Released, Renie fell to her knees and crawled away from the pit, fiery pain coursing along both sides.

The tiktok was now stumbling, blind and beset, but its flailing defense took a toll. One of the monkeys was batted from the air and fell limply to the ground. The tiktok took a few awkward steps, then seemed to find its balance. Another monkey was struck down with a horrible wet crunch as the tiktok began to move slowly toward Renie again. She could not see in the darkened chamber whether either of the two battered shapes was !Xabbu's.

Abruptly, and without warning, the chamber, the struggling tiktok, the monkeys, and the Scarecrow enthroned amid his clutter of life support, all turned inside out.

It seemed to Renie that a million camera flashes all blazed at once. The small pools of light became black, the shadows flared into blinding color, and everything jerked and stuttered simultaneously, as though the universe had slipped a sprocket. As she felt herself wrenched into a thousand pieces, Renie screamed, but there was no sound, only a vast low hum that ran through everything like a foghorn buried deep in the heart of the world.

Her sense of her body was gone. She was whirled in a vortex, then spread thin over a thousand miles of nothing, and all that remained to her was the single point of consciousness that could do nothing more than cling to the bare idea that it existed.

Then, as suddenly as everything had happened, it stopped. The bleeding colors of the universe ran backward, the negative became positive, and the chamber was restored.

Renie lay gasping on the floor. Emily was stretched beside her, whimpering, arms wrapped around her head in a futile effort to keep the chaos at bay.

"Jesus H. Christ," slurred the Scarecrow. "I *hate* when that happens."

Renie dragged herself up onto her knees. The remaining tiktok lay in the middle of the chamber, its arms twitching slowly back and forth, its pocket-watch innards apparently disrupted past recovery. The two surviving monkeys hovered over it, wings whirring at hummingbird speed, staring fearfully around the room as though everything might go mad again any second.

The screen from which Tinman's eyeless face had watched them now displayed only a confetti-shower of static.

"That's been happening too often lately." The Scarecrow propped his head between two hands and furrowed his burlap brow. "I used to think it was Tinman's doing, like the tornadoes—it's a bit too advanced for Lion—but he wouldn't have chosen that timing, would he?"

"What's going on here?" Renie crawled to examine both monkey corpses—neither of them were !Xabbu. "Are you all crazy? And what have you done with my friend?"

Scarecrow had just opened his mouth to say something annoyed when a small shape appeared at his shoulder.

"Stop!" The baboon reached down and grabbed one of Scarecrow's larger hoses firmly in his long fingers, then followed its length until he gripped the tube just where it entered the straw man's body at the neck. "If you do not let my friend go free," !Xabbu said, "and the girl Emily, too—I will pull this away!"

Scarecrow craned his head. "You are *definitely* out-of-towners," he noted pityingly. "Weedle! Malinger! Come get him."

As the flying monkeys shot toward the throne, !Xabbu wrenched the tube free. A wisp of cotton batting floated free of the end; as the monkeys caught him and pulled him up into the air, it swirled lazily in their wake.

They dropped !Xabbu from a few feet up. He landed, crouching, at Renie's feet, baffled and defeated. Scarecrow lifted the tube in his soft fingers and waggled it. "Stuffing refill," he explained. "I was a little less tightly-packed than I prefer. Things have been busy lately, personal grooming suffers—you know how it is." He looked down to Weedle and Malinger, who had landed by his booted feet and now were picking fleas off each other. "Call the other flymonks, will you?"

Weedle leaned back his head and made a high-pitched whooping noise. Dozens of winged shapes suddenly swept down from the darkness overhead, like bats disturbed in their cavern roost. Within seconds, Renie and !Xabbu were pinioned head and foot by dozens of clinging monkey hands.

"Now, leave the emily on the floor—I want to talk to her—and take the other two to the tourist cell, then come right back. Be sharp about it! The tiktoks are going to be out of service, so everybody's pulling double shifts until further notice."

Renie felt herself lifted into the darkness, wrapped in a cloud of vibrating wings.

"Not all of you!" the Scarecrow bellowed. "Weedle, get back here and reattach this stuffing-duct. And change my damn filters!"

THE door clanged shut behind them, a solid, permanent sound.

Renie looked around their new accommodations, taking in the institutional, mint-green paint that covered walls, ceiling, and floor. "This isn't quite how I imagined the Emerald City."

"Ah, look," someone else said from the far end of the long cell. "Company."

The man sitting in the shadows against the wall, who seemed to be their only cellmate, was slim and good-looking (or at least his sim was, Renie reminded herself.) He appeared as a dark-skinned Caucasian, with thick black hair brushed back in a slightly old-fashioned style, and a mustache only slightly less extravagant than the metal ones the tiktoks' wore. Most astonishingly, though, he was smoking a cigarette.

The sudden leap of longing at the sight of the glowing ember did not smother her caution, but as she swiftly reviewed the facts—he was in here with them, so he was probably a prisoner too, and therefore an ally; it wasn't like she was going to trust him or anything, since he might not even be real—she found herself coming to the conclusion she had hoped to reach.

"Do you have another one of those?"

The man raised one eyebrow, looking her up and down. "Prisoners get rich from cigarettes." He seemed to have a slight accent to his English, something Renie couldn't recognize. "What is in it for me?"

"Renie?" !Xabbu, not understanding the treacherous lure of even noncarcinogenic cigarettes, reached up to tug her hand. "Who is this person?"

The dark-haired man did not seem to notice the talking baboon. "Well?"

Renie shook her head. "Nothing. We have nothing to trade. We came here like you see us."

"Hmmm. Well, then you owe me a favor." He reached into a pocket on his chest, pulled out a red pack of something called Lucky Strikes, and shook one out. He lit it off his own and held it out. Renie crossed the cell to take it, !Xabbu trailing behind. "You have the gear to taste that?"

She was wondering the same thing. When she inhaled there was hot air in her throat, and a feeling of something filling her lungs. In fact, she could almost swear she could taste the tobacco. "Oh, God, that's wonderful," she said, blowing out a stream of smoke.

The man nodded as though some great truth had been revealed, then slipped the cigarettes back into the pocket of his overalls. He wore the same factory-issue boiler suit that she had seen on all the other henrys in Emerald, but he did not strike her as one of those domesticated creatures. "Who are you?" she asked.

He looked irritated. "Who are *you?*"

Renie introduced herself and !Xabbu under the same assumed names as she had given in Kunohara's bugworld—after all, she told herself, the stranger had only given her a cigarette, not donated a kidney. "We just stumbled in," she said, assuming that if this man were not one of the bovine residents of the simworld, their outlander status must be obvious. "And apparently that's a crime around here. Who are you and how did you wind up here?"

"Azador," the stranger said.

Confused by his accent, Renie at first thought he had said "At the door," and she turned to look. He corrected the misunderstanding.

"*I* am Azador. And I am here because I made the mistake of offering advice to His Wise Majesty the King." His smirk contained an entire world's worth of world-weariness. Renie had to admit that he had quite a handsome sim. "You are both Citizens, yes?"

Renie looked at !Xabbu, who was sitting on his heels well out of Azador's reach. The monkey-sim's returned glance was inscrutable. "Yes, we are."

The stranger did not seem interested in gleaning more details, which left Renie feeling she had made the right decision. "Good. As am I. It is a shame that, like me, you have had your freedom stolen from you."

"What's with this place?" She suddenly remembered Emily. "The scarecrow-man—the king—he has our friend. Will he hurt her?"

Azador shrugged: he could take no responsibility for the foibles of others. "They have all gone mad here. Whatever this place once was, it has fallen apart. You see this in bad simulations. It is why I offered my advice." He stubbed out his cigarette. Renie recalled that her own was burning down, unsmoked; she drew on it again as Azador continued. "You know the film of Oz, do you not?"

"I do, yes," Renie answered. "But this doesn't seem quite right. It seems much . . . much bleaker. And this is Kansas—Oz wasn't in Kansas, it was somewhere else, wasn't it?"

"Here, it did not start this way." He took out another cigarette, then changed his mind and tucked it behind his ear. Renie found herself watching it avidly, even with one burning between her fingers. She didn't like that feeling. "I told you," Azador went on, "the simulation has fallen apart. It has two connected locations, Oz—which I think was also a book, for reading—and Kansas, the American state. They were like the two ends of the hourglass, you see, with a slender part between them where things could pass back and forth."

!Xabbu was inspecting the cell with solemn attention. Renie thought he seemed upset.

"But something went very wrong on the Oz side," Azador said. "I have heard terrible stories—murder, rape, cannibalism. I think it has been all but abandoned now. The three men—the Citizens—who were first playing the characters of Scarecrow, Tinman, and Cowardly Lion, all brought their respective kingdoms through to the Kansas side."

"So it's some kind of war game?" she asked. "How stupid! Why recreate something sweet like Oz just to make it into another shoot-em-up?" *How typical of men,* she wanted to add, but didn't.

Azador gave her a lazy smile, as though he read her thoughts. "It did not start quite that way. The Tinman, the Lion—they are not those who originally began the game. They came in from outside, just as you did. But they have taken over the simworld, or nearly so. Only the Scarecrow fellow had a strong enough position to resist them, but I think he will not last much longer."

"And that other stuff? For a moment, it seemed like the whole simulation turned upside down or something. Did you feel that?"

!Xabbu had climbed to the top bunk of the bed nearest the wall, and was examining the tiny, screened window. "Do you remember what Atasco said?" he asked. "When that thing ran across the room, that thing made of light?"

Renie went cold at the mention of the murdered man's name, but Azador seemed to be paying little attention. "I don't . . ."

"He said that he thought the system was perhaps growing too fast. At least, that is what I remember. Or growing too big, perhaps. And Kunohara said . . ."

"!Xabbu!"

Now Azador did take notice. "You met Kunohara? Hideki Kunohara?"

"No," Renie said hurriedly. "We met someone who knew him, or claimed they did."

"The bastard found me in a flesh-eating plant—a 'pitcher plant,' I think it is called." Azador's indignation sounded very real. "He lectured me, as though I were a child, on the complexity of nature or some nonsense. And then he left me there, standing in foul-smelling liquid that was doing its best to digest me! Bastard."

Despite her worry, Renie was hard-pressed not to laugh. It did sound rather like the odd, self-satisfied little man they had met. "But you got away."

"I always do." Something dark passed behind his eyes. He changed the moment by taking the cigarette he had stashed behind his ear and elaborately applying the flame of a chunky silver lighter to it. When he had put the lighter back in his pocket, he rose and walked slowly past her toward the cell door, where he stood humming an unfamiliar song. She suddenly felt sure that he had spent lots of time in places like this, either in VR or plain old RL.

!Xabbu crept down from the upper bunk and leaned in close to Renie's ear. "I said those names on purpose," he whispered. "To see what he would do."

"I wish you hadn't." More anger seeped through her quiet tone than she had intended. "Let me handle the cloak-and-dagger stuff next time." !Xabbu gave her a surprised look, then moved to the far corner and crouched there, examining the floor. Renie felt terrible, but before she could do anything about it, Azador had strolled back to their end.

"I will go mad if I stay here any longer," he said abruptly. "We will escape, yes? I have knowledge that will give us our freedom. A plan of escape."

Renie looked around, startled. "Are you sure you should say things like that? What if the cell's bugged?"

Azador waved his hand dismissively. "Everything is bugged, of course. It does not matter. The Scarecrow creature does not have enough subjects left to review the tapes—miles and miles of tapes! The technology of this Kansas simworld is strictly twentieth century—have you not noticed?"

"If you have such a good plan," !Xabbu asked, "why are you still here?"

Renie had been wondering how the stranger knew so much about the Scarecrow's security procedures, but she had to admit that the Bushman's question was a good one too.

"Because this escape needs more than one person," Azador said. "And now we have two people and a very smart monkey!"

"I am not a monkey." !Xabbu frowned. "I am a man."

Azador laughed. "Of course you are a man. I was making a joke. You should not be so sensitive."

"You," !Xabbu suggested darkly, "should perhaps make better jokes."

ALTHOUGH he would tell them no other details of his plan, Azador insisted they must wait until evening before attempting their escape—although how the man would tell the time in a cell whose only window looked out onto a horizontal airshaft, Renie could not guess. But she welcomed the opportunity to rest. Both their tornado-thrashed sojourn in Kansas and their dragonfly-crashing venture through Kunohara's bugworld had entailed one life-or-death struggle after another, all of them exhausting and painful.

!Xabbu was immersed in a self-sufficient silence that Renie knew was in part due to hurt feelings, and Azador was sitting with his eyes closed, whistling tunelessly but quietly. She found herself for the first time in a long while able simply to sit and think.

Not least of what occupied her was their mysterious cellmate. Azador had proved unwilling to be drawn out on the subject of his own background, or what brought him to this simworld or to the Otherland network in the first place. If he was not a living, breathing Citizen, he was a Puppet that had been constructed with great care to seem like one—he spoke of the network and its illusions with every sign of a knowledge so intimate as to border on contempt. He was also quite impressive, in his way, and not just because of his handsome sim—Renie could almost imagine the word "swashbuckling" applied to him—but at times he seemed to show a different side, flashes of someone vulnerable, even haunted.

But why waste time thinking about this stranger when there were so many other things to consider, so many life-or-death problems still unsolved?

Well, for one thing, girl, she told herself, *you're a bit randy. It's been too long between men—way too long—and this constant danger, all this adrenaline, it's getting to you.*

She looked at the bulge of the package in Azador's pocket, was sorely tempted to ask for another cigarette. Surely anything that helped her relax would be a good thing? She felt like one of the Tiktoks, wound far beyond its optimum tension. But she did not like the way she was thinking about cigarettes again, as though they were somehow just as important as the quest to save her brother. She had hardly thought about them in two days—was it going to start all over again now? She hadn't eaten anything since entering the network, and she wasn't obsessing about *that*.

With strong effort, Renie forced her mind away from distractions, back to the problems at hand.

Instead of their entrance into the network bringing answers, the mysteries had only deepened. Who was this Circle group Kunohara had mentioned—were they really the same people who had helped !Xabbu leave the Okavango to attend school? If so, what could it mean? Did !Xabbu know more than he was telling? But if so, why admit he knew anything about the Circle at all? She dismissed this newest line of thought, too. The entire Grail Brotherhood thing was so broad and so confusing, and there was so much she did not know, that at some point it began to seem like someone's street-corner rant, all absurdist self-referentiality and throbbing paranoia. She should stick to the big ideas.

But what *were* the big ideas, exactly? What had they learned? Anything? Kunohara had seemed to insinuate that there was some kind of conflict going on between the Grail people and this Circle group. But he had also suggested that both sides might be wrong, and that the system was somehow more than they realized. Could that, and the other things they had seen—Atasco's scuttling anomaly, the false creatures and effects catalogued at the Hive, the bizarre breakdown in the Scarecrow's throne room—be indicators of a system in trouble?

A sudden thought jabbed her like a long, cold needle. *And if Stephen is tied up in this system somehow, if he's been sucked into it in some way, and the whole thing goes down—what then? Will he wake up? Or will he be trapped in a dying . . . whatever it is? Machine? Universe?*

Without thinking, she looked to !Xabbu as though the little man could protect her from the chilling thought that she had not spoken aloud. He was holding his hands before him, wiggling his fingers—doing the string game without string again, she realized. His thin back was turned toward her.

She needed this man, she realized in a rush of affection, this sweet, clever person hidden behind a monkey's shape. He was her best friend in the world. Astonishing to consider—she had known him less than a year—but it was true.

Renie worked the lace of her boot free, then slid closer to !Xabbu.

"Here," she said, handing him the cord. "It's easier with real string, isn't it?"

He turned it over in his small hands. "Your boot will not stay on. That is not safe." He furrowed his brow in thought, then lifted the bootlace to his mouth and bit it through with sharp teeth. He handed back half the lace. "I do not need a long piece. My fingers are smaller now."

She smiled and retied her boot. "I'm sorry I spoke that way to you earlier. I was wrong."

"You are my friend. You want what is best for me—for both of us." It was astonishing how serious a baboon face could look. "Would you like to see me work the string?"

Azador, seated against the wall a few meters away, glanced over at them for a moment, but his eyes were distant; he seemed lost in thought.

"Certainly. Please show me."

!Xabbu tied a knot in the section of bootlace and stretched it into a rectangle, then his fingers moved rapidly in and out, plucking at the strands like a pair of nesting birds, until he held between his palms a complex, geometrical abstraction.

"Here is the sun. Can you see it?"

Renie was not sure, but she thought the diamond shape near the middle of the design might be what he meant. "I think so."

"Now the sun sinks low—it is evening." !Xabbu moved his fingers and the diamond moved down toward the line of horizon, flattening as it went.

Renie laughed and clapped her hands. "That's very good!"

He smiled. "I will show you another picture." His monkey fingers moved quickly. Renie could not help noticing how much his movements resembled someone using squeezers to input data. When he stopped, he had made a completely different design, with a tight nexus of strings in one of the upper corners. "This is the bird called the 'honey guide.' Can you see him?"

Renie caught her breath, startled. "You said that name before." It seemed important, but she needed long moments before she remembered. "No. Sellars said it. When we met him in Mister J's, and you were . . . unconscious. Dreaming, whatever. He sent a honey guide to bring you back from wherever you had gone."

!Xabbu nodded his head solemnly. "He is a wise man, Sellars. The honey guide is very important to my people. We will follow him for great distances until he leads us to the wild honey. But he does not like to lead humans to the honey—we are too greedy. Ah, see now, he has found some!" !Xabbu wiggled his fingers and the small spot in the corner moved agitatedly from side to side. "He is going to tell his best friend, the honey badger." !Xabbu quickly made another picture, this time with a large shape at the bottom and the small shape at the top. "They are such close friends, the honey guide and the honey badger, that my people would say they sleep under the same skin. Do you know the honey badger, Renie?"

"It's also called a ratel, isn't it? I've seen them in zoos. Low to the ground, claws for digging, right?"

"Mean bastards," Azador said without looking up. "Take your fingers off if you give them a chance."

"They are very brave," !Xabbu said with deliberate dignity. "The honey badger will fight to protect what is his." He turned back to Renie. "And the little bird is his best friend. When the bees have finished making the honey, and it is dripping golden inside the tree or in the crevice of a rock, the honey guide comes flying out of the bush, calling, *'Quick, quick, it is honey! Come quick!'*" As !Xabbu repeated the words, this time in his own clicking language, he made the small upper figure vibrate again. The larger one remained immobile. "Then his friend hears him, and feels that there is no better sound, and he hurries after the bird, whistling like a bird himself, calling, *'See me, o person with wings! I am coming after you!'* That is a wonderful sound, to hear friend calling to friend across the bush." !Xabbu worked the strings with his agile fingers, and now the lower shape was moving too, and as the smaller figure became tiny, so did the larger shrink away, as though the honey badger hurried after its guide.

"That's wonderful," Renie said, laughing. "I could see them!"

"They are the closest friends, honey guide and honey badger. And when the honey badger comes to the honey at last, he always throws some out on the ground for his friend to share." He let the string fall slack between his fingers. "As you do for me, Renie. We are friends like that pair, you and I."

She felt something catch in her throat, and for a split-instant thought they were no longer locked in an institutional cell, but stood again beneath the ringed moon in !Xabbu's memory-desert, exhausted and happy from their dancing.

She had to swallow before she could speak. "We are friends, !Xabbu. Yes, we are."

The silence was broken by Azador loudly clearing his throat. When they turned toward him, he looked up, feigning surprise. "No, do not mind me," he said. "Carry on."

!Xabbu turned back to Renie and his mouth curled in a shy smile that wrinkled the baboon muzzle. "I have bored you."

"Not at all. I love your stories." She did not know what else to say. There were always these strange watersheds with !Xabbu, and she had no idea what they might be leading to—a deeper and more familylike friendship than she could imagine? True love? At times she felt there was no human model for what their relationship might be. "Tell me another story, please? If you don't mind." She looked over to Azador. "If we have enough time."

Their cellmate, now engrossed in his quiet whistling again, made a vague hand gesture, bidding them amuse themselves however they pleased.

"I will tell you another story with the string game," !Xabbu said. "We use it sometimes to teach stories to the children." He suddenly looked abashed. "I do not mean to say that I think you are a child, Renie. . . ." He examined her face and was reassured. "This is a story of how the hare got his split lip. It is also a story of Grandfather Mantis. . . ."

"May I ask you a question before you start? Mantis—Grandfather Mantis—is he an insect? Or an old man?

Her friend chortled. "He is an insect, of course. But he is also an old man, the oldest of his family, and the eldest of the First People. Remember, in the earliest days, *all* the animals were people."

Renie tried to figure this out. "So is he tiny? Or big?" She could not help remembering the terrible, razor-limbed monstrosity that had stalked them through the Hive. From the look that passed across his long face, she could see !Xabbu remembered, too.

"Grandfather Mantis rides between the horns of the eland, so he is very small. But he is oldest and cleverest of the First People, the grandfather of the Elder Race, so he is very big, too."

"Ah." She examined his expression, but could see no mockery. "Then I suppose I'm ready for the story."

!Xabbu nodded. He quickly brought his fingers apart and began to move them in and out, until another many-angled pattern had formed. "In the early days, there was a time when Grandfather Mantis was sick, and almost felt himself to be dying. He had eaten *biltong*—that is dried meat—that he had stolen from his own son, Kwammanga the Rainbow, and when Kwammanga found out it was gone, he said 'Let that *biltong* be alive again in the stomach of the person who has stolen from me.' He did not know it was his own father. And so the *biltong* became alive again in the stomach of Grandfather Mantis, and gave him a terrible pain."

!Xabbu's fingers flexed and the picture rippled. A shape near the middle wriggled from side to side, so that Renie could almost see Grandfather Mantis writhing in his agony.

"He went to his wife, Rock-Rabbit, and told her he felt himself to be very ill. She told him to go into the bush and find water, so that by drinking he would soothe himself. Groaning, he went away.

"There was no water close by, and Mantis walked for many days, until he came at last to the Tsodilo Hills, and in their heights he found the water he had been seeking. Drinking deeply, he felt better, and decided he would rest a while before returning to his home."

The baboon hands moved through a succession of shapes, and Renie saw the hills rise and the water shimmer. A short distance away, Azador had stopped whistling and seemed to be listening.

"But back in Grandfather Mantis' *kraal,* everyone was frightened that he had not returned, and they feared that if he died they would never see him again, for no one of the Early Race had ever died before. So his wife Rock-Rabbit sent her cousin, the hare, to go and look for him."

For just a brief moment Hare made his appearance in the net of string, then bounded off.

"Hare ran in Mantis' footprints all the way to the Tsodilo Hills, for he was a very swift runner, and reached them by nightfall. When he had climbed the hills, he found Mantis sitting beside the water, drinking and bathing the dust from his body. 'Grandfather,' said Hare, 'your wife and your children and all the other First People send to ask how you are. They fear that you are dying, and thus that they will never see you again.'

"Mantis was feeling much better, and he was sorry that all the others were worried. 'Go back to them and say that they are foolish—there is no true death,' he told Hare. 'What, do you think that when we die, we are like this grass?' He lifted a handful of grass. 'That we die and, feeling ourselves to be like the dry grass, turn into this dust?' He lifted the dust in his other hand and flung it into the air, then pointed at the moon, which hung in the night sky.

"Grandfather Mantis himself had caused the moon to be, but that is another story.

" 'Go and tell them,' he said, 'that as the moon dies but then is made new, so too in dying they shall be made new. And thus they should have no fear.' And so he sent the Hare back down out of the hills, bearing his message.

"But Hare was of the sort who believes himself very clever, and as he ran back toward the *kraal* of Grandfather Mantis and his family, he thought to himself, 'Old Mantis cannot be certain of this, for does not everything die and turn to dust? If I give them this foolish message, they will think *me* foolish, and I shall never find a bride, and the other people of the Early Race will turn away from me.' So when he reached the *kraal,* where Rock-Rabbit and all the rest were waiting for him, he told them, 'Grandfather Mantis says that dying we will not be renewed like the moon, but instead like the grass we will turn into dust.'

"And so all the people of Mantis' family told all the other First People what Hare told them Grandfather Mantis had said, and all the First People were filled with great fear, and wept and fought among themselves. Thus, when Mantis himself came back to his home, with his bag of hartebeeste skin over one shoulder and his digging stick in his hand, he found everyone full of sadness. When he learned what the Hare had said, and which was now being spoken as the truth by all the First People in the world, he was so angry that he lifted his digging stick and struck the Hare, splitting his lip. Then he told Hare that none of the bushes or grass of the veldt or rocks of the desert pans would ever keep him safe, and that his enemies would always seek him and find him.

"And that is why the hare has a split lip."

The last string picture vibrated for a moment between !Xabbu's outstretched hands, then he brought his palms together, making it disappear.

"That was lovely." Renie would have said more, but Azador abruptly stood.

"Time to go."

Renie's arms were starting to hurt. "This doesn't make any sense."

"It does not make sense to *you*," Azador said airily. "Just keep your hands pressed flat."

Renie muttered a curse. The position, facing the wall with her arms spread wide, pushing against the cold cement, was unpleasantly reminiscent of being arrested. Azador was lying on his stomach between her feet with his hands also pressed against the wall, parallel to hers but just above the floor. "All right," she said, "you've convinced me you're out of your mind. What now?"

"Now it's what's-your-name's turn—monkey man." Azador craned to look over his shoulder at !Xabbu, who was watching with a certain lack of enthusiasm. "Pick a spot as close to the center as possible— where the middle of an 'x' would be if our hands were on the ends. Then hit it."

"It is a very hard wall," !Xabbu pointed out.

Azador's laugh was a grunt of irritation. "You are not going to break it down with your little hand, monkey man. Just do what I say."

!Xabbu slid in so that his head was against Renie's stomach, just below her breasts. It made her uncomfortable, but her friend did not hesitate. When he had chosen his spot, he struck with the flat of his hand.

Before the smack had finished echoing from the cell's hard surfaces, the section of wall demarcated by their extended arms had vanished, leaving a blank white surface on all the exposed edges. With nothing left to support her, Renie stumbled forward into the next cell.

"How did you do that?" she demanded.

Azador's smile was infuriatingly self-satisfied. "This is VR, Ms. Otepi—all make-believe. I just know how to make it believe something different. Now that part of the wall thinks it is no longer a wall."

!Xabbu had sidled through, and was looking around the empty cell, an exact replica of the one they had just left. "But what good has this done us? Must we do this through every wall until we are outside?"

Azador's pleased expression did not change. He walked to the new cell's door. One tug of the handle and it slid sideways, open to the hallway. "No one bothers to lock the empty cells."

To cover her irritation at the man's success—her first impulse had been to say "That's cheating!", which she knew would have been a marvelously stupid remark—she slid past him and peered into the hallway. There was nothing but mint-green cement and closed doors all the way to the turning of the corridor on both sides, the monotony broken only by posters depicting the Scarecrow—a healthy, vibrant, stern Scarecrow—proclaiming *"10,000 Munchkins Dead—For What? Remember Oz!"* and *"Emerald Needs YOU!"*

"There's no one out there—let's go." Renie turned to Azador. "Do you know how to get out of here?"

"There is a service bay at the back of the cells. There may be guards, but there will be fewer than at the front, where all the government offices are."

"Then let's do it." She took a few steps, then looked at !Xabbu. "What's wrong?"

He shook his head. "I hear something . . . smell something. I am not sure."

A flat *boom* broke the stillness, so faint as to be almost inaudible: someone might have dropped a book on a table a few rooms away. The sound was repeated a few times, then silence fell again.

"Well, whatever it is, it's a long way away," Renie declared. "We'd better not wait for it to get here."

Not only the corridor before their cell, but all the corridors were empty. The sound of their hurrying footsteps—or hers and Azador's, since !Xabbu's feet made only the faintest noise—rebounded eerily from the long walls as they ran, and made Renie uneasy. "Where is everybody?"

"I told you, this place is falling apart," said Azador. "The war has been going on for years—Scarecrow has only a few minions left. Why do you think we were the only prisoners? The others have been set free and then sent to fight in Forest, or in the Works."

Renie did not even want to know what "the Works" was. First Atasco's realm, then the destruction of the Hive, now this. Would these simworlds simply crumble into virtual dust, like the veldt grass of !Xabbu's story? Or would something even more sinister replace them?

"Go slow," !Xabbu said. "I hear something. And I feel something, too—it is tapping in my chest. Something is wrong here."

"What the hell does *that* mean?" Azador demanded. "We're almost at the loading bay. We are sure as hell not just going to stop."

"You should trust him," Renie said. "He knows what he's talking about."

Moving more cautiously, they rounded a corner and found themselves at a nexus of corridors. In the middle of the open area lay a tall man with a long green beard and a pair of smashed green spectacles. An antique rifle of some kind lay beside him. He was clearly dead: several things that should have been inside him had oozed out onto the floor.

Renie fought an urge to vomit. Why did people have innards in this simulation, but not in the bugworld?

Azador took a wide route around the body. "The loading bay is just another hundred meters this way," he whispered, pointing to where the wide corridor bent sharply. "We can . . ."

A scream of pain rattled through the corridor, so fierce that Renie's knees went weak. Even Azador was clearly shaken, but the three of them went cautiously to the bend in the corridor and peered around.

On the wide loading ramp at the end of the corridor, several more men with green beards and spectacles were fighting to the death to keep an army of tiktoks at bay. The greenbeards were supported in their struggle by a few even odder creatures—skinny men with wheels for hands and feet, a teddy bear with a popgun, other soldiers that seemed to be made entirely of paper—but the defenders were clearly outgunned, and several dozen of them had been destroyed. Only one of the tiktoks had gone down, although two or three others were staggering in circles with their insides blown out, but the green-bearded soldiers appeared to have exhausted their ammunition and were now using their long rifles exclusively as clubs. Sensing imminent victory, the buzzing tiktoks were swarming closer to the defenders, like flies around a dying animal.

"Damn!" Renie was almost as irritated as she was frightened. "Games! These people and their bloody stupid war games!"

"It will not be a game if those things get us," Azador hissed. "Turn back! We will go out another way."

As they returned to the places where the corridors crossed, and where the first defender's body they had encountered still lay, !Xabbu reached up to tug at Renie's hand. "Why is this dead one here, when the fighting is still at the entrance?"

It took Renie a moment to understand what he was asking, and by that time they had left the green-bearded corpse behind them. Their cellmate had turned right and was sprinting up the corridor.

"Azador?" she called, but he had stopped already.

Two more corpses lay near the wall at the next corridor branch—two bodies in three pieces, since the soldier's top half had been forcibly separated from his bottom half. Beside him lay the pulped remains of one of the flying monkeys. Loud simian squawking echoed from the side-corridor, more monkeys in pain and terror.

"We do not need to go that way!" said Azador in relief. "I have remembered another route." He started to move forward, and did not turn even when a very human, very female scream came bouncing down the passageway.

"*Emily. . . ?*" Renie shouted at Azador's retreating back, "I think that's our friend!"

He did not turn or slow down, even when she cursed at him. !Xabbu had already started down the corridor toward Emily's voice. Renie hurried to catch up.

They had just caught sight of a battle that, although now familiar, would never be less less than bizarre—flying monkeys and mechanical men, struggling to the death—when Emily's slender form burst from the meleé and came running toward them. Renie grabbed at her as she tried to run past and was almost knocked down. The girl fought like a tail-dangled cat until Renie wrapped her arms around her and squeezed as hard as she could.

"It's *me,* Emily, it's *me,* we're going to *help* you," she said, over and over until the girl stopped struggling and finally looked at her new captors. Her already panic-widened eyes grew wider.

"You! The strangers!"

Before Renie could reply, a monkey flew past them down the corridor, but not under its own power. It smacked against one wall, flopped bonelessly, and skidded.

"We have to go," Renie said. "Come on!" She took one of the girl's hands and !Xabbu took the other as they sprinted away from the unpleasant sounds of buzzing and claw-crunched monkeys. Azador was not in sight, but they turned in the direction he had gone. Emily, as though she had not been under tiktok attack only a few moments earlier, babbled happily.

". . . I didn't think you'd come back—or I didn't think *I'd* come back, really. The king, he had this machine do all these funny things to me—it was worse than anything the medical henrys ever do, made me feel all goosebumpy, and you know what?"

Renie was doing her best to ignore her. "Do you hear anything?" she asked !Xabbu. "Any more of those machine men ahead of us?"

He shrugged his narrow shoulders and tugged at Emily's hand, trying to get her to move faster.

"Do you know what he said to me?" Emily went on. "It was such a surprise—I thought I was in trouble, see, and that they were going to send me to the Bad Farm. That's the place you go when they catch you trying to steal from the food barn, like this other emily I know, and she went there for just a few months, but when she came back, she looked like she was way much older. But do you know what they said to me?"

"Emily, shut up." Renie slowed them now as they turned another corner. This one opened into a wide room with polished tile floors and shiny metal staircases leading to a mezzanine. More monkey corpses were scattered about the floor here, and also the bodies of a pair of tiktoks, which had apparently tumbled through the mezzanine handrail where it was bent like silver licorice. The windup men had smashed like expensive watches dropped onto pavement, but next to one of them, something was moving.

Emily was still prattling. "He told me that I'm going to have a little baby!"

It was Azador. A dying spasm from one of the tiktoks had fastened on his leg, and now he was struggling to pull himself free of the thing's locked grip. He looked up at their approach; his fearful expression quickly turned to one of annoyance.

"Get this thing off me," he growled, but before he could say more, he was interrupted by a shriek from Emily so loud that Renie flinched away from her in pain.

"Henry!" Emily skittered across the room and leaped over one of the smashed Tiktoks, then flung herself onto Azador. Her attack thumped him back against the floor so hard that his leg jerked free of the claw, tearing his overalls and leaving red weals on his ankle. Emily climbed on him like an overstimulated puppy and he could not push her away. "Henry!" she squealed. "My pretty pretty prettiest henry! My pudding-heart lover! My special Crismustreat!" She stopped, straddling his chest, as he looked back at her in stunned surprise. "Guess what,"

she demanded. "Guess what the king just told me. You and me—we made a baby!"

The high-ceilinged room fell silent in the wake of this revelation. After a moment, the dead tiktok made a clicking noise, and the claw that had held Azador's ankle ratcheted one final time, then froze again.

"This," said Renie at last, "is really, really strange."

CHAPTER 16

Shoppers and Sleepers

NETFEED/NEWS: Experts Debate "Slow-Time" Prisons
(visual: file footage of morgue attendant checking drawers)
VO: The UN is sponsoring a debate between civil libertarians and penologists
about a controversial technique known as "slow-timing," in which
prisoners' metabolisms are slowed by cryotherapy while they are
simultaneously exposed to subliminal messaging, so that a twenty year prison
term would seem to pass in months.
(visual: Telfer in front of UN)
ReMell Telfer, of the civil rights group Humanity is Watching, calls this
further evidence that we have become what he terms a "people-processing
society."
TELFER: "They say they want these prisoners to return to society more
quickly, but they just want more manageable prisoners and faster
turnaround. Instead of trying to prevent crime, we spend our money on more
and more expensive methods of punishing people—bigger prisons, more
police. Now they want to take some poor jerk who's stolen someone's wallet
and spend half a million of the taxpayer's credits to put him in a coma . . . !"

ANOTHER pair of the voracious tongs leaped from the water and flung itself at them, the huge jaws snapping like a bear-trap. Chief Strike Anywhere managed to dodge the attack, but the tongs smashed against the birchbark rail as they fell back into the river and Orlando and the others were rattled violently in the bottom of the canoe.

Another shudder rolled Orlando on his belly and onto the knobby hilt of the sword he thought he had lost, then a shout of pain from the Indian made him sit up. One of the pairs of salad tongs had the chief by the arm and was trying to drag him into the river; as Orlando watched in horror, the arm began to stretch like taffy. He snatched up his sword and brought it down on the tongs as hard as he could, just behind the teeth. The impact shook him from his fingers to his spine, but the tongs let go of the chief, sent Orlando an evil look, then sank back into the roiling water.

Chief Strike Anywhere rubbed his arm, which had already snapped back to its former size and shape, then turned to renew the battle. A chorus of thin voices from close by made Orlando wonder if someone might be coming to rescue them, but it was only the vegetables on the shoreline, who had disassembled their conga line to crowd along the water's edge. Most were watching the attack on the canoe in thrilled horror, although some, particularly the stewed beets, seemed to find the whole thing wildly funny, and were shouting out useless, drunken advice indiscriminately to both boaters and predatory utensils.

Something thumped them at the waterline once more and the little boat shuddered. Orlando braced himself, then raised the sword over his head. He knew that any moment now the canoe would go over, and he was determined to take at least one of the hinged, blunt-headed creatures with him. Fredericks rose beside him, trying to fit an arrow to his bowstring even as the canoe seesawed briefly on the handle of one of the attackers, then dropped back into the water.

The ruckus from the shore was suddenly pierced by a scream of anguish.

Some of the vegetables in the front row, jostled by the gawkers behind them and the dozens more hurrying out of the upturned colander to see what was happening, had been forced out into the river. A little cherry tomato was wailing piteously, floating farther and farther from the riverbank. A head of lettuce, a flower lei still looped about its widest circumference, waded out after the tomato, shrieking.

Something split the water beside the lettuce. The head was tossed up into the air, then fell back. More jaws flashed and clacked shut— even at a great distance, Orlando could hear the fibrous crunching. As lettuce leaves flew everywhere, the whole school of tongs hurried to the vicinity. Panicked, the beachfront spectators began to blunder into each other as they fled the feeding frenzy, and in the chaos several more fell into the water. Bits of tomato pulp and bleeding beet now streamed from toothy jaws. A carrot wearing a barbecue apron was lifted up out of the water and snapped in half.

Within moments the water around the canoe had grown calm, while a stone's throw away the river's edge was a froth of snapping tongs and vegetable parts. Chief Strike Anywhere picked up his paddle and turned the canoe again toward the middle of the river. "Lucky for us," he grunted, "them like salad better."

"That's . . . that's horrible." Fredericks was leaning on the side of the canoe, fascinated by the murderous violence. A scum of pureed vegetables was quickly forming along the river's edge.

"It them fault," replied Strike Anywhere coldly. "They get tongs worked up in first place. Smell of vegetables make them crazy."

Orlando could not help feel sorry for the little cherry tomato. It had cried just like a lost child.

"No can take you to land that side," Strike Anywhere told the tortoise later, as they floated in the slow current at midstream. A little mist lay on the river here, so that the banks were almost invisible, the cabinets only dim shapes towering on either side. "Tongs very busy there for long time."

"I perfectly understand." The tortoise had only recently reemerged from his shell, where he had retreated during the attack. "And I have no wish to be deposited on the other side, which is strange to me. Perhaps I will stay with you a while, if you don't mind, and then you can set me ashore later."

Strike Anywhere grunted and began to paddle again.

"We have got to get out of here, Orlando," Fredericks said quietly. "This all just scans too majorly. I mean, it would be bad enough just to get killed, but sixed by something out of a silverware drawer. . . ?"

Orlando smiled wearily. "If we help you find your papoose," he called to the chief, "will you help us to leave the Kitchen? We don't belong here, and we need to find our friends."

The chief turned, his long-nosed face shrewd in the dim bulblight from above. "No can go back up faucet," he said. "Have to go out other end of Kitchen."

Before he could explain further, a sound came to them across the waters, a chorus of piping voices that Orlando thought for a moment might be survivors from the terrible vegetable massacre—except these voices were raised in intricate, three-part harmony.

"Sing we now, we rodents three,"
Sightless all since infancy,
Can't see, but we sing con brio,
A blind, note-bleating fieldmouse trio."

A shape appeared in the fog, long and cylindrical, surmounted by three vertical figures. As it drew closer, it was revealed to be three mice in matching dark glasses, perched atop a bottle—which, with impossibly clever pink feet, they rolled beneath them like a lumberjack's log, never once losing their balance. Their arms were looped about each other's shoulders; the outside mouse on one end held a tin cup, the one at the other end a white cane.

"And ever since our mummy birthed us
We love to clean up every surface
Just pour enough to fill this cup
And wipe those stains and spills right up!"

"Three little mice, we like to sing,
But love to clean more than anything,
And if you use us, we suspect
You'll also find we disinfect!
A one-eyed bat could see it's true—
Blind Mice Cleanser will work for you!"

The tinny barbershop harmonies were so perfect and so completely silly that when the song was finished, Orlando could think of nothing to do but applaud; the tortoise did, too. Fredericks gave him an irritated look, but reluctantly joined in. Only Chief Strike Anywhere remained stoically silent. The three mice, still rolling the bottle beneath them, took a deep bow.

"Now available in Family Size!" squeaked the one holding the cane.

The word "family" may have touched a chord in the chief, or he might only have been waiting courteously for the mice to finish their song. He asked, "You seen bad men on big boat? With little papoose?"

"They could hardly have seen anything," suggested the tortoise. "Now could they?"

"No, we don't see much," agreed one of the mice.

"But we listen a lot," added another.

"We may have heard this particular tot." The third nodded gravely as he spoke.

"A big boat passed us."

"Two hours ago."

"They didn't seem to like our show."

"A baby was crying."

"We thought that was sad."

"And jeepers!—those men sounded pretty bad."

After a pause, the one with the cane piped up again. "They didn't smell too good, either," it said in a conspiratorial whisper. *"Ot-nay oo-tay ean-clay,* if you see what we're saying."

Strike Anywhere leaned forward. "Which way they go?"

The mice put their heads together and indulged in a great deal of quiet but animated discussion. At last they turned back, spread their arms, then began to do a chorus kick while still keeping the cleanser bottle revolving merrily beneath them—a very good trick, even Fredericks had to admit later.

> *"The shores of Gitchee-Goomee*
> *May be shady, green, and nice,"*

they sang,

> *"But except saying 'Hi!' to Hiawatha,*
> *The trip's not worth the price.*
> *The spot you seek is closer*
> *—You can be there in a trice!—*
> *Those kidnapping chaps*
> *Have followed old maps*
> *To the famous Box of Ice."*

The mouse with the tin cup waved it in a circle and added, "Don't forget—it's almost spring! Time to scrub your surfaces daisy-fresh!" Then the trio danced their pink feet so fast that the bottle swung around until its nose pointed away from the canoe. As the current carried them off, Orlando noticed for the first time that not one of them had a tail.

Within moments they were lost in the mist again, but their high-pitched voices floated back for awhile longer, singing some new hymn to the glories of elbow-grease and shiny counters.

"Right, the farmer's wife . . ." Orlando murmured, as the nursery rhyme came back to him. "Poor little things."

"What are you babbling about?" Fredericks frowned at him, then shouted, "Hey, where are we going?" as the chief began paddling with renewed and even increased vigor toward the unexplored farther shore.

"The Ice Box," explained the tortoise. "It is near the far end of the Kitchen, and a place of many legends. In fact, stories tell that some-where inside it lie 'sleepers'—folk who have existed as long as the

Kitchen itself, but always in slumber, and who will dream their cold dreams until Time itself ends if they are left undisturbed. Sometimes these sleepers, without ever waking, will predict the future to anyone lucky or unlucky enough to be nearby, or answer questions that otherwise would go unaddressed."

"Bad men no care about sleepers," the chief said, leaning into each stroke of the paddle. "Them want gold."

"Ah, yes." The tortoise laid a stubby finger alongside his blunt beak and nodded. "They have heard the rumors that one of the Shoppers themselves has left a cache of golden treasure in the Ice Box. This may be merely a fairy tale—no one I know has ever seen one of the Shoppers, who are said to be godlike giants who come into the Kitchen only when night is done, when all who live here are as helplessly asleep as those in the farthest depths of the Ice Box. But whether the gold is a myth or the truth, clearly these bad men believe it to be real."

"Help me out, Gardino," Fredericks whispered. "What the hell is an ice box?"

"I think it's what they used to call a refrigerator."

Fredericks looked at the unstoppable, mechanical movements of Chief Strike Anywhere as he paddled toward his lost son. "This just scans and scans, doesn't it?" he said. "And then it scans some more."

At least another hour seemed to pass before they reached land—or floor, Orlando supposed. Clearly the size of the river bore very little relation to any kind of scale; based on the size of the sink and countertops they had already visited, the Kitchen would have to be a real-world room hundreds of meters wide for such a long water journey to make sense. But he knew it was no use thinking about it too much—the Kitchen, he sensed, was not supposed to be analyzed that way.

The spot the chief had chosen was a small spit of dry space near the base of a massive leg that might have belonged to a table or chair—the piece of furniture was too large to see properly in the dark. This side of the kitchen seemed darker than the other riverbank, as though they were a much greater distance from the overhead bulb.

"You stay here," the Indian said. "Me go to look for bad men. Me come back soon, we make plan." One of his longer speeches now finished, he carried the canoe out until the water was past his perfectly cylindrical chest, then climbed aboard with silent grace.

"Well," said the tortoise as he watched him paddle away, "I can't pretend to be happy I've been caught up in all this, but I suppose we must make the best of things. Too bad we have no way of lighting a fire—it would make the waiting a little less lonely."

Fredericks seemed about to say something, then shook his head. Orlando realized that his friend had been about to ask a question, but had been suddenly embarrassed by the idea of talking to a cartoon. Orlando smiled. It was funny to know someone so well, and yet not to know them at all. He had known Sam Fredericks for years now— since they had both been sixth graders—and still had never seen his face.

Her face.

As always, the realization startled him. He looked at the familiar Pithlit-the-Thief features—the sharp chin, the large, expressive eyes— and wondered again what Fredericks really looked like. Was she pretty? Or did she look like her usual Fredericks sims, except a girl instead of a boy? And what did it matter?

Orlando wasn't sure it *did* matter. But he wasn't sure it didn't, either.

"I'm hungry," Fredericks announced. "What happens if we eat something here, Orlando? I mean, I know it doesn't really feed us or anything. But would it feel good?"

"I'm not sure. I guess it depends on whatever it is that's keeping us on the system." He tried to consider that for a moment—how the brain as well as body might be locked into a virtual interface—but he was having trouble making his thoughts stay together. "I'm too tired to think about it."

"Perhaps you two should sleep," the tortoise said. "I would gladly keep watch, in case our friend comes back, or something less savory takes an interest in us."

Fredericks gave the tortoise a look not entirely devoid of suspicion. "Yeah?"

Orlando settled against the broad base of the furniture leg, which was wide as a grain silo out of one of those old Western flicks and made a reasonably comfortable backrest. "Come on," he said to Fredericks. "You can put your head on my shoulder."

His friend turned and stared. "What does *that* mean?"

"Just . . . just so you'll be comfortable."

"Oh, yeah? And if you still believed I was a guy, would you have said that?"

Orlando had no honest answer. He shrugged. "Okay, so I'm a total woofmaster. So take me to Law Net Live."

"Perhaps I should tell you lads a story," the tortoise said brightly. "That sometimes helps to dig a path toward the Sands of Sleep."

"You said something about the Shoppers." Orlando had been intrigued, although he did not know if he had the strength to listen to an entire story. "Do you believe they're the ones who made you? Who made all the . . . the people in the Kitchen?"

Fredericks groaned, but the tortoise ignored him. "Made us? Goodness, no." He took his spectacles off and wiped them vigorously, as if the mere thought made him jumpy. "No, we are made elsewhere. But the Shoppers, if the stories are true, bring us here from that other place, and thus we spend our nights in the Kitchen, longing always to return to our true home."

"Your true home?"

"The Store, most call it, although I met a group of forks and spoons once who belonged to a flatware sect that referred to the great home as 'The Catalog.' But all agree that wherever that great home is, it is a place where we do not sleep unless we choose to, and in which the Bulb is beautiful and bright through a night which never ends. There, it is said, the Shoppers will serve *us.*"

Orlando smiled and looked to Fredericks, but his friend's eyes were already closed. Fredericks had never been very interested in the hows and whys of things. . . .

As the tortoise droned quietly on, Orlando felt himself sliding into a sort of waking dream in which he and his fellow Kitchen-mates could live their cartoon lives without fear of being put back in drawers or cabinets, and in which all the violences of the night before were gone when darkness returned again.

Kind of like it would be if I lived here all the time, he thought groggily. *It's funny—even the cartoons want to be alive. Just like me. I could live here forever, and not be sick, and never have to go into that hospital again, 'cause I will go there again, and next time I won't come out, maybe I won't come out this time the tubes and the nurses all pretending they're not sad but I wouldn't have to if this was real and I could live here forever and never die. . . .*

He sat up suddenly. Fredericks, who perhaps against his or her better judgment had curled up against his shoulder after all, protested sleepily.

"Wake up!" Orlando shook his friend. The tortoise, who had lulled himself into a kind of gentle reverie, peered at him over the rim of his spectacles as though seeing him for the first time, then slowly closed his eyes again and dropped back into sleep. "Come on, Fredericks," Orlando whispered loudly, not wanting to drag the tortoise into this, "wake up!"

"What? What is it?" Fredericks was always slow as a sloth to wake, but after a few moments he apparently remembered that they were in a potentially dangerous place and his eyes popped open. "What's happening?"

"I figured it out!" Orlando was both elated and sickened. The full import of the thing—the dreadful bargain those people had made—was just becoming clear to him. It could never mean as much to Fredericks as it did to him, never be as personal to anyone else, but even with his own fears and obsessions screaming their empathy, the thought of what the Grail people were doing made him angry to the very core of his being.

"Figured *what* out? You're having a dream, Gardiner."

"No. I'm not, I swear. I just figured out what the Grail Brotherhood people want—what all of this is about."

Fredericks sat up, annoyance turning to something like worry. "You did?"

"Think about it. Here we are, and we've already been in a bunch of these things—these simworlds—and they're just as good as the real world, right? No, better, because you can make anything, *be* anything."

"So?"

"So why do you think they made these places? Just to run around in, like you and I run around in the Middle Country?"

"Maybe." Fredericks rubbed his eyes. "Listen, Orlando, I'm sure this is utterly important and everything, but could you just tell me in a few words?"

"Think about it! You're some majorly rich person. You have everything you want, everything money can buy. Except that there's one thing you can't do, no matter how much money you have—one thing money can't buy, that makes all the houses and jets and everything worthless.

"They're going to *die,* Fredericks. All the money in the world can't stop that. All the money in the world won't help you if your body gets old and dies and rots away. Until now."

Now his friend's eyes were wide. "What are you saying, exactly? That they're going to keep themselves from dying? How?"

"I'm not sure. But if they can find a way to live here, in this Otherland place, they don't need bodies any more. They could live here forever, Fredericks, just like they've always lived—no, better! They can be *gods!* And if they had to kill a few kids to get it, don't you think they'd be willing to pay that price?"

Fredericks gaped. Then his mouth closed and his lips rounded. He whistled. "*Tchi seen,* Orlando, you really think so? God." He shook his head. "Scanny. This is the biggest thing ever."

Now that he understood the stakes for the first time, Orlando was also realizing that he hadn't known how frightened he could be. This was the black, black shadow of the golden city. "It is," he whispered, "it really is. The biggest thing ever."

THE dark-skinned army man behind the desk was not the normal, friendly Corporal Keegan that usually sat there. He kept looking at Christabel like the waiting room of an office was not the place for a little girl, even if it was her dad's office and he was just on the other side of the double doors. Corporal Keegan always called her "Christa-lulu-bel" and sometimes gave her a piece of candy from a box in his drawer. The man at the desk now was all scowly, and Christabel did not like him.

Some people just made mean faces at kids. It was scanny. (That was Portia's word, and Christabel wasn't entirely sure what it meant, but she thought it meant stupid.) And it *was* stupid. Couldn't the man see that she was being extra special quiet?

She had a lot to think about, anyway, so she just ignored the scowly man and let him go back to working his squeezers. A *lot* to think about.

The boy from outside was what she had to think about, and Mister Sellars. When the boy had come into Mister Sellars' tunnel and frightened Christabel so bad, he had been waving a sharp thing and she had been really, really sure he was going to hurt them both with it. And he had even waved it at Mister Sellars and called him bad names, like "freak," but instead of being scared, Mister Sellars had just made a kind of funny quiet laugh and then asked the boy if he wanted something to eat.

Christabel had seen a show on the net once where a bunch of people were trying to catch the last tiger somewhere—she didn't remember if it was the last tiger in the world or just in that place, but she remembered it was the last—because the tiger had a hurt leg and broken teeth and it would die if it tried to live in the outside by itself. But even though the tiger's leg was so hurt that it could barely walk, and they were offering it food to try to get it to go in a special trap, it still wouldn't come near them.

That was the look the strange boy had given Mister Sellars, a you-won't-catch-me look. And he had waved the knife around again and yelled really loud, scaring Christabel so bad she would have peed her pants again if there was anything left to pee. But Mister Sellars hadn't been scared at all, even though he was so thin and weak—his arms weren't any bigger than the boy's arms—and was in a wheelchair. He just asked him again if he wanted something to eat.

The boy had waited a long time, then scowled just like the man at the desk was doing, and said "What you got?"

And then Mister Sellars had sent her away.

That was the hardest thing to think about. If Mister Sellars wasn't afraid of the boy who was named Cho-Cho, if he didn't think the boy would hurt him, why did he send her away? Did the boy only hurt little kids? Or was there something Mister Sellars was going to do or say that he didn't want Christabel to hear, only the boy? That made her feel bad, like the time when Ophelia Weiner had said she could only have three people to her slumber party, her mom's rules, and had invited Portia and Sieglinde Hill and Delphine Riggs, even though Delphine Riggs had only gone to their school for a few weeks.

Portia said afterward that it was a dumb sleepover, and that Ophelia's mom made them look at pictures of Ophelia's family at their house in Dallas where they had a pool, but Christabel had still felt very sad. And having Mister Sellars send her away so he could talk to the boy and give him something to eat made her feel the same way, like things were different.

She wondered if she could take out the Storybook Sunglasses and say "Rumpelstiltskin" and then ask Mister Sellars why he did it, but even though she really, really wanted to, she knew it would be a very bad idea to use them here, right in her daddy's office with that man looking over at her with his face like a rock. Even if she whispered ever so quiet, it was a bad idea. But she really wanted to know, and she felt like crying.

The door to her daddy's office room suddenly opened, like it had been pushed open by the loud voice that was talking.

". . . I don't really care, Major Sorensen. Nothing personal, you understand, but I just want results." The man talking was standing in the doorway, and the man behind the desk jumped up like his chair had caught on fire. The man who said he didn't care wasn't as tall as her daddy, but he looked very strong, and his coat was tight across his back. His neck was very brown and had wrinkles on it.

"Yes, sir," her daddy said. Two more men stepped out of the office and moved to either side of the door, like they meant to catch the man with the brown neck if he suddenly fell over.

"Well, then get it handled, damn it!" the man said. "I want him located. If I have to throw a cordon a hundred miles wide around this base and institute house-to-house searches, I will—I consider finding him that important. You could have done whatever was necessary before he had time to find a hiding place, and I would have made sure General Pelham backed you all the way. But you didn't, and there's not much point in stirring up a hornet's nest now. So, do it your own way . . . but you better get it done. You read me?"

Her daddy, who was nodding his head as the man spoke, saw Christabel over the man's shoulder and his eyes opened wide for a second. The man turned around. His face was in such a frown that Christabel was certain he was going to start yelling at everyone to get this little kid out of here. He had a gray mustache, much smaller and neater than Captain Ron's, and his eyes were very bright. For a moment he stared at her like a bird would look at a worm it wanted to eat, and she was scared all over again.

"Aha!" he said in a growly voice. "A spy."

Christabel pushed herself back into the chair. The magazine she had been holding fell onto the floor with the pages open.

"Ohmigod, I scared her." Suddenly he smiled. He had very white teeth, and his eyes crinkled up when he did it. "It's all right, I'm just kidding. Who are you, sweetie?"

"My daughter, sir," her daddy said. "Christabel, say hello to General Yacoubian."

She tried to remember what her daddy had taught her. It was hard to think with the man smiling at her. "Hello, General, sir."

"Hello, General, sir," he said, and laughed, then turned to the man who had been sitting at Corporal Keegan's desk. "You hear that, Murphy? At least someone connected with this man's army gives me a little respect." The general came around the desk and kneeled down in front of Christabel. He smelled like something she smelled on cleaning day, like furniture polish maybe. From close up, his eyes were still like a bird's eyes, very bright, with pale flecks in the brown. "And what's your name, honey?"

"Christabel, sir."

"I'll bet you are your daddy's pride and joy." He reached out and took her cheek between his fingers, just for a moment, very gentle, then stood up. "She's a beauty, Sorensen. Did you come down to help your daddy work, honey?"

"I'm not quite sure why she's here myself, sir." Her daddy walked toward her, almost as though he wanted to be close in case she said something wrong so he could stop her. Christabel did not understand why, but she felt scared again. "Why are you here, baby? Where's your mommy?"

"She called the school to say Mrs. Gullison was sick, so I should come here. She's shopping in the town today."

The general smiled again, showing almost all his teeth. "Ah, but a good spy always has a cover story." He turned to her daddy. "We're due back in Washington in three hours. But I'll be back beginning of next week. And I'd *love* to have some definite progress. I recommend that to you highly, Sorensen. Even better, I'd like to come back and find you-know-who under full guard in a suicide watch cell, ready for questioning."

"Yes, sir."

The general and his three men headed toward the door. He stopped there after the first two went through. "Now you be a good girl," he said to Christabel, who was trying to get the idea of a suicide watch out of her mind, and wondering who would wear something like that. "You mind your daddy, you hear me?"

She nodded.

"Because daddies know best." He gave her a little salute, then walked out. The scowly man went out last, looking very spyflick, like if he didn't keep watching carefully, Christabel's daddy might run up behind the general and hit him.

After they all left, her daddy sat on the desk and stared at the door for a while. "Well, maybe we should get you home," he said at last. "Mommy ought to be back from shopping by now, don't you think?"

"Who are you supposed to find, Daddy?"

"To find? Were you listening to that?" He walked over and messed up her hair.

"Daddy, don't! Who are you supposed to find. . . ?"

"Nobody, sweetie. Just an old friend of the general's." He took her hand in his. "Now come on. After the day I've just had, I think I can take a few minutes off work to drive my daughter home."

IT was odd, but the thing that awakened Jeremiah Dako was the silence.

The oddity was that as one of only two people roaming through a huge, abandoned military base, he should have been startled by anything *except* silence. Living in the Wasp's Nest with only Long Joseph for company was most of the time like being the last inhabitant of one of the ghost townships that dotted the southern Transvaal, where the Tokoza Epidemic had emptied the shantytowns so quickly that many of the fleeing residents left even their few miserable possessions behind—cooking pots, cardboard suitcases, tattered but wearable clothing—as though their owners had all been snatched away in a second by some dreadful magic.

But even the deserted Transvaal worker stations had been open to wind and rain and the incursions of wildlife. Birdsong could still be heard echoing through the dusty streets, or rats and mice scrabbling in the rubbish dumps.

The Wasp's Nest, though, was a monument to silence. Shielded from the elements by uncountable tons of stone, its machineries largely stilled, its massive doors so tightly sealed that even insects could not slip in and the air vents so finely-screened that no visible living organism could enter, the base might have been something from a fairy tale—Beauty's castle, perhaps, where she and all her family slept, powdered in the dust of centuries.

Jeremiah Dako was not a fanciful man, but there were times in the eternal night of indoor living, when his companion Joseph Sulaweyo had finally slipped into fitful sleep—a sleep that seemed plagued by its own malign fairy folk—when Jeremiah stared at the vast cement coffins that were now his responsibility and wondered what tale he had stumbled into.

He wondered, too, what the Author expected him to do.

I'm one of the ones they don't talk about much in the stories, he decided on a night when the readings were unremarkable and the hours went by slowly. It was only a slightly painful realization. *The man holding the spear by the door. The one who brings in some magical something-or-other on a velvet pillow when someone important calls for it. One of those people in the crowd who shouts "Hooray!" when everything ends happily. I've always been that man. Worked for my mother until I was grown, worked for the doctor for twenty-four years after that. I might have run away from it all for beautiful, beautiful Khalid if he had asked me, but I would have wound up keeping house for him, too. I would have been in his story, that is all, instead of the doctor's or my mother's, or right now this crazy thing with machines and villains and this big empty building under a mountain.*

Of course, a spear-carrier role was not entirely without rewards, and neither was this multistory ghost town. He had time to read and to think now. He had not had much time for either since he had gone to work for the Van Bleeks. All his spare time had gone into assuring his mother's comfort, and although Susan would not have begrudged him the occasional quiet hour spent reading or watching the net while she was deep in her researches, the mere fact of her trust had spurred him on to great—and almost always unnoticed—efforts. But here there was literally nothing to do except to watch the readouts on the V-tanks, and make sure the fluid levels stayed topped up. It was no more difficult than maintaining the doctor's expensive car—which was now parked in the lowest of the Wasp's Nest parking lots, and which would be gathering dust if he didn't go up there every few days to clean it with a soft cloth and agonize over the ruined grill and cracked windshield.

He sometimes wondered if he would ever get to drive it again.

Jeremiah, despite not liking the fellow very much, would have been willing to devote more of his leisure time to conversation with Long Joseph, but Renie's father (who had never been exactly warm) was growing increasingly remote. The man spent hours in brooding silence, or vanished into the farther reaches of the base and returned with his eyes reddened by tears. Jeremiah had liked it better when the fellow was just nasty.

And Jeremiah's every attempt to reach out had been rebuffed. At first he had thought it was only the man's pride, or perhaps his hopeless, provincial prejudice against homosexuality, but lately he had come to realize that there was a knot in Long Joseph Sulaweyo that might never be untied. The man lacked the vocabulary to define his pain except in the most obvious ways, but more critically, he did not seem to understand that there could be an alternative, if he would only try to find the answers within himself. It was as though the entire twenty-first century had passed him by, and he could imagine emotional pain solely in the primitive ways of the prior century, only as something to be raged against or endured.

Lately, as though the inner turmoil were coming to a rolling boil, Long Joseph had taken to walking incessantly, not only vanishing for long journeys through the base—Jeremiah had thought at first he was searching for alcohol, but surely he had given that up by now?—but even pacing in a most maddening way when they were in the same room, always moving, always walking. In the past few days Joseph had even begun singing to himself as he did so, filling the long silences between irregular conversation with a tuneless murmur that was starting to make Jeremiah feel like someone was poking him repeatedly in the back of the head. The songs, if that was what they were, did not seem to have any application to Long Joseph's situation. They were just old popular standards, repeated over and over again, sometimes—bereft of their original melodies and with the lyrics mumbled or even turned into nonsense syllables—just barely, though irritatingly, recognizable.

Jeremiah honestly did feel sorry for the man. Joseph had lost his wife in a horrible, lingering way, his son was all but dead with a mystery illness, and now his daughter had gone away into danger, although she remained cruelly, deceptively near. Jeremiah understood that Long Joseph was hurting badly, and that the absence of anything to drink had removed one of the man's few emotional crutches, but

that did not mean that the mumbling and the pacing and the inces-
sant idiot crooning were not soon going to make Jeremiah far more
crazy than Long Joseph could ever aspire to be.

Thus it was that when he awakened in the middle of the night,
several hours before he was due to take his next shift from Renie's
father, the silence—the absence of even the distant whisper of Joseph's songs—startled him.

Jeremiah Dako had dragged the military-issue camp bed down to
the underground lab in part because he had been working longer and
longer shifts watching over the V-tanks, filling in for Long Joseph
when the man was late returning from one of his rambling walks
around the complex—or sometimes when he did not come back at all.
At least, that was the reason he cited, not without some heat, when
Joseph Sulaweyo demanded to know his reasons for moving a bed
into the lab.

But in a dark part of his imagination, he had also begun to lose
trust in Long Joseph. Jeremiah feared that, in a fit of despondency,
the other man might actually do something to damage the tanks or
the processing equipment that made them run.

Now, as he lay in the darkness of the office he had chosen as his
makeshift bedroom, listening to a very unfamiliar silence, he felt a
cool wind of fear blow through him. Had it finally happened, then?
Or was he just strung too tightly himself? Being trapped for weeks in
a deserted underground base, listening to the echoes of his own footsteps and the mumbling of a crazy man, was not the way to keep
anyone mentally healthy. Perhaps he was jumping at shadows—or at
innocent silences.

Jeremiah groaned quietly and got up. His heart was beating only a
little more swiftly than it should, but he knew he would not get back
to sleep until he saw for himself that Long Joseph Sulaweyo was sitting in the chair in front of the tank readings. Or perhaps off using
the toilet—even Jeremiah occasionally left the room on his own shift
to answer a call of nature or to make coffee, or even just to get a little
cold air in the face from one of the ventilation ducts.

That was probably it, of course.

Jeremiah slipped into the pair of old slippers he had found in one
of the storage lockers—a comfort that made him feel at least a little
bit at home—and walked out to the catwalk to look down at the level
that contained the control panels.

The chair was empty.

Still very deliberately staying calm, he headed for the stairs. Long

Joseph had gone to the kitchen or the toilet. Jeremiah would just watch the tanks until he got back. It was not as though there was ever much to do beyond the quite predictable work of topping up the water and other liquids on schedule, and flushing out the waste system and slotting in new filters. And what could be done anyway, short of pulling Renie and !Xabbu out of the tanks—against Renie's express wishes—unless there were a full-scale emergency? The communication system had gone bad the first day, and had proved itself beyond Jeremiah's skills to fix. So even if Long Joseph had wandered off, it wasn't as though he were leaving the helm of a ship in the middle of a sea battle or something.

All the readings were normal. Jeremiah checked them twice just to make sure. As his eye swept along the station for the second time, he noticed the faint light of the drawscreen. The stylus lay beside it, the only thing on the station not at right angles to something else, a single and minor note of disorder, but for some reason it made Jeremiah shudder as he leaned forward to read the screen.

I CANT TAKE NO MORE, the note read, the labored handwriting black against the glow of the screen. *I AM GOING TO BE WITH MY CHILD.*

Jeremiah read it two more times, trying to make sense of it as he fought the strangling sense of alarm. What did the man mean, *with his child?* With Renie? Did he think he could join her just by climbing into the tank? Jeremiah had to restrain the urge to throw the great lids open, to make sure the madman had not climbed into the plasmodal gel beside his unconscious daughter. There was no need for him to touch the V-tanks, he knew. The readings on Renie's tank, on both of them, were normal—one set of vital signs in each.

A darker meaning suddenly occurred to him. Jeremiah stood up, suddenly very afraid.

If he thought his boy Stephen had died—if he had suffered one of his bad dreams, perhaps, or his depression had just beaten him down until the difference between comatose and corpse seemed nil. . . .

I have to go and look for him, the mad bastard. Jesus save us! He could be anywhere in here. He could just go up to the top story of the lab and throw himself off.

Reflexively, he looked up, but the floors above the lab were silent, and nothing moved on any of them. The great snake-tangle of cables above the V-tanks was also unchanged, although for a moment one of the cable troughs, dangling unused, looked unpleasantly like a hanged man.

There was no body on the floor either.

"Good God," Jeremiah said aloud, and wiped his brow. There was no helping it: he would have to look out for him. It would take a while, but not forever—the base was sealed, after all. But he would have to leave the tanks unsupervised, and that he did not like. Perhaps because of his own apprehension, the sleepers within seemed terribly vulnerable. If something happened to them while he was chasing after that crazy fellow . . . ! He could not bear the thought.

Jeremiah went back to the station and hunted through the settings until he found the one he remembered—something Martine had demonstrated two weeks ago, which felt like years back, now. When he changed the output line, the the sound of twin heartbeats (!Xabbu's slower, but both strong and not unduly agitated) bounced out of the public address system and filled the high laboratory chamber: *bi-bom, bi-bom—bi-bom, bi-bom,* slightly out of synch, with Renie's lapping the Bushman's by the seventh or eight beat.

It would probably send Long Joseph absolutely mad if he heard it, make him positive something had gone wrong, but at this moment Jeremiah did not give a damn.

"Joseph! Joseph, where are you?"

As he searched the huge building, trudging through the deserted halls with the ping-pong of twin heartbeats echoing around him, Jeremiah could not help but remember coming back to the doctor's house on that awful night. The lights had been out, which was normal, but even the security lights along the fence had been dark; from the moment he had turned onto the wide cul-de-sac and seen the house's shadowy silhouette, he had been terrified. And each moment of walking through the silent corridors, calling the doctor's name without reply, had only intensified the fear. As dreadful as it was, finding Susan Van Bleeck lying battered on the floor of the laboratory had almost been a relief—at least the horror had a shape now. It could get no worse.

Except of course it *had* been worse, when he had returned to the hospital after dropping Renie off, to find orderlies around her bedside, unhooking the life support.

And now, forced by that man's idiocy to wander in his slippers through *this* cavernous place, as if reliving that dreadful night, not knowing when he might stumble on a body. . . . He was even more angry than he was frightened. If he found Joseph Sulaweyo, and the man had *not* killed himself, Jeremiah would give him the thrashing of his life, no matter whether the other man was bigger or not.

The idea of giving a man a beating because he had failed to commit suicide pried loose from him a nervous and entirely involuntary gasp of laughter. It was not a pleasant sound.

He checked the most obvious places first. Joseph's own bed in the communal bunkroom was deserted, the tangle of blankets on the floor the only knot of disorder in an otherwise empty place. The kitchen, where the man had searched with such insane diligence for something to drink, was also empty. Jeremiah forced himself to open the pantries and the walk-in freezer, and even to look in the cabinets, despite his fear that he might pull one back to find Joseph's corpse leering at him, mouth foaming with some horrid industrial cleaning fluid. But the kitchen too was silent and uninhabited.

He worked his way systematically through all the living quarters and the offices, opening everything bigger than a file cabinet drawer. It took him the better part of two hours. The sound of Renie's and !Xabbu's heartbeats accompanied him, still quietly calm, but with just enough variation that after a while it became almost reassuring: it made him feel a little less alone.

Bi-bom . . . bi-bom . . .

His search of the living and working quarters finished, Jeremiah continued up to the parking lot, in case the mad fool Sulaweyo had tried to run the Ihlosi's engine and kill himself with carbon monoxide, not realizing that he would run out of gas long before he could fill half a million cubic meters of garage, even were it not ventilated. But the car was empty, untouched since its last cleaning, as battered and useless for the moment as Jeremiah felt. He opened the door and got a pocket torch out of the glove compartment, then continued on through the garage, shining the light up into the dark spaces behind the dangling lights on the extremely small chance that Joseph might have dragged himself up into the girders somehow to hang himself.

The garage levels were much faster to check, and all four were empty. Jeremiah stopped in the uppermost for a rest and a think, listening to the percussive echo of the heartbeats, now quadrupled and more by the stony walls. It made no sense—he had checked everywhere. Unless the man *had* climbed into one of the tanks. If he had drowned himself in the fluid, it would explain the lack of any extra vital signs.

Jeremiah shuddered. The thought of Irene Sulaweyo, unaware in that viscous blackness of her father's body floating only a few inches away . . .

He would have to check. It was horrible, but he would have to look. He wondered if just opening the tank would be enough to pull the sleepers out of their virtual dreams. And if Joseph was not there, and the experiment were aborted for nothing . . . ?

Troubled and still fearful, Jeremiah made his way over to the largest ventilation duct to get some air to clear his head. It worked, but not in the way he had planned.

The ventilator's screen was lying on the floor.

Jeremiah stared at it stupidly for a moment, then up to the open end of the great square tube, a dark hole into nothing. Jeremiah directed the torch beam back to the floor and saw that a handful of bolts had been set carefully in the middle of the screen.

The duct was big enough for a man, but narrow enough that someone, if they went carefully, could use their own shoulders and legs to brace themselves as they climbed upward. If that person were very determined. Or a little mad.

The amplified heartbeats were quieter here at the far side of the garage, away from the speaker. Jeremiah leaned his head into the duct and shouted Joseph's name, and heard his own voice rattle away and die. He shouted again, but there was still no reply. He wriggled his head and upper body into the duct and aimed the torch upward. A few cobwebs trailed at the first juncture, tethered only at one end, as though something had squeezed past them.

As he stared, Jeremiah thought he heard a sound breathe down the duct, a faintly musical hooting—perhaps a muffled voice trying to call out despite an injury. He strained to listen, but the sound was very quiet, and he cursed the heartbeats that had until only a few moments ago kept him such good company. He tucked the torch into his pocket and dragged himself all the way up into the duct so that he could block out the public-address noises with his own body.

And now he could hear it, the murmuring sound. A second later he knew what it was. Somewhere far away, up and along many lengths of plasteel pipe, the wind that swept down the Drakensbergs in the early morning was blowing across the other end of the open duct.

Long Joseph had gone to be with his child, Stephen. Not metaphorically—not by killing himself—but literally. Of course. Joseph Sulaweyo was a very literal man.

Oh, my Lord, what will happen now? Jeremiah climbed awkwardly back out of the duct. The heartbeats of those he guarded still echoed through the cavernous garage, slow and even, as though nothing had changed.

The bloody, bloody fool. . . !

CHAPTER 17

In The Works

IT was hard to have an intelligent thought about the scene before her—the stranger Azador on the floor amidst a wreckage of tiktoks, the girl Emily twittering like a bird as she covered him with obviously unwanted kisses—and Renie didn't have time to wait for such a thought to show up anyway. Corpses from New Emerald City's dwindling army of flying monkeys and green-bearded soldiers were scattered through the corridors of the Scarecrow's headquarters. Other defenders were dying at that very moment just a few hundred meters away, trying to hold the loading bay against rampaging tiktoks, and danger was increasing by the second. Still, she could not simply ignore what she had just heard.

"You . . . you had *sex* with her?"

Azador scowled as he wrestled free of the girl. "Perhaps. What is it to you?"

"She's a Puppet, isn't she?" Although with Emily just a few meters away, as joyful as a puppy to have rediscovered her beau, it was hard to believe that.

"Yes?" Azador climbed to his feet. "So? And what do you care about the sexual habits—or, let us be blunt, masturbatory habits—of others? Would you care to discuss your own sexual life?"

"But . . . but she's just a . . . a *program.* How could you do it? How could you take advantage of her?"

Azador shook his head, recovering a little of his self-assurance despite the girl wrapped around his shin, kissing his knee. "You cannot have it both ways. Is she a program? Or did I take advantage of a young woman?"

Renie turned to !Xabbu for some kind of support, but the baboon was no longer paying attention. "I hear more of those machine men coming." He pointed across the wide, tiled floor. "From that direction."

"We have to go out the front way." Azador tried without success to pull his leg free of Emily's clinging grasp. "God damn it!" He lifted his hand.

"If you hit her," Renie said sharply, "I'll kill you."

Azador stared at her for a long second. "Then you get this silly bitch away from me. Quickly, or we will all be killed."

Renie pulled the protesting Emily loose. The girl wailed, "But our baby . . . !"

"Is never going to get born if we don't move." A sudden thought hit her. "What did that horrible tin man say? 'You've discovered the Dorothy,' something like that? Is that what they were talking about—this baby?"

Azador was not interested in discussion. He was already legging it across the broad room, heading for a corridor at right angles to the one !Xabbu had warned would disgorge attackers. Renie swallowed a curse and jogged after him, with !Xabbu four-legging beside her. Emily needed no urging to follow the mustached man.

It's one thing to say you'd kill him, girl, Renie thought, *but he's big, and you don't have any weapons.* She berated herself for not having pilfered one of the antique rifles from the dead soldiers, although from what she'd seen at the loading bay, she doubted any of them had ammunition left.

Azador was not making the pace easy, and Renie was still sore from the many calamities in Kunohara's world and this twisted version of Oz. He led them on a winding route through the building, down corridors that seemed dead-ends, but which proved to have doors hidden in alcoves. Renie wondered again how he knew so much about this particular simworld. Not to mention his little trick for changing a wall into a door, she remembered.

Who the hell is this fellow?

The Scarecrow's palace, an endless functionalist warren of concrete walls and linoleum floors, could have doubled for a municipal structure in Durban, or indeed anywhere in the Third World. It had clearly once been occupied, even feverishly busy—old-fashioned printouts and other papers lay scattered everywhere, making footing treacherous, and there were enough desks and chairs to seat hundreds just in the sections they traversed, although at least half of them seemed built for people of much smaller than normal size—but now the building was as empty as the Hive after the ant swarm had passed through it.

Entropy, she told herself. *Isn't that the word? As though these things were filled up once, and then just allowed to run down, fall apart.* But they had been in only three simulations so far. It was a bit early to be making judgements.

Azador stopped in front of a wide double-door and strained against it. The doors opened a crack, but something seemed to be blocking them on the far side. Renie fell in beside him to add her strength; even Emily pushed, staring at her beloved as she did so as if he were singlehandedly parting the Red Sea. The image seemed even more appropriate a moment later when the doors suddenly crashed open and a gush of something scarlet poured through. For a moment Renie could only see it as a nightmarish wash of blood, but it was dry, and whispery, and when she scooped it in her hand she found it was . . .

"Confetti. . . ?"

They waded through the drifts of paper dots, then vaulted over the tumbled desks which had been piled on the far side. A banner, which dangled in their faces as they clambered over the furniture, read "We'll Miss You, Jellia Jamb! Happy Retirement!" in huge painted letters.

"This is the reception hall." Azador surveyed the stacks of folding tables which barred two of the room's other three entrances. "Someone's tried to barricade the place."

"Pretty pitiful job they made of it," Renie observed.

"Not many defenders left," Azador pointed out. As Renie started toward the unblocked door, he shouted, "No! Do not do that!"

Irritated, she spun. "Who are you to give me orders?"

"It is not orders. They have pushed things in front of other doors, but not those. We are expected to go through. Perhaps there is a trap on the other side."

Despite her dislike of the man, she was filled with shame. "You're right. I'm sorry."

"Let me go," !Xabbu suggested when they reached the door. "I am light and fast."

Renie shook her head. "Not until we open the door. Azador, is there a way to go around this one, like the way you got us out of the cell?"

He examined the walls in silence for a moment, then shook his head. "Not this room, no. This is not—what is the word?—snap-on code. Someone made this specially. It may have been nice at one time."

Renie looked at the huge, windowless, mint-green space and doubted that was so. Her eyes lit on the banner. "Hang on." She dragged the length of heavy paper from the wall, then approached the door cautiously and looped it through the handle. After giving the ends of the banner to Azador, she took one of the folding chairs—this place really could have been a Pinetown social hall!—and approached the door from the side. She reached out with the folded chair and pushed the latch on the door handle until it clicked, then Azador yanked on the banner and the door swung open.

Nothing exploded. No cloud of gas or rain of needle-sharp spikes flew out at them. !Xabbu approached the doorway cautiously, his muzzle close to the ground, head bobbing like a mongoose stalking a snake. Renie said a silent bit of childhood prayer for the little man's safety.

Seeing nothing immediately wrong, the baboon took a careful few steps forward, out of sight. Renie held her breath. An instant later, he scampered out again, fur erect along his spine. "Come quickly!"

The room was empty except for a pile of old clothes lying in the middle of the floor, festooned with coils of tubing. Renie was about to ask !Xabbu what had excited him when the bundle of old clothes lifted its flat, shriveled head. Emily squeaked and backed toward the door.

". . . *help* . . ." it murmured, a tiny dry sound that faded even before it had finished.

"Jesus Mercy, it's the Scarecrow." Renie took a few steps forward, then hesitated. Hadn't this thing wanted to kill them? But on the other hand, perhaps it could tell them how to get out of this place. Otherwise, they were reliant on Azador, and she was becoming less comfortable with that thought by the minute. "What can we do?" she asked the wrinkled thing on the floor.

A single finger rose and pointed limply toward one of the doors set in an otherwise featureless wall. She could only hope the thing still had enough brains to know which door was which.

"I hear the metal men," !Xabbu announced. "Very loud. Close now."

Renie snatched up the Scarecrow, trying not to trip over the spaghetti tangle of tubing. The King of Kansas twisted weakly in her grasp—a remarkably unpleasant sensation, like cradling a burlap snake.

All this kind of takes the shine off that nice Oz flick, Renie could not help thinking.

The door opened easily; inside, a stairwell led upward. Emily, her face frozen somewhere between awe and repulsion, snatched up a stray handful of tubes and one of the Scarecrow's booted feet, which had tumbled loose during the swift collection, and followed Renie, closely trailed by Azador and !Xabbu.

Something like a boiler room waited at the top of the stairs, pipes cross-connected in a tight grid beneath the ceiling and running up and down the walls. A single chair that might have come from the cockpit of an ancient airplane sat in front of a spot on one wall where all the pipes curved around the imitation wood cabinet of the wall-screen.

Scarecrow's head fluttered. He wobbled his hand toward a pipe that ended at right angles to the rest, its protruding nozzle a little more than a meter off the floor. Scarecrow summoned all his strength to take a breath. Renie leaned close to hear his voice whispering out.

"*. . . in chest . . .*"

She looked at the nozzle, then at the limp twist of overalls and flannel shirt that stretched between ribbon legs and empty head. She slid his nearly empty torso onto the nozzle between two buttons of his shirt, impaling him like some medieval torture victim, then held him in place. Nothing happened. One of the Scarecrow's hands flapped toward a flywheel. When Azador turned it, a hissing sound filled the room.

The Scarecrow's torso began to swell first, then his head slowly inflated, too. His legs straightened, unrolling themselves until his overalls were tight as sausage-skin. At last the King of Kansas forced himself away from the nozzle with jointless, balloon arms, and turned stiffly to face Renie and the others. He took his finger from the hole in his chest and let some air leak out until he was a little closer to his old baggy self, then plugged the opening with some spare straw from his lost foot.

"I've got bladders like you couldn't imagine," he said by way of explanation, his voice high-pitched and tight. "I can fill them with air in a pinch—and it's definitely Pinch City around here." He winked, but his head was so round that the eyelid couldn't fully close. "This won't work for long, but it will last until I can make certain neither of those bastards gets to take over Emerald—unless one of them wants to pitch his pup-tent on rubble and hot ashes, that is."

"What are you talking about?" Renie stepped forward, half-tempted to yank the straw stopper back out again. "You're going to burn the place down? What about us?"

Scarecrow waved a hand. His grin, which pulled his inflated features even tighter, actually squeaked. "Wouldn't be very generous after you saved me, would it? Fair enough, I'll let you get out first. But you'd better go now, because I've got another few minutes, tops. These Farmer John overalls don't make for a real tight pressure seal, if you know what I mean."

"We don't know how to get out of here," Renie said. "Is there . . . is there a crossing place? Like on the river?"

"A gateway?" The Scarecrow's scalloped smile widened. "Don't you even know what they're called? You really are out-of-towners, aren't you?"

"I know what a gateway is," Azador said tightly. "And I know there is one here in your palace."

"Palace!" The Scarecrow wheezed and thumped his knee with a gloved hand. A tiny puff of strawdust flew up. "That's a good one. You should have seen my 'cot in the real Emerald City—that was a palace! This—Christ, I think it's an engineer's rendering of an old National Guard armory or something. We got it cheap when we were setting the whole thing up."

"But there's a . . . a gateway here?" Renie pressed him.

"Was. Or rather still is, if you don't mind wading through about two hundred more of those goddamned mechanical men. It's in my throne room, behind the wallscreen. But Tinman's wind-ups have got it now—they have just about everything. Why do you think I dragged my sorry behind all the way over here?" He lifted a few of his tubes and rattled them sadly. "I can't believe after all this time, it's over."

"I hear the clicking men close by," !Xabbu announced. "In the big room beneath us."

"They won't get in here," Scarecrow said dismissively. "Once those doors are closed, it would take them days to break through."

"So how do we get out?" Renie demanded.

The Scarecrow, his neck still a bit overfull, had to turn his whole body to look at her. "I'll have to think about that. And you want a gateway, right?" He cupped his shapeless chin with one hand and set his forefinger against his pale temple.

"God damn it!" Azador shouted from the corner of the room. "Get this creature away from me!"

Renie turned to see Emily take a step backward, lip quivering. The girl finally seemed to have realized her attentions were unwanted. Renie interposed herself between the two of them. "Just stay close to me," she told the girl.

"But he was my special henry," Emily said tremulously. "He called me a pretty little pudding."

"Yeah?" Renie shot Azador a disgusted look. "Well, here's some news from RL—sometimes men are full of shit."

The subject of this description rolled his eyes and folded his arms across his chest.

The Scarecrow clapped his flabby palms together. "Ah! Of course! You can go to the Works. There's a gateway there, where the River runs through the treatment plants."

"The Works?" Azador asked. "That is where the Tinman is strongest."

"Yeah, but he's not watching his own backyard, he's watching *here*. Where the endgame is playing out." The King of Kansas was beginning to deflate. His puffy features took on a worried expression. "But you can't let him catch this girl. If he gets the Dorothy, the whole game's over."

"This is a *game* to you?" Renie shook her head in frustration. "All of this, people dead, suffering, and it's still just a game?"

Scarecrow was struggling now to hold his head upright. "Just? Are you uttermostly scantagious? I've barely been out of this simulation for two years—long enough to change my fluids and filters back in RL and that's about it. I've lost at least fifteen percent of my bone-mass, for God's sake, atrophied muscles, you name it! I've given everything I had to this simworld, and held onto it even after those whatever-they-are floated in from some other simulation and bumped out my partners. Now I'm going to blow up me and this whole building so that Tinman bastard and his fat crony don't get their hands on it—which means it will take me weeks to figure a way back in—and you say it's 'just a game'?" He rubbed his slack face. "You're the one who's out of her mind."

"Have you been out recently? Offline?"

He squinted at her. "Not for a couple of days. But I guess I'll get a little vacation now, like it or not. Why do you ask?"

Renie shrugged. "No particular reason." But she thought, *You've got a surprise coming, fellow,* then realized how callous that was. This person's life might be at risk—they still had no idea what the apparently changed rules of Otherland meant. "No, that's not true," she said. "There's an important reason. We think something might be wrong with the entire network. People have . . . have been having very strange problems. Unable to go offline. And . . . things that happen here might be affecting them offline, too." There was no way to explain her worries quickly, but she had to try to warn him. "I think if I were you, I would try to get offline the regular way before I committed virtual suicide."

The Scarecrow opened both eyes wide in a look of mock-astonishment, but behind him, Azador appeared disturbed. "Ooh, thank you, little lady. And when I happen into *your* world, I'll be sure to give you a bunch of unneeded advice, too." He turned to Azador, as though deciding that he was the only one worth addressing. "There's an airshaft running above this room—just behind that grille, there. You can follow it all the way to the roof if you want, or down to the basement, although you probably don't want to get stuck in a vertical shaft if you can help it. Got me?"

Azador nodded.

"Once you're out, you can make your way across the city to the river, and reach the Works that way. Or do whatever the hell you want. But you'd better get going, 'cause I can't wait forever. About fifteen minutes after I see the last butt disappear into the airshaft, this place is going to go up like a United Nations Day fireworks show. I can't wait any longer than that. I'm falling apart."

!Xabbu walked forward and stood on his hind legs before the straw man, who was sagging badly. "Can you not breathe more air into yourself?" the Bushman asked.

"I don't think the seams on this body would hold through another fill-up, and if they rip before I do what I want to do, it's all over. So get the hell out of here, will you?"

"Just tell me one thing," !Xabbu said. "What is the Dorothy you spoke of? You said we must keep the girl safe."

"Part of the way this simworld is set up." Scarecrow's voice was growing squeaky and thin. "Post-apocalyptic. Nuclear war. Survivors can't breed. Lots of Auntie Ems, Uncle Henrys, all sterile. So the myth of a girl-child who will be born to one of the emilys. The Dorothy, get it?" He peered from sunken, painted eyes at !Xabbu, who clearly did not. "Oh, go on," he trilled. "Get out of my face." He flicked on the wallscreen, which displayed a vision of New Emerald City under siege, a few of its squat buildings on fire and tiktoks rumbling through the damaged streets like two-legged tanks.

As first !Xabbu then the others struggled into the ventilation duct, Scarecrow raised his flabby arms high. *"I've seen things you people wouldn't believe,"* he declaimed in a helium squeal. He appeared to be talking to himself, or to the screen. *"Attack ships on fire off the shores of the Nonestic Ocean. I watched magic blunderbusses flash and glitter in the dark near Glinda's Palace. All those moments will be lost in time, like tears in the rain."* His head sagged with an audible hiss of escaping air. *"Time . . . to die . . . ."*

Last into the vent, Renie paused to try once more. "Scarecrow—whoever you are—I'm not just making this up. I think people might be dying from things that happen online. Really dying. There's something very wrong with the network."

The straw man had exposed a hidden panel in the wall, and with great effort was using his wobbly fingers to throw toggle switches, one after the other. "Jeez," he sighed. "You sure know how to screw up a good exit speech."

"But this is important!"

He shut his eyes and clapped his gloves over the place where ears would have been. "Is someone talking? Because I'm not hearing anything. . . ."

Renie sighed and turned to crawl after the others.

Minutes later they tumbled out of the vent and onto the gravel-strewn roof. It was day outside, but just barely. The sky was restless with ugly black clouds, and the hot, damp air smelled of electricity—Renie guessed there had been more tornado attacks while they had been inside. A steady trickle of sweat dripped between her breasts and down her stomach.

The river appeared to be a good distance into the Works, a dark clot of storage tanks, industrial piping, and lumpish low buildings. After a hurried argument, they decided to make their way across the railyard and then cross the Works at as direct an angle as possible, spending only as much time on Tinman's territory as they had to on their way to the river. Although they could see small knots of dispirited henrys being herded by tiktoks near the front of Scarecrow's concrete palace, the service yard below them was empty, so they clambered down a drainpipe to the ground and sprinted toward a siding away from the main line where several railway cars had been abandoned.

They were sheltering behind the tall wheels of a flatcar, and had just recovered their breath—or !Xabbu had, and the others were getting closer—when a loud but muffled *whump* knocked the ground from underneath them. Even the massive flatcar bounced, its wheels scraping against the track; for a terrifying moment Renie thought it might tip over and crush them all.

When the earth had stopped shaking, they crawled past the end of the flatcar and looked back. The innermost section of the Scarecrow's headquarters had been completely leveled, and much of the rest was hidden by a rising cloud of dust and dark smoke. Bits of ash and debris were beginning to filter down around them in a fine rain.

"Jesus Mercy," Renie said. "He did it. He blew himself up."

"So?" Azador spat. "Only idiots waste their time on games. We will go now, while Scarecrow's enemy is trying to find out what has happened." As if to illustrate his words, those Tiktoks not caught in the blast had already begun swarming toward the ruined palace, beams from their belly-lamps crisscrossing in the murk. "We will slip through the Works without Tinman even noticing us."

"How do you know about the Works anyway?" Renie demanded. "In fact, how do you know so much about this whole simworld?"

Azador shrugged. "I get around." He scowled. "Enough with questions. If I were you, I would be nice to me. Who took you out of that cell? Who knows the secrets of this place? Azador does." He pulled out a cigarette and felt for his lighter.

"We don't have time for that." Renie pointed at the sky. "Look at those clouds—there could be another tornado any moment, and we'd be caught in the open."

Azador grimaced, but tucked the cigarette behind his ear. "Fine. So lead the way."

Like it's some kind of treat for me, Renie thought. *Thanks so much, Mr. Azador.*

Crossing the vast railyard took more than an hour. The open spaces were particularly perilous, and several times they reached shelter only moments before they would have been spotted by one of the roving gangs of mechanical men. As the sky grew darker, orange safety lights smoldered into life around the yard, throwing boxcars and switching stations and derelict engines into stark relief. Renie could not see why Scarecrow and his friends had wasted processing power on a place like this, even if they did get the ingredients cheaply. She could understand building Oz—but a Kansas railhead?

That was one of the differences between the rich and everyone else, she decided. These Otherland people could lavish money and attention on anything that struck their fancies. Unlike ordinary people, they could afford to be crazy.

The fugitives stopped to catch their breath in a covered freight car. The murk from the destruction of the Scarecrow's headquarters had spread across the horizon, although it was hard to tell where the cloud of dust left off and the threatening skies began. Despite the growing darkness, the air was hotter now than it had been half an hour before.

Shielded from spying eyes by the freight car's walls, Azador had lit a cigarette, and was blowing smoke rings at the low ceiling. He was also pointedly not talking to or even looking at Emily 22813, who crouched a short distance away, watching his every move with naked misery.

"He knows things," !Xabbu said quietly to Renie. "Even if you do not like him, we should discover whether he can help us find our friends. To remain separated from them, I think, will only endanger us all."

Renie watched as Emily sidled over toward Azador, her hand balled in a pale-knuckled fist. At first Renie thought the girl was going to hit him (which did not bother her in the least, except for the possibility of violent reprisals) but Emily only thrust her hand in front of Azador's mustached face. Something glittered in her outstretched palm.

"Do you see?" Emily asked him pleadingly. "I saved it. You told me not to lose it, and I didn't lose it."

"Of course," Renie breathed, staring at the small golden object. "I completely forgot about it. *He* gave it to her, didn't he? That's what she said." She stood. "Where did you get that, Azador?"

He did not look at either of the women. "Get what?"

"That gem. Where did it come from?"

He rounded on her, smoke streaming from his mouth and nostrils. "Who are you? Who are you, crazy woman? I do not have to answer your questions! I go where I want, I do what I please. I am of the Romany, and we do not tell our stories to *gorgio*."

"Romany?" Renie ransacked her memory. "You mean a gypsy?"

Azador snorted and turned away. Renie cursed herself for her impatience. !Xabbu was right—they could not risk losing what he might know. It burned like fire to apologize, but she knew it had to be done. "Azador, I'm sorry—I do ask too many questions. But we are strangers here and we don't know what to do. We don't know all the things you know."

"That is the truth," he muttered.

"So help us! You're right, you don't have to tell us anything, but we need your help. This place—this Otherland network—do you know what is happening here?"

He looked at her from the corner of his eye, then took a long drag on his cigarette. "What always happens. Rich idiots play games."

"But that's not true any more. The system is . . . changing somehow." She wondered how much she could tell him without giving away their own situation—they could not assume he had come by the gem innocently. "You heard what I said to the Scarecrow. I know you did. I'll ask you the same question. Have you tried to go offline?"

He turned to face her. Emily shrank back against the wall of the freight car as if something passing between them might burn her. "I heard what you said to the Scarecrow," he said at last. "Yes, I have tried."

"And?"

He shrugged and brushed his thick hair back from his face. "And it is like you said. I could not leave. But for me it is okay," he added carelessly. "I am in no hurry."

"You see?" She dropped to the floor and sat cross-legged. "We need to share information."

Azador hesitated, then his face seemed to close, like a door shutting. "No. Not so easy. Any anyway, we cannot spend time here talking, talking. Maybe when we are through into the next place."

So he planned to go with them. Renie wasn't sure how she felt about that, but perhaps Azador was keeping his secrets for that very reason, as a bargaining chip against desertion.

"Okay." Renie stood. "Then let's get on the road."

The outer edges of the sprawling railyard gradually became more and more tangled with pipes and tanks and electrical wires, as the yard—unobtrusively at first—metamorphosed into the Works.

The pipes which snaked through the railyard to service the rolling stock with water and fuel, and to draw off or load various fluid cargoes, now became a more prominent part of the landscape. Large pipes became larger still, and systems of ducts and conveyors were lashed together in bigger and bigger aggregations until massive bundles of pipe seemed to replace trains as the things attended, as the object of all fears and desires.

The mottled sky, which sagged above Emerald's railyard like a dripping blanket, was first divided into quadrants by hanging wires and the everpresent pipes, then subdivided into smaller and smaller sections as the infrastructure thickened overhead, until at last it was only a suggestion of fitful movement in the chinks between clustered ducts. Even the ground, which had been flat, heat-cracked muck in the railyard, seemed with each step they took to become something more befitting the Works, first growing a skin of rough concrete, then sweating out pools of stagnant water and rainbow-shimmering oil. The only congruity between what they had left and where they were traveling was how the sullen character of the now almost invisible skies was artificially duplicated in the cavernous Works—the thunder of the deep-gurgling pipes, the water misting down from decaying seals and faulty joints, even blue-white arcs of electricity that mimicked the lightning, spasming where the insulation had worn away from the bundled wires.

Moving into these knotted caverns of dirty plastic cable and corrosion-roughened metal was unpleasantly like being swallowed by something. In fact, Renie reflected wearily, their entire experience in the network had been like that. The problems they thought to solve, the tragedies like Stephen's they meant to avenge, had once seemed such clear-cut things, but instead she and the others had been drawn deeper and deeper into the games and idiosyncratic obsessions of Otherland's builders, until it was hard to tell what was even real, let alone what was important.

The forest of vertical cylinders and the artificial skies of horizontal tubing at least provided many places to hide, which was fortunate: as they learned within a short while of entering the Works, they were by no means its only inhabitants.

Once underneath the tangle of pipes, they saw surprisingly few tiktoks—the large, clumsy mechanical men were perhaps not well suited for maneuvering through the sometimes cramped spaces—but they discovered that the Works was home to many other clockwork creatures, also more or less humanoid, but far smaller and shoddier. Many of these, like antique toys, seemed only a cheap tin shell over gears and springs, split vertically with their two halves held together by bent metal tabs. The crude colors with which their features and uniforms had been painted on made them seem even more unpleasantly soulless than the tiktoks.

As they hid behind a trunk of several intertwined vertical pipes, Renie watched one of the crude toys totter past their hiding place—flat eyes unmoving, mouth drawn as an emotionless line—and could not help shuddering. It was not only the things themselves that disturbed her, but the thought of what kind of person Tinman must be to have such empty, pointless subjects, virtual or not.

There were a few humans, too, henrys and emilys, all shaven-headed and wrapped in oil-stained rags; Renie guessed they had been impressed from the Scarecrow's population. Most of them carried heavy burdens, some laden so terribly that she could not understand how they managed to walk, but even those with nothing to carry looked only downward. They trudged through pools of dirty water and staggered around obstacles without glancing up, as though they had covered their routes so often that vision was no longer necessary.

"Which way do we go?" Renie asked in a whisper, barely audible above the dripping of water on asphalt. They were deep in the shadow of a group of concrete columns, each as wide as a very large, very old tree. The fibrous catacombs of the Works stretched monotonously away on every side. "We need to find the river."

Azador frowned. "It will be . . . that way." He pointed, but he did not sound certain.

!Xabbu was up on his hind legs, sniffing, doglike head bobbing up and down. "I can tell nothing by my nose," he confessed. "It is all too much the same—the worst of city smells. But the wind feels a little more cool from that direction." He gestured, his thin hairy arm at a right angle to what Azador had just indicated.

Renie looked at Azador's slitted eyes and realized they had reached a crisis of leadership. She trusted !Xabbu's instincts and training, but the gypsy, if that was truly what he was, might leave them any moment—might simply, in his irritation, decide to follow his own direction. Could they afford to let him go and give up on what he might be able to tell them? If he had demonstrated only the trick in the cell, she might have said yes, but there was the unexplained matter of Sellars' gem as well.

"Okay," she said to Azador. "Take us there." She hoped !Xabbu would understand.

Outside, the sun had gone down, or the stormy skies had thickened to complete impenetrability, because the Works was growing dark. Beneath the arbors of pipe and twisted cable, sickly green-and-yellow lights glowed into half-life behind cracked panels, augmented by an occasional sparking flash of electricity. Groans and faint shrieks echoed through the damp corridors, ghostly with distance, as though nightfall was bringing the Works to its fullest life.

Renie hated the place. Reminding herself that it was nothing but displayed lines of code did not do much good, since she still did not know whether she and !Xabbu could survive an online death. All she knew for certain was that she had seldom wanted to get out of a place more.

*   *   *

They were in one of the few large and open spaces, a joining of several tunnels, like a catacomb constructed of wires, when the figure stepped out of the darkness immediately in front of them.

Renie's heart, which had threatened for a moment to stop beating, found its rhythm again when she saw it was only one of the henrys, a stumbling, tattered figure with a metal canister slung across his shoulders. Before they could step back into the shelter of one of the cross-corridors he looked up and saw them. His eyes bulged in his pale, sparsely-bearded face. Renie stepped forward, raising a finger to her lips.

"Don't be frightened," she said. "We're not going to hurt you."

The man's eyes grew even wider. He tilted back his head and swallowed, his Adam's apple moving so violently it distended his neck, then he threw open his mouth to reveal some kind of loudspeaker jammed deep between his jaws, and Renie saw with horror that what she thought was beard were silver wires protruding through his cheeks. An earsplitting mechanical siren howled from the speaker, so loud that Renie and the others staggered back with their hands over their ears. The henry stood helplessly, vibrating from the sheer volume, as the sound whooped and screamed out of his throat.

They could only run. All around, answering alarms began to sound, their tones a notch less urgent but still horribly loud. An emily turned the corner in front of them, saw them dashing toward her, and let out her own inhuman shriek, as raucous as the first. Moments later two of the shoddy tin men appeared a little farther down the dripping corridor, and their own warning klaxons rose to a hysterical pitch as well.

Tracking us, locating us, Renie realized. Emily was stumbling; Renie grabbed the girl and dragged her along as she followed Azador into a side-passage. *They'll swarm to where the loudest are, until they have us surrounded.*

Another tattered human stepped into their path, too suddenly for Renie to identify it as male or female. Even as the spectral creature dropped the heavy bag it had been carrying and yawned its mouth open, Azador knocked it to the ground with his shoulder. As they rushed past, skinny arms and legs waggled helplessly in the air, and a broken siren-throat ratcheted instead of screamed.

We're just running, she realized. *Nowhere. This will get us killed.* "!Xabbu!" she shouted. "Lead us to the river!"

Her friend did not answer, but bounded ahead of them, tail high, and began to run on all fours. He sprinted around a dividing of the ways, slowed until he was sure they were still behind him, then accelerated again.

The alarm screams were rising on all sides now, and even though the Works-dwellers who stepped into their path did not try to stop them, or even to avoid being shoved aside, they all shrieked louder when Renie and the others pelted by, a sonic arrow pinpointing the direction of their flight. The din was maddening.

Now there were faces coming toward them at every turning, the haunted stares of the humans, the empty, chipped grimaces of the tin creatures, even the dark bulk of a few tiktoks. Soon the very crush of metal bodies and wasted flesh would seal off the avenues of escape, one by one.

Emily slipped in an oily puddle and stumbled again, this time pulling Renie and herself to the ground. As they struggled upright, !Xabbu hopped frantically in place, swiveling his muzzle from side to side.

"I smell nothing, but I think it is there." !Xabbu jutted his head toward one of the narrow ways. He took a deep breath and closed his eyes for a moment, despite the chaos all around them. He worked his fingers in the air for a moment as though trying to grasp something, then opened his eyes again. "It is there," he said. "I feel it to be true."

The uneven passage was rapidly filling with tin toys, all shambling toward them like sleepwalkers. "They've got between us and the water," Renie said, heart sinking.

Azador looked at her, then at !Xabbu, then spat on the ground. "Follow," he growled. He sprang forward and slammed into the first wave of the metal things. His rush knocked them back like bowling pins, smashing one to the ground where it split into two nutshell halves and a clutter of gears. Renie led Emily forward, trying to keep the girl behind Azador's broad back.

The whining shriek of dozens of mechanical throats was now louder than a jet engine. Renie felt rough, hard hands trying to close on her, and she lashed out in a blind rage, shoving and punching. For a moment Emily went down beside her, but Renie fought her way through the confusion of shapes and found the girl's slender arm, then pulled her onto her feet. Now even Emily was flailing around her in panic, slapping at the tin creatures with open palms, her mouth contorted in a scream that Renie couldn't hear.

Renie staggered forward, numb and depleted, her fists and arms bloody. Yet another flat, enameled face rose before her, buzzing as it gave the alarm. She kicked its rounded midsection and tipped it over. Beyond it was nothing but Azador and darkness.

He turned a face that was now a sheet of red toward them and beckoned with a shaking, bloody hand. The corridor ahead was empty, a trail of dimly flickering lights leading away into darkness. They had broken through.

"Jesus Mercy," Renie choked. "Are . . . are . . . you . . . ?" She heard a clattering noise behind them and turned. The tin things which had not been completely disabled were rocking like overturned beetles, struggling to rise, to resume the chase. Renie's stomach tightened. "Where's !Xabbu?"

"*Hurry!*"

Renie whirled to see the welcome baboon shape, which had appeared like a sacred spirit in the corridor ahead. "We are almost at the river!" he called.

They hobbled after him. Within moments the claustrophobic passages opened out and the conduit columns suddenly stretched dozens of meters higher. The wide, black mass of the river lay before them. The loading dock was empty, the creatures and people who had been there, Renie felt sure, summoned to form part of the mob through which they had just fought. She could hear the survivors behind them, still bent on pursuit, howling and dragging themselves along on bent limbs.

"Is the gateway here somewhere?" she asked, struggling to get her breath back.

"Don't be a fool," Azador growled. "We will never live to find it."

"Then we need a boat."

Two large container ships lay at anchor, one with its cargo nets hanging half-unloaded, bulging with crates of people-feed and crank-case lubricant. Renie and the others ran down the dock looking for something more their size, and found it in the shape of a small river tugboat, not much more than a barge with rubber bumpers. They clambered aboard. Renie found a barge pole and used it to unhook the tie line, then Azador got the engine started and they chugged slowly out onto the dark river.

Behind, a crowd of howling humans and mechanical people had reached the dock, but their dreadful voices were already growing fainter as the barge pulled for the middle of the river.

Azador hung on the wheel, grim and silent, with hands bloodier than his face. Emily collapsed in the bow, weeping. With !Xabbu's help, Renie got her into the cabin and onto the thin pallet which had served as the barge captain's miserable bed.

Even as Renie whispered soft words to the girl, words both of them could barely hear because their ears were still ringing painfully, something crackled beside them. What Renie had thought was a mirror suddenly began to radiate grainy light, then the eyeless face of the Tinman appeared on the screen.

"So," it said cheerfully, "you outsiders are all still alive—and the

special one, the wee mother-to-be? Lovely, lovely. Little bundle of joy
unharmed, too? Excellent! Then I believe my line is supposed to be:
'*Surrender the Dorothy!*' " The gate in its mouth clacked up and down as
the Tinman vented its horrible, buzzing laugh. "Good, yes? But of
course I hope you won't *really* surrender, and spoil the fun. . . ."

Renie snatched up the barge pole and hammered the screen into
shards and powder, then sank to the floor, exhausted and fighting
back tears.

CHAPTER 18

The Veils of Illusion

NETFEED/BIOGRAPHY: "The Man in the Shadows"
(visual: slow-motion footage of Anford speaking at convention)
VO: Rex Anford, sometimes referred to as the "Commander-in-Absentia" or
"The Gray Man," is the subject of this biography, which traces his rise from
small-town obscurity through his emergence in the new Industrial Senate as
a representative for ANVAC, General Equipment, and other low-profile, big-
money corporations, and to his eventual election as President of the United
States. The controversial issue of his health is discussed, and experts analyze
file footage in an attempt to diagnose what, if any, medical problems he
might have . . .

A swirl of colors grew out of the blinding golden light—black, ember-red, and at the last a deep neon blue just shading toward ultraviolet that seemed to enter him like a vibration—then Paul was through, still tangled in the grasp of the man who had kidnapped him. He struggled to protect himself, then realized that his opponent was not fighting, but only holding him passively. He set his hands against the man's chest and shoved. The thin, dark-skinned man stumbled backward, then threw out his arms and regained his balance.

The level ground beneath the stranger's heels extended only another few yards behind him before dropping away down a steep, grassy slope. Far below, a river threaded its way through the narrow canyon, foaming through descending cataracts until it wound out of sight. But Paul did not stop to admire the stunning view of water and hills and tangled trees, the skies so sunny the world almost sparkled. His attention was focused on the interloper who had stolen him from the England of the Martian invasion—a distorted version of his home, but still the closest he had found to what he had lost.

"Now," the stranger began, smiling, "Of course I owe you an apol . . ." His eyes widened and he took a startled step backward as Paul sprang toward him.

Paul did not hit the stranger squarely, but he wrapped his arms around him and together they tumbled down the slope in a single rolling knot. For all Paul knew, they might bounce from some precipice and plunge to the distant valley floor, but he did not care. Chased and mistreated for unfathomable reasons, he finally had his hands on one of his tormentors and would take the man down with him, even if neither of them survived.

There was no precipice. They arrived at the bottom of the hill with a spine-jarring thump, but with several more descending slopes still between them and the valley floor. The impact threw them apart and they lay for a moment where they landed, struggling for breath. Paul was the first to move, rolling over onto his stomach to crawl toward his enemy, who saw him and scrambled to his feet.

"What are you doing?" The stranger danced back from Paul's swiping grab. "Are you trying to kill us both?"

For the first time, Paul noticed that the stranger was no longer dressed in the tattered Edwardian suit he had worn before. Somehow—by magic, for all Paul could tell—he had acquired a shiny waistcoat and pair of baggy pants that might have come from an Arabian Nights pantomime. Paul flicked a glance down and saw that he was dressed the same way, with silky pantaloons and his feet in thin, pointed slippers, but he had no interest in stopping to wonder what it meant.

"Kill us both? No," he gasped, and dragged himself upright. "I'm just trying to kill you." His ribs ached from the fall and his legs were weak. Still, he knew he would fight to the end if necessary, and felt a little pleasure at that realization—the warmth of someone who had not been good at games in school, and who had shied away from fights, realizing that he wasn't a coward after all.

Yes, I'll fight, Paul thought, and it changed how he thought of himself, of his situation. *I won't just give up.*

"Stop, man," the stranger said, lifting his hands. "I am not your enemy. I have tried to do you a kindness, but I have been terribly clumsy."

"Kindness?" Paul wiped sweat from his forehead and took another step forward, but did not press the attack. "You kidnapped me. You lied to me, and then you shoved me through that, that . . ." He waved his hand toward the hill above, and the place they had arrived, ". . . whatever it is. What sort of kindness is that?"

"As I began," the man said, "I owe you an apology, and here it is—I am very, very sorry. Will you strike me once more, or will you let me explain?"

Paul eyed him. In truth, he was not looking forward to grappling with the stranger again. Despite his thin frame, the man's body had felt hard and resilient as braided leather, and unlike Paul, he did not seem injured or even winded. "Explain, then."

The stranger sat himself cross-legged on the ground. "I saw you in that market. You did not seem to belong, and I watched you. And then I saw your companions. They were not what they appeared to be, but you did not seem to notice."

"Not what they appeared to be. You said that before. What does that mean?"

"I cannot say, exactly." The stranger's smile appeared again, a broad and self-effacing thing so sympathetic that Paul felt he should not trust it on principle. "They had the appearance of an average Englishman and Englishwoman, of the type that should be in that place, but something in them, some shadow beneath the seeming, spoke to me also of hunting beasts. My lord Shiva put it in my head that they were not what they appeared, and that you were in danger." He spread his hands, palms upward. "So I took it on myself to get you away."

Paul remembered his own moment of fear. The Pankies had indeed resembled the creatures who hunted him, although they had demonstrated no other similarities. His distrust of the stranger eased a little. "Then why didn't you just warn me? Why drag me through—what was that, anyway? What are these things that take us from one place to another?"

The stranger gave him an odd look. "Gateways? Portals, doors, they are called those things, too. What do you call them?"

Now it was Paul's turn to frown. "I don't call them anything. I don't even know what they are."

The stranger stared at him for a long moment, his deep brown eyes intent. At last he shook his head. "We must speak more. But we must also move through this place to another gateway, for this is the country of the fiercest of my enemies and I cannot stay long." He rose, then extended a hand toward the distant waters. "Will you come with me? There will be boats down below, and we can speak as we go upon the river."

If the man intended to harm him, he was going at it in a very round-about way. Paul decided he would stay on guard, but give him a chance. Perhaps he could give Paul some information. Anything that might dispel the cloud of ignorance and confusion that had been surrounding him for so long would be worth almost any risk.

"Very well," he said. "If you will answer my questions honestly."

"I will answer as much as I am allowed. Some secrets there are that have been given into my care, and those I may not tell anyone, even at the cost of my soul."

Paul had no idea what that was supposed to mean. "Who are you, then?" he asked.

"I am Nandi," the stranger said, and touched his palms together in front of his chest. "Nandi Paradivash, at your service. I am sorry our meeting has been so upsetting. And you are. . . ?"

"Paul," he said without thinking, then inwardly cursed himself for using his real name. He tried to summon another name, but could only think of the madman who had dragged him through the palaces and deserts of Mars; he hoped Nandi had not met him. "Paul Brum-mond. And I have another question. Where the hell are we?"

Nandi did not appear to have noticed anything amiss with Paul's name. "I am surprised," he said. "You are English, are you not? Surely you should recognize one of the catechisms of an English school career."

Paul shook his head. "You've lost me."

"Ah? *'Where blossomed many an incense-bearing tree;'* " the stranger declaimed, " *'And here were forests ancient as the hills, Enfolding sunny spots of greenery.'* You see, there are the forests, there are the trees—sandalwood, spruce—can you not smell them? And we will soon be upon the River Alph, traveling, perhaps, through 'caverns measureless to man. . . .' "

Paul felt something tickling his memory. "The River Alph. . . ?"

"Yes." Nandi nodded, smiling again. "Welcome, Mister Paul Brum-mond . . . to Xanadu."

The hillsides were glorious with wildflowers, tiny static explosions of yellow and white and pale powdery blue, and the soft breezes did indeed waft exotic scents. As they made their way down to the river, from slope to ever-lower slope, Paul found that he was struggling to hang onto his wariness. It had been a long time, if ever, since he had been in a place this lovely, and at least for the moment he felt almost safe. His protective reflexes, coiled like springs, began to relax a little.

"It is indeed beautiful," Nandi said as if reading his thoughts. "Those who constructed it did their work well, but it is not an Oriental place at all. It is a representation of an idea—an Englishman's idea of an Asian paradise, to be accurate."

At first Paul thought that "those who constructed it," was another religious reference, like the man's citation of Shiva, but after a few moments he realized what he had heard. "Those . . . who constructed *this* place?"

Nandi watched a bright green bird streak overhead. "Yes. The designers and engineers."

"Engineers? *People?*"

Now the stranger turned. "What do you ask, Paul?"

He hesitated, torn between the need to blurt out everything, his fear and ignorance, and the urge toward secrecy which was part of his armor—and woefully thin armor it had been. "Just . . . just tell me what this is. This place."

"This simulation, do you mean? Or the network?"

Paul's legs turned wobbly. He took one staggering step, then had to sit down. "Simulation? This is a simulation?" He flung up his hand and stared at it, then took it away and stared at the valley in all its intricacy. "But it can't be! It's . . . it's real!"

"Did you not know?" Nandi asked. "How could that be possible?"

Paul shook his head, helpless, reeling. A simulation. Someone had implanted him, then covered it up. But there were no simulations as perfect as this. It simply wasn't possible. He closed his eyes, half-certain that when he opened them all would be gone, and he would be back in the giant's grinding-house again, or Humpty-Dumpty's Castle. Even those insanities made more sense than this. "It can't be."

Nandi crouched at his side, his face full of concern and surprise. "You did not know you were in a simulation? You must tell me how you came here. This is more important than you realize, Paul Brummond."

"I don't know how I got here—and anyway, it's not Brummond. I lied." He no longer cared enough to deceive. "My name is Paul Jonas."

His companion shook his head. The name meant nothing to him. "And you do not know how you came here?"

Numbed and listless, Paul told him all that he could remember—the worlds seemingly without end, the unanswered questions, the frightening blackness that covered his recent past. It was like listening to someone else talk. When he had finished, Nandi let his chin fall to his chest and closed his eyes, as if for some perverse reason he was taking a nap; when he opened his eyes again, he was clearly troubled.

"And all this time, Paul Jonas, you have been pursued through the creations of my enemy. That must mean something, but I cannot imagine what it is." He stood. "Come. We must hurry to the river. The longer we spend here, the greater the danger, I suspect."

"Your enemy—you said that before, too." Paul began to follow the slender man down the hill again. "Who is this enemy? Do you mean he owns this place?"

"We shall not speak of him. Not here." Nandi Paradivash put a finger to his lips. "Old folktales say that to name a demon is to summon it, and that might prove true for us as well. Who knows what name or words may trigger a search agent?"

"Can we talk on the river? I . . . I have to know more."

"We will speak, but be careful what words you choose." He shook his head in wonderment. "I should have known that He who dances the Dance would not put His hand upon me and point me toward a stranger for no reason. A few moments of Maya, of illusion, and almost I forgot the smoke of the burning-ground that was in my nostrils when I learned truly to serve Him."

The beauty of Xanadu impinged on Paul more than ever as they covered the last mile down to the riverside. Knowing what he knew, he could ignore nothing: this delicately scented flower, that tree, the grass rustling soft beneath his feet—all false. Constructs. But there could be no simulation of life so faultless. He did not consider himself anything like an expert, but he was no hermit either. He had seen the much-touted "photorealistic" VR environments out of China advertised all over the net, and his friend Niles had even let him try out one of the government's better simulation engines, an embassy dinner with lifelike opportunities for political gain or loss. Paul had been very impressed by the experience—the puppet actors who could actually make conversation, the small objects like silverware that vibrated convincingly if you pinged them on the edge of a plate—but even last year's state-of-the-art had been miles, no, light-years behind this!

"The people in these . . . simulations," he asked. "They aren't real either?"

"Some of them are," Nandi said. "This was built for rich and powerful people to use, and they and their friends can appear here like gods taking mortal forms. But most of the people, as you call them, are Puppets. Things without souls. Machinery."

The words of Professor Bagwalter in the Martian simulation came back to him, and now Paul understood them. The man had been a participant—a Citizen—and had wanted to know if Paul was one, too. But if that was true, then maybe the bird-woman, Vaala . . . ?

"Am I the only person you have met in here who has lost his memory?"

Nandi smiled a little. The river was now just before them, submerged stones making lacy white Vs on the rough jade surface. "You are not merely that, you are the only person I have ever heard of who did not know he was in a virtual environment." He led Paul down to a short, sandy stretch of beach. A tiny dock that seemed to have been carved from a single piece of white stone lay partially hidden by a strand of cattails. Tugged by the current, a small but elegant boat bobbed at the end of its painter like a dog waiting to be walked.

Nandi gestured Paul to the seat at the front of the boat. "Please," he said, "I will be your steersman, as Krishna became Arjuna's charioteer. Do you know the *Bhagavad Gita?*"

"I have a copy," Paul said. "Back home, wherever that is." He did not add that it had been a gift from one of his more disastrous girlfriends, shortly before she had tipped over into what Paul considered religious mania. His last meeting with her had been some months afterward, when he had seen her playing a drum and chanting in the Camden Town tube station, blind behind the goggles that flooded her senses with some chargelike mantra.

"Ah, good." Nandi smiled. He unhooked the boat's painter and guided them out onto the flowing river. "Then you will understand me when I compare you to Arjuna, a brave man—a great hero!—in need of advice and wisdom."

"I didn't read it carefully, I'm afraid." In fact, he hadn't read it at all, and the only thing he remembered from the entire episode was that Krishna was a god, or perhaps just God, and he thought that if this Nandi was assigning himself the role of Krishna, he was getting a bit above himself.

Listen to me, he thought. *I sound like my grandmother.*

The landscape slid past, precious and perfect. Far down the valley, past many bends of the river, a cloud of spray lifted high above the water, crowned by a brilliant rainbow. Paul tried to remember the famous Coleridge poem, but could not get any farther than: *"In Xanadu did Kublai Khan a stately pleasure dome decree . . ."*

"Can you talk to me now?" he asked. "The sound of the river should keep anyone from hearing us."

Nandi steered them past one of the rocks and its white arrowhead wake. "It is more than sound we must fear. Every word you speak is translated through several kinds of virtuality engines, and that, too, leaves traces. The people we seek are the masters of this place, just as Trimurti is the master of the real world, and both rule their domains to the smallest mote of dust, the most minuscule flash of subatomic forces. That is why the error of these people is so great—they seek to make themselves gods."

"You keep saying 'they' or 'these people.' Who?"

"A group of men—and some women, too—who have declared themselves the enemies of everything. They name themselves the Grail Brotherhood, misusing the old myth for their own purposes—stealing the story, it could be said. They have built this place, and they live here and disport themselves like the eldest sons and daughters of Heaven. Not all of this network is as pleasant as this—no, much of it is even worse than anything you have seen. Simulations of slavery and cruelty and sexual debauchery, they have made them all."

"But who are you? I mean, how did you come to be involved in all this?"

Nandi eyed him for a moment, considering. "This much I can tell you. The Grail Brotherhood have touched things, harmed things, that they do not even understand. And so it is that some have come to-gether to oppose them. We are the Circle." He held up his hand with his fingers rounded into a ring, and peered through it with one bright, brown eye. The effect was almost comical. "Where you find us, there you will find safety, at least as much as we can give, for clearly you are an enemy of our enemy."

"Why?" The fear that he had suppressed came rushing back. "Why should people like that care about me? I'm no one! I work in an art museum, for Christ's sake."

The boat was picking up speed as the river narrowed, the cliffs now looming high above their heads. Shaded by a drooping willow tree, a deserted teahouse stood on a rock promontory overlooking the water like a piece of delicate jewelry left behind by a giant. It was almost too beautiful, Paul thought, fighting down his panic. For the first time, he saw how this place could be, must be, unreal.

"I do not know why you have drawn their attention," Nandi admit-ted. "It is likely to do with the time you cannot remember. But those who chased you through several simulations—I cannot doubt they are agents of the greatest of the Brotherhood, since those were all his places. As is this."

"They all belonged to one person? Mars, that Alice in Wonderland thing, all of them?"

"Wealth is not one of the things he lacks." Nandi's smile was sour. "He has built dozens of these."

"What is his name?"

The dark-skinned man shook his head. "Not here. When we pass through to another place, I will tell you, but there is no sense in uttering words that surely would be among the first his agents would investigate, since only those from outside the system could understand that this place *has* a human creator." Nandi glanced up sharply at a movement on the heights above, but it was only a shepherd leading a flock of sheep across a high ridge. The man did not look down, although several of the sheep did. Paul realized it was the first person other than themselves they had seen since entering Xanadu.

"Agents," he said aloud. "So those two . . . things following me from one simulation to another were agents? Of this Brotherhood person?" He frowned. "Do you think that couple, the Pankies, were agents, too? They didn't have anything like the same effect on me. And I spent a night sleeping next to them, but nothing happened."

"Again, I cannot say." Nandi spent several moments concentrating on guiding the boat between the rocks, which were growing more numerous. When a clear stretch of water was before them, he continued. "We have studied these people, but still our knowledge is small—after all, they have labored hard and spent much money to keep their works hidden. But something was wrong with those two, that man and woman. I felt the hand of my God touch me." He said this as simply and with as much conviction as he might have explained being the first to see a parking space in front of the off-license. "If you do not trust the gods—if you do not trust God—then you have rejected yourself."

Nandi again devoted himself to his steering. Paul sat back on the polished bench and watched the green hills and raw rock faces slip past. It was difficult to find a place even to begin thinking about all this. It would have made a fairly dubious plot in a flick, let alone being acceptable as the course for his actual and only life. But it made a horrid kind of sense, too: once you accepted a simulation this good, it answered many of his other questions.

He even felt a moment's disappointment as he realized that he had not seen the beginning of history in the Ice Age, but only someone's coded dramatization of it. Still, the People, whatever they truly were, had not only seemed real to Paul, but if they were Puppets they seemed awfully self-sufficient ones, fully engaged with their own pretend world, with their fears and triumphs and folklore. Perhaps, he reflected, even imaginary people just needed a story of their own—something that made sense out of things.

But if it had all been code, all make-believe, then what about the woman who had spoken to him through the sick Neandertal child? The winged woman who came to him in dreams? She had begged that he find her. . . .

It was too much to work out all at once.

"If these people are so powerful," he asked, "then what are you and your friends in this Circle thing going to do? And why do you care, anyway, if a bunch of rich bastards have private orgies on their VR network?"

"If only it were that, Paul Jonas." Nandi lifted the dripping paddle from the water so he could turn to face him. "I cannot tell you all that would answer you properly, but you must trust me when I say that I believe what they are doing threatens everything. *Everything*. And even if you doubt my belief, it is a fact that they have hurt and killed many to build this thing of theirs, this . . . theater of Maya. And they will kill many more to keep it secret as long as necessary. In fact, from what you have told me, they are trying to kill you as well—or to do something worse to you."

The fear came back, goose-pimpling his flesh, and he had to suppress the urge to scream at the unfairness. What had he done to offend people like that? He mastered himself. "You haven't told me what you plan to do about it."

"Nor can I," Nandi said. "And not just for the sake of secrecy. You have enough problems, Paul. You do not need the burden of knowing what we know. It is one less thing they will work to make you confess if you are ever captured."

"You talk like this is a war!"

Nandi did not smile this time. "It *is* a war." After a moment's silence, he added: "But although they think themselves gods, they are merely human. They make mistakes. They have made some already, and they will make more, no matter how many forms they wear, no matter how many lives they build for themselves in this place. It is as Krishna said to Arjuna: *'Do not grieve for the life and death of individuals, for this is inevitable; the bodies indeed come and go, but the life that manifests in all is undying and unhurt, it neither slayeth or is slain.'* This is a central truth of the world, Paul. Krishna spoke of what you might call the soul or the essence. Now these Grail criminals, as they seek to ape the gods, they are caught in a lesser version of this same great truth, a shadow cast by its shining light. You see, they cannot shake off what they are, no matter how many times they change their skins."

"I don't understand."

"Look at this man, our chiefest enemy. You have been in many of his simulations, the dreamworlds that he has fashioned for himself. What do they have in common?"

Paul had thought something similar himself not long ago, and he struggled to summon the memory. "They're . . . they seem very old. The ideas, I mean."

"Exactly." The charioteer was pleased with his Arjuna. "That is because he is an old man, and longs for the things of his youth. Here, I will tell you something. He was born in France, this man I will not name, but was sent to a school in England during the Great War, because his family wanted him away from the fighting that tore France. He was a lonely child in that foreign country, fighting to be like the others, and thus the things of his boyhood are all those bits of Englishness he tried so hard to embrace—Lewis Carroll, H. G. Wells, the comic magazines of travel to other planets . . . ."

"Hold on." Paul leaned forward. "Do you mean to tell me this man was alive during the Second World War?"

Nandi was amused. "I refer to the First World War, in fact."

"But that would make him . . . That can't be. No one's that old."

"He is." The gentle smile vanished. "He has made the preservation of his own life an object of religious devotion, and he treasures his memories as the myths of that religion. He cannot truly share it, though—the childhood to which his virtual worlds are shrines is one that no other living human remembers. If he were not so unreservedly evil, it would almost be possible to feel sorry for the man."

The boat abruptly dropped away beneath them for a moment, and Paul had to stop thinking in order to hold onto his seat and not be jounced overboard when the small craft smacked down into the water again.

"The river is more dangerous here, just before the caverns," Nandi said, backing water furiously with his paddle. "We will talk more when we are in a safer place."

"What caverns. . . ?" Paul asked, then whooped in surprise as the boat dipped again, then slid between two rocks and passed over yet another cataract.

For the next several minutes he clung with both hands to the sides of the boat as Nandi expertly steered them past obstacle after obstacle and the river sank ever deeper into the fold of the canyon. The cliff walls now rose up so steeply on either side that only a sliver of sky could be seen, and its light died a quarter of the way down the rock face.

"We will miss seeing the pleasure dome," Nandi called over the tumult of the waters. "There is a tributary that passes by the front gates, but I assume you do not wish to linger and admire our enemy's handiwork, or meet his henchmen."

"What?" Paul could make out only a few words.

"There!" Nandi pointed. "Can you see it?"

The mist that Paul had wondered at earlier now covered most of the river before them, billowing into the air in a sparkling cloud. Through it, at least half a kilometer ahead and partially blocked from view by the cliffs, he could see a forest of white-and-gold minarets like the battlements of the dream castle he had seen when he climbed the great tree. It was almost impossible not to admire the painstaking artistry that had gone into this place. If it was all the work of human hands, as Nandi had said, then they had been very skilled hands indeed.

"Are there people in there?" he asked. "I mean, real people?"

"Just a moment," his companion called above the noisy river. They rounded a bend and Paul saw a gaping black mouth in the cliff face, swallowing the river down. He had time for only a surprised and wordless shout, then the bottom dropped out from under them again and the boat slid down a roaring flume into chilly darkness.

For long seconds he could see nothing, and could only cling to the bench, positive that they would be smashed against unforgiving stone or upended in the violent currents. The boat surged up and down, and skewed abruptly from one side to the other without warning, and none of Paul's desperate, bellowed questions were answered. The blackness was absolute, and the horrible thought began to grow that Nandi had been thrown overboard, that he was rushing into oblivion alone.

The boat left the water again, free-falling for what seemed to Paul's shrieking imagination like ten seconds, but was probably less than one, then splashed down in a great drenching spume of water. Paul clutched the rail until he could feel that the boat was at last nosing into calmer waters. The rush of the cataract began to quiet behind them.

"Sometimes it is exhilarating to wear flesh," Nandi's voice said in the darkness. "Even virtual flesh."

"I . . . I didn't enjoy that," Paul replied. "Wh-where are we?"

"In caverns measureless to man, as the poem says. But wait. You will see."

"S-see?" His teeth were chattering, and not just from fear: the summery heat outside had not penetrated here. In fact, it was terribly, terribly cold. "See h-how?"

Something made a wet, scratchy sound behind him, then light blossomed out of the void. Nandi had produced and lit a lantern, and now hung it from the boat's high, curved stern, so that it threw its creamy radiance all around.

"Oh," said Paul. "Oh . . ."

The black river had widened again, and now extended an arrow's flight on either side of them, flat as a velvet tablecloth except for the diminishing waves from the cataract. An immense tunnel of ice surrounded the river, its ceiling fifty meters or more above their heads. But this was not just an ice cave—it was a crystalline abstraction of infinite variety.

Huge pillars like translucent candles stretched from floor to ceiling, aggregated from trickles of water frozen and refrozen over the centuries, and diamond-faceted blocks as big as houses lay piled along the bank as though by gigantic hands. Everything was covered by a net of hoarfrost—tiny, delicate traceries of white, draped like the finest spidersilk. Ice bridges stretched across the river in gleaming spans, and where the ice on the tunnel walls had cracked and fallen away, steep ice slopes now angled down to the water's edge. Even as Paul and Nandi watched, a small piece sheared loose from one of the walls ahead of them, rolled slowly down the bank, and splashed into the River Alph; only as they approached it did Paul realize that the chunk bobbing near the frozen riverbank was half as wide as the Islington house that held his flat.

"It's . . . the whole th-thing is m-magnificent," he said.

Nandi heard the shiver in his voice. "There are blankets under the bench, I think."

Paul found two, sumptuous things with a rich sheen, embroidered with fanciful animals playing musical instruments. He offered one to Nandi, who smiled and shook his head. "I do not much feel either cold or heat," Nandi said. "In the place where I last lived, I became accustomed to the elements."

"I don't remember the Kublai Khan poem," Paul admitted. "Where do these caves go?"

"On and on. But the river itself crosses through them and empties into the sea. And long before that, we will have passed through the gateway."

"I don't understand how any of this works." His attention was momentarily diverted as a block of ice the size of a London hovercab fell from the ceiling and splashed noisily into the river a hundred meters ahead. A few seconds later, the ripples set their small craft rocking. "These gateways—why are they in the water?"

"It is a conceit. There are other gateways, too, of course. Most of the simulations have dozens, although they are hidden—only those who travel with the permission of the simulations' owners are given the tools to locate gateways. But the people who built this gigantic network wished to have some common thing that would tie it together, and so through every simulation, the River runs."

"What river?"

"It is different in different places—in some it is not even a river, but part of an ocean, or a canal, or even something stranger, like a lava stream or a miles-wide flow of mercury. But always it is part of the greater River. I suppose it would be possible, given enough time—more than the lifetime of even someone like our chief enemy, though—to pass all the way down the river, crossing through every simulation, until like the famous serpent with its tail in its mouth, the river met itself again and you had returned to the place you started."

"So there's always a gate on the river, in each simulation." Paul, with the blanket wrapped around him, was feeling better, and each piece of information was like food to a starving man.

"Two, at the very least—one at either end of the river's passage through that simulated world."

"But there are others, too—like that one in the Hampton Court maze that you pushed me through."

Nandi nodded. "Yes. I had been there several days, and had seen one or two people go into the maze who never came out again—members of the Brotherhood or their employees, perhaps. So I investigated. All the gates, even the river gates, allow the privileged user to go where he or she chooses, and unlike those at either end of the river, the others do not lead through the network in any particular order. But almost all the gates have a default setting, usually into another world belonging to the same master. However, I am pleased to say, we will reach one soon which will take us out of *this* man's domains entirely."

"How do you know all this?" The frustration was building inside him—there was so much to learn before the most important questions could even be framed.

"We of the Circle have studied these people and their works for a long time. And although I have only entered this network recently, I am not the first of my kind to come here." Nandi spread his hands as if offering Paul something. "Men and women have died to learn the things I am telling you now."

Almost without his knowledge, Paul's fingers had stolen to his neck. "If I'm in a simulation, though, I must be able to go offline. So why can't I find the plug? Why can't I just pull the damn thing out?"

His companion looked grave. "I do not know how you came here or why, Paul Jonas, or what keeps you here. But at the moment, I cannot leave either, and I cannot tell you the reason for that. It does not affect me—I knew I could not leave until I had accomplished what I was sent to do, in any case—but it must be affecting others. But this is part of why we have dedicated ourselves to opposing these people. I know it is a cliché of the worst sort," he made a mocking face, "but the Grail Brotherhood have tampered with things they do not fully understand."

A piece of the cavern wall had slid down into the river in front of them, filling the water with chunks of ice, and Nandi concentrated his energies on steering them through. Paul huddled in his blankets, fighting the vague but definite feeling that time was short—that there were things he should be asking, and that he would regret it greatly later if he didn't think of them now.

He thought of the woman, the only thing that had made sense to him in all this madness until now. Where did she fit into all this?

But should I tell this man everything, absolutely everything? What if he's really working for those Grail people himself, and he's just toying with me? He looked at Nandi's narrow, sharp features and realized he had never been able to tell anything useful about anyone by looking at them. *Or what if he's just a madman? Maybe this is a simulation, yes, but maybe all this Grail stuff is some mad conspiracy theory? How do I know that he's not a Puppet himself? Maybe this is part of the ride.*

Paul tugged the blanket closer around him. That kind of thinking did no good. A few days ago, he had been lost in a kind of fog; at least now he had the basis for rational thought, for making decisions. He could doubt anything and everything, but what Nandi Paradivash said made sense: if he, Paul Jonas, was not stark raving mad, then only some kind of simulation gave a rational framework to all that he had experienced. But simulations of this level, actually indistinguishable from reality, had to be something new. Only people with the kind of power Nandi was talking about could afford this kind of quantum leap.

"What do they want?" he asked suddenly. "These Grail people, what do they want? This kind of thing—it must cost trillions. More, whatever that would be. Quadrillions."

"I told you, they wish to become gods." Nandi reached out with his long-handled oar and poked away a small boulder of floating ice. "They wish to live forever in worlds of their own devising."

"Forever? How are they going to manage that? You, me, we've both got bodies somewhere, right? You can't live without a body, no matter

what your brain thinks it's doing. So what good is all this? It's just an
incredibly expensive game. People like that, they don't need anything,
except for more time."

"If I knew all the answers to what you have just said, I would not
have had to come here." The ice behind them, he resumed his measured paddling.

Paul pulled the blankets aside and sat forward. "So you don't have
answers? What *are* you doing here? I've told you lots of things. What
can you tell me?"

Nandi was silent for a long time, his paddle dipping and emerging,
over and over, its gentle slurp the only sound troubling the air of the
great ice cave.

"I was a scientist," he said at last. "A chemical engineer. Not an
important one. Merely I managed a research department of a large
fibraware company in Benares, which is better known as Varanasi.
Have you heard of it?"

"Varanasi? It . . . it was some kind of important city in India. There
was an accident there, wasn't there? Something toxic?"

"Benares was and is the holiest city of all. It has always existed, a
jewel of sanctity on the banks of the Ganges. But when I was a scientist, I did not care about this. I did my job, I had friends from work
and school, I roamed the streets, both the real streets of Varanasi and
the virtual byways of the net. There were women and drugs, and everything else with which a young man with money can occupy mind
and body. Then the accident happened.

"It occurred at a government lab, but it could just as easily have
happened somewhere else. The lab was a small place by the standards
of government interests, far smaller even than my own corporate facilities. So small."

In the silence, Paul said: "So this was the accident I heard about?"

"Yes. A big, big mistake. But it was really just a small thing that
happened in a small lab. A failure of containment for one viral agent.
The lab worked often with such things, as we all did, and all potentially lethal viruses were engineered to be unable to replicate beyond
a few cycles, enough for study but no more. But an improper proce-
dure had been used in developing this viral agent, or the genetic ma-
nipulation itself was deliberately sabotaged, or perhaps the virus itself
developed a mutant resistance to the safeguards. No one knows. A
centrifuge malfunctioned. A receptacle cracked. Everyone in the lab
was killed within minutes. Containment was broken because one
woman from the front office survived long enough to reach the fences,
within yards of a busy city street. An automatic alarm from the facility

probably saved the lives of millions. As it was, two hundred thousand died in a month, most in the first few days, before a virus-killer could be engineered. The army shot thousands more as they tried to break out of quarantine."

"God, yes, I saw that. On the newsnets. It was . . . it was terrible." Paul was aware of the monstrous inadequacy of the response, but could think of nothing else to say.

"I lived in that quarantine. It was street by street. My mother and father lived only two blocks away—two blocks!—and I could not go to them. They died with the flesh melting from their bones and were burned in a pit with hundreds of others. For one month the block in which I lived became a jungle. People who think they are going to die within hours . . ." Nandi shook his head. There was something terrible in his eyes as they peered from the shadows cast by the lantern. "I saw terrible things. The children, who could not defend themselves . . ." He paused, seeking words; when he continued, his voice was thick and hoarse. "I cannot speak of it, even now. I myself did terrible things as well, greedy, mad things. I did them for fear, for hunger, in what I thought was self-defense. But the worst of my crimes was that I watched what others did, but did not stop them. Or at least I thought that was my worst crime."

The light in the cavern had changed in some subtle way, bringing the other man's face into sharper focus. Paul saw that there were fissures in the ceiling ahead; a few rays of daylight stabbed down from above like searchlights, columns of bright fire dousing themselves in the River Alph's dark waters.

"I had long before rejected the religion of my parents," Nandi abruptly continued. "I had no need of such benighted superstition— was I not a man of science, an enlightened creature of the twenty-first century? I survived the quarantine by existing in a mindless state, throwing off my intellect entirely. But when the quarantine was lifted, and I walked past the bodies stacked on the street corners, waiting for the government to come and haul them away, then my intellect returned and I began to think I might have made a very grave error in how I had built my life. As I continued through the streets, through the smoke of the burnings and the rubble of the fires and explosions— for during the chaos of the quarantine parts of the city had become something like war zones—my heart began to perceive that there was a wound in the material world that no amount of science could heal, that in fact science itself was only the helpful lie told to a dying man.

"Then I reached my parents' block, and the pit where the bodies had been burned. Someone told me what had been done there, and for a while I was lost again, walking in darkness. I cast myself down into the pit and I swam there, weeping, in the ashes of the dead, the stench of their burned bones and fat in my nose, the oil and soot of their carbonized forms painting me black. And then the hand of God reached into me, and touched me."

Paul realized he was holding his breath. He let it out. A vapor, it hung in the air over his head, slowly turning invisible.

"The words of old wisdom came to me then," Nandi continued slowly.

"The world has Maya and its veils, which is to say illusion, as its material cause—the illusion that permits souls to enact their dance of good acts and evil acts, and thus to turn the wheel of incarnation. But that is only the *material* cause of the world. Shiva, he who *is* the dance, is the first cause, that which always was and always will be. It is said: *'Thus it is that as the First Cause—sometimes called 'The Terror' and 'The Destroyer'—dances upon the darkness, demonstrating his five acts of creation, preservation, destruction, embodiment, and release, he contains in himself both the life and death of all things. So for this reason his servants dwell in the cremation ground, and the heart of his servant is like the cremation ground, wasted and desolate, where the self and its thoughts and deeds are burnt away, and nothing remains but the Dancer himself.'* "

His face seemed to have changed, to have become something hard and sharp as a stone knife. His eyes glinted with a cold light that made Paul distinctly uneasy.

"So at that moment, as I lay in the ashes of the dead, I gave myself to Shiva—to God. And by doing it I found a science that all the works of humanity can only approximate. All that happens, happens because God wills it. All is part of the dance. So although it is my lot to combat the Grail Brotherhood, I also know that they can have no success that does not glorify Heaven. Do you understand, Paul Jonas?"

Paul was too stunned to reply for a moment. He could not tell if he had just been told something profound or had endured the ravings of a religious maniac, a man driven mad by tragedy. "I don't think I do," he finally replied. "Not really."

"You are wondering what sort of lunatic accompanies you, are you not?" Nandi smiled a tired smile. In the growing light, he looked a little less frightening. "In the cremation pit where my parents had been burned I learned what my greatest crime had been. My sin had been that I believed that *I* was the measure of the universe. Years later, when I returned to another cremation ground, preparing myself in the Shivaite manner—becoming an *aghori,* we would say—for this task, I came to see that even those children of the quarantine, so horribly abused and murdered before my eyes, were a part of the body of God. Even their *murderers* were God, and thus were doing God's work."

Paul's head felt overloaded, his thoughts heavy. "I still don't understand any of that, or if I do, I don't agree with it. If murder is God's work, then why are you bothering to fight against these Grail people?"

"Because that is my task, Paul Jonas. And out of my actions, my resistance, more of God's wishes will become visible and manifest. The Grail Brotherhood, too, are doing God's work, as am I, although they do not believe it and doubtless think the opposite is true. And I am sure the same is so for you, too."

A short while earlier, miserable at the thought of being hunted, Paul had rejected the idea of his own importance. But now, hearing this man describe him as just another cog in Heaven's implacable machinery, he found himself swinging in the other direction. Some prideful thing in him, something that he could not dislike or even separate from himself, rejected the idea. "Are they all like you, then?" he finally asked. "The people in the Circle? Are they all Shiva-worshipers?"

For the first time, Nandi laughed. "Oh, goodness, no. Or perhaps I should say, 'Oh, heavens, no.' We are from all different faiths and disciplines. All we share is our knowledge of the Eternal, and the will to devote our lives to serving it."

Paul could not help smiling. "Ecumenicals. My grandmother always said that you folks were the biggest danger there was."

"Pardon?"

"Nothing. A bit of family humor." Paul looked up. The ice was growing a little thinner on the cavern walls here, the air a bit warmer. He let the blanket sag and stretched his arms. "So what next? For us, I mean. Where are we going?"

"To the next simulation," his companion replied, still paddling tirelessly, his slender arms moving with an almost mechanical motion. "Where I will tell you the name of the man who is my enemy and, it appears, yours. And then I just go my own way."

"What do you mean?"

Nandi's face was set hard again, locked like a door. "You cannot travel with me, Paul. I was meant to meet you, that I am certain, but we are not to travel together long. You have your own role to play, whatever that may be, and I have mine. None but one of the Circle can go where I am going. I am sorry."

The shock was powerful and surprisingly painful. After a vast stretch of loneliness, he had finally found someone to call a companion, if not yet a friend, and now that human connection was going to be severed immediately. "But . . . but where will I go? Am I just going to roam through these simulations forever?" He felt his eyes filling with tears and blinked angrily. "I'm so tired. I just want to go home. Please, help me. I want to go home."

Nandi's expression did not soften, but he took one hand off the paddle and touched Paul's shoulder. "You will find a way, if it is God's will."

"I don't care about God's will! I don't care about the Brotherhood, or your Circle, or any of this. I don't belong here."

"But you do belong here. I do not know how, but I know." Nandi squeezed his arm, then withdrew his hand.

Paul turned, unwilling to show the other man his need any longer, and stared at the river stretching before them. The tunnel walls glowed in the distance, the ice afire with deep golden light. "Is that the gateway?" he asked.

"No, only the sun of the outside world. But the gate is not far beyond."

Paul cleared his throat; then, still looking out at the dark water and the approaching daylight, said: "There's a woman who comes to me in dreams."

"In dreams you have here? In this network?"

"Yes. And I saw her in at least one of the simulations."

He related all that he could remember, the words spilling out, from the first dreams to the most recent. He described meeting her in the flesh in the Mars simulation. He repeated what she had told him when she had spoken through the Ice Age child. "But none of it makes sense," he finished. *Go to the wanderer's house and release the weaver*—that could mean anything."

Nandi was silent for a long time, thinking. The light began to grow, throwing long stalactite shadows across the ceiling of the cave. Then, for the second time, the dark-skinned man began to laugh.

"What's funny?"

"I suppose it is only that for so long we Indians envied the very Britishness that had been thrust upon us by our conquerors, but which we were never fully allowed to enjoy. Now it seems that an education at the university in Varanasi gives one a better grounding in the classics than an education in England itself."

"What are you talking about?" Paul tried to restrain his anger, but this was his life the man was laughing at. Pathetic though it was, and at the moment full of gaps, it was all he had.

"I suspect you are looking for Ithaca, my friend Paul. The wanderer's house is in Ithaca."

The cave mouth was before them, spilling light, turning the river's surface into gilded foil. Paul had to squint. "Ithaca. . . ?"

"Goodness, man, did you not read Homer? The English school system is in even greater disarray than I thought." Nandi now appeared to be enjoying himself. He applied the paddle to the water with dispatch, slipping them through the rocks that thronged the cave's opening and out into what at first seemed like the brightest, most blazing sun Paul had ever experienced. Moments later, as his dazzled eyes finally began to adjust, he saw the flat plane of the ocean lying dark and still in the distance, at the end of the river's cursive track across a forested plain. He also noticed that something seemed to be wrong with the color of the water just ahead. Then the first arrow struck.

Paul gaped in amazement as the shaft shivered to visibility in the boat's prow, only inches from his hand. It might have been a completely new and original object for all the sense his mind could make of it. A moment later another arrow smacked into the wood next to it, then Nandi cried out behind him.

Paul turned. A side stream, perhaps the tributary Nandi had mentioned earlier, rushed in from one side here, crossing through a forest of pines to join the Alph. Two boats were racing toward them on this smaller river, a hundred meters back but closing fast, each sped by half a dozen oarsmen. The archers standing in the prow of the leading boat wore silks whose bold, shimmering colors reflected the bright sun. One drew his bow, then released the string. An instant later something buzzed past Paul's head.

Nandi was slumped forward on the bench, a slender black shaft jutting from his thigh, his loose pants already sodden with blood. "It appears the Khan was in residence after all," he said. His face had gone yellowish with the shock, but his voice was strong. "These, I think, are after me, not you."

Paul crouched as low as he could without actually hiding behind Nandi. The two pursuing boats had left the sidestream and now coursed down the Alph directly behind them. Several more arrows whisked past, missing only because the current was rough and all three craft were pitching. "What difference does it make who they're after?" Paul demanded. "They'll kill us both anyway! How far to the gateway?"

Nandi clenched his teeth, squeezing his jaw so tight that tendons stood out on his neck and veins bulged in his forehead, then broke the arrow off just above the skin. "It is too far to reach it without being shot like rabbits. But if I am not here, I think things will go differently for you." He crept to the edge of the boat, still holding his head low.

"What are you talking about?"

"I knew we would part, but did not realize it would be so quickly," Nandi replied. "The place you seek is not in the next simulation, or even close, but with luck you will find your way there. It is Ithaca you are looking for, I am almost certain." He lurched over the side, but caught the rail with his hands and hung from the boat's rail with his legs already in the water, tipping the small craft sideways.

"Nandi, what are you doing?" Paul tried to drag him back, but the slender man pushed his reaching fingers away.

"I am not committing suicide, Paul Jonas. The Khan's soldiers will have a harder time catching me than they think. Stay in the boat. The current will take you through." Another flurry of arrows whickered past overhead. "Your enemy's name is Felix Jongleur—do not underestimate him!"

He let go and threw himself backward, flinging out his arms to make a great splash. By the time he surfaced Paul was twenty yards downstream, and could only watch helplessly as Nandi Paradivash swam to shore and limped into the trees.

The first boat backed water furiously when it reached the spot where he had disappeared, then slid to the shallows so the soldiers could leap out to pursue him, but the second boat did not slow. The archers on board, who had waited while those in the first craft tried their luck, now had a chance to demonstrate their own art; as Paul lay huddled in the bottom of the little boat arrowheads spattered against it like hailstones, splintering the wood all around him.

He only saw a brief glimmer of blue overhead, a gleaming, shimmering azure like a cloud of uneven light, then something made the hairs on his arms stand up from his skin, sparking, and he passed out of Xanadu.

CHAPTER 19

A Day's Work

THE suburbs slid past and were replaced by the hills and their towns, commuter havens side-by-side with failed developments empty as museum displays in the white morning. The mild shadows grew ever smaller as the sun climbed toward noon, as though the bright light in the sky could even evaporate darkness.

"So, we couldn't have done this with a call?"

"I need to see this place, Stan. I just do. One of those things."

"Just explain this again—Polly Merapanui came from way up north. She was a street kid in Kogarah, got killed under a Sydney highway. So why exactly are we going to the Blue Mountains, which isn't any of those places?"

"Because she lived there." Calliope pulled around a truck full of broken concrete pieces, which was moving about as fast as might be expected. "For almost a year after she moved down from Darwin. You know that—it's in the files."

"Just trying to get my head wrapped around it." He pursed his lips, watching another dust-dry town slide past the windows. "We couldn't have made a phone call? It's not like I'm desperate for police-related things to do on my infrequent days off, Skouros."

"As if you had a life. Anyway, her stepmother doesn't have a line. No access."

"Quality folk."

"You are a snob, Stan Chan."

"Just trying to entertain myself on the long drive."

Calliope opened the window. The heat had eased a bit; a light breeze riffled the yellow grasses along the hillsides. "I just need somewhere to start, Stan. I need . . . I don't know, a feeling, something."

"These people didn't even see her during the two years before she died. And if her momma don't got no line at the cot, then baby wasn't even calling home, was she?"

"You are the least convincing slang user I've ever heard. No, they didn't see her, didn't hear from her, except for one or two freeline messages to the place where her stepmother worked. But they *knew* her, and nobody we've found in Kogarah could say the same."

"Did you ever think this might be a lot of trouble for a bad case?"

Calliope expelled her breath with an angry huff. "All the damn time, Stan. Just let me try this and if nothing happens, we'll discuss bagging the whole thing. Okay?"

"Okay. Are we there yet?"

"Shut up."

The foothills had become mountains, bold headlands of weathered rock, whiskery with blue gum and evergreen. Calliope's underpowered car had dropped back behind even the cement truck now, and made noises as it climbed like a walking toy trapped in a corner.

". . . Look, Stan, I'm just saying that someone doesn't do what this guy did—the stones in the eye sockets, all those stabs and cut wounds—unless he either had a grudge, or he's a real textbook sadist, and those kind don't stop at one when they've had success. So either there's someone in her past we need to find out about, or we've got an unrecognized serial killer out there. Nobody in Kogarah knows of any grudges there, not even any boyfriends. Checking the IPnet, we've got nothing either." She finished her squeeze bottle and dropped it over her shoulder into the small rear seat.

"So we look for what? Someone who followed her to the big city from out here, stalked her for two years, *then* slashed her? A stretch, Skouros."

"I know it's a stretch. Damn it, was that the turnoff for Cootalee?"

"She mixed on the streets, she fixed on the streets, she got sixed on the streets."

"Christ, Stan, will you quit talking like a cop? I hate that shit."

"How do you want me to talk?" He fell silent as she made what was doubtless an illegal u-turn across two lanes of empty freeway and a dirt center divider. " 'Calliope Skouros, you have captured my heart. I love you madly. Please let me take you away from all this homicide-related sordidness. . .'?"

"Oh, that would work out well—a Greek lesbian and a Sino-Australian fairy-boy."

His bared his very good teeth in his sunniest smile. "I'll have you know that I am exclusively, and perhaps one could even say enthusiastically, *not* a fairy-boy."

"Like that really improves the odds, Chan." She shot him a sudden, worried look. "You were joking, weren't you? You haven't been carrying around some hopeless crush on your unobtainable partner, have you?"

"Joking."

"Oh. Good."

She drove for a while in silence, waiting for Cootalee, advertised but not yet delivered. She fiddled with the car system, but after a while turned the music down again. "Okay, here's an old one," she said.

"Adam and Eve and Pinch Me went down to the river to bathe.
"Adam and Eve fell in and drowned—which one of the three was saved?"

"Are we there yet?"

"Come on, Stanley, which one?"

"Which one what?"

"Which one of the three was saved?"

"What are my choices again?"

"You're just being an asshole, aren't you? Adam and Eve and Pinch Me."

"I would guess . . . Adam."

"No! Pinch Me!—*ouch!* God, you're a shit, Chan."

"You just missed the Cootalee offramp."

"I think it's only fair to tell you," she said fifteen seconds later, as she laid tracks across another center divider, "that the engagement is definitely off."

"She's *gone?*"

The woman peering around the door of the trailer had the aggrieved look of someone unfairly accused. "I told you. She took off a month ago."

"Where?" Calliope looked at Stan Chan, who was inspecting the blocks placed underneath the trailer as though they were a feat of engineering rivaling the Pantheon. The woman, in turn, was watching Stan Chan with great distrust, as though at any moment he might snatch those same blocks of oil-scummed wood and run away with them.

"How should I know? I didn't know the bitch, but her goddamn dog kept me awake all the time. Good riddance."

"You see," Stan said a few minutes later, as they motored slowly out of the trailer park. "Quality folk."

"I hope her employer has some idea," Calliope said glumly. "Or you're going to start looking awfully right about coming up here. For once in your life."

The address from the files, listed as Polly Merapanui's stepmother's place of employment, turned out to be a modest house on the far side of Cootalee. A huge gum tree stretched its branches over most of the yard. A pair of dark-skinned children were squirting each other with a hose in its patchy shade, shrieking, while a small brown dog barked and circled them in a paroxysm of joyful excitement.

The door was opened by an Aboriginal woman wearing glasses and an apron. She wiped her hands dry on the apron as she examined Calliope's identification, then said, "Come in. I'll get my husband."

The man who emerged from the back room buttoning his shirt wore his curly black hair in a puffy, incongruously young style. A long, narrow beard made him look like something out of the Flemish school. "Hello, officers. I'm Reverend Dennis Bulurame. What can I do for you?"

"We have this address listed as the place of employment for Lily Ponegarra, also known as Lily Merapanui. We wanted to talk to her."

"Ah. She's not here, I'm afraid, but she did work for me. Well, for the church. Come into my study. You might just grab that chair and bring it with you."

Reverend Bulurame's study was a smallish room which contained little more than his desk, an inexpensive wallscreen, and a number of posters advertising church events—sales, concerts, carnivals. "Lily cleaned for the church, and sometimes for us, too."

"You say it in the past tense," Calliope pointed out.

"Well, she's gone. Left town. She met a man, is what happened." He shook his head and offered a rueful smile. "There wasn't much to tie her here, anyway. It's not like the church job was making her rich."

"Do you know where she's gone? The name of the man?"

"Billy, Bobby, something like that. That's all I know—probably not too helpful, am I right? And she didn't say where she was going, just that the two of them were going away. She apologized for not giving two weeks' notice, I'll say that. Is she in trouble?"

Stan Chan was examining the posters. He had to step to one side to let the reverend's wife through the door with a tray of lemonade and three glasses. "No. We just wanted to ask her some questions about her daughter."

"Her. . . ?" It took a moment. "Polly? After all this time?" Bulurame shook his head. "Terrible. But I'd almost forgotten. Strange, that something so dreadful could slip into the background. Lily was devastated. That girl was all she had."

"Nobody ever caught him, did they?" said Mrs. Bulurame. "That devil-devil man who killed her."

"Have you made an arrest?" The reverend leaned forward. "Is that why you're here? Preparing a case?"

"No, I'm afraid not." Calliope took a drink of lemonade, which could have used more sugar. She unpuckered and asked him, "Did either of you know Polly?"

"Not really. Saw her in the street or down at the store occasionally, but Lily hadn't come to work for us then. In fact, it was partly because the murder hit her so badly that I decided the church could use some regular cleaning, if you know what I mean. Give her something to do. She wasn't in good financial shape either. There are some people who did well out of the second Land Settlement Bill, Officer, but others like Lily who . . . well, they just let it slip through their fingers." The clear implication was that the reverend and his wife were among those who had done the sensible thing and invested their Settlement money in a nice house and a home station to get them all the netfeeds.

Calliope sighed inwardly. They were going to hear very little of interest from this pleasant, self-satisfied man, she felt sure. She forced herself to work through the rest of the questions as Stan Chan sipped lemonade and acted as though he found nothing more fascinating in all the world than advertisements for bake sales. The results were as disheartening as she had suspected: the Bulurames knew nothing of any boyfriends the daughter might have had, and couldn't even tell them if the stepmother had any friends still in town who would know something of the family's history.

"Lily didn't go out much," the reverend explained. "That's why this man—well, I don't think it was a spiritual relationship, if you know what I mean. She's almost a little simple, Lily is, bless her—I worry that she's easily led about."

Calliope thanked him for his time. He did not get up. As his wife was letting them out the door, and Stan was looking sour at the prospect of having to dodge past the hose-waving children, Calliope turned back.

"You said 'that devil-devil man,' Mrs. Bulurame. What did you mean, exactly?"

The reverend's wife opened her brown eyes wide, as though Calliope had ventured a complete non sequitur—perhaps asked her if she liked to skydive naked. "Oh! Well, it's . . . it's just like that story, isn't it?"

"Story?"

"I heard it when I was a little girl, from my grandmother. About the Woolagaroo. The devil-devil man with crocodile's teeth. Someone made him, carved him out of wood, but he had stones for eyes. Just like what happened to poor little Polly."

An hour and a half later, all other leads dry as the backroad dust that had settled on Calliope's department car, they drove back out of Cootalee.

"Woolagaroo," she said. "Do you know anything about Aboriginal folklore, Stan?"

"Sure. In fact, it was an important part of my police academy training, Skouros. We spent hours every day reading about the Bunyip and How the Kangaroo Learned to Jump. If we had time after that, we sometimes squeezed in a little pistol-range work. Wasn't it like that for you, too?"

"Oh, shut up. I'll take that as a no." She put on the music, a modern piece by someone whose name she could never remember, downloaded off a late-night show. The music filled the car, sparse and bittersweet, like something played beside a Japanese ornamental pool. Stan Chan closed his eyes and reclined his seat.

Woolagaroo. Calliope silently tasted the word. *Devil-devil. Stones for its eyes, just like the old story, she said.*

It was nothing, of course. But it was a little better quality of nothing than anything else so far.

* * *

"**B**UT since you are an attorney, Mr. Ramsey, surely you of all people can understand that we don't give out our performers' home lines or any other private information. That would be unheard of. Impossible." Even as she shot him down, the public relations woman's smile did not change. In fact, with the shimmering, animated Uncle Jingle poster covering the entire wall behind her, and the inset window featuring the live feed from the show, her fixed professional grin was about the only thing on Catur Ramsey's wallscreen that wasn't moving.

"I'm not asking for her home code, Ms. Dreibach. But I have a matter of great importance to discuss with her, and she hasn't answered a single one of my messages through any of the other channels."

"That is her right, isn't it, Mr. Ramsey?" The smile lost a little of the rictus quality—she was perhaps a tiny bit concerned. "If this is a legal issue, shouldn't you be contacting our legal department directly?"

On the live feed, Uncle Jingle was being swallowed by a whale, or something that would certainly have been one if cetaceans were made of bricks. Ramsey had watched enough of the Uncle Jingle show during the past week to know that this creature was called the Walling Whale. Uncle Jingle's melodramatic terror was not entirely comfortable to watch. What did kids really think of this stuff, anyway? "Maybe I haven't made myself clear," he said, tearing his eye away from the miniaturized spectacle. "Olga Pirofsky has done nothing wrong. My clients have no complaint with either Uncle Jingle's Jungle or the Obolos Entertainment Corporation. We simply want to talk to Ms. Pirofsky about something very important to my clients, and I'm asking for your help because she isn't answering my messages."

Ms. Dreibach patted her helmet of glossy hair. She looked relieved, but not entirely convinced. "I'm glad to hear that, Mr. Ramsey. Obolos is the world leader in children's entertainment, you know, and we don't want to see unfounded rumors of some kind of legal problems all over the nets. But I don't think I can do anything to help you. I can't force one of our employees to take your call, after all."

"Look, is there *anything* you can think of? Could someone hand-deliver a message for me? Assure Ms. Pirofsky that she might be able to help my clients with a very important matter, at no cost to herself except a few minutes for my phone call?"

"Well . . ." The public relations woman had weathered her tiny storm of doubt, and now appeared to be thinking about potential tradeoffs down the line. "We'd hate for you to go away thinking that we don't do our best here at "The Happiest Place on the Net." I could give you the office line for the show's director, I suppose. Perhaps she . . . oops, it's a *he* this week!" She made a "silly-me" face that took ten points off her IQ and added almost that many years to her age. "Perhaps he could give your message to Olga. To Ms. Pirofsky."

"Thank you. That would be wonderful, Ms. Dreibach. I can't tell you how helpful you've been."

She went still again as she consulted her directory. On the wall behind her, Uncle Jingle turned a cartwheel that never ended, spinning around and around and around.

The call came in at a few minutes before ten o'clock, just as he was thinking he might actually be ready to go home. He sighed and sank back into his chair. *"Answer."*

The incoming line was voice-only. The voice itself sounded very, very tentative, with a faint trace of accent which he had never noticed on the Uncle Jingle show. "Hello? Is there someone there named . . . Ramsey?"

"Decatur Ramsey, Ms. Pirofsky. That's me. Thank you so much for returning my call. I really appreciate you taking time out of your busy . . ."

"What do you want?"

So much for formalities. The director had as much as said that she was an odd bird. "I'm an attorney—I hope they told you that. I'd like to ask you some questions on behalf of my clients."

"Who are they?"

"I'm not at liberty to disclose that just now, I'm afraid."

"I have done nothing to anyone."

"No one's saying you have, Ms. Pirofsky." *Jesus,* he thought, *this woman isn't just regular odd—she sounds frightened.* "Please, just listen to the questions. If you don't want to answer them, all you have to do is tell me so. Don't get me wrong—you will be doing my clients a huge favor if you do help. They are dealing with a very, very difficult problem, and they're desperate."

"How can I help them? I don't even know who these people are."

He took a breath, praying to the God of Depositions for patience. "Just let me ask you the first question. Are you familiar with something called Tandagore's Syndrome?"

There was a long silence. "Go on," she said at last.

"Go on?"

"Let me hear all the questions, then I'll decide if I'm going to answer you."

Catur Ramsey was half-convinced that he'd stumbled onto some kind of lunatic—the kind who believed that the government had a bunch of little green men stashed away somewhere, or that the intelligence agencies were beaming messages into their brains—but since his clients' own case was pretty damn strange, there was at least a remote chance he might be onto something.

"I can't really ask you the rest of the questions unless I know the answer to the first," he explained. "I suppose they would go something like, 'Do you know someone who has it? If not, why are you interested in this and other related medical conditions?' See, Ms. Pirofsky? Like that. But I need to get that first answer."

There was an even longer silence this time. He began to think she had soundlessly cut the connection when she abruptly asked, in a voice little more than a whisper, "How . . . how did you know I was interested in the Tandagore sickness?"

My God, he thought. *I've scared this poor woman almost to death.*

"It's no secret, ma'am—I mean, Ms. Pirofsky. Nothing shady. I'm researching these syndromes for my clients. I've been contacting lots of people who have asked the mednets for information, or have written articles, or even who have just had undiagnosed illnesses in their family that resemble the Tandagore profile. You're not the only person I've contacted, by any means." *But you're certainly one of the most interesting,* he did not say aloud, *since you work on the net itself, and directly with children. You're also one of the most ridiculously damn difficult to get hold of.*

"I've been having these terrible headaches," she said, then hurriedly added, "oh, God, you're going to think I'm a crazy person. Or that I have a brain tumor or something. But I don't. The doctors say I'm fine." She fell silent for a moment. "You're going to think I'm even crazier, but I can't talk to you about this on the phone." She laughed nervously. "Have you noticed how hardly anyone says 'phone' any more? I suppose that means I'm really getting old."

Ramsey struggled to sort through the clutter of ideas. "You don't want to talk on . . . on the phone. Is that right?"

"Maybe you could visit me?"

"I'm not sure, Ms. Pirofsky. Where are you? Somewhere near Toronto, right?" He had found a newsnet snippet on her from five years back, a minor personality piece from a small net magazine.

"I live . . ." She stopped again, and several seconds of silence followed. "Oh, no. If you saw my name, looking into this Tandagore thing, then that means . . . that means *anyone* can find out." Her voice got smaller at the end, as though she had stepped away from the speaker, or toppled down a hole. "Oh, God," she murmured. "I have to get off. I can't talk."

"Ms. Pirofsky, please . . ." he began, but the connection clicked off.

He sat staring at the dark screen for some moments before he brought his wallpaper back up, wondering what he could give up to make time for a visit to Canada, and wondering how he would feel about that if the woman turned out to be as unstable as she sounded.

Jaleel Fredericks was one of those people who gave the impression you'd just dragged him away from something *really* important—that even if you were calling to tell him his house was burning down, he'd be a little surprised you'd bothered him when there were things that truly deserved his attention.

"Forgive me, Ramsey, but I'm tired," he said. "What this comes down to is that you don't really have anything yet. Am I right?"

"Basically." It was bad strategy to equivocate with Fredericks, but you couldn't let him run roughshod over you, either. He was a good man, Catur Ramsey had long ago decided, but he was used to folding people into shapes that suited him. "But you have to clear the brush before you can start building the cabin."

"I'm sure." He frowned as his wife said something offscreen. "That's not what he's calling about." Fredericks turned his attention back to the attorney. "She says she's been trying to get the authorization for those records you wanted, but it may be a few more days. And did you get that stuff of Sam's she sent you."

"No problem. And yes, I got those files, but I haven't had a chance to look through them yet. I'll get back to you at the beginning of the week, let you know what all this research amounts to."

As he was waiting for the Gardiner family's number to pick up, Ramsey watched the stream of cars sliding past on the elevated freeway three floors below his office window, the rain-slick asphalt streaked with reflections from the headlights. He knew he should have asked the Frederickses to authorize a trip up to Toronto, but the idea of explaining the Uncle Jingle woman to Jaleel Fredericks was less than appealing. He wasn't sure himself why he felt there might be something worth pursuing there.

He only had to wade halfway through the incoming call filter before Conrad Gardiner picked up. He was Ramsey's age, perhaps even a bit younger, but he looked ready for retirement, his face barely animated.

"What can we do for you, Mr. Ramsey?"

"I was just curious about something. Do you still have that problem with your son's agent and the missing files?"

"Yes. We've had two different companies in to see what they can do, but no results." He shook his head slowly. "I can't believe all that stuff has just been mailed right out of our system by . . . by a *program.* Gear, making its own decisions." His laugh was not a happy one. "Well, that's the twenty-first century for you, isn't it?"

"What was its name?"

"You mean Orlando's agent? I don't know. It was 'something something *PsAI*'—a Pseudo-Artificial-Intelligence, you know? Old, but expensive when we got it. I suppose I could look it up."

"Actually, I was wondering if Orlando had a name for it. You know, a nickname? People, especially kids, often do that."

"Jesus, you're kidding." Gardiner was taken aback. "I really can't remember. Vivien!"

His wife walked into the room, just barely visible on Ramsey's screen. She was taking off her coat; he guessed she'd been at the hospital. Her husband passed the question on to her, and she said something Ramsey couldn't hear.

"Beezle Bug," Gardiner reported. "That's right. I'd forgotten. He's had it since he was a little kid." His mouth twitched, and he turned away for a moment. When he had mastered himself, he asked: "What do you want to know that for, anyway?"

"Just wondering," Ramsey said. "An idea. I'll tell you about it another time."

He broke the connection, then sat back to think, watching the cars leave snail trails of light on the freeway below.

It was midnight by the time he got home. Third time that week, and it was only Thursday.

IT was almost worse that he knew it was a dream.

Such visions were all that ever came to him in the bloodless darkness that was now the closest he came to sleep—the same tired images, the same recycled shames and horrors. They might be broken apart and then sifted together in strange combinations, but they were still the very ones that had visited him for years, some for over a century.

Even Felix Jongleur's ghosts were growing old.

The three senior boys stood before him, blocking the stairway and any chance of escape. Oldfield had the collar of his white shirt turned up, and held a cigarette cupped in his hand. Patto and Halsall, who had been waiting for their turn, followed Oldfield's gaze. The three stared at him like Macbeth's witches.

"What are you looking at, Jingle-Jangle?" Oldfield demanded.

"Little sniveler," added Halsall. "Sniveling Frog bastard."

"Juggles wants to join in," Patto said, grinning. "He wants a puff on your fag, Oley."

It was all so predictable—history and fantasy splashed together in an untrustworthy mix. The part of Jongleur's ancient brain that stood at a critical distance from the dream-stage recognized that the stairwell and landing were not from the Cranleigh School residence but his childhood house in Limoux, and that the dream-Patto had almost entirely lost his true features, and looked instead like a man Jongleur had known (and whose business he had ruined) back at the turn of the most recent century, almost ninety years later than these imperfectly remembered school days.

But for all its repetitions, the humiliation of this dream and others like it did not become less.

The English boys were on him now, like jackals on a fallen antelope. Halsall wrenched his arm behind his back while Oldfield grabbed at his crotch and twisted until he screeched with pain and sucked in air and smoke from the stolen cigarette. He could feel it again, that horrible taste; each breath was a red fire going down his throat. He choked until he almost vomited.

"Parley-voo, Juggles." Patto twisted his ear. "Parley-voo, you sodding Frenchie spy."

But instead of kicking him as they usually did, they snatched his elbows and pulled him around, facing him toward the end of the second floor landing. Toward the window.

That doesn't belong here! he thought, and suddenly the tired old dream filled him with a surprising panic. *Not that! Not the window!*

But he was being hurried toward it, his arms pinioned. The window grew larger before him, round and without any kind of grille or crossbars, backed by what his dream-self knew to be a profound blackness, a poisonous dark abyss, from which he was protected only by the thinnest sheet of glass.

He knew that he did not ever, ever, ever want to find out what was on the far side.

They can't do this to me, he thought in terror. *They think I'm a boy, but I'm not, I'm old—I'm old! They can't . . .*

He was shouting it in the dream, too, telling them he was too frail, but Oldfield and the others only laughed louder, then shoved him toward the window. Shrieking, he struck the hard surface, but instead of the glass breaking, it was he, ancient, dry, and brittle, who shattered into a thousand pieces.

The dreams, the truth, his memories, shattered, mixed together, and flung . . .

. . . Showering outward into the sunlight like a spray of water, each piece spinning like a separate planet, the cloud of iridescence a universe that had lost its equilibrium, now flying apart in high-speed entropic expansion.

The cries echoed and echoed, as they always did, but this time they were his.

He awakened in blackness, without even the virtual lamplight of Abydos to soothe him. For a brief moment he was actually in his body and nothing else, but the horror was too much and he plunged back into his system. A blind, helpless thing, a slug wrapped in gauze and mylar, floating in a dark tank—he shuddered at the thought of having to exist as he truly was. He pulled on his machinery as though it were armor.

Once into the system, the world's oldest man did not bring up the full glories of his custom-made Egypt, but raised instead a much simpler virtual world that held nothing but dim and sourceless blue light. Jongleur basked in it, caressed by subliminal sonics, and tried to calm the great fear that gripped him.

The young could not understand the horror of being old. That was nature's way of protecting them from uselessly harmful knowledge, just as the atmosphere around the Earth created a blue sky that shielded humanity from constant exposure to the naked unconcern of the stars. Old age was failure, limitation, marginalization—and that was just the beginning. Because every moment was also a step closer to nothingness, as Death drew ever nigh.

Felix Jongleur had dreamed of a faceless, shadowy figure all through his childhood, the Death that his father had told him "waits for us all," but it was when his parents sent him away to that ghastly school in England that he had finally learned what it looked like. One night, as he leafed through a tattered newspaper one of the upper-classmen had left behind in the dormitory cabinet, he had seen an illustration—*"an artist's rendition,"* the caption read, *"of the enigmatic Mr. Jingo,"*—and had known at once that this was the face of what hunted him through his dreams far more implacably than even the cruelest older boys had ever stalked him in the Cranleigh halls. The man in the picture was tall, wrapped in a dark cloak, and wore a tall, old-fashioned stovepipe hat. But it was his eyes, his mesmeric, staring eyes, and his cold grin which had caused young Felix's heart to race with recognition. The article, the explanation of who the artist's lurid drawing represented, had been gnawed away by rats and would thus forever remain a mystery; only the picture had survived, but that had been enough. Those eyes had watched Felix Jongleur ever since. As all the intervening decades had rolled past, he had lived under the gaze of those amused, soul-empty, terrifying eyes.

They waited. He—it—waited. Like an unhurried shark beneath a failing swimmer, Mister Jingo had no need to do anything else.

Jongleur fought now against the morbidity that sometimes grew on his isolated mind like an opportunistic parasite. It would all be easier if only one could *believe* in something outside oneself—something loving and kind, a counterweight to that hideously patient gaze. As his mother's sisters had done. Positive that Heaven waited for them—a place apparently identical to Limoux, except that good Catholic spinsters no longer had to put up with aching joints and noisy children—they had been the picture of security, even on their deathbeds. Not a one of them had left life with anything other than calm, even cheerful, acceptance.

But he knew better. He had learned the lesson first from his father's sad, tired face, then learned it again and more brutally in the jungle of English public school. Beyond the sky there was no Heaven, but only blackness and abounding space. Beyond one's own self there was nothing to trust, nothing upon which to rely. Darkness waited. It would take you when it wished, and no one would lift a finger to save you. You could scream until you thought your heart would burst, and someone would merely push a pillow over your face to muffle your cries. The pain would go on. No help would come.

And Death? Death, with his top hat and hypnotist gaze, was the greatest bully of all. If he did not take you from behind and unawares, if in some way you managed to avoid him and grow strong, he merely stood in the shadows and waited until time itself dragged you down. Then, when you were old and weak and helpless, he would stalk you as brazenly as a wolf.

And this the young, in their magnificent stupidity, could never understand. For them, death was only a cartoon wolf, something to be mocked. They did not see, could not know, what it would be like in that day when the monster became real—when straw, or wood, or even walls of brick would not save them.

Jongleur shuddered, something his attenuated nervous system reported rather than felt. His only solace was that since he himself had been old, he had watched three generations of youth inherit this dreadful realization and then go before him, dragged screaming out of their shattered houses into the night while he himself still avoided those smiling jaws. Genetic therapy, vitamin-flooding, low-dose triggerpoint radiation, all the tricks available (unless you had Jongleur's almost limitless assets and Jongleur's seminal ideas) could only delay death a little. Some, the luckier and the wealthier, had recently lived into a second decade past their first century, but they were still children compared to him. As the others all fell, as his own grandchildren and great- and great-great-grandchildren had been born, aged, then succumbed, one after the other, he alone had continued to cheat Mr. Jingo's patience.

And God or whatever willing, he would do so forever!

Felix Jongleur had faced night-terrors for more than two long human lifetimes. He knew without looking at the chronometer, without reference to any of the information he could summon with little more than a thought, that outside his fortress the last hour before dawn lay heavy on the Gulf of Mexico. The few fishing boats that he allowed in Lake Borgne, his private moat, would be loading up their nets. Police in surveillance labs in Baton Rouge would be nodding off in front of their monitors, hoping that the morning shift would remember to bring them something to eat. Fifty kilometers west of Jongleur's tower, in New Orleans, a half-dozen or more tourists would be lying in the gutters of the Vieux Carré, missing their money cards, key cards, and self-respect . . . if they were lucky. Some less fortunate might wake up drugged, with a hand gone and the wrist hastily cauterized so the thieves could avoid a murder charge (most rental car companies had abandoned palmprint-readers, but a few still held out.) And some of the gutter-flung tourists would not be lucky enough to wake up at all.

The night was almost gone.

Felix Jongleur was angry with himself. It was bad enough that he should float in and out of sleep without realizing it—he did not remember drifting off—but to wake up, heart aflutter like a frightened child, because of a few familiar and now-tiresome dreams. . . .

He would do some work, he decided. That was the only good solution, the best way to spit in the face of the man with the tall hat.

His first impulse was to return to Abydos-That-Was, to review recent information from the comfort of his god-throne, surrounded by the attentions of his priests. But the nightmare, and especially its unusual juxtaposition of elements, had unsettled him. His home suddenly did not feel secure, and although the great house that his physical body never left was more heavily defended than most military bases, he still felt the urge to have a look around, if only to assure himself that all was as it should be.

Anchored by seven subterranean floors (a hundred-plus vertical feet of fibramic cylinder, which had been literally screwed into the delta mud), Jongleur's tower reached another ten stories up from water level into the foggy air above Lake Borgne, but the great tower was only part of the vast complex that covered the artificial island. An engineered mass of rock about fifty kilometers square, the island housed only slightly more than two thousand people—a very small town by numbers alone, but more influential than most of the world's nations put together. Jongleur was only slightly less a god here than he was in his virtual Egypt: with a subvocalized word, he brought up the battery of video images that detailed every corner of his domain. All over the tower and the surrounding buildings, wallscreens became one-way windows in an instant, and words and numbers superimposed on the surveillance pictures began to fly past him like sparks.

He started on the outside and worked his way in. The east-facing perimeter cameras brought him the first hints of sunrise, a reddish glow above the Gulf, still dimmer than the tangerine lights dotting the oil rigs. The guards in two of the perimeter observation towers were playing cards, and a few were not fully in uniform, but the squadrons in all six towers were awake and alert, and Jongleur was satisfied; he would memo the commanders about keeping a watch on discipline. The rest of the defenders of his domain—the human defenders, in any case—slept in their bunks, row upon row upon row. Their quarters and parade grounds alone took up almost half the artificial island on which the tower stood.

He moved his inspection inward to the tower itself, flitting from viewpoint to wallscreened viewpoint over scores of rooms and dozens of corridors like some magical spirit that lived in mirrors. The offices were mostly empty, although a skeleton crew was in place taking overseas requests and pulling information off the nets for the morning shift to examine. A few custodial workers at the end of their shift, local men and women who had no idea how closely they had been examined before being hired, were waiting on the esplanade for the shuttle boat that would take them around to their quarters on the island's far side.

His executive staff had not come in yet, and their offices stood hushed and dark except for the glow of electronic displays. Above the executive offices were the first of the tower apartments, reserved mainly for visiting dignitaries: the few of these treasured and envied living spaces that had been fitted as permanent residences were awarded to only the very luckiest of Jongleur's entire worldwide operation.

Jongleur's remote eye discovered the bathrobed president of one of his larger Ukrainian subsidiaries sitting on one of the tower apartment balconies, looking down at the lake. Jongleur wondered if the man might be awake so early because he was jet-lagged, and then remembered he had a conference scheduled with the fellow later in the day. It would take place through intermediary screens, of course; the Ukrainian executive, one of the richest and most powerful men in his entire country, would doubtless wonder why, after coming all this way, he should not meet his own employer in person.

The man should count his lucky stars that he didn't have to see his master face-to-real-face, Jongleur thought. The Ukrainian would take away an image of his employer as an eccentric, security-obsessed old man, instead of discovering the unpleasant truth—that their founder and leader was a monstrous *thing,* held together by medical pressure-wrappings, continuously submerged in life-preserving fluids. The visiting executive would never have to think about how his employer's eyes and ears had been pierced by electrodes connected directly to the optic and auditory nerves, how his skin and even muscle grew more jelly-soft hourly, threatening to slide free at any moment from bones thin and weak as twigs.

Jongleur's thoughts did not linger long on the familiar horror of his own condition. Instead, his disembodied inspection flitted up through the private apartments to the lowest floors of his own inner sanctum, where it touched briefly on the quarters of his various bodyguards and technicians, on the hardware rooms where the most important machines were serviced, and on the chamber locked behind three separate pressure-doors and two guard stations where the tanks lay in their padded cradles. His own life-support tank, a capsule of black, shiny plasteel, bulked like a royal sarcophagus at the center of the room, its tentacles of bundled and multiply redundant cables stretching away on all sides. Three other tanks shared the huge circular room with his, the smaller and less central capsules that belonged to Finney and Mudd, and—close by his own resting place—that other and most significant oblong, as large and gleamingly opaque as his own.

He did not want to look at that other tank for very long.

Neither did he wish to carry his inspection any farther. The topmost floor, as always, remained out of bounds, even—perhaps especially—for him. The master of Lake Borgne had decided long before this day he did not ever again want to look into the suite of rooms at the top of the tower. But he had also known that if it remained available to him he would be unable to resist, that just as an aching tooth draws a probing tongue, he would torture himself if he did not do something. He had thus reprogrammed his surveillance system, and locked that part of it away behind a code he did not have. Unless he specifically asked his security manager to reprogram it—and he had fought against that temptation a thousand times—it would remain as black to him as the emptiness between stars.

Reassured to see the rest of his fiefdom safe and secure, and not wishing to dwell any longer than necessary on what floated in the fourth tank, or what remained at the pinnacle of the tower, he called up his virtual domains and continued his inspection there, in the worlds he had created.

On the Western Front near Ypres, the battle of Amiens raged on. The man for whom the trenches had served as a prison was gone now, but the simulacra who fought and died there went on doing so regardless, as they had before the prisoner had arrived. When this most recent version of the battle had ended, the corpses would rise from the mud again, as if in mockery of the Day of Judgment; the shattered bodies would be remade, the shrapnel drawn back together and reassembled into murderous shells, and the battle would begin once more.

On Mars, the warrior Rax people of the High Desert had attacked the citadel of Tuktubim. The Soombar had made a temporary peace with Hurley Brummond in order to employ his fighting legion of Earthlings in the city's defense. It all looked to be great fun.

Old Chicago was celebrating the end of Prohibition with widespread public drunkenness, so that particular cycle was almost over. Atlantis had risen up from its recent watery grave, and was poised to begin anew. Looking Glass had already entered another cycle, red and white pieces at either side of the metaphorical chessboard.

Jongleur flicked through his worlds, choosing vantage points at random, adjusting if the initial view did not give him the information he sought. In one, the Spanish Armada had somehow survived the windstorms in the Channel, and the Spaniards were even now making their way up the Thames to sack London with their superior forces; he promised himself he would check back, perhaps even embody himself so he could see it firsthand, since he had missed the last time this rare outcome had occurred.

Another invasion of England, this one from H. G. Wells' version of Mars, was winding down to its conclusion. It seemed rather depressingly slow there. He wondered whether he would have to recalibrate the simworld.

In fact, he noticed as he moved through several more simulations, his virtual domains seemed in need of more attention than he had given them of late. Xanadu was all but deserted, the gardens of the Pleasure Dome looking particularly untended. Narnia remained under snow, as it had been for months, with no allegorical lion in sight to end the winter. That Hobbit world, constructed as a favor for a great-great grandnephew, had collapsed into total warfare, which was fine, but the technology seemed to have escalated beyond what he dimly remembered was appropriate. Machine guns and jet bombers, in particular, seemed a bit *de trop.*

There were other, more subtle problems in other simulations, but they still troubled him. The Asgardians were drinking heavily rather than fighting, and although it was not uncommon to see the explosive Norse temperament turn suddenly melancholy, even Bifrost looked dusty and untended. Elsewhere, in Imperial Rome, the last of the Julio-Claudians had been usurped by a commander of the Praetorian Guard named Tigellinus, which was an interesting twist, but most of the new emperor's facial features were missing. The leader of Rome's nightmare visage—eyes and nose absent, only smooth skin in their place—was reproduced on all the coins and official statuary, which was unsettling enough, but what was even more bizarre was that no one in Rome seemed to have noticed anything wrong.

Jongleur flicked through his other domains with increasing speed, and found things to concern him in nearly every one: Dodge City, Toyland, Arden, Gomorrah, and many more, all seemed oddly off-kilter, as though someone had minutely changed the essential gravity of every virtual world.

The old man was grimly pleased that he had been startled awake by a nightmare, and that he had made this inspection as a result. These were not simply playthings, these worlds—they were the birthrights of his godhood, the fields of Paradise in which his immortality would be spent. It would not do to let things go to seed.

It was as he flicked through one of the last of his created worlds, a comparative backwater based on a series of English comic stories from the era of his young manhood, that he saw the face that for so long he had hoped he might see, feared he might see.

The face was visible only for a moment, in the midst of a crowd of people in formal clothing, but the image flew to his eye like an arrow. He felt his ancient heart begin to rabbit as it had when he dreamed; more faintly, he perceived his real body thrashing slowly in its restraining harness, disturbing the thick fluids that surrounded it. He stared, forgetting for a moment that he could leap through the view and into the scene, to clutch and catch, but even in that moment of hesitation, the face vanished.

He flung himself into the simulation, snatching the first sim his system offered, but the one he had sought for so long, as if sensing his approach, had already fled the large room and dashed out the door into the crowded streets, there to disappear. He followed, but it immediately became clear there were too many people in the way, and too many avenues of escape. Pursuit was hopeless.

Bertie Wooster, Tuppy Glossop, and the other members of the Drones Club were more than a little startled by the appearance of a seven-foot polar bear in the middle of their annual dinner dance and charity fund-raiser. Discussion of the phenomenon was intense, and calls for bar service were immediately doubled. Several of the fairer sex (and, it had to be admitted, one or two of the manly contingent) went so far as to faint. But even those who had taken in the spectacle with a jaded eye, jiggling neat Scotch not one whit on its journey mouthward as the pale intruder galloped roaring across the floor and knocked half the band flying (gravely wounding a clarinet player in the process), found themselves indescribably disturbed when the polar bear fell onto its knees just outside the door in Prince Albert Road and began to weep.

CHAPTER 20

The Invisible River

NETFEED/ART: Explosive Homage
(visual: wreckage of First Philadelphia Bank)
VO: The guerilla artist known only as "Bigger X" has claimed credit for the
package-bomb which killed three and injured twenty-six at a branch of the
First Philadelphia Bank last month.
(visual: file footage—broken showroom window, floral print body-bags)
The controversial Bigger X, who began by creating special coverings for bodies
he had stolen from the morgue, then started poisoned-product scares in
Florida and Toronto, has now claimed credit for three different murderous
assaults. In the recorded message he sent to "artOWNartWONartNOW", he
claims his work is an homage to such pioneers of forced-involvement
performances as Manky Negesco and TT Jensen . . .

"*CODE Delphi. Start here.*
"This is Martine Desroubins. I am resuming my journal.
Much has happened since my last entry, two days ago.

"The first, and perhaps the most important thing, is that we have
crossed into a new simulation. I will wait to describe this new place
until I have told how we left the old one.

"The second is that I have learned something more about this virtual universe, and every piece of new information may be critical.

"I have reached a stage now where I can 'read' the physical information of our environment as well as I can decipher the signposts of the real-world net, and thus can move around here almost as easily as any of my sighted companions—in fact, in many ways my abilities seem to be blossoming far beyond theirs. Thus, I believe it to be my particular task to attempt to understand the machineries behind these worlds. As I said before, I am not optimistic about our chances of survival, let alone success, but as we improve our knowledge, our small odds at least become slightly larger.

"So much to tell! I wish I had found time earlier to whisper some of these words into the auditing darkness.

"Back in the last simulation, our company—now only Quan Li, T4b, Sweet William, Florimel, and myself—set out after Orlando and Fredericks. A faster pursuit would undoubtedly have been better, but it was almost evening when the river swept them away, and only fools would strike out across unknown territory in the dark—especially unknown territory where the spiders are the size of circus carousels.

"The men—I shall call them that for simplicity's sake—wanted to build another raft like the one which had been lost with our other two companions, but Florimel suggested strongly that whatever we might gain by traveling swiftly on the river would be lost with the time it would take to make the raft. She is clearly someone used to organizing things—in some ways she is like Renie, but without the openness, the willingness to admit fault. I sense that she is constantly frustrated by the rest of us, like someone forced to play a game with a less capable partner. But she is clever, there is no arguing that. She argued that we should follow the beach and riverbank as far as it would take us. That way, if Fredericks and Orlando had managed to get off the river themselves, or had been swept into some backwater, we would not be rushed helplessly past them.

"Quan Li agreed with Florimel, and at risk of polarizing our party along lines of apparent gender, I cast the deciding vote in favor of this plan. So we set out along the line of the river even as the morning sun appeared above the trees on the far bank. I did not see it, of course, but I could sense it in ways far beyond merely its heat on my face—even in a simulated world, the sun is the sourcepoint of many things.

"The first part of the journey went uneventfully, except for some bickering between Sweet William and Florimel, which Quan Li tried to discourage. Florimel said that if we did not find the two young men, we should attempt to capture a member of the Grail Brotherhood—catch one of them within a simulation—and then use force or its threat to gain information about the network, perhaps even to compel the prisoner to assist us. William thought this was asking for trouble—that it was far more likely we would not only fail, since we knew so little about their powers within the network, but that we would bring the entire Brotherhood down on our heads. Quan Li and William both seemed keen not to attract undue attention. Florimel was scornful of what she saw as timidity.

"T4b remained silent and uninvolved throughout, seeming more interested in maneuvering his spiky armor over the pebbles and clumps of dirt which to us were major obstacles. I cannot say I blame him for staying apart.

"Just before noon, after we had tracked the river through several broad curving turns, I found myself distracted by a strange but not entirely unfamiliar sensation. I realized I had felt that unusual vibrancy on the morning we were forced ashore by the feeding frenzy. I had been nearly mad then, overwhelmed by the new input, and so I could not immediately remember what the sensation had heralded.

"As the tingling grew stronger, my companions began to shout that a white figure was hovering above the water just a short distance away. I could not sense anything so mundane as color, and in fact the tingling seemed to be confusing me so badly that I could barely sense the apparition at all.

"Quan Li said, 'It is a man! The one who led us to T4b when the fish spit him out!' William shouted some admonition at the stranger to 'quit acting like bleeding Jesus, for Christ's sake' and to come ashore. I paid only small attention to this because I was trying literally to make sense out of the bizarre input. Unlike the swirl of organized information that characterized my knowledge of my companions' sims, the stranger was more an *absence* of information—like a black hole, which signals its astronomical presence by what does not come from it.

"After our encounter with what we eventually realized was one of the Lords of Otherland, I came to believe that what I sensed, or rather did not sense, was the work of very sophisticated gear—something which negated the signs of the user's virtual existence in much the same way that high-powered sound baffles can counteract noise by broadcasting contrasting, deadening tones. The question still remains why anyone, especially the master of a simulation as complex as the one we were in, should need such doubtlessly expensive camouflage. Perhaps these masters of virtual space do not always stay in their own kingdoms. Perhaps they wish to be able to wander through their neighbors' gardens and harems unnoticed.

"While I was still experiencing him as a puzzling lack of signal, the stranger briskly announced, 'I am Kunohara. You are guests in my world. It is bad form not to introduce yourselves to a host before you walk through his lands, but perhaps you are from someplace where courtesies are unfamiliar.'

"It was strange to me, since his voice seemed to issue from nowhere, like old-fashioned film music. To the others, the strangest thing was his position, floating half his own height above the flowing river.

"Predictably, Quan Li hastened to apologize for any breach of courtesy. The others were silent or subdued—even William, after his initial remark, kept his insolence in check. Kunohara, who the others tell me appeared as a small Asian man, floated toward the riverbank and came to a stop before us, then lowered himself to dry land. He proceeded to make several archly cryptic remarks—enjoying his private knowledge almost as a child would. I was paying less attention to what he said than to what he *was*—or rather, what he seemed to be. If this was one of our enemies, one of the powers of this virtual universe, I wanted to learn as much about him as I could, but most particularly I wanted to know how he manipulated the environment, since all of Otherland's controls were hidden from us. Perhaps he used the aspect-dampening gear just to prevent such discoveries. In any case, I gleaned very little.

"It soon became apparent that although we knew nothing of this Kunohara, he knew something of us. He knew we had fled Atasco's simulation—William, who had appointed himself ambassador, guardedly confirmed it—and alluded to companions of ours in such a way that it suggested he may have met one of our two missing groups, although he claimed to know nothing of their current whereabouts. 'Things are shifting,' he said, seeming to think that explained something. 'Most of the gates are random.' He then posed us a riddle which I shall try to remember verbatim.

"He said, 'The Grail and the Circle oppose each other. But both are circular—both have closed their systems, and would do the same with this new universe. But a place can be found where the two circles overlap, and in that place is wisdom.'

"Sweet William, with a little more restraint than he usually shows, demanded to know what all this meant. I recognized the name 'the Circle,' but with no access to my usual information resources, could only search my own overtaxed memory, without result—and still with no result as of this moment.

"Kunohara seemed to be enjoying his role as mysterious oracle. 'I cannot answer *what*,' he answered William. 'I can suggest a *where*, however. Atop the Black Mountain you will find a place the two circles are very close to each other.'

"Florimel spoke up, quite angry, and asked why he played games with us. Kunohara, who was still to me nothing more than a voice, laughed and said, 'Do not games teach children how to think?' With that he vanished.

"A furious debate ensued, but I did not take part. I was trying both to memorize his words and to think about the voice, hoping I might find some information there the others had not. I can only believe he was what he said—the owner of the world we were in. If so, he must be privy to many of the Grail Brotherhood's plans. He might even be one of them. But if he is one of our enemies, and he knows we oppose the Brotherhood—and if not, why bother to taunt us in such a strange way?—then the question remains . . . why did he take no action against us?

"I cannot make sense of it. These are strange people. It is true that the very rich, as some American writer once said, are not like you and me.

"With Kunohara gone, we continued along the river. As we marched, William pointed out, correctly but with mocking abrasiveness, that Florimel had missed her chance to overpower and threaten one of the Grail Lords. She did not hit him, but to me it felt as though she wanted to.

"The afternoon came on and slid past. I talked with Quan Li about Hong Kong and her granddaughter Jing, who is eight years old. She spoke movingly about the terrible pain Jing's sickness has caused for the whole family—Quan Li's son, who is a transshipper of raw materials, has taken a year's leave from his company so he can share time at the hospital with the child's mother, and Quan Li fears he will never build his business up again. She herself, she said, has been driven almost mad by what has happened to her only grandchild, and her conviction that it was something related to the net was at first looked on by the family as an old person's fear of technology, and later as a deepening and worrisome obsession.

"I asked her how she was able to remain online for such a long time, and she confessed shyly that she had emptied her savings—another sign to her son and daughter-in-law that she was unstable—and checked into an Immersion Palace, a sort of VR vacation spa on the edge of the Central District, for an extended stay. She said with what sounded like a rueful smile that this extra time in the Otherland network must be burning up the last of her retirement income even as we were speaking.

"William and Florimel had argued again, this time over what Kuno-hara had said—William called it 'rubbish' and was convinced it was meant to mystify us or even mislead us, that Kunohara was entertain-ing himself at our expense—and so neither of them was talking to anyone. I attempted to speak to T4b, about whom I feel I know less than any of the others, but he was very resistant. He did not seem angry but distant, like a soldier between one dreadful battle and the next. When I gently questioned him, he would only repeat what he had said before, that a friend of his had been affected by the same thing that had struck Renie's brother and Quan Li's granddaughter. When I asked him how he had found out about Atasco's world in the first place, he was vague, even elusive. He would not even say where he lived in the real world, except that it was somewhere in America. His conversation, though frustrating, leads me to suspect that despite his inarticulate ways, he is quite clever about getting around on the net. He also seems, more than any of the rest of us, impressed with the Grail Brotherhood and the 'strong line' they must have to build a place like this, which I assume means money and power.

"We were fortunate in our encounters with the local wildlife all day. We met a shorebird, an apparition large as an office tower, perched on stiltlike legs, but escaped it by dodging into a natural cave in the river-bank and waiting until it grew bored and crunched away. Later a large beetle of some kind forced us to scramble up the side of a gulley, like people caught in a narrow road when a truck wants to pass. The beetle paid us no attention, but we had so little room that I could trail my hand along its hard, pebble-grained shell as it passed, marveling again at the detail of these worlds.

"Late in the afternoon I began to sense a change in the river. What had been a moving chaos of information, complete with water sounds so complex they might have been the work of hundreds of modern improvisational composers all working simultaneously, began to de-velop . . . structures. It is hard to explain more clearly than that. What had once been almost completely random began to manifest certain congruencies, certain more definite patterns, like veins of crystal em-bedded in ordinary rock, and I had the first intimations of a greater and more complex structure somewhere close by.

"I told my impression to the others, but they saw no difference in the river beside us. This changed within minutes. Florimel was the first to notice the hint of something sparkling in the water, faint at first, like the bioluminescent algae churned up in a ship's wake, but mixed evenly throughout the river. Soon the glow was impossible for the others to miss. As for me, I sensed something very strange, what

I can only call a curvature of space. The openness that I had sensed before me for so long, both on the river and on either side, seemed to be coming to an end, as though we had reached a spot where what lay before us moved into two dimensions. I still could perceive what I must call a metaphorical vanishing point, the sort of thing an artist might use to give the illusion of an extra dimension, but space itself did not seem to continue beyond that point. The others told me that the riverbank and river continued on into the visible distance, although the blue glow, which was now so bright that they said it actually reflected from their features, diminished sharply after a point some few yards ahead.

"When we reached the edge of the space I could perceive, something strange happened. One moment we were moving forward along the stony bank, single file, with Florimel in the lead. In the next step, Florimel was walking in the other direction, moving past Quan Li, who had been in line behind her.

"My companions were astonished, and took turns following Florimel through this strange, topsy-turvy effect. There was no sense of transition, no point at which they could feel themselves turning around. It was as though they had been edited like an old fashioned videotape, between one frame and the next—going, going, going, returning.

"I was less surprised than the rest. I had felt Florimel's essence—her information, as it were—disappear for a split-instant before reappearing in its inverted form. Apparently only my own heightened senses were capable of perceiving the microseconds in which this haunted-house effect took shape. But it made no difference. No matter how many times we tried, at whatever speed and in whichever combinations, we could not go any farther along the riverbank. I suppose that this must be a trick of the designers to limit the need for entry and exit points. I cannot help wondering if the nonhuman Puppets might not at this point receive some prefabricated memory of what had occurred on the far side of a barrier they would never actually perceive.

"This and other speculations, not to mention arguments, took the good part of an hour. Clearly, if we were to cross out of the simulation, it would have to be on the river itself. But just as clearly, if we were to build a boat, we would not be able to leave until well into the next day, since the sun was already setting in the west. We also had to decide whether we believed Kunohara's assertion that the gates— apparently the ways in and out of the various simworlds—had indeed gone 'random.' If so, time was less of a factor, since the chances we would find Renie and Orlando and the others on the far side would be small.

"Ultimately, we decided we could not take that risk. Florimel volunteered to lead us on foot through the shallower waters at the river's edge. Sweet William was not happy with this, and pointed out—with some justice—that we might find the river stronger or wider on the other side of the gateway, perhaps even be swept off to drown. He pointed out that we could not even be sure that the river on the far side would be water and not sulfuric acid, cyanide, or something equally unpleasant.

"I agreed with him and said so, but also said that if we were to have any chance at all of finding our lost companions, speed was the most important thing. I found myself impatient at the thought of another night in that place, although I did not say so. For the first time, I had begun to glimpse some of the structures beneath this new universe, as Kunohara had called it, and had felt a little of my earlier helplessness evaporate. I wanted to be moving on. I wanted to learn.

"The other three agreed with me, and so William reluctantly made it unanimous, with the proviso that he go alongside Florimel, so that if conditions proved hostile, one could help the other.

"We found a place where the bank dipped closest to the river's surface—there were no gentle slopes at our size—and with the aid of a grass shoot, clambered down into the water, remaining within arm's reach of the bank.

"It was no more than knee-deep, but the current was strong, and there was also an odd sensation of liveliness to the water, as though it were full of charged, vibrating particles. Quan Li told me that the visual effect was quite spectacular—'like wading through fireworks,' she said. It was less pleasant for me, since the energies being simulated were uncomfortably similar to the devastating input-overload I had experienced when I first came through into Otherland. I held onto Quan Li's elbow to keep my balance as we moved toward some kind of flat surface, a rippling plane which marked an end to the simulation. William and Florimel reached it and passed through—in an instant they were simply gone, their telltale signatures erased from my perceptions. Quan Li and I stepped through after them.

"The first thing I sensed on the far side, the perception of the very first moment, was a vast hollowing-out of space in front of me. Except for the river, which still flowed strongly beside us, I faced a tremendous emptiness where I had been surrounded by densely packaged information everywhere in Kunohara's world. The second thing I sensed was Florimel standing on the edge of this great emptiness, with William still a step or two behind her. To my surprise, she took several steps to the side, deeper into the river, as if to get a better view. The current yanked hard at her legs. She waved her arms desperately, teetered, and then was snatched away.

"Quan Li shouted in surprise and horror beside me. Sweet William grasped hopelessly at the spot where she had stood. I could feel Florimel's essence being washed down the river, could sense her struggling against the pull, and thus I was astonished to hear William's ragged voice say, 'Look at that! She's flying! What the hell is this about?'

"Even as we all watched, Florimel managed to regain some control and move herself toward the edge of what I still perceived as the river, but no one else seemed able to see. She pulled herself out of the flow into what seemed nothingness to me, and immediately her progress slowed. She began to fall, slowly at first, then faster.

"William screamed, 'Flap your arms, Flossie!', and what I at first thought was unbelievably cruel even from him proved good advice. When Florimel extended her arms, she pulled up, as though she had spread invisible wings. To our growing astonishment, she began banking and diving like a bird, describing great spirals in the apparently empty air before us. By the time a few minutes had passed, she had made her way back to us, and drifted on the wind just beyond where we stood, keeping herself aloft with occasional movements of her arms.

" 'It is wonderful!' she cried. 'Step off! The air will hold you up!'

"Now I perceived that what at first had seemed a great hollow space had its own sorts of information, but was far less static than the world we had just left. It required me to make a certain . . . recalibration, for lack of a better word, and a hurried discussion with the others helped me complete the picture. We stood on a promontory looking down into a vast stony valley, its bottom hidden in shadow far below. It was either twilight here, as it had been in Kunohara's world, or early morning. In either case, only blue-gray sky showed above the peaks that lined the valley. Ahead of us down the canyon we could perceive other small shapes, but distance made them obscure, even to my senses.

"The river had become a horizontal current of fast air, invisible to the others but not to me, a continuous slipstream running right through the canyon.

"After a little discussion, Sweet William and I both stepped off the precipice. As Florimel had found, if we spread our arms and thought of them as wings, we could adjust ourselves to the air currents—there were many breezes less powerful than the river-of-air that were never-

theless very useful—and float or even soar. Convincing Quan Li and
T4b to abandon the safety of the promontory was harder. T4b in particular seemed to think his armor, despite being no more real than the
valley or the air currents, might drag him down.

" 'Well, you should have thought of that before you dressed yourself
up as a workshop bench, now shouldn't you have done?' William told
him.

"At last we lured the other two out onto what seemed like treacherous air, T4b consenting to hold hands with Florimel and myself until
he was certain it would work. This almost proved him right in his
pessimism, because with our hands and his clenched in a human
chain, we could not sail the winds. We began to drop, and had to let
him go. T4b plummeted another hundred meters before he spread his
arms and began to flap wildly, like a farmyard hen. To his immense
relief he proved as buoyant as the rest of us, and within perhaps a
quarter of an hour we were all swooping and playing on the breeze
like angels amid the clouds of Paradise.

"William in particular seemed to enjoy himself. 'Bloody hell,' he
said, 'finally something worth building this ridiculous place for! This
is brilliant!'

"It fell to me to suggest we had better start exploring our new environment, since we didn't know how conditions might change. There
might even be 'wind-floods,' I said, in which the river would overflow
its banks and send us all crashing down the valley, banging against
outcroppings of stone. The others agreed, and we set out like very
unusual migratory birds.

"We did not have wings, invisible or otherwise, but our arms acted
on the environment much as wings would have. However, we did not
disrupt any larger area of information than our physical size war-
ranted, so I concluded at last that our new environment was more a
fantasy than a scientific extrapolation—even if we had been in a place
of very low gravity, we would not have been able to effect such dramatic movement with the body surfaces we could present to the air
currents, and would not have dropped so swiftly on those occasions
when we stopped flapping our arms. This simworld did not attempt
to be realistic. It was a dream of flying written large.

"In fact, I came to appreciate what I can only call the poetry of the
place, and began to agree with William that here was something
worth building such an expensive network in order to have. There
was more to this new world than just stone and air. Unusual trees of
unexpected colors—their leaves heather-purple, bright yellow, or even
pale, heathery blue—grew directly out from cracks in the canyon

walls, some with trunks almost completely horizontal, others starting that way but bending at their midpoint to rise parallel to the cliff face. Some were so broad and many-branched that an entire flock of people could have rested in them—and often did, as we later learned. There were other kinds of plant life as well, flowers as big as serving platters also growing out of cracks in the stone, hollow vines anchored to the cliffs, but with long tendrils which reached to the river, swirling in the wind-currents like ocean kelp. There were even round balls of loose vegetable matter that spun through the air like tumbleweeds, having no contact with the ground at all.

"In fact, the river of air seemed much like a normal terrestrial river, the center of many kinds of life. The floating plants, for instance, seemed most common just at the edge of the air-river—rolling along its 'banks,' as it were. Birds and insects of many kinds also hovered close to the strong currents, which seemed to carry a great deal of living matter in their invisible clutches, much of it apparently edible. I wished many times in those first hours that I had time to study this strange ecology properly.

"It soon became apparent that we had arrived during the morning, for before too long the leading edge of the sun appeared above the canyon-fencing peaks. As the air warmed, more creatures were drawn to the wind-river, and soon we were surrounded by a cloud of insects and birds and even stranger creatures. Some were rodents similar to flying squirrels, but others bore no relationship to any earth animals. One strange creature in particular was very common, a hollow thing shaped like nothing so much as a long furry boat, with tiny black eyes and webbed, paddling feet. Quan Li dubbed it a 'ferryman.'

"We flew for hours, pacing the river. The canyon remained largely the same all along, although we passed a few waterfalls—not air, as the river was air, but actual water spilling down the cliff faces. There were enough holes in the canyon wall that I began to wonder what kinds of larger creatures might also share this world, and in particular if there might be some less harmless than the birds and the ferrymen. My senses had not become familiar enough with this new environment to discriminate the signature of whatever might be lurking in the caves from the chaos of flying things and whirling air currents around me. Although ultimately my senses may prove more trustworthy here than those of my companions—for instance, in my being able to 'see' the river where they could not—I have the disadvantage of having to learn an entirely new set of indicators. This is something I will have to prepare for if we make it into other simulations. Especially in those first hours, I was like a bat suddenly released into a tickertape parade.

"The others, though, had only to depend on their natural senses, and once they had discovered the knack of flight, seemed to be enjoying themselves very much. William in particular was as cheerful in this new place as a small child, and it was he who named it 'Aerodromia.' For the moment, we had almost forgotten the serious nature of our problems, and about our lost companions. In fact, that first half-day in the new world was a bit like a holiday.

"It was late afternoon when we met our first Aerodromic humans. They were clustered on a horizontal tree near a vast waterfall, a tribe of perhaps two dozen. Some were bathing in the water, some were filling skin bags which they wore tied to wide belts. They grew still at our approach, and if I had not been with sighted companions, I might have missed them entirely, since the waterfall was for me a scene of much information confusion.

At Florimel's suggestion, we moved toward them in a slow and indirect fashion, trying to demonstrate that our intentions were peaceful. The people, who I am told have dark brown skins and sharp-boned features, like the Nilo-Hamitic races of Earth, watched us carefully, staring out of the waterfall mist like a troop of solemn owls. Some of the women pulled their naked children close. Several of the men lifted short, slender spears as we approached, but seemed in no hurry to use violence. We learned later that the spears are really harpoons, each one tethered to its owner by twenty or thirty meters of cable spun from human hair, the cables themselves more valuable than the weapons. Altogether, their level of civilization seemed to be somewhere between late Stone Age and early Bronze Age, although it quickly became apparent there was no metal among these people.

"One of the men, a wiry fellow with a graying chin beard, dropped off his branch and skimmed toward us with a grace that suddenly made us all conscious of how little we knew about flying. He spread his arms at the last moment to rise before us like a butterfly, and asked in quite comprehensible English who we were.

" 'We are travelers,' Florimel replied, earning a disgruntled look from William for taking the initiative. I cannot help wondering if this struggle for leadership is to go on forever. I sincerely hope it does not. 'We mean no harm,' she said. 'We are new to this place.'

"The chief or headman or whatever he was seemed to find this acceptable, and a short discussion ensued. Florimel asked him if he had seen any of our companions, and described the four we had lost, but he shook his head and said no strangers had passed through the valley for at least 'a dozen suns,' and none at all who matched the descriptions we gave. Then he invited us to come and meet with his folk. We of course agreed.

"Our hosts, we learned soon, were called the Middle Air People, a decorative rather than territorial description, since everything beneath the clouds and above the farthest depth of the canyons was apparently considered to be the Middle Air. In any case, this particular group of Middle Air People was one of the families of something named the Red Rock Tribe, although they were also a *hunting flight.* Again I had the sense of things it would take me months or years to understand properly.

"We were offered drink and food, and while we gulped the fresh, cold water and pretended to nibble at bits of what William claimed was dried ferryman, we had a chance to study the people more closely. Their clothes were made from skins and furs, presumably from creatures they had hunted, but there were buttons and some obviously decorative stitchery, so they were not primitive.

"When we had eaten, the entire family leaped from the tree near the waterfall and took to the air. We scrambled after them, and were quickly but discreetly shunted to a position near the children and more obviously diminished elders. It was hard to feel slighted. Even a moment watching the graceful, soaring arcs of the adult members of the family showed us how handicapped we truly were.

"We moved in a wide spiral down into the canyon and then downstream beside the river of air, flying for what seemed the better part of an hour. At last we reached the rust-colored outcroppings that were the source of the tribe's name, and found there a more established camp—the hometown of the entire Red Rock Tribe, complete with sleeping caves and the few belongings, such as large cooking pots, that the tribes did not carry with them during the day. I wondered at the paucity of their possessions, but after I watched one man sharpen a stone spearhead by flying swiftly downward while holding the edge of it against the rock face, so that the spearhead left a streak of stone-dust down the vertical cliff, I realized that their environment must give them much that our own ancestors had been forced to do by long, backbreaking effort.

"There were several dozen other family groups already in camp for the night by the time our host led us in—perhaps as many as four or five hundred Middle Air folk altogether. Our family exchanged ritual greetings with many, then spent a long time gossiping with the nearest neighbors. It was something like being on one of those stony islands in the sea where many kinds of birds congregate to nest, chaotic at first inspection, but in reality very highly organized.

"As the sun began to set behind the cliffs on our side of the valley, fires were lit on almost every promontory and families gathered to eat and talk among themselves. Our own family roosted along the trunks and thicker branches of a cluster of trees which grew perpendicular to the cliff face, like outstretched hands. This seemed to be their particular territory here in the larger campground.

"When everyone had settled, and a fire had been lit on a wide slab of stone cradled on the forked trunk of one of the largest trees, a woman of the family sang a song about a child named 'Two Blue Winds' who ran away from home to become a cloud, much to his mother's sorrow. Then a young man did a dance that the other Family members found very funny, but which I found so gracefully athletic—in my mind's eye, I could see his information slithering and jumping like quicksilver on a tilting pane of glass—that I found myself growing tearful.

"As the evening sky lost the last of its color, the stars gleaming now against the black, our host, who is named 'Builds a Fire on Air,' began a long story about a man who ate one of the tumbleweeds—the people here call it 'Air-Spinner-Bush,' which is an accurate if not very poetic name—and was blown away down the river. He had numerous adventures in lands that seemed to be fantasies even in this fantastic place, like the Land of Three-Headed People and the Land of Birds with Eyes on their Wings. The tumbleweed-eater even visited the uncanny Land of Sideways Cliffs—this perhaps a description of real flatlands, perhaps out of racial memory, or else simply the most preposterous geography the Family could invent. At the end he found a beautiful wife and many 'fletches,' a word I still do not understand but which seems to indicate wealth, but was so traumatized by the experience that he swallowed a huge stone so he would never be blown away again, and thus lived out the rest of his life on the ledges of the cliff face, unable to fly.

"I could not tell if this was supposed to be a happy or sad ending. A little of both, perhaps.

"We were fed again, this time with fresh meat and fruits, and we all ate enough to be sociable. It is hard to tell what effect eating has on us in this virtual environment. Obviously it has no real impact on our physical bodies, but so many of our internal systems seem influenced by whatever keeps us here that it is hard not to wonder how complete the mind-body link is. Do we receive energy when we eat here, as in some old-fashioned game where one must not let one's reserves of strength drop too low? It is impossible to say. Sweet William has complained occasionally about missing the *pleasure* of eating, as has T4b in his less articulate way, but none of us has noticed any other physical penalty.

"After the story had ended we were shown to Builds a Fire on Air's cave, where his wives—or sisters, for all I could tell—made us comfortable.

"My companions fell asleep fairly quickly, but I found myself wakeful, thinking of all the things I had learned about myself and the network, pondering questions I still had no answers for. It is apparent, for instance, that we will never force our way back out the way we came in against the current of the air-river, so we are more-or-less doomed to look for another gate. I wondered, and wonder still, whether this is part of the plan of Otherland—whether the river's current is meant to carry visitors sequentially through the network.

"This, of course, leads me to wonder how large the network is, how many simulations all together, and of course, what chance we have of finding Renie and the others if we must search the thing at random.

"Later I had a dream, and thought I was back in the blacked-out corridors of the Pestalozzi Institute, searching for my parents while something in turn searched for me, something I did not want to find me. I woke from that in a cold sweat. When I could not immediately go back to sleep, it seemed a good time to catch up on this journal. . . .

"There is a great deal of noise outside all of a sudden. The others in the cave are rousing themselves. I suppose I should go and see what has happened. I hear anger in some of the voices. I will have to add to this entry later.

"Code Delphi. End here."

It had started in the back of his mind, a slipped rhythm of the kind that gradually takes over a track and turns the music to its own purposes, a rogue vibe hijacking the entire piece. If he had been back in Sydney, he could have hunted in his normal way, and that would have gone a long way toward scratching the itch. But instead he was stuck in Cartagena for at least another week, tidying up the last loose threads of the Sky God project, and he dared not do anything that might draw more attention.

He had already been given cause to regret the cabin attendant, whatever her name had been. One of the other passengers on the plane from Sydney had witnessed their chummy conversation, and when the story of her disappearance had hit the nets, the passenger had felt obligated to call the authorities. Dread had been cool as Andes snow when the police came to the door of his hotel room, but even though the cabin attendant's body was long since disposed of, he had not liked the surprise at all.

The police seemed to have been reassured by their conversation with the man named "Deeds," and found nothing suspicious in either his story or his documentation. (Dread's aliases and documents were as good as the Old Man's money could buy, which was more than good, of course—his false passport was actually a real passport, albeit issued to an imaginary person with Dread's face and retinal prints.)

So nothing had come of it, but it had still been an unpleasant surprise. He was not particularly worried about the possibility of arrest—even if the Beinha Sisters could not pull the proper strings locally, the Old Man's contacts in the Australian Department of State were so powerful that if necessary, they could probably get him released and onto a diplomatic charter flight with a murder weapon still clutched in his bloody fist. But calling for help of any kind would have led to questions he did not want to or could not afford to answer.

The Cartagena police had ultimately taken their investigation elsewhere, but it was clear that no matter how powerful his urge, this was not a good time for Dread to slake his thirst for the hunt. Not in RL, anyway.

He had already tried the best versions of his particular obsession that VR had to offer—MurderWorld, Duck Duck Goose, Black Mariah, among the mainstream attractions, and some simulations that were themselves illegal, floating snuff nodes that were reputed to use involuntarily-wired human subjects. But even if some of the victims were real, as rumor strongly suggested, the output itself was dim and unsatisfying. A large part of the thrill of Dread's hunting was the *feel* of things—the blood-pumping, adrenaline-coursing, heightened reality that brought him the texture of a sleeve like a radar map of a new planet, the echoing, endless rasp of an indrawn breath, the flicker of desperation in the quarry's stare, bright as neon against night, when she saw the first hint of the closing trap. The net could offer only the thinnest, most threadbare imitations.

But the Grail Project . . .

The idea had been forming at the back of his mind since he had stumbled onto the thing, since the moment he had realized there were hundreds, maybe thousands of lands within the network as intricate and sophisticated as the Old Man's Egypt and far less regulated. It had forced its way into his conscious thoughts soon after, and the recent interplay with Dulcie Anwin—Dread would be the first to admit he had enjoyed taking the self-possessed bitch down a couple of pegs—had really made it throb.

The thing was, these Otherland creatures not only behaved as though they were alive, they truly seemed to think they were. That made the whole idea even more delicious. He understood how his own Aboriginal ancestors had felt when they came across the ocean in their canoes and stepped forth onto Australia for the first time. An entire continent that had never known the tread of a human hunter! Creatures who did not know enough to fear man, to flee his stones and clubs and spears. And now Dread had found an entire world like that—no, an entire universe.

Confident, cocky, lazy, dead, a small voice reminded him. It would be a mistake to let himself explode into some *folie du grandeur*—especially when the keys to the whole operation might someday be in his grasp if he only played things right. But that was a long way off—the Old Man would not easily be outwitted or outlasted. And Dread felt such a need right now. . . !

He reopened his connection to the Otherland sim, shutting off Dulcie's loop code and pulling the body on like a suit of clothes. He could feel the stone of the cave floor under his back, hear the breathing of the other travelers on either side of him, even and slow. He flexed his fingers, holding them up before his eyes, but he could not see them move. Very little light. That was good.

He levered himself up off the ground and waited until he was sure he was balanced before stepping over his nearest neighbor. Between him and the mouth of the cave lay the local chieftain, whatever his name was, and several of his immediate family. They, too, seemed to be sleeping deeply, but Dread still used almost a quarter of an hour to cover the hundred yards, a journey as soundless as grass growing.

When he reached the mouth of the cave, he remained in its shelter for long moments as he surveyed the area, trying to make certain no one from any of the other family groups was up and wandering around. The thin crescent moon had already passed beyond the looming cliffs; the campfires had all burned down, and silence hung so heavily on the place that he could hear a bird's wings flapping far out in the darkness above the river of air. He moved quietly to the edge of the nearest promontory, then let himself drop into nothingness, counting to twenty through a heart-stopping freefall before he spread his arms and felt the air lift him.

Chimes, he thought. *I want chimes. And running water.*

The music, quiet splashing and the soft tang of metal on metal, rippled through him. He hovered for some minutes, letting the sound calm and center him, then mounted higher, back toward the roosts of the Middle Air People.

This was an amazing place, he thought. He was glad that he hadn't needed to share it with Dulcie for most of the day, since her next shift wouldn't begin until dawn. It made him feel like a child, this flying, this simworld—although not like the child he'd actually been, who had never experienced a moment of pure joy. Not until the first killing. But here, now, feeling the air wash over him, he felt stripped clean of everything earthly, a perfect machine, a thing of dark light and sweet music.

I'm a black angel, he thought, and smiled through the chimes in his head.

He had seen her as they flew in, a pale-haired womanchild taking care of younger siblings in the boughs of one of the great trees—a mutation, perhaps, an albino, or some other kind of genetic sport. More important than her arresting looks had been her age, young enough to control but old enough to be sexually attractive. Dread had no interest in hunting actual children, and felt a faint scorn for those who did, as though they had failed some test of personal integrity. It was similar to the scorn he had felt for those who pretended to practice his own special art, but who did it only in VR, and with simulated victims—they faced no reprisal, feared no law. They would not be chased, as he always was, by the tame pack mastiffs who hunted the hunter on behalf of the common herd.

He squeezed the chimes into something a bit more emphatic, a theme for a heroic and solitary predator. No, those pretend-killers were not really doing it right. They were broken machines, but he himself was an almost perfect device.

His soft but dramatic searching music had been playing quite a long time when he finally located her family's sleeping cave. He had paid close but unobtrusive attention to where everyone went as the evening had worn down, but the landmarks he had noted—the oddly-shaped outcropping, the stunted sailor's knot of a tree that clung to the cliff face—were hard to locate in full moonless dark. But he was full of the high airiness of the hunt, and that alone had convinced him that he could not fail; that alone had kept him at his task until he found what he sought.

She was sleeping between two smaller children, a faint shape recognizable only by the dimmest starsheen on her hair. He poised himself above her like a spider at the edge of a web, seesawing gently until he had his balance for the one permissible strike. When he was ready, his hands thrust down. One clamped around her larynx, the other dug beneath her and scooped her up, prisoning her arms even as she spasmed awake. His sim body was wiry-strong, and the grip on her throat kept her from uttering even a sound. In three steps he was out of the cave, leaving a cooling space between the two children, who slept on, oblivious.

She struggled in his arms until he slipped his fingers to the carotid and pinched off the blood flow; when she had gone limp, he threw her over his shoulder and stepped out—like the rest of her people, she was inordinately light, as though her bones were mostly hollow. This led him down several distracting avenues of speculation, so that he almost missed his footing in the dark. He ran quickly to the huge outcrop he had noticed earlier, a jut of stone like a broken bridge that stretched far out over the valley, beyond the tips of even the largest horizontal trees, then paused at the base, preparing himself. This was the most difficult part, and if he had miscalculated, any number of dire things might result.

Dread shifted the girl's weight forward a little, then added an insistent backbeat to the ringing music in his head, preparing himself, setting the scene. The sky seemed to crouch lower, expectant, watching.

The star, he thought. *Me. The impossible chance. Backlight. Heroic silhouette.* The camera in his mind saw everything, his poise, his cleverness, his courage. No stunt doubles. He alone.

He flung himself along the length of the promontory, pumping the virtual analogues of his own hard-muscled legs until he had reached sprinter's speed. The stone stretched before him, a dark finger pointing at an even greater darkness. It was hard to guess where the end was. Wait too long—disaster. Jump too soon—the same.

He jumped.

He had gauged it correctly, and sprang off the outcropping's farthest point. As he felt the air beneath him he extended his arms for more glide, doing his best to keep the girl balanced, but he could still feel himself beginning to sink. One person could not fly with the weight of two, even when the other was as small and slender as his captive. In a moment he would have to let her go, or he himself would be dragged down as well. He had failed.

He felt the wind stiffen. A moment later he was forced sideways, knocked head over heels, so that he had to pull his arms in and clutch the girl to him tightly. He had reached the river of air.

Dread's music swelled triumphantly. The river seized him in its grip and dragged him away from the camp of the Red Rock Tribe.

When she began to stir in his grasp, he fought his way out to the slower currents of the air-river, until he felt her weight begin to drag at him. Then, when he gauged the time was right, he let her go, then folded himself up to follow her down.

He had guessed correctly in this, too: Her innate reflexes saved her
even before consciousness had fully returned. As she hovered, disoriented and frightened, trying to understand where she was and what
had happened, he circled her in the darkness and began to talk.

Her throat still too bruised for speech, she could only listen as he
described what was going to happen. When panic at last overwhelmed
her, and she turned and fled away up the canyon, he gave her just a
few moments' head start. A proper chase was one thing, but he knew
it would be a very bad idea to let her actually beat him back to the
nesting place of her people. After all, even bruised and terrified and
confused, she was a better flier than he was.

It turned out to be a glorious chase. If she had kept on a straight
course, she might even have outraced him, but in the dark she did not
know quite who or what he was. As he had gambled, she chose evasive action, hurrying to a hiding spot and then, when he had flushed
her out, swooping off to the next. At times he flew close enough to
hear her terrified, hitching breath, and during those moments he did
indeed feel himself to be a shadow-angel, an instrument of the cold
side of existence, fulfilling a purpose that he alone of all mortals could
even partially understand.

The pale-haired girl was tiring, her movements more and more erratic, but he guessed that they were also drawing close to the encampment. Dread had held his own excitement at bay for almost an hour,
a prolonged foreplay that had pitched him to places that even the
music in his head could only approximate. Images seemed to play out
before his eyes, a reverse virtuality in which his most surreal and vicious thoughts were projected outward, onto the malleable darkness.
Broken dolls, she-pigs eating their own young, spiders fighting to
death in a bottle, butchered sheep, women made of wooden logs split
and smoldering—the mind pictures seemed a halo around his head,
filling his maddened vision like a cloud of burning flies.

The dog people, the screaming men, the child-eaters. Half-remembered
stories told to him in an alcoholic slur by his mother. Faces changing,
melting, fur and feathers and scales sprouting from the skins of people
who had pretended normality, but stayed too long by the campfire.
The Dreamtime, the place where the unreal was always real, where
nightmares were literally true, where hunters took whatever shapes
they wished. Where little Johnny could be whatever he wanted and
everyone would worship him or run screaming forever. The Dreamtime.

As he spun himself above the failing, weeping quarry in a parabola
that exactly graphed his own long-denied fulfillment, as he hung at

the top of his rise and prepared to stoop, a blinding burst of light pierced his mind, an idea that had no words, and which would only begin to make a kind of sense later, in the calm after the killing.

This is the Dreamtime, this universe where dreams are made real.

I will stand at the center of it, and I will twist *it, and all of creation will fall down before me. I will be king of the Dream. I will devour the dreamers.*

And as this thought flared inside him like a fiery star, he plunged down through the black winds and fastened on the flesh and thrilling blood and crumpled them into himself, hot as flame, cold as zero, a dark and forever kiss.

He had just enough presence of mind afterward to hide the body, or what was left of it, in a place that would keep secrets. He retained only her knife, a wicked piece of volcanic glass honed sharp as a straight razor, not out of sentiment—he was not a collector—but instinct. Virtual or not, he had missed having a blade close to hand.

He stopped to bathe in one of the waterfalls, cleaning away the traces and letting the sting of cold water bring him back to something resembling sanity, but as he sailed back through the drying winds he was still amazed by the vague but overwhelming idea that now filled him. When he reached the cavern where his companions slumbered he had a brief lapse of concentration, nudging one of them in the dark as he tried to reach his own sleeping spot. At the protesting murmur he froze, fingers hooked like claws, reflexively prepared to fight to the death—even in this made-up world there would be no net, no cage ever, not for this hunter—but his disturbed companion merely rolled over and went back to sleep.

Dread himself could not even approach the edge of rest. His skull seemed full of glaring light. He left the sim body on autopilot and called Dulcie to take over ahead of schedule.

There was so much to think about. He had found the Dreamtime, the true Dreamtime, not the ghost-ridden bush of his mother's babbled tales. So much to consider. He had no need for sleep, and felt like he never would again.

"CODE *Delphi. Start here.*

"Something very serious has happened. One of the Red Rock Tribe—not a member of the family who found us, but one of the others who shares this system of caves—has disappeared. Builds a Fire on Air came to tell us, and although he clearly regarded us with suspicion, he was courteous enough not to accuse us of anything. A young woman named Shines Like Snow vanished during the night, getting up and walking away from her family, apparently.

"Needless to say, and this Builds a Fire on Air *did* tell us, suspicion has fallen on our company. We are fortunate that such a disappearance is not unheard of—young women have run away with men from other tribes before, or been kidnapped, and sometimes one of the flying people suffers an accident or meets a large predator while out at night—but it is rare, and everyone is very upset.

"Besides my own sorrow on their behalf, I am troubled by what seems to be a half-memory of my own, that someone *did* rise in the night.

"As I think I said already, I lay awake thinking late after we had all bedded down in this cave. When, without noticing, I had finally drifted into a shallow half-sleep, I dimly sensed someone stirring. Later, minutes or hours for all I could tell, I heard movement again. I thought I heard a whispery intake of breath and a murmur that sounded a little like Quan Li's voice, but of course that means nothing, as it could have been her, but caused by someone bumping her, or even just as a response to a dream.

"However, I must think about this carefully because now it may prove significant. But a quick discussion among us after the chief left reveals that none of the other four admits getting up in the night, and there is nothing to suggest any one of them is lying. I may have dreamed it. But the whole thing is troubling, of course. I also doubt now I will get a chance to ask any of the questions I had so longed to have answered, since Builds a Fire on Air and his family are very preoccupied, and in any case it might only draw more attention to us as outsiders.

"As I look out past my companions, who are huddled nervously on the cavern floor, I can perceive the far side of the valley, a stark mass of relatively static information made fuzzy by the variables of morning mist. The stones themselves must be purple with shadow, since the sun has still not risen above the cliffs.

"We have a long way to go just to get out of this world, and if these people turn against us we will not be able to escape them, any more than we could outrace a group of aerialists across a high wire. Aerodromia is their world, not ours. We do not know how far down the river the next gate is, nor do we know where any others might be.

"I think when we first thought of coming to the Otherland network, we—at least Renie and Singh and I—thought that it was like other simulation networks, a place where one learns the rules once, then puts them to use. Instead, each of these simulations is its own separate world, and we are constantly being caught up and held back by the things we find here. Also, we have come not a bit closer to solving the problems that brought us. We were too ambitious. Otherland is having its revenge.

"Builds a Fire on Air is coming toward the cave again, this time accompanied by a half-dozen weapon-bearing warriors—I can feel the dead solidity of their stone spears and axes, different from the signature of flesh and bone—and an agitated man who may be the missing girl's father. The chief is himself uneasy, sorrowful, angry—I can sense these things emanating from him, distorting the information space that surrounds him. The whole thing does not bode well.

"So, again I am interrupted. It is our entire experience here, only written small. If our enemies knew, they would laugh—if they even cared enough to notice. We are so small! And me, storing up my thoughts against oblivion or an increasingly doubtful success. Each time I wonder if this will be the last time, the last entry, and these final words of mine will float on forever through information space, unheeded and unharvested.

"Builds a Fire on Air is gesturing for us to come out of the cave. Others of the Middle Air People are gathering to watch. Fear sours the air like ozone. I must go.

"Code Delphi. End here."

CHAPTER 21

In the Freezer

ORLANDO and Fredericks did not have much time to consider the implications of Orlando's realization. Even as they tried to imagine what mechanism the Grail Brotherhood might have discovered that would allow them to make the network their permanent and eternal home, Chief Strike Anywhere grounded his canoe beside them on the spit of dry linoleum.

"Found bad men," he announced. His dark face seemed even darker, as threatening as a thundercloud, but he spoke as calmly as always. "Time to get papoose."

The tortoise, who had slept through most of the discussion between

Orlando and Fredericks, was roused. After fumbling for long moments in the depth of his shell, he at last located his spectacles and pronounced himself ready to go.

Orlando was less sure. Fredericks' earlier words about risking their lives for cartoons came back to him, made even more daunting now by the idea that he might have figured out something critically important about Otherland and the Grail Brotherhood, and that it would thus be doubly unfortunate if he and Fredericks didn't live to inform Renie, !Xabbu, and the others.

Still, he thought as he clambered into the canoe behind the cartoon Indian, a bargain was a bargain. Besides, if they did not help the chief, they would have to make their way across the Kitchen on foot, an unknown distance through unknown obstacles. They had already met the dreadful salad tongs—he had no urge to discover what other bizarre things stalked the floor tiles by night.

The chief paddled them quickly across the dark waters, the steady movement almost lulling Orlando back to sleep. The tortoise, whose calm might have had something to do with being covered in armor plating, *did* fall back into a thin, whistling slumber.

The river opened wide before them, until it seemed almost an ocean: the far bank was very distant, visible only because a few fires burned there. Orlando did not realize for long moments that the great pale expanse behind the fires was not the kitchen wall, but a vast white rectangle. It stood quite close to the river's edge, but loomed higher than even the mountainous countertops.

"Ice Box," pointed out Strike Anywhere.

"And the bad men are inside there?" Orlando asked.

"No." The chief shook his head emphatically. "Them *there.*" He pointed with his paddle.

Hidden by darkness before, visible now only because the watch fires of the Ice Box threw them into silhouette, a forest of masts had appeared before Orlando and the others, sprouting from a shadowy bulk with a curving hull. Orlando swore quietly, surprised and alarmed. The chief backed water for a moment to slow their progress, then let the canoe drift silently. The huge vessel was mostly dark, but a few of its small windows glowed with lantern light—illumination Orlando had mistaken for reflections of the beach fires.

"It's some kind of pirate ship," Fredericks whispered, eyes wide.

As the chief paddled them closer to the galleon, Orlando wondered at the ship's odd silhouette: the tall masts and the tight-furled sails seemed normal, as much as he could tell, but the hull seemed unusually smooth, and there was a strange, handle-shaped loop near the stern that did not correspond with any representations of pirate ships he had ever seen. It was only when they were so close they could hear the murmuring of voices from the deck above that he could make out the row of ballast barrels hanging along the hull. The nearest read "CORSAIR Brand Condensed Brown Sauce." The smaller letters beneath implored him to "Keep your first mate and crew in fighting trim!"

The pirates' forbidding ship was a gravy boat.

As they pulled up alongside the huge vessel and lay silently against its hull, like a baby carrot or a sliver of turnip that had dropped from a serving ladle, Orlando whispered, "There must be a hundred people on board to crew a ship that big. How are the four of us supposed to. . . ?"

Chief Strike Anywhere did not seem interested in a council of war. He had already produced the out-of-nowhere rope that he had used to save them from the sink, and was making it into a lasso. When he had finished, he cast it expertly over one of the stern lanterns, pulled it taut, then began to make his way up the gravy boat's curving rear end. Orlando looked helplessly at Fredericks, duly noted the scowl, but slid his broadsword into his belt and followed the matchbox Indian anyway.

"I think someone had better stay with the canoe, don't you?" the tortoise whispered. "Good luck, lads, or break a leg—whatever it is one says when someone's going to fight with pirates."

Orlando heard Fredericks reply with something less pleasant than "good luck," then felt the rope go tight behind him as his friend began to climb.

Neither of them could ascend as swiftly as the cartoon Indian. By the time they had reached the stern rail and pulled themselves over, Strike Anywhere was already crouching in the shadows at the front of the poopdeck, fitting an arrow into his bow. Fredericks made another sour face, then took the bow the chief had given him from his shoulder and did the same. Orlando fingered the pitted edge of his sword and hoped that he wouldn't have to use it. His heart was beating faster than he liked. Despite the simworld's complete and total unreality, despite the dancing vegetables and singing mice, this felt a lot more dangerous than any of Thargor's Middle Country adventures . . . and probably was.

Most of the lights and all the voices were concentrated on the main deck. With the Indian in the lead, moving as silently as the best clichés suggested, they slid closer to the edge of the poop where they could sneak a look down.

"What is the range, Bosun?" someone inquired from the opposite end of the ship, in a voice of quite theatrical tone and volume.

A barefoot man in a striped shirt turned from his consultation at the main deck rail with another sailor to shout, "Two hundred, give or take the odd length, Cap'n." Both sailors were of singularly unattractive appearance, clothes stained, teeth few, their eyes glinting with malice.

"I shall descend from the foredeck," the oratorical voice announced. A moment later a shape in flowing black swept down from the forecastle and onto the deck just below their hiding place. The captain's footsteps had a curious syncopation; it was only when he reached the main deck that Orlando saw one of the man's legs was a wooden peg.

In fact, more than the captain's leg was artificial. His left wrist ended in an iron hook, and the other arm had an even stranger termination: as the pirate lord lifted a telescope to his eye, Orlando saw that he gripped the tube with some kind of metal clasper, an object unpleasantly reminiscent of the ravening salad tongs. But even these strange additions were less noteworthy than the captain's huge ebony mustachios, which sprouted beneath his hawklike nose, then corkscrewed down on either side of his sallow face to rest coiled, like weary vipers, on the white lace of his collar.

After having stared through the telescope for a few moments, the captain turned to his men, who stood at ragged attention around the mainmast, watching with gleeful anticipation. "We have reached the appointed hour, my sea-vermin, my filth of the foam," he declared. "Run up the Jolly Roger and then prime the Thunderer—we shall not waste time with smaller guns."

At his words a pair of younger corsairs, no less grimy and desperate for their youth, leaped to the rigging to raise the pirate banner. A handful of other men hurried onto the foredeck and began to roll a huge cannon back out of its gunport—a piece whose carriage wheels were as big as tables, and which looked as though it could fire an entire hippopotamus. As they cleaned the weapon, scouring the barrel with a broom twice the length of the sailor who wielded it, then poured in an entire sack of gunpowder, the pirate ship drifted ever closer to the shore. The Ice Box jutted above them like a high cliff.

The captain threw back his black cloak to reveal its blood-red lining, then stumped to the railing and lifted both his not-quite-hands to his mouth. "Ahoy the Ice Box!" he bellowed, his voice echoing and re-echoing across the water. "This is Grasping John Vice, captain of the *Black Tureen*. We have come for your gold. If you open the great door, we will leave the women and children untouched, and we will kill no man who surrenders."

The Ice Box stood silent as stone.

"We're in range, Cap'n," the bosun called.

"Prepare the boats and the landing crews." Grasping John hobbled a few steps closer to the great gun before striking a pose of stoic resignation. "And bring me the firing match."

Orlando felt Chief Strike Anywhere tense beside him. One of the pirates emerged from a bolthole somewhere with a bundle in his arms, only its tiny red head protruding from the blanket. The bundle was crying, a thin, small sound that nevertheless tugged at Orlando's heartstrings.

"All hands in place, Cap'n," the bosun shouted.

Several of the crew began to dance, arms folded, cutlasses out and gripped in their hairy fists.

> *"Wicked, wicked, wicked, we,"*

they sang, dreadfully out of tune but in a cheerful jig-time,

> *"Bad we are as men can be,*
> *Rotten work, we'll get down to it,*
> *(If it's good, we didn't do it.)"*

> *"Evil, evil, evil us,*
> *Some are bad but we are wuss,*
> *Dread deeds we perform with glee,*
> *We aspire to infamy!"*

The captain smiled indulgently, then beckoned with his hook. The sailor with the crying bundle skittered forward and delivered it into Grasping John's clasper. The bundle's noises intensified.

"Let us see if the Thunderer can melt yon stronghold's icy reserve, eh, my salt-flecked swine?" The captain flung the blanket aside to reveal a squirming, shivering baby match, a miniature version of Strike Anywhere and his wife. He clearly intended to scrape the infant's sulphured head on the rough deck, but before he could do so, something had leapt through the space near Orlando's ear and was shivering in the black sleeve of Grasping John's coat. For a moment the entire foredeck stood frozen and silent. The pirate captain did not drop the baby boy, but he did lower him for a moment to inspect the arrow lodged in his arm.

"A mysterious someone seems to be shooting things at me from the poop," he observed evenly. "Some of you filthy fellows hurry up there and kill him." Then, as a dozen unshaven, scar-faced pirates rattled up the gangway, and Orlando and Fredericks scrambled to their feet in cold-stomached anticipation, Grasping John took the baby and rubbed him down the length of the massive cannon barrel, so that the small head sparked and then flared. As the infant began to cry, the captain lifted him and lit the cannon's great fuse.

Groaning in fury and pain, Strike Anywhere vaulted off the poop-deck. He landed in a group of confused pirates, scattering them like bowling pins. In a moment he had reached the pirate captain and snatched the blazing child from the man's metal hands. He plunged the baby's head into the bucket used to cool the cannon barrel, then lifted out the weeping, spluttering infant and held him close against his chest.

Orlando turned from this drama as the first of the pirates reached the poop, avidly waving his cutlass. Then, in the next five seconds, several things happened.

Thargor-reflexes slowed but not gone, Orlando dodged a cutlass-blow, stepped aside, and swung his broadsword in a flat arc; he smacked the leading pirate in the back and sent him flying off the roof, even as the tattooed buccaneer behind him fell back down the steps with one of Fredericks' arrows in his striped midsection.

Chief Strike Anywhere took his dripping, screaming child and leaped over the railing into the water. Grasping John watched with dark amusement, curling a mustachio with the end of his hook.

The fuse on the Thunderer burned down, vanishing inside the barrel for a split instant before igniting the powder with a roar like Judgment Day. The cannon vomited fire and the carriage heaved backward against its chains. The entire ship rocked, so that Orlando, Fredericks, and their pirate attackers all fell flat.

The massive cannon ball hissed across the water and smashed into the huge handle of the Ice Box, breaking it off and denting the door.

For a moment after all this had happened, as the echoes of the Thunderer's eruption died away, everything was still. Then the Ice Box's massive door, tall as a mountainside, slowly swung open.

They were not, Orlando realized, in a very good position. Although at least half of Grasping John's crew were climbing into the boats, with the obvious intention of rowing ashore to attack the gaping Ice Box, most of the rest seemed content to concentrate on killing Orlando and Fredericks. The original half-dozen had been defeated, but another dozen or so were already scrambling up the gangway, brandishing sharp objects of various sorts.

Chief Strike Anywhere had disappeared over the side, having secured his wounded papoose and presumably no longer interested in the cartoon corsairs or anything else. The tortoise-guarded canoe lay out of sight below the railing of the *Black Tureen,* and even if they could fight their way to it through the mass of ugly buccaneers, the pirate ship had drifted far enough toward the beach that there was no guarantee the canoe was still at the larger ship's side.

Need a new plan, Orlando realized. *Any plan at all, actually.*

One of the last of the landing boats swayed in its davits as a snarling, swearing band of caricature sea-criminals struggled to lower it away. Orlando slammed aside a swiping attack by the first of the new pirates coming up the stairs, then shouted to Fredericks, "Follow me!"

His companion, who had either run out of arrows or the room to shoot them properly, was using his bow as an awkward sort of shield while fighting back with a cutlass liberated from one of their attackers. "Where?"

"The boats!" Orlando paused for balance, reminding himself that although he was much stronger than he would be in his own brittle-boned form, he did not have Thargor's superhuman muscles anymore. He grabbed at one of the mizzen lines and swung out over the heads of their jostling attackers, then dropped to the main deck. In too much of a hurry to see whether Fredericks had indeed followed him, he rushed to the landing boat and managed to shove the nearest pirate overboard before the man saw him. Of the three others, two were steadying the swinging boat, so Orlando engaged the third. Fredericks appeared at his side a moment later, and together they quickly dispatched Orlando's opponent. The other two, armed only with knives, considered the matter for a moment, then sprang down from the boat and disappeared in the direction of the foredeck. As Orlando and Fredericks had discovered, the cartoon pirates were less fearsome than they appeared, but the sheer weight of their numbers still made them dangerous.

"By the Toils of the Tortugas!" Grasping John bellowed from the foredeck, his cloak a-flap in the rising breeze. "They are escaping! Is there not a single man on this tiresome *sauciére* who can fight? Must I do it all myself?"

Orlando and Fredericks moved to either end of the jollyboat, then, at the count of three, both swung their swords and chopped at the ropes that held the boat suspended over the rail. The ropes, as almost everything else in the simulation, did not behave as their real-life equivalents would have, but parted with a satisfying *twang* as soon as the blades touched them. The boat dropped the dozen feet to the river, sending up a splash of white foam.

Orlando could not at first decide whether it would be best to follow the other pirate boats toward the land at the base of the Ice Box, or to strike out deeper into the river. Fredericks pointed out a group of pirates rolling a heavy cannon toward the gunport on their side.

"Follow the other boats—he wouldn't fire at his own men," Orlando declared. They bent over their oars and swept in the direction of the beach, hurrying to catch up with the landing party. A few moments later, with the river's edge still a hundred yards away, a dark something cracked past over their heads and struck the boat just in front of them, flinging pirates and bits of pirates in every direction.

"Wrong again," Fredericks helpfully pointed out.

They sculled on, heads low. The cannon fired, and then fired again, the shells throwing up gouts of water on either side of them. When they saw the waters growing shallow, they tumbled overboard and swam for the beach.

As they emerged from the river, conscious that they were trapped between Grasping John's cannon and his invasionary force, they heard a flare of trumpets and a great shout. The defenders of Ice Box were streaming out through the broken door and onto the beach to meet the buccaneers. Orlando's relief was mixed with a certain amount of amazement, because a stranger force would have been hard to imagine.

The vanguard, a sort of literal cannon fodder, was a squadron of militant vegetables, the very antithesis of the partying tomatoes and beets they had seen earlier. Squash of many colors and shapes waved asparagus spears. Sullen-looking yams were backed by a line of huge eggplants, scowling purple things as terrifying as wild elephants. The leader of this martial salad was a handsome carrot waving a sword in the air and shouting, in a thin but dramatic voice, "For God and Saint Crisper!"

As the first of the vegetables met the pirate assault, more unusual defenders leaped down from the Ice Box, most of them freshly sprung from labels and packages. A pride of Scotsmen with kilts and claymores tootled bravely on bagpipes as they marched, setting the pace for a squadron of clowns (with their companion unit of attack-trained, overdressed poodles) and a horde of shining-eyed, red-cheeked children shrieking like harpies and waving sharpened serving spoons. There were salamis dressed as gondoliers who brandished their poles like quarterstaffs, growling bears off honey jars, and milk-bottle cows of many different sizes and shapes whose glassy fragility was offset by their curving translucent horns and sharp-edged hooves. A camel, a small troop of djinni on a flying carpet, and several others too distant or too obscure for Orlando to make out completed the defending force. There were even several flour-dusted and slightly nervous Quakers, perhaps acting as battlefield observers to make sure the combatants obeyed some Kitchen Conference's rules of war.

Orlando's pleasure at the defenders' emergence was quickly tempered when he realized that the Ice Box residents seemed to consider them just more pirates—he and Fredericks were nearly beheaded by pole-swinging gondola pilots before it became clear that the stripe-shirted sausages were singing *"O sole mio"* as a war cry rather than as a welcome. They decided to retreat to the outskirts of the battlefield, and not a moment too soon, for an explosion that cratered the linoleum in front of the Ice Box announced that Grasping John had resumed his shelling from the *Black Tureen.*

They found a shadowed nook at the base of a cabinet near the Ice Box but well-removed from the hostilities, then settled down to watch the battle in comfort and comparative safety.

Orlando had found it difficult from the beginning to understand the Kitchen's internal logic, and cartoon warfare proved just as incomprehensible. Some things seemed absolutely arbitrary: a hump on the camel's back, when thumped with a pirate's oar, simply popped up elsewhere on the camel, but a yam struck by a similar oar immediately became many little diapered baby yams. The salami-gondoliers, when "killed" by a hard blow or a swipe from a cutlass, fell into a row of neat slices. But the pirates, who were presumably made from condensed gravy, seemed quite solid, even when wet. In fact, there didn't seem to be any consistent order to any of it, which Orlando (who liked to know the rules) found particularly frustrating. People—if you could call them people—stretched or inflated or broke into pieces, but there was no death in the sense of someone being killed in their normal form and staying recognizably dead—even the pirates they had stabbed or chopped on the boat just sort of tumbled away. In fact, Orlando felt sure all these combatants, winners or losers, would be back in their old shapes tomorrow, whenever "tomorrow" came.

This would have been perfectly acceptable, and even quite interesting, but unlike their enemies, he and Fredericks had shown no tendency to stretch or bounce or otherwise adjust to the weirdness of the place and its dangers. Orlando severely doubted they would survive being diced by pirate swords, for instance, as had just happened to one of the eggplants. And if he or Fredericks died here in the cartoon world or in any of the others . . . then what?

It was a question that had to be answered, Orlando decided, but he hoped they wouldn't find out the hard way.

*   *   *

The Kitchen's night crept past and the battle raged on. The defenders at first fought a slow retreat to the very base of the Ice Box, where vegetable pulp spattered the white enamel as the last of the fighting eggplants laid down its life, then the tide turned and the defenders pushed the buccaneers back down the beach until the besiegers were knee-deep in the river, fighting for their lives. For hours neither side could win a decisive advantage. Attack met counterattack, back and forth, until most of the combatants were disabled or as dead as cartoons could be expected to become. The sagging Ice Box door had been pitted by cannonballs until it resembled a map of the moon, but Grasping John had long since run out of ammunition and the guns had fallen silent. Now the last defenders fought the final few pirates hither and thither through the julienned remains of their heroic comrades.

"How are we going to get out of here when this is over, Orlando?" Fredericks asked. "Without that Indian . . . Do we have to go all the way down the river?"

Orlando shook his head. "How would I know? I guess so. Unless there are other ways out. Didn't the tortoise say there are people in the Ice Box who can answer questions? 'Sleepers' or something?"

Fredericks gave him a hard stare. "No, Orlando. Possibility *not*. We're not going into that thing to go hunting for some even weirder cartoon monsters. Forget it."

"But that's how these things *work*, Frederico. You have to figure out what the rules are. You want information, you have to pay a price. Come on. If there was a way out of here and it turned out to be right next to us, wouldn't you rather take a little trouble to find that out than go all the way down to the end of the river, like you said?"

"A little trouble. That's *fenfen*. You always get your way, Orlando, and I always pay for it. You and your utterly brilliant ideas. If you want to go climbing around in that thing, go ahead, but nothing's going to get me in there."

"*I rather think you're wrong,*" suggested a third voice.

Grasping John Vice stepped into view around the edge of the cabinet. The arm struck by the Indian's arrow was bandaged with a wide piece of white cloth, but there was no sign of blood. A flintlock pistol, screwed to his wrist in place of the clasping device, was leveled at the two of them. "You see, in part thanks to you two, I have very little crew left. So I'm afraid I will need some help hauling my gold out of the Ice Box." He leaned toward them with a theatrical leer. Up close, it was easier to see that he was not a real person—the sharp angles of his face were exaggerated, his features unwholesomely smooth, like a doll's.

"So your pirates won?" Orlando asked dully. He was furious with himself at being taken by surprise. The captain would never have gotten within fifty yards of the real Thargor without being noticed.

"It is what is called, I believe, a Pyrrhic victory." Grasping John gestured with his hook at the silent battlefield, littered with the remnants of attacker and defender. Nothing stirred. "Still, it means there will be many fewer with whom to share my rightful booty." He jabbed the pistol at them. "So get up. And you, man," he said to Orlando, "if you have anything warmer to wear than that absurd acrobat costume, I suggest you put it on. It is rather cold inside, I'm told."

As they waded through the slaw of the battlefield, Orlando scavenged a vest—Grasping John called it a "weskit"—and a pair of calf-length trousers whose pirate owner was no longer in the vicinity, having apparently been struck so hard by projectile puffed wheat that he had been blown right out of his clothing. With Captain Vice never more than a meter or two behind them, but also careful not to draw close enough to be attacked and disarmed, they mounted from the floor of the Kitchen onto the bottom shelf of the Ice Box. There the captain's words proved prophetic: The air beyond the door was indeed very cold, and despite his additional clothing, Orlando was shivering before they had been inside a minute.

The bottom shelf was as crowded with dwelling places as any other part of the Kitchen they had seen, but all the boxes, jars, and containers of various sorts were empty—a refrigerated ghost town. As they made their way down the main street between the boxes, the wind sighed through the open door, rustling a discarded napkin. They were able to climb onto the second shelf from the top of the tallest carton, whose now-deserted label read "Ship of the Desert—Fresh Dates," and whose humped resident Orlando had watched meet her tragicomic end on the battlefield below, broken in half when one of the pirates had produced a handful of straw and thrown it on her back.

The second shelf was as untenanted as the first. A row of cardboard egg cartons stood open and deserted, the brave soldiers once housed therein having flung themselves down from this very shelf onto the besiegers, when for a grim moment it had seemed that defense would fail and the pirates would storm the Ice Box itself. Several of the pirate victims of that kamikaze sacrifice still lay at the base of the Ice Box, halted inches short of their goal, embalmed in drying yolk.

They continued up two more shelves without seeing another living thing, a journey that took well over an hour, including several trampoline-hops across cellophane-wrapped bowls and a scary crawl along the loose handle of the meat and cheese drawer. Then, on the top shelf, near the back, Grasping John's quest was at last rewarded.

On a blue china plate lay a paper sack, from which spilled a child's Halloween plunder—gumdrops like brightly colored gems, peppermint sticks, paper-wrapped toffees . . . and a pile of gleaming gold coins. Grasping John staggered forward, his face alight with greed and triumph.

"It's just chocolate!" Fredericks whispered. "Those fake gold coins for kids!"

"The riches!" the pirate captain exulted. "Ah, sweet Fortune, the riches that are now mine! I will buy two ships—three! I will crew them with the worst and most dreadful mercenaries from under the sink and behind the rubbish bins, and we will plunder at will. I will be master of the entire Kitchen!" He used hook and pistol to grip and then lift one of the coins, which was proportionately as large as a manhole cover, and after threatening Orlando and Fredericks with his pistol to keep them crouching where they were, stumbled with it to the edge of the shelf where he could admire its glitter in the light of the Bulb.

"I always knew that a golden destiny awaited me," he crowed. He waved the coin in the air, then clutched it tight against his breast, as though it might sprout wings and try to fly away. "I knew it! Did not a soothsayer tell my mother that I would die the richest and most elevated man in all of the Kitchen?"

As he paused in silent rapture, a single noise broke the stillness, a brief *tump* like a knuckle rapping on a tabletop. Grasping John looked on all sides for the source, then turned his gaze down. A feathered shaft had sprouted from the center of the golden coin. The pirate captain's face wore an expression of mild surprise as he swiveled back to face Orlando and Fredericks. He tried to lift the coin again to examine it, but it was stuck in place. A dawning realization crept over him as he stared down at the butt of the arrow that had spiked the coin to his chest, then he swayed, took a step backward, and fell from the shelf, the gold foil glimmering for just an instant as he spun out of sight.

As Orlando and Fredericks watched in stupefaction, two hands grabbed the edge of the shelf where the pirate captain had stood, then a dark shape pulled itself up and onto the shelf, facing them.

"Bad man dead now," Chief Strike Anywhere explained.

Orlando scrambled to the edge and looked down. Far below, Grasping John Vice was a small, dark, and very still shape on the linoleum at the foot of the Ice Box. With his cape flared beneath him, he looked like a swatted fly.

"We . . . we thought you left," Fredericks stammered. "Is your baby all right?"

"Papoose in boat," the chief said, which didn't really answer the question. "We go now."

Orlando turned and made his way back across the shelf. "First I want to see if there are really any Sleepers, like the tortoise said. I have a question I want to ask them."

The Indian shot him a dubious look, but said only: "Sleepers up there," and gestured with his thumb to the ceiling of the Ice Box above their heads.

"What, up on the roof?" Fredericks asked.

"There must be a freezer compartment or something," Orlando decided. "Can we reach it from here?"

The chief led them to the side of the shelf where a series of small holes in the wall had apparently been designed to accommodate moving the shelf up or down. He led them in a short climb; then, when he was braced against the ceiling, he reached up over the top edge and tapped on something they couldn't see. "Here."

With help from the Indian, Orlando managed to climb past him until he reached a thin ledge that ran the length of a door which seemed only slightly less massive than the front of the Ice Box. As he crouched beside it, he could feel the cold beating out in waves. He looked down at the dizzying view and began to think this might be a very bad idea after all. The pirates had needed a giant cannon to open the big door. How could he and Fredericks hope to budge this thing without at least jackhammers and blasting caps?

With no real hope of success, he braced himself in the corner between the ledge and chilly wall, then inserted his sword into the crack running down the side of the door. The blade crunched through ice crystals, but met no other resistance. He pulled back on the handle, levering it in the crack, and was astonished to feel the door give ever so slightly.

"What are you up to, Gardiner?" Fredericks shouted from below. "We're hanging on the wall here, y'know, and we're about five inches from the edge, so there are utterly more comfortable things we could be doing."

Orlando was saving his breath for another pull. He jammed his heels against the frosty ledge and heaved. For a moment nothing happened except that he felt himself slide toward the rim of the narrow ledge, and had a brief but overstimulating vision of plummeting down to join Grasping John as a splotch on the floor. Then the freezer door creaked open. Its massive edge almost scraped him from his crouching-place as it swung past. A cloud of vapor slowly rolled out and surrounded him.

"I did it!" he shouted, and tried to pull himself in. The metal at the edge of the door was so cold that his skin stuck to it, the pain of tearing his hand free so distracting that he almost toppled over backward into nothingness. When he had his balance again he clung to the ledge, waiting for his heart to slow. "The door's open!" he called down to Fredericks. "Damn! It's *cold!*"

"Well, lock me twice, Gardiner," his friend called back. "What a surprise."

Orlando waved a hole in the unfurling mist. Just inside the door, the freezer floor was covered in an ankle-high layer of frost—cold on knees and hands, but nowhere near as bad as the frozen metal. It was dark inside: only the faintest light crept in from the Bulb suspended overhead. Orlando could not see the depths of the freezer—within a few steps, all was in shadow—but it seemed surprisingly large.

"Are you coming up?"

"All right! All right!" Fredericks' head appeared in the open doorway. "You never stop, do you? Why don't we just be glad we're alive and get out of here?"

"Because I think this Otherland place has rules, just like game worlds." Orlando clambered back to the edge and gave his friend a hand up. "I don't know what they are yet, but I bet it does, in its own way. And we have questions, don't we?"

"Lots of them," Fredericks admitted. "But the first one, which I never see you asking, is 'Why look for trouble?' "

"Where's the chief?"

"He thinks you're impacting majorly. He's not coming—I don't even know if he'll wait for us, Gardiner. In fact, I don't know . . ."

"Ssshhh." Orlando held his finger to his lips. "Not so loud—it doesn't feel right. Anyway, we're here—let's look around."

Fredericks seemed about to argue, but caught a little of Orlando's suddenly somber mood and fell silent. When they stopped moving, the mist rose around them, so that their legs vanished and they seemed to be standing hip-deep in a cloud bank. Fredericks' eyes grew wide as he surveyed the white emptiness. Orlando had already felt it. The freezer was not quite like any other place they had been in the cartoon world. Behind the stillness lurked a sort of quiet attention, as though something, perhaps the very fog and ice, regarded them with dreamy interest.

Orlando began to walk deeper into the freezer, each footstep puncturing the frosty crust, disturbingly loud compared to the previous silence. His friend shook his head, but followed. Within a few steps the light of the open door was only a sheen in the mist behind them.

Fredericks looked longingly back over his shoulder, but Orlando would not be swayed. As he adjusted to the strange twilight gloom, he began to see details he had missed before. He still could not discern either wall of the freezer, and the depths were still lost in fog and shadows, but he could see the roof—a smooth white surface lightly furred with frost, about three times his own height above them—and where all had been a pale blur he could now make out actual shapes in the mist before them, low mounds rising here and there from the icy floor, snow-covered lumps like the cairns of ancient dead.

As they neared one of the mounds, Fredericks slowed, his reluctance plain. Orlando could feel it too, the sensation of trespass. If the rest of the cartoon world seemed primarily designed to amuse its creators, the freezer seemed to be something else, a place that belonged to no one . . . something that had grown rather than been created.

They paused before the icy tumulus, surrounding themselves with a cloud of their own breath. Orlando was seized again by the feeling that they were in someone else's place, that they were aliens here. At last, he reached out and carefully wiped away a layer of rime.

As the popsicle wrapper appeared, it seemed at first a moment of comic anticlimax. The colors burst out as the frost was scraped aside, jarringly bright against the endless white that surrounded the mound. But beneath the words "Lucky Boy Fudge Pop" was a picture of a child, and the terrible clarity of the image made it seem more than just a piece of packaging art, that instead a real body had been pressed into the wrapper. The boy was dressed in shorts and a striped shirt and an odd cap that seemed of some much earlier era. His eyes were closed and his mouth sagged, ever so slightly down. At first Orlando thought this was somebody's dreadful joke—that they had wrapped their product with a picture of a dead child. Then the Lucky Boy moved, a slight flicker of eyelids, a minute flair of nostrils, and a thin, unhappy voice murmured in their ears.

"Cold . . . dark . . . Where. . . ?"

Orlando took a stumbling step backward and almost knocked Fredericks over. Without either of them noticing, they clasped hands and moved away from the tumulus.

"This is horrible," Fredericks whispered at last. "Let's go."

Orlando shook his head, afraid that if he spoke he would lose his nerve. He pulled Fredericks in a wide path around the mound, heading deeper into the freezer, but could not shake off the memory of the sleeping child. At last he disengaged himself and returned to smooth the frost back over the Lucky Boy's pale face, then returned to Fredericks. Silent, they walked on.

The mounds rose higher on all sides now, some as large as the car-ton-houses of the lower shelves, all made impenetrable and mysteri-ous by their covering of ice. In some places, where the frost was thin, faces showed as through thick, dirty glass; they seemed mostly chil-dren, but there were also stylized animals and some less easily identi-fied creatures, all sealed in cold slumber. Voices hung in the air, phantom murmurs that Orlando at first thought were only his imagi-nation—faint cries for absent mothers, protests against the dark, swirling sounds as bodiless as wind crying down a chimney.

Surrounded by these pitiful, terrible voices, Orlando wasn't even sure any more what he was looking for; the thought of trying to ques-tion one of these sleepers, to drag them up into something like wake-fulness, was repellent. He was beginning to think Fredericks had been right again, that coming to this place had been a dreadful mistake, when he saw the glass coffin.

It lay in the center of a circle of mounds, a translucent oblong sil-vered with frost but not sunk in a blanket of white like the rest of the freezer's occupants. It stood out as though it had been waiting—as though it were something they had been meant to find. The other voices grew quiet as they approached it. All of Orlando's hard-earned simworld instincts told him to expect a trap, and he could feel Freder-icks' wire-tight tension at his side, but the place seemed to weave a spell around him. He found himself strangely helpless, unable to take his eyes from the object as he walked forward. It was with no more relief than he had felt on seeing the popsicle wrapper emerge that he realized it was a butter dish, the old-fashioned sort with a glass lid. In raised letters along the bottom, barely legible through the frost, was the legend "Sleeping Beauty Brand—Fine Creamery Butter."

Fredericks, too, seemed lost in a kind of hypnotized state, and did not resist or object as Orlando leaned forward and wiped a clear spot in the glass. Something was inside, as he knew there would be—not a picture, but a shape with all three dimensions. He cleaned a larger space so they could see her whole.

She wore a long, antique green gown trimmed with feathers and pearled with ice. Her hands had been folded on her breast, clutching the stem of a white rose whose petals had tumbled free and lay scat-tered on her throat and shoulders and in her cloud of dark hair. Her eyes were closed, the long eyelashes tipped in frost.

"She . . . she looks . . . so *sad*," Fredericks said in a strangled whisper.

Orlando could not speak. His friend was right, but it seemed a wholly inadequate word, like calling the sun warm, or the ocean wet.

Something about the set of her mouth, the bleak fixity of her ivory features, made her seem a monument to quiet unhappiness; even in death, she was encased in her sorrow far more completely than she was encrypted by glass and ice.

Then her eyes opened—dark, amazingly dark, but occluded by frost, so that she peered through cloudy windows. Orlando's heart thumped. There seemed a terrible distance between those eyes and what they should see.

"You are . . . strangers," a voice sighed, seeming to come from everywhere and nowhere. *"Strangers . . ."*

Fredericks gasped and fell silent. Orlando fought to make himself speak. "We . . . we are . . ." He stopped, uncertain of what mere words could explain. "We . . ."

"You have traveled across the Black Ocean." Her face, like her body, remained motionless, and the dark irises remained fixed upward, starring at nothing, but Orlando thought he could feel her struggling somewhere, a bird trapped in an attic room. *"But there is something in you that is different than the others."* The mist rose for a moment around the glass coffin, obscuring their view. *"Why have you come? Why have you wakened me? Why have you brought me back to this terrible place?"*

"Who are you?" Orlando asked. "Are you a real person? Are you trapped here?"

"I am only a shadow," she sighed. *"I am the wind in empty spaces."* Great weariness dragged at her words, as though she explained something that could not possibly make any difference. *"I am . . . the queen of air and darkness. What do you want of me?"*

"Where . . ." Fredericks was trying hard to master his voice, which wanted to squeak. "Where are our friends? We've lost our friends."

For a long time there was only silence, and Orlando feared she had dropped back into slumber, but the mists eddied a little and he saw that her dark eyes were still open, still staring at something unseeable. *"All of you have been called,"* she said then. *"You will find that which you seek as the sun sets on Priam's walls. But another waits for you, too. He is close, but he is also far away. He is coming."*

"Coming? Who's coming?" Orlando leaned forward, as though proximity could make things clearer. "Coming when?"

"He is coming now." The words, spoken with a distant carelessness, sent a shiver through Orlando that had absolutely nothing to do with the frost. *"He is already here. He is the One who dreams—we are his nightmares. He dreams you, too."*

"What is she talking about?" Fredericks demanded, tugging at Orlando's hand in growing anxiety. "Who's coming? Here?"

"Let me sleep again," the voice said, the faintest tone of petulance creeping in, a child dragged from her bed for some incomprehensible, grown-up purpose. *"Let me sleep. The light is so far away . . ."*

"We'll find our friends at Priam's what?" Orlando asked. "Priam's walls?"

"He comes." Her voice was growing fainter. *"Please let me go. Don't you understand? I have . . . lost . . . my . . ."* The rest of her words were too faint to hear. The lids slid back down to cover the great, dark eyes.

As they stood in silence, the mist rose again until the coffin was completely obscured. Orlando turned, but it was even hard to see Fredericks, though his friend stood only an arm's length away. For a long moment Orlando felt himself weighted down by a crushing sadness, a misery that for once was not his own, and it left him speechless.

"I think we should go," he began at last, then the light changed and things were immediately, inexplicably different.

"Orlando. . . ?" Fredericks' voice suddenly seemed very far away. Orlando reached out but his fingers, first probing, then frantically grabbing, touched nothing. His friend was gone.

"Fredericks? Sam?"

The mist around him began to glow, a diffuse gleam that turned the whole world translucent, as though he were trapped in the center of a piece of quartz. The light, which at first had only been a brighter whiteness, soured into an unnameable color, a hue that on a not-quite-imaginable spectrum where red did not exist would have fallen directly between purple and orange. A horrible electric fear pinned Orlando, sweeping away all sense of up and down, pushing away the walls and the floor so that the light itself became a void, an absence, and he was the only living thing left, falling endlessly in the terrible orange-lavender nothing.

Something wrapped itself around him—something that was the void, but was not the void. It spoke in his head. He became its words, and each word was a thing painful to shape, painful even to think, an inhumanly powerful howl of misery.

Angry, it said inside him. The thoughts, the feelings, became the entire universe, turned him inside-out, raw against the great emptiness. *Hurt things,* it said, and he felt how it hurt, and how it would hurt others. *Lonely,* it said.

The bit of him that still was Orlando understood suddenly, and dreadfully, that there was something more frightening than Death.

Black mountain. The words were also a vision, a black spike that stretched so high the very stars were shoved aside in the night sky, a terrifying vertiginous thing that grew up from impossibility into sheer blasphemy. *Kill everything. My children . . . my children . . . kill everything.*

And then it was gone, and the void turned inside out again with a silent clap like all the thunder that had ever been. Then the mist and the white burst into being around him once more. Orlando fell onto his face in the snowy floor and wept tears that froze hard on his eyelids and cheeks.

After a while, Fredericks was beside him—so abruptly and completely that it made a strong argument that his friend had been quite dramatically *somewhere else.* Orlando stood. They looked at each other. Even though they saw Pithlit and Thargor, the pretend-faces of a children's game, both could tell without uttering a word that the other had heard the same things, felt the same indescribable presence. There was actually nothing that could be said just then, or needed to be. Shivering and silent, they made their way back through the mounds, through the now-voiceless freezer, and at last staggered out to the place where the mists grew thin.

Chief Strike Anywhere was waiting at the freezer door. He looked at them and shook his head, but his large hands were gentle as he helped them onto the shelf below and then assisted them in the long climb down to the base of the Ice Box.

Neither of them could walk very well. The chief kept them from falling until the battlefield was a good distance behind them, then found a protected spot against the base of the counter where they could huddle, and built a fire before it. As they stared in dull stupefaction at the flicker of the flames, he got up and vanished into the darkness.

Orlando's thoughts were at first small and flat and without much meaning, but after a while the worst of the shock ebbed away. By the time the chief returned some time later with the tortoise, and carrying his blanketed baby sleeping in his arms—the top of Little Spark's head was blackened, but he seemed otherwise healthy—Orlando was at least able to muster a faint smile.

He fell asleep still staring at the fire, the flames a curtain that obscured, but did not entirely hide, the darkness beyond.

Third:

GODS AND GENIUSES

The ancient Poets animated all sensible objects with Gods or Geniuses, calling them by the names and adorning them with the properties of woods, rivers, mountains, lakes, cities, nations, and whatever their enlarged & numerous senses could perceive.

And particularly they studied the genius of each city & country, placing it under its mental deity.

Till a system was formed, which some took advantage of & enslav'd the vulgar by attempting to realize or abstract the mental deities from their objects; thus began Priesthood.

Choosing forms of worship from poetic tales.

And at length they pronounc'd that the Gods had order'd such things.

Thus men forgot that All deities reside in the human breast.

—William Blake, *The Marriage of Heaven and Hell*

CHAPTER 22

Inside Out

NETFEED/ENTERTAINMENT: Ronnies Deny Non-Existence
(visual: DYHTRRRAR giving press conference, Luanda Hilton)
VO: The flurry group Did You Have To Run Run Run Away Ronnie? gave
its first ever live press conference in Luanda, Angola, to refute the rumors
that they are in fact software Puppets. The all-female group have been
magnets for rumors ever since their first net appearances, and suspicious
critics have called them "too contrived, too perfect," to be real. Ribalasia
Ronnie, speaking for the group, read this statement:
R. RONNIE: "It's a shame when hard-working artists have to waste their
time trying to prove that they're real people . . ."
But the press gathered in Luanda were not an easy crowd.
REPORTER: "How do we know that you're not lookalikes selected to match
the gear. . . ?"

RENIE leaned on the railing where !Xabbu was perched and watched the dark, faintly oily river.

Another day, she thought, *another world. God help me, I'm tired.*

The Works was slipping away behind them, the tangle of pipe and pylon crowding along the bank infiltrated and then gradually replaced by cottonwood trees and sedge, the flicker of security lights supplanted by a waxing prairie moon. If she ignored the dull throb of pain from cuts and bruises, and the baboon shape her friend wore, she could almost convince herself she was somewhere normal. Almost.

She sighed. "This isn't going to work, you know."

!Xabbu turned, flipping his tail to the outside of the rail so he could face her. "What do you mean, Renie?"

"All of this." She waved her hand, encompassing Azador, sullen and silent at the wheel, Emily in fitful sleep in the cabin, the river and the Kansas night. "This whole approach. We're just being dragged—or chased—from place to place. From simulation to simulation. We're no closer to our goal, and we're certainly no threat to the bastards who got my brother."

"Ah." !Xabbu scratched his arm. "And what is our goal, then? I do not ask to make a joke."

"I know." She frowned and let herself slide down until she was sitting on the deck with her back to the gunwale, staring now at the opposite but equally dark and quiet riverbank. "Sellars told us to look for this Jonas person, but that's the last we've heard of Sellars. So how do we find Jonas, out of millions of virtual people? It's impossible." She shrugged. "And there are all kinds of new questions, too. What's-his-name, Kunohara, said that your friends in the Circle were tied up in this somehow, too."

"They are not my friends, exactly, if he was talking about the same group. They are people for whom I have respect, an organization of men and women who try to help others of their tribes, and who helped me. Or so I believed."

"I know, !Xabbu, I'm not accusing you of anything. I couldn't tell whether he meant they were helping the Grail people or fighting them, anyway. What did he say? 'Opposite sides of the same coin'?" She leaned her head back against the railing, overwhelmed by it all. They had been in this virtual universe so long! How was Stephen? Had there been any change in his condition? And how was her father, for that matter, and Jeremiah? It was almost impossible to consider that they might be only inches away from her. It was like believing in the world of spirits.

"If I would be making a guess," !Xabbu began slowly, "it would be that Kunohara meant the Grail people and the Circle are at war, somehow. But he did not think there was really much difference between them."

"Could be." She frowned. "But I'm tired of guessing at things. I want facts. I need information." Either the river was narrowing, she noted absently, or Azador was steering them closer to the bank: the trees loomed higher than they had only minutes before, their shadowy presence blocking more of the sky. "We need a map, or we need to know where Martine and the others are. Or both." She sighed. "Damn it, what happened to Sellars? Has he given up on us?"

"Perhaps he cannot get back into the network," !Xabbu suggested. "Or he can, but like us, he can only search without knowing."

"God, what a gloomy thought." She sat up, ignoring the protesting ache from her back and legs. "We need information, that's all there is to it. We don't even understand how *this* place works." She swiveled. "Azador!"

He looked up but did not answer.

"Fine, then," she said, dragging herself upright. "As you wish." She limped to the back of the tugboat, !Xabbu trailing after. "It seems like a good time to talk," she told the man. "What do you think?"

Azador took a last drag, then flicked his cigarette over his shoulder. "The river is getting smaller. Narrower, I mean."

"That's nice, but I don't want to talk about the bloody river. I want to talk about you and what you know."

He eyed her coldly. He had found some bargeman's coat, which hid the holes torn in his boiler suit and the dreadful bruises they revealed. Blood had dried on his face in patches. She could not help remembering how he had thrown himself into a crowd of their enemies. He might be irritating, but he was no coward. "You talk," he said. "Me, I don't talk. I am sick of talking."

"Sick of talking? What does that mean? What have you told us about yourself? That you're a gypsy? Do you want a medal for that? Help us, damn it! We are in trouble here. So are you!"

He turned up his collar, then took yet another cigarette and screwed it into the corner of his mouth below his dark mustache. Frustrated, Renie broke her own resolution and extended her hand. Azador smirked, but gave her one. Then, in what seemed an uncharacteristic act of courtesy, he insisted on lighting it for her.

"So?" she tried again. She disliked herself for giving in to her addiction so easily and so quickly. "Tell me something—anything! Where did you find cigarettes?"

"Things, objects, do not travel from one world to another," he said flatly. "I found these on someone's desk in New Emerald City." He smirked. "Munchkin goods are salvage under rules of war."

Renie ignored his joke, if it was one. "Objects do translate—I've seen it. Orlan . . . I mean, one of our friends had a sword in one simulation, then he had it in the next one, too."

Azador waved his hand dismissively. "That was someone's possession—like clothes. Those go everywhere the sim goes. And some of the things that travel," he pointed down to the deck, "like a boat, they go to the next simulation, but then they change. There is another thing like them in the next world, but . . . but different."

"An analogue," Renie said. Like the boat from Temilún that had become a leaf.

"Yes, that. But cigarettes, other small things—money or someone else's jewels that you have found—these you cannot carry from one world to another."

She had little doubt what he meant by "found" but knew better than to say so; it was much better to keep him happy and talking as long as he seemed willing. "How did you learn so much? Have you been in this network a long time?"

"Oh, very long time," he said offhandedly. "I have been many places. And I hear things at the Fair."

Renie was puzzled. "What do you mean, the fair?"

For the first time in the conversation Azador looked uncomfortable, as though he might have said more than he wished. But neither was he the type who would admit to second thoughts. "Romany Fair," he said, in a tone that suggested Renie should be ashamed not to have known already. She waited a moment for an amplification, but none came. Even with his present talkative mood, the man was not what anyone would call long-winded.

"Right," she said at last, "Romany Fair. And that is. . . ?"

"It is where the travelers—the Romany—meet, of course."

"What is it, another simworld?" She turned to !Xabbu, wondering if he were making any more out of this than she was. Her friend was perched on the stern rail. He did not seem to be listening, staring out at the files of trees slipping past on either side as the long, silvery "V" of the river narrowed behind them in the moonlit distance.

"It is not a place, it is . . . a gathering. It changes. The travelers come. When it is over, they leave, and next time it is somewhere else." He shrugged.

"And it's here in . . . in this network?" She had almost called it the Grail Project—she was having trouble remembering what information she had already let slip in front of him. Her head and muscles were still throbbing with the pain of their escape, God only knew what or who would try to kill them next, and she was finding it increasingly difficult to keep track of the lies and evasions that security demanded.

"Of course!" He was full of scorn that she could even imagine something different. "This is the best place—this is where all the rich people have hidden their greatest treasures. Why should we travelers settle for second-best?"

"You mean you and your friends roam around here at will, having little parties? But how did you get in? This place has security that kills people!"

Did she again see a moment's hesitation? A shadow? But when Azador laughed, his harsh amusement sounded genuine enough. "There is no security that can keep out the Romany. We are a free people—the last free people. We go where we want to go."

"What does that mean?" A sudden thought occurred to her. "Wait a moment. If you can all agree on a place to meet, then that must mean you can find your way around—you must know how to use the gates."

Azador looked at her with studied indifference.

"Jesus Mercy, if that's so, you have to tell me! We have to find our friends—people's lives depend on it!" She reached out to clutch his arm, but he shook her off. "You can't just keep it to yourself and let people die—little children, too! You can't!"

"Who are you?" He took a step away from her, scowling. "Who are you to tell me what I can do? You tell me I am a pig for what I did to that silly Puppet in there," he slashed a hand at the cabin where Emily lay, "and then, when I have already told you much, you order me to tell you more—order me! You are a fool." He stared at her, daring her to argue.

Renie tried to bite back her fury, which was as much at herself as at him. *When are you going to learn, girl?* she fumed. *When do you figure out how to keep your mouth shut? When?*

"I do not even know who you are," Azador went on, his accent thickening with his anger. He looked her up and down with insulting slowness. "A white woman pretending to be a black woman? An old woman pretending to be young and beautiful? Or are you even a woman at all? That sickness is common on the net, but not, thank God, among the Romany." He turned and spat overboard, narrowly missing !Xabbu, who stared back at him with an unreadable baboon expression. "What I do know is that you are *gorgio*. You are an outsider, not one of us. And yet you say, 'tell me this, tell me that' like you had a right to our secrets."

"Look, I'm sorry," Renie began, wondering how many times she would have to apologize to this man when what she really wanted to do was slap him hard enough to knock his mustache off his lip. "I shouldn't have spoken that way, but . . ."

"There is no 'but,' " he said. "I am tired, and it feels like all my bones are broken. You are the leader? Okay, then you steer this ugly boat. I am going to sleep."

He let go of the wheel and stalked away around the cabin, presumably headed for the prow. Unpiloted, the boat pulled sharply toward the bank. Within seconds, Renie was so busy wrestling it back into the center of the river that she lost any chance for a parting shot, either dismissive or conciliatory.

"Next time, you talk to him," she suggested to !Xabbu. Her scowl felt as though it had been carved permanently onto her face. "I don't seem to be handling it very well."

Her friend slid down from the railing and padded over, then reached up to squeeze her arm. "It is not your fault. He is an angry man. Maybe he has lost his story—I think so."

Renie squinted. The river and the trees ahead of them were so dark as to be almost inseparable from the night. "Maybe we should stop. Throw out the anchor or whatever you do. I can hardly see."

"Sleep is a good idea." !Xabbu nodded his head. "You need rest. We all need rest. In this place, we never know when something will happen."

A variety of possible replies flitted through her head, some sarcastic, some not, but she didn't have the strength to waste on any of them. She throttled down the boat and let it drift toward the shallows.

Renie could feel the sun broiling her exposed skin. She groaned and rolled onto her side without opening her eyes, questing for shade, but there was none to be found. She threw her arm across her face, but now she was conscious of the sun's glare and could not ignore it. It poured down on her, as though some giant, sadistic child were focusing its rays with a titan magnifying glass.

Renie sat up, mumbling curses. The burning white disk was almost directly overhead, only thinly hidden behind a layer of dull gray cloud—there would be no shelter anywhere on deck. Also, either the anchor had slipped and they had drifted, or the river and its banks had mutated while she slept; Renie did not know which prospect was worse. The river had narrowed dramatically, so that less than a stone's throw separated them from the banks on either side, and the polite forest of cottonwoods had at some point become an insidious mesh of vegetation—a jungle. Some of the trees stretched up a hundred feet or more, and except for the open track of the river, she could not see more than a few yards into the undergrowth in any direction.

!Xabbu was standing on his hind legs by the rail, watching the jungle edge past.

"What happened?" she asked him. "Did the anchor come loose?"

He turned and gave her one of his odd but cheering baboon smiles.

"No. We have been awake for some time, and Azador is driving the boat again."

The man under discussion was huddled over the wheel in the boat's stern, dark brows beetled and a fog of cigarette smoke drifting around him. He had thrown aside the coat. The bottom of his boiler suit was belted with a length of rope, since only a few tattered strands remained from the suit's top part. His sim was very tan and his chest and arms quite muscular. She turned away, irritated by his ridiculous good looks—it was adolescent to pick a sim like that, even if he looked like that in RL, which she firmly doubted.

"Anyway, it is good you are awake," !Xabbu added. "The girl Emily is unhappy, but she does not want to talk to me, and Azador will not speak to her."

Renie groaned again and levered herself to her feet, clinging to the railing for a moment while her calf muscles spasmed. She found it astonishing to contemplate her many aches and realize that what had struck her had not been metal fists and poorly-padded human bones, but a puddinglike substance merely pretending to be those things. Not that the results were any the less painful.

She limped to the cabin. The girl was sitting up on the bed, pressed into the corner of the tiny room as though afraid of small creeping things on the floor. Despite the sheen of sweat on her youthful skin, she was clutching the blanket tightly to her chest.

"Hello, Emily. Are you all right?"

The girl regarded her with wide, worried eyes. "Where's the monkey?"

"Outside. Do you want me to get him?"

"No!" Emily's rejection was almost a shriek; she regained her composure a little and laughed nervously. "No. He makes me go all funny. He's just like the Scarecrow's flymonks—all little and hairy and those pinchy fingers. How can you stand it?"

Renie thought for about two seconds of trying to explain !Xabbu's situation, then decided against it. If this girl was a Puppet, telling her anything about VR or aliases would just be confusing, or even needlessly cruel. Unless . . .

"He's not really a monkey." Renie tried a soothing smile; it made her jaw hurt. "He's . . . he's under a spell. He's really a man—a very nice man—but someone bad turned him into a monkey."

"Really?" Emily's eyes widened again. "Oh, that's so sad!"

"Yes." Renie settled on the edge of the bed and tried to get comfortable, but there didn't seem to be a throbless muscle in her entire body. "Was that all that was bothering you?"

"No—yes. No." As if exhausted by these changes of mind, Emily regarded her for a moment, then suddenly and quite spectacularly burst into tears. "What's g-going to h-h-happen?"

"To us?" Renie reached out and patted the girl's shoulder, feeling her small, birdlike bones through the thin shift. It was strange, finding herself again in the role of reassuring someone, of being a substitute mother; it also made it hard not to think about Stephen, but she didn't need any more pain today. "We've escaped from all those people who are chasing us. Don't you remember?"

"I don't mean that. What about m-me? What about the little baby in my t-tuh-tummy?"

Renie wanted to say something encouraging, but could think of nothing. What could she offer this girl, this creature coded for baby talk and helplessness? Even if she and !Xabbu escaped the simulation, it was almost certain that Emily would not transfer with them. And even if some fluke allowed it, could they afford to take her along? Go off to save the world accompanied by a pregnant, effectively half-witted child who needed constant attention? It didn't bear thinking about.

"It will be all right," was what she came up with at last, and hated herself for saying it.

"But it won't—it won't! Because my henry doesn't love me anymore! But he did, he *did,* and he gave me the pretty thing, and we did all the lover-games, and he said I was his pudding and now everything is . . . is *bodwaste!*" The strange amalgam seemed to be the worst word she knew. Immediately after uttering it, she collapsed face-first onto the bed, wailing.

Renie, with nothing to offer except sympathy and a reassuring touch, at last coaxed the girl back to something resembling normality. "The shiny, pretty thing he gave you," she asked when the weeping had quieted, "did he tell you where it came from?"

Emily's eyes were red-rimmed, her cheeks mottled, and her nose was running, but she was still irritatingly pretty. If Renie had retained any doubt that the creators of Kansas were men, she let it go now. "He didn't tell me anything, except that it was mine!" the girl moaned. "I didn't steal it—he gave it to me!"

"I know." Renie thought of asking to see the gem again, but did not want to excite her further. "I know."

When a sweaty and miserable Emily had finally slipped back into fitful sleep, Renie walked out to the stern. She felt a tug of addiction and wanted to ask for a cigarette, but she had already broken her own rule once. "She's really upset," she reported.

Azador flicked his eyes toward the cabin for a moment. "I noticed."

"These people may be Puppets," Renie added, "but they certainly don't think they are. I mean, that may all be code, but it's pretty damn convincing."

"These rich bastard *gorgios* got too much money for their own good. They hire too many programmers, try to make everything so perfect and real."

"But you liked how real she was before, didn't you?" She heard the anger beginning to creep into her voice and turned to the rail to inspect the ever-thickening wall of jungle foliage on the near bank. There was something faintly unnatural about the vegetation, but she couldn't quite decide why that was so. She turned back to Azador. "Don't you feel sorry for her at all?"

He let his lids droop, so that he viewed the river before him through hired-assassin slits. "Do you feel sorry for your carpet when you step on it? That is not a person, it is a machine—a thing."

"How do you know? This place—this whole network—is full of real people pretending to be characters. How do you know?"

To her surprise, Azador actually flinched. He fought to hold onto his mask of indifference, but for a moment she saw something very different in his eyes before he turned away and fumbled another cigarette into his mouth.

She was struggling to make sense of this reaction when !Xabbu's urgent call from the prow startled her just-settling thoughts into confused flight.

"Renie! Come here. I think it is important."

Her friend bounced excitedly on the railing as she walked toward him. She realized with more than a little worry that his movements seemed to become more simian daily. Was he simply growing more familiar with the baboon sim, or was the constant life and perspective of a beast beginning to affect him?

"Look." He pointed toward the shore.

Renie stared, but her mind was a jumble of confused ideas, all jostling for her attention. There was nothing obviously wrong along the riverbank. "What is it, !Xabbu?"

"Look at the trees."

She applied herself to examining the place he indicated. There were trees, of course, in all sizes, with thick creepers drooping between branches like the survivors of a constrictors' orgy on the morning after. Nothing seemed particularly noteworthy, except for a certain regularity to the forms—which, she abruptly realized, was what had bothered her a few minutes earlier. Although both the trees and vines had the realistic look of nature, they seemed to be spaced and connected at rather mechanical intervals. In fact, there were too many right angles. . . .

"It looks arranged." She squinted against the harsh sunlight, and as she did the shapes became more general. "It looks something like the Works. Except made out of plants."

"Yes!" !Xabbu bounced in place. "Do you remember what the Scarecrow said? That his enemies were in the Works, and in Forest."

"Oh, my God." Renie shook her head, almost—but not quite—too exhausted to be afraid. "So we've just drifted right into the other fellow's kingdom? What was his name?"

"*Lion . . .*" !Xabbu said solemnly.

A thin hissing sounded all along the riverbank, and then a ghostly image began to flicker in the right-angled spaces between several of the trees—a parade of images, duplicated from tree to tree, identical and profuse. Each apparation was little more than a reflection in a rippled pool, so faint and smoky as to be barely visible, but Renie thought she saw a hard flash of eyes and a great, pale face. The hiss turned into a crackling rush, then the images faded, an army of ghosts all put to flight at the same instant.

"What the hell was that?" Azador called from the stern, killing the engine and slowing the tugboat to a drift.

Renie was trying to decide for herself what the hell that had been when she felt !Xabbu's small hand—his 'hairy, pinchy fingers,' as Emily had unkindly called them—close on her arm. "See there," he said, his whisper not quite disguising his wonder and unease. "They come down to the water like a family of elands."

Several hundred yards ahead, a small, stealthy group of human figures had appeared from the shelter of the vegetation beside the river. Not yet having seen the boat, they crept down the bank to the water's edge. Some crouched to drink as others stood on guard against attack, nervously watching the jungle behind them and the nearest parts of the river. They were pale-skinned, dirty, and naked but for the ornaments they wore, which Renie guessed were some kind of hunting trophies: several wore tails swinging at their rumps, while others sported antlers on their brows, or ears dangling down beside their faces.

Renie crouched, then waved to Azador to do the same. He squatted beside the pilot's wheel to watch as the boat drifted nearer.

The tugboat had silently covered perhaps two thirds of the distance when an antler-crowned sentry saw them. He stared gape-jawed at the boat for a moment, then made a strangled barking noise. The other naked humans leaped up in confusion, costume-tails flipping from side to side, and shoved and bumped each other in bleating fear as they retreated into the jungle.

The boat swept on, now almost level with the spot where the humans had vanished. The sentry, last of the group, stopped at the edge of shelter to watch the boat drift past, ready to fight to defend his tribesfolk's retreat. His antlers appeared to be wriggling, which Renie thought at first was a trick of the dappled sunlight where he stood, but then she saw that what she had thought were prongs of horn were actually hands, grafted onto his head at the temples. His arms ended at the wrist, knobbed in scar tissue.

The fingers of these horrid imitation antlers twitched again as she slid past, and the sentry's eyes—all dark iris, with no white at all—met hers with the hopeless, terrified stare of a damned thing scuttling across the rubbish heaps of Hell. Then he showed her his tail of stitched-on skin as he bounded away into the dark dells of Forest.

LONG Joseph Sulaweyo stood at the edge of the trees staring out onto the highway and felt as though he were waking up from a dream.

It had all seemed so simple in the night, with Jeremiah asleep and the high ceilings of that bloody damned Wasp's Nest place echoing back Joseph's every lonely footstep. He would go see his son. He would make sure that Stephen was still all right. Renie had said once that maybe Joseph had chased his son away, scared him into the coma or some foolishness, and although he had furiously rejected this bit of doctor nonsense, it had still sunk its hooks into him.

Stephen might even have come awake by now, he had told himself as he had rummaged together what small bits of possessions he had decided to take. How would that be if he did? How cruel? What if the boy woke up and his whole family was gone? And as Joseph had taken the last few bills from Renie's wallet—she wasn't going to need it, was she, down in that bathtub-with-wires?—it had all seemed to make a sort of magnificent sense. He would go and see the boy. He would make sure Stephen was all right.

But now, in the light of late afternoon, with bits and pieces of Drakensberg vegetation snagged in his trouser legs and fouling his hair, it seemed a different story altogether. What if Renie came out of that machine before he could get back? She would be angry—she would say he had just gone out to find something to drink, and had put them all in danger. But that wasn't true, was it? No, he had a responsibility to his son, and Renie was just his other child. She wasn't her own mother, whatever she thought sometimes. She wasn't his wife, to dog him about how to behave.

Long Joseph took a few steps out onto the hard shoulder. The night seemed to come early here: it was just a couple of hours past noon, but the sun had already dipped behind the mountain and a cold wind was sighing down the slope, strumming the trees and getting in under Joseph's thin shirt to devil his chest. He plucked the worst of the brambles off himself and wandered a little way up the road, stamping his feet to keep warm.

Renie didn't know how smart he was—she thought he was a fool, just like all children did about their fathers. But he would be down to see Stephen in Durban and back before she even knew he was gone. And what did she care, anyway? It wasn't like she was standing around waiting for him. Renie had left him behind, just like her mother and her brother had done. They all expected him to sit around waiting. Like he didn't have a life of his own.

He squinted up the empty hillside road, then down the other direction, as though closer inspection might reveal a bus that he had somehow missed.

The light was almost entirely gone. Joseph had been stamping so long and so hard that he couldn't decide any more which was worse, the cold in his toes or the ache in his feet from thumping them on the road. Only two cars and one truck had gone by, and although all had looked at the man by the side of the high mountain road with surprise, none of them had even slowed. His breath was beginning to show now, a chalky haze that hung before his face for a moment each time before the wind snatched it away.

He was just beginning to think about making a bed for himself somewhere in the brush, out of the chilly downdrafts, when a small truck appeared around the bend of the hill above him, headlamps surprisingly bright against the twilight. Without thinking, Joseph turned in the middle of the road and began waving his arms. For a moment it seemed the driver had not seen him in time—Long Joseph had a flashing vision of his body left broken and unnoticed in the bushes like a dead township dog—but then the lights veered toward the shoulder and the truck stopped, spurting gravel from beneath its wheels. The driver, a stocky white man in a shiny jacket, jumped out.

"What the hell do you think you're playing at, you crazy bastard?"

Joseph flinched at the Afrikaaner accent, but he was too cold to be choosy. "Need a ride."

The driver peered at him, then looked around, clearly wondering if

Long Joseph might have confederates waiting to spring out and hijack his truck, or perhaps do something worse. "Ya? Where's your car?"

Long Joseph had a moment of sheer panic as he realized he'd invented no story to explain being here on this lonely mountain road. That government place—he was supposed to keep it secret, wasn't he?

The driver, worried by his silence, took a step back toward his truck. "How did you get here, then?"

An incident from Joseph's youth came back suddenly, like a blessing sent special-delivery from God. "Fellow was giving me a ride," he told the driver. "But we have a big fight. Argument, I mean, He threw me out the car."

"Ya?" The driver was still suspicious. "What were you arguing about?"

"I told him that rugby football was rubbish."

The other man laughed suddenly, a big deep chortle. "Goddamn! Well, I think you're full of *kak* too, but that's no reason to leave someone out to freeze to death. Get in. You aren't an escaped murderer, then?"

Long Joseph hurried toward the car, blowing on his hands. "No. But I almost kill my brother-in-law once when he wreck my car." It had actually been Joseph who had wrecked his sister's husband's car to start the fight, but it sounded better this way.

"You're all right, then, fellow. I almost killed mine, once, too. I still may do it."

The driver's name was Antonin Haaksbergen, and although he was undeniably an Afrikaaner bastard and therefore by Sulaweyo's Law already proved vicious and untrustworthy and a bigot, Long Joseph was forced to admit that he was not completely without redeeming features. For one thing, his small truck had a very good heater. For another thing, he didn't ask too many questions. But perhaps the most persuasive evidence came almost immediately, as they rounded the bend and left Joseph's hitchhiking spot behind.

"You want a drink, fellow?"

It was as though someone had opened a curtain and allowed sunshine to flood into a long-darkened room. "You have some wine?"

"You're not half-picky, are you? No, but if you're very nice to me, I might let you have a rid illy."

Joseph frowned, suddenly suspicious, wondering if he had exchanged the looming threat of one girly-man for another. "Rid illy?"

Haaksbergen reached into a compartment behind the seat and produced a can of Red Elephant beer. He handed it over to Joseph and took out one for himself, which he opened and placed in the holder on the dashboard. "I've been good all trip, and now I've got company, so I'm entitled, eh!"

Joseph nodded, the can already raised, the cool liquid running down his throat like rain onto parched desert hills.

"You like my truck?" Haaksbergen inquired, taking a sip of his beer. "It's nice, ya? The engine's a hydrogen-burner—quite good, and cheap to run, but I suppose if one of those little gimmicks fell out or something it would all blow up and take us with it. Still, that's life, eh . . . ?

"Good God, fellow, are you done with that already?"

The rest of the journey passed in a glorious, warm, liquid slide. The lights of the towns, more numerous near the bottom of the mountains, floated past the windows like tropical fish. By the time they had reached Howick, Long Joseph and Antonin ("my mother was Italian—what can you do?") were pretty much best friends. Even Haaksbergen's occasional remarks about "you blacks" or "your people," or his quiet disgruntlement at Joseph drinking most of the beer, seemed part of the frank exchanges of newfound brotherhood. Deposited in front of the railway station, the late-night crowd eddying around him, Long Joseph waved a cheerful good-bye as the truck hummed away up the main road.

A slightly muddled thumbing-through of his cash resources made it clear he would never make it to Durban by train, and in any case he had no urge at the moment to go anywhere. He found a bench inside the station, curled up, and fell into a sleep where even the dreams were bleared, as though seen through deep water.

He was rousted firmly but without too much unpleasantness by a private security guard a little before dawn, and when he could not produce a ticket, was herded out onto the street with the rest of the multiracial assortment of dossers and transients. He spent a part of his ready cash on a squeeze-bottle of Mountain Rose from a 24-hour liquor store, in part to kill the deeply unfamiliar feeling of having drunk too much beer the night before, in part to help him think.

The thinking ended in a nap on a park bench. When he woke, the morning sun was climbing overhead and the world had become unpleasantly bright. He sat for a moment, watching people who never looked back at him as they walked past, and rubbing at the sticky ooze which had somehow collected on his chin, then decided he had better get moving. No telling when Renie might come out of that thing and go barking mad if he was still gone.

He returned to the caged kiosk that jutted from the side of the liquor store like a machine gun turret, and passed some bills through the slot in return for another bottle of Mountain Rose, which left him with only enough money to take the bus a few kilometers—far too small a distance to be any help. He had a few swallows of wine, then with magnificent self-control closed the pressure seal, slid the bottle into his pocket, and walked with immense care back to the highway.

His third and last ride of the day was on the back of a produce truck. Squeezed between towers of wrapped and crated greenhouse fruits, he saw Durban rise before him, a cluster of oblongs dominating the Natal coastline. Now his busfare was enough to get him wherever he might decide to go. He toyed with the idea of returning to the shelter where he and Renie had lived and finding some of his cronies, Walter or whoever else might be around, and taking them with him to the hospital, but Renie had made it clear that the shelter was no longer safe, and the last thing Long Joseph wanted to do was get in trouble and have Renie able to tell him later that he was just as stupid an old man as she had suspected he was.

The idea that the trouble might be the sort which he wouldn't survive long enough to be shouted at by his daughter only occurred to him later.

He had walked back and forth between the bus stop and the front entrance of the Durban Outskirt Medical Facility perhaps a dozen times in two hours. It was only when he had actually reached the hospital that he remembered Renie saying there was some kind of quarantine, and indeed, no matter how long he watched the building, no one seemed to be going in and out except doctors and nurses. There were even guards at the door, private security men in padded black firefight suits, the kind of muscle that even the craziest drunk didn't bother to mess with. And even though his opinionated child might think he was a drunk, Long Joseph knew that he wasn't crazy.

He had swallowed down perhaps half the wine, but the rest was still sloshing in the bottle in his pocket, testament to his good sense and powers of restraint. There were other people on the street in front of the hospital this evening, too, so he knew that he wasn't being suspicious. But beyond that, he had reached a sort of blank wall in his own head, a big hard something that kept him from doing anything else. How could he see his son if there was a quarantine? And if he couldn't see him, then what? Go back, and face that womanish Jeremiah and admit it had all been a mistake? Or worse, go back and find Renie up and asking questions, and not even be able to give her news of her brother?

He wandered from the bus stop toward the small cluster of trees that stood on a knoll a few yards down from the medical facility's front door. He leaned against one of them and slapped his hand gently against the squeeze-bottle while he waited for an idea to come. The wall in his head remained firm, as heavy and unyielding as the helmeted men by the entrance. One of them turned in his direction for a moment, the face shield blank as an insect's eye, and Long Joseph stepped back into the trees.

That would be all he needed, wouldn't it? Have one of those weight-lifting Boer bastards notice him and decide to teach the *kaffir* a lesson. All the laws in the world couldn't stop one of those private thugs before he broke your bones—that was what was wrong with the country.

He had just found a safer spot, deep in the tree shadows, when a hand clamped on his mouth. Something hard pressed into his back, nestling against the knobs of his spine.

The voice was a harsh whisper. "Don't make a noise."

Long Joseph's eyes bulged, and he stared at the security guards, wishing now they could see him, but he was too far away, hidden in the dark. The hard thing prodded him again.

"There's a car behind you. We are going to turn around and walk toward it, and you are going to get into it, and if you do anything stupid I'm going to blow your insides all over the sidewalk."

His knees weak, Long Joseph Sulaweyo was spun around so that he faced out the far side of the stand of trees. A dark sedan waited at the curb, obscured from the medical facility by the copse, its door open, the interior dark as a grave pit.

"I'm taking my hand off your mouth," the voice said. "But if you even breathe loud, you are dead."

He still could not see his captor, only a dark shape standing just behind his shoulder. He thought wildly of all the things he might do, all the netflick heroisms he had ever seen, kicking guns out of villains' hands, immobilizing an attacker with a kung fu jab; he even thought for a moment of screaming and running, praying that the first shot would miss. But he knew he would do none of those things. The pressure on his spine was like the nose of some cold, ancient creature, sniffing for the kill. He was its prey, and it had caught him. A man couldn't outrun Death, could he?

The car door was before him. He let himself be bent double and shoved inside. Someone pulled a sack over his head.

My children don't deserve no stupid man like me for a father, he thought as the car jerked into motion. A second later, anger dissolved into terror. He suddenly felt very sure he would be sick, would strangle himself in the sack on his own vomit. *God damn, look at this foolishness!* he mourned. *My poor children! I have killed them both.*

RENIE stood up slowly, fighting an urge to be sick again. When she had thrown up in the insect world, nothing had come out, and thus it might have been interesting or even instructive to consider why the Kansas simulation had provided her with a clear stream of liquid to vomit. Renie, however, did not particularly want to think about regurgitation at all. As it was, the memory of what had made her sick in the first place, those poor mutilated creatures, was still nauseatingly strong.

"What is the problem with this place?" she moaned, wiping her chin. "Are these people completely crazy? Jesus Mercy, and I thought the Yellow Room was bad! Are they all some kind of lunatic sadists?"

Azador restarted the engine and the tugboat began chugging down the river once more. "They were only Puppets."

"You *would* say that!" Only the overwhelming feeling of weakness and despair prevented her from starting another argument.

"I understand what Renie means." !Xabbu was standing upright on the boat's rail, his balance impressive even on the gentle river current. "Are there really so many . . . what is that word, Renie? So many sadistic people that are the masters of this place?"

"They are rich bastards," Azador said. "They do what they like."

"It's hard to believe some of this . . . *ugliness*." Renie had taken a few deep breaths, and was beginning to feel normal again. "Who would want to live with it? Who would want to do it? I mean, the person behind Scarecrow might have been a bastard, but he didn't seem *that* bad. But I suppose if it was all just a game to him . . ."

"Scarecrow had nothing to do with that," Azador said flatly. "He lost his hold on this place long ago. What you saw, those puppets torn up and sewed back together like dolls, that was done by the Twins."

"Twins? What twins?" Renie kept her voice polite—she had made too many mistakes with Azador already.

"They are two men who are found many places in this network. Perhaps they are masters, or pets of the masters. But they move in many simulations, and always they turn them into shit." He gestured at the jungle, which more and more resembled the claustrophobic strangle of the Works, except here trees and vines doubled for the industrial clutter. "I have seen them before, and what they do. When they catch any of us travelers, they do not simply throw us out of the network. If they can, they keep us connected and they torture us." He spat over the side. "I do not know who they truly are, but they are demons."

"And they're . . . twins?" Renie was fascinated. Another one of Otherland's doors had opened.

Azador rolled his eyes. "That is a joke, because they always go around together. And because one is fat, one is thin, no matter where they go or who they become. But they are the Twins, and you can always tell them."

"You don't know if they're real people or not?" Renie had the feeling that Azador hadn't realized yet he was actually communicating—for the second time that day!—and that time to get answers was therefore short. "But how can they be, if they're in more than one simworld?"

The gypsy shook his head. "I do not know. All I know is that they are many places and they are always, always bastards. Here they have become Tinman and Lion."

So some of the owners of this universe were people like Kunohara, Renie thought, content with their own backyards. But others didn't stay in their own simulations, and even vandalized their neighbors' domains. Were they at war with each other, these Grail Brotherhood people? That would make sense—trust the rich to try to screw each other out of something that was big enough for all of them. It would be pleasant to leave them to it, except that one enemy in charge of everything wouldn't make things any easier than a lot of enemies, as far as Renie was concerned. Also, she and !Xabbu would still be un-armed pedestrians in the middle of a war zone.

"Can you tell us anything else about these twins, or the others who own this network?" she asked.

Azador shrugged. "It is too hot to talk, and I am tired of thinking of those people. I am Romany—we go where we want, we do not care whose land we cross." He reached into the coat lying at his feet, mus-cles rippling, and rooted in the pocket for a cigarette.

He was right about the heat—the sun was at full noon, and the trees no longer shaded the river. Renie worried briefly about Emily, still sleeping in the windowless cabin, then caught herself. The girl was a Puppet, wasn't she? And this was her simulation, after all. Per-haps Azador was right—perhaps she was taking these mechanical people, these bits of code, too seriously.

The thought drew out another, something she had forgotten, or from which she had been distracted. "Azador, how are you so certain Emily is a Puppet?"

He looked surprised, but pretended not to have understood. "What?"

"I asked you before, but you never answered me. You said it didn't matter what you did, because she was a Puppet. How do you know?"

"Why does it make any difference?" he growled. His disdain was not entirely convincing. Renie felt sure for the first time that he was not merely angry at being questioned, he was actively hiding something.

"I'm just curious," she said, as levelly and calmly as she could. "I'm ignorant about these things. I haven't been here as long as you, haven't seen as many things as you have."

"I am not a child, to be made to talk by this sort of trick," Azador snapped. "And if you want to be the boss and stand in the sun, asking questions, then you can be the captain of the bloody boat, too." He gave up his search through the coat pocket, left the wheel spinning, and stalked away up the deck.

Before Renie could say anything more, !Xabbu waved urgently for her attention. "Something is wrong," he said, and sprang from the rail down to the deck.

Renie paused. The heat haze shimmering between the tree branches began to thicken, forming pictures in midair in the crooks of branches, a thousand reflections of the same thing. The image that appeared in all of them was much clearer this time, a massive stub of a yellow head with a shaggy, dirt-clotted mane and piggy eyes almost lost in deep, horizontal wrinkles. The jowls drooped around a mouth crammed with huge, broken teeth, which now yawned open. A growling voice blared and stuttered like a bad radio transmission. Renie could only make out a few words—". . . Outsiders . . . Forest . . . terrible fate . . ." Like something in an unvisited museum, the dreadful face chewed on for a few moments, babbling and groaning, then faded, leaving dark spaces between the branches once more.

"Sounds like the alert is going out about us," Renie said grimly. "I think that's what it was saying, anyway. It's hard to tell—this whole place seems like it's falling apart." Or the two different worlds, Forest and the Works, were growing into one blighted whole. Emerald would soon be absorbed, too—she could see how the ruined buildings, fields, and dust that had once been Scarecrow's domain, the last besieged outpost of a lovely children's tale, would now become another analogue of the larger machine, perpetually dying but still full of malevolent life. Was that what would happen to all of the Otherland network one day? Although the great simulation universe was the citadel of her enemies, the thought depressed and disgusted her.

"I am not sure," !Xabbu said, peering over the railing.

"That it's falling apart? Are you joking?" Renie could still taste bile from earlier. She badly wanted a cigarette now. What was the point of abstaining? Might as well take what pleasure she could, while she could. She was about to go find Azador, but saw his coat lying in a tangle on the deck. Yes, it was rude, but the hell with the self-righteous bastard.

As she leaned down to fish in the pockets, she asked !Xabbu, "Didn't you see that transmission or whatever it was? It's like the generator for the whole simworld is running down."

"That is not what I meant, Renie." !Xabbu turned for a moment to survey her fumblings with his close-set brown eyes. "I am not sure that the transmission, as you called it, is what I felt coming, just a moment ago. . . ."

Renie found the cigarette packet; a moment later, her fingers closed on the hard shape of Azador's lighter. It was impressively heavy but still comfortable to hold, the silver sides covered with intricate design elements, like some family heirloom from a century or two back. When she clicked it, a tiny, white-hot ball of burning plasma appeared, floating in an invisible magnetic field above the top of the lighter. So, despite its old-fashioned look, it was meant to be a Minisolar—the kind of expensive modernist accessory that in RL was most often carried by young market bankers or successful charge dealers.

Mildly intrigued by such virtual ostentation, Renie noted the monogram inscribed on its one featureless side, an ornate *Y.* She wondered whether that was one of their companion's initials, and if so, whether Azador was a first name or a last name. Then she wondered if the lighter even belonged to him. Maybe he had "found" it somewhere in Kansas.

"What was that terrible noise?" Emily called from the doorway of the cabin. "That . . . *growling?*" The girl took a few steps toward the stern, her eyes wide but blinking rapidly against the sunlight. Her hair tousled from sleep, her bare feet and simple shift made her look more than ever like a stretched child. "It woke me up. . . ."

As Renie took the still-unlit cigarette from her mouth to answer, the sky abruptly split into component colors, blue, white, and black, and the world shuddered to a halt.

Renie found herself frozen in space, unable to move or speak. Everything she could see—sky, boat, river, Emily—had gone flat, dead, and motionless as printed images on cheap transparencies, but the transparencies all had dozens of ghost images behind them, piled one atop the other and slightly off-center, like a scatter of animation cels that had been carefully aligned and then accidentally dropped.

A second later the images heaved themselves back together, like a fumbled deck of cards run in reverse, and the universe shuddered back into motion.

As Renie stood frozen, unsure whether she herself could move and too stunned to test the possibility immediately, something flared white above the cabin, a brilliant vertical stripe of blankness that hovered above the reanimated river and jungle like an angel, a star, a rip in the wallpaper of reality. It wriggled, creating for itself arms and legs and a faceless splash of white where a head would be.

"Sellars. . . ?" she breathed, but still could not make herself move, although she could feel her body again, feel her arms dangling, her feet flat on the deck. Recognition of that strange shape, that absence of visual information, flooded through her. "Jesus Mercy," she was shouting now, "is that Sellars, finally?"

The white form stretched out its arms as though testing the weather. Renie saw !Xabbu move up beside her, his long muzzle lifted like a dog looking at the moon. Even Emily, who had fallen to the deck in terror after the strange rupture, turned to see what Renie and !Xabbu were staring at.

The white shape spun slowly in the air as though it hung on a string, bouncing in agitation.

"*Chingate!*" it cried out. "What you doing, old man?" Renie did not recognize the voice, childishly high, hoarse and startled. "What is this *loco* place? This ain't no locking net, *viejo*." The figure started to thrash harder, the arms and legs windmilling so that for a moment it seemed a tiny star was going supernova just above the river. "Get me outta here! Get me outta here, you *mentiroso* mother . . ."

The white shape vanished. Once, more, the sky was just the sky, the river was only the murmuring river.

"That was not Sellars," !Xabbu said a few seconds later. In other circumstances, Renie would have laughed at the anticlimactic obviousness of it, but she was as stunned as he was. She saw the edge of Azador's bare shoulder in the prow of the boat, the rest of him blocked by the cabin, and realized she was clutching his lighter so hard it was hurting her fingers, gouging her palm.

"Hey!" he shouted, "what are you doing there?"

What am I doing? she thought, boggled. The world had just been turned into origami, and he was blaming her? Brain still firing but moving almost nothing, like a car in neutral, she looked back to the empty spot where the white shape had hovered.

"If . . ." was all !Xabbu had time to say. Then everything went mad once more.

This time Renie had no stance from which to watch it happen, no separated space in which to be an observer. This time all around her and even inside of her, color, shape, sound, light, folded in on themselves. A moment of anticipatory shudder, then everything collapsed, swift as a whipcrack.

Long seconds in emptiness. Not gray, but empty. Not black, but lightless. Only time to try to remember who she was, but not time to remember why that might be important, then everything exploded, the inside-out almost instantaneously becoming the outside-in once more.

Water was in her mouth, and cool, sludgy river water was all around her, too. The boat was gone. She thrashed, trying to find the sky. She clawed her way to air with one hand strangely paralyzed, doubled in an arthritic fist. She did not know which way to turn because everywhere she moved her head, the river slapped her face. She tried to cry out, got another mouthful of water, choked.

"Here, Renie!"

She foundered toward !Xabbu's voice, felt a small hand grasp her arm and tug her forward, then she touched something smooth and complex and caught it with her arm, hooking her elbow until she felt secure against the two pulls of the river, sideways and down. She lifted her head far enough above the water to see Emily gasping beside her. The girl was clinging to the roots of the same tree, a dead banyan or something like it, which stood, storklike, halfway out into the water. !Xabbu was farther up the curve of the root, staring down the river.

Renie turned and saw what he saw. The boat was chugging on, already twenty or thirty meters downstream and rapidly leaving them behind. She raised her voice to shout for Azador, but saw no sign of him on the deck or at the wheel. Whether he was in the river himself and drowned, translated somewhere else entirely, or even still on the boat, it made no difference. The tug did not slow, did not turn toward the bank, but instead murmured on between the walls of Forest, ever smaller, until a curve of the river took it from their view.

CHAPTER 23

Beside Bob's Ocean

NETFEED/NEWS: New Trial For "Ignorance Abuse" Parents
(visual: Hubbards weeping outside courthouse)
VO: A date has been set for the second child-abuse trial of Rudy and Violet
Hubbard, accused by their adult daughter, Halvah Mae Warringer, of having
created a "climate of ignorance" during her childhood which constituted
abuse. Warringer alleges that because of her parents' prejudices and
ignorance, and their "willful failures to improve," she was exposed to racial
intolerance, health-issues insensitivity, and negative body-images in a way
that has adversely affected her adult life. The first trial in Springfield,
Missouri, ended when the jury was unable to reach a verdict . . .

JUNIPER Bay, Ontario, reminded Decatur Ramsey a lot of the towns he'd lived in growing up, as his staff sergeant father had been transferred from base to base, first with, then eventually without, his wife—Catur's mother. On first inspection, Juniper Bay had the same flatness as those long-ago towns, not just geographical, but . . . Catur stretched for the word as he stopped at an intersection where a young matron attempted to guide two young children across after the light had already turned yellow.

Spiritual, he thought at last. A spiritual flatness. As though the inner life of the city had been pressed down. Not eradicated, just . . . flattened.

It was a bigger city than many he had known as a child, but like so many of those—railroad towns down to a trickle of freight cars on the busiest weeks, factory towns with half the employees laid off—its best days appeared to be behind it. The young people, he could guess, were leaving for more exciting places, for Toronto or New York, or even the metropolis based around D.C. where Ramsey made his own home.

A row of banners hung along the main street, flapping in the stiff breeze, advertisements for some upcoming civic celebration. Ramsey felt a small twinge of shame. It was easy for him to make judgments, a confirmed city convert in a ridiculously expensive car (a rental car too rich for his budget, but an indulgence he had allowed himself.) Was there actually anything worse about a town which had lost its upward thrust, especially when you compared it to the seething pile of conflicting agendas that made a modern city? At least people occasionally saw each other on the street here, maybe even still went to the same churches, to meetings at their kids' schools. To walk on your own feet down one of the sidewalks of the Washbar Corridor metroplex, to linger any longer on the streets than the time necessary to dash from vehicle to door, was to proclaim yourself destitute or suicidal.

The address he had been given was in a small warren of streets behind the business district, an old neighborhood of two- and three-story wooden houses that must have been the previous century's version of an upscale young professionals' neighborhood. Now the houses and their old-fashioned yards lay beneath the sundial stripe of the elevated train track, a band of shadow that darkened a full quarter of the block. He had a brief vision of that great bar of shade rolling across the windows every day, on a schedule as predictable as those of the trains overhead, and thought he could guess why the houses, despite having such unusually large amounts of space around them, *lebensraum* which should have made them valued pieces of real estate, still had an air of seediness, of gradual but inevitable decay.

He pulled up in front of number 74. The parts of the house he could see above the high hedges seemed a little cleaner than its neighbors, or at least more recently painted. He announced himself at the gate, and although no one answered, he was buzzed in. As he walked up the long front path, he found himself impressed by the size of the property. Olga Pirofsky might only be one of twelve Uncle Jingles, but it was an incredibly popular show, after all, and he supposed even the faceless actors must be well paid. The garden had largely been left to grow wild, but was not completely untended. Here in the lee of the thick hedges, it had the feeling of a previous era, of Victorian entertainments and elaborate children's games. The house itself, although small compared to the size of the grounds, had three stories and a number of windows set at a number of angles.

Contemplating how it would feel to sit at one of those windows looking down on one's own garden, a garden you could get lost in, Ramsey wondered how much house the fierce mortgage on his two-bedroom apartment would buy in a town like this.

It took a while for anyone to answer the door, which gave him ample opportunity to examine the dried Christmas wreath hanging there, probably not just months but years out of its original season, and a pair of rubber boots standing beside the mat.

The door opened, but only a few inches. A small, bright eye peered out past the chain. "Mr. Ramsey?"

He tried to make himself look as little like a murderer as possible. "That's me, Ms. Pirofsky."

There was a moment of further hesitation, as though she were still contemplating the possibility of a trick. *My God,* he realized as the moment stretched. *That's just what she's doing—she's that worried.* His small flash of irritation died. "I can show you my driver's license if you'd like. Don't you recognize my voice from our phone calls?"

The door closed, and for a moment he thought he'd made a mistake, but then the chain rattled and the door opened again, wider this time.

"Come in," she said, her faint accent curling the edges of her words. "It's terrible to make you stand on the doorstep like a Jehovah's Witness or something."

Olga Pirofsky was younger than he had expected from the hesitancy of her phone conversation, a fit, square-shouldered woman in her late fifties or early sixties, thick brown hair cut short and largely gone to gray. Most surprising of all was the sharp confidence of her gaze, not what he expected from someone who had been examining him from behind the chain to see if he were some kind of spyflick assassin.

"That's all right," he said. "I'm just very, very glad you decided to meet with me. And if anything useful comes out of this, you'll have done a big favor for some very nice people."

She waved her hand, almost dismissively. "I can't tell you how bad I've felt about all this. But I don't know what else to do." For the first time since he had entered, a little of her self-possession slipped. She looked from side to side as though reminding herself that she was on home ground, then smiled again. "It's all been very upsetting." She backed a few steps toward the stairs and signaled him to follow. "Let's go upstairs—I hardly use this part of the house at all."

"It's a lovely house. I was particularly impressed by the garden."

"It's gone all to rack and ruin—is that the phrase? I used to have a tenant who lived down here on the bottom floor, and she liked to work out there, but she was transferred by her company. It's been years!" She was heading up the stairs now, and Ramsey followed. "There's a gardener who comes once a month. Sometimes I think I should get a tenant again—not for the money, but just to have someone else in the house, you know, in case of an emergency, I suppose—but I think I've become too used to living by myself. Well, except for Misha."

They exited the staircase into what Ramsey supposed was the second floor parlor, a modest-sized room with a fireplace and a few rather spare and artistic bits of furniture. As if in mockery of the rest of the room's simplicity, the far corner was dominated by a huge device festooned with bundled cables, something halfway between a spaceship control module and an old-fashioned electric chair.

"I am babbling, yes?" She saw him looking at the chair. "It's for my work. We all of us—all the Uncle Jingles and the other characters, you know?—work from our homes." She froze in place, then frowned and tapped herself on the forehead, the broad body language of a pantomime artist. "I forgot! Would you like some tea? Or I could do coffee."

"Tea would be fine."

"Just one moment, then." She stopped in front of the inner door. "Something is going to happen now. Are you easily frightened?"

He couldn't puzzle out her expression. "Frightened?" Good God, what was this woman going to show him? Could all this secrecy and worry be justified after all?

She opened the door and a tiny, furry thing rushed out, claws scrabbling on the polished floorboards. To his shame, Ramsey flinched. As though door and mouth were somehow connected, once released the tiny, furry thing began to bark. It had the voice of a much larger animal.

"Misha is very fierce," she said, and he realized that she had been fighting back a smile. "However, he is not as terrifying as he looks." She slid through and the door closed behind her, leaving him alone with the small, bat-eared dog, who darted back and forth just out of Ramsey's reach, emitting loud noises of loathing and distrust.

Catur Ramsey had settled deeply into the couch as the woman told him of her trip from doctor to doctor, of the succession of unsettlingly cheerful reports which did nothing to make the headaches stop. Gaining confidence, she reported the results of her researches as well, another catalog of unhelpful findings; she was clearly trying to work up the courage to tell him something she thought important, just as clearly not quite there yet. His eyes, wandering a bit from time to time, settled on a framed picture turned face-down atop the mantel-piece, and he wondered who it might be. All good lawyers had a little bit of cop in them, a nagging busybody voice that was always asking questions. The really good lawyers, though, knew when to ignore the voice. Olga Pirofsky clearly needed to talk, and Ramsey let her.

". . . And that's when I thought . . ." She hesitated, then leaned down to scratch the dog's head. The tiny black-and-white thing was peering out from between her ankles, glaring at Ramsey as though he might be some kind of advance agent for the canine Antichrist. "It's so hard to say—I mean, it sounds so foolish with you sitting there, and you coming all that way just to see me."

"Please, Ms. Pirofsky. I haven't been out of that office in so long, I'm beginning to talk to the rubber plants. Even if you throw me out right now, it'll have done me good." Which was true, he realized. "So just tell me the story in your own way."

"I thought that it didn't make sense. That no one who had ever participated in the show—we keep that whole database, like I told you—had ever had this Tandagore's Syndrome. That just doesn't seem right. I mean, there have been millions, Mr. Ramsey. I'm not a person who works with statistics, but that doesn't seem right."

"And. . . ?" He wasn't quite sure exactly where she was going, but he was beginning to have an idea. As she hesitated, trying to order her thoughts, Ramsey leaned forward and waggled his fingers in a peacemaking gesture at the dog. Misha's eyes sprang wide in incredulous fury, then he leaped to his feet in the space behind his mistress's ankles and began to bark as if he had been scalded.

"Oh, for goodness' sake, Misha!" She stuck her hand down the back of the sofa cushion and pulled out a small cloth-covered ball. She waved it in front of the dog's nose and then tossed it over to the far corner of the room. Misha sprang after it and chivvied it into the corner by the V-chair, then sank his teeth deep into the ball and began, growling deep in his little throat, to kill it with great thorough-ness.

"That should keep him for a bit," she said fondly. "What I'm trying to say is, does it make sense? That the statistics about *Uncle Jingle's Jungle* should be so different from the averages?"

"So are you saying you think something special the company does is preventing this from happening, this Tandagore Syndrome? But that would be a good thing, wouldn't it?"

"Not," she said carefully, "if they were making sure nothing happened to anyone on the show because they had something to hide." She appeared to have found her confidence at last, and stared at him with something approaching a challenge on her face.

Ramsey was perplexed. If she was right about Uncle Jingle being exempt, it was certainly interesting, although most likely it would prove to be a fluke of some sort. But it was also possible, and in fact much more likely, that she had simply accessed the wrong data, or misread some numbers. That was the great drawback of the net, as well as its glory—anybody could get hold of anything and make whatever they wanted out of it; it was a treasure trove for amateurs, cranks, and outright loonies.

But he had to admit that the woman sitting across from him didn't *seem* like a loony, or even a crank. Also, he liked her, and found himself not wanting to offend her, even if he was beginning to suspect the trip might have been a waste.

"It's a very interesting possibility, Ms. Pirofsky," he said finally. "Obviously, I'll look into it."

The keen look in her eyes faded, became something else. "You do think I'm crazy."

"No. No, I don't. But my clients have a child who seems to have developed Tandagore, and they need facts and figures, not theories. I really will look into what you say." He put his teacup down on the floor. It seemed to be time to leave. "I promise you, I take everything about this problem very seriously."

"This child—is it a boy or girl?"

"I'm not really allowed to talk about my clients." He heard his own stiff tone and didn't like it. "It's a girl. She's been in a coma for several weeks now. That's why we're in such a hurry—the few cases of Tandagore where there's been recovery, it's always been early in the illness."

"The poor thing," Her face held a deep sorrow—far deeper than what he would expect from someone hearing someone else's bad news. "That's why this frightens me so," she murmured. "The children. They are so helpless. . . ."

"You've been working with children a long time, haven't you?"

"All my life, almost." She rubbed her face as if to scour the sorrow away, but was not entirely successful: her eyes were wide, almost haunted. "They are all I care about. And Misha, I suppose." She smiled faintly at the dog, which was celebrating its victory with a nap, head resting on the murdered ball.

"Do you have children of your own?" He still held his briefcase across his knees, unsure of whether to begin the move toward the door, but when he asked the question her whole bearing changed. She visibly sagged, an effect so obvious that he experienced a rush of shame, as though he had deliberately done something to frighten or shock her. "I'm sorry, that's none of my business."

She waggled her fingers, telling him it did not matter, but her cheeks had reddened. She stared at the dog for a quarter of a minute, saying nothing. Ramsey, too, was silent, frozen on the couch by guilt and propriety.

"Can I tell something to you?" she said at last. "You do not know me. You can go if you want to. But sometimes it is good just to talk to someone."

He nodded, feeling any control of the situation he might have had, of his schedule, of his own feelings, sucked away like sand in an ebb tide. "Of course."

"When I was young, I traveled with a circus. My parents were both circus people, and our show, *Le Cirque Royal,* traveled all over Europe and even Asia. You do know what a circus is, don't you?"

"Yes, ma'am. I mean, I've never seen one, but I know what they are. There aren't many circuses left, I don't think. Not in the US, anyway."

"No," she said. "There are not." She sighed. "I do not know why I am telling you this, but I suppose you deserve to know. I was both a clown and a bareback rider, from the time I was a little girl. Much of what I do on the Uncle Jingle show are things that I learned then, from the other circus clowns and performers. Perhaps I am the last who learned these things. In any case, it was a good life, although we did not have much money. We were all together, we traveled many places, saw many things. And when a young man came to join us, a mentalist—do you know that term? Someone who reads minds, or pretends to. It is a very popular midway attraction, like a fortune-teller. I think you see them still sometimes on the net. So when this beautiful young man came to join us, I had everything I wanted.

"His name was Aleksandr Chotilo." She paused, then smiled, a fragile smile but not without pleasure. "I have not said his name out loud for a long time. I thought it would hurt more than it does. I will not bore you with a long story. You are a young man. You understand about love."

"Not that young any more, I'm afraid," he said quietly, but nodded for her to continue.

"We would have been married—my parents liked him, and he was of our people, the traveling life, circus life. When I told my father I was going to have a baby, he set a date very quickly. I was so happy." She closed her eyes for a moment, slowly, as if falling asleep, then opened them and took a deep breath. "But everything went wrong. In the fifth month, the pains came—very, very bad. We were in Austria, outside Vienna. I was taken in a helicopter to the hospital, but the baby was born dead. I never saw him." A pause, jaw clenched tight. "Then, as I was still recovering, my Aleksandr was hit by a car in the Thaliastrasse and killed instantly. He had been on his way to visit me. He was carrying flowers. My father and mother had to bring me the news. They were both crying." With her sleeve she dabbed at her own eyes, pink around the edges but still dry. "I went mad, then. There is no other word for it. I became convinced that Aleksandr had been kidnapped—even after I saw him in his coffin, the day of the funeral, when I had to be carried out of the church. I was certain that my baby was alive, too, that a terrible mistake had been made. I lay in the hospital bed every night imagining that Aleksandr and our son were trying to find me, that they were lost in the hallways outside, wandering, calling my name. I would scream to them until the nurses sedated me." She smiled as if to emphasize her own foolishness; Ramsey found it a very discomforting expression. "I was completely mad."

"I spent three years in a sanitarium—now *there* is a word you do not hear these days—in southern France, where *Le Cirque Royal* had its winter quarters. I did not speak, I barely slept. I do not remember that time now, except in little pictures, like someone else's story, some documentary. My parents did not think I would ever be myself again, but they were wrong. Slowly, I came back. It made them happy, even though it did not make *me* happy. But I could not be in the circus— could not travel the places we had all been together. I went first to England, but it was too gray, too old, like Austria, the people with their quiet, sad faces. I came here. I grew old myself. My parents died, my mother just a few years ago. And everything I do, I do for the children."

She shrugged. The story was clearly over.

"I'm so sorry," he said.

"You deserved to know this," she replied. "It's only fair."

"I'm afraid I don't quite understand."

"That I was mad. That for a long time they all thought I must stay in an institution for the rest of my life. When you are running around trying to discover things, and you are considering the things I have told you, you deserve to know that the information comes from a crazy woman who was in an institution, who has spent her entire life trying to make children happy because she let her own child die."

"You're too hard on yourself. I don't think you're crazy—in fact, I wish most of the people I have to work with were as sane as you are."

She laughed. "Perhaps. But don't say I never told you. I can see you are ready to leave. Let me just lock Misha away, then I will walk you to the door."

As she tried to reconcile the dog, awake again and excited, to being confined to the kitchen for a few minutes, Ramsey sidled toward the mantelpiece and the picture. When he lifted it, the black button eyes of Uncle Jingle regarded him with glee.

"Horrible isn't it, really," she said as she walked back into the room. He started guiltily and almost handed it to her, a child caught with his hand in the cookie jar.

"I was just . . ."

"I don't want to look at it anymore. Bad enough being on the inside of it. Take it if you want."

He tried to refuse gracefully, but somehow, after they had said their good-byes and he was navigating his way through the tree-lined streets, trying to remember the way back to the freeway, Uncle Jingle sat propped on the seat beside him, grinning like a cat that had just broken into an aviary.

THERE was, Yacoubian noted with satisfaction, a certain unease in the air.

"It is scandalous," said Ymona Dedoblanco, the mouth of her leonine goddess-head twisted in annoyance, ivory fangs gleaming. "It has been weeks, and still it is not functioning properly. What if something were to happen?"

"Happen?" Osiris turned toward her, his masked features as always unreadable. He seemed slow, though; Yacoubian thought he could sense a kind of disconnection in the Old Man. If he had been an opposing general—which, in a way he was—Yacoubian would have said this enemy no longer cared to pursue the battle. "What do you mean, 'something were to happen'?"

The lion-headed goddess could barely control her fury. "What do you think I mean? Don't be foolish!"

The lack of obvious reaction to this breach of protocol was impressive: all along the table the Egyptian beast-faces with which their host masked them were carefully neutral, as though they viewed this altercation with nothing more than polite interest, but Yacoubian knew a line had been crossed. He glanced at Wells to share this small triumph, but the technocrat's yellow god-face was as inscrutable as all the others.

"I mean, what if one of us died?" the lion-goddess continued.

"What if there's some kind of accident while we are all forced to stand around, cooling our heels like peasants lining up for bread?" The root of her anger was suddenly apparent. She, like most of the others, probably never left the safety of her stronghold, and had full-time, highest quality medical staff on constant call. She did not fear immoderately for her safety, or her health. Ymona Dedoblanco was furious because she was being made to wait.

The Old Man stirred, but Yacoubian still found his manner strange. Didn't Jongleur realize that many others in the Brotherhood were losing patience, too? The general could barely suppress his pleasure. After all he and Wells had done to unseat the old bastard, notably without success, it seemed now that all they would have to do would be to wait for the chairman to write his own dismissal.

"My dear lady," Osiris said, "you are making too much of a slight delay. There have been a few minor complications—not surprising when one considers that we are creating the greatest forward leap for humankind since the discovery of fire."

"But what are these earthquakes?" demanded Sobek, the crocodile-god.

"Earthquakes?" said Osiris, confused. "What are you talking about?"

"I think Mr. Ambodulu is talking about the perturbations in the system we discussed last time," said Wells smoothly. The lemonskin features of the Memphite creator-god Ptah suited him perfectly, a tiny half-smile permanently on his lips. "The 'spasms,' as I call them. We have had a few more than usual recently, as we've been bringing the system fully online."

"You call it whatever you like," said the crocodile. "All I know is that I am sitting in my palace in your network—the palace that cost me seventeen billion Swiss credits—and the whole thing goes," even in his anger he pronounced the old British phrase with pride, "arse over tea kettle. Inside out. Colors and light and everything breaking up. You cannot tell me that is just a spasm in the system. It is more like a heart attack!"

"We all have quite a bit invested in this project," said Osiris coldly. "Nothing is being taken lightly. You heard Wells—Ptah, I mean. It is part of the growing pains. This is a very, very complicated mechanism."

Yacoubian was almost beside himself. The Old Man had called someone by their RL name instead of his own Egyptian nonsense! He was definitely losing it—there couldn't be any question about it. The general looked around, half-expecting to see cracks in the massive granite walls, bits of the eternal twilight seeping through chinks in the Western Palace's roof, but of course the simworld was as it had ever been.

That's the thing about all this VR bullshit, though, he thought. *It's like one of those Third World armies—lots of brass and parade uniforms, and you don't notice anything's wrong until one day you come in and the barracks and the staff room are empty and they've all gone off to join the rebels in the hills.*

Except for the officers, he thought with a certain grim humor, *who will be heading for the border, one step ahead of the war crimes tribunals. Like all of us will be, if this thing ever comes apart too badly.* It was tempting to celebrate anything that looked like the Old Man foundering, but even a Jongleur-hater like Daniel Yacoubian knew that nothing could be allowed to threaten the Grail Project itself.

"Actually, I'm beginning to wonder if it's all just normal perturbations of the system," Wells said. "There seems to be more turbulence than we expected." He stood and opened a window full of three-dimensional representations of data, an array of colors and strange shapes in slow movement that might have been some surrealist painter's nightmare. "You can see we've had a disturbing jump in system spasms during the last few months, and the trend is continuing to spike upward quite spectacularly."

"Oh, for God's sake," said Osiris in a rare, unintentionally comic remark. "This is the whole point of turbulence, is it not? That it cannot be fully anticipated? You of all people should know this, Wells—and it is your job to administer the Grail System, after all, so you should be very careful about pointing fingers." He turned to survey the table. "The fact is, we have a network more complicated by a couple of magnitudes than anything ever created, and it is up and running, thousands of nodes, trillions upon trillions of instructions per second, and except for the occasional bout of wind, it's working." He waved his bandaged hand in disgust, rattling the flail he usually gripped against his chest.

"Could it be the Circle?" Ricardo Kliment, the solar deity with the head of a dung beetle, rose to his feet, mandibles twitching. "Great Osiris, could it be those sneaking people who are doing this to our network?"

"The Circle?" repeated Osiris, astonished. "What does that have to do with anything?"

"The true question," Wells said quietly, but so everyone at the table could hear, "is whether these problems are connected to the operating system—which, I would like to point out, is still the exclusive province of our chairman, and which none of the rest of us, even my own company, is allowed to work with directly."

"But these people from the Circle," the beetle pushed on, "they are our sworn enemies! They have wormed their way into the network—why could it not be them? They are antitechnologists, socialists and ideologues, opposed to everything we are trying to do!" He was almost yelping. Yacoubian knew that Kliment of all people had reason to agonize over the delays. The general's intelligence told him that the organ-market privateer was in a hospital in Paraguay, his body so riddled with a particularly virulent mutant cancer that transplants and chemotherapy were no longer holding it at bay.

"We are all of us powerful people," said Osiris, his tone making it clear that, as everyone already knew, Kliment was perhaps the least powerful of their number. "We do not need to pretend to care about ideologies. In fact, even if these people and their Circle organization carried certified proof they were Angels of the Lord, I would still sweep them from my path. No obstacle will keep me from the Grail.

"But the truth is, they are nothing. They are petty anarchists and God-botherers, the kind of trash you find howling on soapboxes in public parks, or handing out soiled leaflets in front of train stations. Yes, a few of them have crept into the network, but so what? Just a few days ago, I captured one sneaking across one of my domains. He is being made to talk, I promise you. But he has said nothing that gives me even a moment's worry—he and the other scum do not even know exactly what the Grail Project is. Now, dear Khepera, please stop wasting my time."

Kliment sat down heavily. If a lacquer-shiny insect face could be said to wear the expression of a scolded child, his did. Everyone knew that the South American was one of Jongleur's most ardent supporters—what could the Old Man be thinking?

"You have not responded to me yet, Chairman," said yellow-faced Ptah. "At a time when many in the Brotherhood are nervous about their investment, about the delays, can't you relax your rules a little? I know I for one would feel a lot better if I could actually work with the operating system that maintains our whole network."

"I am sure that you would. Yes, I am certain that you would love to have it in your control," said Osiris stiffly. He turned to the others, birds and beasts arrayed around the long table. "This man has already tried once to take control of the Brotherhood. Just a few weeks ago, you all saw the Americans make a false accusation against me—an accusation of something which proved to stem from an error in this man's own company, a frightening breach of security!" He pushed himself back from the table, shaking his huge, bemasked head, giving every impression of a noble monarch betrayed by the thankless minions of his own court. "And yet here it is again—my fault! Everything is my fault!" He turned on Wells. "You, and your unusually quiet friend," he darted a dead-eyed glance at Yacoubian, "have constantly questioned my devotion to the project—I, who conceived it and began it! You wish me to give up control of the operating system, and then trust you, Robert Wells, to respect my position as chairman? Ha!" He thumped a hand down on the table and several of the beast masks twitched. "You would be at my throat in a second, you treasonous cur!"

As Wells spluttered—rather convincingly, Yacoubian thought—Jiun Bhao in his guise of ibis-headed Thoth rose to his feet. "This is not civil." His calm tones did little to hide his distaste. "We do not speak in this way to each other. It is not civil."

The Old Man looked at him, a little wildly, and for a moment it seemed he might say something rude to the Chinese magnate as well, a flirtation with political suicide so breathtaking that even Yacoubian found himself staring, openmouthed. Instead, Osiris finally said: "Our god of wisdom has proved the aptness of my choice of persona for him. You are right, sir. I was uncivil." He turned toward Wells, whose yellow smile he must have found galling, but now he was all correctness. "As our associate points out, I have been rude, and for that I apologize. However, I would like to add that you, too, have been inconsiderate in your remarks, Ptah, when you suggest that I am hiding something from my colleagues."

Wells bowed, a shade mockingly. Yacoubian was suddenly unsure where things were going. The old bastard wasn't going to get away with it again, was he?

"Just a minute," Yacoubian said. "There are still questions to answer here. Bob says the problems in the system aren't all because of the size of it. He says it's the operating system. You say 'none of your business.' Then how do we get some goddamn answers?"

"Ah, Horus, monarch of the skies," said the Old Man, almost fondly. "You were silent so long, I feared we had lost you offline."

"Yeah, right. Just tell me how we can make sure this whole thing isn't going to come crashing down around our ears."

"This is becoming tiresome," Osiris began, then ram-headed Amon, the owner of six Swiss banks and an island "republic" off the coast of Australia, raised his hand.

"I would like to know more about this, too," he said. "My system tells me that there are regular breakdowns of the machinery in all my domains. We all have more than money invested here, and soon we will have *everything* invested in this project, including our lives. I believe we are due better information."

"See?" Yacoubian wanted the Old Man to squirm some more—there was no telling when he would be this vulnerable again. He turned to Wells to solicit his help. "I think we should have the whole thing out now. Start talking plain facts."

"Stop," said Osiris, his voice tight.

Wells, much to Yacoubian's astonishment, said, "Yes, I think you should leave it alone, Daniel."

If Sekhmet the lioness heard him, she did not seem to agree. "I demand to know what is wrong," she snarled, "and I demand to know how it is going to be fixed." The owner of Krittapong, a technology firm only slightly less powerful than Wells' Telemorphix, and a woman whose name was whispered in respectful horror throughout the secret slavery bureaus of Southeast Asia—she had beaten more than a few servants to death with her own hands—Dedobravo was not good at being patient. "I demand answers now!"

"I will personally assure . . ." Osiris began, but now it was Sobek again, his crocodile snout wagging.

"You cannot take our money and then tell us we have no rights!" he bellowed. "It is criminal!"

"Are you insane, Ambodulu?" Osiris was visibly trembling. "What are you babbling about?"

The entire gathering seemed about to plunge into screaming chaos when Jiun Bhao raised his hand. Gradually, the voices quieted.

"This is not the way to do business," Jiun said, slowly shaking his bird-head from side to side. "Most distressing. Not acceptable." He paused and looked around. The silence held. "Comrade Chairman, several of our membership have asked for more information about these . . . what was the word? . . . these 'spasms' in the system. Surely you do not object to such a reasonable request?"

"No." Osiris had calmed. "Of course not."

"Then perhaps by the time of our next meeting, you could promise them some kind of report? With all respect to your very busy schedule, it would be a useful antidote to some of the overly emotional responses we have seen today."

The Old Man hesitated for only a moment. "Certainly. That is eminently fair. I will have something prepared."

"Something *useful,*" said Yacoubian, and immediately wished he hadn't. The force of Jiun Bhao's irritated stare, even through a virtual interface, was unsettling.

"And," the god of wisdom continued, now speaking to Wells, "perhaps our American comrade could have something similar prepared, detailing what he knows of the problems from his end?"

"Certainly." The yellow smile was ever so slightly smaller than it had been.

"Excellent. Most kind." Jiun Bhao sketched a bow—more a nod of the head—to both parties, and then spread his arms. "We have had a tiring day, and we have discussed many important things. Perhaps it is time to say farewell until our next gathering."

Neither Osiris nor any of the others demurred.

Even as the Western Palace of the Old Man's Egypt winked out, Yacoubian heard Bob Wells' voice in his ear.

"A word with you, Daniel."

The moment of darkness was followed by a flare of light as a vast, sunny room built itself in an instant, a high-ceilinged dining hall with a view through the massive windows to what Yacoubian guessed was the rocky Pacific coast. Despite the room's dimensions, there was only one compact table. Wells sat on one side of it, his sim a replica of his actual body with detail that was just a tiny bit short of Grail-system perfection.

"Are you sure this is a good idea?" the general asked as he joined him. "Wouldn't you rather go somewhere in RL, like we did that other time?"

"Except for your line and my line, this is a dedicated machine, Daniel," said Wells. "And I'll wipe the code after we've finished. Here, let me open it up."

The windows dissolved, leaving nothing but air between the table and the sea below the cliffs. The roar rose until it filled the room. Without moving, Wells scaled it back until it was only a quiet pulse. The smell of the water and the ozone-tang were suitably convincing. "Better than a restaurant, don't you think?" the owner of Telemorphix asked. "Although if you'd like something to pretend with, a drink or something, let me know."

"I'll just smoke," said Yacoubian. "Since this is your place, I'm sure you can make sure the fumes don't blow in your direction." The general took out one of his Enaqueiros. He had spent rather a lot of money making sure the simulation performed properly; as he drew this one beneath his nose, savoring the aroma, he felt once again it had been money well spent. These techno-barons might be able to rebuild Babylon for you brick by brick, but try and get a decent virtual cigar. . . .

After the general had patted his pockets without result for a few moments, Wells raised an eyebrow, then moved his finger. A box of matches appeared in front of his companion.

"So why didn't you jump on the Old Man?" Yacoubian demanded

when he had got the cigar drawing nicely. "It's not like you, Bob. He was on the defensive—a few more shots and he would have lost it entirely."

Wells turned from his survey of the ocean. His eyes, with their strange, antiqued-looking whites, were mild, almost empty. He didn't speak for a long time. "I'm trying to think of a nice way to put this, Daniel," he said finally. "But I can't. You know, sometimes you are incredibly stupid."

Yacoubian belched out pseudo-smoke, which imitated the real thing very well, rising above his head in a billowing blue-gray cloud. When he had caught his breath again, he gasped, "What kind of bullshit is that? You can't talk to me that way."

"Of course I can, Daniel. And, present irritation aside, I still think you're smart enough to listen to me and learn something." Wells fanned reflexively at the smoke, prim as a dowager. "Yes, if we had pushed the Old Man a bit farther, he probably would have said or done something that would have lost him the rest of the Brotherhood's good will. Which is why I did nothing, and why I tried to give you some useful advice about doing the same, Daniel, which you ignored."

"Listen, Bob, I don't care how rich or how old you are. People don't talk to me that way."

"Maybe they should, Daniel. It can't have escaped your notice how Jiun Bhao took control of the meeting there at the end. And what, thanks to you and that Dedoblanco bitch pushing too hard, is the result? We're going to have to match reports on these system problems at the next meeting."

"So?" Yacoubian had the cigar burning fiercely now, jutting erect in his line of sight, obliterating Wells' face in a red glow with each inhalation.

"So, who do you think is going to judge whether either answer is acceptable? Gracefully, quietly, that Chinese bastard is going to make himself the unelected chairman, and he'll show the rest of the group how to vote. If he hands the reins back to the Old Man, Jongleur will owe him. If he hands them to us, and pushes Jongleur onto the sideline, we're in a *de facto* coalition with Jiun—but only so long as he finds us useful."

Yacoubian knew he was sulking, but was reluctant to give it up for something more useful. "I thought you wanted the Old Man out."

"No, Daniel, I wanted me in. There's a difference. And don't forget, Jongleur's still holding a few cards of his own, like that goddamned operating system which no one else ever gets to touch—if we blunder into some three-way struggle with him and Jiun, it's going to be very bloody. And I doubt we'll win."

"Jesus." Yacoubian sat back, still angry but now depressed, too. "You people."

"What does that mean, 'you people'? You were the one who came to me in the first place about edging the Old Man out. 'We don't need him any more, Bob. He's unstable. Foreign.' Have you forgotten already?"

"Enough, already." Yacoubian acknowledged defeat with a wave of his hand. One thing he had learned in his career was that when the situation became untenable, it was a waste of time to dick around trying to save face. "So what do we do?"

"I don't know." Wells sat forward. The noise of the sea dropped another notch, although beyond the windows it was still active as ever, throwing itself against the rocks like a jilted lover. "The fact is, Daniel, I'm worried. These spasms really are a problem. None of my people can make sense of them at all, but even our cloudiest projections don't look good. And there are other things happening, too, as you know—some very bad results on the client nodes, the lease-properties and whatnot. That Kunohara fiasco."

"Tell me about it. But I figured it was just because of the system going online—you know, a one-shot thing. You're saying it's bad trouble, huh? Do you think it could be related to that guy who got away into the system, the Old Man's prisoner? Is he some kind of saboteur?"

Wells shook his head. "I can't imagine how even an expert could hack the system from inside—not as far inside as he is, anyway. And it strikes me as something much larger than that. It's a chaotic perturbation. Don't give me that look, Daniel, I know you're not stupid. When a complicated system starts to go wrong, it can start small, but if it keeps on . . ."

"Jesus." Yacoubian had the sudden urge to hit something. "You mean, all this political shit aside, the whole thing might really go south on us? After all these years of work, all this money?"

Wells frowned. "I don't believe it will actually collapse, Daniel. But we're in *terra incognita* here, almost literally." He put his bony hands on the table and looked at them, examining the tight-stretched skin as though he had never seen it before. "There are some very strange things happening. Speaking of the Old Man's prisoner, you remember that tracking agent that we sent out looking for him—the Nemesis device?"

"Please don't tell me it blew up or something."

"No, no, nothing like that. It's still out there, still pursuing its task. But . . . and I don't quite know how to express this . . . it's not all there."

"Huh?" Yacoubian looked for somewhere to put out his cigar, but Wells was distracted and no ashtray appeared. The general balanced it on the edge of the table. "I'm not following you."

"I'm not sure what's going on myself. The whole Jericho Team is combing the data, but one thing's clear—Nemesis is working far under capacity. Like part of it had been coopted for other tasks. But we can't tell why, or how, or even what exactly is going on."

"It's just a piece of gear. Can't you send another one?"

Wells shook his head. "Complicated. For one thing, we'd like to study this one without confusing the issue. Maybe it will help us figure out what's causing the system spasms—just figuring out what the system spasms actually *are* would be a step forward. Also, because of the way the Nemesis code looks for patterns . . . well, it would be like having so many undercover cops on the same investigation that they started arresting each other."

Yacoubian pushed his chair back from the table, dislodging the cigar which tumbled off the edge; it vanished before it hit the ground. "Jesus H. Christ, I hope you're happy, Wells. You've ruined my day. I think I'm going to go home and shoot myself."

"Don't do that, Daniel. But I do hope you'll check with me before you do anything too drastic at the next meeting. Things are going to be delicate for a while."

The general glowered, but that battle had already been lost. "Yeah, whatever." He patted his pocket again, then remembered. "By the way, Bob, could you give me a gate out of here?"

"Something wrong with your system, Daniel?"

"Yeah. My team's messing around with it. Just a minor problem."

"Certainly. Are you ready to go?"

"I guess so. One other thing—just curious, you understand. Have you . . . has anything turned up missing from your system?"

"Missing?" Wells' pale eyes narrowed.

"You know. Small things. Bits of gear, things like that. Virtual objects."

"I don't think I understand, Daniel. Do you mean there are virtual objects missing from your own system? You . . . mislaid something?"

Yacoubian hesitated for a moment. "Yeah. Just my lighter. Must have left it in one of the domains. I guess that if the simulation's complex enough you can lose something just like you can in RL, right?"

Wells nodded. "I suppose. So you haven't lost anything important, then? Whatever it is, you can just duplicate it."

"Of course! Yeah, it was just a lighter. I'll take the gate now, Bob."

"Thank you for hearing me out. I hope I wasn't too rude."

"Tact isn't your strong suit, Bob, but I think I'll live."

"That's nice to hear, Daniel. Good-bye."

The dining room, the open windows, and the unceasing toil of the Pacific Ocean all vanished in an instant.

CHAPTER 24

The Most Beautiful Street in the World

NETFEED/SITCOM-LIVE: Travels With Invisible Dog "Sprootie"!
(visual: Wengweng Cho's living room)
CHO: Oh, no! Someone has ruined my report for the district governor! It is torn to pieces! But this room has been locked all day!
SHUO: (whispers) Sprootie! You are a bad dog! I should cut off your little invisible stones!
(audio over: laughter)
CHO: I will be executed for this! My family will not even receive my death insurance. Oh, this is terrible!
SHUO: I will think of something to help you, Respected Cho. (whispers) But clever Sprootie will surely make things difficult all over again!
(audio over: laughter and applause)

THE blue neon haze faded. The sparks flickered and died. Flat on his back beneath a starless night sky, Paul tried to make sense of it all—Nandi's revelations, the sudden attack, the escape from the Khan's warriors, the whole incomprehensible mess. And now the River had taken him up once more, carried him yet again from one reality to another, from Xanadu to. . . ?

From where he lay, stretched full-length in the bottom of the boat, he could see only the fat, full white moon, reassuringly ordinary—as if that meant anything. What miserable new place would this turn out to be? An Amazon River full of crocodiles? The siege of Khartoum? Or something even stranger, something he could not guess at, the spawn of a rich old devil's fever dream? An overwhelming sense of homesickness spread through him.

And it's Felix Jongleur who's done this to me.

The name, the last thing Nandi had told him, rang strangely in his mind. He had heard it before, he felt sure—perhaps some mention had been made by the man calling himself Professor Bagwalter on that *Boy's Own* version of Mars. But there was more to it, somehow, a resonance that went deeper and brought with it strangely disassociated images—a cauldron, a window, a room full of birds. The images were as fleeting as they were vague; when he tried to hold them, to form them into something that made sense, they fell apart, leaving only a dull pain not much different than the homesickness.

Jongleur. It was something, though—a name to work with, both inside his own head, and outside, in these strung-together worlds. A tool, perhaps even a compass. Something he could use to begin to find his way.

But this new simulation isn't one of Jongleur's. That's what Nandi said.

The thought gave him the strength to draw himself up, elbows on the gunwale, and look around. The air was cool on his cheeks, the night brisk but not uncomfortable. He seemed to be warmly dressed (the Arabian Nights garb had apparently been left in the Xanadu simulation) but he was far more interested in what lay before him: for some reason it was hard to see clearly, but there was definitely a scatter of lights along the bank—a modest profusion, but enough.

At least I'm not lost in the wilderness, he told himself, *in the middle of nowhere. . . .* Even if he were to pass through the most cheerful, populous virtual city imaginable, however, "nowhere" was still exactly where he would be. In an electronic illusion. Up to the eyeballs in code. Nevertheless, the idea of tasting the more civilized side of virtuality had its appeal. After the Ice Age and the Martian invasion, he was tired of sleeping rough.

The lights seemed to be getting farther away; Paul realized he was drifting. As he felt for the paddle, his boat floated out of the fog bank he had not even known was there, and the city lights abruptly blazed up before him like God's own chandelier.

It was one of the most beautiful sights he had ever seen.

As he stared in amazement, the paddle dangling uselessly above the water, dark shapes began to move past him through the thinning fog, shadows drawn across the array of lights like the track of a brush dipped in ink. As the first boat slid by, too distant for him to make out details before it vanished, he thought he heard a murmur of laughter across the water. Within seconds, half a dozen more had appeared, as if formed directly from the mist. Lanterns swung on their curving prows, and even after the shadowy craft had slipped past him and returned to the fog, he could still see their swaying lamps, like fireflies.

A smaller boat with no lights at all suddenly knifed across his bow, so close Paul could almost have reached out his paddle and touched the shiny black hull. He had a glimpse of monstrous and distorted faces at the rail, and for a moment his heart plummeted: It seemed he had been dropped onto the waterways of another alien planet, Mars again, or worse. Someone shouted at him in what sounded like drunken surprise, then the black boat was absorbed into the mist, speeding toward the city lights. It was only when it had vanished completely, and he was alone with the fog in his gently rocking boat, that he realized that they had all been wearing masks.

The lights were closer now, looming above him like a mountain range made entirely of jewels, but these gems were beginning to change into things more prosaic but no less delightful—torches, streetlamps, windows lit from behind, all smiling at him through the darkness. There were lights on the far side of the water too, just as bright despite the distance, and just as cheerful. The pleasure craft entirely surrounded him now, full of masked revelers, voices raised as they laughed or called to nearby boats. Music floated on the night air, plucked strings and voices, skirling flutes, not always in tune. He believed there was something distinctly old-fashioned in the snatches of sound he heard, but concentration was difficult when one was floating through a dream.

A much larger boat, a barge covered with canopies and lit by dozens of hanging lanterns, floated before him now, tied to a vast dock along the bank. He heard a snatch of raucous singing, and paddled close enough to it that he could see a trio of figures in white masks standing along the railing.

"I'm lost," he shouted up to them. "Where am I?"

The revelers took some moments to locate the source of the voice, down in the darkness beside the barge's hull. "Near the arsenal," one of them finally called back.

"Arsenal?" For a moment Paul thought he had been flung into yet another warped version of London.

"Of course, the arsenal. Are you a Turk?" another asked. "A spy?" He turned and said, "He's a Turk," to the third, silent mask.

Paul thought the man was joking, but he wasn't certain. "I'm not a Turk. Near the arsenal *where?* Like I said, I'm lost."

"If you're looking for the Dalmatian Bank, you're almost there." As he spoke, something fell from the first man's hand and splashed into the water near Paul's boat. "Whoops," he said. "Dropped the bottle."

"Idiot," said the second. "Hey, there. Be a good Turk and toss it back to us, will you?"

"Is it really a Turk?" the third mask asked suddenly. He sounded even more drunk than the first two.

"No," Paul said forcefully, since they didn't seem to like Turks, then decided to gamble. "I'm an Englishman."

"English!" The first laughed. "But you speak like a real Venetian. I thought English couldn't speak anything but that log-sawing tongue of theirs."

"You said the promenade is just ahead?" he called as he pushed himself back from the vast hull. His thoughts were fizzing. "Thank you for your kindness."

"Hey, English!" one of them shouted as Paul paddled away. "Where's our bottle?"

The Dalmatian Bank was a great quay thronged with hundreds of boats of all sizes, moored so closely together that their sides scraped. This night, at least, the bankside was blindingly ablaze with torches and lanterns; the tall, many-arched facades of the buildings seemed lit for some extravagant film premiere. Paul tied his small boat to a mooring post at the shadowy end of one of the piers. It was a poor thing in comparison to the boats bumping against the dock all around it. He doubted anyone would bother to steal it.

So it's Venice, he thought as he made his way through the jostling crowds, a fabulous array of masks and swirling robes in full drunken celebration. He was pleased. His art historian background would actually be of some use. *Can't tell when exactly, especially with everyone in costume, but it looks Renaissance-ish,* he decided. *La Serenissima, didn't they call it?—the Most Serene Republic.*

He was himself dressed in dark hose and something he dimly remembered was called a doublet—neither of best quality, but not embarrassingly ragged either. Across his shoulders lay a cape heavy as an overcoat, whose hem swept just above the muddy ground. A slender, scabbarded sword with a fairly simple basket-hilt rattled by his side, which should have completed the ensemble, but something was bumping at the back of his neck as well. When he tugged the object around so he could see it properly, he found it was a mask, an expressionless face with a cool finish like porcelain, its chief feature a huge beak of a nose. He stared at it for a moment, wondering if he should recognize the character it portrayed, then—remembering that he seemed to have more than a few enemies in this still-strange virtual life of his—he pulled it over his own features and retied it at the back of his head. He immediately felt less conspicuous, and moved forward with no immediate plan except to be part of the crowd for at least a little while.

A woman in a dress whose bodice revealed most of her breasts stumbled and snatched at his arm for support; he held her steady until she had her feet beneath her. She, too, wore a mask, a face of exaggerated maidenhood with pink cheeks and red, full lips. Her male consort tugged her away roughly, but as she turned she brushed her front against Paul's and gave him a wink through the eyehole of her mask, a feathery, slow-motion bat of the lashes, as subtle as a falling piano. Despite the smell of slightly sour wine that lingered after her, he found himself suddenly aroused, a reflex that terror and confusion had for a long time almost completely subsumed.

But what is she? he thought suddenly. *A Puppet, chances are good. And what would that be like?*

He had seen an inflatable sex doll once, part of a twentieth century cultural exhibit at the Victoria and Albert Museum. He and Niles and the others had laughed at the crudeness of the thing, at the sad emptiness of putting it to its intended purpose, of being face-to-face with that astonished stare and lamprey mouth. But how would making love to an imaginary Venetian party girl be any different, really?

"Look here, Signor, hey, look here." He glanced down to see a small, unmasked boy tugging at his cloak. "You looking for women? I can take you to a nice house, a beautiful house, only the finest flesh. Cypriots? Or maybe you like yellow-hairs from the Danube, huh?" The boy, despite being no more than seven or eight and very dirty around the edges, had the hard professional smile of an estate agent. "Black girls? Arab boys?"

"No." Paul was about to ask the urchin where he could find a place to sit down and have a drink, but realized if he did he would be hiring a guide for the rest of the evening, whether he wanted one or not, and he didn't even know yet if he had any money in his pockets. "No," he repeated, a little louder this time, and dislodged the boy's hand from his cloak. "I don't want any. Be a good lad, go away."

The boy regarded him judiciously for a moment, then kicked him in the shins and slipped into the crowd. A moment later, Paul could hear his piping voice as he doorstepped another potential client.

Paul was solicited by several more small boys, of varying degrees of griminess and determination, by a few men, and by a dozen or so women, the oldest of whom, despite her bare shoulders and rouged cleavage, reminded Paul uncomfortably of his own Grammer Jonas. But rather than depressing him, the parade of those who would separate him from his ducats (he discovered he had a few, in a purse on his belt) merely added to the spectacle, part of the same show as the jugglers, fire-eaters and acrobats, the potion-peddling mountebanks, the musicians in grades from dismal to sublime (who nevertheless still muddled each other into a general din), the flags, the wavering lights, and the Venetian citizens themselves out for a good time, a never-ending swarm of masked figures in gowns of glittering, jewel-dotted brocade or multicolored velvets.

He had made his way down the length of the Dalmatian Bank—named, he vaguely remembered, for the ships from the Adriatic that docked there—and was just about to cross the famous *Ponte della Paglia,* the Straw Bridge, when he again felt someone plucking at his sleeve.

"Looking for a nice place, Signor?" asked a small dark figure who had just appeared at Paul's side. "Women?"

Paul scarcely looked at him—he had learned that it was a waste of time even to respond—but as a quartet of wine-addled soldiers stumbled down the bridge and Paul was pushed to one side, he felt something tugging at his purse. He turned and flung his hand down to his side, imprisoning the boy's wrist with his own arm. The would-be pickpocket struggled, but Paul caught at his other arm as well; having learned from his earlier lesson, he held the thrashing boy just out of shin-kicking range.

"Let me go!" His prisoner contorted, trying to bite his wrist. "I wasn't doing nothing!"

He dragged the boy out in front of him and gave him a good shaking; when he had finished, the criminal slumped in his grip, sullen but sniffling.

Paul was just about to let him go—with perhaps a boot up the arse for the sake of education—when something in the face caught his attention. A moment passed. More people jostled by, clambering up the arched back of the bridge.

"*Gally . . . ?*" Paul dragged the resisting boy into the glare of one of the street lanterns, The clothes were different, but the face was exactly the same. "Gally, is that you?"

The boy's returned glance combined fear and ferretlike calculation: his eyes darted back and forth as he looked for a distraction suitable to aid his escape. "Don't know who you're talking about. Let me go, Signor—please? My mother's sick."

"Gally, don't you recognize me?" Paul remembered his mask. As he pulled it off, the boy took advantage of the release of one wrist to make another attempt to bolt. Paul let the mask fall to the mud and caught the tail of the boy's shirt, then reeled him back like a game fish. "Goddamn it, hold still! It's me—Paul! Gally, don't you remember?"

For a moment, as his prisoner stared at him in terrified fury, Paul's heart turned heavy. It was a mistake. Or worse, as with the winged woman, it was only a phantom, a confusion, a deepening of the mystery. But then something in the child's expression changed.

"Who are you?" the boy asked slowly. "Do I know you?" His dreamy tone was that of a sleepwalker describing sights he alone could see.

"Paul. I'm Paul Jonas!" He realized he was almost shouting and darted a worried, shamefaced look around, but the swirling festival crowd seemed oblivious to the miniature drama at the base of the Straw Bridge. "I found you in the Eight Squared. You and the other Oysterhouse Boys—don't you remember?"

"I think . . . I have seen you. Somewhere." Gally squinted at him. "But I don't remember the things you say—well, maybe a little. And my name's not what you said." He pulled experimentally at Paul's prisoning grip, which still held him. "They call me 'Gypsy' here, because I'm from Corfu." This assertion was followed by another pause. "You said, 'Oysterhouse'. . . ?"

"Yes," said Paul, heartened by the boy's troubled, thoughtful expression. "You said you and the others had traveled across the Black Ocean. And you worked in that inn, what was it called, *The Red King's Dream?*" Paul felt suddenly vulnerable—too many names that might mean something to someone else as well, spoken in the midst of a crowd. "Look, take me to the place you mentioned—I don't care if it is a whorehouse. Somewhere we can talk. I'm not going to hurt you, Gally."

"It's Gypsy." But the boy did not run away, even when Paul released his hand. "Come on, then." He turned and trotted away from the bridge, scuttling through the crowds on the Dalmatian Bank like a rabbit through tall grass. Paul hurried to follow him.

They had traveled for some minutes away from the quayside, following the path of one of Venice's many rivers deeper into the Castello district, through narrow streets and narrower alleyways, some scarcely wider than Paul's shoulders, and across small stone bridges when the path dead-ended on one side of the water. The noise and lights of the Dalmatian Bank quickly fell away behind them; soon the boy was little more than a shadow, except when he passed through light pooled below windows or open doorways, and for a moment regained color and three solid dimensions.

"Is it Carnival, then?" Paul asked breathlessly at one point. Gally, or Gypsy, was sitting on the abutment of a delicate bridge, waiting for Paul to catch up; a stone lion's face peered from between his shins.

"Of course!" The boy cocked his head. "Where are you from, that you don't know that?"

"Not from around here. But neither are you, if you'd only remember."

The boy shook his head, but slowly, as though troubled. A moment later he brightened. "It's mad tonight. But you should have been here when the news came in about the Turks. That was a real ruckus! Made this look tame."

"About the Turks?" Paul was more interested in filling his lungs.

"Half a year ago. Don't you even know about that? There was a tremendous huge battle on the ocean, somewhere with a funny name—'Lepanto,' I think. The biggest sea battle that ever was! And we won it. I think the Spaniards and some others may have helped a bit. Captain-General Venier and the rest blew the Turkish navy to pieces. They say there were so many bodies in the water you could have walked from ship to ship without getting your feet wet." He went round-eyed at the wonder of it all. "They took the Turkish pasha's head off and stuck it on a pike, then the fleet came back into the Lagoon with the Mussulmen's flag and all their turbans trailing in the water behind them, and they were firing their cannons until everyone thought the whole city would fall into the water!" The urchin kicked his heels against the lion's stony chest, chortling with pleasure. "And there was the grandest festival you can imagine, with everyone singing and dancing. Even the cutpurses took the night off— but only that one night. The festival went on for weeks and weeks!"

Paul's amusement at the boy's bloodthirsty recitation suddenly soured. "Half a year ago? But you can't have been here more than a few days, Gally. Even if I've lost track of time, it couldn't be more than a couple of weeks. I was with you in the Looking Glass place—with the knights and the queens and Bishop Humphrey, remember? And then on Mars, with Brummond and the rest of them. Just a short while ago."

His guide jumped down from the stone lion. "I don't know what you're talking about, Signor. The names you say, I don't know, maybe." He began to walk again, more slowly this time. Paul followed.

"But we were friends, boy. Don't you remember that either?"

The small, shadowy figure broke into a trot, as though Paul's words flicked at him like a whip. Then he slowed and stopped.

"You'd better go away, Signor," he said as Paul approached. "Go on back."

"What do you mean? Why?"

"Because there aren't any women." He would not meet Paul's eye. "I was taking you to some men I know, down near the Rialto Bridge. Robbers. Bad men. But I don't want to any more. So you should go back."

Paul shook his head, surprised. "But you said you thought you remembered. About when we were together before."

"I don't want to know about it! Just go away."

Paul crouched and again took the child's wrist, but gently this time. "I'm not making this up. We were friends—still are friends, I hope. I don't care about any robbers."

The boy finally looked up. "I don't like those things you said. They . . . it's like a dream. Scares me." He mumbled this last. "How could you be my friend when I don't know you?"

Paul stood, still holding onto the boy's wrist. "I can't understand it all myself. But it's true, and when I lost you before, I felt terrible. Like . . . like I should have taken better care of you. So I'm not going to let it happen again." He released the boy's arm. It was true—he didn't understand much himself. If the boy was a Puppet, he should never have been able to leave his original simulation, but he had traveled with Paul from the Looking Glass World to Mars—and here he was in Venice. But if he was a real person, like Paul, a . . . what was the buzzword? If he was a Citizen, then he should know who he was. He hadn't forgotten everything during the transition to Mars, so why now? Like Paul, the boy seemed to have lost an entire piece of his past.

Another lost soul, he thought. *Another ghost in the machine.* The image sent a chill through him.

He considered explaining everything that he knew, but one look at the child's frightened face defeated the idea. It would be too much, and far too quickly. "I don't know the answers," he said out loud. "But I'm going to try to find out."

For the first time since their meeting by the bridge, Gally regained his street-urchin cockiness. "You? How are you going to find anything out? You didn't even know it was Carnival." He frowned and sucked his lip. "We could ask the lady in the church. She knows lots of things."

"What lady?" Paul wondered if he was going to be taken to pray to the Madonna. That would be a pretty logical fifteenth or sixteenth century Venetian solution to a problem.

"The Mistress," said Gally/Gypsy, then turned and started back in roughly the direction they had come.

"Who?"

The boy looked back. "Cardinal Zen's Mistress. Now come on."

To Paul's surprise, his guide led him all the way back to the *Ponte della Paglia* and then over it, toward the famous fretwork arches of the Doge's Palace and St. Mark's Square. The Carnival crowds were still thick along the waterfront and even thicker in the square itself.

Paul was surprised by how it all affected him: the Piazza San Marco was so familiar from the holidays he had spent here, including a week at the Biennale with a girlfriend just after university (when he had for the first time in his life thought that he, too, might actually get to have the kind of romantic adventures that others always seemed to be having) that now he found himself abruptly falling out of the illusion of Venice-as-it-was. It was almost impossible to look at the palace, the campanile, and the onion-shaped domes of St. Mark's—all the subjects of a thousand calendars and postcards, and which he had photographed exhaustively himself on his first visit—and not feel connected back to his own century, when Venice was a tourist haven, beloved but inconsequential, something more like a theme park than a once-imperial city.

The boy clearly had no such conflicts. Paul had to race to keep up with him as he glided through the revelers, and almost lost him when he zigzagged suddenly to avoid walking between the two great pillars at the entrance to the square.

The body of a hanged man dangling on a gibbet between the pillars—the recipient of a public execution, still serving as an edifying spectacle for the masses—helped to restore Paul's focus on this version of the Serene Republic. Even the bright lights of the waterfront could not illumine the man's face, which had gone swollen and black. Paul remembered his holiday tour, and how things like the Bridge of Sighs, a covered bridge high above the canal, where criminals were conveyed back and forth from the cells to the inquisitorial chambers, had seemed so quaint. *This* Venice was not quaint; it was real and rough. He decided it would be a good idea to remember that.

"Where are we going, Gally?" he asked when he had caught up.

"Don't call me that—I don't like it. My name's Gypsy." The boy screwed up his face, pondering. "This time of night, it shouldn't be too hard to get in." He trotted ahead, forcing Paul to furl his flapping cape and hurry after him again.

Armed guards with pikes and peaked helmets stood outside the main entrance to the Doge's Palace. Despite the freewheeling celebration all around them, Paul thought they looked very intent, not the least bit uninterested in their jobs. The boy sailed by them and into the shadows of the Basilica, then disappeared behind a pillar. When Paul walked past, a small hand snatched at him and pulled him into the darkness.

"This is the tricky part," the boy whispered. "Follow me close, and don't make any noise."

It was only as his small guide slunk away down the colonnade that Paul realized he was planning to break into St. Mark's Basilica, the most important religious building in Venice.

"Oh, Christ," he said quietly to himself, a helpless blasphemy.

In the end, it was not as bad as he feared. The boy led him to a staircase set below street level, at a corner of the church away from the piazza and the crowds. With a boost from Paul, Gally then clambered up the wall beside the stairs to a window, which he pried open; a few minutes later he was back at Paul's level, appearing like a magician's helper through a door under the stairs that Paul had not even noticed.

Despite his acute awareness of danger, Paul still retained enough of his tourist sensibility to be disappointed by the dark interior of the basilica. Gally led him on a long and roundabout but still hurried route through the tapestried nooks and crannies of the great church. There was enough candlelight to lend a small golden gleam to the mosaics on the floors and walls, but otherwise they might have been in a warehouse or hangar where a lot of dim, oddly-shaped objects were being stored.

At last they reached a particular archway hung with an arras. The boy signaled to him to be quiet, then poked his head through for a brisk reconnaissance. Satisfied, he signaled to Paul that it was safe.

The shadowy chapel was a good size, but after the vast, echoing spaces outside, it seemed quite intimate. The altar, which stood beneath a monumental statue of the Madonna, was almost completely covered in flowers and votive candles. In front of the altar another robed and hooded effigy, this one slightly smaller than lifesize, was silhouetted against the flickering candleglow.

"Hello, Signorina," the boy called softly. The smaller statue turned to look at them; Paul jumped.

"Gypsy!" The figure made its way down from the altar steps. When she stood before them and threw back her hood, the top of her head barely reached Paul's breastbone. She wore her white hair knotted close at the back of her neck, and her nose was as hooked and prominent as a bird's beak; as far as Paul could tell, she could have been anything from sixty to ninety years old. "What good wind?" she asked, which seemed to be a Venetian greeting which required no answer, for she immediately added, "Who is your friend, Gypsy?"

Paul introduced himself, using his first name only. The woman did not return the confidence, but smiled and said: "I have done my duty by the Cardinal for the day. Let us go and drink some wine—lots of water in yours, boy—and talk."

Paul remembered the nickname the boy had given her, and wondered what duties the Cardinal might have required of her. As if she guessed at his confusion, she explained as they stepped through a side door in the chapel and into a narrow corridor.

"I take care of Cardinal Zen's chapel, you see—his memorial chapel. It is not a thing a woman would normally be allowed to do, but I have . . . well, I have certain friends, important friends. But Gypsy and his cronies all enjoy the joke of calling me Cardinal Zen's Mistress."

"It is not a joke, Signorina," the boy said, puzzled. "That is what everyone calls you."

She smiled. A few moments and several turnings later, she opened a door off the corridor and ushered them into a private apartment. It was surprisingly large and comfortable, the walls draped with tapestries, the high ceiling intricately painted with religious imagery; embroidered cushions almost completely hid the low couches, and roses drooped in all the vases, loose petals just beginning to accumulate on the tabletops. Oil-burning lamps filled the room with soft yellow light. To Paul it seemed a surprisingly sumptuous, distinctly feminine retreat.

Something of his reaction must have shown in his face. Cardinal Zen's Mistress looked at him shrewdly, then disappeared into a side room and reappeared a few moments later with wine, a jug of water, and three goblets. She had removed her hooded robe, and now wore a simple, floor-length dress of dark green velvet.

"Is there something I can call you, Signorina?" Paul asked.

"Yes, I suppose repeated references to the late Cardinal will become tiring, won't they? 'Eleanora' will do." She poured wine for all of them, holding true to her promise to water the boy's severely. "Tell me your news, Gypsy," she said when she had finished. "Of all my young friends," she explained to Paul, "he is the most careful observer. I have not known him long, but already I rely on him for the best gossip."

Although the boy attempted to honor her request, after he had stumbled through a few stories about duels and surprise engagements, and rumors about the activities of a senator or two, Eleanora raised a hand to quiet him.

"You are distracted tonight. Tell me what is wrong, boy."

"He . . . he knows me." Gally gestured toward Paul. "But I don't remember him. Well, not really. And he talks about places I don't remember either."

She turned her bright, hard-eyed gaze on Paul. "Ah. Who are *you*, then? Why do you think you know him?"

"I knew him from somewhere else. Not Venice. But something is wrong with his memory." Her eyes made him a little uncomfortable. "I mean him no harm. We were friends before."

"Gypsy," she said without looking away from Paul, "go into the pantry and get another bottle of wine. I want the one with an 'S' painted on it—the letter that looks like a snake." She sketched it on air.

When the boy had slipped off into one of the apartment's other rooms, Eleanora sighed and sat back on the divan. "You are a Citizen of some kind, aren't you?"

Paul wasn't certain how she was using the term. "I might be."

"Please." She raised her hand. "No foolishness. You are a real person. A guest in the simulation."

"I'm not certain I'm a guest," he said slowly. "But I'm not just a piece of code, if that's what you mean."

"And neither am I." Her smile was hard and short. "Nor is the boy, if you come to it, but what else he is, I am not sure. Tell me why you have followed him. Be quick—I don't want him to hear this, and although the bottle I asked for is on the bottom of the stack, it will not take him forever to find it."

Paul considered the risks. He wanted to know more about the Cardinal's so-called Mistress, but he was in no position to bargain. She could be one of what Nandi had called the Grail Brotherhood— she might even be Jongleur himself in disguise for all he knew—but he had let himself be brought here and that could not be undone. If she was the master of this simulation, she could likely do what she wished with him, whether he opened to her or not. Ultimately, no matter how many ways he looked at it, everything came down to a gamble.

But I'm not drifting any more, he reminded himself.

"Very well," he said out loud. "I'm putting myself in your hands." He told her what he had told Nandi Paradivash, but in even more abbreviated form. He was interrupted once by Gally, covered in dust, wanting Eleanor to confirm that there really *was* a bottle with an *S* on it, and that she wouldn't settle for one of the other perfectly nice ones with blue dots or yellow *X*s instead. When the boy had grumbled back to his task, Paul told her of his encounter with Nandi; he didn't divulge the Shiva-worshiper's name, but told her everything the man had said about the Grail and the Circle.

". . . If I thought the boy was in no danger, I'd leave him alone," Paul finished. "I don't want to cause him any more misery. But there seem to be people after me—believe me, I have no idea why—and I think if they find him instead of me, they'll . . . they'll . . ."

"They'll hurt him until he tells them everything." Her mouth curled in disgust. "Of course they will. I know these people, or at least their type."

"So you believe me?"

"I believe that everything you say could be true. As to whether it *is,* I must consider. Where would you take the boy if he agreed to go with you?"

"Ithaca—or at least that's what the man from the Circle told me. That I would find the Wanderer's house there." Paul swirled the lees of wine in his cup. "And, how, if I may ask, do you fit into all this?"

Before she could answer, Gally reappeared, even more dusty than before, triumphantly bearing the snake-marked bottle.

"Let's go up to the dome," Eleanora suggested suddenly. "It's a bit of a climb, but a beautiful view."

"But I just brought you the wine!" Gally almost stuttered with indignation.

"Then we will take it with us and toast the *Stato da Mar,* my dear Gypsy. I'm sure your friend Paul will not mind carrying the bottle."

If there had been an inconspicuous way to drop a large bottle of wine down a stone stairwell, Paul would have happily let it go somewhere around the hundredth step. He was glad that he had at least left his sword belt behind and did not have to keep the long scabbard clear of the walls while struggling up the narrow stairs. Gally was bounding ahead, frisky as a mountain goat, and even Eleanora, who had to be twice Paul's age, seemed to find the climb comparatively easy. For Paul, it seemed like the cross-country runs at his childhood school—he was last and struggling, and no one bothered about him.

Right, well, it's her world, isn't it? he thought grimly, ducking beneath ever-lower arches that gave his two small companions no problems. *She's probably got some kind of antigravity effect or some other cheat built into her sim—if that's what these people call them.*

At the end of a vertical journey that seemed to take hours, Paul stumbled out onto a narrow walkway to find cold air on his face, the slope of the basilica's Ascension Dome curving outward beneath him, and all of Venice—at the moment it seemed like all of Creation— glittering at his feet.

"There isn't a walkway here on the real one," Eleanora whispered to him, then giggled as she patted the waist-high railing, a superannuated schoolgirl confessing a prank. "But it's worth the sacrifice of a tiny bit of authenticity, isn't it? Look at that!" She pointed at the boats tethered at their mooring posts along the front of the quay. "You can see why a French ambassador once called the Grand Canal 'the most beautiful street in the world.' And busy, too—the sea-empire of the Republic all begins here at San Marco. Where's that bottle?" She worked the lead seal off the neck and took a healthy swallow. "Ships going to Alexandria, Naxos, Modon, Constantinople, Cyprus, coming back from Aleppo, Damascus, and Crete. Holds full of things you can't even imagine—spices, silks, slaves, frankincense and Spanish oranges, furs, exotic animals, metalwork, porcelain, wine—wine!" She hoisted the bottle again. "A toast to the Most Serene Republic and her *Stato da Mar!*"

When she had finished, she passed it to Paul who echoed the toast, not quite sharing her enthusiasm but caught up a little despite himself. He even handed the bottle to Gally and let the boy have a short drink, most of which he coughed and sneezed back up when he got some in his nose.

"When the blind Doge Dandolo helped to carve up Byzantium," Eleanora said, "he took for Venice's share 'one quarter and half of one quarter of the Roman Empire.' You or I wouldn't be so stuffy in the way we put it, perhaps, but think about it! Three-eighths of the greatest empire the world has ever known, controlled by a tiny nation of merchants and seafarers."

"Sounds like Britain," Paul suggested.

"Ah, but this is *Venice.*" Eleanora was swaying just a bit. "We are not like Britain, not at all. We know how to dress, we know how to fall in love . . . and we know how to cook."

For the sake of amicable relations, Paul swallowed his few vestiges of national pride, chasing them with more wine. Eleanora fell silent as they passed the bottle back and forth, glorying in the view. Even as midnight neared, the lanterns of hundreds of boats still bobbed on the Grand Canal like embers drifting on a breeze. Beyond the canal the islands were each afire with their own Carnival lights, but past them lay only the dark sea.

As they were trooping back down the stairwell, Eleanora paused before one of the slit-windows which offered a view into the interior of the basilica.

"There are quite a few people down there," she said bemusedly. "Someone in the doge's family must be attending a mass."

Paul was immediately on guard. He pressed his eye against the narrow aperture, but could see nothing except a few shadowy blobs disappearing into one of the chapels. "Is that normal?"

"Oh, yes, quite. I just hadn't heard about it, but sometimes I don't."

After half a bottle or more of good Tuscan wine (and effects of same that seemed more than simply virtual), Paul now felt emboldened to ask, "What is your position here, exactly?"

"Later." She nodded toward Gally, several steps ahead of them. "When he is asleep."

They had only been back in her apartment for a few minutes before the boy, sitting on the floor with his back against the divan, began to nod. "Come, child," Eleanora said. "You will sleep here tonight. Go on back to the room there. Stretch out on the bed."

"On your bed?" Despite his fatigue, he was clearly uncomfortable with the idea. "Oh, no, Signorina. Not for a person like me."

She sighed. "Then you can make yourself a nest in the corner. Take some blankets from the chest." When he had stumbled off, she turned to Paul. "I wish I had coffee to offer you. Would you like some tea?"

"Information would suit me better. I've told you my story. Who are you? Are you going to turn me over to the people who built all this?"

"I scarcely know them." She folded her legs underneath her on the divan with impressive flexibility. "And from what I do know, I would not give even my worst enemy into their hands." She shook her head. "But you are right—it would be more fair if I tell you something of who I am.

"I am a Venetian, for one thing. That is more important than what century I was born. I would rather live in this Venice, even knowing it to be a beautiful sham, than any other city in the so-called real world. If I could have built this myself, with my own money, then I would have done it in an instant. But I had no money. My father was a scholar. I grew up in the Dorsoduro and waited tables for tourists, idiot tourists. Then I met an older man, and he became my lover. He was very, very rich."

After the pause had lasted a while, Paul decided that he was supposed to ask something. "What did he do?"

"Ah." Eleanora smiled. "He was a very high chieftain of the Camorra. A well-known Neapolitan criminal organization, as they call it on the newsnets. Drugs, charge, prostitution, slavery, that is what their business was and is. And Tinto was one of their leaders."

"He doesn't sound like a very nice person."

"Do not judge me!" she said sharply, then composed herself. "We make bargains. We all do. Mine was that I stayed ignorant as long as I could. Of course, after a while, you are in too deep to change things. When Tinto joined the Grail Brotherhood, and I saw what amazing things they could make, I had him build me this place. He did—it was nothing to him, with all his riches. For himself, he repopulated Pompeii and rebuilt much of the Roman empire, and also made himself some dreadful spies-and-speedboats holiday worlds as well. But what he really wanted was to live forever—to become Jupiter Ammon on a throne of brass, I suppose. He didn't mind making a little gift for me. He was paying a hundred times what this Venice cost to the Grail Brotherhood, helping them build their immortality machines. Crime, despite the old saying, pays very well."

"Immortality machines," Paul murmured. So Nandi had been right: these people wanted to become gods. The thought sickened him faintly, but it was exciting, too. Not to mention terrifying—what had he done, anyway, that people so powerful and so mad were searching for him?

"But that is the funny thing, do you see?" Eleanora went on. "He did everything he could to keep himself alive until the treatment was perfected—he was old when he first discovered the Brotherhood. He had organ after organ replaced, machinery added to keep his parts functioning, fluids from a dozen laboratories pumped through his veins, radiation therapy, engineered repair-cells, everything. He was desperate to survive until the machines worked and his investment would pay off. Then one of the other Camorra warlords bribed someone on Tinto's medical staff to introduce a special recombinant into his system—a handmade, delayed-action, killer virus. He died choking on his own blood. His body devoured itself. I had been his mistress for fifty years, but I can't say that I cried."

She rose and poured herself more wine. "So here I am, like a guest staying on in a flat whose owner has died. The bills are paid, although I do not know for how long. The Brotherhood received billions from my lover, but he can no longer use their service, so they are ahead of the game. As far as the Grail people are concerned, his relatives can squabble over the estate forever. God! His last wife, those children of his—they are like a nest of serpents."

Paul absorbed this information as Eleanora added a little water to her wine. "Do you know anything about a man named Jongleur—Felix Jongleur?" he asked. "He seems to have it in for me."

"Then you are in trouble, my friend. He is the most powerful of the lot, and a man who makes my Tinto look like a mere schoolyard bully. They say he is approaching two hundred years old."

"That's what the man from the Circle said, too." He closed his eyes, overcome for a moment by the impossibility of his predicament. "But I don't know why he's after me. And I can't get out of these simulations." He opened his eyes again. "You said that Gally—Gypsy—is a real person too, but you also said you weren't sure about him. What did you mean?"

The Cardinal's Mistress sucked on her lower lip, thinking. "It is hard to explain how I know he is a Citizen. I just do. After so many years spent living in a simulation, I can nearly always tell, I think. But although I had never seen Gypsy until recently, he has fully formed memories of being here."

Paul frowned, thinking. "Then how can you be sure that he *isn't* from here—that is, that he's not a Puppet you just hadn't encountered yet? Is there a list of Citizens and Puppets?"

"Oh, no," Eleanora laughed. "Nothing like that. But I was interested in him, so I have done some checking. You see, the Puppets here have evolved within this simulation. They are like real people in that way—they have parents and homes and ancestors. Midwives and priests know of their birth, even if everything is virtual. Some of what Gypsy says about his past makes sense—that is, it could be true. But other things do not hold up. At some level, he knows enough about my Venice to seem a part of it, but he has no real roots here." She finished her wine with a single swallow. "But whatever he is, he is a good boy. He is welcome in my home."

"If your . . . if your lover is dead, then you must be in charge here." A thought was beginning to form.

"No one is in charge. Is a gamekeeper in charge of a forest, just because he kills a deer, chases away a poacher? He does not make the trees grow. He does not teach the birds to nest."

Paul wagged his hand impatiently. "Yes, but you must have the ability to go online and offline, just for instance. Could you send me back to . . . to whatever system has put me on in the first place?"

She considered for a moment. "No. I could not send you back to your own system. But I could throw you out of the simulation. I have that power."

"Where would I go?"

"The entry level—the platform level, as I think Tinto's engineers called it. It is a sort of gray emptiness where you can choose different options."

Paul's heart was beating very fast. "Send me there. Please. Perhaps I could find my way out from there, or at least get some real answers."

Eleanora looked at him closely. "Very well. But I will go with you." She sat straighter on her divan and reached her hand up to the emerald pendant that dangled at her neck. When her fingers touched her throat, her body froze. Paul stared at the unmoving form as long seconds passed. Optimism slowly curdled into a sense of defeat.

When nearly a minute had gone by, Eleanora twitched back to life. "It does not work." She was clearly surprised. "You did not come with me."

"I noticed," he said mournfully. "But you went there yourself?"

"Of course." She sat forward. "We will ask Tinto. But first let me check on the boy." She stood and slipped through an arras into the back room, leaving Paul feeling more than a little stunned.

"What do you mean, ask Tinto?" he said when she returned. "I thought he was dead?"

"He is. Follow me." She led the floundering Paul out of the apartment and back down the dark hallway, raising a finger to her lips to signal for silence. A few voices murmured from the chapel on the far side of the basilica, not-quite-comprehensible snatches of speech floating through the vast, echoing room. Paul's sense of failure had deepened. A claustrophobic certainty that he would never escape began to rise, until he was fighting back real panic.

Eleanora's small, shadowy form led him back into the room in which he had first met her, Cardinal Zen's chapel. "He is a nasty old bastard, my Tinto," she said quietly. "That is one reason I don't want the boy wandering in."

Paul tried to push the fear aside long enough to concentrate. "Please explain."

Her smile was sardonic. "Tinto is dead. But in his last year, they were trying to prepare him to be able to live full time on the system. Don't ask me how—I wanted nothing to do with such ghoulishness. They made some kind of, I don't know, copy of him. But it was flawed. The equipment was not working correctly, or they did not finish the copy. Again, don't ask me, because I don't know. But it is accessible through his system. I only let it . . . manifest, I suppose . . . here." She gestured around her, indicating the chapel. "I could not bear to have it roam freely. You will see what I mean."

"It's . . . is it a person?"

"You will see." She moved forward, then pointed to the chairs facing the altar. "Sit there. It's better if he doesn't notice you."

Paul took a seat. He expected Eleanora to do something complicated—a chant of invocation, or even something a bit more modern, like pushing some hidden buttons—but instead she only mounted the steps before the altar and said, "Tinto, I want to talk to you."

Something flickered atop the altar, then a quiet voice murmured words Paul could not understand. The volume abruptly rose, but he could still make no sense of what was being said.

"Ah, I forgot." Eleanora turned toward Paul with a strangely unstable smile. "Everything here except Tinto is running through translation software. I imagine you are not a scholar of Neapolitan dialects, are you?" She moved her hand; a moment later comprehensible English was rasping out of the flickering light atop the altar.

"How long have I been on this table? God damn, I told you idiots I had work to do today. Get me off here or I'll tear your balls off."

"Tinto." Eleanora raised her hand again. "Tinto, can you hear me?"

The shimmer of light above the altar grew until Paul could see the head and shoulders of the dead man who had been Eleanora's lover. His heavy features sagged with age; his head wobbled. Beneath a nose that had obviously been broken several times was a thick, draggled mustache that, like his hair, had been dyed an unnatural black. The lower half of his virtual body was entirely hidden by the casket-shaped altar, so that he seemed a corpse that had sat up in the middle of its own funeral.

Tinto flickered a little, his resolution poor. Paul could see the candles through his chest. *"Eleanora? What are you doing here? Did Maccino call you?"*

"I just wanted to ask you some questions." Eleanora's slightly shaky voice suggested she was not as cold-blooded about the whole thing as she had led Paul to believe. "Can you answer some questions?"

"Where the hell am I?" The ghost, or whatever it was, brought up two gnarled fists to rub at its eyes. For a moment it distorted, narrowing until it almost disappeared, then sprang back into its original shape. *"My legs hurt. I feel like shit. These doctors—they're useless, eh? Did Maccino call you? I told him to send you some flowers, nice roses like you like. Did he call you?"*

"Yes, Tinto. I got the flowers." Eleanora looked away for a moment, then looked back at the altar. "Do you remember my Venice? The simulation you had built for me?"

"I ought to. Cost enough." He pulled at his mustache and looked around. *"Where am I? Something's . . . something's wrong with this room."*

"What should I do if I can't get offline, Tinto? What if it doesn't work, and I can't get offline?"

"Did those bastards screw it up?" He scowled, a toothless tiger. *"I'll have their balls. What do you mean, can't get offline?"*

"Just tell me. What can I do?"

"I don't understand." Suddenly, it seemed he might cry. His bony face wrinkled around the eyes and mouth, and he shook his head like someone trying to wake up. *"Goddamn it, my legs hurt. If you can't get out the normal way, Eleanora, you just walk out. Get to someone else's territory, use their gear. Take the canal—you can always get to the next place along the river. Either that, or . . . let me think, Venice . . . yeah, you go to the Crusaders or the Jews."*

"You can't think of another way to get offline? More direct?"

He stared, trying to focus. *"Eleanora? Did you get the flowers? I'm sorry I couldn't come see you, girl. They have me in this goddamned hospital."*

"Yes," she said slowly. "I got the flowers." She took a long, deep breath, then lifted her hand. "Goodnight, Tinto."

The image convulsed once, then vanished.

Eleanora turned to Paul, her jaw set, her mouth a thin line. "He always asks about the flowers. He must have been thinking about them when they made the copy."

"But you got them—the flowers."

"To tell you the ruth, I don't remember." She shrugged, then turned away as if she did not want Paul to look at her any more. "Let's go back. Sometimes he's more useful than others—he wasn't much help tonight, I'm afraid."

In the corridor, Eleanora stopped suddenly and drew Paul into the shadows at the back of the passage. Framed in the archway before them, on the far side of the basilica, a solemn-faced group of men was filing out of one of the chapels. They were dressed in heavy robes, and each wore what Paul guessed was some kind of chain of office around their necks.

"That's the Council of Ten!" Despite her almost inaudible whisper, she sounded very surprised. "I can't imagine what they're doing here in the church at this time of night." She took his arm and drew him along the passageway. A few silent steps and they had reached another archway, this one mostly hidden by a tapestry from the basilica floor. She peered around the hanging, then beckoned Paul. "Those are the leading senators of Venice—the ones who hold the Inquisitions," Eleanora whispered.

Paul watched with a mounting sense of unease as the group stopped in front of the chapel door, conversing in quiet tones. His earlier panic was returning, even stronger now. How could Eleanora not know about something happening in her own simulation? His stomach knotted and his skin went cold. He suddenly felt as though he should run as fast as he could, in any direction at all.

The last of the Ten emerged from the chapel, followed slowly by numbers Eleven and Twelve. This pair, unlike the others, were dressed simply in dark, hooded robes. One was very, very large. The other—although it was hard to tell for certain through the loose robe—seemed exceptionally thin.

The slender one said something and the nearest senators shook their heads, but it seemed more a frightened attempt to placate than true agreement.

"Oh God." Paul's knees were shaking. He gripped the railing to keep from falling. "Oh, God, they're here." The words were little more than a murmur—Eleanora beside him might not have heard—but to Paul in his terror they seemed to rattle and echo through the cavernous, high-shadowed room. His throbbing heart felt like a drum in his chest, announcing *Here I am!*

On the basilica floor, two hooded heads turned toward him in unison, scanning the darkness like hounds sniffing for the scent of their quarry. Now he saw that they both wore Carnival masks, stark white shapes that peered out from the shadowy hoods like skulls. The thin one was masked as Tragedy, while his fat companion sported the empty grinning face of Comedy.

His pulse pounded in his head so hard that Paul thought he might faint. He reached out a hand to the woman beside him, but felt nothing. The Cardinal's Mistress had gone, leaving him alone.

"Yes, we know you're there, Jonas," called the voice that had once belonged to Finch; the words drifted toward him like poison gas. *"Oh, yes. We can smell you, and we can hear you—and now we're going to eat you up."*

CHAPTER 25

Red Land, Black Land

NETFEED/ENTERTAINMENT: ANVAC Sues Griggs

(visual: Griggs House, gun turrets in foreground)

VO: Bell Nathan Griggs, creator of "Inner Spies" and "Captain Corpse" and other top-rated net programming, is being sued by ANVAC, the world's largest security corporation. ANVAC charges that Griggs violated the security agreement by opening his Isla Irvine home to the "Cot n' Cave" net program, thus exposing ANVAC security equipment and procedures.

(visual: ANVAC corporate headquarters—featureless wall)

ANVAC would make no comment on the lawsuit, but Griggs has gone into hiding, although he has made a statement to the media.

(visual: Griggs as anonymous human figure)

Griggs: ". . . Damn right I'm scared. These people are going to make sure I have some kind of accident. I thought it was my own house—my home. Hah! Talk about naive."

THEY slept that night in a camp on the linoleum at the base of the counter. A space of greater darkness ended when the bulb high overhead began to glow again. The Kitchen, it seemed, existed only as a nighttime world. Now the bulb was alight again, and Night, which was the Kitchen's "day," had returned. Orlando and his companions rose.

He and Fredericks helped to load the Chief's canoe in depressed silence. The Indian hardly ever spoke; his child, even with burns on its head, was no less stoic. After a while, even the talkative tortoise sensed the mood of the group and gave up his attempts at conversation. Orlando was relieved. At the moment, conversation of any kind seemed like work. He was mourning, though he didn't know why.

It didn't really make sense at all. He and Fredericks had helped save the Indian's child in as neatly-constructed an adventure as any Thargor had ever had, albeit in a world that made Thargor's Middle Country look as sensible and normal as the most sedate RL suburb. He and his friend had journeyed into the depths of the freezer, and had gained what was undoubtedly an important, if cryptic, clue to the whereabouts of their companions. His game-world instincts had all proved correct. Why then did he feel like someone he knew had died, and that it was his fault?

Fredericks was morose, troubled by the same experiences, which was another reason not to waste strength on communication. But when they had boarded the canoe and Chief Strike Anywhere was vigorously paddling them out into the deeper, faster waters of the sink-overflow river, Orlando at last felt compelled to break the silence.

"Where are we going?"

"Downriver," the Indian said.

Orlando looked at Little Spark, strapped to his father's back. The infant, whose features were as cartoonish as its sire's, wore a blanket tied around its tiny red head which the chief had dipped in river water. Black scorch marks peeped out from the edges of the makeshift dressing, but the child showed no sign of discomfort, staring back at Orlando with unnervingly serious black eyes. "Downriver?" Orlando asked. "Is there something else we still have to do?"

"Take you to end of river," the chief explained. "You no belong here."

He said it so matter-of-factly, and it was so manifestly true, that Orlando was surprised to realize that it stung a little. As shattering as their experience in the freezer had been, he felt like he was happier in the world of the Kitchen, or in any of the virtual worlds they had visited, than he had ever been in RL.

"I am not in a hurry, you see," the tortoise offered. "The chief has promised to drop me off on his way back to the river's source. I am not sorry to spend a little more time with you folks. Pirates, kidnapping, a great battle—we have had quite an adventure together, after all!"

"Adventure. . . ?" Orlando couldn't begin to explain why what the tortoise was saying seemed like such a devastating understatement, nor did he want to try. Beside him, Fredericks was staring forlornly out at the passing riverbank, at the cabinets like a row of tall bluffs. Orlando turned back to the tortoise and manufactured a smile. "Yeah, I guess we have, haven't we?"

By the end of the long, twilit day they had still not reached the end of the river.

The cabinets first gave way to the soapy, frothing swamps around the base of what Orlando guessed was an old-fashioned washing machine. From the center of the river they saw huts on stilts spread out through the swamp. Some of the denizens emerged onto their porches to watch the strangers pass, but although all of them seemed to be armed with spears—they were mock-African tribesmen, as far as Orlando could tell, actually bleach bottles with embarrassingly caricatured black features and brilliant white teeth—none of them did more than wave lazily at the canoe.

As the hours wore on, the swamps gave way to meadowlands, which seemed to be some kind of mat on the floor, grazed by scouring-pad sheep, each one a puff of pure, unsoiled white. There were a few scrubbing-brush giraffes as well, that stretched high up to polish the ceramic mugs hanging from the cup trees dotting the sisal plain.

Orlando's critical faculties had not been suspended, even if his enjoyment had taken a battering. He noted with admiration how the Kitchen idea had been stretched to cover a whole world, with ample space and plenty of things to experience, while still remaining fundamentally a kitchen. The sleight of hand concerning distances continued to intrigue him, too. He could still see the kitchen sink where they had entered the world, faint as a distant mountain in the half-light and ridiculously far away. If he and Fredericks and their companions were really an inch or so tall, as seemed true when he measured himself against the various objects and inhabitants . . . Orlando did some quick mental arithmetic and decided that by that standard, an entire Kitchen of normal proportions would only be perhaps a quarter of a mile from one side to the other. And yet they had paddled with the current for almost two full days, and hadn't reached the end of this one yet.

For the first time, Orlando wondered who owned the Kitchen—was it one of the Grail Brotherhood? Or were there other types of landlords in the network, ordinary rich people who rented space from the Brotherhood and then built their own worlds? It was hard to imagine the Kitchen's creator being one of the rich monsters that Sellars had described. The simworld seemed too . . . *whimsical,* if that was the right word. (It was one he'd seen many times, but he wasn't entirely positive what it meant.)

The bulb overhead was beginning to dim. The chief found a shallow backwater along the edge of the sisal fields and they all waded to shore. Strike Anywhere then made a fire, using the odd method (considering he was himself a kitchen match) of rubbing two sticks together. Or perhaps it was not such an odd method, Orlando reflected, thinking of the cruel way the infant Little Spark had been used by the pirates.

As they sat, watching the fire burn down from a roaring blaze to a flicker of orange flame, the tortoise recited the tale of Simkin Soapdish, a foolish young man who, because of his purity of heart, saved a bird (apparently the Icing Sugar Fairy in disguise) from a hunter. Because of the fairy's help, Simkin was later able to solve the deadly riddles of King Karpet and marry the monarch's daughter, Princess Potholder. (Orlando was fairly certain those were the names, but he was still depressed, and tired now, too, and thus finding it hard to keep his attention focused.) It was apparently a familiar Kitchen folktale: all seemed to end happily, with evil thwarted and virtue triumphant, although some of the details seemed inexplicably strange, like the frightening Voice of the Disposal, an all-devouring monster in the sink which recited the king's riddles. As he was sliding into sleep, Orlando wondered idly if this was a story that had been programmed in by the Kitchen's designers, or whether the Puppets had invented it themselves.

But Puppets can't invent anything, can they? At least, Orlando didn't think that was possible. Surely only things that were alive could make up stories. . . .

A cool breeze was sweeping off the river and across the Kitchen, and the brisk touch of it on his face woke Orlando. Fredericks was sitting up, staring at the fire, which had burned down to a pile of coals that rippled with tiny, dying flames. Someone—Orlando at first thought it was his friend—was whispering.

". . . You're going to die here . . ."

He sat up. A face moved in the embers—the cartoon devil they had seen before in the potbellied stove. As it leered and winked, Fredericks watched it with a solemnity that made Orlando nervous.

"You should never have come to this place," the demon declared, chuckling unwholesomely. *"It will be the end of you. . . ."*

"Fredericks?" Orlando moved forward and shook his friend by the shoulder. "Are you all right?"

"Orlando?" Fredericks shook his head as though he had been napping. "Yeah, everything's chizz, I guess."

"You shouldn't be listening to that *fen.*" Orlando poked angrily at the coals with a stick. The image deformed for a moment, then popped back into shape and laughed at him.

"That?" Fredericks shrugged. "Problem not. It's like watching some old flick—it just goes on and on, saying the same things. I wasn't even paying attention."

The devil, as though it had heard and understood this, scowled fiercely and dissolved back into the flames with a bold hissing laugh that nevertheless sounded slightly disappointed. For some moments, the only noise was the crackle of the exorcised campfire.

"That thing in the freezer," Fredericks said at last. "After the Sleeping Beauty. That . . . other thing. It was real, wasn't it?"

Orlando did not have to ask what his friend was talking about. "Yeah. I guess so. I don't know what it was, exactly . . ."

"But it was real." Fredericks rubbed his eyes. "It's . . . it's too far scanny, Orlando. How did we get into this? What's going on? That thing—that was the *real* devil, I think. Like, locking medieval. The actual factual."

"I don't know." Orlando felt it again, but at a distance now. Something so bizarre, so total, could only be summoned up in memory as a dim copy. "It felt like it was everywhere. More like God."

"But, see, I never understood before." Fredericks turned, his thin Pithlit-face almost sick with distraction. "I mean, even when I found out we were stuck here . . . even when I went offline, and it . . . *burned* like that . . ." Fredericks searched for the words. "I didn't think there was anything like that thing, not anywhere, not in RL or VR or anywhere. That was *evil.* Like something from the Middle Country, but for real!"

The experience had felt more complicated than that to him, but Orlando didn't want to argue. He knew what Fredericks was talking about—a part of him, too, had continued to think of this all as some game. Now he knew to the very marrow of his bones that something existed that was more frightening than he could have ever imagined—that the fear it created was worse even than his terror of death.

"Yeah. It was . . ." There weren't really words. "It was the most major thing ever," he said finally. "I thought my heart was going to explode."

Silence fell again, except for the fire noises and the tortoise's pennywhistle snores.

"I don't think we're going to get out of this, Orlando. Something's gone utterly major wrong. I want to go home—I really, really do."

Orlando looked at his friend, doing his or her best not to cry, and suddenly, unexpectedly, felt something open up inside him. It was as though a door, long shut, its hinges gone rusty with disuse, had suddenly been kicked wide. What lay on the other side wasn't a bright spring day, but it wasn't darkness either. It was just . . . something else. The door had opened inside him—in his heart, he supposed—and beyond that door the rest of his life, however long or short, was waiting.

It was all quite stunning, and for an extended moment he thought he might faint, or fall over. When he was himself again, he felt compelled to say: "I'll get you out of this somehow. I swear, Sam—do you hear me? I promise that I'll get you home."

Fredericks turned, head cocked to one side, and surveyed him. "Is that some kind of boy-girl thing, Gardiner?"

Orlando laughed, although it hurt a little, too. "No," he said, and it was the truth, as far as he could tell. "I don't think so. It's a friend thing."

They lay back down to sleep, side by side. By the sound of his breath, Fredericks seemed to fall away quickly, but Orlando lay for a long time looking up into the dark recesses of the Kitchen's ceiling, wishing there were stars.

They had only been on the river for an hour again when Strike Anywhere nosed the canoe toward shore. He clambered out with his papoose in his arms, and waved for the tortoise to follow him, but when Orlando and Fredericks began to do the same, he shook his head.

"No. You take canoe." He pointed downstream. "End of river that way. Very close."

"But what will you do?" Orlando looked from the Indian to the deceptively placid river, narrow here and meandering through a grove of bottle brushes. "Your home . . . your wife . . ."

The chief shook his head again. "I make new canoe to go back. You take this one. Gift from me, squaw, and papoose."

Fredericks and Orlando thanked their benefactor. They changed positions, and Orlando took up the paddle. The tortoise, in an excess of emotion, had steamed his spectacles and was trying to rub them clear with his thumbs. Ultimately, Orlando decided, you had to treat them all as people, whether they were or not.

"Good-bye," he said. "It was nice to know you."

"Be careful, lads." The tortoise was sniffing a bit. "If you get into difficulty, remember Simkin Soapdish, and do what's right."

"Do right for your people, your tribe," Strike Anywhere elaborated. He held up Little Spark; the baby, as ever, looked serious. "Be brave," the chief added.

Orlando worked the boat out into the current and they began to drift downstream. "Thank you!" he shouted.

The tortoise had found its handkerchief and was trying to wave it and use it to wipe its glasses at the same time. "I will pray to the Shoppers for your safety," he called, then was overcome by another wave of snuffling sobs. The Chief, no emotion visible on his broad red face, watched them until a bend of the river and a stand of bristling bottle brushes blocked their view.

Fredericks seemed content to watch the spiky forest drift past. Orlando paddled lazily, letting the river do most of the work. He was trying to make sense out of all the different things in his head, and it wasn't easy. Oddly, the chief's words were stuck in his mind.

"Do right for your people, your tribe." That was all well and good if you were a cartoon Indian, but what the hell was Orlando's tribe? Americans? Kids with weird medical problems? Was it his family, Conrad and Vivien, who were now so inexplicably far beyond his reach? Or his few friends, one of whom was stuck in this scan factory with him? He had no idea what the Indian's words meant, if they meant anything, but somehow the exhortation seemed to resonate with the strange feeling of a new life begun that he had experienced the night before, although he could not yet understand why.

He shook his head in frustration and began to paddle a little harder.

They came upon it at the end of the forest—a wall that rose before them, high as the sky, a vast vertical field of slightly faded flowers. The wallpaper was peeling in places, and in the middle, skyscraper-high above their heads, hung a framed picture of people in straw hats boating on a river, the colors dim in the twilight. The river itself narrowed into a thin stream along the linoleum and vanished into a hole in the baseboard.

"What's on the other side, you think?" Fredericks asked loudly. The hole in the baseboard was closer every moment, looming now like a highway tunnel. The wall itself had begun to shimmer, as though a heat haze were rising from the Kitchen river's surface.

"Don't know!" Orlando found he was shouting, too. The canoe was moving faster now, the water noises growing more clamorous by the instant, rapidly becoming a roar in his ears. "But we're going to find out!"

The current snatched at them and yanked them forward, sweeping them into the opening. The sudden darkness began to spark gas-ring blue.

"We're going too fast!" Fredericks called. Orlando, who had put down the paddle and was clutching the sides of the canoe for dear life, did not need to be told. The bursts of blue light whirled past like tracer fire out of an air warfare game. Daylight vanished, leaving only blackness spattered but not illuminated by the angry sparks. Then the nose of the canoe tipped downward, and blue fire streamed past them in a continuous, boiling cloud as they began to drop. Orlando struggled for breath.

The splash was nowhere near as large as he expected. At the last moment, something seemed to ease their fall and slide them safely onto the river, which was horizontal again. The sparks were fading, and now they could see an irregular opening through which streamed bright, red-golden light. Orlando squinted against the glare, trying to make out what lay before them.

Fredericks, looking back the way they had come, went goggle-eyed. "Orlando!" he cried. His voice was almost inaudible—the rush and tumble of the river had taken on an additional sound, a chorus of chanting voices that boomed and echoed, the words incomprehensible in the tumult. "Orlando!" shouted Fredericks, "Look!"

He turned and looked over his shoulder. Fading rapidly into the darkness of the massive cavern behind them, but unmistakable, was a gigantic figure a hundred times their size. It glowed with a blue light of its own, but the river pouring out of the jar it held sparkled even brighter. The giant had the rounded breasts and hips of a woman, but wore a stiff beard on its chin, and was muscled like a man. Above the great head nodded a crown of lotus flowers. For a moment the giant seemed to see them, and the huge, black-painted eyes blinked once, but then they were swept out of the cavern into the sunlight, and there was nothing visible behind them but the red stone of a mountain and the crevice out of which the river flowed into the hazy morning.

Orlando turned to face downriver. His pilfered pirate clothes had vanished. Their boat had changed too, becoming something wider and flatter, and their paddle was now a crude bargepole, but he barely noticed. Before them, the river threaded away through an immensity of desert. Except for mountains faint and gray-blue in the distance on either side, only a few lonely palm trees shimmering in the heat broke the plane of the horizon. The morning sun, still low, was already a blazing white disk that dominated the wide, cloudless sky.

Sweat was already beginning to bead on the Thargor sim's dark skin. Fredericks turned to him, the look on the thief's face one that clearly presaged another statement of the incredibly obvious.

"If you tell me it's a desert," Orlando warned him, "I'm going to have to kill you."

"Priam's walls," Orlando said, breaking a long silence. "That Sleeping Beauty said we'd find Renie and the others at 'sunset on Priam's walls.' Whatever that means."

"It's weird major not to be able to look something up on the net." Fredericks leaned over the boat's low side to trail fingers in the slow-moving water. "Not being able to get any information."

"Yeah. I miss Beezle."

They had been drifting for the better part of a day. The great red desert had remained changeless on either side, and only the occasional palm tree sliding past on the riverbank demonstrated that they were moving downstream. The long steering pole was useful when they occasionally drifted into the shallows and lodged on an invisible spit of sand, but was no use whatsoever when it came to increasing their speed. They had discovered what appeared to be a sail and two sections of a mast lying rolled in the boat's flat bottom beneath their feet, but they were using the sailcloth as a makeshift shelter against the blazing sun, and were not in any hurry to give up its shade for the dubious benefit of sailpower, since the day was as windless as it was stiflingly hot.

"So what is it with you and that bug, anyway?" Fredericks asked lazily. "How come you don't have one of the newer agents?"

"I don't know. We get along." Orlando frowned. "It's not like I have so many other friends or anything."

Fredericks looked up quickly. "Sorry."

"Problem not. How about you?"

"How about me what?" The tone was slightly suspicious.

"Do you use a personified agent on your system? You never mentioned one."

"Nah." The thief's fingers dipped back into the water. "I think I had one, once. It was one of those *Miz pSoozi* things—you remember those? My father thought it was embarrassing, though. He gave me some professional daemon gear when I turned twelve and Miz pSoozi got sixed."

Orlando wiped sweat off his face and flicked it into the dark green waters. "What's your dad like? You never really told me."

"I don't know. Like a dad. He's really big. And he thinks everyone should be like him and never be wrong. He always says, 'Sam, I don't care what you do, as long as you do it well.' But I always wonder, I mean, what if I want to be majorly bad at something? Everybody can't be good at things, can they?''

"How about your mom?''

"Nervous, kind of. She's always worried things will go wrong.'' Fredericks snatched at a shining fish, which dove beneath his grasp. "How about your parents? Are they normal or what?''

"Mostly. They don't like it that I'm sick. They're not mean or any-thing—they try really hard. But it makes them utterly unhappy. My father hardly even talks anymore. Like he might blow up or start cry-ing if he wasn't careful.''

Fredericks sat up. "Is there . . . isn't there anything they can do?'' he asked shyly. "About that disease you have?''

Orlando shook his head. For the moment, the edge of his bitterness was gone. "No. You wouldn't believe how many things they've tried already. You haven't had fun until you've had cellular therapy—I couldn't even get out of bed for about two months. Felt like one of those S&M simworlds. Like someone was shooting hot rivets into my joints.''

"Oh, Orlando! That's horrible.''

He shrugged. Fredericks was staring at him, his expression suspi-ciously close to pity, so Orlando turned away.

"So where do you think we are now?'' Fredericks asked at last. "And what do we do?''

Orlando thought this practical question might be a clumsy attempt to distract him, but he had enough problems dealing with his own illness without expecting everyone else to be able to do it perfectly. "Where we are, you can guess as good as I can. But we have to find this Priam's Walls place—we need to find the others. I have to tell them what the Brotherhood is trying to do.''

"Do you think they really can?'' Fredericks asked. "Live forever? Isn't that, like, scientifically impossible or something?''

"Don't tell me, tell them.'' Orlando stood and pushed the boat, which had been slowing, out into a deeper part of the channel. "*Fen-fen*, I'm sick of water. I swear, I'd be happy if I never saw another river.''

A faint thump and grumble of thunder rolled out of the cloudless, pale blue sky; it murmured echoingly along the sides of the distant mountains before the valley grew quiet again.

Orlando had his stars this time, but they did not give him much joy. After the long sunset, during which the waters of the river had first turned a molten gold, then darkened to black as the shadow of the western mountains crept across them, they had poled to the sandy bank and dragged the boat onto the shore, making camp in the symbolic if not actual shelter of a small stand of palms. With the sun gone the desert soon grew cold. Fredericks, wrapped in half the stiff sailcloth, had managed to fall asleep fairly quickly. Orlando had not been so lucky.

He lay staring upward, half-convinced he could see movement in the black sky, ripples passing through the pinpoint stars as though they were sequins on the costume of a dancer engaged in some incomprehensibly langorous movement, but he was unable to concentrate, and was instead being irritated and engaged by his own body. The distractions of daylight gone, he could feel his heart beating in his chest, and it seemed to him to be beating too swiftly. He was short of breath, too, as far as he could tell between bouts of shivering when the breeze freshened.

I don't have that much time left, he thought, for perhaps the dozenth time since the sun had gone down. He could feel his own fragility quite distinctly, his slow-slipping grasp on health. Beneath the excitement of this strange place, these unexpected adventures, his physical self was growing ever wearier. *The real me is in a hospital somewhere— and I wouldn't be getting any stronger even if I wasn't. I might even be in a coma by now, like Renie's brother. And if they decide to pull my connection, like they did with Fredericks . . .*

He considered it only a moment, his heart rabbiting in his chest— the overworked heart that he could feel, but which was not actually in this marionette body.

If they do that to me, and the pain is as bad as Fredericks said, I won't make it.

In the hour before dawn he slipped into a half-dream, a place of long, dark halls. The sound of a softly crying child was always around the next corner, somewhere in the blackness. He knew it was important he find the child—who was frightened and lonely—but he did not know why. He hurried on, feeling his way through unfamiliar spaces, while the quiet sounds of loneliness and heartbreak remained always just ahead.

It was only as he realized that the sound had become more like the harsh breathing of an animal that he remembered where he was, and suddenly came awake, still in the blackness behind his own tight-shut eyes but with the cold desert night on his skin. The sounds continued, now near, now a little farther. Something was sniffing its way around the camp.

Orlando opened his eyes just a slit, his heart again pounding in his chest. A strange, hunched shape was silhouetted against the stars, bending and then straightening; when it stood upright, moonlight reflected from bright, animal eyes. Orlando reached for the Thargor-sword lying at his side. Long campaigns in the Middle Country had taught him always to sleep with it within reach.

With his fingers curled around the hilt he paused, willing his pulse to slow, composing himself for the conflict to come. As though it suddenly sensed his waking presence, the thing froze, becoming just another shadow. The snuffling noises stopped. Orlando leaped to his feet and shouted a warning to Fredericks even as he brought the sword around in a sweeping arc. The first blow landed, the flat of the blade thumping against something solid, and he was raising the sword for another cut when a very human-sounding shriek stopped him dead.

"Don't kill him! Don't kill him!"

Orlando wavered. The dark shape was rolling on the ground before him. He looked around wildly, wondering who had spoken. Fredericks was struggling out of the sailcloth, clearly still confused and half-asleep. It was only when the thing cried out again that Orlando realized that the intruder he had struck was talking about itself.

"Don't hurt him any more! Poor fellow! Poor fellow!"

It writhed at his feet, making little whimpering noises into the dirt. Orlando wished again they had Chief Strike Anywhere with them, or at least his fire-making expertise. He lowered the point of his sword until it touched the intruder, who stiffened and fell silent.

"We're going to wait until it's light," he said slowly and clearly. "You are not to move until then. Do you understand me?" Without thinking about it, he had fallen into Thargor's gruff, commanding tones.

"Most generous, that is," the dark shape said eagerly. "Upaut, it hears you."

"Right. Well, Oopa-oot, if that's your name, just lie still. The sun will be up soon."

Fredericks, his face a pale blur, remained a healthy distance away from the prisoner. As they waited, he and Orlando (in an old trick from their adventuring days), talked calmly of all the prisoners over the years who had tried to escape them and who had been skinned or otherwise mutilated in reprisal for the trouble of catching them again. Upaut, whatever it was, seemed to take them at their word: although it begged them not to say such terrible things, it remained huddled on the sand until the first light began to brighten the eastern sky.

In the gray dawn light, their prisoner was revealed to be essentially human, tall and ropy and with mottled gray-brown skin, wearing nothing but a grimy loincloth. But instead of a man's head it had doglike, pointed ears that been shredded at the tips, and a gray, furry snout. After it revealed impressive yellow fangs, which winked into view when it unfurled its long tongue to lick its lips, Orlando kept his blade even closer to the prisoner's throat.

"It's a werewolf," Fredericks said calmly. They had both seen far worse in the Middle Country. "Pretty sad-looking one, too."

"Do not kill it!" The creature rubbed its muzzle in the sand at Orlando's feet, making the rest of its words hard to understand. "It will go away, back into the hot Red Land! It has promised never to haunt the Black Lands again, and it will go back into the desert, even if it is hungry and lonely!" It rolled one amber eye back to see the effect this plea was having. "It only came down to see who the powerful strangers were, who float so bravely in the sacred waters of Father Nile."

"The Nile?" said Orlando. "So we're in Egypt, then." He looked at the bony creature kneeling before him and felt the tug of memory. He had not spent his young life studying fatality in all its variations for nothing. "And this has to be what's-his-name with the jackal head— Anubis, the Death God."

"*Noooooooo!*" The prisoner began to roll on the ground, throwing handfuls of sand over itself, like a crab trying to dig its way to shelter. "Do not say that cursed name! Do not talk of the one who stole Upaut's birthright!"

"Jeez, sorry," said Orlando. "Bad guess."

The thing that called itself Upaut rolled onto its back, its long arms and legs curled protectively over its belly. "If you spare its life, it will tell you the secrets of the Red Land. It has been living here for many moons. It knows where the fat beetles hide. It knows where the flowers bloom at midnight, the tasty flowers."

Fredericks was frowning. "I've seen this type before. He'll wait until we're asleep, then slit our throats. Let's just kill him or something and get going."

"No, this reminds me of something. In Tolkien—you really ought to read that, Fredericks, I keep telling you. Text. The interactives miss all the good stuff."

"Words, all those words," said Fredericks with lofty disdain. "Utterly slow."

Orlando would not be deterred. "See, someone said they were supposed to kill a guy like this, but Frodo the Ring-bearer said not to do it. 'Pity stayed his hand,' or something like that. And it was important." He couldn't remember just at this moment what the situation had been, but he knew he was right.

"This isn't a game and it isn't a story, Gardiner," Fredericks pointed out crossly. "This is our lives. Look at the teeth on that hairy mama-locker. Are you crazy?"

"If we spare your life," Orlando asked the kneeling prisoner, "will you be our guide? Promise not to try to hurt us?"

"It will do just as you say." Upaut sat up, his long torso gritty with sand, his eyes bright. "It will be your slave."

Orlando was certain there was something else he needed to do; after a moment, he remembered. "You need to swear on something important. What is the most sacred thing you can swear on?"

For a moment Upaut straightened; a distant look clouded the yellow eyes. "It will swear on its godhood."

"You're a god?" said Fredericks, lip curling.

"It is most definitely a god," their prisoner declared, a little huffily. "Of course it is. Once, before it earned the anger of the Lord Osiris, it was a great warrior-god, one of the chief protectors of the dead." Upaut stood, achingly scrawny, but taller by the height of his long-eared head than even the Thargor sim. In the blue dawn light, he looked quite spectacularly alien; even his voice grew deeper. "Once," the creature declared solemnly, "it was known to all as *Khenti Amenti*—'He Who Rules the West'."

Upaut stood, staring at the mountains, rose and orange with the light of the morning sun, clearly remembering better days. Then the moment passed; tattered ears sagged and shoulders slouched. "And which of the one thousand and nine hundred gods are the glorious masters?" he asked them pleasantly.

"Us?" said Orlando. "We . . . we'll tell you later."

Upaut was very excited by the boat. "It had a boat once," he told them, sniffing the prow appreciatively. "Long and beautiful, it was—rowed by a dozen lesser gods while Upaut itself stood before the mast. It towed the sun's royal barque when it went aground on the rough parts of the sky. Great was Upaut!" He threw his lupine head back, as though he might howl. "Great in reverence among the Lords of the Black Land. Another of its names was 'He Who Opens the Way'!"

Orlando wasn't quite sure how to respond. In this place, it could all be true—or as true as anything else was. "So what happened?"

The wolf god looked around in some confusion, as though it had forgotten others were present. "What?"

"He asked what happened," Fredericks said. "And why do you always call yourself 'it'?"

"Poor fellow, poor fellow!" Upaut was clearly moved by his own predicament. He folded his long legs so he could sit down in the middle of the boat. "Let us go upon the beautiful river and it will tell you the sad tale."

As Orlando poled the boat out into the slow current, he wondered how it had happened that they had gained a slave, but he was still doing the work himself. But before he could point out this seeming incongruity, Upaut was in full flow.

"Once Ra, the sun, was pharaoh of all creation, and all was as it should have been. But in time he became old and full of trembling, and wished to give up the burdens of kingship. His sons and daughters by then had duties of their own—Geb the earth, Shu the air, Hathor the night sky full of milky stars—so Ra gave kingship over gods and men to his grandsons, Osiris and Set.

"Set ruled these red southern lands, Osiris the black and fertile lands of the north. Set was great in magic, but Osiris, too, was great in magic, and he was also great in cleverness and very jealous. So he set a trap for Set. He invited his brother to a banquet, and had his artisans make a great chest of cedar wood, covered in gold. When the banquet was finished, Osiris said that the wonderful chest should belong to whoever it fit. Set climbed in, and Osiris and his warriors fell upon him, closed the chest, bound it, and threw it into the waters of Hapi the Nile, so that Set was drowned. But this you must know already, brother gods, and Upaut will hurry to tell of how it was itself brought low." The wolf god shook his long-snouted head.

Orlando had made a bit of a study of Egyptian mythology, unpleasantly fascinated with its death-cult reputation; now he was puzzled. The Osiris myth was the best-known bit of the whole thing, but he would have been willing to bet that it was the other way around—Osiris betrayed and murdered by Set. He shrugged. Who knew how things worked here? Maybe someone had spent a zillion credits and then messed up the easy bits, got the story wrong. It wouldn't be the first time.

Upaut was declaiming again. "So Osiris became Lord of the Two Lands, and declared himself King of the Dead as well, so that Set's body was given into his keeping. The grandson of Osiris—some even say his son—Anubis, the jackal-headed one, became Osiris' chief minion, and to him the Lord of Life and Death gave the duties that had once been mine, that of protecting the dead on their journey to Ra's blessed bosom, which we call 'The Rites of Coming Forth by Day'." The wolf god paused and shook his head; there was a glint in his eye which belied his next words. "But Upaut was not bitter, although Upaut's offerings were taken away, and all its duties and honors and titles, until it was little more than another servant in the palaces of the dead, with few worshipers or houses of its own. But then other servants of Osiris, even less exalted than Anubis, began to plague Upaut. Tefy and Mewat, they were named, called by some 'the Twins,' and they were not even gods, but spirits of the darkest sort, demons from the Underworld. But they were favored servants of Osiris, and they took what they wanted, giving back nothing.

"From Upaut they stole the final prizes of godhood, Upaut's last temple, last few priests. They destroyed that place of worship, threw down Upaut's standards, broke in pieces Upaut's armor and chariot, bespoiling everything for no greater reason than that Upaut was now weak and they were strong in their lord's favor.

"When Upaut, who had once ruled the kingdom of the dead, went to Osiris asking that the lord's servants be restrained, that there be some recompense, Osiris became angry. 'How dare you come to me and tell me what you deserve?' he said, growing in might and stature until his crown touched the ceiling of his throne room, his eyes burning with fire. 'Who are you? What are you? You are no god anymore. You are less than a mortal man, even. Go into the Red Lands and live like a beast.' So Upaut was banished. And the Lord of Life and Death declared also that if it calls itself anything but the name of a beast, even the life it has will be extinguished, and it will squeak and flutter in the Great Darkness forever."

Anger and despair made Upaut's voice tremble. The great amber eyes closed and the wolf's head drooped to his chest. Orlando, poling the barge off a sandbar, found himself sympathetic enough that he resented having to steer the boat a bit less than he had before the story had begun, but he also thought the onetime Lord of the West was a bit prone to melodrama. Still, it couldn't be easy to lose your godhood.

Fredericks, as if thinking along the same lines, said quietly: "It's kind of like it was for you when Thargor got killed, maybe."

There are things I'm a lot more worried about losing than Thargor, Orlando thought, but said nothing. As the wolf god clenched and unclenched its clawed hands, making little sounds of self-pity, Orlando turned his attention back to the wide river and the seemingly boundless desert.

Upaut roused himself from his misery eventually, and spent the rest of the long, hot day regaling them with stories of his god-days, at least half of which seemed to revolve around his constant battles with the arch-serpent Apep, the monster whose mission in life seemed to be daily attempts to devour the sun god Ra and his celestial barge. When

Upaut had not been flinging spears at Apep, he had apparently been entertaining a ceaseless parade of females, both goddesses and mortal priestesses. While the first few descriptions of these particular types of worship piqued Orlando's adolescent interest, and the constant use of the phrase "it revealed its glowing godhood" had a certain amusement value, by the fifth or sixth he had begun to notice a sameness to the tales—in his own memory, Upaut was as stalwart and inexhaustible as any fertility deity—and by the time the wolf god had begun the dozenth tale of amatory conquest, Orlando was ready to brain him with the barge pole.

Fredericks had fallen asleep beneath the shelter of the sailcloth some time earlier, leaving his companion stuck as the god's sole audience, a maneuver for which Orlando was already planning several intricate schemes of revenge.

"Do you know where Priam's Walls are?" Orlando asked suddenly, more in hopes of forestalling the tale of Upaut's seduction of Selket the Scorpion Goddess than in expectation of information. If the wolf god was a creature of this simworld, it wouldn't know about any other, and the chances they had stumbled immediately into the one they were seeking had to be at least a thousand to one.

Still lost in a reverie about Selket's exoskeletal charms, Upaut took a moment to respond. "What is that? No, that is not a name it has heard, therefore it doubts such a thing exists. There is the temple-palace of Ptah, which is known as Ptah-Beyond-the-Walls. Ptah the Artificer is another one who has risen high during Osiris' reign, although he is true friend to no one, not even the Lord of the Two Lands. Is that what you mean?"

"No, I don't think so." Orlando's back was beginning to hurt. Whatever kept him in the simulation seemed also to have assigned him a fairly arbitrary level of health and strength—far greater than his own, but quite a bit less than what the tireless Thargor would have received in any simulation that recognized the Middle Country's ranking system. "Maybe you should handle the boat for a while."

Upaut's eyes grew wide. "May it do so? It has not been allowed to steer a craft since Osiris cast it down." He stood, towering and spindly, and took the barge pole in trembling hands. As he set the pole for the first time and pushed off, the wolf god began to sing under his breath, a simple, up-and-down melody that in other circumstances Orlando would have found almost pleasant.

He crawled under the sailcloth, nudging the protesting Fredericks until his friend moved over. Orlando felt terribly hot, and now that he had stopped moving, his head was beginning to pound.

"Where are we going anyway?" Fredericks asked drowsily.

"I don't know. Downstream." Orlando squirmed, trying to find a position that would allow his back muscles to unkink.

"And then what? Keep going in and out of different simworlds until we get to this Priam place?"

"That could take us years," Orlando said dully. It was a horrible problem, but he couldn't think about it with his head throbbing like this. He felt a flash of anger at Fredericks, who always had to be told, never just thought things through by himself. Herself. "We have to come up with another way to find it," he said. "We can't just go on like this until we get lucky, Fredericks. I won't last long enough."

"What do you mean. . . ?" the other asked, then broke off and fell silent. Orlando rolled on his side, turning his back on his friend, and tried to find a comfortable position against the hard deck.

Upaut's voice rose, a dreamy singsong, chanting the same words over and over until Orlando had no choice but to listen.

> *"Supreme one, beautiful in adornment,*
> *Your armor bright as the barque of Ra*
> *Mighty in voice, Wepwawet! He Who Opens the Way,*
> *The master in the West,*
> *To whom all turn their faces—*
> *You are mighty in majesty!*
> *Wepwawet, hear now this prayer.*
> *Khenti Amenti, hear now this prayer.*
> *Upaut, hear now this prayer. . . !"*

It was with a slightly uneasy feeling that Orlando realized the wolf god was singing his old hymns to himself.

When he wakened from a brief nap, sweaty and with his head still throbbing, Orlando was glad to see that Upaut's strange mood had passed. Their prisoner was poling the barge down the middle of the Nile, which had swelled here until both banks were quite far away. If the water was wider, though, the sandy face of the desert had not changed, still mile after mile of rusty sand stretching away into the distance. Only a jumble of fallen stones along the river bank broke the monotony, the vast but long-abandoned remains of some structure that Orlando did not want to ask about, for fear of provoking more of Upaut's tedious stories.

"Yes, as you see, the sands are spreading," the wolf god said. "It has been a dreadful time, since Set was killed by Osiris. The season of Inundation comes, and there is not enough water to overflow the banks and darken the fields. Going Forth comes, but in that season the ground is dry and the seeds are uncovered by hot winds. Harvest season comes, but the earth is barren. Then, when Inundation returns, Hapi's waters remain low and sullen. The desert, the Red Lands, have grown. The Black Land itself is threatened, and even Osiris in his great house at Abydos must be fearful."

Orlando wondered who this Osiris was, whether he was the human master of this place, maybe even one of the Grail Brotherhood. "If the drought's so bad, why doesn't the Lord of the Two Lands, or whatever you called him, do something about it?"

Upaut looked around nervously, as though watchers might be hovering overhead in the flat blue sky. All Orlando saw was a vulture, spiralling lazily in the superheated air on the far side of the river. "It is said that Set's curse defies him. That is why he took back the Lord of the Red Land's body, so that he could threaten Set with the loss of it, which would leave his *ka* floating in the final, forever darkness." Upaut shuddered, and the great pink tongue moistened the black lips. "But the curse of Set has not abated, and all the lands suffer."

Fredericks had been stirring, and now sat up. He looked around and made a sour face. "Sand, sand, sand. This locks. I mean, utterly."

Orlando smiled. In an upside-down universe, Fredericks' grumpiness was something to depend on.

"I'm serious, Orlando. If something doesn't happen, I'm going to scan out from all this sun."

"Perhaps," said Upaut, who had not had the benefit of shelter or a nap and might have been a little touchy, "Ra, in his great wisdom, is trying to speak to you. You should open your heart."

"Ra is speaking to *you*," Fredericks snapped. "He's telling you to shut up and steer the boat."

Upaut gave him an inscrutable look, but fell silent.

Orlando wiped sweat from his forehead and wondered what his real body was doing with this simworld information. *I hope the doctors don't think it's a fever. Then they'll just fill me full of more contrabiotics. But I suppose the extra fluids they'll give me couldn't hurt.* It was strange to think he even *had* another body. He had been living in this particular Thargor-sim for so long now, his other existence had begun to seem like the pretense.

"What if we swim a little?" he suggested to Fredericks. "It would cool us off."

Upaut looked at him as though he had gone completely mad. "But the favorite food of Nile crocodiles is godflesh."

"Ah," said Orlando. "Then I guess we won't swim."

*   *   *

In the night, in the dark, he did not realize at first where he was,
nor even quite *what* he was. The blackness had taken on dim form, a
shape of ancient desolation, massive columns tumbled in the sands,
huge granite blocks lying scattered like dice. The stars in the night sky
were unnaturally bright, and gave the uppermost faces of the stone a
sheen like silver.

"*. . . I'm still trying,*" a voice was saying. "*Can't you hear me? Tell me you
can hear me.*" The tones were familiar, and the urgency made Orlando
curious, but he had to fight a great lethargy before he could move
farther into the ruins. It came to him, as he floated forward between
the flat or rounded faces of the intricately carved, fallen stones, that
he was dreaming.

"*Boss? Just say something. I'll pick it up.*" The voice was faint, but since
it was the only noise in the great emptiness of the night, he could
hear it clearly, as though it whispered into his ear. "*Boss?*"

An obelisk lay on its side before him, all but a portion of its uppermost face and one sharply angled edge buried in sand. A carving of a
beetle drew his attention: of all the thousands of images cut into the
black granite obelisk, it alone gleamed, as though animated by starlight, and it alone moved.

"*I'm running outta time.*" The carving squirmed as though trying to
escape its stone prison. He felt himself drawing near, his memory
faintly pricked. "*If you can hear me, just let me know. Please, boss!*"

"What is it?" he asked. "Who are you?"

"*It's you! But I can't make out what you're saying. This talking-in-your-
ear bit ain't working—I'm going to stick a probe up against your earbone,
boss. No offense meant.*"

The little gleaming scarab moved convulsively on the obelisk. When
it spoke again, he could hear it much more clearly. "*Say something,*" it
directed him.

"Who are you?"

"*Beezle! Your agent—don't you remember? I know, you're pretty much
asleep, boss, so this must be hard for you to grasp. Just listen, 'cuz I don't want
you to wake up, neither. You're dreaming, see, but that's the only time I can
reach you. There's a certain REM frequency you hit on the way up and the way
down, and it kinda works like a carrier wave. But it's hard to figure, and
sometimes there are people here in your hospital room, so then I have to lay
low.*" The shimmering beetle was motionless on the obelisk now, as
though concentrating. "*So just listen for a minute, okay? On your direction,
I dumped everything off your system and hid it.*"

He was beginning to make a little sense of what the thing was saying, and although he did not think of himself as specifically Orlando Gardiner, he now knew more or less who he was and who this strange-sounding creature was. But it was hard to engage fully with what the thing was telling him. "I told you to do that?"

"Yes, you did! Now, shut up, boss, if you don't mind me saying it. Let me get on with what I gotta tell ya.

"I can only reach you like this at certain times, and you've been sick again, so it's been even harder. Your temperature's really high, boss. The doctors and your family are worried. So take care of yourself, if you can, okay? I've checked out this Atasco guy who got sixed in Colombia, like you asked me, and I tried to get to his system, but it's really, really weird, boss—all locked up, security everywhere, but not the kind you'd expect. Hard to explain, I'll give you a full report if you want." It paused for a moment; when Orlando did not speak, it hurried on. *"He was a member of something called the Grail Brotherhood, according to the information I've searched. Lot of weird little things in the news about them right now, rumors and like that. Lot of stuff about Atasco too, 'cuz he's dead.*

"But I need you to tell me if I'm going down the right alleys, boss. There's all kinds of information on the nets about TreeHouse now, too—rumors, a little hard news, everything. Some people died, some kids are in comas. Is this the kind of thing you want me to do? I can't do anything but audit-mode right now, no touching, just research. If you want me to be more active, tell me to do it—it's gotta be an order, boss. I can't do anything else unless you tell me to . . ."

Orlando tried to gather his thoughts, which were drifting like seaweed in a deep current. The ruins seemed to have shifted, edging closer, so that stone now loomed over him on every side. "Do it," he said at last. He couldn't remember the creature's name. "Beetle. Do it. Everything." He mused for a moment longer, trying to put words to the thoughts that were still swirling, still without coherence. "Come. Come and find me." He tried to think of where he was, but could not. A place? "Egypt," he said at last, although he knew that did not sound right. "I am . . ." For a moment it was almost there, a word, a thought . . . another land? It slipped free and was gone. "Egypt," he said again. "Online."

"I'll do my best," the silvery shape told him. The glow began to fade. *"I'll try to get to you . . ."*

The voice dwindled. The starlight dimmed. Orlando felt his name come back to him, clear now, but somehow unimportant. A moment later he realized he had been dreaming, and as he tore through the last gauzy veils of sleep, he struggled to remember what he had dreamed about.

Beezle . . . he faintly remembered. *In the ruins. Said he was looking for me—didn't he?*

It was already hard to summon up the details. He opened his eyes to find the broken stones in whose circumference they had made camp still around him, but instead of the silvery starshine of his dreams, they were touched by a faint pink glow—the first light of dawn. A rustling noise nearby reminded him that the wolf god Upaut had been terribly restless during the first part of the night; his mumbling had kept Orlando from falling asleep for a long time . . .

A shadow abruptly loomed over him, dark against the dark sky. Yellow eyes burned like lamps. Something cool and sharp touched Orlando's throat—Thargor's sword.

"The greatest of all spoke to it." Upaut's voice, so mild and reasonable as they had made camp, had regained the triumphal tone of his self-hymn. "Spoke through you as you slept, because he knew Upaut was listening. He spoke to it . . . to . . . to *me.*" The wolf god uttered the personal pronoun with trembling pleasure. "Me! Upaut! And Ra spoke forth in his scarab-form, Khepera, Beetle-of-the-Morning! *'Do everything,'* he said. *'Come and find me,'* were his words to faithful Upaut. *'I am Egypt,'* he said to me, me, me!"

The wolf god did a strange dance, kicking up his long legs like a stick insect on a griddle, but kept the point of the sword near Orlando's face.

"My time of exile is over," Upaut crowed. "And now I will go to Ra's temple, and he will give back to me my birthright! My enemies will be brought low, they will rub their faces in the dust and make great lamentation. Again I shall be Khenti Amenti, He Who Rules the West!"

The blade was waving uncomfortably close to his face; Orlando pushed himself back a few inches. Beside him, Fredericks had just awakened, and was lying beside him in wide-eyed alarm. "What about us?" Orlando asked.

"Ah, yes." Upaut nodded gravely. "You have served as the Mouth of Ra. I will not shame myself by injuring his messenger. You may both live."

Relief turned to indignation. "What about your promise?" Orlando demanded. "You swore on your godhood!"

"I promised not to harm you. I have not. I promised to guide you. I have, if only for a short time." Upaut turned on his heels and strutted down to the beach, the early light picking him out, slender as a lotus-stalk against the dark river. Orlando and Fredericks watched helplessly as the wolf god pushed their boat out into the shallows and climbed in. When he had poled it out into the current, he turned to look back at the bank. "If you come before me when I am again master of the West," he shouted to them, "I will be merciful. I will grant your souls honor!"

As the boat began to drift away, the wolf god threw back his head and began to bay out another hymn to his own godliness.

Orlando clutched his head in his hands. "Oh, God. We're locked, now."

"I told you we should have killed him." Fredericks looked more closely at Orlando and saw his misery. "Hey, it's not that bad." He patted his friend's shoulder. "We'll just make another boat. There are palm trees and stuff like that."

"And cut them down with what? Chop them up how?" Orlando jerked away from Fredericks' attempts to soothe him. "He took my sword, remember?"

"Oh." Fredericks fell silent for a moment. The sun was clearing the eastern mountains now, the sands beginning to burn red. "How far do you think we have to walk before we get to another whatever you call those things . . . another gate?"

"Through a thousand miles of desert," said Orlando bitterly. It wasn't, he felt sure, much of an exaggeration. The shocked expression on his friend's face didn't make him feel the least bit better.

CHAPTER 26

Waiting for the Dreamtime

NETFEED/NEWS: "Data Terrorists" Broadcast Manifesto
(visual: three human figures sitting on pile of toys)
VO: At noon yesterday, GMT, a brief and bizarre manifesto broke into most
commercial net channels, from a group calling itself the Dada Retrieval
Collective.
(visual: trio wearing animated Pantalona Peachpit masks)
DRC 1: "The sea squirt is a marine animal that starts out with a
rudimentary brain, but once it stops moving, affixes itself to a rock, and
begins simply to filter seawater, it doesn't need its brain anymore, so it digests
it."
DRC 2: "We have formed the Sea Squirt Squad to commemorate, protest,
and celebrate this fact. We will dedicating ourselves to the destruction of
telecommunication wherever possible."
DRC 3: "No dupping. S3 is real. We're going to kill the net. You'll thank us
someday."

STAN Chan stuck his head around the partition. "Got something
for you. Woman out at UNSW with the rather fabulous name of
Victoria Jigalong. She's supposed to be first-rate, top of the field, like
that. I sent you the name and number."

"So why are you standing there, bouncing around like a jack-in-the-box?"

"Because I wanted to see the shining look of gratitude on your real, live face. I'm going to get lunch—coming?"

"No, thanks, I'm having a no-lunch day. Girl has to watch her figure, you know."

"And you call *me* old-fashioned." He disappeared; she heard him joking with a couple of the other detectives on his way out.

Calliope Skouros called up Stan's memo and settled back to read through it, wondering if discipline could be relaxed enough to allow for the packet of biscuits stashed in the bottom drawer. After all, starving yourself was not the way to diet properly. On the other hand, if she wanted to keep her already broad-shouldered, wide-hipped figure in what she considered reasonable shape, she had little margin for indulgence.

She scowled and left the biscuits where they were. It was all about "looking like a police officer," wasn't it? Which, if you were a man, could include a gut and a fat behind. But if you were a woman fighting for promotion, and queer to boot. . . .

Chan's hasty dossier on Jigalong did make her sound like a good source. She had several degrees in Aboriginal Folklore and Comparative Anthropology, and had served on more commissions than Calliope could imagine without a shudder. She also seemed to have involved herself with quite a few specifically woman-oriented causes, which seemed like it might be a good sign.

The call to the University of New South Wales, after an endless series of facades, eventually presented her with the Anthropology Department associate. He had been offline for a few moments when the picture suddenly changed.

Calliope's first impression of Professor Jigalong was that she was very, very dark-skinned, almost literally black, so that until she surreptitiously adjusted the contrast of her screen, there was only a mask with unnervingly white eyes in the center of the display. The woman's head was shaved, and she wore vast hoop earrings and a necklace of chunky stone beads.

"What do you want, Officer?" Jigalong's voice was smoky and deep, her entire presence quite overwhelming, even over telecom lines. All Calliope's thoughts of appealing to sisterhood had evaporated. The woman was . . . well, witchy.

In her best professional manner, and trying to show proper respect (for some reason she thought that might be an issue) Detective Skouros introduced herself and quickly explained that she was looking for information on the Woolagaroo and any related myths.

"There are many collections of myths suitable for beginners," the professor replied, cool as a misty morning. "They are available in several media. I'll be happy to have someone send you a list."

"I've probably seen most of them. I'm looking for something a little deeper."

The woman's eyebrow rose. "May I ask why?"

"It's a murder investigation. I think there's a possibility that our killer may have been influenced by Aboriginal myths."

"In fact, you think the murderer is probably a black man, don't you?" The professor's tone remained flat and unbending. "It has not occurred to you that he might be a white man imitating something he has seen or heard or read about."

Calliope felt a flare of irritation. "First off, Professor, I'm not positive that the killer is a *he* at all. But even if it is a man, I don't care what color he is, except so far as it helps us catch him." She was angrier than she'd realized at first. Not only didn't this woman want to acknowledge sisterhood, she saw Calliope as just another white cop. "In fact, the most important thing here is the poor girl he killed, who happens to have been Aboriginal herself—a Tiwi—not that it makes her any more or less valuable. Or any less dead."

Victoria Jigalong sat silently for a moment. "I apologize for my remark." She didn't sound exactly sorry, but Calliope had her doubts this woman could manage such a thing. "Why do you think this has something to do with native myths?"

Calliope explained the condition of the body, and the remark the reverend's wife had made.

"Mutilations of the eye are not uncommon in other countries, in other cultures," the professor said. "Places where they have never heard of the Woolagaroo myth."

"I realize the Aboriginal folklore angle is only a possibility. But someone killed Polly Merapanui, and someone did that to her, so I'm going to follow up any lead I have."

The dark face on the screen was carefully quiet for several seconds more. "Is this going to be one of those tabnet field-days?" she asked at last. "You know, 'Cops Seek Abo Myth-Killer'?"

"Not if I can help it. It's a five-year-old murder, anyway. The sad truth is, no one cares but me and my partner, and if we don't come up with anything soon, it's going back into the *Unsolved* file, probably for good."

"Come to my office, then." Having made up her mind, she spoke briskly. "I'll tell you everything I can. Fix a time with Henry, the one you spoke to first. He has my schedule."

Before Calliope could protest her own busy calendar, Professor Jigalong had ended the call.

She sat staring at the screen for half a minute, full of useless frustration, then called back the associate and arranged a meeting. Furious at her own malleability—she, the one her father had called "Ox" because of her stubbornness—she scrabbled in the bottom desk drawer for the biscuits. Diet, hell. She would eat herself huge, until the Jigalong woman quailed at the sight of her.

What she found at the bottom of the drawer, after a long and fruitless search, was an IOU from Stan Chan dated two days earlier, a chit for the packet of biscuits he'd stolen.

The biscuit thief was doing legwork for another case, so Calliope went to the university by herself. She missed the shuttle from the parking lot, and decided to walk across campus instead of waiting for another hoverbus.

The students seemed uniformly well-dressed—even the clothes that imitated gutter fashion were expensive and finely tailored; Calliope was more conscious than she wanted to be of her decidedly unglamorous suit and flat, practical shoes.

Most of the young people she saw were Pacific Rim Asians, and although she had already known that many mainland Chinese were enrolled at UNSW (one of the school's nicknames was "BUSX", which stood for "Beijing University, Sydney Extension"), it was still a bit startling to see it in person. The entire country was really half-Asian now, she reflected, although most of the Asians, like Stan, whether their grandparents had been Chinese, Laotian, or Korean, were now as Australian as Waltzing Matilda. They had joined the mainstream—or rather the mainstream had broadened. Funny how that happened. But, of course, not everyone was part of it: some, like the Aboriginal peoples, remained largely excluded.

Professor Jigalong's earlier reaction reminded Calliope that only a few generations ago, her own Greek immigrant ancestors had been the funny foreigners, the butt of jokes and sometimes the target of uglier treatment. But in fact, if you looked at it from the Aboriginal point of view, Calliope and her Greco-Australian forebears had never been that different from any other whites.

Victoria Jigalong's office was no bigger than most academic holes-in-the-wall. What was surprising about it was its austerity. Calliope had been expecting to find it filled with Aboriginal art, but instead, except for a cabinet with several shelves of old paper books, and a not completely tidy desk, it was as stark as a monk's cell. The professor's shapeless white dress, revealed as she stood up from behind the desk, its muslin length emphasized by her height, suddenly seemed a kind of ecclesiastical garment. Calliope exited the firm, dry handshake and lowered herself into the only other chair, caught between hops again.

"So." The professor donned a pair of almost antique spectacles. With the lenses over her eyes, and with her shiny, hairless head, she now seemed a thing entirely made of reflective surfaces. "You want to know about the Woolagaroo myth."

"Uh, yes." Calliope would have preferred at least a bit of humanizing small talk first, but was clearly not going to get it. "Is it well known?"

"It is one of the more common. It appears in different forms in the story-cycles of quite a few Aboriginal peoples. Most have the key elements in common—a man takes it into his head to build an artificial man and give it life. He constructs it from wood, and gives it stones for eyes, but his attempts to breathe life into it by magic fail. Then, when he has walked away in disgust, he hears something following him. It is the Woolagaroo, of course, the wooden devil-devil man, and it chases him. Terrified, he hides, and the Woolagaroo continues on its way, over stones and thorns and even walking on the bottom of rivers, until it disappears." She steepled her fingers. "Some folklorists do not believe it is truly a myth from the Dreamtime. They think it is more recent."

"I'm sorry, slow down for a moment, please." Calliope pulled her pad from her bag. "Do you mind if I record?"

Professor Jigalong looked at the device with distaste, and for a bizarre moment Calliope thought she was going to be accused of trying to steal this very modern and impressive woman's soul. "If you must," was all the professor said.

"You said 'the Dreamtime.' That's a myth, too, isn't it? That there was a time before time, when all the Aboriginal myths were actually true?"

"It is more than that, Detective. Those who believe, believe that it can be accessed. That in dreams, we still touch the Dreamtime."

She had spoken with a peculiar emphasis, but Calliope did not want to get embroiled in some kind of academic crossfire. "But you said some people think this Woolagaroo myth is, what, modern?"

"They believe it is an allegory of the first contact with the Europeans, and with their technology. It is a myth, they say, that warns the native people that machines will destroy their makers."

"But you don't think they're right."

"The wisdom of so-called primitive people runs deeper than most of those who call themselves civilized can understand, Detective Skouros." The harshness of her tone seemed almost automatic, the fossil rigidity of an old argument. "One does not have to have seen a gun or a motorcar to think that humanity should not rely too greatly on that which it makes, as opposed to that which it *is*."

Calliope did her best to draw the woman back to specifics; the professor, as if realizing that the detective in front of her was not part of the debate she herself felt so strongly about, relented. She filled up fifteen minutes of the pad's memory with citations of different versions of the folktale, and of various expert commentaries written about it. Professor Jigalong's gestures were concise but subtly theatrical, her deep speaking voice almost hypnotic, and even her casual conversation gave the impression of being long-considered. Once more Calliope had the sensation of being overwhelmed by the professor's peculiar magnetism. At first she had thought it was sexual—Professor Jigalong was a handsome and very impressive woman—but more and more it seemed she was fascinated by the woman's sheer presence, her own reaction more like the awe of a potential devotee.

Calliope didn't like that. She didn't see herself as a fan, let alone a cult follower, of anyone or anything, and she couldn't imagine changing that for a professor of folklore with a chip on her shoulder. But it was hard not to react to the woman.

As she was listening (or half-listening, in truth, because the wealth of detail was beginning to overwhelm her), Calliope let her gaze drift around the office. What had seemed a monastic blankness to one of the walls was now revealed to be a very large—and, it appeared, fairly expensive—wallscreen, resting now in a neutral flat white tone. And there was a single ornament too, which she had missed against the multicolored spines on the bookshelves.

The object on the wooden stand was quite simple—a slightly irregular circle of yellowed ivory or bone, stood upright like the mouth of a tunnel, the whole thing including its almost invisible support bar no more than a hand's length high. Had it not been the only adornment in that otherwise purely functional room, Calliope would barely have noticed it. Instead, she found it hard to look away.

". . . and that is why, of course, I find your suggestion that this particular myth may be part of a ritualistic killing very unpleasant."

"Oh! I'm sorry." To cover her embarrassment at having stopped listening, Calliope shook her pad slightly, as though it had frozen up. "Could you just say that again, please?"

The professor gave her a hard-edged look, but her voice remained even. "I was saying that there is a sector of native Australian society that believes the Dreamtime is coming again. Like most fundamentalist movements, it is a reaction to suffering, to political disenfranchisement. And not all who believe this are fools or dupes, either." Here she paused for a moment, as though for the first time considering what to say next. "But there are some who believe that they can hasten this return of the Dreamtime, or even shape it to their own ends, and they are quite willing to pervert the rituals and beliefs of their own people to do so."

Calliope felt a rising spike of interest. "And you think the killer might be someone like that? Someone who's trying to perform some ritual, some magic, to bring back the Dreamtime?"

"Possibly." Victoria Jigalong looked far unhappier than seemed appropriate. Calliope wondered if it pained her to speak of what seemed an example of her own people's gullibility. "The Woolagaroo is a potent metaphor in some quarters—and not just an example of technology's troubling side. There are those who see it as a metaphor for how the white man's attempts to remake the native peoples in his own image will eventually backfire. That his 'creation,' if you will, will turn on him."

"In other words, some people use it as an incitement to racial unrest?"

"Yes. But remember, even in these unsettled times, it is a myth, and like all my people's myths, what is beautiful in it—what is *true* in it—is not to be confused with what sick or unhappy minds might make of it." Oddly, this stern woman almost seemed to be asking the policewoman for understanding.

After Calliope had thanked her and was standing in the doorway, she turned and said: "By the way, I couldn't help noticing that ring of bone on your bookshelf. Is it a piece of art, or an award of some kind? It's really quite beautiful."

Professor Jigalong did not turn to look at the shelf; neither did she answer the question. "You seem like a good woman, Detective Skouros. I am sorry for my earlier sharpness."

"That's all right." Calliope was flustered. The professor's tone had gone strange and hesitant again. Was it going to turn into a come-on after all? Calliope didn't know quite how she felt about that.

"Let me tell you something. Many people are waiting for the Dreamtime. Some are trying to make it happen. These are strange days."

"They certainly are," she said quickly, then wished she had kept her mouth shut. The woman's stare was very, very intense, but that was no reason to babble.

"Stranger than you know." Victoria Jigalong now turned and walked to the bookshelf. She took the bone circle down and ran a reverent finger around it, like a nun telling the rosary. "And in these strange days," she said at last, "do not underestimate someone who summons the Woolagaroo magic. Do not take the Dreamtime idea lightly."

"I don't take anyone's beliefs lightly, Professor."

"We are not talking of beliefs any more, Detective. The world is coming to a great change, even if most cannot see it yet. But I should not keep you any longer. Good afternoon."

Half an hour later, Calliope was still sitting in her department car in the parking lot, playing back the interview as she stared at her notes on the Woolagaroo myth, and trying to figure out what in hell *that* had all been about.

CHRISTABEL waited and waited outside the metal door, trying to make herself not be afraid any more. It seemed like there was a dragon behind the door, or some other kind of monster. She was afraid to knock, even though she knew it was only Mister Sellars on the other side. Mister Sellars and that bad, scary boy.

When she finally felt brave enough, she banged on the door with the stone, the little code that Mister Sellars had taught her, *bump-bumpa-bump-bump.*

The door opened. The boy's dirty face looked out at her.

"I want to see Mister Sellars," she said in her most serious voice.

The boy opened the door to let her through, and she crawled past him. He smelled. She made a face at him and he saw it, but he only laughed, a little hissing sneaky sound like Mystery Mouse.

Inside the tunnel it was hot and wet and cloudy, and at first she couldn't see very much. There was a little stove on the floor, and a pot bubbling on top of it, making the steam that made it so hard to see. The air smelled funny, not sour like the boy, but like something from the medicine cabinet at home or one of the things her daddy drank.

When she was inside the door, she stood up. She couldn't see much because of the cloudy air and she didn't know where to go. The boy gave her a little shove, not too hard, but not very friendly, making her trip and almost fall. She was scared again. Mister Sellars always called out hello to her, even when she came without talking to him on the Storybook Sunglasses first.

"You bring some food, *mu'chita?*" the boy asked.

"I want to see Mister Sellars."

"*Ay, Dios!* Go on, then." He walked up behind her like he would push her again, and Christabel hurried along the wet concrete so he wouldn't touch her.

Mister Sellars' chair was standing empty in one of the wide places in the tunnel, which made her even more scared. Without the old man in it, it looked like something from the news on television, like one of the spaceship things that landed on Mars and began making little machines like a mama cat having kittens. She stopped and would not go near it, even when the boy came up behind her. His breathing seemed very loud. So did her own.

"This little bitch all crazy," the boy said.

Something stirred in the shadows beyond the chair. "What?" asked a quiet voice.

"*Mu'chita loca*, seen? She say she wanna talk to you, but she jumping all around. I don't know." The boy made a snorting noise and went to do something with the pot full of boiling water.

"Mister Sellars?" Christabel was still scared. He sounded funny.

"Little Christabel? This is a surprise. Come here, my dear, come here." She could see something waving just a little, and she walked around the chair. Mister Sellars was lying down on a pile of blankets, with another blanket over him so that only his head and arms stuck out. He looked very skinny, even more than usual, and he did not lift his head up when she came close. But he did smile, so she felt a little better.

"Let me see you. You will forgive me for not getting up, but I'm afraid I'm rather weak just at the moment. The work I'm doing is quite tiring." He closed his eyes, almost like he was going to sleep, and waited a long time before he opened them. "Also, I apologize for the atmosphere. My humidifier has malfunctioned—that means it stopped working—and I've had to improvise."

Christabel knew what 'malfunction' meant, because Rip Ratchet Robot said it on the Uncle Jingle show whenever his rear end fell off. She wasn't quite sure what Mister Sellars meant, though, since his humidifier didn't have anything to do with his rear end, as far as she knew. She wasn't sure about "improvise" either, but guessed it had something to do with boiling water.

"Are you going to get better?" she asked.

"Oh, I expect so. There's a great deal to be done, and nothing will be accomplished with me flat on my back. Well, actually I could be standing on my head and it wouldn't make any difference, but I need to be stronger." He opened his eyes wide for a moment, as though he were really seeing her for the first time. "I'm sorry, my dear, I'm bab-bling. I'm not feeling very well. What brings you to see me? Shouldn't you . . ." he hesitated for a moment, as though looking at something invisible, "be in school?"

"It's over. I'm going home." Christabel felt like there were secrets to tell. She didn't want to talk about school. "How come you haven't called me?"

"As I said, my dear, I'm working very hard. And I don't want you to get into any trouble."

"But why is *he* here?" She was whispering now, but the boy still heard her, and laughed. For a moment she wasn't scared of him, she just hated him, hated his stupid face always hanging around when she came to see Mister Sellars. "He's not good, Mister Sellars. He's bad. He steals things."

"Yeah, s'pose you go to *la tienda* and buy all that soap, then?" the boy said. He laughed again.

"That's not necessary, Cho-Cho." Mister Sellars' trembly hand came up like a branch blown by the wind. "Christabel, he stole because he was hungry. Not everyone has a nice family like you do, and a warm place to sleep and plenty to eat."

"*Verdad,*" said the boy, nodding his head.

"But why is he your friend? *I'm* your friend."

Mister Sellars slowly shook his head, not saying no, but sad. "Christabel, you are still my friend—you are the very best kind of friend anyone could have. The help you gave me is more important than you could ever know—you're the hero of a whole world! But right now I have to do the rest of my work, and Cho-Cho is better for that part of things. And he needs a place to stay, so he's staying here."

"And if I don't stay here, I tell those army *vatos* that there's a crazy old man living under their base, seen?"

Mister Sellars' smile was not a happy one. "Yes, there's that, too. So that's all, Christabel. Besides, you can't keep sneaking out. You'll get into trouble with your parents."

"I won't!" She was angry, even though she knew he was right. It was getting harder and harder to think up reasons to go off on her bicycle alone so she could bring bags of bread and half-sandwiches and pieces of fruit from her lunch to the boy and Mister Sellars. But she was afraid that if she stopped coming, the boy would do some-thing bad—maybe take Mister Sellars away somewhere, or hurt him. Her friend was very thin and not very strong. Right now, he looked really sick. "I don't care if I get in trouble, anyway."

"That's not a good way to think, Christabel," Mister Sellars said gently. "Please, I'm very tired. I'll call you when I want you to come, and you're definitely still my friend. Your job right now is to be Christabel, and make sure your parents are happy with you. Then, if there's something big and important I have to ask you to do, it will be easier for you to do it."

She had heard this kind of talk before. When she wanted to have her hair cut in the same style as Palmyra Jannissar, the singer she saw all the time on the net, her mother had said, "We don't want you to look like Palmyra, we want you to look like Christabel." Which meant N-O spells "no."

"But . . ."

"I'm sorry, Christabel, but I really must rest. I've worn myself out working in my garden—it has grown so tangled! . . . and I must . . ." He let his eyes close for a moment. His funny, squishy face looked empty in a way she hadn't seen before, and it frightened her all over again. She felt very worried—he didn't *have* a garden anymore, now that he lived in a hole, not even one plant, so why would he say something like that?

"C'mon, weenit," the boy said, standing over her now. "*El viejo's* sleepy. Leave him alone."

For a moment, because he said it strange, she almost thought he cared about Mister Sellars. But then she thought about how he lied and stole, and knew he didn't. She got up, and for the first time she knew what it meant in her stories when it said "her heart was heavy." Something inside her felt like it weighed a million pounds. She walked past the boy and didn't even look at him, although she could see out of the corner of her eye that he was doing a stupid bow, like someone in a flick. Mister Sellars didn't say good-bye. His eyes were already shut, his chest going up and down, up and down, fast but gentle.

Christabel did not eat much of her dinner. Her daddy was talking about bad things at work, and about pressure he was under—she always imagined it like the roof that came down and squished people in *Kondo Kill,* which she saw once at Ophelia Weiner's when all the parents were having a party downstairs—so he didn't notice that she just kind of rearranged her food on her plate, pushing her mashed potatoes into a funny skinny shape that sort of looked like she'd eaten some.

She asked to be excused and went to her room. The special Storybook Sunglasses that Mister Sellars had given her were sitting on the floor near the bed. She looked at them and frowned, then tried to do some of the arithmetic problems in her school workbook, but all she could think of was how sick Mister Sellars had looked. He had seemed crumpled up, like a piece of paper.

Maybe the boy was poisoning him, she thought suddenly. Like in Snow White. Maybe he was putting something bad in that boiling pot, just like the poison that the bad queen dipped the apple into. And Mister Sellars would just get sicker and sicker.

She picked up the Storybook Sunglasses, then put them down again. He had said he would call her. He would be angry if she called him, wouldn't he? Not that he had ever really been angry with her, but still . . .

But what if he was going to get poisoned? Or maybe even just get sicker from something else. Shouldn't she bring him some medicine? She hadn't asked him because she was so unhappy, but now it seemed like he might really need some. That boy would never be able to get medicine, but Christabel's mommy had a whole cupboard full of things—patches and bottles, painblockers, all kinds of things.

Christabel put the sunglasses on and stared into the black that was inside them, still thinking. What if Mister Sellars did get angry, and then told her not to talk to him or come see him any more?

But what if he was really sick? Or getting poisoned?

She opened her mouth, thought about it for a just a little longer, then said *"Rumpelstiltskin."* She didn't say it very loud, and she was just wondering whether she should say it again when a voice spoke to her, but not a voice from the glasses.

"Christabel?"

She jumped and pulled off the Storybook Sunglasses. Her mother was standing in the doorway with a funny look on her face, her eyebrows squinchy. "Christabel, I was just talking to Audra Patrick."

Christabel had been scared that Mommy knew she was calling Mister Sellars with their secret word, and for a moment she couldn't understand what her mother was talking about at all.

"Mrs. Patrick, Christabel? Danae's mother?" Her mother frowned even more. "She said you didn't come to Bluebirds today. Where did you go after school? You didn't get home until almost four. In fact, I asked you how Bluebirds was, and you said 'fine'."

Christabel couldn't think of anything to say. She stared at her mother, trying to think of another lie, like all the others she had been telling, but this time she couldn't think of anything, of anything at all.

"Christabel, you're scaring me. Where were you?"

Down in the tunnel, was all that was in her head. *With the boy with missing teeth, and the poison clouds, and Mister Sellars all sick.* But she couldn't say any of that, and her mother was staring at her, and there was a feeling of Really Big Trouble starting to fill up the air, just like the steam filled up the tunnel, when all of a sudden the Storybook Sunglasses in her hands made a little crackling noise.

"Christabel?" said Mister Sellars' little tiny voice. *"Did you call me?"*

Christabel stared at the sunglasses for a moment, confused. She looked up at her mother, who was staring at the sunglasses too, her face almost completely without expression.

"Christabel?" said the tiny voice again, but it seemed very loud.

"Oh . . . my . . . God! What is going on here?" Her mother took two steps into the room and snatched the sunglasses from Christabel's hand. "Don't you move, young lady," she said, scared and angry together. She turned and went out, slamming the door behind her. A moment later, Christabel could hear her talking in a loud voice to Daddy.

Alone in her room, Christabel sat without thinking for a few moments. The bang of the door closing still seemed to be going on and on, a booming noise like a cannon, like a bomb. She looked down at her hands, empty now, and burst into tears.

CHAPTER 27

The Beloved Porcupine

NETFEED/NEWS: "Diamond Dal" Dies
(visual: Spicer-Spence meeting Pope John XXIV)
VO: Dallas Spicer-Spence, known to the tabnets as "Diamond Dal," was
found dead in her Swiss chateau, a victim of heart failure. She was 107.
Spicer-Spence won and lost several fortunes and several husbands during her
colorful life, but she was probably best-known for her legal battle during her
residence in Tanzania to make a chimp named "Daba" the executor of her
estate, an attempt to dramatize her concern for the rights of the country's ape
population, sold by the hundreds every year for biomedical research.
(visual: Daba sitting at desk, smoking a cigar)
Spicer-Spence succeeded in her legal challenge, but Daba the chimpanzee
predeceased her by more than a decade. The disposition of her estate is now
in the hands of several human lawyers . . .

RENIE was finding it hard to move. Her entire body throbbed with pain and fatigue, but that pain was nothing compared to the greater weariness which gripped her. She had no strength to go forward, and no belief left from which to draw more strength. The world had become a solid, resistant thing, she herself as boneless as the river she had escaped only minutes before.

!Xabbu had just finished arranging the firewood in a neat cone at the center of the forest clearing. Emily, the refugee from New Emerald City, sat shivering in a swiftly narrowing patch of sunlight and watched without interest as the nimble baboon fingers drew two more pieces of wood from the place they had been collected. The Bushman-baboon fitted the tip of the smaller stick into the hole in the larger, then steadied the larger log with his feet and began twirling the smaller piece between his palms, as though he meant to enlarge the hole.

Renie felt a reflexive jerk of guilt watching her friend do all the work, but it was not enough to overcome her misery. "You didn't need to pull out the Aboriginal Camping Kit, !Xabbu," she said. "We've got Azador's lighter." She handed him the lighter, which she had been gripping so hard in the river that there were still marks on the virtual skin of her hand.

How about that Otherland VR technology, she thought sourly. *Pretty impressive, huh? Hooray, hooray.*

!Xabbu studied it for a moment, his raptness of attention almost comical—a monkey, by all appearances, trying to make sense of something clever and human. "I wonder what this letter 'Y' stands for," he said, studying the design engraved on the lighter's cover.

"It's probably that bastard's name—I mean, we don't know if Azador's a first name or a last name, do we?" She hugged her knees as the beginning of what promised to be a stiff evening breeze swept down the riverside, rattling the jungle foliage.

!Xabbu turned the lighter over, then looked up at her. "He said to me that his name was Nicolai. That Azador was his last name."

"What? When did you talk to him about that?"

"While you were sleeping. He did not say very much. I asked him what country his name came from and he said it was Spanish, but that his people were Romany, and to the travelers Spain was just a country like many others. He said his first name was Nicolai, which was a good Romany name."

"Damn." Despite her dislike of the man, Renie could not help being irritated that the mysterious Azador had told !Xabbu more about himself in a five-minute conversation than he had shared with her over several days. "Well, then we'll never know what the 'Y' is for, will we? Maybe it was his father's. Maybe he stole it. I'm betting on the second."

!Xabbu found a way to flick the button with his not-quite-human thumb; the tiny nova blazed just above the end of the lighter, and did not move even when the breeze strengthened. When the kindling had caught, !Xabbu handed the lighter back to Renie, who stuck it in the pocket of her tattered jumpsuit.

"You seem very sad," he said to her.

"Should I be happy?" It seemed a waste of time, explaining the obvious. "Azador's real name is the least of our problems. We're stuck in the middle of this bloody simulation without a boat, surrounded by God knows what kind of homicidal monstrosities, and just to keep things interesting, the entire network seems to be falling apart."

"Yes, it was very odd, very frightening, the way the whole world . . . changed," !Xabbu said. "But that is not the first time we have experienced such a thing. Emily, what happened to us on the river and in Scarecrow's palace—has it happened here other times?"

The girl looked up miserably, her huge eyes full of the need to surrender. "Don't know."

"You're not going to get anything out of her," Renie said. "Trust me, it's happened here before. And it will happen again. Something's wrong with the whole system."

"Perhaps they have enemies," !Xabbu suggested. "These Grail people have hurt many—perhaps there are others who are fighting back."

"I wish." Renie tossed a fallen seedpod onto the fire where it blackened and curled. "I'll tell you what's going on. They've made themselves a big network, and they've spent billions and billions to do it. You remember how Singh said that they employed thousands of programmers? Well, it's just like building a big skyscraper or something. They've probably got Sick Building Syndrome."

"Sick Building syndrome?" !Xabbu had turned his back to the fire, and was waving his tail slowly back and forth as he warmed himself, as though conducting a symphony of flames.

"When someone makes a complicated system and seals it up, little things begin to turn into big things just because the system is closed. Over time, a tiny flaw in a skyscraper ventilation system becomes a very serious problem. People get sick, systems fail, like that." She didn't have the energy to crawl nearer the fire, but it cheered her the smallest, smallest amount just to see its movement and feel the pulse of its heat. "They've forgotten something, or one of those early programmers sabotaged it, or something. It'll all come apart."

"But that is good, is it not?"

"Not with us stuck inside it, !Xabbu. Not if we can't figure how to get offline. God knows what a system collapse would do to us." She sighed. "And what about all the kids—what about Stephen? What if the network is all that's keeping them alive, somehow? They're locked into it, just like us." As soon as she had said it, a chill that had nothing to do with the wind on the river gripped her. "Oh, my God," she moaned. "Jesus Mercy. I'm an idiot! Why didn't I think of it before . . . ?"

"What, Renie?" !Xabbu looked up. "You sound very upset."

"I've been thinking all along, well, if worst comes to worst, someone will open up those tanks and pull us offline. Maybe there will be pain, like that kid Fredericks talked about, but maybe not. But I've just now realized that . . . that we must all be like Stephen."

"I do not understand."

"We're comatose, !Xabbu! You and I! Even if they pulled us out of those tanks, we wouldn't be awake, we'd be . . . just there. As good as dead. Like my brother." Tears came—unexpectedly, because she had thought she had cried them all.

"Are you sure?"

"I'm not sure about anything!" She rubbed at her eyes, angry with herself. "But it makes sense, doesn't it? Something that pulls you in and won't let you get back into your physical body—doesn't that describe just what happened to Stephen, and Quan Li's granddaughter, and everyone else?"

!Xabbu was silent. "If that is so," he said at last, slowly, considering, "then does that mean Stephen, too, is here? In the Otherland network somewhere, with a body, like the ones we have?"

Renie was stunned. "I never thought of that. Oh, God, I never even thought of that."

Her dreams were fretful and feverish. The last was a long, disjointed epic, which began with her chasing Stephen through a house of endless branching tunnels, his footsteps always ahead of her, while he remained only a shadow or a blur of motion disappearing around a corner, always just heartbreakingly out of reach.

The house itself, she slowly realized, was alive—only the fuzziness of dreaming had prevented her from seeing the sweaty elasticity of the walls, the intestinal roundness of the corridors. She could feel its monstrously drawn-out breathing, inhalation and exhalation minutes apart, and knew that she had to catch Stephen before he went deeper into the thing and was lost forever, absorbed and digested, irrevocably changed.

The twisting passageways came to an end in front of an immense darkness, a chasm that fell away, ever narrowing, like a huge black mountain of air turned upside down. There were voices in the depths, forlorn cries like the lamentation of birds. Stephen was falling—she knew that somehow, and also knew she had only an instant to decide whether to leap after him or let him go. !Xabbu's voice was on the path behind her, telling her to wait, that he was coming with her, but !Xabbu did not understand the situation and there was no time to explain. She moved to the rim and, with her toes at the very edge of the precipice, had tensed to throw herself outward into the whispering darkness when someone grabbed her arm.

"Let go!" she screamed. "He's going down! Let me go!"

"Renie, stop." The pulling grew more insistent. "You will fall into the river. Stop."

The darkness stretched away before her, the pit abruptly becoming longer and narrower, until it was a black stream, a Styx rushing past. If she could only get into it, she would be carried after her brother. . . .

"Renie! Wake up!"

She opened her eyes. The true river—for nothing in this experience could be called "real"—burbled only a few feet below her, almost invisible in darkness but for the shimmer of the current and the undulating reflection of the moon. She was crouching on her hands and knees on the edge of the crumbling riverbank, with !Xabbu clinging to one of her arms, his small legs braced against a root.

"I . . ." She blinked. "I was dreaming."

"So I guessed." He helped her straighten up before releasing his grip. She stumbled back toward the fire. Emily lay curled in a fetal position near the coals, breathing softly, her elfin face deformed against her pillowing arm.

"Isn't it my turn to take watch, !Xabbu?" Renie asked, rubbing her eyes. "How long have I been asleep?"

"It does not matter. You are very tired. I am not so tired."

The temptation was strong to let go, to slide back into dreams, however disturbing. Anything was better than this grim, waking reality. "But that's not fair."

"I am very good at waiting for sleep. That is the way of a hunter, as my father's family taught it to me. In any case, you are important, Renie, very important, and we can do nothing without you. You must have some rest."

"Me, important? That's a good one." She slumped. Her head seemed made of concrete, her neck too weak to hold it up for more than a few moments at a stretch. Nowhere to go, nothing left to do, and nothing even to distract her from her misery. She newly understood her father's habitual urge toward oblivion. "I'm about as much use as . . . as . . . I don't know. But it isn't much use, whatever it is."

"You are wrong." !Xabbu had been poking up the fire, but now he turned, his posture strange even by baboon standards. "You really do not know, do you?"

"Know what?"

"How very important you are."

Renie did not want to hear a pep talk from anyone just now, !Xabbu included. "Look, I appreciate it, but I know what I can and can't do. And at the moment, I've run way beyond my areas of competence. In fact, we all have." She tried to summon up the passion to explain it to him properly—to let him know just how hopeless things were—but there were almost no reserves left. "Don't you see? We're up against something far bigger than we ever guessed, !Xabbu. And we've done exactly nothing—nothing! Not only haven't we made any inroads against the Grail Brotherhood, they don't even know we're here. And they wouldn't care if they did know. We are a joke—a bunch of fleas making plans to wrestle an elephant." Her voice sounded dangerously uneven. She bit her lower lip, angry now and determined not to cry again. "We've been so . . . so *stupid.* How could we have thought we could do anything against an enemy this big, this powerful?"

!Xabbu sat on his heels for a long silent time, the fire-poking stick clutched in his small hand. He stared at the flames, as though reading a particularly difficult passage in a textbook. "But you are the beloved Porcupine," he said finally.

The unexpectedness of it startled Renie into laughter. "I'm the *what?*"

"Porcupine. She is the daughter-in-law of Grandfather Mantis, and in many ways his best-beloved of all the First People. I told you once I would tell you the final story of Mantis."

"!Xabbu, I don't think I have the strength. . . ."

"Renie, I have not asked you for anything. Now I am asking you. Please listen to this story."

She looked up from the embers, struck by the urgency in his voice. There was obvious silliness in a begging baboon, the small hands raised in supplication, but she did not—could not—laugh. He was right. He had asked nothing of her.

"Right, then. Tell me."

!Xabbu bobbed his head, then pointed his muzzle at the ground for a moment as he thought. "This is the last tale of Mantis," he said finally, "not because there are not other stories to tell—there are many, many I have not told you—but because it is of the last things that happened to him in this world."

"Is it sad, !Xabbu? I don't know if I can take a sad story right now."

"All the most important stories are sad," he replied. "Either what happens in the story, or what happens after it." He reached out a paw and touched her arm. "Please listen, Renie."

She nodded wearily.

"This is a story from late in the life of Grandfather Mantis—so late that black people, and perhaps even white people, had come to the lands of my ancestors. We know that because it starts with sheep, which came with the black herdsmen. These men brought their sheep in great flocks to eat the thin grass that sustained all the animals Grandfather Mantis and his hunters loved—eland, springbok, hartebeeste.

"Mantis saw these sheep and recognized that they were a new kind of animal. He hunted them, and was both pleased and worried that they were so easy to kill—there was something wrong about creatures that waited so passively for their deaths. But when he had shot two with his arrows, the black men who owned them came upon him. The men were as numerous as ants, and they beat him. At last he pulled his cloak of hartebeeste hide around him, so that his magic blinded them, and made his escape. Although he was able to take the two sheep he had killed, the herders had beaten him badly. By the time he had limped back to his camp, his *kraal,* he was so tired and sore and bloody that he felt himself to be dying.

"Mantis told his family, 'I am unwell—they have killed me, those men who are not of the First People.' And he cursed the newcomers, saying 'My word upon them. They shall lose their fire, and they shall lose their sheep, and they will live only like ticks, on uncooked food.' But still he was unwell, and felt that the world had become a place of darkness. He felt it to be true that there was no more room for the First People."

Renie understood that here was the first of the parallels that !Xabbu intended to draw, between her own helpless despair and the misery of Grandfather Mantis. She was almost annoyed at what felt like cheap psychology, but something in the high seriousness of !Xabbu's voice undercut it. He was preaching to her from the Old Testament of his people. This meant something.

"He called all his family before him," !Xabbu continued, "his wife Rock-Rabbit, his son Rainbow, his beloved daughter-in-law Porcupine, and their two sons, the grandsons of Mantis, who were named Mongoose and Younger Rainbow. Porcupine, with her great heart and sympathetic eye, was the first to see that something was very wrong with her father-in-law. Neither did she like the sheep, which were strange to her. 'Look,' she said to her husband, Rainbow, 'look at the creatures your father has brought back.'

"But Mantis told them all to be quiet, and said, 'I am weak with pain, and my throat is swollen so that I cannot speak proper words or eat these sheep. Porcupine, you must go to your father, the one called the All-Devourer, and tell him to come and help me eat up these sheep.'

"Porcupine was fearful and said, 'No, Grandfather, for when the All-Devourer comes, there will be nothing left for anyone. He will leave nothing behind under the sky.'

"Mantis was stubborn. 'Go to the old man yonder, the All-Devourer, and tell him to come that he may help me eat up these sheep. I feel that my heart is upset, so that I want the old man yonder to come. When he comes, I will once more be able to talk properly, for my throat is swollen now and I cannot talk in the way that I should. Let us lay out the sheep and welcome your father.'

'Porcupine said, 'You do not want that old man to come here. Let me give you some springbok meat, so that you can fill your belly.'

"Mantis shook his head. "That meat is white with age. I will eat these sheep—this new meat—but you must tell your father to come and help me.'

"Porcupine was sad, and full of a great fear, for Mantis had never before been so sick and so unhappy, and something terrible was bound to happen. 'I will go to fetch him, and tomorrow he will come. Then you will see him for yourself, that terrible old man, with your own eyes.'

Mantis was satisfied with this and fell asleep, but still he cried out in his pain even as he slept. Porcupine told her sons Younger Rainbow and Mongoose to take the springbok meat away and hide it, and to take their father Rainbow's spear and hide that as well. Then she set out on her journey.

"As she traveled, she looked on everything she passed with the eye of her heart, and said to herself, 'Tomorrow this thing will be gone. Tomorrow that thing will be gone.' When she reached the place where her father lived, she could not face him, but from a distance shouted out: 'Mantis, your cousin, bids you to come and help eat up the sheep, for his heart is troubled.' Then she hurried back to her family at the *kraal* of Grandfather Mantis.

"Mantis asked her, 'Where is your father?'

"Porcupine said, 'He is still on the way. Look at that bush, standing above us, to see if a shadow comes gliding from on high.'

"Mantis looked but saw nothing.

"Porcupine said, 'Watch for the bush to break off. Then, when you see that all the bushes up there have disappeared, look for the shadow. For his tongue will take away all the bushes even before he has come up from behind the hill. Then will his body come up, and all the bushes around us will be devoured, and we will no longer be hidden.'

"Mantis replied, 'I still see nothing.' Now he, too, was frightened, but he had invited the All-Devourer, and the All-Devourer was coming.

"Porcupine said, 'You will see a tongue of fire in the darkness, for all that stands before him he destroys, and his mouth engulfs everything.' And she went away then and took back the springbok meat that had been hidden and gave it to her two young sons, that they should be strong for what lay ahead.

"And as Grandfather Mantis sat waiting, a great, great shadow fell upon him. He cried out to Porcupine, 'Oh, daughter, why is it so dark when there are no clouds in the sky?' For in that moment he felt what he had done, and he was very afraid.

"The All-Devourer said in his terrible hollow voice, 'I have been invited. Now you must feed me.' And he sat down in Mantis' camp and began to eat everything, for within the great mouth, in the heart of the shadow, there was a tongue of fire. First he ate the sheep, and chewed their bones, and swallowed their fleeces. When he was done, he ate all the other meat, and the *tsama* melons, and the roots, and every seed and flower and leaf. Then he devoured the shelters and the digging sticks, the trees and even the stones of the earth. When he swallowed down Rainbow, the son of Mantis, Porcupine took their two children and ran away. As they escaped, the All-Devourer swallowed down Mantis' wife, Rock-Rabbit, and then even Grandfather Mantis himself disappeared into the stomach that now stretched from horizon to horizon.

"Porcupine took the spear which her sons had hidden and heated it in the fire until it glowed, then she tested her sons to make sure that they would be fit for what lay ahead. She touched Younger Rainbow and Mongoose with the hot spearpoint, pressing it on their foreheads, their eyes, their noses and ears, to make sure they would be brave enough to see and understand the way ahead. The eyes of Mongoose filled with tears, and she said 'You are the mild one—you will sit on my father's left hand.' But the eyes of Younger Rainbow only grew drier the more she burned him, and she said, 'You are the fierce one, you will sit on my father's right hand.' Then she took them back to the fire and they seated themselves on either side of the All-Devourer, who was still hungry, although he had eaten nearly everything under the sky.

"In a moment he would eat them up, too, but instead the two brothers grabbed his arms and pulled him back, dragging him down to the ground. As they held him, fighting against his great strength, and while the tongue of flame in his black mouth was burning them, Younger Rainbow took his father's spear, and at his mother Porcupine's bidding, sliced open the stomach of the All-Devourer. He and Mongoose pulled the stomach wide open, and everything that the All-

Devourer had eaten came rushing out in a flood—meat and roots and trees and bushes and people. Even Grandfather Mantis came out at last, changed and silent.

"Porcupine said, 'I feel that everything has changed. Now is the time when we must go away and find a new place. We will leave my father the All-Devourer here, lying in the *kraal*. We will go far away. We will find a new place.' And she led her father-in-law and all her family away, out of the world and into a new place, where they still live.'"

Renie had been so struck by the idea of little Mantis crouching in fear as the sky turned dark and the All-Devourer came upon him that at first she barely realized the story had ended. In his folly, the Bushman's god had called down the ultimate horror—how was she any different herself?

"I . . . I'm not sure I understood the story," she said at last. It had not been as sad as she had feared, but the ending did not seem to outweigh the terror of what happened to the characters. "What was it supposed to mean? I'm sorry, !Xabbu, I'm not being difficult on purpose. It's a very impressive story."

The baboon sim looked tired and dejected. "Do you not see your own self in this, Renie? That you, like Porcupine, are the one who we depend on? That like Mantis' beloved daughter-in-law, you are the one who has taken action when all seemed hopeless? It is you that we rely on to bring us out of this place again."

"Don't!" A flash of anger took her. "That's not fair—I don't want anyone relying on me! I've spent all my life picking other people up, carrying them around. What if I'm wrong? What if I'm too weak?"

!Xabbu shook his head. "We do not need you to carry us, Renie. We need you to lead us. We need you to look with the eyes of your heart, and to take us where they direct you."

"I can't do it, !Xabbu! I'm out of strength. I can't fight any more monsters." The All-Devourer story was becoming jumbled in her head with her own dreams and the shadow-creatures of these unreal worlds. "I'm not Porcupine. I'm not sweet and sensible. My heart doesn't have any goddamned eyes."

"But you do have prickly spines, as she does." The baboon's mouth quirked in a slightly sour smile. "I believe you see more than you know, Renie Sulaweyo."

Emily had woken up, and was lying quietly on the ground watching them, the whites of her eyes bright parentheses in the predawn light. Renie felt bad about waking her—they were all tired and needed rest,

God knew—but even that brief moment of guilt sent off another sizzling spark of irritation. "Enough of the mystical foolishness, !Xabbu. I don't get it. I never have got it. I'm not saying you're wrong, but you're speaking a language I don't know. So instead of waiting for me, what are *you* going to do about all this—the Grail Brotherhood, this network we can't get out of, all this? What's *your* plan?"

!Xabbu was quiet for a moment, as if shocked by her vehemence. She was embarrassed at how hard she was breathing, how much her control had slipped. But instead of retreating or arguing, !Xabbu only nodded gravely.

"I do not want to make you angry, Renie, by saying things you do not believe in, but once again you have seen with the eyes of your heart. You have spoken a truth." A heaviness as dreadful as her own seemed to come over him. "It is true that I no longer know what I am meant to do. I tell you stories, but I have forgotten my *own* story."

She was suddenly frightened that he might leave them—leave her—and set off on his own into the river-jungle. "I didn't mean . . ."

He raised a paw. "You are right. I have forgotten the purpose I was given. In my dream, I was told that all the First People must come together. That is why I am in this shape." He gestured at his furred limbs. "So I will dance."

This was the last thing she had expected to hear. "You . . . you'll what?"

"Dance." He turned in a circle, inspecting the ground. "It will make no noise. You can go back to sleep if you wish."

Renie sat and stared, not sure what to say. Emily, too, was watching warily, but there was a light in her eyes that had not been been there previously, as though in some way the Mantis story had touched her. !Xabbu walked in a circle, dragging one of his hands to make a line in the dirt, then stood and stared at the sky. A glimmer of dawn was just appearing on the horizon. He turned slowly until he faced it, and Renie recalled another one of his stories. !Xabbu had told her that his people believed the first red light of morning was the hunter Morning Star returning to his camp, hurrying back to his bride, Lynx.

And the reason Morning Star hurried, she now remembered, was that he feared the hatred and jealousy of Hyena, a lost creature of the darkness, almost as frightening as the All-Devourer.

As he began the shuffling steps of what he had once called the Dance of the Greater Hunger, !Xabbu seemed focused on something beyond the camp, perhaps even beyond Otherland itself. Renie's own despair had settled into something viscous, a heavy, sticky netting that exhausted her and held her down. So this was what her scientific investigation had become, she thought—half-baked answers to impossible questions, dancing monkeys, magical worlds along an endless river. And somehow they would sift this endless desert of sand for the one grain that would bring back her brother?

!Xabbu's dance continued, a throbbing, rhythmic movement that carried him gradually around the circle he had drawn. A few birdcalls enlivened the dawn, and the jungle trees rustled and shivered in the breeze, but in the camp the only movement was the baboon pacing *step, shuffle, shuffle, step,* bending toward the ground and then straightening to stretch his arms high and wide, eyes turned ever outward. He completed the circle and kept going, now a little faster, now slowing once more.

Time slid by. A dozen circuits became a hundred. Emily's eyes had long ago trembled and fallen shut, and Renie was half-hypnotized with fatigue, but still !Xabbu danced, moving to music he alone could hear, tracing steps that had been immeasurably ancient when Renie's own tribal ancestors had first come to the southern reach of Africa. It was the Stone Age she was watching—the living memory of humankind, here in the most modern of all environments. !Xabbu was aligning himself, she realized—not with the material universe, with the sun and moon and stars, but with the greater cosmos of meaning. He was relearning his own story.

And as the dance went on, and the jungle began to ripen into full dawn, Renie felt the cold hopelessness inside her thaw just a little. It was the story that mattered, that was what he had been telling her. Porcupine, Mantis—they were not just quaint folktales, but ways of seeing things. They were a story that gave life order, that taught the universe how to speak the words that humans could understand. And what was anything, any human learning or belief, but just that? She could let chaos swallow her up, she realized, as the All-Devourer swallowed everything—even Grandfather Mantis, the spirit of first knowing—or she could shape chaos into something she could understand, as Porcupine had done, finding order where only hopelessness seemed to exist. She had to find her own story, and she could make it whatever shape she thought best.

And as she thought these things, and as the little man in the baboon's body danced on, Renie felt the thaw inside her spread and warm. She watched !Xabbu drawing his careful repetitions, as beautiful as a written language, as complex and satisfying as the movement of a symphony, and suddenly realized that she loved him.

It was a shock, but it was not a surprise. She was not certain whether it was a man-woman love—it was hard to get past the antipathy of their different cultures and the strange masks they now wore—but she knew beyond a doubt she had never loved anyone more, nor had she ever loved anyone in quite the same way. His monkey form, which disguised but did not truly hide his bright, brave spirit, was transformed from a subject of bemusement into a shining clarity of meaning, as powerful as a drug experience, as hard to explain as a dream.

I'm the one who has to see that we are all connected, she thought. *!Xabbu's dream told him that all the First People needed to come together, like in that story about his ancestor and the baboons. 'I wish there were baboons on this rock,' wasn't that it? But that story isn't really about him—it's about me. I'm the one the hyena has been chasing, and !Xabbu has offered me his shelter, just like the People Who Sit on Their Heels did for his ancestor.*

"There *are* baboons on this rock," she whispered to herself.

And, discovering this truth, she felt it burning inside her. It was so *right*. She had turned away from a gift, thinking it did not matter, but in fact a gift—and specifically the gift of love—was the only thing that *did* matter.

She wanted to grab the little man, pull him out of his trance and explain to him all that she had just comprehended, but his concentration was as great as ever, and she understood that these revelations were hers—!Xabbu was searching for his own. So instead she fell into step behind him in the circle, hesitantly at first, then with ever-growing confidence, until they moved in parallel, the diameter of the circular track always between them, but the circle itself always connecting them. He gave no sign he knew she had joined him, but inside her heart, Renie felt sure that he did.

Emily woke up again, and this time, seeing both her companions treading the circle, her eyes went even wider.

They danced on as dawn crested and morning took possession of the jungle.

Out of silence, a story. Out of chaos, order. Out of nothingness, love . . .

Renie had been in a sort of trance herself for a long time, and it was only when weariness made her stumble that she saw the world around her again. It was a disturbing transition: she had been somewhere else, and knew in an inexplicable way what !Xabbu meant by "the eyes of the heart." He himself was still dancing, but slower now, with great deliberation, as though he were approaching a moment of reckoning.

Something else was moving in the corner of her vision. Renie turned to see Emily crouching like a frightened animal, waving her hand as if to drive something away. At first, Renie thought that the sight of her and !Xabbu dancing so long and so single-mindedly had unnerved the girl. Then she saw a face peering in at them from the undergrowth, a scant half a dozen yards away.

Renie stumbled again, but out of caution forced herself to dance on, although her heart was no longer in it. She examined the spy as best she could without obviously staring. It was one of the patchwork monstrosities they had earlier disturbed drinking at the river. The face was human, but only barely. The nose looked like something else that just happened to be in the middle of the face—formerly a toe, perhaps, or a thumb; the creature's ears jutted from its neck, which made its naked head seem stark as a battering ram. But despite these terrifying abnormalities, the creature did not seem threatening. The cowlike eyes watched !Xabbu's dance with a yearning that was almost pathetic.

But that doesn't mean anything. Renie's revelatory trance was shattered, her internal alarms jangling. *Those creatures have been altered— expressions, body language, none of those things can be trusted.*

She slowed her own dancing as naturally as she could, then stepped out of the circle as though she had finally tired. It was not altogether false—she was panting and soaked with sweat. She stole another look as she wiped her forehead. A second face had appeared beside the first, this one with its eyes set far too low in its cheeks. A third freakish countenance followed, then a fourth, all now jostling in the undergrowth to watch the baboon dance.

Emily had fallen to her hands and knees and was pressing her face against the ground, her thin back quivering with barely-suppressed terror. Renie was worried, but there was something so timid and helpless about the creatures that, altered or not, she had begun to feel they offered no immediate danger. Still, she called out to her friend.

"!Xabbu. Don't do anything sudden, but we have guests."

He danced on, *stamp, shuffle, shuffle, stamp.* If he was only pretending not to hear her, it was a brilliant piece of acting.

"!Xabbu. I wish you would stop now." Behind her, Emily made a little choking noise of fear. Her friend still did not seem to notice anything outside himself.

More of the damaged people were becoming visible. At least a dozen had formed a semicircle in the thick vegetation at the edge of camp, cautious as deer, and Renie heard a faint rustling behind her as well. She and her companions were slowly being surrounded.

"!Xabbu!" she said, louder now. And he stopped.

The baboon tottered for a moment, then fell down. By the time

Renie reached his side he had struggled back up to a sitting position, but the way his head wobbled on his neck frightened her, and although she held him and spoke his name, his eyes would not focus. A stream of clicking, unintelligible speech came out of his mouth, dumbfounding her, until she realized that the networks' translation gear must not know any Bushman dialects.

"!Xabbu, it's me, Renie. I can't understand you." She fought against rising panic. !Xabbu engrossed in dancing and meditating was one thing, but !Xabbu unable to communicate at all was a lonely, terrifying thought.

The baboon eyes rolled back under his lids and the incomprehensible language, fluid and yet laced with percussive sounds, trailed away to a whisper. Then, weakly, he said, "Renie?" Her name, that single word, was one of the most wonderful things she had ever heard. "Oh, Renie, I have seen things, learned things—the sun is ringing for me again."

"We don't have time to talk about it," she said quietly. "Those creatures we saw earlier—they're here. All around the camp, watching us."

!Xabbu's eyes popped open, but he did not appear to have heard anything she'd said. "I have been foolish." His evident good cheer was startling. Renie wondered if he had gone a little mad. "Ah, it is different already." His eyes narrowed. "But what is it I am feeling? What is different?"

"I told you, those creatures are here! They're all around us."

He clambered out of her arms, but only flicked a glance at the ring of half-humans before turning back to Renie. "Shadows," he said. "But there is something I have missed." To her astonishment, he put his long muzzle close to her face and began sniffing.

"!Xabbu! What are you doing?" She pushed him away, terrified that the watchers might turn violent now that the Bushman's dance had ended. !Xabbu did not fight her, but simply walked around her and resumed sniffing her from the other side. His monkey hands moved delicately across her arms and shoulders.

The audience moved closer now, sliding out of the vegetation and into the circle of the camp. There was no threat in their movements, but they were still a frightening sight, a catalogue of malformation— heads set too low, arms growing from rib cages, extra legs, a row of hands running down a back like a dinosaur's crest, and all the modifications done with what appeared to have been clumsy carelessness. Worst of all, though, were the patchwork people's eyes—stupefied by pain and fear, but still aware of their own suffering.

In desperation, Renie tried to grab at !Xabbu, but he eluded her, continuing instead to sniff and pat and ignore her questions. Her terror and confusion were already threatening to overwhelm her when a loud sigh rippled through the monstrous human herd. Renie froze, certain that the creatures were about to charge, which allowed !Xabbu the freedom to thrust his hand into her pocket.

"I should have known it," he said as he lifted Azador's lighter up to catch the morning sun. "It was speaking, but I was not listening."

The crowd of watchers began to move again, but instead of attacking, they stepped back into the undergrowth so quickly that their misshapen forms almost seemed to have liquified and flowed away. Renie was stunned, both by the apparently causeless retreat and her friend's even more incomprehensible behavior.

"!Xabbu, what . . . what are you doing?" she gasped.

"This is a thing that does not belong," He twisted the lighter from side to side as though hoping to see some secret mark. "I should have known it before, but I have let myself become confused. The First People were calling to me, but I did not hear."

"I don't know what you're talking about!" The deformed creatures were gone, but her sense of tension had not diminished. A branch snapped nearby, loud as a firecracker. Something was crunching toward them through the jungle, careless of stealth. Even as Renie reached out to her distracted friend, a group of dark upright shapes shambled through the line of trees and stopped at the edge of the clearing.

There were perhaps half a dozen of them, huge, shaggy, bearlike creatures that were nothing so simple and clean as bears. Livid patches of moss grew on their pelts, and vines rooted to the sides of their necks coiled down through the fur, as writhingly alive as worms, to burrow in again at crotch and knee. But worse of all, where their heads should have been they wore instead the mindless smiles of carnivorous plants, great shiny purple and green pods which sprouted directly from their short necks, the mouthlike openings edged with toothy spines.

As these monsters waited, chests jerking with heavy, uneven breaths, another figure shambled out of the trees and took up a position in front of the plant-bears, a shape that although shorter, bulked even wider than its massive servants. Its tiny eyes gleamed with pleasure, and its flabby mouth stretched in a grin that revealed broken tusks of different yellowed lengths.

"Well, well, well," rumbled Lion. "Tinman has been a bad little machine, letting you get away. But his bad luck is my good, and now

the game is mine. Ah! This must be the Dorothy, and its
. . . container." He took a waddling step toward Emily, who scuttled
away across the dirt like a wounded crab; Lion laughed. "Congratula-
tions on your pregnancy, little Emily-creature." He rotated his knobby
head toward Renie and !Xabbu. "Some sculptor once said that the
statue is already inside the marble—that all the artist is doing is cutting away what is unnecessary." He laughed again. Spit glistened on
the distended lower lip. "I feel the same way about the Dorothy."

"What is the point of this?" Renie demanded, but she knew how
small and unconvincing her voice sounded, how insignificant her
strength was compared to even one of the massive and hideous plant-
bears. Hopelessness washed through her. "It's all a game, isn't it? Just
a cruel game!"

"But it is *our* game—my game, now." Lion smirked. "You are the
intruders. And, as someone once said . . . *trespassers will be eaten.*"

Renie wracked her mind for anything about Lion or his Twin that
might help, but nothing came. They were fearsome, Azador had told
her. They were unimaginably cruel.

"I can feel something," said !Xabbu brightly, startling Renie so that
she turned to stare at him. He still stared at the lighter cupped in his
hands; Lion, his mindless slaves, everything else might not have existed. "Something . . ."

"!Xabbu, they're going to kill us!" At Renie's words, Emily whimpered on the ground at her feet. Renie's terror was leavened for a
moment by a flash of anger—could this girl do nothing except whine
and cry?

"They?" !Xabbu looked up, still distant, still thinking of something
else. "They are meaningless. They are shadows." He caught sight of
Lion, and his lip curled in disgust. "Not all shadows, perhaps. But still,
they mean nothing."

Lion saw the lighter and his predator's eyes narrowed. "Where did
you get that?"

"!Xabbu, what is going on?" Renie demanded under her breath.

"And I misjudged other things, too." !Xabbu reached down with
his free hand and urged Emily to her feet. She resisted, but he planted
his splayed toes and kept tugging until she got into a crouch. "I will
explain later," he said; then: *"Run!"*

He jerked at Emily's arm again and got her stumbling toward the
river bank. Renie stared dumbfounded for a split-instant, then
sprinted after them. Lion shouted no orders, but within moments she
could feel the thunderous tread of the bear-creatures lumbering in
pursuit.

!Xabbu led the staggering Emily all the way to the bank and out into the river shallows, until the water reached his own simian shoulders. Renie thought he was going to swim for it, but instead he turned the girl downstream and pushed her ahead of him before swinging around to look for Renie.

"Just keep going that way," he urged. When Renie splashed past him, he swam back to the bank.

"What are you doing?"

"Keep Emily going downstream," he called back. "Trust me!"

She thrashed to a halt and almost lost her balance. "I'm not going to let you kill yourself to save us," she shouted. "That is old-fashioned bullshit!"

"Renie! Please trust me!" he cried from the scrub covering the bank. Already the trees were crackling a short distance away as Lion's servants crunched closer.

She hesitated for an instant. Emily had fallen down; shoved and pulled by the current, she was having trouble getting to her feet again. Renie cursed and waded after her.

They made slow, agonizing progress through the mud and high water, but Renie saw that !Xabbu's first idea at least had been good—they were still making better time than Lion and his huge creatures, who were forced to tear their way through the thick jungle foliage. She also knew that it was ultimately useless. She was gasping for breath already, and Emily would not last more than another few minutes, while their pursuers, she had no doubt, were virtually tireless. If !Xabbu hoped they would be able to wade all the way to the next transition point, which might be ten or twenty miles away, it was a brave but hopeless thought.

Lion had taken notice of their strategy. One of his bear-monsters crashed out of the undergrowth and down onto the bank, which crumbled beneath its weight and toppled the creature into the river, but it came up quickly, mossy fur streaming, eyeless vegetable head snapping spiny jaws as it set out through the shallows in disheartingly swift pursuit. Renie dug on even faster, half-carrying Emily, who was having trouble keeping her balance, but she could hear the wallowing noises behind her growing closer, paced by the thunder of the bankside pursuit as it plowed through jungle.

Her legs had grown dangerously rubbery when she spotted a thin gray-brown arm waving from a tree branch just ahead.

"This way!" !Xabbu called. As they stumbled to the branch he grabbed at Emily and helped her up onto the bank. The creature behind them did not roar or hiss or otherwise show emotion, but it dropped forward so that it could wade on all fours, increasing its speed. The horrid vegetable head furrowed the water like a tanker's prow.

Renie and Emily staggered after !Xabbu, up the bank and through the clinging branches.

"I thought I would be able to travel more quickly through the trees than you could," he explained as they fought their way into the jungle.

"But where are we going? We'll never outrun them."

"Just here," he said as he stopped to help a weeping Emily untangle herself from a vine. He was panting himself, but his voice was oddly calm. "Only a few steps more. Ah, this is it."

They limped into a small, empty clearing covered with tumbled branches and a mulch of fallen leaves. Light arrowed down through the trees and the hanging creepers as through the window of a cathedral. The noise of pursuit was terribly close.

"But there's nothing here." Renie looked at her friend in despair, wondering if the strain had finally driven him mad. "Nothing!"

"You are right," he said, raising his small hand. The first of Lion's plant-bears reeled into view, smashing its way toward them through the trees. "There is truly nothing here at all . . . if you only look."

A column of golden light flared in front of them, a tight helix curling endlessly on itself like a molten barber pole. An instant later it flattened and spread into a perfect rectangle. Renie could see nothing within the four straight sides except shifting colors, like the imprisoned rainbow of a radioactive soap bubble. !Xabbu took Emily's hand in one grip and Renie's in the other and led them toward it.

"How did you. . . ?" she began, almost beyond the point of surprise.

"Later I will tell. We must hurry now."

Two more plant-bears had appeared behind the first, and the dimmer but no less menacing figure of their master was right behind them; Lion shouted something at the fugitives, but his words were lost in the distorted, animal roar of his voice. "We can't take Emily out of her simulation," Renie said, frantic with the dwindling moment. "But if we leave her, they'll get her. Hurt her, take her baby."

!Xabbu shook his head, still pulling them both along. Renie caught Emily's eye, wanting to say she was sorry, but the girl was gray with fatigue, head down and stumbling. Renie hoped that whatever the system did to a Puppet when it tried to leave the simworld, it would be quick and painless. Perhaps it would even move Emily to some other part of Kansas.

Then the glow of the gateway was all around them, a flaring plasma sunspot that gave off no heat, and Lion's rising bellow of frustration was silenced.

They tumbled to a stop on a solid something which would have been the ground in a sane universe. Instead, it was a bumpy planar surface, angled like a hillside. The land, if it could be called that, was a curious patchwork, with all manner of colors moving in sluggish animation from surface to surface, slashed with jagged veins of flat, unreflective white, like bone showing through lacerated skin. But most disturbingly of all, in many parts of this surreal environment— particularly unsettling all across the expanse of what should have been sky—there was simply *no* color. But no color, she realized before her mind revolted and she had to shut her eyes, was not black, or white, or even the gray of a lost signal. It was simply . . . no color.

"Jesus Mercy," groaned Renie after a long moment, half-reverent, half-terrified. "Where are we, !Xabbu? And how did you make that happen?" She opened her eyes a slit, looking for her friend. What landscape she could see on the periphery of her vision was uneven, with suggestions of blocky, malformed things that might have been mountains, or trees, but trying to see them made her head hurt.

!Xabbu was lying on his side, his narrow chest barely moving. His pupils had rolled back under his eyelids.

Renie crawled to his side. The ground beneath him had visual depth, as though the baboon were stretched on a pane of glass over a cloudy sky. For a moment she had the dizzying certainty that she and he would both fall through it into nothingness, but the invisible earth was as solid as packed soil.

"!Xabbu?" He did not answer. She shook him, gently at first, but with increasing firmness. "!Xabbu, talk to me!"

Something made a noise behind her. Renie spun, ready to defend herself.

Emily 22813 was pulling herself up to a sitting position, her eyes wide.

"But . . . but how can you be here?" Renie demanded of the girl. In a day full of astonishments, this seemed one too many. "Unless . . . unless we're still in Kansas . . . but I don't think we are." She could make sense of none of it. "Jesus Mercy, it doesn't matter. Help me with !Xabbu—I think he's hurt, or sick."

"Who are you?" Emily sounded honestly curious. The voice was the same, but something in the intonation had changed. Her eyes narrowed in her pretty, childish face. "And what is wrong with your little monkey?"

Renie whirled to see !Xabbu's limbs stiffening in swift jerks. He was convulsing.

"Oh, my God," she shouted. "Someone, help!"

Nothing else moved anywhere in the unfinished landscape. They were alone.

CHAPTER 28

Darkness in the Wires

ANNELIESE said: *"Someone is calling you."*

Her soft Virginia drawl was so familiar that for a little while it became part of Decatur Ramsey's dream. His onetime assistant joined him on the hillside, looking out over the foggy valley. Something lurked down there in the gray-shrouded hollows. Ramsey knew only that it hunted him, and that he did not much want to meet it. He wondered whether that was what Anneliese was trying to tell him, but when he turned to ask her, the fog had risen, obscuring his vision.

The dream ended quickly, collapsing into the prosaic darkness of his bedroom, and with it went Anneliese's round, serious face. But her voice remained, and told him again that someone was calling. Ramsey sat up and snapped his fingers for the time, which his system obligingly threw onto the wall in glowing blue numerals—03:45.

Anneliese's tone grew a little sterner, exhibiting that steely sweetness that ran like a freshet of cold water through generations of southern womanhood. It was strange to think that her voice was still alerting him to messages and other household information, years after she'd left his employ. He didn't even know where she was any more—married, moved to another state, dim recollection that she had sent him a birth announcement for her first child . . .

Ramsey pawed at his eyes. His face felt like an ill-fitting mask, but he was finally awake. Almost four in the morning—who the hell was it? *"Answer."*

Anneliese's voice cut out in mid-remonstration, but nothing replaced it. Or at least Ramsey heard nothing—no voice, no hum or whispery *tick-tick* of static. But he still *felt* something, as though he stood before a window opened to the vacancy of deep space.

"Olga? Ms. Pirofsky? Is that you?"

No one spoke, but the feeling of waiting emptiness would not go away. It was as though the void itself had called him, the darkness in the wires trying to find a voice with which to speak.

"Hello? Is anyone there?"

Another hovering span of time, second stretching into second. Ramsey was sitting upright now in bed, staring into the almost total darkness above him, at the ceiling he could not see when his blackout blinds were shut, no matter the time of day or night. A knifepoint of fear touched him.

The voice, when it finally came, was an incongruous surprise. *"Ramsey, Decatur?"* A fruity, nasal Brooklynese, but oddly hesitant, as if it were puzzling out the pronunciation by phonetics.

"Who is this?"

"Ramsey, Decatur?" it asked again, and then it spewed out what at first seemed a meaningless run of numbers and letters. It took long moments before his sleep-addled mind began to recognize node and message codes, addresses. His heart quickened.

"Yes, yes. This is Catur Ramsey. I left those messages. Who is this?"

A long silence. "Not authorized," it said at last. "Whaddayou want?"

The cartoonish voice was quite difficult to take seriously, but he suspected he had very little room for error. "Please, stay connected. Is this Beezle Bug? Orlando Gardiner's agent? Can you at least confirm that?"

There was another long silence as it sorted through nesting permission hierarchies. He could almost feel its fuzzy logic overheating. "Not authorized," it said at last, but the lack of a denial was as much admission as Ramsey needed.

"Listen to me," he said slowly. "This is very important—important for Orlando, especially. Whatever permissions you need to talk to me, is there any way they can be obtained? If not, you're in a loop—do you understand? I want to help him, but I can't do anything if you won't cooperate. If I can't help him, he won't come back, and if he doesn't come back, he won't ever be able to give permissions for anything again."

The cab-driver voice on the other end took on a strangely aggrieved tone. "I know what a loop is. I know lots of things, Mister. I'm good gear." Ramsey could not help but be impressed by the responsiveness, especially for such an early generation of Pseudo-AI. Beezle *was* good gear.

"I know. So listen to me, then. Orlando Gardiner is in a coma—he is not conscious. I am an attorney for his friend Salome Fredericks— Sam, I think Orlando calls her. I want to help."

"Fredericks," the agent said. "He calls her 'Fredericks.' "

Ramsey had to suppress a whoop of triumph. The thing was talking to him. There must be more flexibility in its programming than he had thought. "Right, that's right. And to help them both, I need to have information, Beezle. I need access to Orlando's files."

"Orlando's parents tried to drezz me." It sounded almost sulky.

"They don't understand. They can't understand why you won't let them see Orlando's files. They want to help, too."

"Orlando told me not to let anyone see them, or change anything, or delete anything."

"But that was before his . . . his accident, his illness. Now it's important you let me help. I promise I won't let the Gardiners turn you off—drezz you. And I'll help bring Orlando back, if it can be done." He had a sense of Beezle now as a live thing, albeit of a strange sort. He could almost feel it out there in the darkness, a creature of legs and hard shell and skittish, fixated thoughts. He felt as though he were reeling it in from a great distance on a very, very thin line. "You can't wait for Orlando to give approval for things any more," he added. "You have to honor the original spirit of his commands."

God, he thought. *If anything's going to singe its logic, that will. I don't know many humans that wouldn't have trouble with a concept like that.* And as if to prove his worries prophetic, the darkness remained alive but depressingly silent for a long time.

But when the thing spoke, it was not to announce a fuzzy logic meltdown, or to protest improper authorization. What it said startled him so that he forgot the silly voice and the strange circumstances entirely.

"I'll ask him. Back in a couple of minutes."

Then the agent was gone. The line into the void was a broken string.

Ramsey lay back, confounded. Ask him? Who? Orlando? Had the little software agent somehow gone mad? Did gear do that? Or did it mean something else he could not understand?

He lay in the dark for a long time, his brain infested with noisy uncertainties. At last he got up and made himself a sandwich, took the milk accidentally left on the counter to warm since evening, and went to the living room to eat, look at his notes, and wait.

When Anneliese's disembodied voice announced the call, it startled him from a half-doze. His sheaf of papers—Ramsey had never shed the old-fashioned habit, learned from his father—slid to the floor with a dry splash.

"Someone is calling you," Anneliese reminded him as he fumbled after his papers, sounding disappointed with his tardy response.

These things, these machines, he thought—*what would we do without them? If all the real people disappeared, how long until some of us noticed?* More likely, but no more pleasant, what if his ex-assistant died but he did not hear of it? Her voice would still be waking him up, but from beyond the grave, as it were.

"Answer," he said sharply when he had captured his notes, irritated with himself, but also full of confused apprehensions, as though he had never entirely left his earlier dream.

"It's okay—I can talk to you," the cab-driver voice told him without preamble. "But don't think you're getting everything, 'cause you're not."

"Beezle, who did you just speak to?"

"Orlando." The agent said it with calm authority.

"But he's in a coma!"

Quickly, but with what sounded suspiciously like pride, Beezle Bug explained about its midnight forays and its stolen audiences with its master. "But it only works at certain stages of his sleep cycle," it went on. "Kinda like a carrier wave, see?"

Ramsey realized he had his first major ethical dilemma on his hands. If this was true, Orlando's parents should be told. Keeping them ignorant of a line of communication to their comatose child wouldn't only be unprofessional, but inhumanly cruel as well. But even if he could believe a chunk of code over all the doctors, the decision was still not simple. Olga Pirofsky's story had sent Catur Ramsey down some disturbing pathways in the past few days, and he was beginning to be frightened by what he had stumbled into. If his suspicions were correct, anything that punctured the general belief that Orlando Gardiner and Salome Fredericks were unreachable would put them and their families in real and terrible danger.

He weighed the problem, then decided that the middle of the night, with only two or three hours' sleep behind him, was not the time to make a decision.

"Okay, I believe you," he said aloud. His laugh was shaky. *I'm talking to an imaginary cartoon bug,* he thought. *Who's my only contact with a witness to what may be an ongoing crime of something like genocide. Oh, and that witness is for all intents and purposes dead.* "I believe you. Millions wouldn't. So let's talk."

And somewhere, in the darkness that was not a place, in the hours when most people were walking the farthest corridors of dream, they talked.

DULCIE put the loop program on, leaving the sim to sleep—or rather to counterfeit it—as she prepared for the transfer. The uninhabited body's twitches and fitful breathing mirrored her own discomfort, as though the tool had absorbed some of the feelings of its wielder.

Wielders, she reminded herself—*plural.* The sim had two masters, after all.

In what she had told herself was the spirit of good organization (but also, she secretly knew, in an effort to keep some kind of distance between herself and her employer's invasive presence) Dulcinea Anwin had constructed a virtual office space for the Otherland Project—or "Project Dread," as she thought of it to herself, with the pun fully intended. It was mostly snap-on gear, a standard workspace with picture windows that looked out on Dread's choice of scenery, a cold, sharp-edged version of nighttime Sydney that rather depressed her. She could have lobbied for a different view, and could certainly have replaced it with anything she wanted during her solo shifts, but as with so many other things lately, she found herself acceding bonelessly to her employer's whims.

She reviewed her mental notes (those which could safely be shared) and spoke them aloud to update the diary file. There was more to say than usual: their puppet sim, along with the rest of the little traveling company, was in a difficult situation. The local tribespeople were upset because there had been a kidnapping, and as strangers their group was automatically suspect.

She wondered for a brief moment if there was a chance one of their number might actually be involved in the disappearance, but it seemed unlikely. They were an odd and secretive group, but it was hard to conceive of any of them as kidnappers or rapists. In fact, she had begun to feel something sneakingly like fondness for them as traveling companions. No, if anyone was capable of doing something drastic, it was her own boss—but that was impossible. Dread had rock-solid reasons for not attracting notice to their virtual persona or the company in which it traveled.

Dulcie stared at the display, the virtual city spread below her like an old-fashioned circuit map, millions of little routines flickering out their individual messages, each oblivious to the larger picture. No matter how she tried, she could not entirely dismiss the worry that Dread might have something to do with their current virtual dilemma, although she also felt certain she was just being thin-skinned. Yes, he had snapped at her, threatened her, but that didn't make him an idiot, did it? He would kill, of course he would—she had seen a dozen or more people snuffed out in the commando raid on Bolivar Atasco's island, and had herself shot someone at his orders—but those were armed soldiers and hardened criminals, and that had been war. Of a sort.

As for what he had said to her . . . well, some men just liked to threaten women. She had met the type before—had even once been forced to rearrange the face of one, a drunkenly aggressive Russian mercenary, with a rock crystal ashtray. But Dread wouldn't piss in his own punchbowl, as her father had liked to say. He was far too smart for that.

But that was the problem, wasn't it? That was why she couldn't think straight about any of this. She'd never met anyone quite as smart as Dread seemed to be, or at least she hadn't met any who also had his weird animal charisma. Her earlier dismissal of him as a self-aggrandizing lowlife, a death-and-destruction fanboy, of whom she had met far too many, now seemed facile: there was something other than the normal mercenary brutalism going on behind that strange dark face, and Dulcie had to admit she was beginning to get interested.

Oh, please, she told herself. *It's bad enough you chose to work with people like that. You don't want to get involved with one again, too. How many times do you have to make that mistake?*

But of course, it was the excitement of real danger that had brought her out of her old job in international banking—through a financier boyfriend who dabbled in, but was ultimately afraid of, the actual hardcore stuff—into the world of black ops. There was still a part of her that ached to go back to her high school reunion one day and tell all those girls who used to call her "Dulcie Android" and "Gearhead" the truth about where life had taken her. *"What do I do for a living?"* she would say. *"Oh, overthrow governments, smuggle weapons and narcotics, you know, just . . . stuff. . . ."* But it was a useless fantasy. Even if they believed her, they would never understand, those ex-cheerleaders and proud PTA presidents whose idea of being really bad was fudging their taxes or having a meaningless affair with the pool cleaner. They would never understand the giddy high, the no-hands, terrifying exhilaration of a big op. And she, Dulcinea Anwin—the same little Dulcie Android, with her math books and her glasses and her one-year-late crop haircut—was now a serious player.

A chime sounded. A moment later Dread appeared in the middle of the office, his sim dressed in the black shirt and pants he favored, his hair pulled into a horsetail that vanished into the color of his shirt at the back. He sketched a little bow. Dulcie could not help wondering how closely the sim's rangy but muscular frame mimicked his real-life shape. He appeared no taller than she, perhaps even a bit shorter, but could easily have corrected that on his sim if it were an issue. She liked that it wasn't.

"Asleep?" he asked. He seemed very smiley, bubbling over with happy secrets.

"Yeah. Some of them are talking, but at least one other person was sleeping, so it seemed okay to slide offline and catch up on some notes. It's been a busy day in Flying Caveman Land."

"Ah." He nodded, almost too gravely, as though he were getting ready to tell a joke. "Still that kidnapping thing? No change?"

"Not really. They're still being held—there's supposed to be some sort of tribal gathering or something where the crime will be discussed." She couldn't get a fix on him today. Something was definitely up—even his sim seemed to crackle with electricity. "You seem very cheerful. Did you get some happy news?"

"Did I. . . ? No. I suppose I'm just in a good mood." He grinned, a shark-flash of white. "You're looking very good yourself, Dulcie. Is that a real-time sim, or have you sculpted it a bit?"

She looked down at her virtual self quickly, then realized he was teasing her. "It's real-time, as you damn well know. Just plain old me." Even the way he admired her was strange—predatorily sexual, but also somehow nonsexual at the same time, like a sultan with a hundred wives trying to decide whether to make a well-connected young noblewoman his hundred and first. Again, she was seized by conflicting impulses, the need to put distance between herself and this man countered by the mesmeric effect he had on her.

Schoolgirl crush, she thought, half-amused, half-disgusted. *You always did like the bad boys, Anwin.*

"Well, I'm sure you have things to do," he said abruptly, almost dismissively. "Feed your cat, whatever. And I'd better get to work." He held up his hand to forestall her next remark. "I'll go over the notes after I check in." He paused, thinking. "You know, you've been working really hard lately. Why don't you take twenty-four hours off? No, make it forty-eight. Paid, of course. Give you a chance to catch up with things at home. I haven't been giving you much time for that lately."

He had wrong-footed her again—she had never met anyone who could do that so consistently. What was this about? Was he trying to get her out of the way, afraid she would bungle this business with the tribal council? Or was he genuinely being nice? It was true, she had pulled so many twelve-hour shifts lately she hadn't had time to do more than shower and sleep and review her crisis-mail in between. There were still things on the home front to be taken care of that had gone untouched since she had returned from Colombia.

"That's . . . that would be fine, yeah." She nodded her head. "Are you sure it won't be too much for you?"

"Oh, I'll rest when I need to." He smiled confidently, and she was struck yet again by his energy. She'd never seen him quite like this.

"Okay, then. Chizz. I'll see you. . . ."

"This time, day after tomorrow. Enjoy your days off."

She left the virtual office, disconnected, and sat on the couch for a while, letting her confused thoughts run freely, go skittering without rhyme or reason. Jones vaulted up into her lap and butted her hand, asking to be petted.

Dulcie could not get the memory of Dread's bright, bright smile out of her head, of the energy coiled in his virtual frame. Or the look on his face the other time, when he had threatened her, his eyes dark as stones. She could not stop thinking about him.

God help me, she thought, tugging absentmindedly at Jones' collar. *I'm either falling for him . . . or he scares me to death.*

If there's even a difference.

WITH Dulcie gone, the man who had once been the boy named
Johnny Wulgaru cranked up his internal music—polyrhythms, mostly
tuneless, but energetic as locusts feeding—and contemplated the virtual city spread beyond the windows of the imaginary office. It was so
like a woman to want a *place* to do things. That was one of the ways
you saw the animal in them, that deep nesting urge. Even his whore
mother had liked to drape colorful scarves across the broken furniture
every now and then, sweep up the ampules and the empty squeeze-
bottles and "make the place nice"—which was like gilding a dog turd,
but try telling that to the stupid bitch. Women didn't float, like men
did. They were rooted, or they wanted to be. You didn't see many
women following the road, drifting from place to place. Of course,
perhaps that was because they didn't want to be with the kind of men
who did.

But it was also why, since he had learned to control anger, he killed
men only for money, or occasionally out of practical necessity. Because
women were close to the ground, close to the machineries of life, there
was a vitality in them that men lacked. Men would throw their lives
away, often as not in a futile gesture, in some preprogrammed rage-
loop that meant nothing, that was only Nature's way of tidying up the
board. But women clung to life—they were of it completely, in it from
their soiled feet to their life-extruding loins to their wary eyes. They
were life, in some way he could not explain, and thus it was more than
simply a job to hunt them and snatch it from them. It was a shout
against all the world. It was a way to make the universe itself take
notice.

Dread snapped his fingers and the cityscape shifted. The Sydney
Opera House appeared from one side of the window and glided into
the center of his view, as though the office itself were rotating. The
city lights streamed past, glittering, each and every one of them a sort
of star, each illuminating its own dependent worlds. But Dread was
the Destroyer of Worlds.

He brought up the polyrhythms until he could feel them cascading
through him like pachinko balls, rattling the bones of his head and
tightening his skin. He felt good—very good indeed. He had a plan,
still largely unformed, but even in its embryonic form it burned inside
him and made him quiver with energy. At moments like this, he felt
himself to be the only truly living thing in existence.

The hunt had been good—very, very good. The pale-haired creature in the flying world had acted just as prey should. She had wept. She had bargained. She had cursed and then wept again. She had fought until the very last moment, and then accepted his black kiss with a broken, pained grace that no male victim, real or virtual, could ever match. The memory of it all still rolled through his veins like the purest opiate, but it did not suppress the excitement of his burgeoning plans: in fact, the memory of his own mastery made the contemplation better, laying the cool hand of practical possibility across the fevered brow of ambition.

Of ambition? No, say it, tell the truth—of godhood. For this must be the way that the gods felt, all those raping, murdering, lightning-flinging, shape-changing monstrosities that used to rule the world. His mother's Aboriginal tales, the Greek myths in school books, the tattered comic books he had found in wards and children's homes, all sources agreed: the gods were powerful, and thus could take anything they wanted, do anything they chose. In no other ways were they different from humans. But where humans wished, or envied, or wanted, gods *took* and *did*.

Well, he was halfway to godhood already, wasn't he? The rest couldn't be too hard.

Dread entered the sim and lay for a while in the shared darkness, listening to his own breath, feeling the chill air creep in from the mouth of the cave. Some people were whispering close by—his companions, perhaps, or their captors. He kept his eyes closed. He was in no hurry. There was suspicion among the members of their little company now, but it was still muted. Other than that glorious hunt, he had done nothing, nor had Dulcie, to draw unnecessary attention.

But Dread was beginning to wonder if that even mattered anymore. What was the value of passing for one of these stumbling fools, when they seemed incapable of doing anything? There were countless worlds here, each exciting in a million ways, and they had explored barely any of them. Worse, they had discovered nothing useful about what the Old Man and his colleagues planned. Dread had committed himself to this horribly dangerous bit of treachery largely because he suspected it would be his best (and perhaps only) chance to send the ancient bastard down the road to painful obliteration, but nothing was coming of it.

He had been cultivating patience so carefully—somehow, at some point, he knew he must be rewarded for it. But not, it had begun to seem, if he yoked himself to these shuffling oxen. Except for the Martine woman, they seemed to have no grasp of the underlying rules of the place, could not feel its movements as he could. They had no rhythm, that was the pathetic truth—no sense of the music of being.

So what to do next? How to move closer to the prize he sensed beat at the heart of this man-made universe? Perhaps it was time to shed these losers and move on.

As he lay in the dark, pondering, one of his companions rolled over and touched his shoulder. Dread had been so far away, so wrapped in complex, exultant thoughts, that at first he could not remember who he was supposed to be, and even after his own false identity came back to him, a few more long seconds passed before he recognized who was whispering to him.

"Are you awake? I need to talk to you." The voice was very close to his ear. "I—I heard one of us come back last night, after we all went to sleep. When that girl disappeared. And I think I know who it was."

Dread rolled the sim body over, keeping the muscles loose and ready. "Oh, no!" He tried to sound what he hoped was the right note of whispered fear. "You mean you think . . . you think one of us . . . is a murderer?"

But inside he was laughing, laughing.

Fourth:

BEDLAM'S SONG

. . . With an host of furious fancies
    Whereof I am commander
With a burning spear and a horse of air
    To the wilderness I wander.
By a knight of ghosts and shadows
    I summoned am to tourney
Ten leagues beyond the wide world's end,
    Methinks it is no journey.

Yet I will sing: Any food,
    Any feeding, drink or clothing?
Come, dame or maid, be not afraid,
    Poor Tom will injure nothing.

        —Tom O'Bedlam's Song (Traditional)

CHAPTER 29

Imaginary Gardens

NETFEED/NEWS: Parents Cannot Implant Without Court Order
(visual: Holger Pangborn and lawyer getting out of car)
VO: The US Supreme Court upheld a lower-court decision that the father
and stepmother of Holger Pangborn violated his civil rights when they had
the Arizona teenager implanted with a behavior-monitoring device similar
to the mod-parole chips used on criminals in Russian and some other Third
World countries. The senior Pangborns have said they will take the case to
the human rights court of the UN.
H. PANGBORN'S ATTY: "Not only did they literally violate his body, they
did so in an appallingly dangerous, slipshod manner. The implant was
performed by someone who wasn't even a doctor, someone whose license to
practice medicine had been cancelled by the State of Arizona two years earlier
for gross malfeasance . . ."

IN his native language, there had been words that came closer than any English phrase to explaining how Sellars thought of this place—the spot where all that he planned and did could be properly considered.

Technologists had their own terms for such things, prosaic if not downright embarrassing, on very rare occasions inspired. But whether it was called an interface, a data display, or a dream library, what had begun a century before as an attempt to conceptualize information in ways that people other than engineers could understand, starting with crude images of the most mundane business objects—file folders, in-boxes, wastebaskets—had expanded along with the power of the technology, until the ways in which information could be ordered and acted upon were as individual, even peculiar, as the people who used it. And Sellars was a peculiar individual by any standards.

As he did every day soon after waking, he closed his eyes and sank deep into himself, into the depths of his distributed system, which was hidden in the interstices of countless other systems, a series of tiny parasitic nodes feeding unobserved on the thick hide of the vast terrestrial datasphere. Sellars had learned this trick of distribution from TreeHouse and similar bandit sites, but had made it his own, carrying it to an extent that no one could have imagined a single individual could accomplish. At first the largest part of his tendrils had siphoned resources directly from his captors, the United States military. In anticipation of changing times, he had later begun to transfer linkage to scores of other networks, but there was no little satisfaction in knowing that he had engineered his escape with the tools of the very people who had held him prisoner. He had done it right under their noses, too, using access methods they had not guessed at, leaving no traces to be found by the intelligence sweepers, who routinely combed his small house on the military base for pro-scribed objects or other indications that he was less resigned to his fate than he seemed, or by the military surgeons, who for years had examined him in the most intimate, unpleasant ways on a frequent but unscheduled basis.

Sellars was patient in ways his opponents could not understand, and subtle beyond their best guesses. He had been playing a long game, and almost five decades of apparent resignation had lulled even the most suspicious minds. But they had missed the most fundamen-tal fact: although he had recently completed his physical escape, and was hiding, like Conan Doyle's purloined letter, in what was nearly plain sight—just a yard or two beneath the very feet of the men who were hunting him, in the disused utility tunnels of their own base—he had escaped into the information sphere years earlier. And since the moment when he had first found his way there, springing from the trap of his crippled body and his house arrest into the free-dom of the net, Sellars had never again considered himself to be a prisoner.

*   *   *

He sank into his system and then summoned his information like Prospero calling a trillion Ariels from a trillion cloven pines. Whether his warders had been correct, or he had—whether he had been a prisoner, or only appeared to be one—his actual departure from the little house and their immediate scrutiny had been a necessary step in his campaign, which now entered its most difficult phase. Unlike the skirmishes with his outmatched captors, his true task had been nearly hopeless from the very first, and teetered minute by minute on the brink of failure. Failure, though, was not an acceptable option: its consequences would be terrible beyond imagination.

Sellars could feel the information gathering thick and lively around him now. In the depths of his own thoughts, submersed in *on* and *off* in their potentially infinite patterns, he began to examine the most recent changes in his information model. Although he had never spoken of it to anyone, he thought of it as his Garden.

On occasions, when he had been happier and more optimistic than he was now, Sellars had even thought of it as a Poetry Garden.

His information model was a profusion, a struggle, a violent but paradoxically controlled exchange of subtleties. It had the look of a jungle, a place where things grew and fought, altered, adapted, where strategies blossomed spectacularly then failed, or bloomed and survived, or simply absorbed the moisture of informational existence and waited. "Garden" was more than just his name for it—Sellars had shaped the indicators in the form of plants, although few of them resembled anything found in a botanist's field manual. The virtual flora altered with the information they symbolized, changing shape and habit as the database relations shifted.

The Garden presented itself as a great sphere. Sellars' bodiless point-of-view floated at its center, able instantaneously to see larger patterns of growth, or to move microscope-close—near enough to count individual grains of pollen on a symbolic stamen. Once upon a time the Garden had represented the full diversity of his interests, all his pastimes and fascinations, the dreams which he could pursue unfettered only in the ether of information space. Now those other functions had shrunk to a few representative images, a bare fraction of the whole—a moss of infrastructure control functions, some vines that marked various telecommunication strategies, and here and there the fading flower of an ignored but not yet officially discontinued project.

These days a new ecology held sway in the Garden. What had started years before as a sifting of new spores, a heliotropic tug on a

few of the existing data plants, had become the dominant paradigm.
Just as hardier species might invade and eventually supplant a frail
indigenous population, Otherland now dominated Sellars' Eden.

He had chosen this form for his model because he had always loved
gardens.

During his long years as a pilot, his epic, lonely journeys, he had
lived only for the times when he could tend to growing things and see
them responding to his care—changing, elaborating, *becoming.* Sellars
could think of no happier human metaphor for God than that of Gardener. In fact, he secretly sympathized most strongly with Him in His
decision to send the angel with the flaming sword to evict the first
man and woman when they proved unworthy of the home He had
given them. To the extent that he indulged the metaphor, Sellars did
not believe that Adam and Eve had been corrupted by knowledge,
but by misunderstood knowledge: something, whether serpentine or
otherwise, had led them to believe—as humans still tended to do—
that they were not simply part of the Garden, but rather its owners.

He sometimes thought of his data model as a Poetry Garden because Sellars could not help bringing poetry into everything he cared
about. In his long years of imprisonment he had sought it out as other
prisoners sought out drugs or religious certainty, and he had used it
to shape everything he made and everything he thought. He absorbed
the Garden's changing states as a lover of haiku contemplated poems
about rain, and listened to its soundless voice as another might feel
the perfect rhythm of a descending line. As with any good poem, Sellars felt the Garden's life more than he thought about it, but as also
with the best poetry, when he did choose to apply rational thought, it
yielded more than he could have dreamed.

An American poet named Marianne Moore, writing about the duties of poets, had once suggested that they should present for inspection, "imaginary gardens with real toads in them"—that the
substance of art, as Sellars understood it, had to be leavened with the
art of substance.

But now the study of Otherland had changed his Poetry Garden
into something barely comprehensible—a swirl of fantastical plants
which seemed almost to have no end or beginning, as though the
information symbolized in the model was growing into one maddening, infinitely complex, infinitely interlinked thing. The Otherland
model represented a conspiracy so intricate and yet apparently absurd
that even the most eagerly delusional paranoid would take one look
at it and return in disgust to normality. It threatened the entire world,
and yet it made no sense.

Sellars was beginning to think that his imaginary Garden could use a few good toads.

He had been staring at the latest version of the information for a long time without really seeing it, he realized. His body meant little to him, but it was hard to deny that the discomfort of his current situation, physical and otherwise, was having an effect on his thinking. In the past days he had found it very hard to wake up, and even after he did, it took him a long time to think clearly—to *see* what was needful to see. He had hoped that the luck of encountering the homeless boy might bring him some respite, but so far the Cho-Cho experiments had been notable failures.

Sellars envied the precision of mechanical operation. Sometimes it seemed that being an organic life-form was a hindrance at best. He had slept for long hours the night before, but he was still not rested, yet the ever-changing patterns in the Garden were crying out for attention. He did his best to push back the fatigue and disappointment of the past week.

One frustration could not be ignored, and it struck him afresh every time he entered this metaphorical place. The people within the Otherland network—those he had summoned into risk, and to whom he had spoken in the Atascos' simulation—were almost completely hidden from him. Since they were at the center of his hopes, any representation which did not show something of their situation was hopelessly flawed. But in the last few days there had arisen a happier but no less maddening paradox: if not for the emergence of what now seemed his greatest enemy, he would have no information about them at all.

Sellars had thought, as he had built his knowledge of the Grail Brotherhood and their insanely ambitious network over the years, that the one who would require the greatest attention and care was Jongleur. The oldest man alive was still a terrifyingly powerful and subtle enemy, but anyone that important in the real world could not help leaving indicators of his actions. A vast, bushy plant with poisonous-looking white flowers near the center of the information model stood as testament to all that Sellars knew about Jongleur. Its stems might stretch astonishingly wide, prying like thin fingers into the Garden's farthest reaches, its roots might bulge the mossy soil in every direction, but the plant itself was at least an individual entity, available for examination and theoretically, if not practically, knowable.

But more and more, as Sellars had fought against the resistance of the Otherland network, desperate to reach the volunteers he had deserted so suddenly, he had come to realize that the network itself, or something that had grown because of it, was his greatest and most worrisome problem. The virtual plant that represented Jongleur and his actions was comprehensible—just like a real plant, it fed itself and fought for sunlight, struggling for survival in the same way that Jongleur bent all his power in pursuit of what might currently be obscure, but were in all likelihood sensibly self-serving goals.

But the operating system, or whatever it was that so fiercely guarded the network, the thing which had already killed several people and had almost killed Sellars himself more than once, was far less comprehensible. In his Otherland-dominated Garden, it manifested as a kind of fungus, one of those primitive organisms that in the real world could grow rapidly and invisibly beneath the earth, expanding for thousands of yards until it had become the largest of all living things. The actual phenomenon this virtual fungus represented—"the Other," as some of the more secretive communications of the Grail Brotherhood referred to it—was clearly an intimate part of the network itself. In Sellars' Garden model, based on all the information he had gathered about its nature and its actions, it sent saprophytic tendrils of interest everywhere, in almost incomprehensible profusion, but the fruiting bodies of its actions came to the surface in only a few places.

But here was Sellars' relatively happy paradox: its near-ubiquitousness had become a major practical boon to him.

In the early hours of being forced out of the network after the Atasco sanctuary had been attacked, and in countless cautious experiments since, Sellars had learned that the Other, whatever it truly was, seemed to be drawn in some way to the people he had smuggled into the network. On those few occasions he had managed temporarily to fix their position (all but once too briefly to make contact of any kind) he had also discovered that position to be surrounded by a whorl of Other-related activity. It was strange—almost as though his volunteers held some kind of fascination for the network itself. If it had been the straightforward fascination that a foreign object inspired in an antibody, as would seem logical, he felt sure they would long ago have been eliminated, as the old man Singh had been, slain by a massive coronary in his South African convalescent hospital room.

But as far as Sellars could tell, during the brief moments of investigation he had snatched between skirmishes with the Other, most of his small company still seemed to be alive within the network. Even more surprising—but his one real ray of hope—was that since this strange and protean enemy was so drawn to them, almost everything he could not discover of their position and situation from direct observation he could infer from the profusion of Other-related actions.

In other words, he had discovered that where the Other was most active on the network, the chances were good that Sellars' own people were nearby.

Not all of the centers of the Other's most frantic activity would be Renie Sulaweyo, Orlando Gardiner, and the others, but many of them clearly were. This was very good for Sellars, but he could only hope that Jongleur and the other Grail members had not noticed the anomaly.

As the mists of his fatigue began to thin a little, Sellars saw that there had been several changes in the Garden since his last connection. Several fungal traces of the Other had broken the surface, and in one place several distinct subsets had come together overnight, localized now in an obscure and heretofore untouched section of his inside-out, green world. He wondered briefly if this new aggregation meant that some of the individual groups, who had been inexplicably separated a short time back, had found each other again. If so, that too might be a cause for hope. He also wondered if it was time to try to use the boy Cho-Cho again. He had not prepared the youth properly the last time, it was now clear—the first emergence into the network had shocked him so badly there had been no point in going forward with the experiment—but it had still been Sellars' greatest success since the Temilún fiasco, since the boy's description of the people he had seen had sounded very much like Irene Sulaweyo and her Bushman-baboon companion.

Sellars put the possibility aside for later consideration. Distracting the security system and then holding and hiding an access line long enough to get the boy through was horrifyingly hard work. He wasn't sure whether he was up to it again just yet.

He moved his focus on the Garden in and out, looking for patterns. The Other's latest fruiting bodies were also interesting. He could not tell yet what they symbolized, but it seemed to be moments of large expenditure of energy on the part of the network. He would run some analysis on them later, when he had finished with the larger picture.

Sellars moved with relief from the obscurities of what was happening within the Otherland system to the section of his Garden that represented things happening outside the Grail network, in RL, where information was more reliable and easier to interpret. Just in the last days there had been a rash of deaths and other occurrences, all related in some way to Otherland, so there was much new growth on those parts of the model.

A reasonably famous, but long-retired inventor of role-playing gear, rumored to have been given his own simulation on the Otherland network for services rendered, had been found dead of apparent heart failure; a group of children from the TreeHouse technocommune had fallen victim to Tandagore Syndrome; but most significant—and perhaps most troublesome for the Grail people—was that a dozen research scientists in almost as many different countries had all been killed within a single eight-hour period.

The scientists had been felled by a variety of causes from cardiac failure to brain aneurysm, but Sellars knew (although the authorities had not yet admitted it) that each of them had been logged into an entomology facility sponsored by Hideki Kunohara—a man with so many connections to Otherland that he himself had become a species of lichen within Sellars' Garden. Kunohara's online facility had experienced some kind of massive failure, although even the investigators' private conversations Sellars had managed to monitor suggested they had no idea how that collapse might be linked to the scientists' deaths.

The various propaganda arms of the Brotherhood were already moving to isolate and confuse the investigations, and with their immense resources might very well succeed, but even the fact of the failure having happened, with such spectacularly newsworthy results, was curious. Why would the Brotherhood allow so many prominent people to die on their network? Were the Grail brethren losing control of their own system? Or were they now too powerful, too far advanced in their plan, to care?

Each of these small botanical newcomers considered, both for itself and within the greater ecology, Sellars moved on.

As his systems collated information from the vast legion of resources he had linked to his Garden, new plants had sprouted and begun to grow almost unnoticed, but some had recently developed such robust size that he could not ignore them.

One represented a lawyer in Washington, affiliated to the Garden model through Salome Fredericks and Orlando, whose vegetable avatar was busy sending roots in all directions. Some of these roots had extended so fast and so far that Sellars himself was being constantly surprised by the new places he found them. This lawyer, Ramsey, was extending a search of his own through the information sphere almost as fast as Sellars could track him, and seemed to have made a large and symbiotic connection with the plant that symbolized Orlando Gardiner's own real-world system.

There was also mysterious activity flowering in Australian law-enforcement networks, which interacted both with the subgarden that represented the Circle—Sellars knew he had a lot of thinking to do as far as the Circle were concerned, perhaps a day's gardening just for them alone—as well as Jongleur, and even the fungal threads of the Other. He had no idea why that would be. More questions.

Irene Sulaweyo's real-world plant, far more available to observation than the one which symbolized her activities inside the Otherland network, had developed some disturbing tendencies as well—stems extending at odd angles, leaves dying as the information they represented suddenly dried up. He dimly remembered that she had a dysfunctional family, and of course it had been her brother's coma which had brought her into this in the first place. Sellars could do nothing more for her online self than he was already doing, but he hoped that her physical body was safe, and made a note to see what he could learn about her situation.

Last, and most worrisome to him personally, was the shiny pale flower that represented little Christabel Sorensen. Until twenty-four hours ago, for all that he had put her through, despite all the risks he had brought to her, her blossom had been thriving. But he had been unable to contact her for two days, and she had not donned the access device he had given her—the replacement Storybook Sunglasses—to answer his last call; his readings suggested they seemed to be broken or decommissioned. It might be something as simple as equipment failure, he knew, but a check of military base records showed that she had not been to school yesterday, and her father had called his own office to excuse himself for the day because of what the system listed as "family problems."

It all worried him very much, not only for Christabel's sake, but for his own. He had exposed himself by being so dependent on the child, although he had seen no other option at the time. It was a grave weakness in his security.

The drooping petals of the Christabel-flower reproached him. The problem required a delicate investigation, and perhaps an equally delicate solution, but he did not have enough information yet about what had changed. He shifted his focus away.

Sellars was tiring now. He looked only briefly to the single green shoot that represented Paul Jonas. For a while, right until the moment Sellars had succeeded in his audacious plan to free Jonas into the system, the Jonas-stem had been the center of a tangled thicket of plans and actions. But now the man was gone, lost in the system beyond any of Sellars observational capabilities, and could no longer be acted upon. But the central Paul Jonas questions remained unanswered.

How could one man so endanger the Brotherhood that they would keep him a prisoner on the system and eradicate all proof that he had ever existed in the real world? Why would they not simply kill some-one who was, for whatever reasons, such a threat to them? They had killed hundreds of others that Sellars knew of with certainty.

He felt a headache coming on. Still too much Garden, not enough toads.

It was all in flux, and although new patterns were forming he could not make sense of them yet. Some were cause for hope, but others filled him with despair. His spherical Garden represented the hopes and fears of billions of people, and the gamble Sellars had undertaken was a desperate one. A week from now, a month, would it still be a vigorous jungle? Or would rot have struck down all plants but the Brotherhood's, tumbled all other stalks and stems and leaves to the ground to become mulch for the venomous blooms of Felix Jongleur and his friends?

And what of Sellars' own secret? The one that even his few allies did not suspect, the one that even in the event of a most improbable and miraculous victory against the Grail, could still turn the Garden into a wasteland of ash and tainted soil?

He was only tormenting himself, he knew, and to no purpose: he did not have a moment's extra time or strength to spend on pointless worrying. If he was anything, he was a gardener, and whether the future brought him rain or drought, sun or frost, he could only take what was given to him and do his best.

Sellars pushed away the darkest thoughts and returned to his tasks.

CHAPTER 30

Death and Venice

NETFEED/NEWS: Chinese Say "Fax You!"
(visual: Jiun Bhao and Zheng opening Science and Technical Campus)
VO: Chinese Minister for Science Zheng Xiaoyu announced today that the
Chinese have taken a huge leap forward in the race to perfect "teleportation"
technology—the spontaneous transmission of matter, a favorite device of
science fiction flicks. In a press conference during the opening ceremonies for
the new Science and Technical Campus in T'ainan—formerly the National
Cheng Kung University—Zheng announced that Chinese researchers were
close to solving the "antiparticle symmetry problem," and that he had no
doubt matter transport, also known as teleportation, would be a reality
within a generation, perhaps as early as the middle of next decade. Doctor
Hannah Gannidi of Cambridge University is not so optimistic.
(visual: Dr. Gannidi in her office.)
GANNIDI: "They haven't let us see much, and what we've seen has a lot of
questions attached to it. I'm not saying they may not have made some
important progress—some of Zheng's people are really excellent—but I
wouldn't be planning to fax yourself home for the holidays just yet . . ."

THE masks of Comedy and Tragedy bobbed toward him through the darkened basilica, but when he most needed to move, fear seemed to have pulled the bones right out of Paul's legs and back. The terrible pair had found him again—would they hunt him until the end of time?

"Don't move, Jonas," narrow-faced Tragedy crooned. "We have lots of lovely, squeezy things planned for you."

"Or we might just rip you apart," suggested Comedy.

A third voice, a silent compulsion which brushed along his nerve endings like a chill breeze, urged him to give up—to fall where he stood and let the inevitable happen. What was the point of flight? Did he really think he could elude these two tireless pursuers forever?

Paul clutched at the wall for support. Some force that emanated from these two was poisoning him, slowing the heart within his chest. He could feel his fingers, his hands and arms and legs, all growing cold, stiff . . .

Gally! The boy was still sleeping in the woman Eleanora's rooms. If they captured Paul, what was to keep them from taking him as well?

The realization sparked something at the base of his brain and sent a charge of rigidity down his spine. He staggered back another step, then found his balance and turned. For a moment he could not remember in which direction Eleanora's apartment lay; the enervating dread that seeped from the pair behind him threatened once more to pull him down. He chose what he thought was the right direction and flung himself forward down the shadowed corridor. Within seconds the compulsion to surrender became less, but he could still feel the pair following behind him. It was terrifying and yet also strangely unreal, a nightmare of flight and pursuit.

Why don't they just capture me? he wondered. *If they're the masters of this network, why don't they surround me, or turn off my sim, or something?* He ran faster, risking a fall on the slippery floors. It was stupid to torment himself with unanswerable questions—better to snatch at freedom while he could.

But they're getting closer each time, he realized. *Each time.*

Paul recognized a familiar wall hanging: he had guessed correctly. A moment later he was pounding on the apartment door, which fell open a few inches before hitting some obstruction. He heard Gally's voice inside, a rising sound of confusion and question, so he put his shoulder down and shoved as hard as he could. The door held for a moment, then the impediment slid to one side, scraping on the flagstones, and Paul tumbled into the room. Eleanora huddled in a corner with wide-eyed Gally pulled close against her.

"You left me!" Paul shouted. "You left me to those . . . things!"

"I came to save the boy," the small woman snapped. "He means something to me."

"You think piling . . . furniture against the door is going to . . . to keep them out?" He was breathing so hard he could hardly talk, and already the sense of imminent attack was growing again. "We have to get out of here. If you can't get me offline, can you at least get us to another simulation? Make a . . . a gateway, whatever those things are called."

"No." She shook her head, her wizened face tight. "If I summon an emergency gateway to interfere with Jongleur's agents, the Brotherhood will know. This is not my fight. This Venice is all I have left. I will not risk it all for you, a stranger."

Paul could not believe he was standing there arguing, while Death and Destruction breathed down his neck. "But what about the boy? What about Gally? They'll take him, too!"

She stared at him, then at the child. "Take him and run, then," she replied. "There is a hidden doorway that will let you out to the square. Tinto said the nearest gateways were with the Jews or the Crusaders. The Ghetto is a long distance—all the way to the middle of Cannaregio. Better to go to the Crusader hospital. If you are lucky, you can outrun those things long enough to get there and find the gate."

"And how am I supposed to find this Crusader place?"

"The boy will show you." She leaned down and kissed Gally on top of his head, mussed his hair with an almost fierce affection, then shoved him toward Paul. "Through my bedchamber. I will make it look as though you forced your way in."

"But you own this place!" Paul grabbed the boy's arm and pulled him toward the chamber door. "You sound as though you're afraid of them."

"Everyone is afraid of them. Hurry now."

They came out of the constricted passageway bent almost double, running so low that Paul was practically on all fours. As they burst out into the lampbright confusion of St. Mark's Square, Gally careened into a crowd of revelers, which caused much staggering, cursing, and spilling of drink. Following close behind, Paul ran into one of the reeling strangers, tumbling both the man and himself to the ground.

"Gally!" he shouted, struggling to rise. "Gally, wait!"

He and the stranger were entangled in each other's cloaks. As Paul tried to fight free, the other man clipped him on the ear, crying, "Damn you, leave off!" He shoved the man back to the ground, then bounded over him, but the man grabbed at his foot and tripped him. He did not regain his balance for a dozen steps; by the time he did, the crowd had closed in around him once more and he could see no sign of the boy.

"Gally! Gypsy!"

As he shouted, an invisible *something* touched him, raising his hackles like a cold hand on the back of his neck. He whirled to see movement in the dark arches along the side of St. Mark's church—two white faces swiveling in the shadows. The masks seemed to float bodiless above the dark robes, like will-o-the-wisps.

A hand closed on his wrist, real flesh this time, and Paul gasped. "What are you doing?" Gally demanded. "You can't fight. We have to run!"

It was only as he clamped shut his sagging jaw and followed the boy into the festival night that Paul realized how true the boy's words were: he had left his sword behind in Eleanora's apartments.

Gally led them north across the square, around or sometimes straight through knots of merrymakers. Where the boy could force his way through to no more reaction than a curse or a half-hearted kick, Paul was not so lucky; by the time he reached the edge of the square he had been forced to flee several offers of violence, and had lost track of his small guide once more. Also, a look back for their pursuers provided new worries: a group of armed pikemen were spilling out of the Doge's palace at a swift trot, and had already begun to fan out across St. Mark's Square with a very purposeful air. It seemed the dreadful two were not going to rely solely on their own stalking skills.

"Paul!" the boy called from a colonnade near the great clock tower at the edge of the square. "This way." As Paul followed, he slipped down a narrow passage, through a courtyard, and then out onto a winding street where rows of market stalls were still lively with custom despite the hour. Several hundred meters from the square, Gally at last ducked into an even smaller alley. On the far side, he crossed the dark street and clambered down to a path along the bank of a canal.

"They've sent soldiers after us, too," Paul panted as he scrambled down a stone staircase and joined him. He dropped his voice as a group of shadowy figures floated past in an unsteady boat, singing. "It's a good thing there are so many people out." He paused. "You called me by my name, didn't you? Do you remember me now?"

"A bit." The boy made a fretful noise. "Don't know. I suppose so. Come on, we have to hurry. We can double back to the Grand Canal, find a boat no one's using . . ."

Paul put a hand on his shoulder. "Hang on a bit. That's the main route through this place, and it's also the one certain way out. They'll be looking for us all along that canal. Is there another route we can take to this Crusader hospital?"

Gally shrugged. "We can go more or less straight across the city—cut through the corner of Castello district and into Cannaregio."

"Good. Let's do it."

"It's pretty dark through there," Gally said dubiously. "Rough, too, you know? If we get killed in Castello, it probably won't be the duke's soldiers who do it."

"We'll take the chance—anything's better than getting caught by those two . . . things."

Gally set out at a near-sprint, with Paul just behind him. The boy turned east along the small canal, and followed it until it curved away north again, then led them across a bridge over the river that flowed behind the ducal palace and St. Mark's. A few people were still making their way in toward the heart of Carnival, the square and the Grand Canal, but the boy had been right—the streets in this part of the city were emptier and darker, with only an occasional lamp to be seen burning in a window. The narrow, cobbled byways seemed too tight here for a deep breath, the buildings looming close on both sides as though threatening to tumble in and crush them. Only occasional faint voices and the smells of food cooking spoke of life hidden behind the walls, but the fronts of the houses were as secretive as masks.

As Paul struggled to stay close to the boy, who moved through the alleys and along the canals with the surefootedness of a cat, he fought to make sense out of what was happening. Those two creatures, Finch and Mullet, as something in him still wanted to call them, although his memory of those incarnations was dim, had followed him from one world to another—no, from one simulation to the next. But they clearly did not know where he was within any given simulation, nor was merely locating him—making visual contact—enough for them to capture him.

So what did that mean? For one thing, their powers, even as servants of the Grail Brotherhood, were not limitless. That much was clear.

In fact, the Grail people don't seem to have much of an advantage over anyone else in these simulations, he reflected. *Otherwise, they could have just found me a long time ago, done some kind of search through their network and pinpointed me, like a lost file.*

There was something there, something to give hope. The lords of the Brotherhood might be terrifyingly rich and ruthless—gods, in a way—but even within their own creation, they were not all-powerful. They could be fooled or eluded. That was more than merely something, he realized: if true, it was a very important idea.

He was jogging along on autopilot, hardly aware of his surroundings, when Gally stopped so suddenly that Paul almost knocked them
both down. The boy waved his hands violently, demanding quiet. At
first he could not understand why they had stopped. They were a few
hundred meters east of the Palace River and had just turned into what
by Venetian terms was a fairly wide street, but silent and with only a
single lantern hanging above a door at the far end to ease the darkness. A thick, ground-level mist made the buildings seem to float, as
though Paul and the boy stood in the middle of one of the canals
instead of a cobbled street.

"What. . . ?"

Gally slapped at his arm to silence him. A moment later Paul heard
a slurry murmur of voices, then an array of distorted shadows suddenly appeared between them and the lantern, several figures walking
abreast, moving with a certain unhurried precision.

"Soldiers!" Paul hissed. "There must be a side street in the middle."

Gally tugged at his arm, pulling him back the direction they had
come. When they reached the end of the street, the boy hesitated for
a moment, then drew them down another alley to let the soldiers pass,
but instead of continuing on toward St. Mark's, the small troop swung
into the alley as though magnetized to the fugitives. Paul cursed silently. The odds were quite hopeless—at least a dozen soldiers in helmets and breastplates filled the passage, pikes on shoulders, boots
kicking eddies in the mist.

Gally darted ahead, but the alley ended on the bank of one of the
canals, the only way forward a stone bridge arched like a cat's backbone, hung with lanterns at each end. If they tried to cross, the soldiers would certainly spot them, but there was no place to hide in the
narrow alley—the armored troop filled it wall to wall. Gally hesitated
for only a moment, then swung down over the wall beside the bridge.
Paul was glad he had been watching—if he had blinked, the boy
would have simply vanished. He scrambled over the low parapet behind him. The tramp of booted feet and the men's voices were so loud
that it seemed a miracle they had not yet been spotted.

They found perhaps a meter of vertical space beneath the bridge,
and half that distance in front of them before the ground fell away in
a straight drop, too far down to the canal for them to go in without a
splash. Repository of many of the wastes of the Most Serene Republic,
the water stank, but that was the least of their worries. They crouched,
Paul with his head pressed painfully against the underside of the
stone bridge, and listened to the soldiers trudge up the span. Then,
maddeningly, the footsteps stopped. Paul held his breath. He could

barely see the boy in the shadows, but he could tell by the tense stillness that Gally was holding his breath, too.

Something splashed into the water an arm's length away from them. Paul held himself firmly, resisting a violent flinch. Whatever it was continued to patter the canal, and then another splashing began beside it. The smell of urine wafted to them.

". . . Tried to kill a senator," someone said above them. His companion mumbled something and they both laughed; the arcs of the streams jiggled and the pattering changed rhythm for a moment. "No, I would, too," the first one said, "but you don't want anyone to hear you say that, do you? Wouldn't want to wind up in the Room of the Cord."

"Mother of God," a voice shouted from further up the bridge, "what, are you two sweet on each other? Hurry it up—we've got two assassins to find."

"Did you hear?" the first man said. "One of them's a boy, a street urchin." His stream dwindled and then stopped. "They should round up those little dockside crabs and boil the lot of 'em, that's what I say." His companion was also finishing, but his words were still inaudible. "Yes," the first added, "but at least we'll get to have some fun with this one when we find him."

Paul could not believe these soldiers could have heard so quickly by any normal means—it was only a quarter of an hour since he and Gally had fled the cathedral. Somehow, Finch and Mullet had manipulated the simworld, moved information across the city at greater-than-Renaissance speed. As ridiculous as he knew it to be, Paul was outraged at the unfairness of it.

The soldiers tramped down the far side of the bridge. Gally put his hand on Paul's arm to keep him in place and still. The soldiers' voices and footfalls grew faint, then were gone. The seconds stretched. Everything was silent except for the almost inaudible lapping of the canal against the bank.

"I . . . I don't remember anything before the Black Ocean," Gally whispered at last, invisible in the shadows.

Paul, thinking only of escape, could not immediately make sense of the words. "Before. . . ?"

The boy spoke clumsily, as though something squeezed his throat. "Corfu, all that—I don't remember it, not really. I just *know* it. But I'm starting to remember other things—the Oysterhouse, like you said, and traveling with Bay and Blue and the others. I . . . I think I even had another name at first, before I was Gally. But I don't remember anything from before we came out of the Black Ocean." His voice

hitched. He was weeping. "I don't remember my mother or my father
. . . or . . . *anything.*"

Even in the midst of danger, Paul could not help wondering who
Gally and the other Oysterhouse children really were, what their place
in all this might be. Were they escaped prisoners, as he was? "You've
talked about this Black Ocean several times, but I don't know what it
is," he told the boy. "Was it a place like this. . . ?" He realized that
the concept of a simulation would probably mean nothing. "Was it a
country, like the Eight Squared or here—like Venice?"

There was a pause. "Not really." Gally had stopped crying, but still
spoke haltingly. Paul suddenly remembered being startled to discover
that the sleeping boy did not breathe. He touched his own chest now,
felt its slow, regular motion. Even taking simulation into account, why
should he breathe, as though he were in his real body, and Gally not?
"It's hard for me to remember good," the boy went on, "but it was
just . . . just dark. Not like this, but dark forever. And for a long time
there was nothing except me and God."

"You and . . . God?"

"I don't know. Somebody was there in the dark, but all around me,
sort of, and I heard the voice talking in my head. One voice. It told me
who I was. It told me I was going to live in a new place, and . . . and
. . . that's all I can remember." Gally's wistful tone vanished. "We
should get moving."

"Christ, you're right." Paul crawled out from beneath the bridge
and almost slipped down the muddy bank into the canal. The night
sky seemed strikingly close, the stars bright as frozen fireworks. "I
almost forgot," he muttered, astonished at himself. All these mysteries, however fascinating, could wait until they were safe. Gally clambered out past him and jogged back up the alley. Paul fell into step
behind him.

But safe where? he thought. *The bird-woman told me to find the Weaver.
And where did Nandi say that would be—Ithaca? Which would be Greece, I
guess, some Greek myth or other. But isn't there an Ithaca in America, too?
Little town in New York or somewhere?*

They hurried through the streets. The few people they passed here
were uncostumed, and seemed to have little to do with the festivities,
except that a few of them were the worse for drink. Twice more they
had to hide from soldiers, but their pursuers never came as close as
they had the first time. Even the Doge's troops seemed to have decided
there was little chance of capturing fugitives in the confusion of Carnival night.

"We're in Cannaregio now," Gally whispered after another long jog, barely audible over the sound of their feet on the stones. "Not too much farther."

The boy led him through back alleys and across empty squares with the nimble certainty of a fox trotting home to its den. Paul could not help thinking how lucky he was to have Gally here to guide him. In fact, he had been lucky in all the simulations, and that was another . important thing to remember. Like the real world, this network could surprise you—there was good to be found, real kindness. It seemed the Brotherhood couldn't make their VR worlds truly realistic without bringing along at least a few of reality's happier chances. That would be something to cling to when despair gripped him again, as he had a feeling it almost inevitably would.

The fog grew thicker as the night stretched into the last dead hours before morning. Paul waved at it but it did not disperse, and when he stopped waving it flowed back in to fill the same spaces again.

"Brine mist," Gally explained, barely visible through the murk. "From the sea. They call it 'Bride's Veil,' too."

Only a people who considered themselves wedded to the ocean, Paul decided, could give such a romantic name to such dire, dank stuff.

In fact, the brine mist turned midnight Venice into something even more surreal than before, which hardly seemed possible. With a church seemingly on every corner, the faces of monsters and saints loomed out of the fog without warning; the statues, whether pious or grotesque, all seemed to stare out and up, gazing eternally at something beyond even Venice's grandeur.

"That's the Zen Palace over there," Gally whispered as they passed a building which stood high above the swirling mists. Their pace had slowed with fatigue, or at least Paul's had, to something scarcely more than a swift walk. "You know, where the Cardinal's family lives."

Paul shook his head, too exhausted and frightened to care, but Gally took it as a sign that he didn't understand. "You know, the one whose tomb the lady takes care of. Cardinal Zen."

Beside feeling profoundly uninterested in tourist information at the moment, Paul was still feeling bitter toward Eleanora for deserting them, however sensible her reasons. He slowed and then stopped in order to suck in a larger amount of the sea-scented air than he had been getting. "Where's this hospital?" he wheezed.

"Just ahead. Past the Jesuits." Gally gently took his arm and got him moving again.

Paul's legs were rubbery and his lungs were burning. It was very difficult to run for half an hour without stopping, another piece of

information left out of the adventure stories and flicks he had seen.
In fact, adventuring in general was ridiculously hard work.

If I'd known I was going to be doing so much of this running for my life,
he thought miserably, *I'd have gotten myself in better shape first. . . .*

As the boy led him past the Baroque facade of the church he had
called "the Jesuits," and out into a public square, Paul felt a sickening
lurch in the pit of his stomach: the unreasoning fear, the chill that the
Finch and Mullet creatures induced in him, had returned. He looked
around, wide-eyed. Perhaps a dozen people bundled against the cold
were finishing out Carnival night in the small square. None of them
bore any resemblance to their pursuers, but although Paul's sensation
of dread was fainter than it had been back in the cathedral, it was
undeniably the same.

"Oh, God," he gasped. "They're here—or they're close."

Gally's eyes were wide. "I can feel them, too. Ever since they
touched me when we were in that . . . that dream-place, I can feel
them."

"Dream-place?" Paul frowned, trying to remember. He and the boy
crept across the square like soldiers on patrol, watching every shadow.
The Venetians loitering near the steps of the Jesuits called after
them—slurred, incomprehensible jests.

"In that castle in the sky," Gally explained quietly.

"You remember that?" Paul had half-believed the castle *was* a
dream, that and the machine-giant he had met there the first time—it
had been so palpably different from his other experiences.

Gally shuddered. "They touched me. It . . . it hurt."

Like a ghost ship sliding out of the fog, a small dark building with
four tall chimneys sprouting from its roof was becoming visible on the
far side of the square. Gally took his hand to hurry him forward, letting him know that this was the place they sought, but Paul found
himself suddenly unwilling to enter. There was something about its
brooding shape that unnerved him, and the sense that their pursuers
were near had grown stronger. Perhaps they were even waiting
inside. . . .

A tall shape materialized out of the mist. Gally squeaked.

"What good wind?" asked a deep, quavering voice.

The unsteady figure was shrouded in a threadbare cape that flapped
like ragged wings. With his long-nosed, almost chinless face and
bright eye, the old man resembled nothing so much as a dirty harbor
bird. "What good wind?" he demanded again, then squinted at Paul
and the boy. "Strangers!" he said loudly, making Paul extremely uncomfortable. "Do you bring wine? It is hard times at the Oratory. We

guests of the Crusaders are forgotten—and on Carnival night, of all nights!"

Paul nodded in what he hoped was a pleasant fashion and tried to step past the stranger, but the ancient creature caught his cloak with a surprisingly firm grip. Gally was almost dancing in his hurry to move on.

"Come," said the old man, tainting the mist with his sour breath. "Just because we are old does not mean we should be forgotten. Do we not fast, just as other Christians do? Should we not then celebrate, too?"

"I have no wine." Paul could feel the shadow of their pursuers moving over them, darker and darker, wider and wider. An idea came to him. "If you take us into the hospital, help us find what we're looking for, I'll give you some money and you can buy yourself wine."

The old man swayed as if amazed by such good fortune. "Into the hospital? That is all? You want to go into the Crusaders?"

"We want to visit someone."

"No one comes to visit us," their new guide said, lurching back toward the four-chimneyed building. He was not contradicting Paul, but stating a mournful fact of life. "We are old. Our children are gone away or dead. No one cares what happens to us, even during Carnival." He spread his arms like an albatross banking on the breeze as he led them around the side of the building, then through a door that Paul would have never seen in the mist and on into the dark, echoing interior. "The front is barred tonight, to keep us out of trouble," their guide said, then tapped with his finger on the side of his nose. "But they cannot keep old Nicoló inside. And now I will have wine, and drink until my head is full of songs."

Paul's first impression was that the Crusader hospital was rather lavishly haunted. A dozen silent forms, wrapped in blankets and sheets, shuffled across landings and up and down the stairs; others stood in doorways, staring at nothing as fixedly as the statues on the churches outside, mumbling or crooning wordlessly. The Oratory was a refuge for the old, Gally whispered, clarifying Nicoló's complaints—especially for those who had no family to take them in. Not all were senile; many turned sharp eyes on the newcomers, or questioned Nicoló about them, but their guide only waved his arms grandly and led Paul and the boy deeper into the building, until they stood at last before the candlelit chapel. A relief of the Madonna and her child stared down at them from above the doorway.

Paul stared at the Savior's infant face, suddenly at a loss. They had no idea where in the hospital the gateway might be, and it seemed unlikely Nicoló or any of the other residents would know—why should the sims know anything about the network's infrastructure? So it was up to him to decide what would be the most likely spot. He thought desperately, but could only think of the river crossings he had made. What about when there was no river? Was there some other way to recognize an exit door, or were the indicators visible only to the people who had built these worlds?

He turned to Gally, but before he could speak the boy went rigid, his face white with fear. Then Paul felt it, too: the terror reached out and closed on him, making his heart hammer and his skin go cold and damp. Their two pursuers were close—very close.

Adding to his dread, at that instant a disembodied voice spoke in his ear. In his confusion and fright, he did not at first recognize it. *"The catacombs,"* it told him. *"You must go down."*

Gally had gone even more wide-eyed. "The lady!" he said.

Paul nodded, a little dazed. She had spoken to them from out of the air, invisibly, but it had been Eleanora.

Old Nicoló watched this exchange with distrust written clearly on his seamed face. Vulture-like, he leaned forward. "You said you'd give me money."

"Show us where the catacombs are." Paul struggled to sound normal, but his insides were turning to ice, and every instinct screamed at him to climb into the nearest crevice and hide. "The catacombs? The underground bits?"

"There's no one down there but dead Crusaders," Nicoló whined. "You said you wanted to visit someone."

Paul tugged his purse free of his belt and held it out. "We didn't say it was anyone alive."

Nicoló licked his lips, then turned and tottered into the chapel. "This way."

The old man led them to a spot behind the altar, to the first steps of a stairwell that, in the dimly lit chapel, seemed little more than a square black hole in the floor. Paul tossed him the purse; Nicoló's expression softened into stupefied glee as he poured the ducats into his trembling palm. A moment later he was hurrying away across the chapel, presumably to spend his earnings while Carnival still lived its final moments. At any other time, Paul would have found the sight of all that creaking avarice funny; now he could barely keep himself standing upright, so powerful was the feeling of a closing trap. He sprinted to a wall sconce, but could not reach the candle. He lifted Gally so the boy could pluck one free.

Even with the candle clenched in Paul's fist, spreading thin light before them, the stairwell was treacherous. The steps were narrow, and worn into a smooth hollow in the middle by generations of monkish feet, all those who had descended to bless the remains of Christendom's protectors and then ascended once more, holy day after holy day, year after year, for centuries. They wound down to the bottom of the stairs, where the catacombs opened out, and there was suddenly far more shadow than candlelight. The flickering glow revealed a row of dark openings in an ancient stone wall, with no sign of which to choose. Paul wiped chill sweat from his forehead and cursed to himself. It was like some horrible role-playing game. He'd never liked those at all.

"Eleanora?" he asked quietly. The sense of menace hung so close now that it seemed even a whisper might reveal them to their enemies. "Are you listening? Which way do we go?" But there was no response. The holes in the walls gaped like idiot mouths.

Gally was pulling at his sleeve, desperate to move on. Paul turned his attention to the floor. Generations of footsteps had also rubbed away at the stone flags in front of each opening, but the section on the far right had the most polished approach, as though most started their pilgrimage there, while the tunnel nearest the far left wall seemed by far the least-trafficked. Paul hesitated only a moment, then chose the left.

The niches in the tunnel walls held sleeping shapes, cold marble hands clasped in prayer on chests, marble faces gazing up through the layers of stone toward a sky they would never see again. As the tunnel wound inward and down, marble gave way to less costly stone, the effigies grew more crude, and even the niches shrank. At last, when they must have long left the underground confines of the Oratory and have covered in mazey wandering much of the area underneath the square, the images of the dead and their individual burials came to an end, replaced by tall stacks of undifferentiated skeletal remains. Paul felt Gally's hand clench his own as the boy shuddered.

The ossuary walls grew higher, until the tunnel was completely banked by bones. Here and there, at turnings of the corridor, skulls were piled like cannonballs, or built into the bone stacks as decorative elements, zigzag lines of unfleshed faces. Hundreds of empty eyesockets stared at them as they passed, near-endless pockets of shadow.

For a moment, even in the midst of despair and great dread, as he stared at the skeletal walls and the ultimate futility of human action they represented, Paul found himself almost admiring the Grail Brotherhood. Cruel, criminal bastards they might be, but there was something almost noble about any human beings who were willing to thumb their noses at the Great Eraser himself—Death, the black vacuum into which all life was inevitably sucked.

His thoughts slid from the general back to the specific, and he was just realizing that there was something profoundly unreal about a Venice in which one could travel so deep beneath the ground and not be up to the nostrils in seawater, when the tunnel abruptly opened out into a wide underground chamber. The roof and floor were held apart by a thousand pillars, great batons of stone carved into the shapes of even more bones, a forest of tibia and femur. The candle could illumine only a part of the chamber—its shadowy recesses fell away without visible ending on all sides—but straight ahead of them was an open place where no pillars stood, a piece of empty floor covered with dusty mosaic tiles. As Paul took a few steps forward, the candle now burning hot and low in his fist showed that the tiles made a picture of a vast cauldron carried by angels and demons, out of which streamed rays of shining light.

The faint sound of shuffling feet whispered from the tunnel they had just left. A jolt of dread went through Paul as though he had stepped on a live wire; beside him, Gally made a weak sound of desperation.

Without warning, a smear of pale golden fire appeared before them in the center of the open space. The glow deepened until the gateway burned so brightly stripes of black shadow leaped out from the bone pillars, and the mosaic on the floor became invisible in the glare. Paul felt a moment of hope, but as he pulled Gally toward the shimmering rectangle two shapes stepped out of it, one mountainously fat, the other starvation-slender. Choking, Paul staggered back in stunned horror, yanking the boy with him.

Tricked! We've been tricked!

As they turned and took a few wobbling steps back in the direction they had come, something new flickered into existence between the pillars. Eleanora's small form hung just above the floor, her wizened face alarmed.

"Do not go back!" Her voice seemed to come not from her mouth, but from somewhere near Paul's head. "It is not what you think—the greatest danger is still following you!"

Paul ignored her. There could be no greater danger than the shapes that had just stepped from the gateway. He pulled Gally with him, back toward the tunnel. Eleanora's hands stretched toward them, beseeching, and the boy hesitated, but Paul would not let him go. Then, even as they had almost reached the door back into the catacombs, two shapes identical to those behind them stepped out of the tunnel and into the pillared room. Reflecting the spreading light of the gateway, the masks of Comedy and Tragedy seemed made of molten gold. A wave of dread rolled off the two figures, paralyzing Paul.

For a moment he thought his brain would stop, jammed like a broken machine. Finch and Mullet were in front of them. Finch and Mullet were behind them. The burrow was stopped at both ends, and they would die like poisoned rabbits. The bird-woman had deserted him, all of her words meaningless now. There was no feather to clutch.

"Turn around!" Eleanora cried. "Run to the gateway! That is your only hope!"

Paul stared at her, speechless. Didn't she understand their enemies were on both sides? To turn to the gateway would be to meet them there as well. . . .

He backed away from the oncoming masks, dragging the boy with him, but as he did he became more and more concerned with what he knew lurked behind him. At almost the point where Eleanora's image hung in the shadowy crypt, still trying to convince him to flee toward the gateway, he turned again. The two disparate shapes were still advancing out of the golden light. For a moment his legs threatened to buckle and drop him and the boy to the floor, to be fallen upon from both sides by mirrored sets of enemies.

The gateway figures were so close now that he could see eyes gleaming in what had only been black silhouettes. He stood helplessly as one of them extended a massive arm toward him.

"Mr. Johnson? Is that you?" Undine Pankie took a few heavy-footed steps forward into the candlelight, holding the hem of her tent-like gray dress so that it did not trail in the dust of the crypt. "Oh, goodness, it is. Sefton!" she called over her shoulder, "didn't I tell you we'd find that lovely Mr. Johnson here?"

Paul was certain he had gone mad.

Her matchstick husband came up beside her, blinking like an owl in daylight. "So it is, my dear. A very good day to you, Mr. Johnson!" They might have been meeting him at a church tea.

"Perhaps he's seen something of our Viola," Mrs. Pankie suggested, and gave Paul a winsome smile that under any other circumstances would have been monstrous and alarming, but at this moment was merely incomprehensible. "And who is that little angel with you? Such a charming lad! Surely you will introduce us. . . ."

All Paul could do was cling tightly to Gally's hand despite the boy's efforts to break free—God only knew what was going through the child's head—and stare. The Pankies looked him up and down, apparently bemused by his attitude, then the cowlike gaze of Undine Pankie moved past him to the pair of approaching shapes, the mirrored image of large and small. She trailed off in mid-platitude, blanching across her entire huge, doughy face. She turned to exchange a swift look with her bespectacled husband, an expression on both their faces that Paul could not begin to make sense of; then, as if in silent agreement, they turned their backs on each other and disappeared into the shadows on either side, leaving Paul with a clear path to the gateway.

"Hurry!" Eleanora cried behind him. "The way is open. Where do you want to go?"

Paul tugged at Gally, who would not move.

"Come, Jonas," hissed Finch from behind him. "Do not prolong this game—it has gone on far beyond amusement."

Paul continued to struggle with Gally, who was resisting him in some paroxysm of unreasoning fear, eyes half-shut, as though he were on the verge of a seizure.

"Where?" demanded Eleanora.

He could barely think. American place-names careened maddeningly through his mind, exotic, foreign names which he had dreamed over in his youth, but which now might, in their clutter, kill him— Idaho, Illinois, Keokuk, Attica . . .

"*Ithaca!*"

She nodded, then raised a hand to clasp the emerald dangling at her throat. The gateway's energies rippled like a wind-raked campfire. Just beyond her, Finch and Mullet had doffed their masks: their true faces remained hidden by the shadowed hoods, but Paul could see the glint of Finch's stare and the lopsided sheen that was Mullet's toothy grin. The force that washed out from them turned his bones to paper.

As the two figures approached to within an arm's length of Eleanora, Gally abruptly regained his wits. "They'll hurt the lady!" he shouted, and began to thrash with renewed, frenzied strength, this time not to resist being carried, but to run to the woman he considered his friend. "They'll kill her!"

"Gally, no!" Paul tried to gain a better grip—it felt like his fingernails were being torn loose—but in the demi-instant he relaxed his clutch, the boy broke free and bolted back toward Eleanora's hovering image.

"*No, Gypsy!*" she cried, "they cannot even . . ."

The pair stepped through her.

". . . Touch me," she finished, full of hopeless misery. "Oh, Gypsy . . ."

Mullet reached out a broad, shapeless hand and snatched the boy up into the air. Gally dangled helplessly from the fat creature's fist, wriggling like a fly in a web.

Paul stopped. The warmthless golden radiance of the gateway was only a few steps away, but it suddenly seemed miles distant. "Let him go!"

Finch chuckled. "Of course we will. He is not the child we truly seek, only one of the vermin of the network. But it's you we want now, Jonas. So step away from there and come with us."

Paul could not fight any longer. Everything had come to the end he had always feared. They would take him down into darkness, down to worse things than death. He looked at Eleanora, but she still hovered in the same spot, a helpless ghost, her face sagging. "Do you promise to let him go?" he asked. "You can have me if you do."

Finch looked at the small boy struggling in Mullet's grip, and Paul could hear the smile in his cold voice. "Certainly. He is nothing. A crack-dweller. A crevice-haunter."

Paul fought a terrible numb listlessness. "Very well," he said hoarsely, and took a step back toward them.

"No!" Gally screamed. The boy kicked out against the giant Mullet, swinging his feet up against the vast, robed belly and pushing as hard as he could, and simultaneously grabbed and bit hard at the restraining fist. Mullet let out a surprised, outraged bellow. He lifted his other hand and pulled the boy away, then flung him down to the ground with astonishing force. Paul heard bones snap, then there was a terrible silence.

Mullet leaned and picked up the limp form, shook it once, then grunted and tossed it aside. The boy's body skidded across the tiles like a rag doll—utterly, utterly lifeless.

"Gypsy!" Eleanora's scream, a long, keening note of agony, ended as though cut with a scalpel in the instant her image vanished. A moment later the crypt began to bend and deform, twisting inward as though crushed in a giant fist. Finch and Mullet and Gally's limp body all disappeared from sight as the vast room collapsed and swallowed them.

Blasted to his core, emptied of everything, and so stunned he could not even weep, Paul turned and flung himself into the doorway made of light.

CHAPTER 31

The Voice of the Lost

NETFEED/NEWS: *Marine Farmers Say Krill Scare Unreasonable*
(visual: sloop "Johanna B." casting sound-nets)
VO: Marine farmers are furious with the wildfire rumors of a parasite in
harvested krill that causes a disease called Tandagore Syndrome.
(visual: UOF's Tripolamenti on dock)
Clementino Tripolamenti, head of the multi-national Union of Ocean
Farmers pointed out that many doctors have already said that Tandagore
Syndrome, a mysterious neurological disorder, has no connection to diet.
TRIPOLAMENTI: "People can say anything. Have you seen this? They call
it "Mad Krill Disease," like it's a joke. We harvest millions of tons of this
healthy marine protein, and it gets put into thousands of healthy products,
and all someone has to do it put some stupid joke on the net and our lives
and livelihoods are threatened . . ."

"CODE *Delphi. Start here.*
"There is so much to tell, so much that is sad and strange
and terrible, that I do not know where to begin. I suppose whoever
plucks these words from the air will not understand unless I explain
everything. I have a moment to speak now—to mumble to myself as
it must seem to anyone else—before the madness begins again. I will
try to tell all that has happened in order, no matter how frustrating I
find it.

"We were among the flying people in Aerodromia, as we had named the place. A girl disappeared, and as strangers we fell under suspicion. We had been befriended by the head of one of the families, Builds a Fire on Air, and when he came for us, grim-faced, and with armed guards, I thought we were to be executed for the crime or perhaps sacrificed to some god of theirs. I was not far wrong.

"The prison-cave to which they brought us was not as pleasant as the one we had shared with Builds a Fire on Air's family. It was cold and damp and spattered with the excrement of bats and birds. Quan Li wept quietly by the small fire, the light rippling on her nondescript features—like Florimel and me, she still wore the generic, vaguely Amerindian female sim she had been given on her entrance to Temilún. T4b, sullen and uncommunicative, was making and then leveling piles of stones on the cavern floor, over and over, like a child kept after school. Florimel and William were engaged in yet another argument, Florimel as usual angry because she felt we were too passive in all we did. I moved to the other end of the cavern to avoid listening to them.

"The Aerodromic tribespeople did indeed suspect us of having something to do with the disappearance of the girl named Shines Like Snow. We were to be put through some kind of ordeal, beginning at the first shadows of evening, to determine our guilt or innocence. When Builds a Fire on Air told us that the few who survived this ordeal usually became insane, I could not help feeling a touch of nostalgia for the old Napoleonic Code. We were miserable and unhappy and frightened, every one of us. Even though we did not know for certain that we could die from what happened in these simulations, we knew already that they could cause us pain.

"As I looked around at my companions, observing their now quite distinct manifestations and feeling the dull throb of their fear, I suddenly perceived that I had shirked my responsibilities.

"I have had the inarguable excuse of my blindness since I was a child, and sometimes have used it in a manipulative way. I would be furious if I were given a job or invited to a party solely because I was blind, but I must admit there have been times the reverse was true—when I told myself *I am allowed,* and begged off from some gathering, or avoided someone, or failed to do something I did not want to do, making my blindness my excuse.

"In that same way, I now realize, I have let my problems shield me from my current situation. I have not suffered less than my companions—in fact, my peculiar circumstances meant I lived with terrifying, overwhelming agony for the first several days after we entered this network. But I have not suffered like that lately, and I have abilities here no one else can even approach, yet I have avoided taking a larger role in guiding this group.

"I did not make a life and career in the real world that most sighted people would envy by being so pliant, so without force. Why should I do so here?

"Ah, but I have already begun to wander away from the events I wish to describe. This is another thought, another debate, for another day. It is enough to say that I have resolved that I will no longer be so aimless. Whether or not I can help these frightened people, I certainly do not want to confront my own obliteration and think, 'I could have done more to help myself.' Call me selfish, but it is my respect for myself that most concerns me.

"The day of our imprisonment wore on, and even Florimel and William finally lost the strength to argue—something they had been doing more to keep the illusion of self-determination than anything else, I guessed. I tried to make conversation with Quan Li and T4b, but both were too depressed to say much. Quan Li in particular seemed convinced that we would be executed, and that her comatose granddaughter would lose her one slim chance. The person in the spiky warrior costume did not even try to communicate. He responded to my questions with grunts, and I at last left him making his endless piles of stones.

"We were finishing the meal our jailers had given us—a small pile of berries and one piece of flat, unleavened bread each—when Sweet William came to sit beside me. Although the others were several meters away, each in his or her own small world of miserable apprehension, William whispered as he spoke. There was something odd about his manner which for all my newfound abilities I could not understand or name. He was agitated somehow, that alone was clear—the information by which I perceived him had a strange vibrational quality, as though he were excited rather than depressed.

"He said, 'I suppose it's time I told you something about meself.' I regarded him with a little surprise—he had always been one of the most reticent about his real situation—but supposed it had to do with the 'death row' feeling we all shared.

"I said, 'If you wish, of course. I would be lying if I said that I have not wondered. But you do not owe me anything.'

" 'Of course I don't,' he said with a little of his old snappishness. 'Don't owe anybody anything.' But instead of reacting to his asperity, I noticed for the first time that something in his accent—an accent I have heard many times used for comedic effect in dramas based in Britain, where apparently they find the mere sounds of Northern England humorous—seemed inconsistent. The vowel sounds were a little awkward, and the two *any*s on his remark were subtly different.

"He was quiet for a moment. Then, as if he had sensed my thought, he said, 'I don't always talk like this, you know. In real life, I don't.'

"I stayed quiet. Was he explaining, or making some kind of excuse? I couldn't understand why he seemed to buzz so, although people respond to stress and unhappiness differently.

" 'I'm not really like this at all, y'see. In RL.' He flapped one of his arms, the batlike cape billowing. 'It's just, what, a bit of glamour. Trying to have a bit of fun.'

"For the first time in several days I wished I could see as other people see. I wanted to look into his eyes, see what was hiding there.

"He leaned closer to me. 'In fact, I'll tell you something funny. Promise you won't tell the others.' He did not wait for me to assent or decline. 'I'm not anything like this at all—this vampire stuff, the deadly-but-beautiful kit and everything. For one thing, I'm *old*.' He laughed quietly, nervously. 'I'm really quite old. Eighty, and a few months past it. But I like to have a bit of fun.'

"I thought of him that way, as an old man, and could make some sense of it, but still was not entirely certain what was going on. For one thing, I wasn't sure he *was* a he, so I asked him.

" 'Yes, yes. 'Fraid so. Nothing so exciting as a full-scale tranny. I haven't been out of the house in years, so I don't know that you'd label it anything at all—I mean, who *cares* what someone is on the net?'

"I had to ask him. I felt I was being manipulated in some way. 'If no one cares, then why are you telling me, and why do you seem so ashamed, William?'

"This caught him by surprise. He sat back—I could feel him folding into himself, like some winged thing huddling on a rainy branch. 'Just wanted to tell someone, I guess,' he said. 'In case something happens to us. You know what I mean.'

"I felt sorry for having pushed him. On the eve of battle, they say, men in the trenches tell their life stories to strangers. There is nothing so intimate and yet so bonding, perhaps, as the approach of death. 'What brought you to the network?' I asked, a little more kindly.

"He did not answer right away, and I had the strange sense that he was preparing to tell a story and making sure he had the details right, as one might when about to spin a tale for a small child. But when he spoke, it sounded genuine.

" 'I'm not a young person,' he said, 'but I like young people. That is, I like the freedom I never had that they have now. I admire that they can just be who they want—make a new sim, join a new world, be anything. When I was young, you still had to do everything face-to-face, and as faces go, I've never liked mine much—know what I mean? Not horrible, don't get me wrong, but not exciting either. Not . . . memorable. So when I finally left the postal service—I was an inspector, ran the regional inspection center actually, retired about ten years ago—I made a life for myself on the net. And no one cared who I really was, only who I was online. I made this character for myself, Sweet William, and made him as outrageous as I could. Sexual roles, social niceties, I bent them all until they screamed, I guess you'd say. I memorized obscure poets, some of those NewBeat folk, some of the Quiet Apocalypse geezers, too, and passed it off as my own. I was having the time of my life, and wondering why I didn't retire earlier.

" 'Then a few of the younger members of my online crowd got ill and disappeared from the net. It was this thing that we all recognize now, this coma thing, but all I knew then was that some nice young ones were gone, as good as dead, and no one knew why. And I was shocked that some of them were so young, too. Like me, they had been pretending to be something they weren't—one of them was only twelve!

" 'So I began to look into all this, these illnesses, whatnot.' He smiled a little. 'I suppose it was a bit like the work I used to do, and I admit I got a touch obsessed. The more I searched, the more questions I had, until I ran into the first of Sellars' little clues. Eventually I used a tip from a mate of mine pretty high up in UNComm and hacked into the Otherland network, looking for Atasco's city. And that's that.' He nodded, his tale told. I felt a certain dissatisfaction, not with the story itself, but with the way he had suddenly told it, after being so secretive for so long. Was it simply fear of what was to come? It seemed odd—we had faced danger almost continuously since we had entered the network. Perhaps, as it seemed, he was reaching out to me in a search for human contact. If so, I was not giving him what he needed. Perhaps I was being unfair to him, I thought. Many have said I am cold, detached.

"But whatever his reasons, and whatever my responses, Sweet William seemed to want more than simply to share his own confession. He asked me about my own background. I told him about where I had grown up, and that I had lost my sight in a childhood accident, which was not the entire truth, but I was not sure why he was asking. He was still strangely elevated, and I found his energies disturbing. William also wanted to know what I thought about the crime of which we'd been accused, if I had any idea what might really have happened.

The whole conversation had an unusual tone to it, as though there were a subtext I could not quite understand. After another quarter-hour's worth of seemingly unrelated questions and small talk, he gave me a jaunty little farewell and went to go sit by himself in the corner of the cave.

"As I was pondering all this, Florimel came to ask me what Builds a Fire on Air had told me about the missing girl. Since I had seen her and Sweet William speaking animatedly earlier, I said, 'William is surprisingly talkative tonight.'

"She looked at me with even less expression than usual and said, " 'Well, I am not,' then turned and walked back to her place a short distance from the fire. Perhaps she thought I was trying to draw her out. Perhaps I was. Meanwhile, I was left to wonder again just what sort of group of misfits I have fallen in with.

"When a blind woman who has spent several days in convulsive madness asks that question, anyone could guess that such a group is in trouble."

"Builds a Fire on Air and other Red Rock Tribe members I did not recognize—most of the local families seemed to be involved—came for us as sundown approached. We were taken to the base of a huge horizontal tree, on which sat a trio of the tribe's eldest men. The father of the missing girl spoke vehemently about her abduction. Her necklace, something she always wore, had been discovered near the mouth of her family's cave, which seemed to suggest that Shines Like Snow had not left of her own will. Other families said they had seen nothing and heard nothing, and spoke of how long it had been since any of the other tribes of the valley had come raiding. When Florimel demanded we be able to ask questions and speak in our own defense, she was refused. The frailest of the three elders, a man so shrunken he seemed to have not just hollow bones but hollow everything, told us courteously but firmly that since we were outsiders, nothing we said could be trusted. He also pointed out that if we were allowed to query witnesses, we might use the opportunity to put a spell on those we questioned.

"Thus our judges arrived at the foregone conclusion—we would undergo an ordeal to test our truthfulness. We would be taken, they declared with great solemnity, to something called The Place of the Lost.

"None of us liked the sound of this. I could see that under other circumstances Florimel or T4b might have been in favor of trying to fight our way out, but we were outnumbered by a hundred to one and the long day's imprisonment had weakened our resolve. We allowed ourselves to be handled, less roughly than we expected—the Middle Air folk were decent at heart, I think—and led away through the day's dying light.

"Although prisoners and guards had to walk, we nevertheless went to the place of our ordeal as a veritable aerial parade, since an army of onlookers swooped and hovered just behind us, like gulls following a garbage scow. We were forced to march for the better part of an hour, climbing at last to a hollow in the cliff face several hundred meters across—a natural bowl where Aerodromians a thousand generations or so in the future might one day attend symphony concerts. This scooped-out space, no doubt the work of some glacier, was empty but for a talus slope that carpeted most of the bottom, and one large round rock in the middle that to my senses seemed ominously like a sacrificial altar.

"I imagined our virtual bodies being tested by the Thousand Cuts or something similar, and for the first time the likelihood of torture and death truly struck me. I began to sweat, though the evening breeze was cool and pleasant. A sudden and oddly horrifying thought came to me—what if they did something to my eyes? The idea of an assault on these—the most useless organs in my body, and virtual besides—nevertheless filled me with a terror so great I writhed in the grip of my two guards, and would have fallen had they not held me up.

"Two dozen or so of the younger and stronger men glided to the ground beside the stone. They put their shoulders against it, grunting and even shouting in their exertion, until at last the stone trembled and slid a meter or two sideways to reveal a blackness beneath. One by one we were dragged to this opening and thrown in. Sweet William went first, and with surprising dignity. When it was my turn, I made myself as small as possible. When I had dropped through, I spread my arms and hovered. I had not known for certain that we would still be able to fly in the cave, but the place was full of strange updrafts—unpredictable, yet enough to keep us floating in one place if we worked at it.

Quan Li had not yet mastered the art of staying upright, and I sensed her now a short distance from me, struggling for equilibrium. Before I could say anything to ease her fears, the vast boulder slid back across the hole and we were plunged into complete darkness.

"Of course, Unknown Listener, as you must have guessed if you have heard my other journal entries, the situation was not as bad for me as it was for the rest of my companions—not at first. Darkness is my element, and the disappearance of light registered to me only as a shift in what the simulation itself was allowed to show in the visible spectrum, not in what I could actually perceive. I could sense the convoluted space of the cave around us, even track the intricate, fluted walls and spiky stalactites as whorls in the flow of information, much as someone watching a river might discern the position of hidden stones by how they deformed the river's surface.

"I had promised myself that I would take a more commanding role in my own fate, so as the others cried out to each other in terror, I calmly absorbed the details of our surroundings, trying to create a mental map.

"Calmly? Actually, I am not sure of that. It was one of my lovers in my university days—before I retreated to my home beneath the Black Mountain and metaphorically sealed the tunnel behind me—who said I was cool and hard as titanium, and just as flexible. He was referring to my habit of standing back from things. It must sound odd to one who does not know me, to hear me speak of the horrors I have already described, and the greater and stranger ones to come, in my detached way. But although that man's words hurt me then, I asked him, 'What do you expect? Do you think a woman who cannot see should dive into things headfirst?'

" 'Dive?' he said, and laughed, genuinely amused. He was a bastard, but he did enjoy a joke. 'You, dive? You cannot even enter a room without examining the blueprints first.'

"He was not entirely exaggerating. And as I listen to myself now, I hear that Martine speaking, the one who must research everything, catalogue everything, perhaps because I have always had to make a map for myself just to move through a world in which others simply live.

"So it is possible that I am making it all sound too cold, too certain. My companions were lost in the dark. I was not as lost. But I was still fearful, and quickly learned that fear was justified.

"The cave was a vast thing like a broken honeycomb, full of pockets and twisting tunnels. We hovered in the empty space beneath the opening, but all around us in the darkness lurked razoring stone corners, knifelike edges, and deadly spikes. Yes, we could fly, but what good was that when we could not see, and a few inches away in any direction there might be an impediment that would main or kill? Already Quan Li had torn her arm on a ragged piece of stone. Even the voice of bold, self-sufficient Florimel quavered with a panic that seemed about to twist out of control.

"Also, although none of the others had realized it yet, we were not alone.

"With some idea now of the shape of the space around us, I called to my companions to stay in place if they could. As I told some where to move so they would be in less immediate danger, I began to perceive a shift in the information field—only tiny ripples at first, but rapidly becoming larger and more pervasive. Of the rest, Quan Li was the first to hear the voices.

" 'What is that?' she cried. 'Someone . . . there is someone out there. . . .'

The sounds grew louder, as though they came whispering toward us from all corners of the labyrinth—a flurry of invisible things, filling the darkness with what at first seemed just moans and sighs, but from which words began to emerge.

" '. . . No . . .' they whispered, and 'Lost . . .' Others sobbed, 'Help me . . . !' and wailed, 'Cold, so cold, so cold . . . ,'—a thousand quietly weeping ghosts, murmuring and rustling around us like the wind.

"But I alone could see them, in my own way. I alone could sense that these were not whole creatures, that they did not have virtual bodies as my companions did, flexible, locked sets of algorithms moving with purpose. What surrounded us was a fog of emergent form, humanlike configurations that arose out of the information noise and then dissolved again. None were complete in themselves, but although they were partial and ephemeral, they were also as individual as snowflakes. They seemed far more than just a trick of programming—each phantom, in its moments of quintessence, seemed somehow undeniably real to me. I already find it difficult to distinguish between the realism of my companions and the realism of the network's simulated people, but these phenomena were even more complex. If such richness can be engendered purely by mechanical means, even by a system as magically capable as Otherland, then I have much to consider.

"But the most undeniable thing about these phantoms was that they filled us with terror and pity. The voices were those of lost and miserable children, begging to be saved, or crying out in the helplessness of nightmare, a chorus of bereavement and pain that no sane mind could ignore. Every nerve in me, every cell of my real body, yearned to help them, but they were as insubstantial as smoke. Despite whatever rationale as code they might have had, they were also ghosts, or the word has no meaning.

"T4b suddenly began shouting, hoarse with rage, the closest to adult I have ever heard him. 'Matti?' he screamed, 'Matti, it's me!

Come back!' Far more blind than me at that moment, he nevertheless flung himself forward and tumbled awkwardly into the cloud of information, clawing at the nothingness with his fingers. Within an instant he was drifting helplessly down a side tunnel, thrashing as he tried to capture something that was not there. I alone could pierce the darkness and see him, and I flung myself into pursuit. I grasped one of his spike-studded ankles and let out a shriek of my own as I felt the sharp points score my flesh. I called for the others to help me, shouting so that they could follow my voice, and I clung to him even as he fought me.

"Before the others reached us, he landed one maddened blow to the side of my head which fired my interior world with a lightless blaze. Knocked almost senseless, I could not tell who captured him or how. He fought them, fought all of them, and was still weeping and calling out to someone named Matti as they dragged him back to the central open space. I was disoriented, spinning slowly in the air where I had been struck, like an untethered astronaut. Quan Li came and took my elbow and drew me back to the others.

"For a while we simply hovered there as the cloud of mourning spirits breathed around us. Shadow-fingers touched our faces, voices murmured just below audibility at our shoulders, behind us, sometimes it almost seemed *inside* us. Quan Li heard something that seemed to make her weep—I felt her begin shaking beside me, convulsive movements, helpless sobs.

" 'What are these things?' Florimel demanded. 'What is happening?' But there was no righteousness, no strength in her voice. She had surrendered to confusion.

"As my wits came back, I thought of the people of Aerodromia, the Stone-Age tribesfolk outside the cavern. No wonder this was their ordeal for suspected criminals, I reflected—if it could fill us with such fright, when we knew it was not real, how much more terrible must it be for them?

"I suddenly realized that I was feeling pity for fictional creations. The reality of this unreality had conquered me.

"Even as I thought these disordered things, I perceived that the insubstantial host keening around us had begun to draw us out of the central chamber. The feathery touches, the whispering voices, were urging and leading us. I alone could sense our surroundings, and understood that they were taking us through spaces large enough that we would not be injured, and so I did not resist. The others, far more disoriented than I was, did not even realize that they were drifting farther and farther from the spot where we had entered the Place of the Lost.

"Florimel floated closer to me, and above the windy murmuring of the voices, asked: 'Do you think these are what we're looking for? Are these the children, the lost children?'

"Despite my mind still working slowly after the blow from T4b's hammering fist, I could not help feeling like the world's greatest idiot. Until she spoke, I had not considered what his outburst might have meant. Was she right? Could this be a place where the comatose victims of the Brotherhood had their virtual existence? Were the chittering spirits around us more than simply an artistic effect in a magical simworld? If so, I realized, we were indeed surrounded by ghosts—the restless spirits of the good-as-dead.

"My last structures of detachment crashed down and I felt myself go cold. What if one of these was Renie's brother Stephen? How much more dreadful for him than the dreamless sleep of coma that would be. I tried to understand such an existence—to live as little more than a cloud of information, semi-coherent, struggling and lost. I tried to imagine how it might feel to a little boy as he fought to maintain the knowledge of his individuality, as he struggled to stay sane in endless, chaotic darkness while all that remained of his true self, like a single ice cube floating in the ocean, threatened at any moment to dissolve and disappear.

"Tears started in my eyes. Fury made me ball my fists and clutch them against my belly, so that for a moment I began to fall, and had to spread my arms again. Even summoning this image for my journal fills me with sick anger. If those few words from Florimel—or whoever she actually is—prove true, I cannot imagine telling it to Renie Sulaweyo. Better to lie to her. Better to tell her that her brother is dead. Better to tell Renie anything at all, rather than even let her guess at such a horrible truth.

"The ghosts led us onward, and as we moved through the cramped spaces of night, their voices grew more comprehensible. Whole sentences floated up from the cacophony, snatches of thoughts and bits of lives as apparently meaningless as a phone line accessed at random. Some spoke of things they had done, or of things they meant to do. Others simply babbled strings of apparently meaningless words. One, a breathy, lisping voice that sounded like a very young girl's, recited a nursery rhyme I remembered from my youth, and for a moment I almost believed I was hearing my own ghost, the shade of the child who had been as good as murdered the night the power went out in the Pestalozzi Institute.

"We came at last to an open place, a great underground cavern like the hollow in a fruit that holds the stone. But this fruit was rotten and the stone was gone. The empty space was filled with buzzing, twittering things, with breezes and soft sighs and touches like trailing cobwebs. Where before a thousand voices had surrounded us, now it seemed a hundred times that number, a thousand times, filled the emptiness.

"As we five living things hovered in the midst of that infinite replication of loss, shivering despite the warm updraft, confused and tearful and frightened, the voices began to find a resonance with each other. Patterns gradually arose out of the chaos, as they had arisen in the great river when we neared the edge of the last simulation. I heard the million voices slowly grow less complex as they tuned themselves individually up or down, slowed their babble or sped their stuttering hesitancies. So bizarre and captivating was the process that I almost lost track of my four companions altogether—they became distant clouds on the horizon of my attention.

"The voices continued to shed their individual characteristics. Screams were muted. Low murmurs rose in pitch and volume. It all happened in moments, but it was as complex and fascinating as watching an entire world being created. I absorbed it with more than just my hearing, perceived the spikes and whorls of conflicting information slowly begin to share a vibration. I tasted the growing coherence, smelled it . . . felt it. The chaos of Babel finally resolved into a single wordless tone, like the quietest note that could possibly be played on the universe's largest pipe organ. Then it stopped. For a long moment echoes still boomed and hissed in the chamber's far corners, ripples of reaction fizzing away like fireworks down the branch tunnels. Then the silence. And out of the silence at last, a voice. All the voices. A single voice.

" 'We are the Lost. Why have you come?'

"Florimel, William—none of my companions spoke. They hung in the darkness beside me, limp and helpless as scarecrows. I opened my mouth but could not make a noise. I told myself that none of it was real, but was unable to believe my own declaration. The presences that filled the cavern held their peace as they waited for an answer, like a hive full of bees anticipating the sunrise—a million individuals so attuned at that moment as to be one thing.

"I found a voice at last—one that stammered so badly that it was hard for me to believe it was my own. But I made words. 'The Middle Air People have condemned us . . .' I began.

" 'You are from beyond the Black Ocean,' chanted the voice of the Lost. 'You are not from this place. We know you.'

" 'Kn . . . know us?' I choked.

" 'You have Other Names,' the Lost said. 'Only those who have crossed the Ocean possess such things.'

" 'Do you . . . do you mean that you know who we . . . really are?' I was still finding it almost impossible to speak. I felt rather than heard a small, sharp movement close beside me—one of my overwhelmed companions whimpering, I thought, or signaling to me, but I could not make sense of it or even try. I was deafened, for lack of a better word, by the power of the voice of the Lost, as helpless as someone trying to remember one tune while standing in front of a full symphony playing a different one.

" *'You have . . . Other Names,'* the Lost said, as though explaining something to the slow-witted. *'You are Martine Desroubins. That is one of your Other Names. You come from a place called LEOS/433/2GA/50996-LOC-NIL, on the other side of the Black Ocean. Your number to call in case of emergency is . . .'*

As the hive-voice went on to recite the number of my storefront office in Toulouse, and that of the company that operated the randomizing resat which Singh and I had rigged to bring us untraceably into the Otherland network, all in the grave tones of God speaking to Moses on the Mount, I had an instant in which the entire world turned topsy-turvy. Had all the horrors we had suffered in the past weeks only been the setup for a bizarre joke, I wondered—had we been brought through all this only to be delivered a lame but still astonishing punchline? Then I realized that whatever the Lost were, they were simply reading my incoming data. The world turned right-side-up again, or as close as possible under such mad circumstances. To the Lost, no part of my "Other Names" as they called them were trivial. They were naming me with my details, as ignorant of context as a dog following its master through every room of a house while the master hunts for its leash.

" *'And you are Quan Li,'* the voice went on. We listened, stunned by the triviality of detail, as numbers and codes representing Quan Li's access path marched past, ending *'. . . From a place called Waves of Gentle Truth Immersion Palace, Victoria, Hong Kong Special Administrative District, China, on the other side of the Black Ocean . . .'*

" *'Florimel Margethe Kurnemann . . . Stuttgart, Germany.'* It ground on, reciting Florimel's data now, a flurry of numbers and account information that seemed to have no ending. We all listened helplessly.

" *'Javier Rogers,'* the voice intoned, *'from a place called Phoenix, Arizona . . .'* It was only when I heard his whimper of surrender, as though something had been torn from him, that I realized I was hearing T4b's real name.

The voice of the Lost rolled on for long minutes, listing a series of way stations as arcane and tangled as a sixteenth-century journey of exploration which constituted T4b's tortuous route to the Otherland network. When it stopped at last, we were silent, overwhelmed. A dim thought plucked at my attention, but before I could make sense of it the voice that was many voices spoke again, and what it said drove other preoccupations from my mind.

" 'Why have you come? Are you meant to lead us across the White Ocean?'

"I did not understand this. 'The White Ocean?' I asked. 'Not the Black, as you just said? We do not know such a place. We are trapped in your network.'

" 'We have waited,' it said. 'We are the Lost. But if we can cross the White Ocean, we will be gathered. We will be home. All will be made right.' There was a dreadful, hollow longing in the shared voice that made me shudder.

" 'We know none of this,' I said helplessly. We were wasting time, my senses screamed now—something was happening, or threatening to happen, while this madness distracted us. I did not know from where that feeling came, but it was there and growing stronger every moment. 'Who are you?' I asked. 'What has brought you all here? Are you children—the children who have been captured by the network?'

" 'We are the Lost!' the voice said, loudly, almost angrily. 'You are all Other, and you must help us. The One who is Other has abandoned us, and we are lost . . . lost. . . !' The single voice frayed then, and I could hear resonances of its individual strands.

"One of my companions was tugging at my arm now, but I was struggling to wring sense out of the situation and could not afford the attention. 'What do you mean, we are Other, but the One who is Other has abandoned you? That is meaningless to us!'

" 'The One who is Other brought us here,' the voice said, but it was voices now, ragged and tuneless. 'It brought us out of the darkness of the Black Ocean, but it abandoned us. It is disordered, it no longer knows us or cherishes us . . .' Component parts almost seemed to argue within the greater chord of the voice. 'We must find the White Ocean, beyond the great Mountain—only there will we be whole again. Only there can we find our homes. . . .' The voice was full of interference now, breaking up like a distorted radio transmission. Someone was still tugging at my arm. I turned, and sensed the information-shape of Florimel.

" 'Martine—William is gone!'

"I was baffled, overloaded. 'What are you talking about?'

" 'William has disappeared! The voices, they did not name him— you heard!' Florimel, too, was struggling not to fly into madness. 'And now he is gone!'

" 'S'her name, the Chinese lady, too,' T4b added in a voice shaky with terror.

The unified chorus of the Lost had almost completely degenerated again, but my sense that something terrible was about to happen grew stronger every moment.

" 'No, I am here!' Quan Li shouted. I could sense her energy signature rising up into our midst. 'William—he pushed me. Hit me!' She was terribly agitated. 'I think he wanted to kill me.'

"My misgivings from earlier now surged to the top. Whatever he was, William had been hiding a secret. Perhaps he *had* harmed the girl of the tribe. 'He ran because he did not want the Lost to name him,' I said. 'I let myself be distracted—me, the only one who could have seen him flee!'

"Before any of the others could reply, several disparate voices came together out of the cacophony to make a single voice, not the great whole, but still vibrating with urgency. *'The One who is Other,'* they shouted, full of fear that was also hopeless joy. *'The Other is coming!'*

"Then the temperature in the great cavern fell, and *it* was there—rather, it was everywhere. The information, all the information, stuttered and went rigid for a moment. I felt a terrible *something* leaning close, the same terrible thing that had nearly crushed the life from me when we entered the network. I could not help myself—animal terror made my entire nervous system convulse. I had only the sense to grab Florimel as I screamed 'Fly! Fly!' Then I threw myself forward. Florimel clutched at me in what for her must have been complete darkness. As she shouted for help, the others grasped at her in turn as I careened forward, trying to break away. I am ashamed to say that I had no thought for any of them as they struck obstacles, as they scraped flesh and bruised bones in an attempt to stay in contact with me—my terror of that Other was simply too strong. I would have thrown my parents to it, my friends, to save myself. I think I would have sacrificed my child, if I had one.

"I could feel it pervading the space behind us like a supernova of ice, like a great shadow under which nothing could grow. Tendrils of its questing thought reached out toward me, and I know now that if it had truly wanted me, physical flight would have been useless. But I had no thought in my head at that moment except a screaming need to escape.

"Somehow the others managed to follow me, although they suffered doing so. We flew like wounded bats—catching ourselves on each other, on the cavern stone, sprawling and cartwheeling through the dark in search of freedom from the growing chill behind us. We

were trapped in the endless, branching tunnels of the Place of the
Lost, and we ourselves were also lost, in every way.

"We burst into a new and open place, another great hollow in the
darkness. For a moment I spun in place, flapping my arms in reflexive
panic. The cacophony of the voices and the deadening horror of the
Other were a little less, but we were still lost in the catacombs. The
cavern's information spun around me, meaningless unless I interpre-
ted it, and it took all the self-possession I could muster just to slow
my rabbiting thoughts and try to consider where we were, what we
could do.

"The others crashed to a halt around me, catching at each other like
drowning swimmers. I silenced them with a sharp, trembling cry, then
fought to concentrate. The structured hierarchies of information
around me would not yield to my panicked mind—it was all tunnels,
all holes, and every hole seemed to empty back into another, a squirming mass of nothingness without outlet. I squeezed my head in my
hands, trying to shut out the clamor of memories, the dull echo of the
voice of the Lost, but the picture was muddy. Where was my mind?
What was happening to me?

"And ever, flickering in the back of my thoughts, a tiny place that
somehow even survived the terror of that Other, was the shocked unhappiness of realizing that someone who had been a good companion,
almost a friend, had proved a traitor. If the nameless terror was not
enough, we also shared the catacombs with our former ally, now
grown inexplicably murderous. Or had he been that way all along, but
only pretending? Had someone set William to spy on us? The Brotherhood? Was everything we had learned, discussed, planned, being reported to them even as we stumbled through this new universe?

"We had suspected things were not going well. We had been wildly
optimistic.

"My thoughts abruptly jerked as though something had smacked
against them. Somewhere, at the farthest reach of my internal darkness, I felt something new. It remains impossible to explain with mere
words, the input from these changed senses of mine, but I was feeling
a distortion in the patterns of information, a tiny flaw in the space
itself—a weak point, as though something had scraped away at the
reality of it from the far side until it was almost transparent. But what
did it mean? It was all so new, *still* is so new, that there are scarcely
patterns even in my own head that can encompass it. Something was
altered, that was all I could tell—something was making a hole in our
space.

"Conscious thought more or less returned to me then, and I wondered if I had discovered one of the places where gateways formed. I could not ponder too long—something greater and more alien than we could imagine was hunting us. I had been touched by it once. I did not think I could survive a second handling.

"Even as my companions gasped for breath, tight-chested with exertion and terror, I struggled to concentrate on that flaw in the imaginary universe that surrounded me, but no matter how I examined it, poked at it, tried to manipulate it, the quirk remained only potential. I went into that darkness so deeply that my head began to throb, but there was nothing to access, no seam or crevice deep enough for my poor understanding to exploit. It was like trying to open a bank vault with my fingernails.

"The pain in my head seemed like the beginnings of a stroke, and I was just about to give up when I saw something—the tiniest, tiniest flash of imagery, as though someone had projected a single microsecond of visual input onto the end of my optic nerve. Yes, I saw it—*saw.* The image was bizarre—a distorted, not-quite-human shape silhouetted against gray nothingness—but even in that sub-instant, it was more vivid to me than the remembered sights which compose the things I see in dreams. I have not seen that way for decades, and for a moment I believed it *was* a stroke, an illusion born out of collapse— that in my straining concentration I had burst a blood vessel in my brain—but I clutched at it anyway. Then I heard a voice, whisper-faint, as though a fluke of acoustics wafted it across miles of distance on a clear night. It was Renie's voice—Renie's voice!—and it said, '. . . find them? Can they . . . ?'

"Stunned, I cried out, 'Renie?'

"The others must have been certain I was going mad. One of my companions pulled at my arm again. 'Martine, someone's out there!' Quan Li wailed. 'I think it's William—I think he's coming after us!'

"I shook her off, desperate to maintain the contact. The silhouetted shape danced before me, but it was tenuous beyond belief, vanishing into fractal fuzziness at the edges, and the more I concentrated on it, the blurrier it became. The weird gray sky behind the moving shape was the only light piercing my inner darkness, so I reached out toward it, tunneling through the hole in the information, trying to touch whatever was on the far side. 'Renie,' I implored, '!Xabbu, if you can hear me, it's Martine. We need your help. Can you feel me?'

"The gray sky grew larger and more brilliant, until its pale light made the emptiness behind my eyes as bright as the moment of a camera flash. Through my ears I heard my companions shouting in alarm, but I could not listen to them. One of them screamed out that

William was coming, and the warning rose to a scream, but I was utterly absorbed in reaching through that impossible pinhole, that single black speck in endless whiteness. I struggled until I thought my head would burst to make my thoughts thin enough to pass through, stitching two sides of the universe together with a thread fragile as cloudsilk, as delicate as imagination itself.

"Something touched me then—touched the inner me. Something unfolded in the information like a budding flower opening into an entire galaxy. I reached out my real hand for my companions, to bring them through with me. The radiance grew until I could perceive nothing else.

"But as we flung ourselves through the light, a shadow came with us. . . ."

CHAPTER 32

Feather of Truth

NETFEED/PEOPLE: Barnes' Legacy Of Scary Fun
(visual: Barnes' face over Fire Tunnel sequence from Demon Playground)
VO: Elihu McKittrick Barnes, who died from heart failure yesterday at age 54, will be remembered by most for the high-speed, thrill-a-second gameworlds he authored, such as the bestselling Demon Playground and Crunchy, but he was also one of the world's leading collectors of Wizard of Oz memorabilia.
(visual: file footage—characters from W. of Oz on Yellow Brick Road)
The 20th century film is still popular over a hundred years after its creation, and royalty and other celebrities have had memorabilia from the film in their collection. Barnes was only the most recent to own a pair of sequined shoes known as the Ruby Slippers, worn by one of the characters in the film, but he considered them to be the gem of his collection. Barnes died alone and without heirs, so it seems certain to be a while before the Ruby Slippers find a new owner.
(visual: Daneen Brill, CEO of The Gear Lab)
BRILL: "He lived like a programmer, he died like a programmer. It's lucky the cleaners were handprinted for the door, or we still might not know . . ."

STAGGERING through the red desert, Orlando came to under-stand beyond any doubt why the ancient Egyptians had made the sun their lord. The white blaze of its eye saw everything, and its fiery touch was equally inescapable. The sun's heat surrounded them, squeezed them; when they stumbled in the red dunes, it was a mighty weight on their backs which tried to prevent them from rising again. The Egyptian sun was a god, beyond question—a god to be propitiated, to be worshiped, and most especially to be feared. Every time he inhaled, Orlando could feel its avid presence lean close and send its searing breath down his throat. Every time he exhaled, he could feel the same entity sucking the moisture up from his lungs, leaving the tissues dry and cracked as old leather.

The whole experience was curiously intimate. He and Fredericks had been singled out for extraordinary attention, and just as a victim of torture begins after a while to feel a deep, indescribable relationship with the torturer, so Orlando had come to feel a curious connection to the very elemental force that was killing him.

After all, he realized, there was a kind of honor in being murdered by a god.

All this wisdom came in only a half a day. With the sun still high overhead, they admitted defeat, and dragged themselves down the bank to soak in the shallowest part of the Nile, heedless of the danger from crocodiles, until their temperatures came down and something like sanity returned. Afterward they sat sharing the thin line of shadow from the area's lone palm tree. Although the river water had evaporated from his skin seconds after he had returned to the bank, Orlando was shivering, so overheated he was beginning to feel chilly.

"If we only had some . . . I don't know, some shelter," Fredericks murmured listlessly. "A tent or something."

"If we only had an air-conditioned jet," Orlando said through clenched teeth, "we could fly to Cairo eating little bags of peanuts."

His friend gave him a hurt look. "Chizz, then. I'll just shut up."

"I'm sorry. I don't feel so good."

Fredericks nodded miserably. "It's just so hard to wait. I mean, it'll be hours until it's dark again. I just wish we could lie down." He examined his ragged Pithlit-robes, which had lost a wide strip near the bottom to make a sort of *keffiyeh* for Orlando's head. "No, all I really wish is that I had more cloth we could use for things. And your sword back to cut it with." Fredericks frowned. "I mean, that seems more fair than wishing for a jet."

Orlando's laugh hurt, like part of him had gone rusty. "Yeah, Frederico, I guess so." He looked down at his tanned, muscular legs. If he were in his old battle-garbed Thargor sim, the one he was used to, he would at least have his skin covered.

Yeah, in black leather, he reminded himself. *That would be a treat, wouldn't it?*

Fredericks had fallen silent beside him. The heat haze warped the monotonous red landscape and flat blue sky, as though they sat in an isolation booth made of antique glass. It *was* odd about the clothes, Orlando reflected. He still didn't have any idea why he was wearing a sim of the young Thargor, rather than the mature warrior of Orlando's later years in the Middle Country. It seemed so—arbitrary. It would have made sense if the Otherland network had disallowed Thargor entirely and replaced him with some other sim, but to find an earlier version of Thargor and substitute that instead? What the hell was *that* about? And how could it happen? If the Otherland people could do something as fine-detail as finding his old Thargor records, either by hacking into Orlando's own system, or into the Middle Country, why would they bother to do so and change his sim accordingly, but then leave him loose inside the network?

The thought was vague, and the crushing heat made it hard to think. For a moment the whole idea threatened to spin away and disintegrate, like one of the dust devils that sprang up from time to time in the sands, but Orlando fought to retain it.

It's as though someone's watching us, he realized at last. *Taking an interest, somehow. But is it a good interest, or a bad one? Are they trying to help . . . or are they just playing some kind of really cruel game with us?* He found it quite easy to imagine the Grail Brotherhood, or his own cartoonish mental version of them, sitting around a corporate boardroom and thinking of ways to torture Orlando and his friends—a bunch of monstrous old men laughing uproariously and slapping each other on the back every time some new twist of agony made itself felt. He decided not to share this new suspicion with Fredericks.

His friend was surveying the river, face slack with exhaustion. From where they sat in the single palm tree's lengthening shadow, there was nothing to see between the slow-flowing Nile water and the mountains on either side except endless, uncaring sands.

"How far do you think it is to a city?" Fredericks asked. "I mean, it can't be that far, can it? If our real bodies are in hospitals, we're not going to die of thirst or starve, so we just have to reach someplace with a roof." He frowned. "I wish I'd paid more attention in the class when we did Ancient Egypt."

"I don't think this has much to do with what you would have learned in school," Orlando said grimly. "I think you could have studied for years, gone off to college and studied there, and it still wouldn't tell you anything about how to deal with this place."

"Come on, Gardiner." His friend was fighting irritation without much success. "There have to be cities! That's what Oom-Pa-Pa the Wolf Boy said, remember? That Osiris lived in a big city."

"Yeah, but this isn't historical Egypt," Orlando pointed out. "I mean, just seeing Upaut should have made that utterly locking clear, right? This is some weird mythological Egypt, you know, gods and magic and *fenfen* like that—if the people who made this decided to put twenty thousand miles of desert into it, they could. A loop-program would do the job pretty well, don't you think? It wouldn't be anything really tricky to design—'Add one thousand miles sand. Add one thousand miles sand. Add one thousand miles sand.' A chimp could do it." He scowled.

Fredericks sighed in despair and collapsed backward, then pivoted to get his head back in the single stripe of shade, where the air temperature was a minute fraction farther below the boiling point. "You're probably right, Orlando. But if we're going to die here, do you have to keep pointing it out to me?"

Orlando almost laughed again. "Guess not, Frederico. As long as you're clear on the concept."

"We're doomed, right?" Fredericks rolled his eyes melodramatically, as though his friend had made the whole desert thing up just to be irritating. "Utterly?"

Now Orlando did smile a little. "Right. Utterly."

"Okay, then. *Doomed.* Got it. Wake me up when it's dark." Fredericks draped his forearm across his eyes and fell silent. The brief moment of cheer had ended.

Orlando felt himself drifting in a kind of half-sleep. The shadow of the palm tree had expanded, somehow, so that even though the sky was still a powdery blue and the sun still blazed above, the land itself had turned dark and the tree was now only a silhouette. Something moved in the branches, a shadowy something with many legs.

"*Boss?*" The fronds rustled. "*Boss, you hear me?*"

He could not remember the name, but he recognized a friend. "I . . . I hear you."

"*Okay. Don't get your skinware in a bundle, just listen. There's a guy who says he wants to help you. He says he's the lawyer for Fredericks' parents—his name is Ramsey. He wants access to your files, if we'll let him. I told him I'd ask you.*"

Beezle. The thing was named Beezle. Orlando worried a little about Beezle's well-being—the wind was starting to blow, riffling the fronds. But wait—how could that be? The day was hot, wasn't it?

Hot and without any wind at all. . . ? "I'm sorry," he said slowly. "Fredericks. . . ?"

"This guy says he's the lawyer for Fredericks' parents." For gear, Beezle could do a good imitation of impatience. *"I've checked him out, and there is such a guy, and he does work for Fredericks' folks. We could swap some information, him and me, but I need your say-so. The files are all under name-security, which means no one but me and you can see 'em unless you spring 'em."*

The sky was losing its color, and even the sun was beginning to darken as a shadow spread quickly across the scalding white face of the disk. "Whatever you think is best." Orlando was finding it difficult to follow the conversation. If something was happening to the sky, didn't he need to wake Fredericks?

"Look, I know you think you're dreaming, Boss. This is really tough. If you want me to help the guy, tell me 'Ramsey can see files.' Just say that, unless you really don't want me to share anything. But I've pretty much run outta ideas, myself. This might be our last chance."

The sun was passing into full eclipse: only a sliver of brightness showed along one rim. The palm tree had begun to sway as a wind rose and flew across the darkening desert. Orlando hesitated. He wasn't sure what exactly was happening, but didn't he have enemies? Could they be tricking him somehow?

"Boss? I'm gonna lose you in a second. Tell me what to do."

Orlando watched the small dark thing moving frantically in the crotch of the palm tree. It seemed easier not to do anything. The clouds would come soon and cover everything over, and it would all mean nothing. . . .

"Say 'yes'," a new voice told him. It came from nowhere, but it was as clear as Beezle's—a woman's voice, one he recognized, although he could not say from where. *"Say 'yes',"* it urged again. *"Ask for help. Before the chance passes."*

The woman's words touched him all the way through the mists of dream, which seemed to be covering him over now, swirling, obscuring all, blanketing him in darkness. She sounded kind. She sounded sad and frightened, too.

He forced himself to concentrate. "What . . . what do you want me to say, Beezle?"

"You gotta tell me, 'Ramsey can see files,' okay?" Beezle's voice was getting harder to make out, but the urgency was clear. *"Please, boss. . . !"*

"Okay, Ramsey can see files." The wind was so loud he almost could not hear himself. *"Ramsey can see files!"* he shouted, but he could not tell if it had made any difference. The many-legged shape in the palm branches was gone. A cloud had obscured the sky, and now was filtering down atop him, covering the tree, covering Orlando, covering everything.

He caught a brief glimpse of a woman's form—a quick, shining moment like the kindling of a flame. She held something in her hand, as though she were offering it to him. Then the clouds blew in and covered her, too.

"Jeez, Gardiner, wake *up!*" Fredericks was shaking him, his voice faint, as though it came from a distance. "It's a sandstorm. Come on, wake up!"

Orlando could barely see his friend. They were in the midst of what seemed a visualization of pure white noise. Sand seemed to be flying at him horizontally, from every direction, spraying into his eyes and nose and mouth. Orlando spit wet grit and shouted: "We have to find some cover! Down to the river!"

Fredericks shouted something back, but Orlando could not hear it. He grabbed his friend by the sleeve and together they staggered toward the Nile, first leaning into the piledriving wind, then tumbling when it switched direction and pushed them from behind. They had started only a few steps from the river, but after a minute or two had passed with nothing beneath their feet except for the slithering, unforming dunes, Orlando knew they had somehow turned in the wrong direction.

His makeshift *keffiyeh* was pulled so tight he could barely breathe, but without it he would be blinded in seconds. This was doing them no good at all, he realized—if they went farther, they might lose the river entirely. He caught Fredericks by the shoulders and turned his friend toward him, pressing his forehead against Fredericks' so he could be heard over the roaring of the wind.

"We missed the river!" he shouted. "We have to stop and wait it out!"

"I can't . . . I can't breathe!"

"Pull your hood over your mouth!" Orlando let go of his own flapping head-cloth for a moment to help. "Just keep it like that, and keep your eyes closed! You'll still get air!"

Fredericks said something that was almost entirely muffled by wind and his hood. Orlando thought it might have been, "I'm scared." He knelt, pulling Fredericks down, then clung to his friend and pulled Fredericks' forehead against his neck, hugging him, struggling to keep his balance against the furious wind and the needle-sharp sprays of sand.

They remained that way for what seemed like hours, a clumsy, four-legged structure, holding together with panicked ferocity, their faces pressed into each other's shoulders. The sand sprayed them like a shotgun blast, and burned like rock salt where it found exposed flesh. The wind howled on and on; Orlando thought he could hear voices in it, condemned spirits and lost souls wailing like abandoned children. At one point he even heard his own mother's voice, weeping and trying to call him home. He clung to Fredericks and told himself it was all imaginary, knowing that to take even a step away from his friend might mean death for both of them. At last the storm blew itself out.

With dwindling strength, they dragged themselves down to the river, which turned out to be only a few yards away—sand-blinded, they had been stumbling along parallel to its course—and washed the dust and blood from their abraded skin. Then they crawled back onto the bank and fell asleep in the full late afternoon sunlight. Orlando woke long enough to rub mud on his legs, which even with Thargor's dark tan were beginning to feel as though they were being broiled, then he slid back once more into a vertiginous and unrestful sleep.

"Everything, everything hurts," Fredericks groaned. The sun had dipped behind the western mountains, and although the sky along that horizon was now the same spectacular color as the desert itself, the heat was much less. The first few stars were agleam in the darkening sky. "We need to rest tonight, Gardiner. I don't think I can walk."

Orlando scowled. He was exhausted, too, aching in every muscle and across every inch of skin. He hated having to be the drill-sergeant. "We can't rest. If we stay here all night, what happens in the morning? The same thing all over again, but twice as bad. I don't know if I can even make it another day without some shelter to get out of the sun." The first chill of evening—still a warm summer night in any other environment—had set him shivering again. "So get up. Come on, or we'll be locked majorly."

Fredericks let out a great sigh of misery, but did not argue. He climbed shakily to his feet, wincing and moaning, and fell in behind Orlando as they began to follow the course of the river.

"So if this isn't the real Egypt," Fredericks rasped after some time had passed, "where are we going?"

"Out of here." Talking split his cracked lips. His legs and head throbbed, and his sunburned, sandblasted skin felt like it had been scoured with a wire brush. For the first time in a long time, it hurt as much to be Thargor as it did to be Orlando Gardiner in RL. "We need to find another way out of here—one of those doors, or gates."

"Do you mean we're walking all the way to the end of the river?" If Fredericks had been in better shape, his voice would have quivered with outrage. As it was, he just sounded horribly depressed.

"Only if we have to. There should be some other way out. I don't believe the people who built these places have to go all the way through them every time."

Fredericks lumbered along beside him in silence for a long moment. "Unless they can just pop in and out anywhere they want. You know, because they're members or whatever."

Orlando pushed this depressing possibility away. He owed something to Renie and the others—and to Sam Fredericks, too. He wasn't going to die in some imaginary desert. Whatever his own story was, it couldn't end like that. It just . . . couldn't.

"We'll find a way out."

When the moon had already passed across the night sky and vanished, perhaps an hour before the sun's return, they found another set of ruins, a cyclopean tumble of stones on a bluff overlooking a wide spot in the river. He and Fredericks found a spot where one massive stone had fallen against another, leaving some small distance between the wide rock faces, and crawled into the gap to sleep.

If Orlando dreamed, he did not remember any of it when he woke in late afternoon with the sun beating down on the sand a few inches away and his head pillowed against Fredericks' leg. After going down to the river to splash themselves with lukewarm Nile water, they drowsed in the shady refuge of the ruins until the sun finally dropped behind the western mountains once more and they could resume their journey.

It was a little easier going the second night, if only because they were better rested, but it was still a mean, joyless trudge. The stars, despite a certain animation they did not display in RL—at times the constellations almost seemed to arrange themselves in the moving, living shapes of humans and animals—were still out of reach, and a night desert was no more interesting than the daylit variety. Somewhere after midnight, Fredericks began singing some dreadful summer-camp song whose main feature was adding a single item to the contents of a suitcase every verse before running through the entire list from beginning to end, and by the time he had reached *a tse-tse fly, round rocks, Jewish rye, padlocks, a bow-tie, some old socks, blueberry pie, three clocks, Dad's left eye, a young fox, octopi, and a small black box,* Orlando was ready to murder his companion and bury his despicable, camp-song-singing body under the ubiquitous sand. His exasperated scream ended the recitation.

Fredericks arched his eyebrows. "What's *your* problem, scanmaster?"

"Could you do something besides sing that song?"

"Like what?"

"I don't know. Talk to me. Tell me something."

Fredericks tramped beside him for a while in silence. The sand rasped and crunched beneath their feet. "Something like what?"

Orlando made a noise of frustration. "About your school, about your family, about anything—just don't sing. What do you do when you're not on the net? Girl things? Boy things?"

Fredericks frowned. "This another one of your what-are-you-really conversations, Gardiner?"

"No. But if it were *me* who was a girl pretending to be a boy, *you'd* want to know what it was all about, wouldn't you?" He waited for an answer, but an answer did not seem to be coming. "Wouldn't you?"

"Maybe." Fredericks shot him a quick glance, then returned to contemplating the featureless dunes. "I don't know, Orlando. What do I do? Just . . . things. I play soccer. I hang around. I used to play *BlueBlazes Collective* all the time. . . ."

"I said when you're not on the net."

"Not much. That's why I'm on the net a lot. The kids where I go to school, they're all doing sex and stuff. Passing around chargers in the restroom. Doing ultravile interactives. Talking about the parties they're gonna have when their parents go out of town. And they listen to all this utterly slumped music. It's just . . . boring. They don't read or anything—not even as much as I do!" Fredericks made a face for effect: it was a standing joke between them that Fredericks thought only a mutant could read as much text as Orlando did. "They don't talk about anything real."

To Orlando, whose few offline friends were other chronics with whom he had shared hospital support groups, this seemed as wild and fascinating a group of options as the jet-setting life of an international master spy, but he tried to make sympathetic noises.

"That's why you're my best friend, I guess," Fredericks went on. "I mean, you were more interesting than all those impacted idiots, even though I never met you." Fredericks walked another two dozen paces before adding, "—of course, if I had known this was the kind of place I'd wind up, I probably would have been better off doing T2 chargers with Petronella Blankenship."

It was meant as a joke, but surrounded at they were by miles and miles of featureless, moon-silvered sand, it carried a certain sting.

* * *

They made camp just after dawn in a tiny oasis comprised of a few date palms and some low, scrubby bushes. As the Nile began to shift from black to a metallic blue, they fell asleep huddled against the west flank of a fallen palm. They were awakened at mid-day by another sandstorm, which not only stung them with choking sand, but shifted enough landscape to reveal that they had been sharing the oasis with the corpses of three camels. The beasts, on closer inspection, proved to be really only camel-shells, since insects and other scavengers had long since devoured everything but bones and skin, and the desert air had then cured the latter so that they still seemed stuffed with the original goods. Orlando found it an incredibly depressing sight, and forced Fredericks to begin their nightly march even before the failing sun had reached the western horizon.

The trek across the sands had now become a familiar but no less miserable routine. The hours seemed to ooze past. Fredericks no longer sang, not even to annoy Orlando.

When the heat began to rise even before the sun had appeared above the eastern mountains, Orlando knew they were going to be in for a bad day. There was no obvious shelter in sight, no trees, no convenient ruins. He and Fredericks decided to dig in.

They scraped a pit for themselves in the damp sand close to the river. When they had dug down a foot or so, they shored the walls of the excavation as best they could with small stones, then Fredericks took off his robe. They lay down side by side, then stretched the robe over the top of their shelter and waited for sleep. Already the early morning sun was beating on the fabric, and despite the river-moisture seeping from the walls, the pit was beginning to warm.

Fredericks managed to fall asleep fairly quickly, as he usually did. Orlando was not so lucky. Sweat dripped into his eyes and pooled on his chest. Sleep would not come. His brain could not let go of things.

They had been walking for days now, but he could see no particular effect in relation to the distant hills. He half-wondered if he had jinxed them by suggesting twenty thousand miles of desert. Perhaps the system had heard him and adjusted itself accordingly. . . .

Fredericks shifted against him, rubbing skin on sweat-soaked skin. Orlando was uncomfortably aware of his friend, who was naked but for a loincloth, and felt confused and oddly shamed. Fredericks was wearing the thin, male body of Pithlit; his chest, while small around the rib cage, was unquestionably male. And yet, even though how the sim was dressed had no bearing on what the real Fredericks was wearing, it was hard not to remember that at least in some sense, this was Salome Fredericks, an actual girl, lying half-naked beside him.

But Fredericks thought of himself as a boy, at least when he was on-line. So what did that make Orlando at this moment, shrinking away from more contact with his friend's virtual flesh because it made him so uncomfortable—because it excited him? Straight? Queer?

Desperate, Orlando told himself. *I'll probably never have sex with anyone unless I pay for it, VR or RL. And time is running out on that particular project, anyway.*

There was a certain type of hero for whom virginity was a source of great power. Given a choice, Orlando hadn't really wanted to be that kind of hero.

He didn't sleep well through the long, hot day. The pit was like a sauna, his mind unquiet. When they clambered out onto the river-bank at nightfall, Orlando felt tired and not very well. Within the first mile, he began to wonder whether he could get through the night's walking.

Fredericks recognized that something was wrong, and although Orlando snappishly refused help several times, his friend adjusted his pace so that Orlando wouldn't have to struggle too hard to keep up. It was hard to disguise this, and for Orlando it was almost worse than falling behind.

He wasn't exactly sure what the problem was. His joints ached, but that was normal for him. He felt hot, but after another hellish desert afternoon, the evening air was still warm enough to make both friends sweat as they waded through the unstable sands, so there was nothing surprising there. The worst thing was that he could not seem to get enough air into his lungs. No matter how deeply he breathed, there always seemed to be pockets of carbon dioxide in the bottom of his chest he could not shift, and he was running out of energy before he had even reached the next inhalation.

He had stopped for perhaps the two-dozenth time, and was bent double, leaning on his knees, struggling to draw in air. "Bad, huh?" Fredericks asked. There was a nervous quaver to his voice he could only partially hide.

Orlando nodded. The effort made him cough, and for a moment fireworks exploded across the blackness of his closed eyelids. Even after he opened his eyes again, the night sky swam and sparkled. "Yeah. Bad . . ."

"We don't have to go any more tonight," Fredericks said carefully. "We could start looking for a camp. Maybe we could build a fire this time—you know, rub two sticks together or something."

Orlando shook his head, trying to ignore the swollen way it felt when he did. "We have to keep going. We have to . . . have to tell the others . . ."

"I know. We have to tell the others what you guessed about those Grail guys."

"So we need to . . ." Orlando drew a ragged breath, ". . . we need to get to Priam's Walls."

"Yeah, but it's not going to help if you kill yourself!" Fredericks was clearly hurting; he sounded almost defiant.

"Look, Frederico," he said, straightening from his crouch. "I *am* going to die. It's not your fault, and there isn't anything you can do about it."

"We're all going to die, Orlando."

"That's not what I mean and you know it. I'm probably not going to make it out of this . . . this network. It's too much for me. I'm used to getting twelve hours of bed rest a day, even when I'm not sick." He raised his hand to forestall Fredericks' objection. "I can't do that here—I just can't. We have work to do. I have this healthy Thargor-body, and I'm going to use it the best I can. If we don't get that information to Renie and !Xabbu and the others, they might not be able to get out of here themselves. They could all die here—half a dozen people! Not to mention all those little kids like Renie's brother. As for me, if there was some kind of Nile General Hospital right here I could check into, with little pyramid-shaped bedpans, it might buy me a few more months at the most." He began to walk along the line of the river, slowly at first, conscious that Fredericks was still standing and watching him. "So thanks for the good thoughts," he called over his shoulder. "But I just don't have any choice."

Fredericks caught up with him before a minute had passed, but seemed to have run out of things to say.

After that, Orlando was determined not to stop again for a while, and they made better time. He needed oxygen, but deep breaths made him cough, so Orlando went back to an RL trick he had developed through numerous bronchial illnesses, breathing shallowly through his nose. He slowed his pace, conceding a little to practicality, but tried to keep his progress steady to make up for it. The moon floated along the horizon and vanished behind a wall of clouds, the first clouds they had seen since reaching this Egypt.

"Do you think it will rain?" Fredericks asked hopefully.

"No. Upaut said it hadn't rained in years in this simworld."

When the sky began to lighten they made camp in a jumble of boulders a hundred meters up from the river. Relieved of the need to be as strong as his healthy companion, Orlando collapsed immediately. He barely felt Fredericks pulling the Pithlit-robe over him like a blanket before sleep dragged him down.

The woman who had urged him to tell Beezle what the agent wanted to hear appeared in the shadow-lands of his dream. She wore only a skirt of some transparent material, but even with her small breasts and gently rounded, almost childlike stomach presented unselfconsciously to his view, and despite his own frustrations and longings, her presence was not sexual. Her eyes, thickly outlined in black, seemed to gaze through him rather than at him. She held something against her bosom, but her dark hair, which hung down in long thick plaits, at first obscured it. It was only when she floated close enough that in waking life he could have touched her (but in the dream he seemed quite immobile, a bodiless observer) and extended her hand to him, that he saw she held a feather, an iridescent plume as long as her forearm which was no color he could name.

Who are you? he asked, or thought he asked.

I am Ma'at, she said. *Goddess of Justice. When your soul is weighed in the final accounting, it is this feather, the weight of Truth, which will be placed in the other balance of the scale. If your soul is heavier, then you will be cast into outer darkness. If your balance rises, you will be taken with the other just and good ones into the barque of Ra, and conveyed to the West to live in bliss.*

She stated this with the kind of calm certainty exhibited by tour guides, or documentary voice-overs. Although he had never seen her before, there was something familiar about her, but his dreaming mind could not summon the memory.

Why are you telling me all this? asked Orlando.

Because that is my task. Because I am one of the gods of this place. She paused, and for the first time seemed thrown out of her rhythm, as though Orlando's question had raised unexpected problems. *Because I do not know who you are, but you are wandering in and out of the borderlands,* she said finally. *Your presence disturbs me.*

Borderlands? Orlando tried to make sense of what she was saying, but the goddess Ma'at was fading into shadow. *What borderlands?*

She did not answer. He woke to find the late afternoon sun still blazing in the sky. He was wheezing, and the effort to fill his lungs drove the dream-goddess from his mind.

Halfway through the fifth night in the desert and the sands showed no signs of ending, or even changing in character. The Nile wound through the empty lands, dwindling into the starlit distance until there was nothing to see but a slack black string. The dunes stretched on and on before them, reshaped by the flurrying wind, constantly changing, constantly the same.

But something was different.

Fredericks noticed it, too. "Do you . . . hear something?"

Orlando, slogging grimly through the ankle-high sands, shook his head. "It's not a sound."

"What do you mean?"

"It's not a sound." He took a deep breath and slowed his pace to an even more deliberate trudge. "I've been feeling it for a while. It's a vibration, kind of, but it's almost a smell, too. It's a lot of things, but at first it just seemed like some noise to me. It's been in front of us for a while, and it's getting stronger."

"Yeah, I'm beginning to see what you mean." Fredericks winced. "What do you think it is?" He was struggling to keep his voice firmly in the deeper registers.

"I don't know. It's not good, whatever it is."

"What do we do?"

"What *can* we do? Keep going. We don't have any other choices, Frederico, remember?"

The sensation continued to grow and deepen. Soon what once had been no more annoying than a buzzing insect, or the faint whiff of something sour, was beginning to dominate Orlando's thoughts. It felt as though he had a throbbing headache, but one that was located somewhere out in the distance rather than inside his head.

Deciding that, whatever it might be, it was definitely the kind of thing they should avoid, if just for their own comfort, they altered their course. The Nile was broad here, the opposite bank invisible even by bright moonlight, so instead of trying to cross the river they swung wide into the western desert. But changing the angle did nothing: however broad their turn, the sensation still seemed to wait just ahead. It filled the night with its presence now, cold and dreadful and inescapable.

It feels like that death-row simulation, Orlando thought, remembering the days when he sought out such things voluntarily, in the hope of desensitzing himself. *Like waiting for them to come get you for execution, and knowing there's absolutely nothing you can do about it.*

"It's the thing from the Freezer," he said out loud. "Waiting for us. It's that thing that you called the devil, the real devil."

Fredericks just grunted. He knew.

Orlando wanted nothing more than to be able to call his parents to come and save him. In fact, he realized, he wanted his mother. At another time, that realization would have shamed him, but not now.

He just wanted to be held and told everything would be all right. But the hell of it was, Vivien might be only real inches away, but she was simultaneously on the other side of the universe. It hurt, it hurt.

Beside him, Fredericks was suffering too, fighting back tears, determined to play the masculine role in just as stupid a way as any boy.

They changed direction yet again, doing their best to double back on their own tracks, although the sands had shifted and it was hard to tell, but it made no difference. The cloud of dread still hung before them.

We have to go to it, Orlando realized dully. *We don't have a choice.*

Beside him, Fredericks' face had lost its usual stolidity; his eyes showed white all around, the stare of an animal at bay. "I don't want to be here—*don't want to be here,*" his friend babbled quietly. "Don't want to do this . . ."

Orlando reached out and touched Fredericks' shoulder, trying to give his friend strength, but his own voice was dense with despair. "We might as well take the direction we were going." He turned, parallel once more to the flow of the Nile. "It won't make any difference even if we go all the way back to where we started."

Fredericks had no strength to argue; he dropped his head and followed Orlando. Something was actively pulling them forward now, sucking at them as though they were planets fallen into the grip of a dark star. Stiff-legged, fighting for balance, they felt it waiting, but could not stop.

As they crested a long rise, they finally saw it. To Orlando, just reaching it was like being punched in the stomach, a sickening thump that drove out his breath.

Nothing about it should have been so terrible. The temple lay nestled in a desert valley, lit more brightly than moonlight alone should have accomplished, surrounded by low cliffs and a vast, uneven ring of broken stones. Along its facade stood an unbroken line of columns, a bleak brown grin like a skull's that seemed to stretch for miles. Although Orlando and Fredericks looked down on the valley from the top of a tall dune, some trick of perspective made the temple simultaneously seem to tower above them, as though the night itself had been bent inward, distorted by the temple's dreadful gravity.

Orlando had never seen anything that looked so completely dead and deserted as that place, so bleak and empty and lifeless; but at the same time, he knew that something lived within, something they had felt for hours before reaching this place, a life so profoundly *wrong* that just looking at its den made every cell in Orlando's body, every electrical impulse of his thought, scream for him to run away. And despite the fact that he knew running would be useless—that any path they took would simply curve through simulation space and bring them back to this high place again—if not for the spell the temple cast, the numbing, paralyzing field of misery that was turning him into unmoving stone, he would still have run away if he could, run until he collapsed, then crawled until his heart stopped.

At least a minute passed before either of them spoke, but every second was a struggle to resist the valley's pull.

"It's . . . it's a really bad place," Fredericks finally rasped, words catching in his dry mouth. "Worse . . . th-than the freezer. Oh, God, Orlando, I want . . . Oh, please, God, I want to go home."

Orlando did not respond: he knew he would need every bit of his strength for what he was about to try. He stared at his foot, then leaned against the temple's compulsive force and watched as his foot slowly lifted free of the sand. He was far, far away, watching something happening on a distant planet through a powerful telescope, and it needed all his concentration to keep that foot (which seemed only faintly his own) moving. He turned it a little to one side, then planted it again. He lifted the other and did the same thing, a painstaking, remote operation. Every second that he resisted the black gravity of the valley felt impossibly tiring.

As he inched himself away from the temple, he reached out a cement-heavy arm toward Fredericks; when he touched his friend, it seemed to transfer a little energy, a spark of life. Face screwed up in an expression of painful, fearful concentration, Fredericks too began to pivot in a small circle, fighting for every degree. When they had turned far enough that the temple finally disappeared behind them—disappeared from vision, but not from their senses: they could feel it at the end of every quivering nerve they had—the pressure became a little less. Orlando was even able to take a first full step away from the valley, muscles quivering and sweat streaming from every pore.

He staggered a few more meters, each pace an agony, as though he were detaching himself from some horrible, many-tendriled plant which had sunk fibers into his very cells. Then, when perhaps half the rise lay between him and the view of the temple, he felt the directional pulse begin to shift, as though the whole massive complex and its ghastly aura of attraction were floating free. In this moment the pressures were abruptly equalized, behind and before, but he knew that if he continued on, no matter which direction, he would again find the temple valley and its nameless inhabitant in front of him. Limp, but drawing on a reserve of strength he had not known he had, he dropped and began to dig.

Fredericks caught up with him, and after a moment tumbled to the sand and began to help, scraping in the clumsy, damaged fashion of an animal that had survived a lightning-strike. When they had dug down a couple of feet into the sand, Orlando let himself roll into the shallow pit. Fredericks crawled in after him, and for a long time they simply lay in a tangled heap, gasping for breath.

"We'll never get around that thing." Fredericks' voice sounded squeezed, as though something had collapsed his ribcage. "It's going to pull us in. It's going to get us."

Orlando could not think about it any more. He had used all his strength just to break the circuit for a moment and bring them this temporary respite. Fredericks was right, but Orlando simply could not think about it. Exhaustion was pulling him down as surely as the temple had, but this time he did not resist.

It was so preposterous that even the logic of dreams was insulted.

The matte-black pyramid stretched so high that it had no visible apex, so wide that it was literally impossible to look in another direction. The visible slivers of night sky on either side of it, though lit only by a few faint stars, seemed almost bright blue in comparison to the pyramid's profound blackness.

He knew he could not deal with this heart-stopping thing alone, and called for the beetle who had spoken to him in other dreams, but he was afraid to raise his voice, and although he called for a long time, the creature did not answer him. But someone did.

He cannot come, your servant. I do not feel him here. She said it as someone who carries sad news for which she feels a small responsibility. *He is in other dreams, perhaps.*

Orlando turned and found her hovering beside him, a shadow barely distinguishable from the night, the feather still clasped in her hand as though it might be some defense against the impossible black pyramid.

Can't you help me? He turned back to the shape which spread so high and so far to either side there seemed nothing else on that side of the world. *I can't get past this thing. We're going to die here if no one helps us.*

You cannot avoid him, she said, not unkindly. *There is no story like that. He is at the center of all of this. He must be faced.*

Is it . . . is it Osiris?

Her face, although hard to see in darkness, seemed to twist as if in pain. *No,* she said. *No, the one who wants your life is something far stranger than that. He is the Lord Set, the sleeping one who rules the Red Lands. He is the one who dreams—we are his nightmares. He dreams you, too.*

He had heard those words before, somewhere. *Who are you?* he demanded.

Ma'at, the goddess of Justice, she said.

I mean really.

I am a voice, she said, *—a word. I am a moment. It does not matter.*

And suddenly it came to him. *You're the woman from the freezer. Sleeping Beauty. You talked to us before. You told us to find our friends at Priam's Walls.*

She did not speak, and now her face was entirely veiled in shadow.

But why don't you help us? You must be trapped here, like us! If we don't get around this temple and out of this desert, we'll die, and so will a lot of other people. And all the children, the lost children!

She had drifted a little way back, and when more silence followed his plea, he was sure he had lost her. He could see only an outline, a hole in the night sky, the silhouette of an angel.

Please? He reached out a hand. *Please?*

Remember, this is a dream, she told him, but it sounded as though she were the one half-asleep.

I know you can do something, Orlando said, and suddenly it did not matter whether this was a dream or not. Something important was within his grasp, perhaps for the last time, and he could not afford to let go. *You know things. Help us get out of here.*

There are balances you cannot understand, she protested, her voice faint as a wind that did not move even the most powdery sand. *Things you do not know . . .*

Please?

She bowed her head then and raised one hand, showing him her palm, ghost-pale against the darkness. He could see a star right through it. *Go forward until you see my sign,* she whispered. *I pray that I do the right thing. We are too many, and there is no single one to guide us.*

What are you talking about? She seemed willing to help him, but he could make no sense of what she was saying. He felt the chance slipping away. *Go forward. . . ?*

Walk into the darkness, she said. *You will see my sign. . . .*

Then she was gone, and the great pyramid shredded like smoke, and all that remained was the black sky and a single bright star.

His cheek pressed flat against the sand, his mouth half-full of grit, Orlando opened his eyes. The star and its dimmer kindred were all that remained to light the night. The moon had gone long ago. The sense of what lay just the other side of the dune was undiminished: the temple was a whirlpool, and they were already in its vortex. No matter which way they turned, they would not escape it.

Walk into the darkness . . .

But she couldn't have meant . . .

Walk into the darkness . . .

Orlando sat up, heart speeding. If he thought about it too long, even in the midst of all this other madness—this virtual universe, this imaginary Egypt, this temple with the awful vitality of a vampire's secret resting place—he would not be able to believe it. She had come to him in a dream. She had told him what to do. The fact that it was the thing he least wanted to do made it all the more critical he not waste time thinking any longer.

He shook Fredericks awake.

"What? What?"

"Come on. Follow me." He scrambled up the side of the shallow pit and then stood. Every joint burned like fire and his breath smoldered in his lungs, but he could not afford to think about those things, either. "Come on."

"Where are we going?"

"Just come with me. Just . . . follow."

Fredericks watched Orlando's first hobbling steps with astonishment all over his sleepy face, an astonishment which turned swiftly to terror. "What are you doing? That . . . that *thing's* over there."

"That thing's everywhere."

"Orlando! Come back!"

He ignored his friend and kept moving forward. The last thing he could afford to do was listen to sense.

"Gardiner, you're scaring me! Are you scanbarking beyond the uttermost, or what? Orlando! Come back!"

One foot in front of the other—*left, right, left.* He felt the horrible magnetic tug of the temple, and suddenly the struggle was not to limp forward, but to keep from running toward it. Something had its grip on him now, a clutch so powerful that if his legs had fallen off he would have dragged himself ahead with his arms alone. The presence opened before him like a poisonous flower calling to a small crawling thing, offering a voiceless, formless, but virtually irresistible invitation. It wanted him. It wanted his life.

"Gardiner!"

Fredericks' cry seemed quite distant. The part of Orlando's brain that was still his own felt sad; he knew that his friend was hesitating, torn between Orlando and his own safety. A moment later, he heard Fredericks' footsteps crunching through the sand behind him, and knew that his friend had made a choice. If Orlando was wrong, or the woman with the feather had been wrong, Orlando had now doomed them both.

But what had she said? *"You will see my sign"*—what did that mean? What kind of help could she give to him?

He was past the crest of the hill now, and moving swiftly downward with the clumsy articulation of a malfunctioning toy. Twice he fell and rolled, but the force that had him in its clutch did not allow him to discover whether or not he had hurt himself; it yanked him to his feet and drew him onward.

Fredericks had quit calling out, but Orlando could hear his friend's harsh, frightened breathing close behind. They stumbled and crawled off the sand hill and onto the valley floor. The temple simultaneously squatted and loomed before them, the columnar teeth smiling wide in anticipation of a coming meal. Orlando could sense that the thing that lived behind that dead grin was sleeping, or partially absent in some other way, but as though he were a flea on a dog's back feeling the first tremors of movement, he could also feel the massive presence beginning to rise toward wakefulness. He stumbled beneath the weight of that terrible sensation and fell, but the pull did not slacken. He could not even take the time to rise, but was forced to crawl forward over the uneven ground.

Some of the sand on the valley floor had been fused into hard lumps and ridges, as though some terrible heat had turned it into crude glass. Boulders and raw shards of stone were everywhere, pieces torn from the distant mountains then crumbled and dropped around the temple. The smaller fragments cut his knees and palms, and Orlando's breath now came out in a continuous moan of pain. Behind him, Fredericks was crying, too. Orlando tried to crawl on the places where the sand was still loose and granular, but his compulsion did not always allow that.

So overwhelming were the sensations that he did not notice the different surface of the object as it passed beneath his hands. The valley floor had gone blurry and black-spotted before him, so he stopped for a moment to suck air into his raw lungs, then coughed until he thought he would pass out. Wheezing, he hung his head to bring back the blood. As his vision cleared, he saw that he was kneeling on the rounded side of something buried in the sands that was not a stone.

It was a piece of pottery, he realized slowly, its exposed surface hard as brick. In the midst of the abstract diagonals which had been cut into the clay was a single pictogram, set apart from the rest of the design by a lozenge-shaped outline—a feather.

You will see my sign . . .

The temple was dragging at him once more, but he fought against it for the first time since leaving their refuge. As his blood surged and throbbed in his head, he scraped at the clay with his fingernails, trying to uproot it from the sand. Fredericks crawled level with him, slack-mouthed and fever-eyed.

"Help me," Orlando gasped. "This is it!"

Fredericks stopped, but for a moment could do nothing else. Orlando dug into the sand, but could not find the edge of the clay. He scraped and scattered, but there was no place to get his fingers under his prize and pull it from the sand.

Fredericks lurched toward him and tried to help. Within moments they had uncovered a large stretch of the curving surface, but still they found no edge. The unceasing demand of the temple, which jutted so starkly above them now that it might have been a mountain, urged Orlando to crawl on his belly, to hasten forward, to ignore everything else. . . .

He groaned. Tears made his vision blur. "It's a jar or something. It must be huge!" He knew they would never be able to resist the temple's force long enough to excavate it. The woman with the feather had tried, but he was not strong enough to use her gift, whatever it was.

The clamor to go forward rose in his skull.

"I wanted to help . . ." he murmured. "I wanted to save them. . . ."

Fredericks had left his side. Orlando sensed his absence and his heart grew colder. He could not let his friend continue on alone. The gamble had been lost.

He raised his head just in time to see Fredericks stumbling back toward him, on his feet by some astonishing effort of will. He was clutching a large chunk of stone in his two hands, and as Orlando stared in stupefaction, Fredericks heaved it up over his head and brought it down onto the sigil of the Goddess of Justice.

There was no noise but the rush and roar in his head as the clay collapsed inward. For a moment Orlando and Fredericks both stared at the jagged hole, then something flickered in its dark depths. A pale cloud whirled up out of the shattered jar and spun wildly past them. It shot into the air, twirling so fast that for a moment it disappeared against the dark sky, then descended again and enveloped the two of them. Orlando flung up his hands to protect his face. When he opened his eyes, a tiny yellow monkey was clinging to his finger, inspecting him with squinting interest. A dozen other of the minute creatures had settled on his arms and on Fredericks.

"Hey, Landogarner!" the thing on his finger said, its piping voice surrealistically cheerful. "Where you go? Why you leave Wicked Tribe in that dark room for so long?"

Two more microsimians rose and hovered. "Tribe angry!" they cried. "Boring room, boring, boring!"

"But now," the first announced smugly, blithe as a gnat hovering at Hell's doorstep, "now we have total big fun!"

This is what was supposed to save us? Orlando thought helplessly, hopelessly. *This is the best she could do?* Rage and exhaustion beat at him like hammerblows. The last of his strength was gone, but the temple still exerted its unanswerable pull. This time, he knew, he would go to it meekly.

Perhaps sensing something, the monkey on his finger turned to look over its shoulder. When it saw the pile of grinning stones it shrieked and clapped two tiny hands over its face.

"Yick!" it said. "Why you bring us here? That not fun *at all.*"

CHAPTER 33

An Unfinished Land

NETFEED/NEWS: Cult Mass Suicide in New Guinea
(visual: smoke victims being helped from Somare Airport)
VO: Twenty-six members of a Papua New Guinea religious sect died after
setting themselves on fire in the airport of the capitol city of Port Moresby.
The sect, linked to the cargo cults which were once a mainstay of island life,
doused their clothes and bodies with gasoline and set fire to themselves in the
main boarding area of Port Moresby's Somare Airport. They made no
announcement and left no explanation.
(visual: Kanijiwa in front of NU of L backdrop)
Professor Robert Kanijiwa of Tasmania's New University of Launceston
claims this mass suicide is part of a frightening trend.
KANIJIWA: "This can't be written off as just another crazy cult—this
particular sect had been around since the 18th century. There's a lot of this
going on just now, and not only in our part of the world—it's like the fever
at the end of the millennium a few decades ago, but without that obvious
explanation. A lot of people seem to feel something strange and apocalyptic is
about to happen, and I'm afraid there's going to be more of this kind of
thing . . ."

SOME of the colors had no names. Bits of sky were embedded in the ground for no apparent reason. Even the presence of Emily, a Puppet who should have been left behind in the simulation for which she was built, was a puzzle that Renie could not solve. But one glimpse of her friend convulsing on the not-quite-ground made all the questions instantly meaningless.

Terrified, she pulled !Xabbu's small monkey-shape close against her chest, trying to slow the horrid jerking motions by simple pressure. She knew it was not the way to treat a seizure, but she could think of nothing better to do. When his convulsions grew so strong that he nearly wriggled from her grasp, she wrapped herself even more closely around him, as though mere stubbornness might save his life. At last his muscles slackened and his movements grew less frenetic. For long seconds she was too frightened to look at him directly, certain that his heart had stopped. Then his muzzle moved against her neck.

!Xabbu's eyes blinked and fluttered open. His gaze wandered for a moment over the mismatched sky and unfinished landscape, then stopped on her, eyes round and solemn. "Renie. It is good to see your face."

"What is going *on?*" demanded Emily 22813 from behind her. "Why won't anyone tell me? Is the monkey sick? Where are we? Who are you?"

Renie could not have replied at that moment even if there had been answers to give. She clutched !Xabbu tightly, tears of relief running down her cheeks and pearling in his fur.

"Oh, I thought . . ." she forced the words out between shudders, ". . . I was sure you were . . ." She found she did not want to say it. "Are you all right now?"

"I . . . am tired," he said. "Very tired."

She let him pull himself free. He crouched beside her, his small, doglike head hanging. He was still quivering, the muscles of his legs weak, his tail tucked between his legs.

"What happened?" she asked. "How did you do that—find the gate and open it?"

"I will tell," he said. "But I must rest for a moment."

"Of course." She stroked his back. "Can I do anything to help?" The relative calm seemed quite surreal. Just moments ago they had been inches from capture by Lion and his hybrid plant-creatures. Now they were . . . somewhere else. And it was a somewhere that made Lion's warped Oz seem the summit of normality.

"Do you people have anything to eat?" Emily asked, as though nothing else were happening. "I'm really hungry."

"I'm sorry, we have nothing." Renie wanted to be patient with her, but it was difficult. Emily had lost some of the most extreme childishness of her behavior, but still seemed to be living in a world of her own. "Later we can go and look, see what might be around."

!Xabbu stood and stretched, then sat on the ground beside Renie and yawned, briefly displaying his impressive canines. "I am feeling a little better," he said. "I am sorry if you were frightened." He gave her the closest thing to an embarrassed baboon smile she had yet seen, and she wondered what her grief had shown him—what things she did not yet herself entirely understand.

"I was frightened because . . . because I thought you were dying." Now it was spoken. She sighed. "But *everything* is so strange. How did you know about that golden light—that gateway thing? And what's she doing here?"

"Emily is not a Puppet," !Xabbu said. "I could not tell you how I know, but I do. After I had danced, I saw things differently."

"Are you saying she's like us? Someone trapped in the network?"

He shook his head. "I do not know. But she is not a . . . what is that word? A construct." He rose to stand on his hind legs. "I should probably explain all that I can." Renie could not help admiring the quickness of his recovery—a legacy of resilience from ancestors who had fought the desert for their survival every hour of every day, for thousands of generations.

"Shouldn't we get out of this place first?" she asked. "Can you open that thing again, that door? It feels so strange here. So . . . *wrong.*"

"I do not know whether I have the strength, or even the ability, to do that again," !Xabbu said. "Let me tell you what happened."

Renie settled herself into something resembling a comfortable position, but the texture and resistance of the ground, or what should have been ground, was disturbing in its variety. At least, she noted gratefully, they were not freezing or burning up. For all its other freakish extremes, the new simworld seemed as weatherless as a business office.

"I told you last night," !Xabbu began, "that you needed to see with the eyes of your heart. And that was true, Renie—you are very important to all of us, even if you do not know it."

She wanted to tell him about her own revelation but knew it was not the time. She also wanted answers to her own most immediate questions. "Go on, please."

"But when you asked me what *I* was doing to help, I realized that you were seeing things very, very truly. Since I had come here to this network, I had lost the vision my people gave to me.

"Renie, my friend, I have been trying to see things with the eyes of a city dweller. I have ignored that which was given to me by Grandfather Mantis, all the wisdom of my own people, and I have tried too hard to be like you, like Martine, like poor Mister Singh. But I am a child in your world, the world of machines. When I try to see that way, I can only have the visions a child can have." He nodded, gaining confidence.

"I told you a story once about the People Who Sit on Their Heels, the baboons—do you remember? How they killed one of the sons of Mantis, and then threw his eye back and forth as though it were a ball? And I told you that when I chose this body, it was because Grandfather Mantis spoke to me in a dream. But I did not understand how it all should fit together. I had lost my people's wisdom. So I danced, for that is what I do when my spirit is hungry.

"When I was in that place, the dancing-place, it came to me. The baboons were at war with Mantis, and they tossed the eye as though it were a child's toy because they did not understand how to look and see with their hearts. That eye was Mantis' own eye, through his son, and they rejected it. They were at war with that vision.

"This is what I learned, as I danced. It was given to me to wear this body, I believe, that I should have to discover and understand this truth. The baboon, he who talks and argues and always jostles with his neighbors for a share of things, does not see with the eye of Mantis—the eye of the spirit. I do not say that they are wicked, the People Who Sit on Their Heels. They have lessons of their own to teach, of friendship and family, and the strength that comes from it, of solving things using busy thoughts and clever fingers. But I had to learn my *own* lesson, Renie. As I danced, I came to understand that I must learn to see again with the eyes that were given to me, to see with the heart of my people—something I have not done since we have been in this place, in this . . . mirage.

"When the dance ended, Renie, it was as though I had walked into daylight after long weeks in deep evening. The things I could see! How can I explain it all? Often your people, the city-people, think that there is a right way and a wrong way to see. They hear old stories like the kind my people tell, old songs, and say, 'Oh, listen to them, they are like children, those Bushmen. They think there are faces in the sky, they think that the sun makes a sound.' But there *are* faces in the sky, if you have the eyes to see them. The sun has a song, if you only have the ears. We are simply different in how we know the world, Renie, your people and mine, and I have ignored the knowing I was taught for too long.

"So when I stopped dancing, when the head-clearing magic of that was upon me, I had a feeling that nothing could be hidden from me any more. You will call it the subconscious at work—that things I had noticed but not understood became plain to me. It does not matter. I know what I know. And the first thing I knew was that something had troubled me, but with all that had happened, in my own preoccupation, I had ignored it, forgotten it.

"It was the lighter, of course, but I did not realize that until I found it in your pocket. You asked, why should Azador carry such a thing, since the letter on it was neither of his names. And Azador himself said that things made for one world could not be brought to another— that is why you were surprised to see Emily had come here with us!"

"But that still doesn't prove anything," she pointed out. "He could have stolen it from someone in the Kansas simworld."

!Xabbu, whose guess had already been proved right, only shrugged.

"Wait a moment," she said. "No, it *couldn't* have come from Kansas, because it's a copy of a modern lighter—one of those stabilized-hydrogen Minisolars. And all the technology in the Kansas world was from the last century."

"I did not know those things," !Xabbu said. "But when I looked at it after I had danced, compared it to all the other things around us, the boat, our clothing, it felt more *real*. I can explain it no better than that, I am afraid. This is what the eyes of my heart saw. Perhaps if I say it was the difference between seeing a white squiggle of line on a rock, and seeing a painting of an antelope on a rock. The difference of . . . *content*, I think, is the word you would say . . . is very, very big. And when I held the lighter, I could see it was more even than that. Another way to say it is that it was like looking at one of my people's digging sticks. You or any other city-person would see a piece of wood, crude, sharpened at one end. To a Bushman, it would have all the meanings a gun or a sea-going ship would have for you, and would speak from its very being of all the ways it could be used, had been used, was meant to be used." He tipped his head toward her quizzically. "Am I making sense, Renie? I am tired, and these are hard thoughts to speak."

"I think so." She turned to see what had happened to Emily, who was being unusually quiet. The girl, apparently as self-absorbed as ever—or perhaps, like an animal, dimly cognizant she was out of her depth—had simply curled up on the not-ground and gone to sleep. "I'm trying to understand, !Xabbu. So, you could tell that the lighter was . . . was *something*."

"Yes. And when I handled it, touched it, I could feel that there were things waiting to happen. Certain bumps, certain faces, had a feeling of rightness. When I stroked it or squeezed it a certain way, I could tell that its maker had intended I do just that. And then one set of the things I did suddenly opened up a gateway. I could see it, shining in the distance."

"But *I* couldn't see anything. Not until we got there."

"I do not think you would have been able to. That tool, that thing that looks like a cigarette lighter, belongs to one of the Grail Brotherhood, I am sure. The person who holds it can see things others cannot—can act as gods act. I do not doubt that if we could make it work properly, we would find many wonderful things we could do."

Renie's heart quickened. This was good news—no, this was excellent news! They might be able to take their destiny back into their own grasp. She looked at the lump of shiny metal still clutched in !Xabbu's skinny fist, and for the first time in days, felt hope return.

"But I saw other things, too," he continued. "No, not 'saw'—that is a misleading word. Knew? Felt? I am not sure. But I could see that Lion's creatures, those sad and torn people, were nothing more than shadows, no more alive than the trees or stones or sky in that place. Lion, though, was alive as Emily is alive," !Xabbu flicked a glance at the sleeping girl, "a real person, or at least a force—not just a part of the simulation."

"And you can tell that now? What's real and what's not?"

He shook his head. "It was in those minutes only, when the feeling was strong in me. Sometimes, after we dance, it as though we stand in a high place and can see great distances, or with great sharpness. But not always, and even when it happens, it does not last." He turned toward the sleeping girl. "Emily looks no more or less real to me now than she did when we met her."

"But you could do it again!"

He made a little barking sound, a tired laugh. "It is not something you can turn on and turn off, Renie, like one of your machines. I had a great need, and I danced to search for answers. For a moment, I had many answers. I saw what was real and what was not, and I summoned a gateway. But even while it happened, I had no idea of where the gateway might lead, which is why we are in this strange place. And I might dance every night for a year and never have that happen again."

"I'm sorry," she said, and meant it. "I just . . . I was just hopeful."

"But there is reason to be hopeful. We have this thing that Azador carried. It opened a gateway. I cannot promise to understand its working as well as I did when the trance was still on me, but it is of your machine world—it has rules. Something we can do will make it work again."

"May I hold it?" She took it from him as carefully as if it were a soap bubble. Despite all the rough handling it had survived just since she had known of its existence—dropped on a cement cell floor and on the tugboat's deck, submerged in the river—it was suddenly a precious object; she did not want to risk anything going wrong.

It looked no different than it had before, a chunky, old-fashioned lighter, its raised "Y" monogram ostentatiously over-elaborate. Even knowing what she knew, there was nothing to suggest it was more than what it appeared. "How did you . . . what did you do to it?" she asked him, running her fingertip along the raised surface of the monogram. "To make it work."

"It is hard to explain." !Xabbu yawned again. "I was seeing with my truest eyes. But there are ways to move your fingers on it."

Renie examined the object in the way her own training had taught her, trying to see what its maker had intended, but it was not a device normally meant to be understood by anyone other than its user—no normal standards of interface design had been employed. It was a rich person's key, the secrets it unlocked meant for that person alone.

Or in certain circumstances, she reflected with sour amusement, *Aboriginal trance-dancers or gypsy thieves.*

For the briefest instant she thought of Azador, and even felt a twinge of sympathy for the man, although it didn't last long. If he had been using this pilfered object to find his way around, he was now part of the common herd again.

Trying to imagine how !Xabbu had seen the thing during his moment of clarity, Renie continued to turn the lighter in her hands, kneading it like a lump of dough, squeezing, stroking, twisting it in her fingers. Once she almost thought she felt it shudder ever so slightly, a tiny vibration like the beating of a moth's wing under velvet, but it ended almost immediately. No matter what else she did, it remained an obstinately unmagical object. She handed it back to !Xabbu, who took it gently, sniffed it, then weighed it in his palm.

"So where do you think we are?" she said. "And who or what the hell is Emily, if she isn't part of that simulation?" She had a sudden thought. "Azador must have known, the rapist bastard! But he kept pretending she was a Puppet."

"Perhaps," !Xabbu said. "But remember, my knowing was only because I had been given a moment of understanding. Perhaps this object can tell such things, and so he did know . . . but perhaps not. In any case, if he stole the lighter, Azador himself may not have understood all the ways of its working." He considered the heavy, shiny object. "As for what Emily is, I cannot say. She is a person, and must be treated as one. Perhaps she is a ghost—you said once there were ghosts on the net."

Renie shivered, despite the nonclimate. "I didn't. I said that some people *believed* there were ghosts on the net—the same people who probably used to believe in the other kind of ghosts, or that if you step on a crack, you'll break your mother's back—and all that kind of nonsense."

!Xabbu tipped his head sideways, which often meant he was considering some polite way to say he disagreed, but if he meant to dispute her, he changed his mind. "I do not know what she is, in any case. As to this place, I suspect it is something unfinished, do you not think?"

"Maybe." She looked around, frowning. "But it seems strange that they wouldn't just finish it before they turned it on, if you know what I mean. There might be bugs in the gear, but most of it would work, and the engineers would fix whatever didn't. But Atasco said they *grew* these places, so . . ." She shrugged. "Whatever, it doesn't matter. But I don't like it here. All the funny reflections and colors make me feel sick to my stomach. Hurts my eyes, too. Is there any chance we could go somewhere else?"

"Do you mean find another gateway?" !Xabbu sniffed the lighter again. "I do not know, Renie. I really am tired, and I do not have the feeling that I had earlier—the true-seeing."

"But like you said, it's just a machine. I don't want you to exhaust yourself, !Xabbu, but give it a try, anyway. See if you can remember what you did."

"What if we open a gateway to somewhere much less pleasant than this?"

"Well, then we turn around and come back to Patchwork Land. Those gates must work both directions, don't they?"

"I am not sure." Nevertheless, he handled the lighter with a bit more intention now, sliding it between his palms like a bar of wet soap. After a moment, he stopped. "I feel that I might be able to do it again, Renie, but I am truly very tired. I do not think this is the best time."

She had a sudden vision of him convulsing, not half an hour before, and cursed her own heedlessness. "I'm sorry, !Xabbu. Of course it can wait. You need rest. Come here—put your head in my lap."

She settled herself back against an irregularity that had the blurred-edges look of a bit of VR sketchwork—more a statement of intent than an actual object, in this case something that planned someday to be a tussock of grass on this potential hillside. It was not tremendously comfortable, but she'd been in worse places lately. !Xabbu crept over and stretched his torso lengthways along her leg with his tail tickling under her chin. He folded his arms across her knee, then rested his head on them, a curious mingling of animal and human postures. He was asleep within seconds.

Renie herself lasted several minutes longer.

She did not know how long she had slept, since there was no way to mark time in this completely timeless place, but she felt as though she had gone fairly deep. As her eyes opened, she had a certain confusion about what she was looking at, which quickly became a feeling that something important had been turned inside out.

Her first coherent recognition was that the no-color sky now had a color. It was not much of a color, rather a slight curdling from its previous nameless shade toward something more like faint gray, but it was a change. Other colors had changed, too, as though some global filter had shifted one notch to the side, rendering most things in the unfinished simworld a shade darker and more solid. But all of the changes were not toward solidity: a few other things seemed to have slipped back toward unbeing, phantom versions replacing objects that had previously been fairly solid features of the landscape, other objects simply gone, swallowed back into nothingness. Perhaps the whole environment was in slow transition, she thought—was on its way to becoming something else.

But transition from what to what, exactly? And why should it seem slow? What was the benchmark? The massive and instantaneous alteration of the entire landscape when they had lost Azador and the boat, the mind-warping upheaval, seemed to be the answer to her second question. Were the fast changes there and the slow changes here simply different versions of the same process? Was the network breaking down, as she had suspected? Or could it be building itself into something else instead?

Bedeviled by unanswerable questions, she had just realized that !Xabbu's head was no longer resting on her knee when she heard him speak.

"Do you know, Renie, I woke up with a thought." He was crouching a few paces away, examining Azador's lighter once more.

"Did you get some good sleep?"

"Yes, I did, thank you. But I want to tell you my thought. I spoke of this thing as if it were a tool, like a digging stick. But what if it is more than that?"

"I'm not following you." Renie saw that Emily had disappeared from the spot where she had been sleeping, but since !Xabbu did not seem concerned, she let it go. "More than. . . ."

"What if this is more than a tool. What if it is a Name? One of the things my people believe—most so-called primitive people believe, in fact—is that there is a great power in names. To know something's true name is to have power over it. Well, what if this does belong to one of the Brotherhood?"

"Then we can use it to get around, go from place to place," she said, considering. "Maybe actually plan where we want to go instead of just winding up there."

"Ah, but if this is something that belongs to one of the Grail people, perhaps it will do for us what it does for that person—perhaps it will be a Name."

"Like an access key, you mean? Get us into places we couldn't get to without it? Maybe get us off the network entirely?"

"Or into the files and information of the Grail Brotherhood." He bared his teeth. "If so, there is much mischief we could do them."

"Oh, !Xabbu!" She clapped her hands together in pleasure. "That would be better than I've hoped for in a long time! Maybe we could finally get some information about Stephen and all the others. . . ."

Her moment of euphoria was interrupted by the arrival of Emily, who came running down the hillside, all legs and flailing arms, as though pursued by demons. "Help me!" she shouted. Renie jumped to her feet.

Emily skidded to a halt, her face contorted into a mask of pain and fury. "I *told* you, I'm hungry and I need something to eat! You said you'd look, but you didn't, and I'm starving! There's nothing around here anywhere!"

Renie was startled by how upset the girl was. How could they know whether Emily really needed to eat or not? They didn't even know what she was, let alone what kind of way she might interact with the network. Maybe she was truly hurting. "We'll help you look . . ." she began, but was interrupted by a scream of frustration.

"I already *looked*, I told you, and there's *nothing anywhere!* And it's not just for me, you think I'm selfish and stupid, but you don't even know me! It's for my *baby!* I have a baby in me!"

"Again?" was all Renie could think of to say, and then added, "I mean, still?"

"You don't know anything about me," Emily wailed, then sank to the ground, weeping bitterly.

"We may really need to find something for her," Renie said to !Xabbu, and sighed. "Maybe there's some, I don't know, fruit-in-progress or something we could pick around here." She stared at the girl. "She's still pregnant. What is this all about?"

!Xabbu was working the lighter in his deft fingers, tracing his way around it as though reading a long poem in Braille. "Perhaps we do need to find another place," he said. "A place more like we are used to, a place with food for Emily, and shelter and familiar things."

Yes, familiar things like obstetricians, Renie was about to say, but she was struck by a new and worrying thought. "When is your baby coming?"

Emily's sobbing had abated somewhat. "Don't . . . don't know."

"When did you last have your period—your time of the month?"

The girl frowned. "I'm six weeks late. That's how I know." She dropped her voice to a whisper. "And I feel . . . funny."

Renie sighed her relief. Sometimes it was hard to tell with the skinny ones, but it sounded like even accounting for distorted network-time, Emily was not due for a while. "We'll do what we can to help," she said, her tone a little softer now. "We'll find you some food . . ." She broke off. !Xabbu had become very quiet, his hands moving very slowly now. He was no longer looking at the lump of metal in his hands, but rather off into the indeterminate distance; he almost seemed to be listening for something.

"Renie," he said calmly, "I think I have found an opening, and it is very close to where we are. Perhaps it is the one through which we came. . . ."

"That's good—that's very good!" Emily's problems aside, if the Bushman could make the lighter work under normal circumstances, then many things would be resolved for the better.

". . . But there is something strange happening. I can feel someone out there."

"What do you mean?" A sudden interior chill made her voice sharp. "What are you talking about, someone? *Who?*"

!Xabbu closed his eyes and was silent for long moments, holding the lighter so carefully in his small dark fingers he might have been a gemcutter preparing to place a master-stroke. "This will sound very mad," he said at last. "It feels like someone is standing on the other side of a pan, a desert pan. When the breeze is blowing true, I can hear the voice very close, although I cannot see the person at all." He made an oddly human face, wrinkling his brow and frowning, and for the first time in hours she was struck by the incongruity of her best friend being a baboon. "Renie, I think it is Martine."

"*What?* You're joking!"

"I can hear her, or feel her. There are no words. But she is just on the other side of something, and she is looking for a way out." His head snapped back, as though he had been startled by a blast of noise. "She is very close!"

Renie crawled toward him, but stopped a few inches away. She was unwilling to touch him, afraid that she would somehow disrupt this incomprehensible circuitry. "Is she with the others? Can you find them? Can they find us?"

"I do not know. I will try to open the gateway, if I can remember what I did before." His frown became a scowl of pained concentration. "It is so hard this time—I am doing something wrong."

But even as he spoke those worried words, an invisible hand abruptly peeled a piece out of the air just a few meters away, letting golden light leak through. Within a second the rip had lengthened into a glimmering horizontal streak about the span of a human's extended arms. Twin lines of fire began to crawl toward the ground. A moment later a membrane of shimmering golden radiance connected them, a light that could be called nothing less than brilliant, but which also seemed strangely confined by its own outline.

Emily stared, gape-jawed. Renie, too, was helplessly fascinated. It was only the second time she had seen this happen, and it was just as impressive an effect as it had been in Forest. Only !Xabbu was not captured by the unearthly look of the thing: his eyes were tight shut and his lips moved in some silent invocation.

The brilliance became a little less. The curtain of flame darkened a fraction toward amber, and Renie was struck by the dreadful certainty that the experiment had failed, that if Martine had actually been somewhere on the other end, they had missed the connection.

A rush of noise erupted from the glow, a roar so sudden and immense that Renie could not hear her own shout of astonishment. Several shapes fell out of the gateway in a tumbling mass and knocked her and !Xabbu to the ground. The noise dropped away, and as it did, Renie saw the golden rectangle flare, then die. She could see little else, because something very heavy and spiky and sharp was lying on top of her, pressing her face into the unfinished ground.

"Martine?" she shouted as she struggled to squirm out from beneath the painful mass. "Is that you?"

T4b, the Goggleboy robot in his attack-armor, rolled away with a bellow of surprise. He landed on his backside and sat for a moment, staring at her, as though she were something quite impossible to believe.

One of the other shapes detached itself from the tumble of bodies. "Renie! My God, it is you!" The sim was still a nondescript Temilúni woman, but the accented voice was unmistakable.

"Martine!" She scrambled to her feet, ignoring the bruises she had gained cushioning T4b's landing, and caught the other woman in such a powerful embrace that she lifted Martine Desroubin's feet from the ground. "Oh, Jesus Mercy, how did this all happen? We thought we'd lost all of you forever! Is Orlando with you?"

Florimel's voice cut across everything like a buzzsaw. "William came through with us, Martine." Renie took this to be good news. "He has hit his head on something, though. He is unconscious."

"Thank God," Martine murmured, and then astonished Renie by asking, "Do we have something we can use to tie him?"

"Tie him?" said Renie. "You mean, tie him *up?* Are you talking about the same William. . . ?"

"Yes. He is . . . I do not know what he is," Martine said. "But he is not what we believed. He tried to kill Quan Li."

"I don't understand." Renie shook her head, helpless before this onslaught of strange new information. "Who all is here? What has happened?" This new world, preternaturally still only moments before, now seemed a hive of activity. T4b had regained his feet and was wiping his handspikes clean of not-ground—several of them were darkly streaked. He was also examining Emily 22813 with interest, although Emily looked at the armored man in turn as though he might be some kind of huge and particularly unpleasant insect.

Quan Li and Florimel (it took a moment to recognize which was which, since Renie had not seen them in a while, and both still wore similar Temilún bodies) were crouched over Sweet William, whose long limp figure, dressed in the familiar black, lay near the spot the gateway had opened. A rill of blood seeped from under his hood and down across his pale face. Florimel was tearing strips off her ragged peasant blouse to bind him; Quan Li was doing the same, somewhat angrily, as though she resented the other woman's help and would have preferred to tie the prisoner herself. Renie wondered how badly William had hurt her, to make retiring Quan Li so fixed and militant in her purpose.

There was no sign at all of Orlando or his friend Fredericks.

!Xabbu climbed to his feet, still holding the lighter. He watched all this activity with a kind of bemused detachment, as though in a shallower version of the trance he had summoned earlier.

"Did you find us, or did we find you?" Martine asked. She seemed quite ragged, able to keep on her feet only with Renie's support. "It was all so confusing. There is so much to tell!"

"We found something," Renie explained, "a key or a remote trigger, something like that. An access device of some kind, anyway—it looks like a lighter, see? !Xabbu used it to open a gate. Two gates, now! We think it belonged to one of the Grail people, but this other man stole it . . ." She realized she was babbling with relief and happiness. "No, forget it, I'll explain all that later. But I don't understand this bit about William. He attacked Quan Li? Why? Is he mad?"

"I fear he is a spy for the Grail Brotherhood," Martine replied. "When we were in the Place of the Lost—but I forget, you do not know where we have been, what we have done." She shook her head and laughed a cracked little laugh. "Just as we do not know what has happened to you! Oh, Renie, how odd it has all been!" She wagged her head in exhaustion. "And this place! What is it? It feels very bizarre to me."

Emily's sudden shriek startled both Renie and Martine so badly that they jumped. "Is he dead?" the girl squealed. "There's so much *blood!*"

Renie turned to look. While attempting to put some space between herself and T4b, Emily had almost tripped over Sweet William, but the girl was not the only one caught by surprise. Kneeling beside him, Florimel held up her hands and stared wonderingly at the scarlet that slicked them both to the wrists. Quan Li's hands were also streaked in blood; she shrank back from William with her eyes wide.

"He does have a head wound," Florimel said, but she sounded uncertain. "They bleed very badly . . ."

Renie reached them in a few seconds, and with Florimel's help turned the long figure over. As William flopped onto his back, Renie let out a gasp of surprise. His black outfit was in ribbons across his belly, and all the creases were awash in blood. A puddle was forming beneath him on the oddly-colored ground, changing color where it had lain for more than a few moments, swirling with pale blues and greens and sickly grays in those places, but still bright red in the wounds and on his garments.

"Jesus Mercy." Renie felt sick just seeing it. "How did this happen? It looks like an animal got him."

!Xabbu bent close. "He is still alive. We must make more bandages and wrap him quickly." He squatted, then took strips of cloth from Florimel and Quan Li that had been meant for use as restraints and began to pull them tight across the ugly wounds. T4b stood over them, absurdly out of place beside the monkey and the two peasant sims, like some offshore-factory children's toy dropped into a classical painting. Nothing on his costume would make suitable field dressings, that much was obvious.

Renie felt a tug on her arm, and allowed Martine to draw her to one side. Instead of asking for reassurance, Martine brought her mouth close to Renie's ear. Her whisper was so quiet that at first Renie was not sure she was hearing correctly, because the blind woman's words were shocking.

"One of them did it," Martine said. "I'm sure that one of them must have tried to kill him. Something else could have attacked him in the cavern—the place where we were—but I felt some act of violence occur just as we entered the gateway, and we were all bunched in a group by then. I cannot tell who is guilty, though—which one of our number is only pretending to feel shock and sadness. Something in this new simulation, some distortion, is blurring my senses."

Martine was talking as though she could read minds, and Renie had no idea what that was about. In fact, she had very little idea what *any* of this was about. "I don't understand." She took a breath, then forced herself to speak quietly. "William is a spy, but one of us tried to kill him?"

"One of the people who came through with me," Martine replied. "I believe that to be true—whatever the cause, it must have happened there, just before we went through the gateway. I am frightened, Renie."

"What can we do?" She stole a quick look. Everyone except Emily seemed actively concerned for William's life, whatever he had done. And how could they be certain that Martine was right—that the blind woman's other senses were reliable? Just days ago she had been so overwhelmed by the network that she had been almost catatonic.

Martine abruptly turned to the others and said in a loud, shaky voice, "I know that one of you has done this to him."

Everything stopped. Florimel and Quan Li's hands halted above Sweet William, still holding bandages torn from one of their shrinking garments, so that they seemed arrested in some staged tableau of mummification. T4b also seemed surprised, but his expression was hidden by his buglike mask.

Emily had been backing away from the bloody scene, hands clutched protectively over her stomach, but the girl from New Emerald City froze like a rabbit at Martine's shout. "I didn't do anything!" she howled, then bent double as though to get between the accuser and her unborn child.

"Not you, Emily," Renie assured her. "But, Martine, we can't just . . ."

"No." Martine shook her head. "What we cannot do is live with doubt. If I am wrong, I am wrong, but I do not believe it. And in a moment I will have an answer." The small woman marched toward the startled group like a sheepdog trying to intimidate a pack of its feral cousins by sheer force of personality. "You know that I have ways of seeing things that you others do not—those who traveled with me know that, anyway."

"What, because something attacked William, and you think it is one of us, you are to be the judge and jury?" Florimel shook her head in disgust, but there was a strange hint of fear and anger in her eyes as well. "That is madness!"

"It will not take much judging," Martine snapped back, showing an aggressive force Renie had never seen from her. "It must be either you or Quan Li—you are the only two who have blood on you, and whoever did this would not come away clean."

Florimel only scowled her contempt, and Quan Li made a weak protest, but Renie had a sudden flash of memory. "Martine, I saw *him* . . ." she pointed at T4b, ". . . cleaning those spikes of his right after you all came through."

"Saying what?" T4b bellowed. "That's far crash—calling me duppy? Sixes, gonna be sixes on everyone!" He raised his armored fists and flared his body-spikes like the spines of a blowfish, making himself a truly frightening package. Renie was forced to consider the fact that without Orlando and his barbarian sim, they would have trouble defending themselves against the Goggleboy if it did come to a fight.

Martine was unswerving. "Then T4b is a suspect, too. If the rest of you do not trust me, let Renie judge."

"Zero be judgin' me," T4b warned. "Far-scanning, you think that. You not, nobody not . . . !"

"Stop!" Renie bellowed as loud as she could, desperate to keep things from running out of control. *"Stop it, all of you!"*

In the near-silence that followed, !Xabbu's quiet voice cut through everything, startling as a gunshot. "He is trying to speak," the baboon said.

Everyone turned to look; all saw Sweet William's black-painted eyes flutter open. Then, in that instant of expectant stillness, a figure abruptly leaped across William's body and attacked !Xabbu.

The attacker was one of the Temilúni sims, but at first Renie could not tell which—was not even sure for a confusing second or two that it *was* an attack, since assaulting the baboon made no sense. The whole thing seemed to unfold in slow time, without obvious logic, like some kind of drug experience. Only as the dark-haired woman raised herself to her knees, unpeeled !Xabbu from her arm, then flung him aside with surprising strength, could Renie see that the aggressor was Quan Li.

Something shiny had bounced away from the scene of their struggle and come to rest only a step away from Renie. It was Azador's pilfered lighter. As she belatedly realized that Quan Li had only attacked the baboon so she could snatch the device, Renie bent and grabbed it, then squeezed it tight in her fist.

Quan Li climbed to her feet, rubbing her bloodied arm. "Damn," she snarled, "that little bastard can bite!" She saw Renie's bulging hand and took a surprisingly quick step toward her, but when T4b and Florimel moved up to take defensive positions on either side of Renie, Quan Li stopped. Her first flash of rage abruptly mutated into a disconcerting, lazy smile that stretched the features far more than seemed natural. "Why don't you just give me that and I'll be on my way, no harm to anyone."

The Hong Kong grandmother's voice and posture had both changed dramatically, but the metamorphosis of her familiar face was even more terrifying. Some new soul had sparked to life inside her—or had finally been set free.

!Xabbu reappeared, limping back to stand near Renie's feet. Reassured that he did not seem seriously hurt, she had just opened her mouth to demand answers when Quan Li sprang with terrifying speed to one side, grabbed Emily, then jerked the girl close to her body in a single, continous movement as lithe and deadly as a snake strike. The grin widened. "If any of you takes another step toward me, I'll snap her neck. That's a promise. Now, let's talk about that lighter, shall we?"

"Emily's a Puppet," Renie said desperately. "She's not even real."

Quan Li raised one eyebrow. "So you wouldn't care if I pulled her apart right here in front of you, is that right? Bones and strings everywhere?"

"Tryin' it, and you six-meat," growled T4b.

"Well, dang it, podner." The harsh new timbre made Quan Li's imitation cowboy-drawl sound even more bizarre. "Guess we got us a Mexican stand-off, then."

Despite this person's matter-of-fact tone, the entire situation felt fatally unstable to Renie. She struggled to keep the panic out of her voice. "If we give you the lighter, then you promise you'll let her go?"

"Happy to. Plenty more where she comes from."

"Answer some questions first. That will be part of the bargain." *If we can keep whatever or whoever this is talking long enough,* Renie thought, *perhaps one of the others will think of something.* Her own mind was churning, but nothing useful was coming. She was furious with herself for being tricked, furious with Emily for being captured. She did not want to risk the girl's life any more than necessary, but they could not just let the lighter go: the idea of giving up that precious device, when they had only just discovered it, was devastating—unthinkable.

"Questions. . . ?"

"Who are you? You can't be Quan Li."

"You are a clever girl, aren't you?" said the person in the peasant sim. "So clever you think you can convince me that you wouldn't care if I skinned this child alive." Emily yelped and struggled a little, but was silenced with a squeeze. "But the truth is, you don't know much about anything—like what's happened to your brother, just for instance. Well, I do, and it's pretty bloody funny, in a sickening kind of way."

"Do not listen!" Martine put a hand on Renie's shoulder. "She is lying—she is just trying to hurt you, to make you angry!"

Staring at the contorted, hateful face that had lurked inside a shape they trusted, Renie felt sick. *It's the Wolf,* she thought. *All that time, it was the Wolf dressed up like sweet old Grandmother. . . .*

"Lying, am I?" The Quan Li thing abruptly turned and hissed a warning at T4b, who had moved a step closer, and pulled the arm around Emily's neck tighter. For a moment the girl's feet lifted from the ground, kicking. "Why would I bother? Why on earth would I care what a gang of hopeless losers like you lot thinks or doesn't think?" The lupine smile crept back. "But since you're asking for the latest news and sports, you might be interested to know that your original Chinese grandmother is very definitely dead. Atasco guested her in— that's how I got onto her line. Granny Quan pretended to be a hacker, but I'm sure some Hong Kong contact got her onto the network. And wound up getting her killed, for that matter." The laugh was febrile, excited. The monster was *enjoying* this.

"Are you working for the Grail Brotherhood?" Renie asked. "Is that why you have been spying on us?"

"Spy for the Brotherhood?" the creature said slowly. "Do you really think this is about you? You don't know *anything.*" The expression changed again, slackening into a cold emptiness which was somehow more terrifying than the demonic grin. Emily appeared to have fainted in the stranger's arms. "Enough talk. I'm calling your bluff, bitch. Either give me the lighter or I start taking pieces off her."

Renie could not doubt it—the eyes that glared back at her out of Quan Li's face were as untroubled by human scruples as those of some elemental spirit—like the Hyena of !Xabbu's stories. She badly wanted someone else to make the decision, to take some kind of control, but none of her companions moved or spoke. It was down to her, and she could keep one or the other—little whining Emily, only debatably human, or the key to a universe, and perhaps to her brother's life.

She handed the lighter to !Xabbu. "Open a gateway."

"What are you up to?" the stranger snarled.

"I'm not just going to hand it to you," Renie said scornfully. "God knows what you could do to us with it. When !Xabbu opens the gateway, you release Emily and we hand over the lighter. Then you step through and leave us alone, like you said."

Florimel was astonished. "You are just going to *give* it to this monster?"

"I wish we had a choice." Renie turned back to the Quan Li thing. "Well?"

It hesitated for a second, then nodded. "Right. But no tricks. Things will get very ugly very fast if you try anything."

!Xabbu had closed his eyes in concentration, and was paddling his fingers atop the lighter's shiny surface. For a moment Renie was afraid he would not be able to make it work again, but then a glimmering curtain of fire kindled in the air behind the stranger. The Quan Li thing maneuvered back toward it carefully, keeping Emily outward as a shield, until the golden rectangle was only a step away.

"Toss me the lighter," it said.

"Let go of the girl"

"It's not your call any more." The flat, emotionless tone was back. "You could even kill me and I'd just drop offline, which is more than you can do—I'm not stuck here the way you are. But I'd rather have the lighter, so throw it to me."

Renie took a deep breath, then nodded to !Xabbu, who pitched it to him. The stranger caught the lighter and examined it quickly, then smiled as it took another step back to the very edge of the golden light, dragging Emily along. The mouth that had been Quan Li's puckered; the spy leaned and placed a kiss on the unconscious girl's cheek. "Come on, sweetness," it said to her. "Let's go find ourselves somewhere to play."

"No!" Renie screamed.

Something leaped onto the stranger's leg and clung. The spy shouted in anger and pain, then Renie and Florimel and T4b were all wading in together, slapping and gouging and trying to drag Emily and her abductor back from the shimmering gateway. Quan Li's Puppet was slippery and shockingly strong, and even with superior numbers they might not have been able to save the girl, but the Quan Li thing could not hold her and pry !Xabbu's teeth out of its thigh as well. With a screamed curse it let her go, then thrashed its way free from the confusion of clutch and tumble.

It paused, the gateway so bright that the stranger was little more than a silhouette as it pointed a trembling finger at Renie and the others, but when it spoke, the tone was eerily calm. "Now it *is* bloody personal. I'll see you lot again, every one one of you."

"Too right you will," Renie muttered.

It brandished Azador's lighter as if to mock their loss, then stepped backward into the light. A second later the gateway went out like a snuffed candle.

For the space of several heartbeats, the silence and stillness seemed to have choked everyone. Renie suddenly thought of something: "Where's !Xabbu? He was holding onto that . . . thing!"

A small hand took hers. The baboon stood by her knee, looking up, his muzzle scratched and bloody. "I am here, my friend. When Emily came free, I let go."

"Oh, thank God." Renie's legs had been threatening to give way, and now they did. She sat down with a bump beside !Xabbu. "Twice in one day."

Martine and Florimel were kneeling beside the pregnant girl, who appeared to be regaining consciousness. T4b stood over them, his arms outstretched, his gloved fingers clenching and unclenching, helpless once more after his brief moment of heroism. No one remembered William until he coughed and spat out blood.

"Is . . . there . . . any water?" His voice was as scratchy as wind in leaves.

Renie crawled across the ground to his side, quickly joined by the others. Her momentary hope evaporated. William's eyes were wandering, unfixed, and his breath made a terrible bubbling sound.

"We have found no water in this place, William," !Xabbu said. "I am sorry." He hesitated for a moment. "Have this water from me," he said, then bent close and let a stream of saliva run from his mouth to William's.

The pale, bloodied jaw clamped, then the gorge rose and fell as the injured man swallowed. "Thank you," he sighed.

"You should save your strength," Florimel told him sternly.

"I'm dying, Flossie, so belt up." He took another liquid breath. "You'll be rid of me . . . soon, so . . . the least you can do is hear me out." For a moment William opened his eyes wide; they lit on Renie, then he winced and let the lids fall shut again. "I thought I heard your voice. So . . . so you're back, are you?"

She took his hand. "I'm back."

His eyes opened again at a new thought. "Quan Li! Watch out for Quan Li!"

"She's gone, William," Martine told him.

"She tried to kill me, the miserable . . . old bat. Didn't want me . . . comparing notes with anyone . . . about that night in Aerodromia. I told her I heard . . . someone come back." He fought for breath. "She said she did, too, but she said it was . . . Martine."

The blind woman leaned close to him. "Is that why you came to me for that strange conversation? Why you told me all those things?"

"I . . . wanted to see how you responded. I told you the truth about me, though. I thought you would . . . know if I lied." He laughed a little, a horrible sound. "Granny played me like a . . . frigging violin, didn't she?" His face contorted, then relaxed. "God, this hurts. It's slow, though. Feels . . . like I've been dying . . . for days."

Renie didn't know anything about the night he was referring to, and it hurt her to see him struggle for speech. Martine could explain it all later. "It doesn't matter, William. Quan Li's gone."

He appeared not to have heard her. "Guess this answers . . . any questions about . . . dying online, eh, Flossie? No one . . . could fake *this* feeling. You . . . drop off the perch here, it's for . . . for real."

Florimel's face was still set in its usual hard lines, but she was clutching William's other hand in hers. "We are all with you," she said.

"Martine, I didn't tell you . . . the whole truth," the dying man murmured. His eyes were again open, but now he seemed to be the blind one, unable to find the Frenchwoman. "I told you that . . . friends of mine, online friends . . . that some were in comas. But, you see . . . there was one in particular. I was . . . I was in love with her. I didn't know that she was so young. . . ! I never met her in real . . . real life." William's face contorted with pain. "I never touched her! Never! But I told her . . . how I felt." He moaned, and there was a terrible harmonic from his punctured lungs. "When she . . . got sick, I thought it . . . was my fault. I came here . . . because I wanted to find . . . find her and . . . tell her I was . . . sorry. Because I thought she was . . . a grown woman, truly I . . . did. I would never . . . ." He gasped and then fell silent but for labored breathing.

"It is all right, William," the blind woman said.

He shook his head weakly. He opened his mouth, but it was a while until the words came. "No. I was . . . a fool. Old fool. But I tried . . . to be . . . a good man. . . ."

He went on breathing raggedly for a time, hitching and gasping, but no more words came. At last he shuddered and went still.

Renie looked at his stiffly unoccupied sim, then pulled a corner of his black cape over his face and sat up. She blinked away tears and wiped her cheeks with her hands. Long moments passed in silence before she said: "We have to bury him. After all, we may be here a while."

"Have you no decency?" Florimel demanded angrily. She still held William's hand. "He is only just dead!"

"But he *is* dead, and the rest of us are alive." Renie stood. *Have to be cruel to be kind,* she thought. They had lost William and they had lost the access device. It was important to have something to do—not just important for her, but for everyone. Even a funeral was better than nothing. "And the thing that killed him might come back any time. We have a lot of other things to talk about, too." She pointed to a spot where the strange landscape had moved a little closer to normality, its gray, protoplasmic color at least formed into shapes that resembled rocks and earth and grass. "If we pick one of the solid spots, like that, we won't have to keep looking at his empty sim for however long we're here. You don't really want to do that, do you?"

"Renie, we are all very tired and upset . . ." Martine began.

"I know." She turned in a slow circle, surveying, taking stock of things. "Which is why there are some things we have to do now, so we don't wind up in this situation again." She heard herself sounding imperious and softened her voice. "By the way, Martine, I was impressed with the way you went after everyone. You can be a bit of a bulldog when you want to."

The Frenchwoman strugged awkwardly and turned away.

!Xabbu came to stand beside her. "Tell me what I can do to help."

Emily 22813, awake again, but deserted by her rescuers, sat up. "That woman tried to kill me!"

"We know," Renie said. "!Xabbu, if there is any way to make a fire in this place, I think it would be a very, very good time to have one."

"I will see what I can do." He loped away up the patchwork hillside.

"She tried to kill me!" the girl howled. "Me and my baby!"

"Emily," said Renie, "we all know what just happened, and we're sorry about it. Now, we've got a lot of problems to solve, so just for once, would you please *shut up!*"

Emily's mouth snapped closed.

!Xabbu found some of what Renie could only think of as non-wood—wire-framed deadfall, like tree branches made of stiffened fishnet. He stacked them in a careful pile, and managed by dint of hard work to induce frictional sparks to ignite this fictional kindling, resulting in a remarkably healthy non-campfire. The flames shifted color and texture in some very disconcerting ways, and sometimes became holes which seemed to show depths not present in the environment, but whatever it looked like, it *was* a campfire: it persuaded the environment to supply them with a node of warmth and a focus for their attention, which was what Renie had wanted.

It's like what !Xabbu said about finding your story, she thought as she looked around at the dazed, fretful faces. *If you can't have a real fire, you have to agree on a fire.* She fought off another great wave of exhaustion. There was work to do that was more important than sleep. In any case, they would need sentries now, which meant she would have to pull first shift, even though she was so tired she felt she might collapse like a wet sack any moment. *If you want to be the hero of the story,* she told herself—*and apparently someone has to be*—*then you have to do the work.*

T4b, glinting with the light of the strange flames; Emily, small face full of self-absorption, far more mysterious than she appeared; !Xabbu, his brown eyes warm in his monkey face as he watched her; stubborn Florimel, her own sim features set like a mask, but her shoulders slumped in weariness; and Martine, face lifted, listening to something no one else could hear—Renie looked at each in turn, considering.

"Right," she said at last. "There's a lot to talk about, and a lot of frightening things have happened. We've lost at least one of our company, and Sellars hasn't reached us—may *never* reach us, for all we can tell. But we're here, we're alive, and we know more than we did. Am I right?" The nods and murmurs were not stirring votes of support, but they were a better response than she would have received an hour earlier. "We managed to find each other across the network, and not all of that was because of the Grail people's access device—!Xabbu and Martine both had a lot to do with it, yes? Isn't that true?"

"Are you trying to make yourself the leader, Renie?" Florimel asked. There was a touch of her normal belligerence in the question, but only a touch.

"I'm trying to tell you what I think. Everyone else is welcome to talk, too. But am I going to stand by, listening to people bicker while we fall apart? No. No, I'm not."

Florimel smiled a little, but said no more. The others nodded and murmured, sad but not hopeless. Everything seemed alloyed in this place, in this gray hour; even the smoke rising from the alien fire was a shimmering combination of solid and unsolid.

"There are things we can do," Renie went on. "Listen to me! Good things, starting here, starting now. We can go forward. But first we truly have to talk." She looked at them all once more, feeling for the word, the tone, that would bring them with her. She had a direction now she could sense—perhaps what !Xabbu had meant by "seeing with the eyes of the heart"—but the endpoint was as faint and theoretical as a distant star, and without help she would lose it again. "And we can't have any more secrets from one another," she urged.

"Do you understand? More than ever, our lives are in each other's hands. *No more secrets.*"

Fire could be made to burn, in that unfinished land, but night could not be made to come. They spoke and argued for long hours, even laughed and wept a little, then lay down to sleep with the light still unchanged.

As she sat through her sentry shift, Renie watched the oddly neutral sky and thought about her brother Stephen.

I'm coming, my little man, she promised him. Her silent declaration was not just for Stephen, but for herself, too, and as a warning for all those things and people which still stood in her way. *I'm coming to find you.*

From now on, she swore, she would keep her eyes wide open.

Afterword

HE found himself on a beach, face down in pale sand. After the long, long night of Venice, it was strange to feel the sun shining on his skin again, especially this bright sun that bleached the sand pale as snow and turned the blue ocean into a shining enamel plate.

Paul stood, muscles aching, and looked up and down the deserted beach. Even the sky was empty except for a few ragged tufts of clouds, and the monogram silhouettes of seabirds wheeling slowly from the cliffs to the sea and back again.

A vast, low house stood high atop the headlands, a thing of stone and wood, surrounded by a gated wall. Shepherds, tiny smears through the heat haze, were driving their flocks out of its gates and down the hill paths and a wagon piled high with earthenware jars was being wheeled in past them into the courtyard. Paul looked along the beach again, then out at the sun-painted ocean, then turned and began to walk toward the house on the cliffs.

Something even whiter than the sand caught his eye. He squatted to examine it and found the half-buried skeleton of a bird, translucent bones disarranged by wind or scavengers. Paul felt a dim empathy. That was how he felt inside—bleached, scoured, dry. There would be worse things to do than lie beneath the sun and let the sand bury him, the tides wash him.

If he had owned a coin, he would have tossed it to decide his fate, caring so little whether he went on or lay down that he was willing to let the gods choose for him. But the rags that clothed him held nothing but salt and sand fleas.

Not drifting any more, he told himself, making a bleak joke. He continued up the beach, toward the bottommost of the hill paths.

None of the sandaled, bearded men at the gates tried to stop him entering, although several made rude comments about his filthiness and age. Incapable of caring what anyone thought, especially shadows like these, puppets unaware of the strings that made them dance, he trudged past. Goats and a few pigs nuzzled his tattered robes, searching for food, but none of the human inhabitants paid him even that much attention until he stopped in the shadow that lay along the threshold of the great house to look back at the wide, flat blue ocean.

A woman in a hooded garment, her hands cracked like leather and twisted by age and hard work, offered him a bowl of wine. He thanked her and raised it to his lips, still watching the endless flight of seagulls out over the water as they circled, dipped, then rose to circle once more.

The old woman seemed very taken by his face. Paul watched with a certain sense of detached curiosity as tears came to her eyes, and then the gnarled hand which a moment ago had been reaching for the dipper took hold of his own hand instead.

"My lord," she whispered, voice as rough as her skin, "my lord, you have come back!"

Paul nodded wearily. If that was the game, then so be it, but he could not become excited at the acting out of yet another scenario. He had done what he had been told. Nandi had said that the Wanderer and the Weaver would be found in Ithaca, and so he was here.

"Come," she said, "oh, come!" She smiled broadly, excitement making her almost girlish. "Follow me, but do not speak a word. The house—your house, my lord—is full of evil men. I will take you to your son."

He frowned. He knew nothing about any son. "I was told to look for the Wanderer's house. I was told that I must release the Weaver."

The serving woman's eyes grew wide. "Has some god put a spell upon you? You are the wanderer, my lord, and this is your house." She looked around worriedly, then turned her teary gaze back to him. "I will take you to her—but please, my lord, on your life, you must go quietly, and speak to no man!"

He allowed himself to be led around the wall of the great stone and wood house, then in through a side door and into a smoky kitchen. The women working there eyed his rags with distaste and shouted ribald questions at his guide, who seemed to be named Eurycleia. He was beginning to suspect what story he inhabited. When an old dog rose from its place near the hearth and limped toward him, growling, then sniffed his hand and began avidly to lick his fingers, he was certain.

"Odysseus," he said quietly. "King of Ithaca."

Eurycleia turned to him in alarm and made a terrified warning gesture at her lips. She sped her pace to lead him through a great hall whose walls were hung with spears and shields. Outside the hall's open doors, a score or more of men lolled in the shadows around the courtyard, their clothes and weapons clearly those of nobility. They seemed to be having a party. Meat was being roasted over pits full of coals, and servants too slow to serve were being cursed at and kicked and smacked with fists. One of the guests was singing an obscene ballad, his bearded chin jutting toward the sky, the object of his attention a darkened window overlooking the central yard.

"Hark how sweetly Antinous sings, Lady!" one of the others yelled hoarsely, a man drunk before midday. "Will you not let him up to sing to you privately?"

Nothing moved in the window. The men laughed and returned to their amusements.

Paul was numb inside. Even as he followed the old woman up the creaking ladder to the upper floor, moments away from something he had sought for a very long time and through at least a handful of different worlds, he was finding it difficult to care.

They killed the child. The thought had been there, wordless, since his eyes had opened, but he could not keep it at bay any longer. The memory of the boy's limp body, and of his own helplessness, had burned inside him until there was nothing left to burn. He had led the boy to his death. He had sacrificed him like a pawn, and then he had escaped.

He was empty.

Eurycleia stopped at the chamber door. She pushed aside the hanging and gestured Paul to step through. As he did, she caught at his hand again and kissed it, then pulled the knuckles against her forehead in a gesture of willing servitude.

The Weaver looked up at his entrance. Her loom, from which she was even now plucking threads, undoing a picture which she had all but finished, stretched before her like a harp made of colors. The tapestry was all birds—birds of every sort, doves, crows, lapwings, and all in motion, walking, pecking, flying with wings outstretched. Their feathers were of every hue, furiously bright.

The woman at the loom stared back at Paul. He had half-suspected the face he would see, but even with his heart a bleached bone inside him, it still made his breath quicken. She was older here than in her other guises, but she was also somehow startlingly young. Her thick, glossy hair spilled on her shoulders and hung down her back like a dark curtain. Her eyes were as deep and haunted as the stares of dead strangers in old photographs. But she was no stranger—she was something much less explicable. She knew him. And although he could not name her, he knew her too, in every cell of his being.

"You are here," she said, and even the voice was like coming home. "At last you have come." She stood and spread her arms, her robes billowing like wings. As she smiled, her face suddenly seemed that of a young girl. "There is so much that we must talk about, my long-lost husband—so very much!"